Flashing downhill on her sure-footed silver mare, beautiful Anna Smith was proving once again what a magnificent rider she was. Today she would teach arrogant Arthur Kincaid a lesson!

Her turquoise eyes sparkled; her gray-plumed hat had long since blown off, her bright hair had come unloosed and streamed behind her as she fled before him, daring him to catch her.

Behind her, Arthur had a vision of what he would do to lustrous young Mistress Smith if he caught her. He could see himself dragging the laughing wench from the mare's back and flinging her down on the ground where he would fall upon her and take what he wanted. His breath sobbed in his throat—she would find him an impatient lover! Her struggles would be a delight, only adding to his pleasure as he tore that blasted riding habit from her back! And then her chemise—ah, he could hear the fabric rip like sweet music in his mind.

She would pay a price for inflaming him—by God, she would learn he was master!

Novels by Valerie Sherwood

This Loving Torment
These Golden Pleasures
This Towering Passion
Her Shining Splendor
Bold Breathless Love
Rash Reckless Love

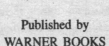

Published by
WARNER BOOKS

Valerie Sherwood

Rash Reckless Love

WARNER BOOKS

A Warner Communications Company

WARNING

The reader is specifically warned against using any of the cosmetics or medications mentioned herein. They are included only to give the authentic flavor of the times. Ceruse, one of the most popular cosmetics of the day, contained white lead and can well be deadly—how much mischief it must have caused! Although common sense would normally restrain the reader from using such unappealing items as "woodlice steeped in wine," a popular asthma "cure" of the 1600s, or "puppy dog urine" to clear the skin, or slaked lime and lye to remove warts, readers are implored to seek the advice of a doctor before undertaking any "experiments" in their use.

WARNER BOOKS EDITION

Cover design by Gene Light

Cover art by Elaine Duillo

Warner Books, Inc., 75 Rockefeller Plaza, New York, N.Y. 10019

 A Warner Communications Company

Printed in the United States of America

First Printing: June, 1982

10 9 8 7 6 5 4 3 2 1

AUTHOR'S NOTE

No era in our history is more colorful or entrancing than the 1600s, when fast-moving events outstripped valiant efforts to record them. It is in these violent times that I have set my story and while the characters and events herein are truly fictional and of my own invention, the seventeenth century backgrounds against which the story is set are real enough. From Bermuda's long-gone forests of giant cedars and ancient cross-shaped houses with their flaring "welcoming arms" front steps, their quaint fireplace doors, and the unusual life-style and early marriages these houses knew, to the wild buccaneer ports of Port Royal and Tortuga and the great plantations of Jamaica and Carolina, the backgrounds are as authentic as I could make them. I may have anticipated the Jamaica Squadron by a few years and of course it was the redoubtable Dutchman, Piet Pieterzoon Heyne, and not van Ryker, who captured the Spanish treasure fleet entire; but history does record a destructive hurricane that raced across the Antilles in 1660; there *was* a famous woman poisoner who was executed in Bermuda in that century for her crimes—but she was not golden-skinned Doubloon; and fierce wreckers did ply their cruel and profitable trade in the reef-strewn islands of the sun.

But most of all, I have tried to recreate the spirit of an age, the wild, wonderful, romantic, swashbuckling 1600s; when nations clashed, new worlds were won, lean pirate ships prowled the seas, and a man might clasp his woman in his arms and sail away to distant uncharted shores—a time in which the America we know and love had its real beginnings.

And to the stouthearted men of that century and their brave and dazzling women, let me now propose a toast:

> *Here where the wild winds have blown,*
> *Where the reckless lovers have played,*
> *Here where their wild oats were sown,*
> *Let us drink to the man and the maid!*

Valerie Sherwood

CONTENTS

Rash Reckless Love

Prologue

St. George, Bermuda, 1673

The girl in the stranger's arms, the slender girl with the burnished gold hair who was about to lose her virginity to this tall man who had sailed in from the north only today, stared for a wild hypnotic moment into his flickering gray eyes and told herself this night was forever.

The stranger had a look of great purpose and an arresting hawklike face but the girl was a strange contradiction: beneath her worn homespun dress and plain petticoat was a chemise incredibly fine and trimmed with fabulous lace. Her delicate white hands—one with a recent burn on the back from contact with a hot saucepan—had obviously never known work. She stood on tiptoe in the dark-haired stranger's embrace, and one of her scuffed shoes, made of fine leather, sported a broken heel. Resting against the nasty bruise just turning blue beneath her right eye—a bruise the stranger had so recently avenged—were long dark curling lashes framing eyes of an unbelievable clear turquoise, deep and brilliant and changeable as the sea itself. As her excitement mounted, so had the color deepened in her peachbloom cheeks. Now her softly parted lips trembled with an unspoken promise and the man who held her so lightly, so caressingly in his arms—as if she were a little bird he had caught in his hands and must not frighten—tightened his grip as he bent his dark head and claimed her mouth with hard, demanding lips.

Now the girl's bright head was bent back, her throat a white curve in the moonlight, her slender back arched as she strained against his deep, throbbing chest. Her palms, at first pressed flat against his chest to restrain him, had been replaced by her ardent young breasts, their delicate curve flattened by their pressure against his strong form. Almost unconsciously, her hands had slipped across the smooth leather of his doublet and her arms had crept luxuriously around the sinewy muscles of his sun-browned neck.

Now his impudent tongue was probing, probing—he was taking liberties with her that she had never allowed, not from any of the many suitors who had once—it seemed forever ago—pleaded with her earnestly on bended knee to marry them.

Her breath sobbed in her throat as new, undreamed-of yearnings rose and shimmered within her. Like wildfire in her blood, this bold stranger's touch had set her aflame. She wanted the unimaginable and felt for a reckless moment that nothing was beyond her reach, *nothing* was beyond her grasp.

In the seawind the girl's light skirts blew and twined around the stranger's long legs. They swirled around his lean thighs, encircled his wide-topped boots. A swatch of lace edging from her chemise skirt caught in his spurs and tore as, poised on the brink, the girl gasped and took a swift, involuntary step backward toward innocence.

So rapt were they that neither of them noticed the tearing lace.

To them the night wind had its own song, its own resonance, for behind their swaying forms the lapping surf rolled in sonorously across the white beach of Bermuda's north shore. Farther along waves crashed against the old, sea-scarred rocks—but not so loudly as they crashed in the girl's ears, for her whole being was taut as a drawn bowstring with the arrow about to fly.

She felt giddy and light-headed, for so much had happened in the short space of a few hours—more it seemed than in all her life before—although that had been eventful enough, heaven knew! But this—this giving of herself, about which she had thought so much, woven so many golden dreams—overshadowed everything: the night, the island, the beauty of the scene—everything. It seemed to her as she looked up into the stranger's intent smiling face, shadowed now, for the wind had blown his thick dark hair like a silken screen between them and the distant moon, that all her life she had waited for this moment and that what was about to happen was inevitable, immutable as if the event had been long ago predicted and carved into stone.

She would be his, this man from the north who had winged south on white sails to claim her, she would belong henceforth to a man she knew nothing about save his name—and in that tense moment in a lost wondrous world with the sea crashing about them, she did not care.

Silently she had pledged her troth. This then was to be her destiny. . . .

Here in the arms of a stranger on a windswept night of stars, the girl was about to become a woman—and she might have drawn back and considered if she had known the real truth about herself and all that had brought her here.

But hers was a reckless heritage, so she did not draw back. Instead, with all her sweet untried passion she embraced her newfound lover.

For she was Georgiana, daughter to the legendary Imogene van Ryker—and like the blazing beauty who bore her, she had been born to flame and torment, to a destiny of doubt and passion, of tumultuous fulfillment and aching desire.

Her mother had been such a woman, and all the Caribbean had echoed with her name.

BOOK I
The Buccaneer's Bride

Her courage, ah, she'll need it....
Come, can't you shed a tear
For lost and lovely Imogene,
Bride to a buccaneer?

PART ONE
The Toast of Tortuga

Golden and tempting and wanton—
That's what they'd like to believe,
A woman of passion, a woman of fire—
Yet a girl with her heart on her sleeve!

The Island of Tortuga, 1660

CHAPTER 1

On the quay at Cayona, under the burning Caribbean sun, a spectacular event was shaping up and sunburned men with cutlasses were nudging each other and edging forward through the outdoor marketplace the better to watch. For that golden beauty, Imogene van Ryker, intent on her shopping among the diverse wares of this crowded buccaneer port, had just been seized around her delectable waist and soundly and publicly kissed—and that by a towheaded half-fledged cabin boy whose cheeks, even as she struggled free from him with delft blue eyes snapping, turned fiery red at this contact with the fabled beauty.

A breathless hush descended upon the crowd. For nineteen-year-old Imogene was bride to the best blade in the Caribbean, the famous buccaneer Captain Ruprecht van Ryker, whose ship of forty guns now rode Cayona Bay, and that same Captain van Ryker, some distance away, had stiffened upon hearing his bride's angry exclamation. Now his big dark head, bent in inspection of a captured shipment of wine, came up and swung around eaglelike to survey the scene.

What he saw caused him to break off his conversation and bound forward just as golden-haired Imogene, with the speed of a spitting cat, pulled free. Her slender body pivoted, her lemon satin skirts gave a devastating swish as she drew back her right arm and brought her palm with a sharp crack across the tall lad's flushed face.

A moment later van Ryker, whose forward rush had led him to knock over an unsteady pile of oranges and three neighboring kegs of salt, and thus brought down on him the deprecations of a gaudy waterfront bawd whose purchases they were, reached the scene. He seized the big lad by one homespun-shirted shoulder and swung him around ungently to face him. The boy's sly impudent face whitened as he found himself looking up into the angry gray eyes of the tall buccaneer and heard the rumbling growl that issued from van Ryker's throat.

Even the angry bawd held her breath.

"*That's* for your temerity." The sinewy buccaneer hurled that homespun figure backward upon the quay, where he landed with a hard thump. "And *this*—!" His sword snaked out before the lad could scramble up.

"No! Van Ryker—don't kill him!" It was Imogene's voice, rising above the sudden mutter of the crowd.

With the point of his blade pinioning down the youth's doublet in the general vicinity of his breastbone, van Ryker paused and studied his victim. He stood above him with his long leather-clad legs planted firmly upon the quay. In his loose white cambric shirt with its flowing sleeves, open to the waist to reveal a heavily muscled sun-browned chest, with two big pistols stuck into his belt, he looked the very picture of vengeance and the crowd held its breath to watch him. Actually the lean buccaneer had no intention of killing the lad, but he intended to strike such terror into his young heart that Imogene would be safe from any further assaults as she strolled through this buccaneer marketplace, even if she walked alone.

"And why should I not?" he drawled.

Her beautiful worried face intent, she moved toward him

with a silken flutter of her yellow skirts. "Because he's so young and—"

"We're all *young*," van Ryker interrupted sardonically, but his saturnine gaze swung toward her. " 'Tis well known buccaneers don't live to be old!"

A general rueful chuckle greeted that remark, but Imogene shrank back, repelled. "He's only a boy," she protested desperately. "And drunk."

"Drunk, is he?" That deadly blade toyed with the braid that decorated the youth's homespun doublet, idly slicing off a piece here and there. White-faced now, the lad stared up in horror along the sharp silver glitter of that shining blade that seemed to lead directly up to the buccaneer's dark face frowning down above him.

"Yes," cried Imogene. "I could smell the wine on his breath when he seized me. Oh, van Ryker—don't hurt him! He couldn't have known who I was. He must have thought me—" she had been about to say "one of *those* women," including with a sweeping wave of her arm the sultry harlots of all nations who sidled about among these dangerous sea rovers and the sharp-eyed traders who dealt with them in Cayona's marketplace. Instead she finished in confusion, "someone else."

Van Ryker shot her a brief glance. She was a woman not easy to mistake. For in all this world, he asked himself, where would one find her peer? Golden and glowing she stood there with the sunlight shimmering on her bright hair and racing in sunlit rivulets along the tempting contours of her tight low-cut satin bodice down into the folds of her billowing lemon satin skirts. She was leaning toward him with a look of mute appeal that would melt stone, and a man could lose himself forever in the depths of her delft blue eyes.

"And *did* you know who this lady was?" wondered the lean buccaneer, flicking off yet another bit of braid.

The boy at his feet gulped—and nodded. He was past lying—and almost past speech.

An even deeper frown descended upon the buccaneer's dark visage. His thick shoulder-length dark hair flowed down around a face that had turned better men than the lad who now lay beneath his sword to trembling jelly.

"You *knew?*" Silkily.

"No!" Imogene saw the danger and sprang forward, seizing van Ryker's arm. "I tell you, he's drunk."

"Not so drunk he can't answer," said van Ryker coldly. With a shrug of his wide shoulders, he shook off his bride's restraining grasp. "Now tell me, lad, what ship are you off of?"

The boy moistened his dry lips and his eyes rolled about him before he spoke. Above him a flight of seabirds banked and swooped and called to one another with raucous cries. The sky was a vivid uncaring blue, that diamond-hard blue of the tropics that had seen so much of death.

"*What ship?*" Van Ryker leaned closer, his face exceedingly evil.

"The *Barracuda*," whispered the youth, his eyes round and staring.

There were indrawn breaths. The *Barracuda* was Captain Flogg's ship, and there had been bad blood between Flogg and van Ryker ever since van Ryker had gone to Flogg's aid in an action against a Spanish squadron, and the *Barracuda*, out of immediate danger, had swiftly sailed away, leaving the *Sea Rover* to finish the engagement alone.

Van Ryker straightened a bit, staring down at the lad. "Then if ye ship aboard the *Barracuda*, ye know the temper of my steel. What madness induced ye to seize my lady here upon the quay?"

The boy swallowed. His terrified eyes rolled this way and that, seeking escape—and found none. "It is a message," he croaked.

"'A message'? What message? Quick about it!" That wicked point left the doublet and played about the lad's terrified face.

"A message from Captain Flogg," choked the boy. He looked about to suffocate.

"And it was to be delivered *thus?* You were to affront my lady?"

Miserably, the boy nodded.

Shoulder to shoulder now, the crowd pressed forward in a circle around them. All knew the *Barracuda* had departed Cayona Bay on yesterday's tide and her captain must have left this arrogant message as a taunt for Tortuga's leading buccaneer. If van Ryker chose to storm out of port after Flogg, and if men began to choose up sides, it could mean the breaking up of the Brotherhood—that Brotherhood of Buccaneers who had built the town of Cayona and the frowning Mountain Fort, with cannon pointed out to sea, that protected their perilous stronghold.

"Well, stand up," said van Ryker, stepping back. "Undoubtedly there's more to this message. I doubt me Flogg would leave you in Tortuga just to buss my lady. What word does he send me?"

The terrified lad scrambled up and stood poised for flight. Imogene looked on in terror.

"He said—Captain Flogg said that I was to seize your lady and throw her skirts over her head in public," he gulped. "And I was to tear off her petticoat and save it and give it to him when he returned to port."

There was a general gasp at such insolence.

"But I couldn't do that," the lad added hurriedly, for some leaping expression in the tall buccaneer's face had led him instinctively to throw up an arm to shield himself. "So I had me two tankards of rum in a tavern and I found her here and I kissed her instead. And he said"— he backed away from van Ryker as he spoke—"Captain Flogg said that I was to tell her she'd soon be in his bed aboard the *Barracuda* and you in no case to stop him!"

"Flogg can't have liked you much," said van Ryker in a conversational tone. "Else he wouldn't have sent you to bear such a message. He can't have expected you to survive it?"

The boy's white face went a shade paler. He looked about to expire. "I didn't see *you,* Cap'n," he blurted. "I thought the lady was alone."

Van Ryker's dark head went back and he gave a short laugh that chilled the nearest onlookers. "Turn around," he said coldly.

The lad cast him a look of utter terror, but turned reluctantly around. He stood hunched over and trembling in his worn homespun. Imogene lifted her arm in a gesture of mute appeal, but van Ryker brushed it aside.

"What's your name, lad?" he asked. "I like to know the names of those I kill."

"Lark Saxon," came the mumbled answer.

"Well, Lark Saxon, let this be a lesson to you not to bear other men's messages if they involve a lady!"

Imogene gave a short sharp scream as van Ryker brought up his sword. She could not stop him now. That swinging blade glinted in the sunlight, and as one man the crowd gave a deep sigh and surged forward to see the insolent youth die.

But the shining blade did not follow its expected course. Instead, with a sudden loud whack, the flat of van Ryker's sword landed stingingly across the seat of young Saxon's trousers. The startled youth leaped in the air and broke into a run. To the accompaniment of deep bellows of laughter from the crowd and shouts of approval, van Ryker pursued the lad all the way to the bay, giving him a last hard spank that toppled him into the water.

"When Flogg returns, ye can give him a message from me." Van Ryker leaned over the edge of the quay, looking down into the splashing water where the youth was just surfacing. "Tell him my sword is at his disposal. I'll be delighted to rid the world of him. And tell him that he'll ne'er touch my lady while I'm alive and if he's lucky enough that I die at my trade, there'll be others rise up to defend her."

"I'll tell him. Thankee, sir!" The lad, no great swimmer, took a gulp of salt water that ended his words and, much relieved, struck out for an arm that was proffered to him from a longboat just pulling in.

"'Tis not enough punishment for so impudent a puppy!" cried a harsh voice behind van Ryker, and the crowd's attention was suddenly focused on a newcomer—a dark Frenchman, clad in handsome maroon ornamented with gold braid, who had stepped from the crowd and was now aiming a heavy pistol at the swimming lad. "I'll give him what he deserves!"

Van Ryker whirled. Instantly his sword snaked out and

knocked the long-barreled dueling pistol from the hand that held it. "I'll fight my own battles, Captain Vartel, and mete out my own punishments."

The Frenchman scowled and bent to retrieve his pistol. His long body came up and he thrust the pistol back into his scarlet baldric. "I should think ye'd have done more to avenge an insult to your lady, van Ryker." His hot gaze wandered over Imogene, who had followed van Ryker to the bayside, stripping her casually as it moved along her body. "And such a lady," he added softly. His arrogant head lifted and he smiled directly into her eyes.

Imogene had felt herself flushing under that penetrating inspection and now she stiffened. The deep breath she took strained her already tight satin bodice to the utmost.

"Captain Vartel." She acknowledged the Frenchman's compliment coolly. "I thank you for coming to my defense but—I need no other champion than my husband."

"My lady is safe," said van Ryker crisply. "Next time I won't be so lenient!" His voice carried to the crowd and held a warning for any who might seek to emulate the lad and steal a kiss from the Caribbean's most fabled beauty.

With a curt bow, Vartel turned on his heel and left them, disappearing into a crowd that went back to haggling and dickering over barrels of captured wine, and kegs of gunpowder and salt pork, and limes and spices and perfumes and jewelry—and haggling, too, for the favors of seductive waterfront bawds who sidled up to buccaneers and traders, sometimes reaching out to stroke a lean sleeve or brushing a tempting breast clad in brilliant captured silks against a strong arm more used to swinging a cutlass than holding a woman. It was once again an ordinary day on Tortuga.

But not for van Ryker. And not for Imogene. The incident had brought them face to face with their world and neither of them liked what they saw.

It was suddenly borne in upon nineteen-year-old Imogene how tawdry and violent was this new world into which her love for the lean buccaneer van Ryker had thrust her . . . and how perilous. On any voyage she might lose him. How had he put it? *Buccaneers don't live to be old. . . . .* And then what? It came to her forcefully how rash and reckless was her love for the strong man beside her. Prevented by some shadow, some blot upon his past, from ever returning home again, something he had not told her and perhaps never would, he must needs live out his life in some buccaneer port like Tortuga among men hunted like himself.

And if he died at sea? Would word of his death be brought to her by a sudden crash as her door was broken in and Captain Flogg—or another like him—stormed in to take her and carry her off to his ship? A fallen buccaneer's share of the spoils was scrupulously sent to his widow in England or Holland or wherever may be. *But what of a widow on Tortuga? What of a widow men's eyes followed greedily as if she herself were a prize to be fought for?*

Beside her, van Ryker was thinking his own dark thoughts. Forgotten now by the onlookers, he stood beside his golden woman and watched the dripping lad being pulled over the side of the longboat. There was a frown upon his keen, hawklike face. The incident had sobered him. Of no great moment in itself, it had brought to him forcefully the position of his young bride on this isle of dangerous men. She was beautiful as the sunlight and there was the challenge of the sea itself in her delft blue eyes with their dark-rimmed irises and long sweeping dark lashes. Her every fluid movement was feminine and alluring—enticing as Eve. She was the kind of woman men fought for, died for—without counting the cost. He should know. He was one of those men.

And he had brought her here . . . here into the path of danger. His soul squirmed at the thought.

Flogg, but half a coward and entirely vicious, a pirate in a land of buccaneers, was not the only one who wanted Imogene. Although assuredly he must have been drunk when he flung this challenge, for he had shown no desire ashore to challenge van Ryker's possession of her. Perhaps someone had twitted him about running away from the Spaniards and leaving the rescuing *Sea Rover* to her fate.

No . . . Van Ryker's heavy frown remained as he sheathed his blade and turned away from the sea. Flogg had flung this

challenge for some deeper reason. He wondered what treachery awaited him out there past the bay.

"Come," he told Imogene gently. "It is over. And"—there
was a grimness to the smile he gave her—"it will not happen
again."

He took her hand and shouldered his booted way through
the crowd, which parted silently to let him pass. Men sporting
gold earrings and cutlasses, hard-faced sun-bronzed men from
a dozen countries, glanced up speculatively as he brushed by
them, then turned back to their inspection of the wines and
brandies, silks and laces, oranges and bananas, weapons and
leather goods, perfumes and spices—all captured booty displayed for buyers from everywhere in the marketplace of this
buccaneer stronghold. Van Ryker glanced up once, speculatively, at the great Mountain Fort that loomed above them, its
guns pointed toward any who dared to question here the
absolute power of the buccaneers.

There was much force here, he mused, but little law. The
governor sent by France was a friend of his, but the governor
had at best a tenuous hold on the place. Mainly he was useful
for issuing—for a price—letters of marque, which turned
buccaneers into privateers. Spain rarely honored those letters
of marque, choosing instead to hang the bearers with the
letters hung derisively around their necks. For himself, van
Ryker had never bothered with them.

No, here the power rested with the buccaneers themselves
and if there was a lord mayor of Cayona—as there was
not—he supposed he would be that lord mayor.

And now Flogg, of all men, chose to challenge his authority. The question was, why?

They had reached an empty space between the clots of
wandering customers that dotted the quay.

"I am glad you spared him." It was Imogene's hurried
voice, speaking quickly before they reached earshot of another group. "For a moment there I was afraid . . ." She let
her voice trail off and he stopped and turned to study her.

"Have ye ever known me to skewer an unarmed man, let
alone a lad?" he asked her gravely.

She flushed and looked uncomfortably away. Of course she
had not! But these last months she had seen so much. Cayona
was a wild town, the wildest in the Caribbean. Here had
drifted the dregs of many nations, here the political outcasts,
murderers, thieves, graduates of many jails rubbed elbows.
Even in broad daylight they were a murderous lot.

"No," she said softly. "I have never known you to do a
dishonorable thing."

The sudden smile that split his dark countenance reflected
his pride in her. "Nor, God willing, will you ever do so.
Although"—his tone changed, lightened—"I've pondered
doing so from time to time! Come, you were considering that
shipment of laces and stuffs over there when the lad seized
you. Let us go back and resume our shopping as if nothing
had happened."

As if nothing had happened . . . . But something *had* happened.
She had come to realize her position here. She had of a
sudden lost her taste for shopping in Cayona's marketplace.

Nevertheless, she offered no resistance as van Ryker urged
her back to her former inspection of the wares of a grinning
giant in leathern breeches. In the heat she saw that he had
stripped off his shirt, which was flung carelessly atop one of
the piles of bolts of materials.

"Taken off the *Santa Cecelia* out of Barcelona," the giant
assured her with a wheezy lisp. She guessed the lisp might be
a token of that engagement, for most of his front teeth were
missing. "Good merchandise all, m'lady—fit for a queen it
is."

"So you told me," she said, restlessly pulling out a bolt,
pushing it away again.

"You were lookin' at this one here," said the lisping giant
helpfully, thrusting a length of blue silk toward her.

"I was just—looking at it." She pushed it away.

"'Twould become you well," observed van Ryker, reaching
out to take the length of blue silk. "D'ye not want it?"

Imogene fingered the shining cloth he held out to her. It
had attracted her by its color—her favorite color, the color
she had worn on a soft night in the Scilly Isles . . . the night

she had lost her virginity to a copper-haired lover who had soon left her.

Her lovely face saddened, for she had borne a child of that event and that child had been wrested from her arms, and had gone down with a ship sunk by the Spanish. Little Georgiana, her daughter, and Elise, the maidservant who had been almost a mother to her, both lost when the *Wilhelmina* had dipped beneath the waves. Imogene had nearly died of grief when she heard it and it was van Ryker who had dragged her back to life, van Ryker who had got her through the worst of it, who had carried her to Tortuga in his ship, the *Sea Rover*, van Ryker who had married her in a "buccaneer's wedding," a sword marriage. How proudly she had walked beside him beneath that arch of crossed cutlasses! How she had sworn— silently of course—to love him forever and to give him, no matter what that doctor had said about the danger of having another child, the night Georgiana was born, children of his own. She had vowed in her heart to be forever faithful, forever true, and her whole being had thrilled to the deep-throated song of the buccaneers—that unforgettable music of her wedding night that still sang through her mind when the moon was high, just as it had on her wedding night when she went into the arms of her dangerous lover.

But that particular shade of blue reminded her of other days, of a copper-haired lover who had proved untrue, and of the aching loss of her baby daughter.

"No," she said, pushing the blue silk aside. "I think I would prefer something else."

Van Ryker sighed, for he privately thought that shade of blue became her well, and she wore it so seldom these days.

"Perhaps this length of gray silk," she suggested, snatching up the nearest thing that came to hand.

"You are gone suddenly demure," he said regretfully. "I think I prefer you as a bird of plumage. Even without your whisk."

His voice was droll and Imogene shot him a sudden look through her lashes. For like the ladies of the English court, she had an old habit of tossing aside her whisk and baring her bosom, despite her deep-cut necklines. A habit that had been thought shocking in the Scillies, where modesty bade young women of fashion to fill in that space between tight bodice and neck with a lawn or cambric scarf or whisk. What fun it had been to shock them!

She laughed, her brooding mood broken. "Wait till you see what I do with it, van Ryker!" she promised him gaily. "Loaded with silver lace and silver tissue and with black velvet ribands catching up the flowing lace cuffs of my virago sleeves—ah, I'll be something less than demure, I promise you! And you in your silver-shot gray doublet and red satin baldric—ah, we'll cut a figure at the governor's next party!"

"No doubt we will," he grinned, letting the sky blue material go with a sigh. "We'll take the gray silk, friend— and anything else my lady takes a fancy to."

He was generous always with his gold, with his kisses— but he had told her so little of himself, of his past, she thought. For instance, although he had once told her he was English, he had never told her his real name. He had married her under the Dutch name he sported aboard the *Sea Rover* and in the Caribbean, where men knew him as a dangerous buccaneer . . . Ruprecht van Ryker.

"Shall I call you Rupert?" she had asked him two days after their marriage, Anglicizing his Dutch name of Ruprecht.

He had hesitated. "No—van Ryker will do well enough for now."

She had asked him then point-blank what his real name was. And he had frowned.

"I'll tell you soon," he had said evasively. "And"— he swept her up and kissed her—"marry you again under that name if you like."

At the time, melting under his hot kisses, it had seemed enough. But now she was suddenly restive after the boy's swift unwarranted attack. Slight though it was, it had served to remind her that she was a woman in a buccaneer port and that there were hot-blooded men about who would seize her from van Ryker if they dared.

She had little to say as she accompanied him through the waning afternoon sunlight as he inspected wines, bought some and had them sent to his house. She was choosing from an enormous pile of fresh limes when he came up and offered her a small silver-chased pistol.

"It seems small enough to fit a woman's hand," he said nonchalantly.

Imogene gave him a troubled glance as she took the pistol. "Yes, it fits my hand nicely," she agreed. "But—" she had been about to say, "do you think I will need it?" when he turned away and bought the gun, stuck it into his belt, where it looked quite small beside the other two, which she privately considered monstrous large.

"I will need a basket if I am to carry these limes home," she told him, and he set off to purchase her a basket, woven from pale green palm fronds.

"There is no need for you to carry fruit home," he observed, taking the basket from her. "The servants enjoy doing the marketing."

"I know they do," she said. "And they probably haggle better and buy for far better prices than I!" Her voice held a tinge of bitterness, for she felt she was no use here—a doxy only, not a wife.

"They would not do it half so well," he said staunchly. "But I would prefer you to let them do it when I am not around to escort you."

"But you have always let me go to the market with Arne," she protested. "You have said he would lay down his life for me!"

"I am aware that he would lay down his life for you, Imogene. I would prefer that he not have to do it."

She stared at him, realizing that the incident on the quay had disturbed him as much as it had her. "I would go mad if I could never leave the house, van Ryker."

"Of course. And when I am not available, on occasion Arne will escort you—perhaps in the company of the governor's wife and some other women."

Safety in crowds . . .

"I see," she said dully. "I will do as you wish, van Ryker."

Around them the shadows were lengthening now and the

raucous dockside crowd was thinning out as men sought drink
and dinner in the many taverns and inns that dotted the town.

Imogene's bright head was bent as if to inspect her satin
slippers.

Van Ryker reached out and took her arm gently in his big
hand. "What is it?" he asked quietly. "What is bothering
you?"

How could she tell him it was this life they led? When she
knew it was the only life he could ever give her. . . .

"What will happen to him?" she asked soberly.

"What will happen to who?"

"To the boy, of course. The one who kissed me."

"If you mean what will he make of his life, he'll become a
buccaneer, I suppose—he's near old enough. And that life
will be shorter than most if he carries many messages of the
kind he carried today!" His voice was grim.

Imogene shivered. His life could be short in any case if,
like the tall man beside her, he followed the trade of buccaneer.

She was silent and sad as she accompanied van Ryker
home to their white-stuccoed house down Tortuga's sun-
baked streets.

CHAPTER 2

At their heavy iron grillwork doors the familiar figure of
big Arne greeted them. He looked a very cutthroat, she
thought, with one gold earring and that red rag tied around
his head to hold in place a shaggy head of graying, sand-
colored hair. He hacked that hair off from time to time, she
knew, with the knife that was stuck casually in his belt
between a brace of pistols. The cutlass that rested against his
thigh was full of nicks from his days of hard fighting against

the Spanish, and his wooden leg sparkled with the pieces of eight—all won at cards—that he had pounded in. Arne was sentry and loyal servant and friend—ever since the raid on Maracaibo had cost him his good right leg and van Ryker, seeing the old sea dog's predicament, had taken him into his household.

Arne swung the big grillwork doors wide and they went through them and on through another set of doors, which stood open—this last pair constructed of thick black oak and garnished with heavy nailheads, for van Ryker had kept his lawless profession in mind when he had built this house. Someday the Spanish might storm Tortuga, silence the guns of the frowning Mountain Fort, and fight a grim battle for the town of Cayona, house by house, street by street. Van Ryker had built his house with that in mind. If the worst happened, he meant this Spanish-style white-stucco residence— stuccoed over heavy stone—to be the last holdout. As unofficial lord mayor of Cayona, he would sell his life dear!

Imogene, preoccupied with the perilous life van Ryker led, had never given a thought to this last extremity. Now, as they entered the cool whitewashed interior, she looked past Arne down the broad, stone-floored hallway to the tinkling fountain in the central open patio around which the house was built. The fountain was of faded rosy stone and had come, she knew, from the raid on Maracaibo, when it had been used, along with the handsome carved stone fireplaces that graced the house, for ballast. The fountain was fed by a spring that also provided water for the house—another reason why van Ryker had chosen this location; he could not be cut off from water.

She would have strolled on toward that fountain but that van Ryker's low voice behind her, speaking to Arne, froze her in her tracks.

"I want you to stay very near my lady, Arne, while I am gone," he was telling the old buccaneer gravely.

Imogene gave a start and turned with a swish of lemon satin skirts. *Gone?* He was voyaging somewhere then? In the delights of her golden honeymoon, which had hung on for months now, she had half forgotten that a buccaneer must eternally scour the seas for his living. She had thought his profession a fearsome one—but one that could be postponed, perhaps indefinitely.

She heard Arne grunt. "Somethin' happen, Cap'n?"

Van Ryker nodded soberly. "Aye. Captain Flogg has this day sent me a message via a half-fledged cabin boy—that he means to take her."

Arne gave his captain a look of disbelief. *"Flogg?"* He whistled through yellow teeth. "He wouldn't dare cross swords with you!"

"That's what I thought—at first. Now I'm wondering what's afoot, for it isn't like Flogg to tell you in advance what he's planning."

"Now, that it isn't, Cap'n. Most likely he was drunk at the time and will regret it when he sobers."

"Let us hope so. For I've no mind to sail away and leave my lady at the mercy of Flogg and his pack of cutthroats."

Big Arne gave his captain an injured look. "I'd let nothing happen to your lady, Cap'n."

"Not while you lived, Arne," said van Ryker gently. "But suppose he means it? Suppose his crew stormed the house? How long could you hold out?"

There was a moment's silence. Past the doors to the left and right that led respectively to the chart room where van Ryker kept his maps, and a large reception room, the rose stone fountain taken in the raid on Maracaibo tinkled. And that tinkle sounded at the moment very loud.

"I take your meaning, Cap'n." Arne stroked his stubbled chin thoughtfully. "Wouldn't your friend the gov'ner send help?"

"If he could do it," sighed van Ryker. "But suppose his own house was encircled? Who knows what's afoot? Remember that pack of Portuguese pirates that just made port here—and we gave them sanctuary even though they're not members of the Brotherhood, but just as a courtesy to passersby? I hear they're friends of Flogg, and who knows what devil's pact they might make?"

Imogene felt a chill go over her as they talked about it,

calmly, as if cutlasses would not clash and echo through these halls, as if blood would not flow over this well-scoured stone flooring beneath their feet if what they feared came to pass. She looked about her at the white plastered walls of this house she called home. For all its dangerous setting, it had a certain barbaric splendor—that unlit torch thrust carelessly into an iron bracket on the wall might have graced a courtyard in Barbary—and she had known happiness here—and love. It seemed ridiculous for them to be talking about the storming of this house where she was mistress.

Feeling unreal, she listened. A few good men, van Ryker was telling the attentive Arne, those he could best trust to hold their liquor and guard their posts, would be left ashore when he sailed and quartered in the smaller house next door he'd built against just such a contingency. Their shares of the booty would have to be paid out of his own share, of course, Imogene knew. For the first time, she felt she was shackling him.

"You did not tell me you were leaving," she said in a subdued voice as they left Arne and made their way into the open courtyard around which the house was built. Behind them the iron grillwork front doors had already clanged shut and Arne was now engaged in locking the second set of doors, of nailhead-garnished solid oak. It would take a battering ram to penetrate those doors. . . . She had not really thought of the house as a fortress before; now she began to realize it was one and to consider—as van Ryker had when he built it—the solid thickness of its stone walls, the massive weight of its iron grillwork, the heavy interior shutters that could close off the windows in the event of storm—or fighting.

She gave an involuntary shiver.

Van Ryker noted that. "I thought 'twould worry you," he admitted, setting a wide-topped boot upon the flight of stone stairs that led up to the encircling covered gallery off which the bedroom doors opened.

"You are right." She accompanied him up the stairway. "It does."

"You are not to worry," he said quickly. "I should not have let you hear our discussion, but you may be certain that Arne will protect you with his life. As will the others that I leave here to guard you."

It was not the possible danger to her life that Imogene was thinking of just now. She was thinking what it would be like to wake without that saturnine face beside her, to lie in the big bed alone and not feel his lean loins brush her naked hip.

They had reached the top of the stairs now and she turned to him with a swaying, seductive gesture. Her head was tilted and her delft blue eyes shadowed by her dark lashes. Below them in the fast fading light, the rose-colored fountain tinkled and burbled. The air was filled with flower scents and the swift velvet night of the tropics was fast closing down. With a swish of satin she moved temptingly closer.

"If 'tis so dangerous a place, why leave me here? Why not take me with you? Surely I'd be safe aboard the *Sea Rover.*"

His gray eyes mirrored his amazement. "And risk you, with the guns of some great Spanish galleass possibly raking me broadside?" He snorted. "For rumor has it the Spanish treasure *flota* is preparing to sail, and they'll not be taken without a fight."

"The *flota?*" Alarm rushed through her. "But there'll be many stout warships in their fleet and you are but one!"

"No, this time I sail with two captured prizes—the galleass, *La Golondrina*, which you'll remember—I've renamed her the *Hawk*. And a caravel I've been outfitting—*La Garza*, which translates to the *Heron*, and I like that well enough."

"Three ships against the mighty *flota?* And one of them a little caravel with lateen sails? You cannot do it!"

He grinned. "That's what they told me when I raided Maracaibo. 'A town so strongly fortified? You cannot do it!'" He mimicked that remembered dismay. "But the stone mantel in your bedroom testifies that they were wrong." His searching hand found the back of her neck and his long fingers combed into her hair.

"Oh, do not tease me, van Ryker!" In her anxiety, she shook free of him. "Maracaibo is a town and you were lucky then, but the *flota* has all the warships Spain can muster!

They are ready to repel an entire foreign fleet! No one has taken them—*no one!*''

"Then pray that I may be the first." With one long arm he drew her closer and bent his head into the heady lemon scent of her bright hair.

"Van Ryker!" She stamped her foot in its satin slipper. "Promise me you will not attempt it. I would never sleep at all if I thought you were out there fighting the entire *flota!*''

"Perhaps I can cut one ship from the pack," he murmured lazily into her lemon-scented golden tresses. "And bring you golden earrings and emeralds that would weigh down a queen!"

"Do not try to lure me with jewels," she pouted, pushing away from him again. "I want to be with you. Not stuck here being guarded." And in a sudden reversal. "If *you* are not afraid of the *flota*, why should *I* be afraid of it? Take me with you!"

He shook his dark head decisively. "You'd get us all killed, Imogene. For I'd forget my seamanship and my good sense—if I thought you were in danger."

She could not help but smile. How much more plainly could he have told her that he loved her?

"Then don't hurry away," she suggested archly. "There are always rumors about the treasure *flota*—you have said so yourself." *And please God, let him not meet up with that fleet of some twenty-odd galleons and galleases, for valiant buccaneer that he is, they would surround and destroy him!* To emphasize the advantages of lingering ashore, she stretched in a seductive way that showed her delightful figure to its best advantage.

"The men grow restive," he muttered, his gray eyes kindling at the sight of her breasts rippling slightly beneath her tight bodice as she flexed her slender arms. "Too much shore duty is making them soft. And besides"—he drew her toward the bedroom door as he spoke—"there is no longer any excuse. We have finished careening and outfitting the ships. If we tarry now, the stores will spoil."

She supposed she might have expected it. A buccaneer cannot stay in his home port forever. . . .

"Make it a short voyage," she whispered, twining her arms around him as they reached the privacy of their bedroom and van Ryker closed the door and shut out the world.

"As short as may be," he promised huskily, eyes glinting, for the touch of her sweet flesh, the soft crushing of her round breasts against his doublet, was anguish and delight. He was only too well aware of all he would be leaving behind him.

"You'll not be leaving until after the governor's party tomorrow night?" She was panicky at the thought that he might sail on tomorrow's tide.

"No, no," he soothed her. "Not till the following day. There are still matters to see to."

So soon . . . She shrank against him, as if she would hold the world at bay in his arms.

He held her gently away from him, seeking to take her mind off partings, for it hurt him to the heart to feel her shuddering in his arms.

"Tell me how you spent your day," he said. "Before I came home from provisioning the ships and took you shopping."

"I will not tell you—I will *show* you." She gave him a challenging look. Swiftly she opened a carved mahogany box, took out a deck of well-thumbed playing cards and tossed them onto the table. "Come, I will challenge you." She began to shuffle the cards and then riffled them flashily. She slapped the shuffled deck down on a table that sometimes served her as a desk. "Cut!"

Van Ryker sighed, for he had no doubt what would come next. He joined his beautiful young wife at the table, where she leaned upon her elbows, studying the cards with apparent fascination.

"I am sure you have seen them before," he said ironically.

"Oh, yes," She flashed him a brilliant smile. "What shall we play for? My petticoats? Or shall we begin with my stockings?"

"I would as soon cut the cards for all your clothes at once and have done with it!"

"Ah, you shall not get off that easy, van Ryker," she admonished him with a wave of her fanned-out hand of cards.

"Make me a wager—and it should be a good one, matched against my petticoats."

"If I win, I shall remove them myself," he warned.

"*If* you win!" she mocked him.

"Very well, a dozen gold doubloons against your petticoats." He had meant to leave more than that with her anyway, for he was certain she would want to shop and buy pretty things from the market while he was gone.

She won the doubloons.

"Would you like to try for my petticoats again?" she taunted.

"De Rochemont is teaching you too much," he muttered.

"He says I am a very apt pupil. He is proud of me!"

"Very well. A casket of coins for the petticoats." He indicated a little wrought silver chest that lay upon the table near his bed.

Imogene's blue eyes widened. That little silver chest was full of golden coins. She bent in concentration upon her cards.

Suddenly his long arm shot out and seized hers in a paralyzing grip. He smiled into her eyes. "Let us see what is in your sleeve," he said softly.

Imogene flushed and bit her lips as he pushed back her big flowing oversleeve and removed the clip with the extra aces attached to it.

"So now you cheat as well," he said coldly. "Do not tell me you did not learn *that* from de Rochemont!"

Imogene's flush deepened. "He has been tutoring me," she admitted with a haughty lift to her chin. "And I find it very interesting. You see, if you press the clip just right, a spring releases a card into your hand—if you wish, you can end up with four aces."

"And what if somebody riffles through the deck and finds there are three more in it?"

"But I am not planning to become a card cheat, van Ryker! I am simply entertaining myself—and you!"

"There are other ways I would prefer to be entertained," he said, drawing her toward him. "In bed, for example."

She would have pulled away from him but he kept a firm hold on her. "I don't know why you are not pleased," she complained. "I have learnt so many tricks from de Rochemont—how to palm cards and deal from the top of the deck or the bottom as I please, how to feel for thick and thin spots and how to mark the cards—I thought you would be amused by it!"

And yesterday he had come home to find big Arne down on his knees on the stone flooring of the courthouse teaching her how to roll out the dice and make her point, how to box the dice, how to hold them up to the light and see small differences, how to detect weighted dice and how to shave off the corners almost indiscernibly so that they would roll predictably. For van Ryker was well aware that cards were not Arne's only game. The pieces of eight he won at cards he dutifully pounded into his wooden leg for his "old age," but the coins he won at dice—and they were numerous—he squandered on tavern slatterns, who picked his pockets while he was drunk, and sometimes even tried to pry loose the coins he had pounded into his wooden leg.

Still—one thing at a time.

"Imogene," he began. "You must know that de Rochemont was run out of France as a notorious card cheat."

"Everyone is on Tortuga for *some* reason!" she flashed. "And Raoul de Rochemont is not only your ship's doctor—he is your friend as well."

"True," van Ryker acknowledged gravely. "Raoul is all of those things. And Arne is my good right hand when I am gone and I would trust him with my life—and yours. But you are not in training to become a tavern wench, Imogene, or a waterfront gambler."

She gave an angry sniff. "But there is nothing to do here on Tortuga," she complained. "I have five servants—more than sufficient to run the house. You cannot expect me to spend every day calling on the governor's wife. Over time, she becomes very boring."

Van Ryker could not but have sympathy with her there. He found the governor's wife abysmally boring.

"Social life here is not—normal," she explained lamely,

"I know you have interesting friends who have sought out this island as a place of refuge but—who among them has brought along a wife? And you do not wish me to associate with their 'light women.' "

It was true enough. He thought over his friends, fine for him because they had intellect and humor and strength. Men with murky pasts, men who had been driven from their own lands, their own kind and found their way to Tortuga, which shared with Port Royal the lamentable distinction of being the most sinful cities of the New World.

He looked at his lovely bride. For all she had been widowed from a disastrous marriage and lost her only child to a ship that had been sunk by Spanish guns at sea, she was but nineteen—and she was bored.

"If only we could be—somewhere else," she said wistfully. "London or Paris or Amsterdam—especially London. So much is going on there!"

Van Ryker winced inwardly. *If only we could be in England,* he thought. Not necessarily in London— *anywhere* in England. But he knew, even as the thought passed painfully through his mind, that he was a marked man and could never go home. Imogene did not know of that other thing in his past, she thought buccaneering his only crime.

" 'So much going on there' . . . " he echoed, studying her.

"Yes, especially now that the king has been restored to his throne."

Ah, that was it, he mused. Reports had just reached them of the three-day carouse that had accompanied King Charles's triumphant return to London. Fountains had run wine and there had been dancing in the streets. The whole city had gone mad with joy, perhaps not so much at Charles's return as in sheer relief at being set free from the grip of Cromwell's fierce puritanical regime. And there were dazzling rumors floating about Tortuga of theaters being reopened, of music halls running again, of public dancing, of light and laughter and parties and people strutting about in fine silks and laces that had been banned by Cromwell. Many of those who remembered the old dreary days under the Puritans were wishing themselves back in an England that was merry again.

It was no wonder Imogene, who had never been to London, yearned to go there, he thought. Her early days in the Scilly Isles had been filled with balls and parties, and she had made a great marriage—even though it had failed miserably, that was not *her* fault. She had lost her baby to the deep, again through no fault of her own, and now she had thrown in her lot with him in Tortuga in a "buccaneer's wedding" of a magnificence that would be talked about as long as men could remember here in sinful Cayona.

But all of that was not London . . .

"Ye *would* have won the gold, Imogene," he sighed, and reached over to hand her the little chased silver casket.

She shrugged away from it irritably. "Gold means little to me, van Ryker—you of all men should know that."

Yes, he knew it. He knew that this fiery woman was not to be bought for gold. When the Dutchman had died in New Netherland—that first husband from whom she had fled in terror—she had not even bothered to claim his vast estate of Wey Gat, preferring that the world think her dead. Hers was a free and roving spirit kindred to his own—and he had cooped her up here in his fortress of a house with a household of servants and every luxury that could be snatched from a passing Spanish galleon. His friends were the best Tortuga had to offer—doctors to treat the ever-brawling buccaneers, keen-eyed traders, resplendent go-betweens who carried ransom demands back to Spain, even a governor and his lady sent from France. But the keen-eyed traders made murky business dealings and many were not welcome in their own countries, the doctors were usually scandal-ridden practitioners who had come here as a last resort, the flourishing go-betweens were to a man—like his ship's doctor, Raoul de Rochemont—disgraced members of the aristocracy. And the governor's wife was boring. . . .

Privately he admitted to himself that Tortuga was no place for a restless, hot-blooded woman—a woman like Imogene.

"I'll *dice* you for the casket." Her eyes narrowed.

He laughed. "With dice you've spent long hours shaving, no doubt. Come, I'll teach you a few tricks myself!" He rummaged in a trunk, pulled out a large pair of dice, tossed them up and caught them. "The casket against your petticoats, Imogene!"

Her blue eyes gleamed. "You're on, van Ryker! Roll out the dice!"

He rolled a five, rolled again—this time a two and a three.

Imogene gave a little sigh and unfastened her pair of yellow petticoats, let them slither to the floor. Her long legs gleamed through her almost transparent white chemise.

"And now for your stockings—which *I* will remove, if I win them." He rolled a nine.

"You'll not make it," she mocked.

He gave her a very steady smile and let the dice roll from his big bronzed hand.

A six and a three.

Imogene gave him a slanted look.

Van Ryker grinned and took his time about removing her stockings. He left her garters around her white legs. "We'll play for those next," he murmured. But he reached up lingeringly around her white thighs and slid his hands down along with the stockings, letting the silk rasp against her skin so that she gave a little unconscious gasp at his touch.

She might have been willing to stop playing then, but he gave her a little push.

"The garters for the casket," he said—and won again.

In quick succession, Imogene—looking rebellious now—lost her shoes, her garters, her lemon satin overdress and her big detachable sleeves and stood there facing him, flushed, in her sheer chemise through which her pale body gleamed delectably.

"And now for your chemise," he said inexorably—and made his point.

With a little exclamation, Imogene snatched up the dice. "I can't tell what you're doing with them," she cried, vexed, and tossed them out, tried to make the point. "They're too big," she muttered. "It makes me clumsy—I can't box them right."

"Ah, but *I* can. My hands are much larger than yours." He tossed the dice away and pulled her toward him. "Just a

gentle reminder, Imogene, that there are many tricks to the
trade you're so intent on learning—and you can come to grief
if you try to take on any of the notorious card sharps that
populate Tortuga."

Breathlessly, she tried to twist away from him, for she was
irritated by her defeat and was not ready to be taken just yet.
"I did not know you could box the dice like that, van
Ryker!"

"Another memento of my misspent youth." He grinned
lazily, reaching up with his free hand to pull the drawstring of
her chemise and then easing the smooth light fabric down
over her white shoulders and round throbbing breasts, stroking
the tingling bare skin of her stomach as the fabric slid down
away from her, caressing the soft outthrust line of her hips.
"You're a sight to drive a man mad, Imogene," he said
hoarsely, and pulled her to him.

The silver buckle of his belt cut into her stomach but she
did not care. She went into his arms in a silken gesture of
surrender and pressed her slight body against his. She loved
this tall buccaneer, loved him with all her heart and soul and
being. She had cast in her lot with him, caring not where his
path might lead her. Other women had respectability, position, power—*she* had van Ryker and she would not have
exchanged him for any prince of the land.

"Van Ryker," she whispered urgently, her lips hot against
his ear, "take me with you."

So that was what all this mocking display had been about.
He realized suddenly that she had hoped to win from him all
his worldly goods and force him to take her along. Beautiful
rebellious Imogene. A great tenderness came over him for
this reckless woman he loved so much and he held her to him
wordlessly and stroked her smooth back and buttocks with
long, roving fingers. Those fingers wandered down her spine
and slid around her slender waist. They found her quivering
breasts and stole along her thighs, lazily probed into silky
depths and then, questing upward, explored the length of her
body again and ended up holding her lovely face uplifted that
he might smile down into her eyes and kiss her tempting
parted lips.

"There's better for us to do this night than gambling," he murmured, and carried her to the big square bed and laid her down upon it. She crossed her arms behind her head and lay there looking up at him, the very picture of desirability. He kept his approving gaze on her as he quickly divested himself of his weapons, his doublet and shirt and trousers and boots, and stood before her in his smallclothes and stockings.

"You're a handsome beast, van Ryker," she sighed, watching him remove the last vestiges of his garments until he stood before her a naked giant, powerful, intent. "Back in England you must have driven the wenches wild. I marvel you should insist on using a Dutch name."

The shadow of a frown passed over his dark countenance. "There's a good reason for me not to be known as an Englishman these days."

"I don't see why," she said, as he lowered his big body onto hers. "Dutch buccaneer, English buccaneer—what can it matter? There's no war between England and Holland—at least not at the moment." For relations between England and Holland were always degenerating into war, it seemed.

"There are—other reasons." He silenced her pouting mouth with a kiss and gathered her in his right arm. Perhaps, he thought, perhaps this was the night to tell her. . . . No, it could wait a little longer. For what would she think of him when she knew the truth about why he could never go home? Even if he managed to buy a king's pardon for buccaneering—and such pardons were to be had for a price—there was another charge against him. He opened his mouth to say *Imogene, I am under sentence of death in England. A jury in my absence adjudged me a murderer. That is the real reason I have masqueraded as a Dutchman and have taken the name van Ryker.*

But he could not do it. On the verge of confession, he stared down into the blue eyes of the woman on the bed—his woman. She was looking back at him proudly—with complete trust.

"Imogene," he murmured, and as if to wipe out the past, to cleanse his sins in the purity of his love for her, he brought his long lithe form down upon her slender naked body in a

sudden sensual onslaught that overwhelmed her, scattered her
defenses like matchsticks, caught her in an onrushing tide of
feeling and drove her onward to heights of passion. Sure of
his manhood, sure of her, he swept her with him up and over
peaks of desire and down rushing rivers of ecstasy and
fulfillment.

For Imogene it was a swift and dazzling journey of shooting
stars and joined bodies and scorching moments.

"Van Ryker," she murmured contentedly as he slid away
from her at last, "you are destroying me. I think I am become
part of you and no longer myself at all . . . soon I shall lose all
identity!"

He did not answer, but he reached out to press her hand as
he lay beside her. Playfully his hand encircled her wrist and
he could feel her racing pulse. He lifted his head and leaned
over and brushed the crests of her breasts with his lips, felt
her sudden start and heard her little gurgling laugh.

"Now you know all my secrets," she sighed, moving
luxuriously closer so that her naked body rippled along his
own. "But do I know all of yours?"

Again he did not answer, but her nearness, her slight,
sensuous movements against his hard frame, set him afire. He
turned toward her with a hoarse inarticulate murmur. Then
gently, elegantly, he took her again in a thrilling silence with
their bodies rippling and straining in perfect rhythm. No
words were needed to enhance that silken joining. It was a
perfection of the senses, poetry in motion. So responsive was
she to his touch, so certain was he of her desires, so deft his
timing, so right each move, each gesture, that they seemed
really to have become one, and as one their passions crested,
as one they went over the brink to fall endlessly, softly into a
vivid afterglow of feeling.

Afterward, still touched by the wonder of it, he lay with his
head resting on her quickly rising and falling breast and felt,
along with her, still wordlessly, that they had reached their
heaven and touched their stars—if only for a little while.

No, he could not bring himself to tell her his dark past—
not yet.

The moon, rising over Tortuga, found them waking, stretching luxuriously, thrilling again to the feel of their naked bodies sliding past each other in the big square bed.

"Would you like some food?" he asked huskily. "Or—?"

She threw a graceful bare leg over the edge of the bed. "We'll order dinner, I think—the servants will still be up. And *then,* after we've eaten..." She gave him a slanted look that promised much and he grinned back at her, seeing her as a white wraithlike shape in the darkness. His lady...his valiant, lovely lady....

CHAPTER 3

True to her promise, Imogene had the gray silk stitched up into a gown she designed herself for the governor's party. All the clever female fingers in the house had worked on it, and although it was hastily done, it had her usual flair for style. She looked ravishing in it.

The party was to be held in the evening—"when it is cooler," the governor's wife had panted when she proffered the invitation—and that morning Imogene washed out her long fair hair in preparation for the event. Van Ryker was gone, somewhere in the town, seeing to the last details of provisioning his ships, for he was meticulous in these matters. To dry her hair, Imogene sat on the iron railing of the balcony outside her bedroom, combing out the thick golden mass with a repoussé silver comb and shaking her head to let the trade winds blow it dry.

Afterward she took a nap and woke to take a luxurious, hot, scented bath—the water perfumed expensively with attar of roses. The soap had been brought from France and it added its own mixed flower scent to the damask rose of the water. Imogene lingered in the tub, lifting the big round sea sponge and letting the warm soapy water cascade down over her wet shoulders and breasts. When she was quite done, one of the maids brought more scented water in a big earthenware pitcher and poured it over her body to rinse her. The maid left and Imogene stepped out upon the tile flooring and toweled herself dry on big linen squares made of the finest flax Holland had to offer.

Buccaneers and their women lived well. . . .

Naked now, she padded to one of the two great round-topped chests that held her petticoats and underwear and night things and chose with care her best white chemise. It was a delicate lawn creation, semi-sheer, with enormous puffed sleeves that she caught gracefully at the elbows with black velvet ribands so that they would spill out a torrent of white lace down over her slender forearms.

Next, critically considering her reflection in the tall pier glass, she put on a stiff pewter satin petticoat heavily worked in silver threads in a rose design. And over that, the shimmering gray silk dress the household had worked so hard to finish in time. The tight bodice with its breathtakingly low square-cut neckline gleamed as she moved, the big flared oversleeves edged in black velvet set off to perfection the huge white virago sleeves of her chemise, the wide rippling skirt overlaid with silver tissue was a silvery haze as she moved. In front the bodice was laced with black velvet ribands, shepherdess style, and above it the white lawn and lace of her low neckline barely covered her nipples.

Her delft-blue eyes narrowed as she studied her reflection in the mirror. She would give van Ryker a tormenting vision to remember while he was at sea! *And a reason,* lurked a tempting little thought at the back of her mind, *for hurrying back to her.*

It was very satisfying to see van Ryker, striding into the room at that moment, catch his breath.

"Was I not right about the gray silk?" she demanded, turning to him with a brilliant smile.

"Aye," he said soberly. "You will sweep all before you, Imogene."

"What is there to sweep—in Tortuga?" she scoffed.

He frowned, for he recognized painfully the truth of what she said. "You knew I was a buccaneer when you married me, Imogene."

"Yes." She gave her elaborate coiffure a last pat. "I knew that." Artfully she inserted a black velvet riband ablaze with brilliants into her curls and turned to give him a defiant look. "But I thought then that you would take me with you, where you went."

"You could not have thought that." He stated it flatly, his mind on decks slippery with blood, and masts shattered and falling upon those decks to crush men locked in battle. He thought of screams and dying men and the boom of heavy cannon. The stuff of nightmares.

"Ah, but I did," she insisted, with a toss of her golden curls that set the brilliants dancing.

His sword swung against his thigh as he crossed the room to her, stood behind her fondling those curls and studying the beautiful rebellious woman reflected in the mirror. As he touched her, his hard face softened. Rash, lovely Imogene . . . With big competent hands he caressed her neck, her shoulders, and their very touch maddened him.

"You could not have thought I'd risk you," he said hoarsely.

She shook free and turned to face him. "And what of me, if the *Sea Rover* is blown out of the water? Have you thought about that?"

He sighed and nodded, taking her silver silk waist in both his hands. His hands could span it. "I am a buccaneer, Imogene. My share of any spoils—just as all who sign the Articles—will be delivered to you. You can sell this house and go to London. There I've left my will with a London agent, whose name you will find in my papers. It was made some time ago but it has ample provisions if I should marry. You will be taken care of handsomely."

"I don't *want* to be taken care of handsomely after you're dead, van Ryker," said Imogene perversely. "I prefer to share your fate."

He brushed her neck with a light kiss.

"No." He turned away, his face as adamant as she had ever seen it.

She knew there was no use arguing with him when he was in this mood. "Wear your silver-shot doublet," she called after his broad departing back. "We will look like a couple of pewter spoons!"

"Sterling," he corrected cheerfully, turning to grin at her. Then his long russet form disappeared down the hall to his own room, where he kept his clothes in a big press. It was the room he'd occupied before she came here and although he now spent his nights in her bedroom, he still dressed in his own.

They made their entrance into the governor's green-shuttered white house that night with style, she thought.

Indeed it was a dazzling entrance. The tall buccaneer in his wide-topped boots with their frosty lawn boothose edged in heavy point lace—his broad chest aglitter in the silver-shot doublet Imogene had recommended, a wide gray satin baldric reaching from shoulder to hip, and the serviceable basket-hilted sword he always wore, brushing his pewter silk trousers. The golden-haired woman with her lissome figure a miracle of silver silk and silver tissue. A vision of silver and gold they must have seemed to the governor's guests, who turned to regard them as they entered the spacious high-ceilinged room.

The governor, a short voluble dark little man, perspiring profusely in a black velvet suit encrusted with gold braid, greeted them effusively as did his wife, Esthonie. Gauthier Touraille might be governor of Tortuga but he was himself governed by his wife. Esthonie never let him forget for a moment that she was the daughter of a chevalier of France, while he was the son of a brewer. She criticized his manners, his dress, his friends. She redecorated his spacious house thrice a year and called it oversmall—not half so large as Imogene van Ryker's, and should not a governor have a better house than a buccaneer? Nightly she bewailed the fact that they and their two daughters had been "banished to this Godforsaken place to live among thieves and pirates!" Gauthier

sometimes reminded her that they were growing rich from the
letters of marque he sold these "thieves and pirates," that she
could shop here in Tortuga in a way a woman in Paris might
well envy, for were not the world's finest goods spread out in
the marketplace on Cayona's quay? And these buccaneers she
railed against were generous—indeed, was not the material of
the very gown she wore tonight—a stiff black silk glittering
with gold points, a part of the lot from a Spanish galleon
bound for Cartagena—a gift of Captain van Ryker, whose
house she envied so much? But the governor might have
saved his breath, for Esthonie pish-tushed everything he said.

"You look ravishing, Madame van Ryker." The governor
bent his flushed face over her hand. Secretly he wished
Imogene looked a shade less ravishing, for Esthonie did not
like to be outshone at her own parties. He had no doubt he
would hear tonight that it was *his* fault she had been overshadowed by the dazzling Imogene.

"Thank you," smiled Imogene, who liked the perspiring
little governor.

"Captain van Ryker! And Imogene! It was so good of you
to come." Esthonie, beaming at the tall captain, held out her
fat black-gloved hand to be kissed.

Van Ryker took it gallantly. "You are a handsome bird of
plumage as usual, Madame Touraille," he said with a smile.

Esthonie bridled, for she loved a compliment. "Ah, but the
plumage would not be so handsome were it not for you,
Captain!" She struck him roguishly with her fan and turned
about for Imogene's approval of her gown. "Is it not a lovely
piece of cloth? So generous of your husband!"

Imogene, who had turned down that same "lovely piece of
cloth" as too garish, smiled and murmured what sounded like
agreement. She was not overfond of Esthonie, who seemed to
her both shallow and pettish, but Esthonie went with the
territory. Here on Tortuga her company must be endured.

"How do you like the room, *ma chère?*" demanded
Esthonie with a wave of her ebony-feathered fan, which
brought to Imogene a whiff of the cloying musklike scent
Esthonie always affected. "I had it done in green especially
for the party."

Imogene, who in these last months on Tortuga had already seen this room done in "ashes of roses" and in ivory, cast an uninterested look about her. "Very nice, Esthonie," she said. "And the flowers are lovely."

"Yes," sighed Esthonie, looking at the massed roses and bougainvillaea, the garlands of green vines that even now were dropping an occasional small spider upon unwary guests. "That is the only good thing I can think of about living in the tropics—flowers all year long."

"Oh, come, Esthonie," laughed Imogene. "There must be *something* else to recommend the tropics?"

"Nothing that I could name." Esthonie's tone grew tragic. She held up her fan to hide her mouth and spoke only for Imogene's benefit. "I fear, *ma chère*, that if we live long enough on this terrible island that my daughters will become strumpets and my husband a hopeless tippler. Look at him, he is toasting somebody's eyelashes again! And he has been drinking steadily all day!"

"He holds it well, Esthonie," said Imogene tolerantly, for she had learned to take with a grain of salt Esthonie's exaggerations.

"And look at Virginie!" hissed Esthonie. "Why, that young buccaneer is all but pawing her! Forgive me, *ma chère*, but I must attend a mother's duties—I must go over and break up that duo! At once!"

Imogene watched with amusement as her stout hostess churned away from her on a direct path for her errant daughter. Dark Virginie, with a figure far overblown beyond her fourteen years, was leaning seductively against the newly painted green wall, giggling as a rugged young French buccaneer toyed playfully with one of her dark curls. Virginie, thought Imogene wryly, was not aptly named, for her virginity was a doubtful matter indeed; there were tales circulating about Tortuga of handsome buccaneers who on occasion climbed in the night hours up the wall of the governor's house to Virginie's balcony.

And Georgette—Imogene's interest quickened. Young Georgette, a two-year-younger version of Virginie and clad in one of the simple white dresses her mother thought suitable to her youth and innocence, was talking to the French buccaneer, Captain Vartel, who had paid her a compliment on the quay yesterday as he put away his pistol. If I were Esthonie, I would be more alarmed about *him,* she thought, and her face broke into a smile as she saw a determined Esthonie, having successfully routed Virginie's admirer, already bearing down on the pair.

But that smile swiftly left her face as Vartel, finding his young target spirited away by her mother, turned restlessly, and Imogene found herself looking directly into a pair of cynical dark eyes in a swarthy face topped by a head of curls the color of dark honey. Those eyes were very keen and they had narrowed at sight of her so that she looked into smiling slits that casually raked her gleaming figure up and down. She felt herself flushing under that bold appraising gaze and turned regally to acknowledge the greeting of one of Tortuga's numerous doctors, who had ambled up.

"Are you acquainted with Captain Vartel, Dr. Argyll?" she found herself asking.

"'Vartel'? Yes, of course, although his ship, *Le Sabre,* has not frequented our port much lately."

"Do you know him well?"

"Oh, my goodness no. Who among us knows him well? Never talks about himself at all. Not surprising—his past may not bear talking of!"

"Nor his present! He nearly shot a boy on the quay yesterday."

"Yes, I heard about that." The plump, balding doctor gave her a droll look. "See what mischief beauty makes?"

Imogene ignored his raillery. "You don't know Vartel's background, then?"

"Only that he admits he's French. Probably can't go home, I'll wager! I treated him last fall for a knife wound that festered, asked him how long he'd been in Caribbean waters— said he'd been here a couple of years. Didn't want to discuss it." His pleasant pink face beamed at her roguishly. "Why?? What've ye heard about him?"

"Quite a bit," said Imogene.

"And nothing good, I imagine," chuckled the doctor.

"You are right," she said shortly. "Nothing good." Cruel tales danced about the lean French buccaneer. Tales of plank walkings, of ravished women, of ransoms collected from Spain for women who disappeared never to be seen again. "What does he do with them, those women?" she wondered. "I'm told he goes on long voyages with them aboard. Does he murder them?"

The plump doctor wagged a cheerful finger at her. "Ah, you've been listening to tales again! Ye must remember tongues always wag in Tortuga and take with a grain of salt what ye hear!"

"I am surprised Esthonie invited him."

"You forget they have something in common—they are both French. And our good governor, I'm told, sells Vartel letters of marque—so there's a profit angle involved."

"I am surprised you stay here in Cayona, Dr. Argyll," she said soberly. "I mean—"

"Ye mean," he said shrewdly, "that unlike so many other members of my profession here, there's naught in my background to keep me from returning home?"

Imogene flushed a little, for that was indeed what she had meant. There were half a dozen doctors here tonight, and of them all she guessed that only plump Dr. Argyll would be welcome in his native land.

"Ye're right, lass," he agreed with a sigh. "I left a good practice in Edinburgh—and could go back to it, I suppose, and build it up again. But a nephew of mine—unruly lad always—fell out with the law. He had to flee the country and when his mother—my favorite sister, lass—learnt he'd become a buccaneer and was sore hurt and like to die here in Tortuga, nothing would do but that I take ship and try to save the lad. I got here too late—he'd already been buried, and I ne'er could bring myself to go back and look into her disconsolate face. So I suppose," he added cheerfully, with a glint in his blue eyes, "that you could call that—like others here—my reason for staying away from my homeland. Not so bad a reason as Dunster's there, of course." He nodded at a thin fellow with a greasy smile. "Dunster murdered his wife and children, I'm told—couldn't be proved on him, but his neighbors in Nottingham would have lynched him, so he fled. Or Provence over there''— he turned to view a lecherous-looking fellow in pink satins—*"he's* supposed to have raped an earl's daughter right after he delivered her of a child. Naturally he couldn't stay around after that, and won't be welcomed back to the area!'' His gaze was reflective, but Imogene shuddered.

"This is a terrible place,'' she muttered. "We should both leave it.'' And remembered suddenly what van Ryker had told her—the *real* reason Dr. Argyll stayed on in Cayona. He had taken up with a woman in one of the brothels, a pretty young red-headed slip of a thing from the London streets. *She,* being giddy, refused to leave her profession; *he,* being stubborn, refused to leave *her.* Stalemate, on Tortuga.

Her suddenly guilty gaze flashed at the doctor, who gave her a rather sorrowful smile. "We all have our reasons,'' he told her. "Yours is van Ryker.''

"Yes,'' sighed Imogene. "Mine is van Ryker.''

"A fine fellow, your Dutchman,'' he murmured. "And of good reputation too.''

My *Englishman,* she thought, feeling irritated that she and van Ryker must ever sail under false colors, even with this ingenuous Scotsman. Aloud she declared, "I am proud of him.''

"As well you should be.'' Dr. Argyll wagged his head in approval. "Though de Rochemont tells me he's not so proud of himself, to have brought you here.''

So de Rochemont, the *Sea Rover's* mustachioed and gallant ship's doctor, was telling tales out of school. "I doubt Raoul would know,'' she said distantly.

"Oh, methinks me he would,'' chuckled the doctor. "Van Ryker brought you here with misgivings and why d'ye think he's not left port all these months? He can't take you with him and he fears to leave you here.''

"He *could* take me with him,'' she said in an argumentative voice.

"And risk having you killed, crippled, scarred for life, taken by the Spanish, burned as a heretic, enslaved? He'd have nothing but nightmares!''

Imogene was about to make the tart answer that all of those things could scarcely happen to one person, when the doctor excused himself as one of the dissolute rakes who frequented Tortuga sidled up. This one was named Carmier—he'd given so many last names one never bothered to remember any of them. Men like Carmier drifted in and out of Tortuga on their way to oblivion. Men with shadowy pasts and watchful eyes, often well-read men whose accents and manners bespoke better days. This particular drifter was an officer on board Vartel's ship, *Le Sabre*.

"Madame." He paused dramatically before her and bowed.

"Yes?" Imogene's lashes fluttered disinterestedly.

"I have the honor to present Captain Vartel."

"Captain Vartel and I have already met." Imogene looked past Carmier, who was already beating a retreat, at the tall Frenchman, who was even now sweeping her a bow that let his dark honey hair brush the tile floor. "As recently as yesterday," she added with some irony.

"But I feared you would have forgotten!" Vartel protested innocently.

"Not really." Imogene extended a gloved hand, which he kissed with a flourish. She wondered if van Ryker was watching.

"Madame van Ryker." Vartel continued to hold on to her hand. "You never cease to amaze me." His bold gaze wandered over her in admiration. *"Mon Dieu*, to find such beauty on Tortuga!"

Imogene managed, with some difficulty, to wrest her hand away. "I don't know why you wouldn't, Captain Vartel." Her smile challenged him. "Some of the loveliest ladies of Spain are taken from their galleons and ransomed from this place. Even by you . . . And some . . . " she gave him a veiled look, "are not seen again."

His answering smile was guileless as he shrugged his fawn satin shoulders. "Is it not sad? Such storms beset these waters! The bones of countless beauties as well as gold and treasure and broken ships lie in the deep."

"I had heard that some ladies had disappeared on clear

nights," said Imogene genially. "Beneath skies laden with stars."

"Ah, there you have it," he breathed, and leaned so close she could catch the rich scent of his pipe tobacco and a musky perfume such as the French affected.

"How? How do I have it?" she demanded with asperity.

"The answer, *ma beauté!* Even straitlaced Spanish ladies, so strictly brought up, bound in by iron stays, so guarded in Spain, must sometimes succumb to the languorous air of the Indies. And here on Tortuga in a port aswarm with fiery rogues—*mon Dieu,* do you think they do not feel it?" His French accent thickened perceptibly as his voice grew richer. "Do you think there are not times when a buccaneer storms a balcony, and a lady of Spain prefers to 'disappear' quietly with her lover rather than return to Spain for reshipment to some dull husband or betrothed in the Colonies? Think on such ladies kindly, madame, for perhaps your own reckless heart would have led you in much the same direction."

That *could* be the way it happened, Imogene realized. She stared at this magnetic man before her, feeling the dark concentration of his gaze as if his strong hands were pressed against her face, willing her to do his bidding. And yet, she sensed they were cruel hands—easy to imagine them round one's throat. . . .

"*You* would best know their fate," she murmured, and would have excused herself and gone to find van Ryker but that Esthonie Touraille bustled up.

"Captain Vartel," Esthonie cried in a twittering voice—for now that Georgette was safely out of the way Esthonie could indulge her own tastes—and the governor's wife was ever taken by a handsome face. "You must know all the latest dances, for I am told you are but recently from Paris!"

"I visited there briefly," admitted Vartel, dismissing Paris with a negligent gesture.

And beat a hasty retreat from there too, I'll wager, thought Imogene, with a scathing look at Vartel. *You arrogant French pirate!*

"Of course," cried Esthonie, clapping her hands in de-

light. "Ah, how we envy you. Paris!" The deep breath she
took almost burst her stays. "Lights from a thousand chandeliers, gilded coaches, the *world!*" She paused rapturously.
"But you can bring us a bit of that world, Captain Vartel. I
have arranged for Claude to play the harpsichord and Virginie
and Georgette will sing—if you will only show us the new
dances?"

"But for that I must have a partner." Captain Vartel's hot
gaze rested on Imogene. "Madame van Ryker, would you do
me the honor?"

When Imogene hesitated, Esthonie gave her an irritable
little push, for she herself had hoped for that honor. "Oh, do
go on, Imogene." She waved a fat, black-gloved hand. "For
we are all desperate to learn them."

Claude, who in better days had played church music—
before the vicar's wife had proved irresistible and he had
run from a mob—seated his velvet trousers at the harpsichord
and Virginie and Georgette sidled over to lean against it.
They had a music hall look to them, the governor's daughters, thought Imogene whimsically. With their heavy drooping
lips and dark-lashed eyes, their cheeks artfully reddened with
Spanish paper, one might almost have expected jugglers and
acrobats to swarm after them onto the floor.

Over Captain Vartel's lean shoulder as he led her out onto
the now cleared floor around which people had clustered to
watch, Imogene caught van Ryker's eye. He was frowning.
Undoubtedly he did not approve of her association with
Vartel, who, he had once told her through his teeth, was "a
bad one."

Imogene shrugged and gave her husband a blithe, lighthearted smile as the wiry Frenchman swung her into some
new dance steps that had the women oohing and aahing. Let
van Ryker see what her life would be like if he left her on
Tortuga!

CHAPTER 4

"What brought you to these waters, Captain Vartel?" she asked as he showed her a step, then swung her out to try it beneath the hanging garlands Esthonie had devised.

With arrogant stance his fawn satin figure took a couple of prancing steps, which Imogene imitated faultlessly. "You mean, madame, why did I become a buccaneer?"

"A pirate, I think." She held that steady smile.

He grinned down at her delightedly. "A nice distinction, that! Well, call me what you will. Like your husband"—his lightly accented voice held a slight but meaningful taunt—"I came to these waters for gold."

Her silver satin skirts flew out as she pirouetted in an elaborate step. "And have you found it?"

"A bit." He shrugged. "Not as much as I desire. Nor any so tempting as the gold of your hair. Will you not call me Jacques, that I may call you Imogene?"

She was about to deny him when again she thought of van Ryker, standing across the room with the governor. A good lesson it would be for him to find her already on first names with a man he despised. For still in the back of her mind lurked the possibility that he might relent and take her with him.

"All right—Jacques," she murmured.

He looked very pleased. "Yes—ah, you did that step perfectly, Imogene. This one is a bit trickier. Turn—now your foot so. And turn again. Ah, Imogene, you are an apt pupil!"

"And you, Jacques, are an excellent teacher," she countered, matching him step for step in what was really an elegant new dance. "So good in fact that I am tempted to believe you

61

must have been a dancing master at some time in your checkered career.''

A slight frown of annoyance passed over his dark face, for in his native France dancing masters were not "gentlemen" and although his world had long since turned its back on him, he still jealously guarded that distinction. "Just a frequenter of balls," he corrected her a shade coldly. "Lured there by beautiful ladies like yourself."

"This is as near as we will come to a 'ball' on Tortuga," said Imogene. There was a touch of bitterness in her voice, for she missed the polite society she had known in her native Scilly Isles, the balls at Star Castle when she had stood on a torchlit parapet and looked out over a waste of moonlit islands and rocks stretching far away.

"You sound," he said softly, "as if you too have known better days."

She gave a little start. Her attitude *could* be adjudged a criticism of the man who had brought her to Tortuga, and she had no mind to criticize van Ryker to this Frenchman. "I was young then—and foolish. I am married now." Her voice was stiff.

He chuckled. "You must indeed have been very young then, for I judge you now to be all of eighteen!"

"Almost nineteen." Haughtily. "And I have seen much in my nineteen years."

"Oh, yes," he grinned. "I am sure you have! But you fancy a ball, you say? Would you permit me to give one for you on board my ship, *Le Sabre?*"

Imogene caught her breath. She remembered how van Ryker, in those first days after he had caught up with her, having pursued her across an ocean, had given an improvised "ball' in her honor on board his ship, the *Sea Rover.* She remembered the gaily colored paper lanterns strung above the deck, the creaking of the great ship as it cut the waves heading for America, the music of the violas that went right through you, and the deep full-throated song of the buccaneers. With a tug of her heartstrings, she remembered dancing with van Ryker beneath the stars and thrilling to his touch.

"I—I could not let you give a ball for me," she said on a caught breath. "But *Le Sabre* is indeed a beautiful ship. I have seen her in the harbor."

"Yes, a ship of thirty guns—while your husband has forty." Regretfully. "But she is well named, don't you think? In your language, the *Broadsword*—and with her I sweep the seas!"

"You are also wearing out Georgette as you sweep me about the floor," laughed Imogene. "She is straining so for high notes, her voice nearly cracked on that last one." Her amused gaze was on the girl in the white dress who leaned against the harpsichord.

"The little Georgette has no voice—she should not sing," frowned the dark Frenchman.

"Oh? I thought you were closely closeted with the little Georgette," sparkled Imogene. "At least, your face was very close to her ear when I first saw you and she was giggling like the schoolgirl she is."

"Georgette fancies dangerous men." He shrugged. "She has a wild nature. I think she yearns to run away to sea."

"Her mother will soon scotch that!" Imogene executed an intricate turn and swirled back to face him.

"Who knows?" He smiled and lifted his head so that his dark honey hair swung about. "Georgette is very young, very enticing. A captain such as myself might be persuaded to take the little baggage aboard."

"Oh, you would not!" she gasped, missing a step. "Georgette is only a child!"

His hard dark eyes met her own. They had a steely look. "Girls younger than Georgette are walking to the altar every day," he pointed out.

It was true but—it was wrong, she thought. Little girls, betrothed as children by their parents, to little lads they scarcely knew, walking up the aisle at twelve. Her gaze shot to Esthonie Touraille's youngest daughter, piping her heart out in this smothering hot room. Foolish little Georgette, starry-eyed over every good-looking buccaneer captain, was too young to wed, too young even to know her own mind. If Georgette chose life beside this dark elegant Frenchman today, how would she feel tomorrow when the glamour had worn off?

"You are thinking dark thoughts of me, Imogene," Vartel accused with a chuckle.

"And of myself," she said suddenly. For it came to her with sudden force that she was one of this company—rakehells all. Who was she to criticize? Was she any better? Her past was as stormy as any of theirs.

The dance came to a close amid hearty applause. Imogene's silver satin skirts swept into a deep curtsy and the Frenchman's dark honey locks brushed the floor as he bowed deeply to acknowledge the acclaim of the company.

"We must all try those steps!" cried Esthonie, surging forward to embrace them both.

"I am sure Captain Vartel will be glad to be your tutor," smiled Imogene, pulling away. "While *I* would welcome this chance to teach them to my husband."

Vartel gave her a regretful look. "I have taught lovely women many things that they have later no doubt taught to their husbands," murmured his outrageous voice in her ear.

"I don't doubt it," said Imogene tartly. "Van Ryker." She beckoned the tall silver-clad buccaneer, who was already striding toward her.

"I see you have discovered one of our worst citizens," was his low-voiced comment as the music struck up again and he whirled her out upon the floor.

Imogene shrugged as she matched her step to his. "But then we are renegades all," she said carelessly. "There— with that foot. There, you've got it! And now whirl me around."

But van Ryker had studied the steps as Captain Vartel trod his measure with Imogene, and needed little coaching. "I do not like to hear you describe yourself as a renegade, Imogene," he said soberly. "Nothing in your life warrants it."

"Does it not?" She gave him a bleak look. "Are you saying that I am better than these—renegades of Tortuga?" She faced him frankly and her blue eyes held a tortured look. "No, perhaps I am worse. For I caused so much trouble for so many people who loved me."

A muscle in his jaw worked, and he swung her around with more force than was necessary. "You must not feel so," he told the silver-clad woman. "You were bruised by fate. None of it was your fault."

Automatically, Imogene executed the next step, which brought her satin skirts swirling around his boot tops. "It was *all* of it my fault," she said reflectively. "I have told myself that I could not help it, that circumstances drove me on, but for Bess Duveen there would have been a way." Her voice softened as she named her old friend, now living on Barbados.

"But Bess Duveen would not have been offered your chances," he reminded her.

"I suppose you are right." Imogene sighed. It would have been so good to see Bess again—indeed she might have asked van Ryker to let her visit Bess while he voyaged, but of course she could not. Because Bess was now married to Stephen—and Stephen was Imogene's copper-haired lover of the Scillies. Life tangled you up so. She supposed she would never see Bess again.

She gave van Ryker a melancholy look. Tomorrow or the next day he would depart. God only knew when she would see him again—maybe never. "Are you not afraid to leave me here in this place, van Ryker?" she demanded, her golden curls bouncing with her dance steps. "Surrounded by so many men of"—her soft lips twitched—"unbridled lust? Like the 'worst citizen' you speak of?"

"Vartel is skating on thin ice," van Ryker told her. "If his crimes can be proved against him, he may be cast out of the Brotherhood."

Cast out of the Brethren of the Coast . . . denied the buccaneer stronghold of Tortuga. A chilling thought.

"And who will cast him out, van Ryker?" she asked soberly. "You?"

"If I had proof."

And that would mean, at the very least, a duel between him and the dark Frenchman—at worst a pitched sea battle between the *Sea Rover* and *Le Sabre*. Her heartstrings tightened—she did not want either to happen.

"Those women who disappeared, you mean?" she asked

argumentatively. "Because nobody knows what happened to them? I charged him with it and he told me they had run away with buccaneer lovers. Suppose it is true? They *could* have disappeared in that fashion so word would not get back to shame their families in Barcelona or Madrid."

Van Ryker snorted. "A persuasive talker is Jacques! And did you believe him?"

Before the hot force of his gaze, she felt herself flushing. If Vartel *had* spirited away those women, of course he must be brought to account for it.

"Did you believe him?" repeated van Ryker harshly.

"I don't know," she admitted thoughtfully. "Yes, I think I did when he said it, but now across the room from him, I am not so sure." She gave her tall buccaneer a slanted look. "Jacques has asked if he might not give a ball for me on board his ship. . . ."

She could feel the sudden tension in van Ryker's body. "You will of course refuse," he said firmly.

"Oh, I have not given him my answer yet," shrugged Imogene, whirling back to face him in the dance. "Who knows, the days may grow very long without you. . . ." It was a desperate thrust to get him to change his mind and take her with him, but it did not work. His face went cold and he bowed and relinquished her without comment, as the music crashed to a close, to his ship's doctor, de Rochemont, who was an expert dancer.

"What do *you* think of Jacques Vartel, Raoul?" Imogene asked him frankly, after Claude had wiped his perspiring face and begun to play again.

De Rochemont's mustaches swayed as he laughed and led her out on to the floor. "I think Jacques is a liar and worse," he said. "He comes of a fine old French family. 'tis rumored— and Vartel is not his real name. He is what you English would call a 'black sheep.' He has fled from his debts and misdeeds in half the cities of Europe, falling ever deeper. I suppose it is only natural that he would end up here—like the rest of us."

"And the women whose ransoms he received and who never reached home again?"

De Rochemont frowned as he executed a difficult step.

"*That* I do not understand," he admitted. "A Frenchman might have kept a likely *jeune fille* around as a mistress, but kill them—not likely. I disagree with your husband about that. Van Ryker believes that Vartel, for reasons of his own, may have caused their disappearance."

Imogene glanced over de Rochemont's brocade shoulder at the swarthy Frenchman, who at this moment was teaching Virginie Touraille the new steps—to the accompaniment of many giggles and stepped-on-toes. He was dangerous, he was attractive, he had turned on her the brilliance of his charm. And there was an innate cruelty she had sensed in him. But was he a murderer of women? Remembering the caressing touch of his hand as he led her out on the floor, she could not believe it.

The evening had progressed and Imogene was dancing with van Ryker again when Captain Vartel, now teaching the new dance steps to young Georgette, who laughed aloud as she trod on his toes, looked over her tossing dark curls and studied the pair narrowly.

Of solid silver, they seemed—glittering, unique. The tall buccaneer with his thick shock of gleaming shoulder-length dark hair and his strong silver-clad body built for battle. The woman, delectable in her silver tissue, a woman of tinsel and fire, moving like a moth in the candlelight, with the same candlelight dancing in her delft-blue eyes as she looked up at van Ryker and turning her fair hair to glowing gold.

Handsome, well matched, a *set*. The Frenchman's dark eyes glittered. This was a set he was determined to break up.

Imogene, meeting his hard gaze suddenly as van Ryker spun her out into the dance, lifted her chin and gave the Frenchman back an insolent stare.

Vartel inclined his head in a slight but wicked acknowledgment of that stare and his bold gaze traced the outlines of her lovely figure meaningfully.

Imogene turned her head away irritably. Vartel's intentions seemed to her clear enough, even though unwelcome.

But she would have been startled had someone told her that it was Vartel himself who had sent yesterday's "message" from Captain Flogg, he who had offered a poor and desperate

young Lark Saxon money to do it—although that bit of
bravado on the quay when he had drawn his dueling pistol
and aimed it at Lark had caused the terrified lad to flee
without trying to collect. And she would have been stunned to
learn that Vartel had brought his ship, *Le Sabre,* to Tortuga
for reasons that had nothing to do with buccaneering, reasons
that involved only her—and van Ryker.

No hint of any of that crossed her mind of course.

But van Ryker, with that sixth sense that came of surviving
many a battle, was warned. Something deep inside, some
note of caution was struck. For van Ryker had seen the way
the dark Frenchman had looked at Imogene. He had seen the
rapier-thin Vartel smile that wide wolfish smile in admiration
of her beauty—and then turn to him with a narrow appraising
glance. That look of Vartel's had had the quality of a narrow
blade sliding in between his shoulder blades.

Suddenly, for no reason that he could pin down, he questioned
Vartel's eagerness to shoot down that lad on the quay yesterday. At the time he had assumed it was only a stage gesture
designed to impress Imogene. Now suddenly he was not so
sure.

And when Imogene was claimed for the next dance by a
puffing but merry Dr. Argyll and van Ryker sought the garden
as a relief from the oppressive heat of the dance floor, and
found himself brushing inadvertently against Vartel, who was
of like mind, he gave the French pirate a sudden challenging
look. "D'ye know Captain Flogg?" he asked innocently.

Captain Vartel's dark eyes went wary. "Not that I remember," he said innocently. "Isn't he a tall, slender reed of a
fellow?"

"No, he's built like a bear with a grizzled black beard,"
said van Ryker.

"Is there some special reason why I should know him?"
drawled the Frenchman.

Van Ryker knew he had nothing solid to confront him
with—naught but an unfounded suspicion. "No," he said
reluctantly. "But from something that happened yesterday, I
thought you might."

Vartel's dark eyes widened. He was damnably clever, this "Dutch" buccaneer who spoke perfect English! Plainly, he'd have to watch his step. He did not inquire what that "something" was, for that might have provoked a quarrel and he was not ready for that—at least not yet. Instead, he tried an angled thrust.

"I've offered to give a ball on board *Le Sabre* in your lady's honor," he said, eyes glinting. "She mentioned the lack of luster in Tortuga society and it seemed fitting."

"Fitting or not, she must refuse you," said van Ryker, giving the Frenchman a level look. "For she sets no foot off dry land when I'm not with her."

"Oh, I could guarantee her safety," said the Frenchman impudently.

"I've no doubt of it." Van Ryker's tone was ironic. "But she still regrets."

The tropical night hung heavy around them. Music from the harpsichord drifted out. Through the open door they could see Imogene's silvery form drifting by in the throng.

"You're sailing shortly, I hear?" The question was couched in a tone faultlessly correct but the implication was still there. *You will be gone and I will still be here. We will see what happens then!*

That implication was not lost on van Ryker.

"Yes," he said shortly. "I will be sailing soon." His cold gray gaze raking the Frenchman said that sailing or not, he would keep his woman!

"A long voyage?" pursued Vartel insolently.

"A short one. I find myself eager to return to my bride even before I have left her."

"Spoken like a Frenchman," murmured Vartel with a smile, and broke off as Esthonie Touraille erupted through the doorway, bore down on them.

"Ah, here you are!" she scolded Vartel. "Hiding in the garden, when every lady here is anxious to be taught the new steps. Come along!"

Vartel shrugged and let himself be tugged away by Esthonie.

But van Ryker stood thoughtful and alone in the tropical

darkness, looking after the departing pair. A clever cutthroat that one, and after Imogene—obviously. And she was young and would be alone and bored.

He frowned into the darkness, realizing forcibly the kind of company in which he left her: The governor's guests came from half a dozen nations. Many had been gentlemen—once. But among them were men who could be bought to do anything—for money. Women who had sold themselves to the highest bidder, even though Esthonie did make an effort to keep *those* out. There were tough grizzled bandits like the absent Flogg who'd grow bolder once the shrouds on the *Sea Rover's* tall masts disappeared over the horizon. And worse— there were men like Vartel waiting like spiders to lure lustrous Imogene into deadly danger.

He was silent on the way home.

"What are you thinking about?" asked Imogene, picking her way carefully beside him over the uneven street.

He was thinking in fact of a letter that had come only this week—and another two months earlier. Between them, they had altered the course of his life.

For van Ryker had made a deep internal vow when he had married Imogene that he would give up buccaneering, that he would make a settled home for her. It was to have been his great surprise as he settled his affairs here in Tortuga.

Those letters, both urgently demanding money, had changed all that. Now he must make at least one more run, hope for some gilded Spanish galleon to come beneath his guns, some treasure ship from the *flota*. He could not stop. Not just yet.

"Nothing," he lied. "I was not thinking of anything. Did you enjoy the party?"

"It was above average for one of Esthonie's parties," she admitted, thinking how dull those parties would be after he sailed. "I suppose it was the new dance steps Captain Vartel brought from France that made the difference," she added flippantly.

He let that pass, but once they were home and in their big square bedroom and Imogene, with her back to him, was slipping out of her silver gown, he gave her a tormented look, strode over to her.

"Imogene," he said, "you must promise me that when I leave, you will not accept Vartel's invitation to give a ball for you on board his ship."

Imogene stepped out of her stiff pewter satin petticoat before she answered. Now she straightened up and turned her fearless gaze upon him.

"If you will not take me with you, van Ryker"—the hardness of her voice matched his own—"and you object to my little . . . *pleasures*" (he guessed she was speaking of cards and dice) "why, then I must entertain myself as best I can. With Captain Vartel—or someone like him."

"By God, you will not."

His hand closed over her wrist so hard it cut off her circulation. She winced but kept her back erect, her face haughty and unyielding. She shrugged.

"I must needs while away the time some way," she said bitterly. "You *cannot* expect me to spend all my time with the governor's wife!"

Van Ryker was bending over her now, his dark hair falling down over his hawklike face, his gray eyes dangerous and wild. "Swear. *Swear* you will have nothing to do with Vartel while I am gone—good God, don't you know he could spirit you away as he did those other women?"

"You don't know he did that!"

"Swear," he said violently.

She shrugged again. "Very well, I swear." As his grip on her wrist relaxed, she massaged it and gave him a slanted, malicious look. "Someone else of interest will doubtless come along. . . ."

They stared at each other, two violent people each bent on having their own way—well-matched antagonists.

"You are determined to go with me, aren't you?" he said at last, studying her.

"At any cost," Imogene told him calmly.

"Have you no conception what my fate could be?"

Her chin went up. "I want to share that fate." In that moment she looked as proud, as inflexible as he. Outside their window a snatch of drunken song drifted up as a buccaneer unsteadily made his way home from a tavern. The trade winds were blowing and the tropic night closed soft about them. "Oh, van Ryker." There was real pain in Imogene's voice. "Don't leave me behind—I couldn't bear it."

That soft wail had touched him and now he enclosed her in his arms. "Imogene, Imogene," he murmured. "What am I to do with you?"

"You should have thought of that," she said half humorously, "before you chased me across an ocean."

"Yes," he said. "I should."

She laughed softly against his chest. "You should have taken one look at me and escaped while you could."

"That too," he agreed.

"I was not meant to languish alone."

"No," he said. "Any fool could see that." He stepped back and considered his lustrous bride. His gaze was speculative, somewhere between anger and amusement. He began to pace about the room.

Suddenly he turned to her with a grim expression. Imogene held her breath.

"So you do not wish to stay on Tortuga?" he said. "Very well—pack!"

"Oh, van Ryker!" She threw her arms around him joyfully. "You are going to take me with you!"

Captain Vartel was delighted when he heard that van Ryker had taken Imogene with him when he sailed. Everything, he told himself contentedly, was working out exactly according to his plan.

PART TWO:
The Hidden Past

Not to have known, nor cared to know—
Far happier she'd be!
But the lid of Pandora's box is breached
And its secrets all flown free!

The High Seas, 1660
CHAPTER 5

"What do you *mean* you're leaving me in Carolina?" demanded Imogene, aghast. She was leaning against the taffrail of the *Sea Rover's* swaying deck as she spoke and a brisk wind was blowing her bright hair and yellow linen skirts. "You told me you were taking me with you on this voyage!"

"Only a part of it." Van Ryker stood solidly before her, surveying her calmly with his steady gray gaze. "I never told you you could go buccaneering with me—only that I'd be taking you with me when I sailed. We're making a fast run to Carolina."

She stared at him in dismay, for it had been so wonderful to be back aboard the familiar *Sea Rover*, to taste the salt air and see above her the whipping white shrouds as the big ship flew before the wind. She had not even questioned where they were going.

Now her mind raced back, remembering that the *Hawk* and the *Heron* had been left behind when they sailed. Both were waiting for some foodstuffs that were slow in coming, van

Ryker had said carelessly. The *Sea Rover* would rendezvous with them later.

Of course she had imagined that rendezvous would take place far to the south, since the gold-filled galleons of the treasure *flota* would be beating their way from Panama northeastward out of the Caribbean into the North Atlantic in their bid to reach Spain. But she had paid little attention when the *Sea Rover* drove north—even less when her great prow swung to the west. Ah, she thought bitterly, she should have been warned!

But of course her mind had not been on their destination—she had really given no thought to that. All her being had been concentrated on the love she bore him.

That first night out with Tortuga behind them, she had leaned against van Ryker on the twilit deck and watched the silvery phosphorescence of the sea and marveled at its beauty.

"I wish we could sail to eternity like this," she had murmured wistfully.

The strong arm that was thrown lightly about her shoulders tightened and the tall buccaneer looked down tenderly upon her. "I wish we could, Imogene—but all voyages must end."

She had not asked him where theirs would end, content to lean against his hard chest and feel the steady rhythmic rise and fall of his leathern doublet, to smell above the salt wind the faint pleasant scent of Virginia tobacco.

"Esthonie Touraille won't believe it when she finds I have gone," she laughed.

"Esthonie Touraille is a woman of sense," he said grimly.

"But boring."

"As you say—boring."

"I will have so much to tell her—to tell them all. Of how we sacked some Spanish town, or brought some great golden galleon to heel."

He did not answer but continued looking out into the glow of the sea, and she was reminded that all week they had sighted but one ship—and that an English merchantman, which they had saluted as they passed her by. No Spanish sails had darkened the horizon. Imogene was secretly glad, for she dreaded the battle that must come—not for herself but for the tall man beside her.

It was a magic evening. The sun's last rays had departed in rosy splendor and now the moon was tracing a pale wake across the ocean's shining surface. They might have been alone in the world, for van Ryker's men had tactfully left him and his lady to their enjoyment of this part of the deck. It was a definite mark of respect. To the buccaneers who sailed with him van Ryker was more than human—almost a god, for he had led them through dangers they felt must have laid low an ordinary mortal. And his golden lady was to them an angel.

Imogene would have been surprised and touched to know how they felt about her.

"When I was a little girl in the Scilly Isles, I used to dream of sailing away in some great white ship," she laughed.

"Where were you bound—in your imagination?"

"Oh, nowhere. I think I planned to leave land far behind and sail forever."

"Weren't you happy in the Scillies?" he asked thoughtfully.

"Not really. My guardian worried about my future and was always thrusting some unattractive suitor at me. And then— well, you know how I fled to Amsterdam and met you there the very day I sailed for America."

"I am not apt to forget that day," he said gravely. He was remembering her as he had first seen her there, gloriously beautiful and on the arm of her betrothed, who heartily disapproved of buccaneers and their ilk. "I chased you half across an ocean, Imogene."

"The surprising thing is that you caught up with us on the high seas."

"You were never far from my sight."

"And yet you waited. . . . Why was that, van Ryker?"

"I think I was fighting it," he sighed. "For I knew you belonged to another man who could give you more—so much more."

"Nonsense," she scoffed. "He gave me a terrible time. Of course, it was my own fault—I should never have married him."

"We are all the product of our mistakes—I as well as you."

"Barnaby and Raoul tell me you never make mistakes. They sing your praises."

The look of melancholy in his gray eyes deepened. "Then they are wrong," he said sardonically. "Barnaby, as ship's master, approves my seamanship. Raoul, as ship's doctor, delights that I heal fast!"

He felt the slight shiver that went through her at this reminder that where he sailed there was not only golden treasure but fighting and death. And once again he cursed himself—as he had so many times before—that he had brought the woman he loved into this dangerous way of life. She would be furious, he knew, when she learned his plans for her but he was hard-pressed to think of a safer place for her than Carolina.

"Was your boyhood happy, van Ryker?"

"Part of it." He thought of hawking through the woodlands and riding across the meadows under a blue sky, he remembered the halls of home when he had confidently expected to grow up a respected gentleman of Devon and take to wife a lady who would sire his sons at a hearth like his father's . . . all that life he had left behind him forever when he became a buccaneer.

"You never tell me about it," she said, idly stroking the smooth leather of his doublet.

"That is because I find I have forgotten it," he lied—because it hurt him even now to think about those golden days of his youth before his world had turned against him.

"But I would like to know what the world was like that shaped you, the places, the people you knew. . . ."

"They were like any county gentry in Devon, good and solid. My father was an honorable man, my mother came of a good family in Somerset. I expected a goodly inheritance to start me out, even though I was a younger son, born of my father's second wife." Suddenly he could not face telling her all those things. "I would rather you spoke of your own beginnings," he said softly, burying his face in her hair.

"I was born a flirt," she laughed. "As well you know!"

His strong features relaxed into a grin. "Flirts come to grief," he warned. "They find rovers and buccaneers!" He swept her up into his arms and carried her, laughing, into his great cabin, kicked the door shut behind him, and began to undress her.

Imogene gave a little gasp as he slipped her bodice expertly down from her shoulders, cupped each breast and kissed it. "I am a lucky man, Imogene," he murmured. "And I intend to enjoy that luck!"

"Van Ryker," she protested. "Every time I want to talk, you cut off the conversation by making love to me!"

His answer was to murmur, "You don't need these," as his hands, reaching beneath her skirts, brushed the tops of her stockings. "Here, I'll help rid you of them."

Imogene fought back little bursts of feeling as he eased the stockings luxuriously from her legs, flung them away. She squirmed in his arms.

"I want to know more about you!" she protested.

"You know all that's important."

"Why can't I be the judge of that?"

He stepped back and looked at her steadily. The only sound was the creaking of the great ship's timbers as she cut the seas. "What is it you wish to know, Imogene?"

Beneath that sudden intent scrutiny she felt nonplussed. "I—suppose nothing special. Just—everything."

A smile broke over his face at her answer and he began swiftly to divest himself of his clothing. His sword clattered as he flung it aside. "Everything. Well, that should take a deal of telling. Have you thought where I should begin?"

"When you were born, of course," she said comfortably, moving away from him—for she fully intended that she should know more about this man she had married before she removed her petticoat and chemise.

"When I was born? Ah, that's a good time. I was born in a coach on the way to Taunton, for my grandmother had taken ill there and naught would have it but my mother must go to her. Halfway there, she was delivered of me."

"How dreadful!" gasped Imogene, thinking of the discomforts of a coach—especially for giving birth. "Did she go back?"

"No, she went on to Taunton."

A determined woman, who had given birth to a determined son. "And your father?"

"He was at sea then. He came back to find me the terror of my nurses—and later the terror of the neighborhood. As I grew up I took up dangerous sports and excelled at them—the most dangerous was wenching." He made a dive for her. She yelped and tried to sidestep him, but she was too late. He swept her inexorably backward upon the bunk and pulled off her petticoat and chemise while she resisted playfully.

"What you really want to know"— his voice was muffled as his lips caressed her neck—"is, did I ever love another woman?"

"And did you?"

"Hundreds," he said comfortably, and moved his long body in one lithe movement so that he rested above her, lying on his elbows, looking down smiling into her face, with his hips resting lightly on her own.

"Be serious!" She gave his shoulder a playful cuff and the motion made her hips slither sensuously beneath his and brought a fiery light into his gray eyes.

"I am always serious about so serious a subject!" He nuzzled her breasts impudently and felt them quiver beneath this sweet assault.

"Van Ryker!" she gasped, trying to pull away. "Did you really ever love another woman?"

"I thought I did once—but that was a long time ago."

She felt a stab of bright burning jealousy of this unknown woman who had had first chance at him. "What happened to her?"

"I don't know. I left."

She was about to ask. *Why? Why did you leave?* But his hips moved subtly above hers and his sudden expert thrust into her loins left her senses atingle so that she melted against him, moving as he moved, in silken ecstasy. Passion clouded her mind and made her forget all those things she wanted to know, all those things he had never told her and about which she was so curious. She was one with him now, moving through a silvery phosphorescence of their own, just as the tall ship glided through silver seas, a shimmering world of racing senses and mad delight.

When he had finished, he lay caressing her, bringing back to her tingling body little bursts of after-feeling that made her skin seem to glow and her heart to race. She lay beside him, lazy and content, forgetful of all her questions.

It was always that way.

Until this morning when he had calmly announced that they were on their way to Carolina, that he would leave her there and continue his venture and pick her up later.

"But—what's in Carolina that you would leave me *there?*" She was baffled.

"My plantation," he said, astonishing her by his answer. " 'Tis called Longview, and I'm leaving you there—in care of my brother."

"Your brother? But I didn't know you had a family!" Somehow, since he never talked about them, she had assumed they were all dead.

"Well, I do. I've two half-brothers and a half-sister."

Above them the shrouds crackled as they stared into each other's eyes.

"When did you buy this—plantation?" she asked in an altered voice.

She had expected him to say, "After I married you," but his answer surprised her. "Several years ago. And I have not one but two plantations. One is in Carolina. The other, which I call Gale Force for the winds that were blowing when first I saw it, is in Jamaica. It is under the supervision of my elder brother, Anthony. Longview in Carolina is under the supervision of my brother Charles."

"Your half-brothers, you say?"

"Yes."

"And what of your half-sister?"

"Esme is married and living in France."

"Two plantations," she murmured. "I can hardly credit it!"

"It was meant to be a great and happy surprise for you," he told her ruefully. "For after we were wed I had meant to give up this buccaneering life and settle down as a planter."

"Then why do you not?"

"Neither of my brothers is well suited to the life," he told her reluctantly. "They are not the best of managers—although Anthony is somewhat better than Charles."

"Then why do you not employ a good factor?"

"I have a good factor named MacDermott at Longview, and I had another good factor named MacNaughton at Gale Force."

" 'Had'?"

"I've received word that MacNaughton died recently of a long illness of which I was not apprised. Now I fear me things may have gone sadly amiss at Gale Force. 'Twas the reason I decided not to leave you in Jamaica."

There was another reason, one he did not tell her, and that was Gale Force's proximity to Port Royal—a wild town, frequented by buccaneers, such men as Vartel and Flogg. Imogene's beauty was a challenge to any man—let alone a hot-blooded buccaneer. It had seemed safer to hide her away in Carolina.

"MacNaughton and MacDermott," she mused. "You trust the Scots, I see."

"Yes, I trust the Scots. And good men both—but frequently overriden by my brothers, usually to everyone's regret."

"Why have you made this arrangement?" she asked bluntly. "And why have I not heard of it before?"

Footsteps were approaching. Barnaby Swift, striding about the deck, taking the air. "Come to the great cabin and I will tell you about it," van Ryker muttered. "For my men do not know about it."

"None of them? Not even Barnaby and Raoul?"

"De Rochemont knows, for I babbled once in delirium when I had sustained a deep wound—but he is sworn to secrecy."

"But *why?*" she demanded, when the door to the great cabin had closed behind them. "For I know you would trust Barnaby with your life!"

"That is true," he said, moving restlessly over to the bank of slanted windows in the stern. He ran a hand through his dark hair, staring out to sea. Imogene sank down on a bench adorned with a garnet velvet cushion, tasseled in gold. She leaned her elbows on the massive black oak table that graced the center of the room and waited. She had long wondered about van Ryker's past and now, she sensed, he was about to tell her.

"Because I had thought one day to change my life around—even before I met you. I had thought when I found the right woman that I would cause word of my 'death at sea' to be circulated and retire to my plantations—which is difficult, for I am a man with a price on his head."

"Van Ryker," she said softly. "Come here and sit down and tell me all about it."

He did not stir from his place at the bank of windows. He looked very solid standing there, tall and purposeful. The ship's lamp swung gently overhead. "Once I tried to tell you my real name," he said. "Only then you did not wish to hear."

"I was a fool," she said bitterly.

He ignored that. Whether he agreed with her or not, she was never to know. "Later I told myself that I would tell you my real name only when I had cleared it, when I could offer it to you like a bright sword in the sun."

She drew in her breath. She had not known he felt about it like that.

"But now I must tell you, for tomorrow if this wind holds we will reach the Carolina coast and perhaps be dining with Charles. At Longview only Charles knows that I am the infamous buccaneer Ruprecht van Ryker. At Longview, I am myself again—Branch Ryder, late gentleman of Devon."

"And I will be—"

"Imogene Ryder."

" 'Imogene Ryder.' " She savored that. It had a lovely sound to it but then—so had van Ryker. "But if there is a price on your head," she pursued, "how do you dare—?"

"How do I dare to use my real name there? I am wanted in England, not the Colonies. And I am seldom at Longview.

Charles fronts for me in Carolina—just as Anthony does in Jamaica. As far as the world knows, Charles owns Longview and Anthony owns Gale Force."

A little pang went through her. So much, so much had been denied him. "But you are known there," she murmured.

"Yes, but only as a brother who has visited but twice in these years: once when the deal was concluded, and once to bring plans for the house."

That quickened her interest. "Are they nice houses?" She had been almost afraid to ask.

"The house at Longview is built of logs. I will add to it later. Eventually it will have a broad sweeping front and tall white pillars to shade a veranda down the front and around the four sides. It is not large, but with verandas sweeping all the way around it, there will always be shade even in the hottest weather."

"And Gale Force?"

"There the house is of stone with a patio, much on the same plan as my house in Tortuga."

So she was destined to become mistress of far-flung plantations. It came as something of a shock to a woman who had placed her hand in a buccaneer's and half expected to finish with him on the gibbet!

"Is there much land?" she asked.

"Vast," he assured her. "Both are large estates and will need years of developing. I fear me neither Charles nor Tony are the men for it, but—" He shrugged.

"Then why don't you do something about it?"

"I had meant to buy them both other plantations, of course, when I returned and took over—to show my gratitude. I had hoped to buy me a king's pardon, but at the moment that is difficult. I have not the right friends to sue for me at court. And—" How could he tell her of the frenzied letters that were always coming his way, letters telling him crops had failed, woodlands burned, ships foundered, slaves sickened and died, bondservants deserted and fled? "This seems not the time," he said a bit sadly.

"Why did you bring your brothers here?" she marveled.

"Since you say they aren't suited to it? Why didn't you just use factors?"

"Because I owe them something, Imogene." He turned to her morosely. "I have tried to pay my debts."

"You owe them?" She was puzzled.

"Yes." He began to walk about the room with his hands clasped behind him, moving restlessly as he talked. "I told you once how my father, a shipowner, was taken by the Spanish on the high seas, thrust into a dungeon and left to rot?"

"Yes, and how your mother ransomed him. And that he died from his maltreatment on the way home." Imogene shuddered.

"Yes." Grimly. "My mother ransomed him—and it took all we had. She sold the family home—a gracious mansion set on broad acres in Devon, and named Ryderwood—and all its furnishings to raise the ransom for him. She was his second wife and loved him well. I was her only child. The children of his first wife—Anthony and Charles and Esme— were all away visiting their kinsmen at the time. They knew nothing of the sale until they returned to find everything swept away from them. They took the loss very hard and accused my mother and me of keeping it from them—and causing their ruin. Shortly afterward my mother died and I took to the sea. Anthony and Charles and Esme became wards of their dead mother's kinsmen and an unhappy life it was from what they tell me."

"You blame yourself for—through your mother—costing them everything?" she divined.

"Yes. For the sale of Ryderwood did no good. My father died anyway before he could reach us. We were all left destitute and that was very hard on his older children, who had expected to inherit his lands and his honors."

"*You* did not expect to inherit these things?"

"I suppose I never thought about it," he muttered. "I felt I would be taken care of, of course—but since the sale of Ryderwood, which I advocated to my mother in their absence, I have always felt that I owed my brothers a living. To my sister I have paid my debt—in other coin."

" 'Other coin'?"

"Yes, I want you to know the truth, Imogene—but I forbid you to speak of it. Charles may speak about it, but even he has not the real facts. Esme was but a little older than myself, and of slight build—about like yourself. I grew up feeling protective toward her, as if she were a younger sister instead of an older one—you must understand that for what I am about to tell you. Esme always turned to me rather than to Tony or Charles when she needed protection."

Any woman would turn to you for that, she thought proudly.

"I did not remain at sea long when first I went buccaneering— indeed it was never my intention. I meant to revenge myself on Spain for killing my father, get myself a tidy sum to start me out and become a planter in one of the Colonies. But I wished to return home first. No one in Devon knew I had become a buccaneer, there was no great danger. So I hied me to Dunworth Hall, where my brothers and sister were then living. It was a great pile of a place and I found my brothers living there as near-servants and my sister pushed into the background by her wealthier cousins."

How angry that must have made you! thought Imogene.

"Worst of all, Vincent Dunworth, eldest of their cousins, was a notorious lecher. He had cast his eye on Esme and meant to have her. The night I arrived, he had raped her—and she had killed him."

Stunned, Imogene stared at him across the black walnut table. Around them the great timbers creaked.

"She was near hysterical and threw her arms around me and babbled that I must save her from jail and worse—for Vincent had been a careful lecher and had scrupulously kept from the servants his intentions on Esme. She feared a trial and hanging."

"I can see she might," murmured Imogene.

"I had some money with me. I gave it to Charles and told him to take Esme and spirit her away into France, where she would be safe from English law. And I made Anthony promise to swear he had seen me kill Vincent."

Imogene leaned forward. "But even so, the law would have been on your side! For you had but defended your sister from a rapist!"

He shook his dark head. "I had to protect Esme's reputation. A woman with a sullied reputation and no money has little chance to marry in a world where women so outnumber men." That was true, she knew—*thirteen women for every man in London,* some said. "So I left a note admitting the deed—and fled."

Imogene's heart sank in her chest. He had condemned himself by his own hand.

"So after that there was a price on your head?" she said dully.

"Yes, for the murder of Vincent Dunworth—a man I had never laid eyes on whilst alive. The Dunworths are a vengeful clan. A trial was held in my absence and I was condemned to death. That sentence will be carried out if I return to England."

"And in the Colonies?"

"Perhaps. If word reached the Dunworths—perhaps. But word may never reach them. I told Anthony to meet me in Jamaica, and as Charles left, I told him after he had gotten Esme settled in France, to join us there. Charles had no trouble getting Esme settled, it seems. She had beauty and a Frenchman named Ribaud saw it. He had wealth to offer her—at least he would one day inherit a large fortune. Charles saw them safely married and joined us on Jamaica, where I had scraped up enough to buy Gale Force. With my buccaneer ventures, I managed to raise a house there and enough to settle Charles in Carolina on large lands at Longview. Understand that my brothers were destitute, and I a bachelor."

"Are either of them married now?"

"No. Only Esme."

"And has her marriage worked out?"

He hesitated. "Esme has married a wastrel, as it turns out. Her Jules is currently estranged from his family and I have twice sent money to keep him from debtors' prison. Jules gambles," he added wryly.

What would they all do without you, van Ryker? she wondered silently. *These half-relations hung around your neck like a millstone?*

Van Ryker's face was grave. He rested his knuckles on the black walnut table and stood looking down at her. "Should I die, you will inherit the plantations, the house in Cayona, everything, It is my intention after this voyage to resettle my brothers on smaller, more manageable plantations of their own—estates more suited to their capacities. But if something should happen to me in the meantime, I would ask that you make a fair distribution among them."

Imogene swallowed. "I would do that, of course," she told him softly. "For I know they mean a great deal to you."

"They are all foolish," he said. "They said wild vengeful things when they returned to find themselves destitute—and by my mother's hand and mine. But I am convinced they were in a state of panic and did not mean the things they said. You see, Esme's mother died bearing her and Esme never would accept my mother's teachings—she went her own precocious way. As for my half-brothers, my father was gone during much of their formative years and they learned to be foolhardy and vain. But they are the only family I have, Imogene—and at heart they are good."

Imogene hoped that was so. She gave van Ryker a tender smile. A man so gallant deserved unshakable loyalty.

The Carolina Coast,
1660

CHAPTER 6

Morning found them on the Carolina coast, the pink dawn
picking out features of a smooth and pleasant landscape, the
mouth of a river and a white beach. Van Ryker chose to cast
anchor at the mouth of that river, which he told her was the
Cooper River, and traverse the short distance upriver by
longboat.

The rowing crew seemed not much interested in the terrain,
rowing along stolidly, thinking this just another call at a
plantation making a deal to barter goods. Imogene realized
van Ryker had probaby chosen them for their lack of imagination.

Only de Rochemont, who sat in the stern with his doctor's
bag, showed any interest, looking about him brightly but
without comment. Barnaby had been left with the ship, for
any emergency could arise and van Ryker trusted Barnaby to
meet it, but de Rochemont, she guessed, had been brought
along not so much because he was in van Ryker's confidence
but because he was a doctor and there was always need of
doctoring among bondservants and slaves in these isolated
places.

She herself sat with van Ryker in the prow and stared about

her at this wild new land that was to be her home until he came for her.

Seabirds—black skimmers, gulls, and brown pelicans—wheeled overhead as they progressed upriver past banks lined with live oaks and magnolias and hickories, and hung with luxuriant overhanging vines. Gray Spanish moss festooned some of the huge trees, hanging down like long gray beards. At times palmetto clumps seemed to overpower the other growth, giving a rich tropical look to the landscape. At other times pond pines and tall cypresses reared their heads among the jessamine and sweet bay and smilax. They saw deer and marsh rabbits come down to the water's edge to drink and twice snakes floated by in the water. This land abounded in game, van Ryker told her proudly, and a dinner of wild turkey or venison was to be expected.

But Imogene was not looking for wild game. She kept looking for signs of civilization—and saw none.

"Longview will be around the next bend," he told her, and she strained forward.

As the wooden pier came into view around the bend of the river, she shaded her eyes and bent forward, trying to make out the house. Ah, there it was, among the trees. It was set well back, she could see that, and the land sloped gently up to it. As they came closer she saw that it was constructed of cypress logs and was large by log-house standards, but to her disappointment it was not beautiful.

"One day I will have me here a house of stone," murmured van Ryker as they disembarked. "Built around this that you see."

Imogene tried to imagine it and could not. The tall heavy old trees with their luxuriant foliage pressed in close, the yard was uncared for, there was a complete lack of landscaping—not a rosebush, not a shrub had been planted—and even from here the small-paned windows looked dirty and she could see that several were broken.

But van Ryker, she knew from his stance and the way he took a deep expansive breath as he looked about him in a proprietary way, saw sweeping lawns and well-tended gardens and a sturdy pier and a grand house rising gracefully in the background—the world that was yet to be.

"Be warned, they will call my brother the landgrave," he murmured as he helped her from the boat.

" 'Landgrave'? What does that mean?"

"Owner of forty-eight thousand acres," he told her laconically.

She gave him a look of shock. *Forty-eight thousand acres?* Could there be that much land in all of the Scilly Isles? And *he* was the landgrave—not his brother. *She* was the landgrave's wife!

"I wonder where everybody is." He was looking about him, frowning. Around them the stillness was oppressive.

Imogene cast her glance toward the house. Nothing had moved there.

It was their first hint that something was wrong.

Now van Ryker was striding toward the house and she was hard put to keep up with him. De Rochemont had hurried up and was sprinting along beside him with the buccaneers straggling after. De Rochemont, she noted, had his hand upon his sword.

Van Ryker threw open the front door—which was unlocked—and she and de Rochemont followed him into the large main room of the log building. Chairs and tables were over-turned, a big cupboard lay face down among broken dishes. Pots and pans and other household implements were tossed about on the hard-packed earthen floor. Now she saw that there was an arrow stuck in the cupboard and that the leg had been slashed from a bench. Plainly there had been fighting here.

Van Ryker was cursing under his breath.

Suddenly Imogene gave a little cry. A man's foot was sticking out from the doorway that led into the next room—and that foot had just moved.

" 'Tis MacDermott!" Van Ryker bent over the fallen man, who was clad in buckskins and had a shock of graying hair. "What happened, man?"

The Scot lifted his head a little. He had a ruddy face gone ashen. There was a bloody gash in his cheek and his voice

was weak. One of his legs seemed to be broken. Beside him
lay a long musket and a sword.

"Your brother—Charles," he gasped.

"What about Charles? Is he dead?"

"No—fled."

Van Ryker's shoulders rocked as if he had been struck a
solid blow. He stepped aside that de Rochemont might tend
the injured man. "We will get ye to the ship, MacDermott,"
he said in an altered voice. "After the doctor here takes care
of your wounds. What of the others?"

MacDermott rallied but his voice was faint. "I think Will
Canady is dead and the slaves have all run off. I've lost a bit
of blood and my leg pains me—I think it's broken. 'Twas
Canady and I fought off the war party and though I tried to
stop him, Canady would run off after them, shooting at them
with arrows when his ammunition ran out. I heard a terrible
howl after he disappeared in the woods and then—nothing. I
fear they got him."

"We'll send a search party. Which way did he go?"

MacDermott nodded inland and his head lolled. He had
passed out.

"Do what you can for him," van Ryker told de Rochemont
morosely. "He's a good man—better than my brother, apparently."

"I'll need bandages," muttered de Rochemont. "I won't
have enough."

"I'll tear off strips from my chemise," offered Imogene.

"Good." De Rochemont smiled at her, then turned to van
Ryker. "These Indians, do you think they'll come back in
force?"

"No way of knowing," muttered van Ryker. He cast a
worried look at Imogene. "In case they do, I wouldn't want
Imogene here."

De Rochemont gave him a sympathetic look. "It must have
been a small war party for two men to fight them off almost
single-handed."

"Yes, but I can't understand what happened—it was so
peaceful here. The Indians were very friendly."

"Times change," said de Rochemont cynically. "Could ye heat me some water?" he asked Imogene.

Quickly and efficiently—for she was always cool in emergencies—Imogene went to work. Van Ryker was off with the search party, but with the help of the guard he had left, she got a fire going. She helped de Rochemont bathe MacDermott's wounds and stanch the flow of blood, and tried to make him as comfortable as she could.

"All the beaver skins were stolen from the dock," MacDermott was saying disconsolately as he came to.

"It's all right," soothed Imogene. "Just lie quiet."

"And the logs that had been cut for shipment were set adrift."

Imogene remembered seeing logs floating by them as they came upriver. "It just happened then?" she asked quickly.

"Yesterday, I think," he said weakly. "I have drifted between sleep and waking since Canady left and could not count the passage of time."

"Don't talk," admonished de Rochemont. "You'll open up your wounds."

The search party found Will Canady's body with a number of arrows sticking out of it. The top of his head had been severed by a tomahawk blow and his scalp was missing. They brought him back and buried him in a little grove behind the house with only a few hurried words said over the body. Imogene had to turn her head away, for the sight of his torn body made her feel ill. Van Ryker snatched up the plantation papers and account books, Imogene seized what silver and pewter she could find, MacDermott was carried carefully down to the longboat, and they all tumbled in and made their way back downriver.

That night aboard the *Sea Rover*, shaken by her experience, Imogene held van Ryker with a special tenderness and there were tears wet upon her cheeks as their bodies locked together in the moonlit great cabin—tears she was quick to brush away, for she did not want to explain to him why she was crying. She had never, before the revelations of these last two days, realized quite what a man he was—a man who shouldered everything, who tried to solve everybody's problems. He had flung his young life, his career, his good name, all at Esme's feet, to save her in her hour of trouble. Imogene imagined Esme, seeing her as fragile and helpless, a timid girl who had struck back blindly at an attacker and by accident killed him.

And the gold he had won by blood and suffering had been invested—part of it at least—with a fool who ran before the foe! And even back on Tortuga, van Ryker had stood ready to defend all those shadowy Spanish women who had disappeared from aboard *Le Sabre*.

Van Ryker, she thought tenderly. Brave and daring, trying to right all the ills of the world!

For the next three days search parties were sent out combing the woods to look for Charles, but he seemed to have disappeared. None of the slaves were found, either. All on the ship were of the opinion that the Indians had carried them off—perhaps they would even be marched to the big slave market the northern Indians operated up on one of the great northern lakes.

MacDermott, worse hurt than he had realized, had lapsed into delirium, but on the night of the third day he was able to tell them more coherently what had happened.

" 'Twas over an Indian woman that the trouble came about," he said. "I warned your brother—I warned the landgrave it would bring trouble but she was young and pretty and he would not let her alone. The woman was married, but she kept coming to the house on one excuse and another. She would stay closeted with Charles for several hours and when she left he would give her little gifts."

"Charles was ever a wencher." Van Ryker sighed.

"Came the day the wench stole something the landgrave valued," continued MacDermott. "A snuffbox, I think it was—anyway they had a falling out about it. The landgrave demanded it back, she clawed at him, he struck her in the face and drew blood and she ran away screaming that he would be sorry. I do not know what she told her people but that night a small party attacked us. We were holding out pretty well until the landgrave panicked." MacDermott threw van Ryker an apologetic look. "Bent low, he ran down to the water and cast off in our only boat. The slaves saw him making his escape and went crazy. They broke and ran for the woods. Some of them were killed. Others disappeared into the trees. Canady and I were left to fight the Indians off alone and we did. If only Canady had not pursued them, he would be alive today."

"We did not find the bodies of any slaves," interposed van Ryker.

"They may not have been dead. The Indians may have dragged them off in the night."

Imogene shuddered. "Are there no neighbors who could help?" she wondered.

"Too far away," van Ryker told her morosely. "And with troubles of their own."

"I am sorry about your loss," said MacDermott, for he knew very well whose money had financed Charles's venture.

Van Ryker ran a hand through his hair. "The place can be rebuilt—but that will not bring back Will Canady nor mend your wounds, MacDermott."

"I'll be all right," said MacDermott. "But I'll miss Will. He had five years to go on his indenture and we planned to buy a place together once his time was over."

Van Ryker cast a look at that injured leg that might never be right. "I'll see you get your place, MacDermott," he promised quietly, and the man on the bunk gave him a grateful look.

Imogene leaned forward. "You said the place could be rebuilt?"

"Someday—the time is not now."

Imogene went on deck and looked back upriver in the gathering darkness. The landscape looked strange and deserted and alien now that the light was going. An alien shore . . . And yet in her heart she could not but believe that van Ryker would return here someday, that he would carve an estate out of this wilderness, and turn his wild holding into civilization. It was hard *not* to believe in a man like van Ryker.

He joined her, there on the deck. Around them the night was very still. She saw that he had posted a double watch in the event of Indian attack—not that a buccaneer ship of forty guns was much troubled by that, but a sneak attack could wreak havoc, even setting the ship afire.

"I am sorry for what has happened," she told him sincerely.

"Worse for Canady and MacDermott than for me." He dismissed it tersely.

"But it means the end of a dream."

"Only for now. Someday I will return—and take over myself. *I* am not apt to run away in the face of danger." His tone was ironic.

"What do we do now?" she asked.

"Now I will take you to Jamaica," he said. "To Gale Force. My brother Anthony is cast in a tougher mold."

"But you have already lost so much time sailing to Carolina," she pointed out, hoping to divert him from leaving her in Jamaica. "Shouldn't we—"

"Imogene," he cut in. "Save your breath. I will *not* take you buccaneering with me. You saw the results of a small Indian raid—imagine if you will what it is like on the decks of shattered ships, locked together, awash with blood!"

She winced. "So we are going to Jamaica?"

"Yes, we are going to Jamaica."

"But what about your brother? You cannot just leave him here!"

He turned on her fiercely. "Have you seen a boat? Can you yourself ferret out where he can be?"

"No, but—"

"For once, Charles will have to take care of himself," said van Ryker bitterly. "I have looked for him long enough. I consider that by his selfish action in running away he got Canady killed and probably a number of slaves—those the Indians do not choose to enslave themselves—and near did for MacDermott. A man must pay for something like that."

In her view of Charles, Imogene was getting a picture of someone soft and unable to cope. She had a nightmarish vision of him lurking in tatters near the shore, his flesh torn by brambles, peering out fearfully through the brush, hoping for sight of a sail.

"But he is your *brother*," she said unhappily.

"He is also a man and should act like one. Perhaps I have coddled him too much."

It was strange, she thought, that van Ryker—youngest of the clan—should seem like the older brother. It was because he accepted responsibility, she supposed, and wondered what his other brother, Anthony, would be like.

But for all his callous talk, she noticed that van Ryker sailed carefully up and down the coast once more, studying the coastline through a glass. "There is another plantation far to the northward," he told her. "And another to the south. If Charles reaches either one, he will be safe."

And with those words, he set sail for Jamaica.

She became friends with MacDermott on the voyage and was sorry to learn that he would not be accompanying her to Gale Force, but would voyage on with the buccaneers until he could be landed somewhere to proceed on to Barbados, where he had a sister. There he would convalesce at his leisure, having promised van Ryker that he was "his man" whenever he wished to try to rebuild the plantation. "For there's a great future in Carolina," he told van Ryker earnestly. "Your brother, he knew not how to run a plantation, nor would he take sound advice."

"So I've discovered." Grimly.

"But with you at the helm," said the old Scotsman, "we could steer a clear course."

Imogene thought so too.

Only one thing happened to mar their trip to Jamaica. And that was their first night out, when Ryker was busy in the great cabin going over the plantation papers under the light of a swinging ship's lamp. Imogene, looking out the windows in the stern, turned as he tossed down what looked to be part of a letter with an irritable exclamation.

Curious, she crossed the room and picked it up.

"Do not read that," he said tersely.

"Why not?" Her interest aroused, she moved away from him, holding the paper up to the lamp.

"Very well, read it," he sighed. "But it will not make you happy."

It was obviously a page from a letter of which they had

neither the beginning nor the ending sheets, for it began in the middle of a sentence at the top and ended the same way at the bottom.

"*...and by now you will probably have heard from Anthony and I am sure that like me you can hardly believe it,*" the letter began in a large flowing scrawl, "*but although Anthony says it is only a rumor so far, it is obviously a very well-founded rumor, for it resounds everywhere—*" Imogene looked up. "Who wrote this?"

"It is Esme's handwriting. Charles was using it for a bookmark in his account book." He looked grim and would have again reached for the letter but that she held it back from him.

"What is Esme like?"

"She is foolish and headstrong."

"No, I mean—what does she look like?" For somehow a disturbingly dominating vision had arisen from that snatch of sentence. This was not the way she had pictured Esme.

Van Ryker frowned. "Esme is very striking. Perhaps a little taller than you, of delicate build. She has an oval face and lavender eyes that sometimes change to tarnished silver. She has a high light voice and charming mannerisms."

"And she is very fashionable? Very—proud?"

"Yes, I suppose so. Why do you ask?"

Something in the letter...something that she felt lay just ahead, something she dreaded, had prompted her to ask that. Perhaps something in the word "rumor." She felt she was marking time, putting off something unpleasant.

"Do your brothers resemble her?"

"Tony does. Both Anthony and Esme look like their mother, who was the beauty of the county and swept all before her. I never saw her of course. She died giving birth to Esme."

"And Charles?"

He gave a wry laugh. "Save that he is dark like the others, Charles resembles nobody—unless it be his mother's great uncle, who is supposed to have died of a heart attack when highwaymen attacked his coach near Salisbury. Charles is plump and easygoing and slovenly in his ways."

"You do not look like them, then?"

He shook his head. "No, I look like my father."

She looked down at the letter again, almost tempted to give it back to him unread, but something drew her to it.

" . . . *but if Branch has really been fool enough to marry some dockside whore in Tortuga,*" she read, "*then I suppose we must live with it, although I cannot believe he has forgotten Elinor, who you'll remember he was so hot to marry!*"

Her head lifted. "Who is Elinor?"

His face was grim. "The girl who threw me over when Ryderwood was sold."

"Oh." She returned to reading the letter. The next line cut her to the heart.

"*But there is some comfort at least in what Anthony says,*" it went on, "*that a 'buccaneer marriage' would count for little save on Tortuga, that the 'minister' who married them*"— the word "minister" was derisively in quotes—"*is probably some outcast from the church and the 'governor' of Tortuga probably has no authority to issue a license anyway, so I suppose it is no legal marriage at all and we can forget about it, as Branch undoubtedly will when—*"

There the page ended.

With shaking fingers Imogene laid the letter back on the table.

"I told you it would make you unhappy," growled van Ryker. He was watching her keenly.

"Is it—true?" she asked painfully. "That the governor of Tortuga has no authority, and we are not legally married?"

"I do not know," he scowled.

"I think—I need some air," she choked, turning away from him.

"Imogene." Van Ryker rose from the table. His dark face was concerned. "I have not written to them about you—indeed, I had hoped to bring you together in some more joyous way than this on which we are embarked. But 'tis only natural that wild rumors would spread. I am a man who gathers rumors as a ship gathers barnacles. You are not to mind what Esme has written; she is an impetuous woman and not in possession of the facts. When Anthony meets you, he will write and tell her what you are like." He tossed down his quill pen and closed the account books. "I am tired of reading about losses and mismanagement," he said, taking her hand. "It is time for bed."

But although he cajoled her as only a lover could, although as always she found herself thrilling to his touch, swept to heights by the insistent urging of his strong masculinity, long after he was sleeping soundly beside her Imogene lay awake staring at a crescent moon through the bank of windows at the stern.

For something told her, some deep inner voice, that nothing was going to be right with Esme or with Anthony—or with Charles, if he turned up.

Nothing would be right because—now she knew what they thought of her.

Jamaica, 1660

CHAPTER 7

Growing larger on the horizon hour by hour, the tortoise-shaped island of Jamaica stretched green before them, rising out of the turquoise sea.

"Are we going to land at Port Royal?" wondered Imogene. She was leaning on the taffrail beside van Ryker, her hip in her lightweight sky blue linen dress pressed companionably against his lean thigh. He had insisted she wear it, for he loved her in blue.

. "No, we'll land at a sheltered bay some distance up the coast."

Imogene was disappointed. From what she'd heard about Port Royal, it was as bad as Tortuga and she'd hoped to convince van Ryker that it would be even worse to leave her in Port Royal than to take her with him. Now her mind raced ahead to the plantation where they were bound. Doubtless she'd discover some good reason why he could not leave her there—dangerous Indians, fever, imminent attack by the Spanish . . . she'd think of something.

"Where is your plantation, van Ryker?" she asked innocently.

"You'll have to remember to call me Branch Ryder when we reach Gale Force," he reminded her. "The house is situated some miles inland. It lies up the Cobre River beyond Spanish Town. But the land stretches from the bay to the Cobre. The shortest route would be up the Cobre, but that would take us past Port Royal and I don't want my face to become too well known there—against the day when I retire to Gale Force and forget I was ever a buccaneer."

"I had wondered why you never sailed into Port Royal," she murmured.

"Now you know."

"What bay is it that your land fronts on?"

"It is an unnamed bay." He turned to her, leaned down and breathed deep of the perfume of her golden hair. "But now I would christen it Lemon Bay—for the scent of your hair this day."

"It is probably ringed by lemon trees—and that is why you would name it Lemon Bay!" she scoffed, laughing.

"*And* limes and bananas and pimentos and coconuts," he grinned. "This is a fruitful land, as you will soon see."

Imogene smiled back at him. Fruitful—as she would be, she hoped. For some day, regardless of the doctor's warning, she intended to give van Ryker a son, a lad who would grow strong and tall like his father and be—like his father—a leader among men.

Van Ryker was looking around him with satisfaction. The voyage had been made swiftly, cleanly. They had not encountered any Spanish vessels—and that was a godsend, with Imogene aboard. Indeed, it had been an uneventful voyage—and that was what van Ryker had earnestly desired it to be—uneventful.

They cast anchor in a small secluded bay, clear as glass and ringed about by an overwhelming variety of trees and climbing vines that threatened to smother them.

"I keep it wild here," van Ryker chuckled, seeing Imogene's surprise that a plantation would be allowed such disorder. "For I wish to discourage visitors to this place. The heavy undergrowth discourages callers."

"I should think it would." Imogene stared at the wild shore, rising up like a green wall before them.

"There is a spring just a short walk from here," he told her. "Up that way." He nodded toward the heavy foliage on the bank.

"'A spring'?" Somehow she was surprised. So many of these islands, she'd been told, had little surface water.

"Yes. The Arawak Indians, who once lived here, called this the 'island of springs.' And this particular spring forms a clear blue pool set in a cleft of rocks. The water is delicious—and fine for swimming. Would you enjoy a swim?" He gave her a lazy look.

"You are not in a hurry to reach Gale Force, then?"

"I would spend a last day with you," he said, reaching out to push back a tendril of her fair hair that had blown across her face. His touch was gentle, his gaze reflective. In truth, having brought Imogene safely here, he was in no great hurry to reach Gale Force. After the debacle at Longview, he had an uneasy feeling that some new unforeseen disaster might greet him at his Jamaica plantation and he wanted to hold his lovely bride in his arms one more night before he faced that. "We could spend the night ashore if you liked and go on to Gale Force tomorrow."

"Yes," she whispered, gazing up starry-eyed into his dark face. "Yes, I would like that."

She, too, had another reason. Because now she knew what they must think of her at Gale Force, and she was in no hurry to meet the rest of the Ryder clan.

They set out in a small boat over water so clear it seemed

as if the boat must drop to the bottom as through a sea of air. Below them brilliant tropical fish flashed and a sea urchin drifted. On the bottom she could see waving lacelike fronds and brilliant shells lying on the white sand.

A magical world . . . easy to lose one's self here, easy to forget there was any other life but this.

Van Ryker pulled the boat up on a narrow rim of white beach and held up some of the great overhanging vines so that she might duck beneath them and make her way into that green world before her. Sea grapes and banana leaves brushed her hair, coconut palm fronds sighed overhead, as they made their way through the rustling green jungle.

Before long they came out into a jumble of rocks and she saw as she clambered over the last one a brilliant blue pool below her. Cloistered as some chamber carved by giants long ago, the blue depths were fed by a delicate little waterfall from the spring that tinkled merrily.

Wordlessly she looked up at van Ryker, and he thought her eyes were both bluer and more beautiful than the depths of the water below. In the tropical heat he reached out to help her with the hooks of her dress. Once she had removed it he spread it out for her to sit on as, now clad in her chemise, she removed her shoes and stockings.

She sat for a few moments leaning back upon her hands, with her neck arched and the soft trade winds blowing her fair hair. She could hear the slight metallic sound as van Ryker divested himself of his sword and pistols. Other familiar sounds as he removed his boots, his doublet and shirt, his trousers and smallclothes. She reached out a foot and with her bare toes tested the temperature of the water in the sparkling pool at her feet. Where the sun struck it, it was tepid, warm as milk. It would be cooler over there where the little cascade tumbled down.

Past her, van Ryker's lean naked body suddenly knifed gleaming into the pool. He cut the water cleanly with hardly a splash and struck out with strong sure strokes, making a swift circle of the little pool. He looked up, dashing his dark wet hair back with one hand and smiled at her, a swift white flash in his dark face.

"Come on in," he said. "The water's fine."

Lazily, Imogene rose to her feet. Across from her, swinging on a low-hanging branch, a red and green parrot squawked and scolded and spread its brilliant wings. But Imogene's gaze was not on the parrot; it was riveted on the man in the water.

Slowly, indolently, teasing him, she pulled the drawstring of her chemise, let it glide halfway down her body so that her round white breasts were exposed to his gaze. She tossed back her thick golden hair with a ripple of her shoulders and set her breasts dancing—and watched the flickering light kindle in his gray eyes.

With even more maddening slowness, she eased the soft white cambric down around her silken hips and let it glide feather-light to the ground, to mound around her slender ankles.

And then she stretched her arms far above her head, stretched her whole slim body luxuriously, like a cat.

It was a beautiful display, her alluring white form graceful against the dark green dappled backdrop of sun and shade, her smoothness contrasted against the rough gray limestone of the rocks that surrounded the pool.

"Imogene." Van Ryker's voice reached her hoarsely. "Come in. I can stand no more."

She gave him a sweet enigmatic smile. There were witching impulses in her today. She was frankly luring him to her arms and she knew he felt she was teasing him unmercifully. She did not quite know why she was doing it—perhaps because she felt she was arriving friendless in a strange land and he would soon be leaving her; she would be cut adrift.

But whatever drove her, she tormented him a little longer. She lifted a bare ankle and inspected it, her bright hair cascading around her shoulders and down her naked body. And then she straightened up and ran her fingers comblike through her hair, and then smoothed her hands down her hips as if to smooth a skirt down over them—but there was no skirt. Her hips were smooth and silky to her touch—and now van Ryker was swimming toward her.

She laughed as he reached up and seized her by her slender

ankle, made a playful effort to kick at him and a soft protest
that ended in a gurgle as he suddenly pulled her into the water
with him.

The warm clear water closed over her head and she came
up laughing and gasping, pulling back the hair that had
formed a wet curtain over her eyes and sending it behind her
in shining strands. She seized his dark head and pushed it
under and broke away from him, still laughing—for she was
an expert swimmer, a skill learned by night along the rock-
studded beaches of the Scillies when her guardian had thought
her fast asleep.

In the clear blue depths she could see him dive under, see
him knife toward her feet. As she tried to escape in mock
panic, he pulled her straight under, caressing her body as it
was pulled by him, first the shapely calves of her legs, and
then her thighs, and then her hips brushed thrillingly past and
her squirming torso was sweetly tormented before he let her
rise, gasping, to the surface.

"So you'll play games with me, my lady?" he grinned.
"Or are you by chance a water sprite?"

"Had the water been less clear, I'd have eluded you!"

"No, had the water been less clear, you'd not have seen
me—and then you'd have wondered what sea monster had
grabbed you!"

"This pool is wonderful," she murmured. "But it's mar-
velous small—I'm used to swimming in the ocean."

"But here you can drink," he reminded her, and swam
over to where the water cascaded down, lifted his head and
let the cool water splash down into his open mouth.

Doubting the wisdom of that, Imogene tried it—and strangled
as the water struck her nose.

"It takes a bit of practice," he laughed. "But you'll
learn."

"Will I have time to learn?" Her eyes were suddenly
shadowed as she looked up at her tall buccaneer.

"Time enough," he said, leaning over to kiss her wet
mouth. The pressure of his lips was very reassuring. And
exhilarating. Imogene felt a tremor go through her. Which
annoyed her—she wasn't ready to make love just yet. She

wanted to torment van Ryker a bit longer first, to make him
realize what he'd be missing if he went away to sea and left
her.

"I am still surprised." She twitched an arrogant bare
shoulder at him. "I'd have thought you'd have wanted to
dash up to Gale Force immediately—after what happened at
Longview. Instead of tarrying with me here. I'd think you'd
be anxious to know how things are at Gale Force."

He sighed and gave her a rueful look, lifted up her dripping
hair and cupped the heels of his hands around her chin.
"Perhaps I'm as well not knowing if Longview's any sample.
Who knows, the Spanish may have taken Port Royal, swept
up the Cobre River, burned Spanish Town to the ground and
swept the plantation clean out from under Anthony!" At her
look of alarm, he grinned. "No chance of that, I'd say. I'd
have seen boats scudding along the coast, people trying to
escape with their goods. No, 'tis a day and a night of love
I'm inclined to, Imogene. A little time of our own together—
without any problems pressing in on us."

There was another reason too, but he did not tell her that.
For hardly had they cleared the beach before de Rochemont,
whose face was less well known than van Ryker's, had set
out in the dinghy for Port Royal on a secret mission for his
captain. Van Ryker had to give him time to accomplish that
mission.

But Imogene, treading water in the deep blue pool, knew
nothing of that. She gave van Ryker a happy smile and shook
her head to shake the water from her eyelashes.

"Perhaps we've swum around enough," she murmured,
gliding nearer and letting her naked nipples slide along his
wet chest.

He was quick to respond to that invitation.

"Perhaps we have," he muttered, and swept her in close to
him so that his manly hardness caressed her wet thighs.

Laughing now, Imogene tried to wriggle away from him,
but he held her fast. He pressed a kiss on her wet lips and as
she struggled, teasing him, their dripping hair tangled and
twined like silken ropes, binding them together.

"Van Ryker—we'll drown!" she protested after they went under and came up again, sputtering and laughing.

"Someday perhaps—but not yet!" He swept her up in his strong arms and splashed out, lifting her onto a stone ledge that stuck out over the pool. There he set her down so that her bare legs could dangle over the edge.

She watched him stride forward. Still naked and gleaming with rivulets of the cool spring water that dashed off him as he moved, he seized his sword and began to hack off fronds and great clumps of tropical grasses. He was piling them up now—making a bed for them to lie on.

Imogene smiled and stretched luxuriously. It was such a wonderful unreal place he had found for them. She felt as if she—who had once long ago in the Scillies asked those great standing stones they called Adam and Eve to send her a lover—had been granted an Eden as well. For that was what this lost primeval green world with its deep blue spring-fed pool seemed to her—Eden. With van Ryker its Adam and herself its Eve. She leaned back dreamily and watched her buccaneer swiftly construct such a bed as Eve herself might have lain upon back in that long-lost Eden.

"I thought we'd—rest," he grinned, his gaze hot upon her face. "Before we eat."

"Ah?" she said, as if that were very instructive. "So you brought food in that great knapsack you carried here over your shoulder?"

"I am a man of many resources," he told her, still grinning. "Come over here and find out."

"No, thank you," she said perversely. "I have not yet completed my swim!" And turned and knifed cleanly back into the water.

Van Ryker was not long in following her. Chuckling, he seized her and teased her into passion, stroking her slim body underwater, impudently poking into secret spots, tickling her where she was most vulnerable. His long arms now held her, now let her go gliding away from him. But always he pursued her through the blue pool, a lean Neptune ever on the chase. And she, a tempting mermaid, now laughing, now pouting, held him off until their desire for each other reached dizzying heights and he seized her again, fiercely, and once again carried her out of the water.

This time he did not let her go but carried her, dripping and cuddled against him, to the pile of fronds and grasses and gently laid her down upon it.

"Van Ryker," she whispered, her soft hands caressing his damp, lightly furred chest, "promise you'll come back to me."

His arms tightened about her and his voice was low and hoarse in her ear, and rich with feeling. "You have my promise, Imogene. I will come back. You may count upon it."

A little thrill went through her at the way he said it. It was a commitment more meaningful than the words themselves, a kind of felt violence. *I will return to you,* she felt he was saying. *Neither heaven nor hell shall stand in my way.*

"I'll hold you to your promise," she warned in a smothered voice, and let her words trail off indistinctly as his warm mouth found hers. She was surrendering herself even as he lowered his big body onto hers, resting lightly on his elbows and cradling her so that she seemed to float upon the fronds. She gasped, for in elegant fashion he was stroking and teasing her pliant torso, driving her onward in sweet rapturous torment. Now his hips were moving in sinuous motion across her own, his manliness was seeking and finding her innermost secrets. And she was once again, with wild little bursts of passion throbbing through her veins, thrilling in delight to all his arts as a lover.

Across the fronds they tumbled, laughing and gasping. They clutched and hugged and trembled and whispered wonderful, unreal, and instantly forgotten promises, and led each other upward on fiery trails that made the world seem lost and far away and only love important.

Theirs was a perfect joining, and their bodies that day in their ecstatic mingling had the sweet impassioned fury of lovers who might be clasping each other for the last time. For who could know if a buccaneer would ever return to his love? Who knew what fate might await him?

Perhaps he would not be joined in battle for a week or even a month, but Imogene kissed him as passionately, held him as fiercely close as if this were the last time her arms would hold him on this earth. And together they knew splendor—and fulfillment.

When at last he released her, they lay for a long time companionably together on their bed of fronds and grasses, while he gently stroked her throbbing body in the afterglow of passion.

"You are not to worry," he said, for he had felt the desperate urgency of her lovemaking. He was stroking her breasts so that she trembled as if shaken by a strong wind.

"I cannot help but worry when you are away," she said in a small, hurried voice, twisting away from his fingers. "For those I love have always seemed to vanish away from me. Like water, they slipped through my fingers." She shivered.

"But *I* will not." The tall buccaneer looked deep into her anguished blue eyes and let his lips trail fierily down her white throat and over her breasts to worry a pink-crested nipple to hardness. He lifted his head and smiled at her. That smile had a steely quality. "Indeed, you would be hard put to try to rid yourself of me!"

"Oh, van Ryker, let it be so!" There were unbidden tears on her lashes as she flung herself against him. Her twined arms brought his head down against her face. She had not meant to let him see how deeply this parting affected her, she had meant to flirt and tease and tempt him to speedy return—or not to leave her at all—but now it all washed over her that he was really going. She began to weep.

"Imogene, Imogene." He cradled her in his arms. "One would think I'd be gone a year—'twill be no long voyage, I promise."

"How can you know that?" she choked. "You said the men were restive."

"Aye, they've been on shore a long time—and they're fighting men, eager to be at their trade again."

"And suppose you don't find rich hauls? Suppose you find galleons with empty holds? Or worse yet, none at all? Will you not stay out, then?"

"Nay, then I'll be tempted to raid some town on the Spanish Main," he said coolly. "The faster to return to you."

She shivered in his arms, for that was an even more dangerous undertaking potentially than attacking a galleon at sea. For the towns were alive with shore batteries, and garrisoned with soldiers against just such emergencies.

"You're not to think on blood and battle," he told her, gazing down on her fondly as his questing fingers stroked her tense back muscles. "Think on my return and how we'll sail back to Tortuga in triumph—and much richer!"

"Van Ryker!" Her voice broke. "You don't need riches to make me love you. I only want you to come home safe!"

"Come," he said in mock alarm, pushing her away. "Food is surely the only answer to these doldrums! And I've brought aplenty. Look in my knapsack there and see what you can find."

She gave him a rueful look, for she knew she could not move him nor change him nor sway him from this voyage. The die was already cast and they must play the game out. Sighing, she pushed back her tumbled hair and got up and went to the knapsack. She exclaimed as she took out of it meat and cheese and bread and a bottle of wine.

"And there's fresh fruit nearby," he said, walking a few paces and returning with a handful of fragrant mangoes. "So we will have us a feast."

The soft air dried their naked bodies as they sat cross-legged and ate their meal. Somehow food had never tasted so good as that snack they enjoyed between lingering bouts of lovemaking. It was as if they were giving themselves a last bit of heaven to remember in the hard, lonesome days ahead—a last kiss, a last clasp, a last sip of wine. . . .

The sun sank red in the west and the swift velvet night of the tropics fell over them like a curtain. Brilliant white stars glowed out of the velvet blackness overhead and a pale golden moon came up and bathed the jungly undergrowth in its silvery light. The trade winds rustled the palm fronds and the noises of little night creatures sang and murmured about them. Lying there beside van Ryker, now soundly sleeping, Imogene's senses were lulled.

It was hard somehow to believe this lovely existence would ever end.

But morning came and with it the sun rose, a brilliant golden ball that lit a hard blue sky and beat down mercilessly over the rich green vegetation. They made love again, gracefully, almost wistfully—and with a kind of longing, for they both knew it would be the last time for a long time to come.

And then they bathed in the clear blue pool and lay lazily side by side on the warm stone ledge above the pool and dried their bodies in the morning heat. It was with reluctance that they finally dressed and turned their faces inland.

"There is a tributary of the Cobre River a little ways from here," van Ryker told her. "It is seldom used because there is a chaotic jumble of rocks that makes it unnavigable by boat just past the point where we will join it. But at that place I keep a small boat always secreted. We will row upriver almost to the main part of the Cobre. There I will again secrete the boat and use it on my return journey."

"How can you be sure the boat will still be there?" she asked breathlessly as she followed him, ducking and weaving through the heavy matted undergrowth.

"Because no one knows it is there but me," he said tersely.

"Not even your brother?"

"Not even Anthony."

"Why?" she wondered. "Don't you trust him?"

"A fox needs two entrances to his hole," he told her. "Just as I felt I needed two plantations because something might happen to one—as indeed it has already. So I felt I needed a secret way to escape Gale Force, if I should be ambushed there."

"'Ambushed'?"

"A man collects enemies in a life such as mine," he told her with a shrug. "And what Anthony does not know, he cannot tell to others, in case of trouble."

Van Ryker thought of everything, she thought in wonder. Perhaps that was part of the secret of his success—magnificent planning, taking the long view.

The boat, a slender dugout, was just where he had left it.

He pulled it out of the undergrowth by main strength and set it afloat upon this relatively smooth portion of the Cobre. Downstream she could hear the sound of rushing waters as the current cascaded over the treacherous jumble of rocks he had described, but she could not see it for the dense thicket that separated them from it.

He steadied the boat for her as she climbed into it and spread out her blue linen skirts.

"You're a lovely sight, Imogene," he said softly. "A man could fill his eyes with you."

She smiled back. "Perhaps we could tarry another day?" she suggested with a tantalizing look.

He hesitated, giving her a yearning look. "There is a place along the bank halfway between here and Gale Force that has grass as soft as cotton and tall trees that overarch it like a green cathedral. . . ."

He was loath to let her go. She could feel it and it gave her confidence. "Surely we do not need to arrive too early," she agreed cheerfully, and cast her eyes modestly down before his suddenly ribald grin, and trailed her fingers in the clear water.

She was thinking that she had left her luggage—all of it—on board the *Sea Rover*. Another delightful reason for delay while he sent downriver for it. She must be careful not to draw attention to that lack until they reached Gale Force. Her blue eyes sparkled with well-controlled glee. For once even van Ryker, that Great Planner, had not thought of everything!

But even as van Ryker bent his sinewy arms to the oars, sending their frail craft upriver, another traveler, this one wild-eyed and dirty and with a two-weeks' growth of beard, burst through the front doors of Gale Force.

Anthony Ryder, an elegant figure in plum silks ornamented with lavender rosettes, was just striding toward those doors on booted feet, riding crop in hand. He broke stride and the dark brows above his murky amethyst eyes drew together in a frown at sight of this barefoot, unkempt stranger with the touseled head of dark hair. Instinctively his hand fell to the sparkling hilt of his handsome dress sword. He was about to hail the stranger and demand that he account for his presence when suddenly he gasped and thrust his sword back into its scabbard and strode forward to grasp the newcomer by his shoulders.

"Charles!" he cried. "What brings you here in this condition?"

"Don't ask, Tony," groaned this slack-mouthed refugee. He sagged on his feet. "Just find me food and some clean clothes—I had to trade my boots and clothing and ring for passage on the dirtiest boat afloat and these rags are crawling with vermin."

Anthony gave an astonished exclamation but he stepped back warily at this threat of vermin. He beckoned the thicker-bodied Charles outside and bade him strip. There, a big impassive black woman dressed in green and scarlet cotton, with a big red turban surmounting her regal head, tossed his filthy clothing onto an open fire and burned them.

Next Charles was led to an open wooden tub of hot water, and the big woman, her sleeves rolled up, thoroughly scrubbed him from head to toe. He gasped and protested as she ducked his dark head under again and again in her earnest effort to rid him of his vermin. Finally he stood erect and dripping and was toweled dry. Clean and naked he padded back into the house to find clean clothes of Anthony's laid out on a guest room bed and his elegant brother lounging indolently against the door with a silver goblet in his hand, regarding him with lifted brows and again asking the question, "What happened?"

"Pour me a glass of what you're drinking," sighed Charles, "and I'll tell you."

Silently Anthony proffered his goblet. He was taller than Charles and much more forceful-looking. He had narrow chiseled features and long thin hands and feet. His clothes were a fit tight to bursting on that shorter blockier figure before him. He listened intently, inclining his handsomely periwigged head as Charles poured out a shameful story of deception and cowardice.

"Does Branch know about this?" he asked at last.

Charles shuddered. "Not yet—he couldn't. For I made it through that blasted forest to the coast and was lucky enough

to find a fishing boat that had been swept off its course by a
gale to the north of us. The crew had put ashore for fresh
water—and a barefoot raggedly lot they were. For the price of
all I was wearing they agreed to set me ashore in Port Royal
and I begged of the minister there, Mr. Gibbons, enough
money to get me upriver to you. I promised you'd recompense him.''

Anthony sighed.

"What do you think Branch will do about it when he
learns?'' Charles's eyes were dark with fright.

"He'll kill you,'' said Anthony conversationally. "But perhaps he won't learn. Ask yourself, how often does Branch
take himself to Carolina?''

"Almost never,'' whimpered Charles. "But twice, as I
remember.''

"Good. And until he ventures there again, ye are safe. You
can write to him occasionally, complaining of how bad things
are going—as I do.''

"But things must be going well here!'' protested Charles.
"Everything's neat as a pin, there's a new wing for the house
going up, and I could see the new lime and pimento trees that
have been planted as I came upriver—and the cane. The cane
looked to be doing well, Tony, and that means sugar—and
rum.''

"Aye.'' Anthony nodded coolly, the motion setting the frosty
lace at his throat astir and causing the big amethyst that held
it to flash suddenly, like his eyes. "In truth, things do proceed
well here. But there's no need for Branch to know of it, any
more than he need know of your debacle. When we tell him of
our disasters, he sends money. Ask yourself, do we want him
to retire? No! 'Tis by these constant infusions of new money
that things can proceed apace.''

"Ye were always of a better wit than me.'' Charles shook
his touseled dark head and looked baffled. A few drops of
water from his damp hair dribbled on his borrowed silk
doublet and Anthony frowned. "My troubles were all real,
Tony—yours only imagined. I had no idea!''

That long oval symmetrical face of Anthony's favored him
with a sour smile. "I've been thinking a deal since I learnt

about this woman Branch has married in Tortuga. It seems she's beautiful and reigns over his household there. I wouldn't like to see her come to Jamaica, Charles."

"No—nor would I." Charles looked frightened again. "For she would puzzle and ask questions and ferret out everything. She would tell Branch he's being cheated!"

Anthony sighed and looked pained. "I dislike that word, Charles. I am merely being paid, let us say, an extra bonus for my devotion here. After all, is it not I who have raised this house? These buildings? Planted these crops, harvested them?"

"Yes, but it was Branch's money bought the place, workmen *he* paid raised the house, for you and I had nothing and ye know it."

His tall brother gave him an impatient look. "What we *were* counts for nothing, Charles. 'Tis what we *are* that counts. And I, as you can see for yourself, am a successful planter here in Jamaica. I've no mind to be dispossessed."

Plump Charles fell silent.

Anthony's voice grew harsh. "So, are you for me or against me? Declare yourself now, Charles!"

"I know not what you mean, Tony," stammered Charles. He pulled at his borrowed collar. "Lord, this is tight." And as his brother's frown deepened, "I'm for ye, of course, Tony. But what am I against?"

Anthony seized Charles's empty goblet and set it down with a bang upon a nearby rosewood table. "Would that ye had Esme's brain!" he muttered. "The pity of it, that I must try to get through that thick skull of yours. . . . Well, listen to me, Charles, and I'll explain it to you. Branch is a buccaneer, right?"

Bewildered, Charles bobbed his head.

"And buccaneering is a dangerous business, right? So Branch could lose his life on one of these sorties into the Spanish Main?"

Again Charles bobbed his head. At least he could agree to that.

"So long as Branch remained single, that would mean that we would inherit, for the will he had drawn up and told us about, the will he left with a London solicitor named Talmadge, left Longview to you and Gale Force to me. But the will has yet another provision—that if Branch married, all would go to his wife. D'you get the drift of what I'm saying, Charles? If Branch dies now, we're dispossessed!''

"But ye wrote me 'twas some defrocked priest who performed the ceremony, and that the license could not be valid because the governor of Tortuga is not truly a governor! I wrote Esme about it.''

"Yes, yes,'' sighed Anthony. "I wrote her too. And I believe that is true, this 'buccaneer's wedding' was no true wedding at all and twas not even under his right name that he married her, as I heard it—he married her as 'Ruprecht van Ryker.' *But suppose he has married her again, Charles? And this time under his real name?* How do we know he has not? And where do we stand then?''

"I see what you mean.'' Charles's brow was furrowed and he sounded quenched. "Then we are in terrible case, Tony— we could be cast out!''

Anthony's face took on a look of infinite malice.

"Perhaps things are not so bad after all,'' he soothed. "I'm mindful that 'twas whilst we were gone that Branch and his mother gave away our patrimony to save a father who was already as good as dead. They should have had better sense! Had I been at home, I'd never have allowed it.''

"I doubt ye could have stopped them.'' Charles shook his head. "When Branch sets his mind to do something. . . .''

"Ye have no force,'' sneered Anthony.

Charles was nettled. Also his tight doublet was all but cutting his stomach in two. "Would *you* care to go against Branch?'' he asked bluntly. "He's deadly with a sword!''

"There's no need to go against his blade,'' Anthony shrugged. He took out an enameled snuffbox and studied it thoughtfully. " 'Tis but necessary to do a bit of fast thinking. I've been in touch with Esme and we've got it all worked out.''

"With Esme?'' cried Charles. "But—but Branch is all that keeps her husband's head above the water! Jules is sinking in a sea of debts! I can't think *she'd* help you, Tony.''

"Esme does not view the situation as you do," said Anthony coldly. "Esme—like me—remembers that she would have had a patrimony of her own but for Branch. And she's in danger of financial ruin again. That French husband of hers has gambled. away everything but her petticoats. She wrote me for money but of course I couldn't help her."

Wouldn't, more likely! thought Charles, squirming in trousers that were cutting off the circulation in his legs. He jumped up, unable to stand it.

"Where are you going, Charles? I tell you that Esme and I have devised a plan that will give Esme the money she needs and I will have Gale Force—which I rightfully deserve anyway, for I've made it what it is. Longview could be yours, Charles, if that plan works out."

"What's left of it." Charles's voice was rueful. "The buildings are probably burnt to the ground by now, and everyone there dead."

"'Tis still a great and saleable holding," said Anthony impatiently. "There's many a man of means would be glad to snap up forty-eight thousand acres of Carolina land and call himself a landgrave to boot!"

"You're right." Charles brightened, for he had just felt a seam in his trousers' waistband split. If that seam opened up a bit more, he'd be able to take a breath! "I could sell the miserable holding for a deal, were it mine!"

"Yes—and settle here with me." Anthony's shrewd eyes considered his brother more kindly. "Take off those trousers, Charles. There's a woman here who's fairly deft with a needle—she'll let them out a bit for you."

"Oh, would she?" Charles was already hastily divesting himself of the tight trousers, puffing as he did so. "And d'ye think a stitch or so to the doublet?"

Anthony nodded and called over his shoulder. He went back to the main topic after a slender golden-skinned woman in brilliant calico had come softly in and taken the clothing away. "Your money could be put to good use expanding this place and eventually we could both die rich—or else sell out ourselves and hie us back to merrie olde England, where the claret flows now that Charles is king and making up for his years of exile! What say ye, Charles? Are ye with me?"

"I know not exactly what ye intend," said Charles cautiously, happier now that he was down to his more loose-fitting smallclothes. "But if it involves no danger, then, yes, I am with ye."

"No danger to *you*," scoffed Anthony. " 'Tis Branch must face the danger!"

"Then I'm your man!" cried Charles recklessly. "For I'm in sore need of a fortune after the battering I took at Longview!" Still in his smallclothes, he accompanied Anthony downstairs. There Anthony refilled his goblet and they clinked goblets merrily. Indeed they might have been discussing the pursuit of some ruffled petticoat and not the destruction of the man to whom they both owed all they possessed.

Charles' mind was still muddy and his brow furrowed again. "I still don't understand how ye'll do it."

" 'Tis easy," said his older brother scornfully. "We'll make all places seem unsafe for his woman so that he'll send her to one of us—to me, since Longview no longer exists, as you tell it. We'll keep him believing we're both in urgent need of money, keep him hurling himself against the Spanish. How long does a man last in his profession, Charles? I can tell you, few live to be old! And if something *does* befall our dear brother, we'll make sure his young widow never inherits!"

"Oh, ye wouldn't kill her!" Charles shrank back in alarm.

"No, no, not with my own hands," said Anthony absently. "But I'll think of something. I'll find a way to rid us of her for all time—and yet not have her blood on our hands."

But even though Charles pressed him, he would not reveal what it was he intended.

The brothers drank on, talking in a low murmur that would not carry to the servants working outside. Anthony kept painting glowing word pictures of the world that awaited Charles once Branch was out of the way, for he knew well his brother's wavering nature. It would take a strong man to hold Charles to the right path—and to Anthony's scheming mind, the right path for Charles was the one down which he would drag him. For once Branch was out of the way, Charles was a chicken ripe to be plucked. He glanced from the glittering alexandrite on his carefully manicured hand to slovenly Charles, slumped there in his smallclothes. He'd invest Charles's money in Gale Force—gentleman's agreement, of course, no papers need be signed. And then some dark night . . .

He crossed his silk-clad knees decorously and continued sipping the excellent Canary he'd purchased in Port Royal, booty from some Spanish galleon long sunk beneath the waves. Outside, the bright Jamaican sun beat down.

But it was not a pretty picture on which the sun shone at Gale Force.

PART THREE
The Deadly Plot

Far from the man who would save her,
Far from his sheltering arms,
Alone, let her courage not waver—
'Tis herself she must save from harm!

Gale Force, Jamaica, 1660

CHAPTER 8

Their white bodies glistening like silver fish in a deep green pool in the afternoon sunlight that filtered down through a cathedral dome of tall branches that rose above them, Imogene and van Ryker lay happy and spent on a bed of soft grass, their bare hips and shoulders touching in wordless communion.

Van Ryker had rowed hard to reach this place and now the slender dugout was secreted in the bushes and the lovers occupied a silent bower. Beneath them was a thick carpet of lush green grasses—soft as van Ryker had promised. Around them rose verdant walls ablaze with the wild beautiful flowers of the tropics, roofed over with swaying fronds and branches. Somewhere unseen a bird sang.

Lying beside him, every nerve still atingle with the passion of his lovemaking, Imogene thought dreamily that she had never seen a dell more sylvan, a place so private, so remote, so lost to the world.

"We'll be late in arriving, you know." Van Ryker rose on an elbow and ran light, experimental fingers along the soft resilient mounds of her breasts. "Darkness may overtake us."

The afterglow of deep emotion burned in the brilliant blue of the wide expressive eyes she turned toward him. "I don't care," she said softly. "I don't care if we never arrive. We can stay here forever."

He gave a rueful laugh and sat up, flexed his big shoulder muscles and tossed back his dark hair with a shake of his head. "You do tempt me too much, witch!"

"'Tis true." She lay there untroubled in her nakedness, glad to be beautiful in his sight, glad to be a woman, glad to be alive. "I *do* wish to cast a spell on you—that you may never leave me."

"Imogene . . ." Van Ryker's voice hoarsened. "I would *not* leave you save that my affairs are in a precarious state. Anthony has written me that Gale Force is near going under and you saw for yourself how things were with Charles in Carolina."

"Yes." She sighed. Wickedly she wished that he would throw it all away, abandon it, sell the land for what he could get and sail away with her on some endless voyage. "You are right." She sat up. "We must hasten away else we will doubtless upset Anthony's dinner plans."

"No need for flippancy," he reproved her as he rose to his feet, the long length of him towering above her. "I have promised to return to you as soon as may be. Meantime, it will hearten me to know that you are cared for, protected."

"I know that, van Ryker." In a sudden excess of affection, she threw her arms around his knees, clasping them to her bare breast. "Pay no attention to me. I keep scheming to find ways to keep you with me."

"That fact had not escaped me, Imogene," he said humorously. He bent down and lifted her gently to her feet, dragging her upward against his long form. He let her naked body sway against his, moved her lightly, delicately from side to side so that her smooth tingling skin rasped softly against his own. "No." He gave a groan. "Ye must get dressed. Any more contact with that sweet body of yours and we'll be here all night!"

She pouted but she got dressed, pulling on the blue linen once again, and the boat was slid once again into the stream.

She leaned back lazily in the dugout as van Ryker once more bent his strong sinews to carry them upriver.

Darkness had fallen when they arrived at Gale Force. They had left the boat secreted and made their way through a jungly stretch of woods before they came out into a small clearing above the Cobre River. Imogene paused and stood for a moment looking upward at the house, which stood on a commanding rise, white in the moonlight.

"At least it's still standing," muttered van Ryker, and there was that in his voice that told her he had had no real certainty that that would be so.

"It's lovely," she said critically, studying the pale glow of its terra-cotta roof tiles in the moonlight and the expansive windows with their heavy iron grillwork. "Tell me, did you lift that grillwork from some Spanish ship?"

"Ye're a wicked wench to suggest it," he chuckled. "I bought it in Tortuga, where I'm tempted to believe it was sold after being lifted from some Spanish ship, and had it transported here. As for myself, I seek gold upon the seas—not iron!"

His step was light as he led her up a path between thick bushes, for the development of Gale Force had not yet reached a point where lawns were being cultivated, although she was to learn there was an overgrown garden in the back.

"Is that not a wing to the house I see?" she asked, peering at a dark shape rearing up. "It looks to be under construction."

Van Ryker stopped for a moment in surprise. "It is indeed a new wing. Anthony had not told me. I see he has been working hard in our interests."

"They keep no very good watch," she complained. "No one has hailed us. The only light in the house comes from that one window."

"Visitors do not approach from this side," he said carelessly. "We are coming at the house from an angle. The front lies in that direction, facing down on the Cobre." He nodded his head and she followed him silently around the corner of the stuccoed stone house, smelling the heady scent of the flowering vines that spilled in profusion everywhere.

They had reached the front of the house now, which

sported heavy iron grillwork doors, and behind them thick wooden ones. But all stood open to the gentle night air.

"Anthony must not have an enemy in the world," she murmured.

The man beside her frowned. Suddenly he moved ahead of her and she fell back a pace, followed as he made his way silently into a shadowy hall with a tiled floor, padded across it, his boots as soundless as if he had been walking barefoot.

Those boots carried him across an open courtyard toward a murmur of voices and moments later they stood in the doorway of a long, high-ceilinged dining room, where a long table was set for two.

At either end of that table sat a well-dressed man whose coloring superficially resembled the other, but Imogene saw that the taller and thinner of the two—the one resplendent in plum silks beneath an elegant dark periwig—had a long oval face of such symmetry that it would have become a woman. His skin was of a delicate ivory hue, almost pallid, which seemed strange in this climate, his lips were full, his head long and narrow. His hand, at that moment reaching for a chased silver goblet, had long sensitive fingers such as might strum a lute, and a large purple alexandrite flashed from a gold setting on his middle finger. This, she assumed, was Anthony, who so resembled Esme. . . .

The other man was shorter, built more solidly, but his body in its fox-hued silks looked flabby, unused, as if he never exercised save to push back from the table or drag a chair up to it. His face was sallow, his eyes, which were of a purplish gray, were dull by comparison with the other man's and his lips were full and pouting, like his cheeks, which puffed out at the jowls. He was not wearing a wig and his dark touseled hair was carelessly pulled back and tied at the back with a riband. There was neither grace nor style to the way he sat slouched in his tall-backed carved chair, there was no elegance in the way he wore his embroidered silk doublet. The lace at his throat hung crooked and a pearl ornament that had been stuck in to hold it looked in imminent danger of falling off. His pudgy hands were lifted to refill his goblet from a wide-mouthed decanter of chased silver. Imogene thought he looked both spoiled and petulant, and guessed at once that this was Charles.

At their silent entrance both men sprang up and their faces both lost color.

"Branch!" cried the taller of the two. His hand had fallen to his sword at their sudden appearance and now it came away as he moved forward to greet the newcomers.

"Tony." Van Ryker acknowledged his older brother's greeting but his hard gaze was fastened on the other. "And *Charles*," he drawled.

"Branch!" Charles echoed his older brother weakly. Halfway to his feet, he looked as if he might collapse back into his chair.

"I had not expected to find you here, Charles," said van Ryker. "Are things, then, coming along so well at Longview that you can go a-visiting as you please?"

"Things are—are moving along," muttered Charles in a suffocated voice.

Van Ryker studied his brother's cringing mien and dismissed him with a scornful smile. "Imogene," he said abruptly, "let me present my brothers—Anthony and Charles. Ye'll not have expected me to arrive with a bride, Tony."

"No, 'tis the first we've heard of it," said Anthony hastily, and swept the floor with his courtly bow. Hastily Charles followed suit. "Have ye eaten, Branch? No? There, Charles, give the lady your chair and bring us a couple of others." He clapped his hands and a brilliantly garbed, turbaned black servant appeared, stood silently with hands clasped. "There'll be two more for supper, Yamsy."

The turbaned head disappeared with a swish of bright skirts.

"Well, well, ye've married a beauty, Branch." Anthony looked at Imogene in some surprise. He had expected a good-looking woman, but this blazing beauty was something of a shock—and she had the bearing and manner of a lady as well. Where had Branch found her? Surely such women had no need to seek the brigands and renegades of Tortuga—they could take their choice of dukes and earls and live lives of silken luxury!

"Did ye expect less?" wondered van Ryker ironically, seating himself in the chair Charles hastily brought.

"No—no, of course not," agreed Anthony instantly. " 'Tis good to see you, Branch. Will ye be staying with us a while?"

Van Ryker shook his dark head. "I will not be staying, but I must leave Imogene for a while in your care, Tony. For I must go a-voyaging and I liked not leaving her in Tortuga."

"She's more than welcome," purred Anthony, regarding Imogene with barely concealed glee. He looked about him and his brows elevated delicately. "Your luggage?"

"Will be along," said van Ryker, and Imogene frowned. She had hoped her lack of luggage would prove a stumbling block to leaving her, but apparently van Ryker had thought of everything. She accepted the wine Anthony poured for her and sipped it.

"How do ye fare here at Gale Force?" asked van Ryker bluntly, holding out his goblet that Anthony might pour him some wine. "When last I heard from you, ye were in bad case."

"Things have improved a bit," said Anthony cautiously. "We are still in dire need of money if the plantation is to improve on schedule, but I have tried to manage wisely."

"And you, Charles?" Van Ryker's big head swung to gaze across the table at his shrinking brother. "How did ye leave Longview? Well, I trust?"

"Aye, very well," lied Charles glibly. He was still pale but he had decided to brazen it out. "We, too, are in need of an infusion of money."

Van Ryker's gray eyes glittered. "And Canady and MacDermott, what of them?" he asked softly.

"Both well." Charles took a gulp of wine.

"Ye lie!" In a single supple gesture, van Ryker gained his feet. Before Charles could move, his towering form had swooped across the table and seized Charles by the lace at his throat, sent the pearl tumbling as he jerked his brother from his chair. "I have just been to Carolina and ye left Canady dead and MacDermott nearly so. 'Twas your cowardice in running away under fire that made the slaves break and run—and they are all dead or taken by now, I've no doubt! What have ye to say for yourself?''

"But the day was already lost, Branch!" Looking near death, Charles found his voice. He was scrabbling at the hands that held him fast. "The savages had overrun us!"

"Again ye lie!" The tall buccaneer shook his cringing brother as a terrier might shake a rat. "Is there no truth in ye, Charles? Ye left them all to die—admit it!"

Charles's smoky-purple eyes were near bulging from his head. He cast a wild look of appeal at Imogene and found her stony-faced. Suddenly he seemed to crumple, hanging limply from van Ryker's fierce grip. "All right, I admit it, Branch!" he wailed. "I thought the day was lost and I ran for my life. A man cannot be faulted for trying to save his own life!"

With a low-voiced oath, van Ryker flung Charles away from him. Skidding backward, Charles's thick figure collided with the carved arm of his tall-backed chair and both he and the chair went crashing to the floor.

"Get up," ordered van Ryker. "Stop sniveling." And as Charles scrambled to his feet, righted the chair and sank down upon it, he turned to Anthony. "What did Charles tell you when he arrived?"

Anthony's murky lavender eyes were very bright. They glittered like amethysts. He saw at once the danger to both himself and Charles—thieves must hang together. "He arrived in scruffy shape, dirty and unshaven. He told me the Indians had attacked them in Carolina and that he had been lucky to escape with his scalp, that he had managed by a miracle to gain the coast and had the luck to chance upon a fishing party who—at the price of all he had on him—brought him to Port Royal, where he borrowed money from the minister, Mr. Gibbons, to get him upriver to me. That's about the size of it, Branch. He arrived only today."

"I see." Van Ryker was studying both brothers under lowered brows. "Well, I think I'd best leave Charles in your charge, Tony. Perhaps you can make a man of him. He's not fit to run a plantation and I feel sick to my heart that I left good men to die under his command."

"But you said MacDermott did not die," squeaked Charles.

"No fault of yours that he didn't," said van Ryker shortly. "Twas mere happenstance that I arrived in time. And the plantation's gone. I've no doubt 'twill have been burned to the ground when next I see it."

"You're going back, then?" Anthony pricked up his ears.

Van Ryker nodded carelessly. "When I've a mind to. But 'twill no longer be left to Charles! Faith, I should have set MacDermott to run it and let Charles be the factor!"

Charles was red to his ears. He began to look resentful, now that he no longer feared for his life. "We were outnumbered," he muttered.

"One of you should have been able to handle ten of them," said van Ryker coldly. "Give me no excuses, Charles." He looked back at Anthony. "Has no one else arrived this day?"

"No. Should someone have arrived?" Anthony looked alarmed.

"Yes. They should be here soon."

"Ah—you mean the luggage, of course." When that remark brought no answer from van Ryker, Anthony watched the turbaned black woman he called Yamsy bring in two plates, which she set before the guests. Trying to assume the role of gracious host, he turned back to van Ryker. "What news do ye bring us from the outside world, Branch?"

"I would expect ye'd have more news for me than I for you, for I've been at sea these past weeks. I was sorry to hear of MacNaughton's passing—a good man."

"Aye." Anthony heaved a deep sigh. "He was a good factor. I'll miss him—but he was ill for a long time. He wanted me to keep it from you, for he feared you'd replace him."

"Did he leave any kin?"

"None we could find. We buried him in Spanish Town, since that was his wish."

There was a moment of silence. Then van Ryker gave his brother a keen look. "What happens at Spanish Town, Tony? I heard the old governor was ill."

"And like to die." Anthony nodded. "Word is, the king is sending out a new governor for Jamaica—Lord Marr."

"I don't know him."

"London family, long at court. Old Lord Marr was the king's staunch ally all through his exile. But the word is"—Anthony's full lips curved slyly—"that he's being sent out to rid the seas of the buccaneers."

"Nonsense," said van Ryker briskly. "Without the buccaneers, Jamaica and all the other English colonies in the Caribbean would lie open to Spanish attack. They'd overrun Barbados—only a fool of a king would want to rid himself of the buccaneers."

"I know ye do consider yourselves privateers, Branch, but the word at court—if I'm to believe the gossip that comes my way from what few visitors we get here—is that King Charles does not share your view. He regards ye as denying the royal coffers much needed revenue."

Van Ryker gave a short laugh. "Ye mean he wants a tenth share of all treasure taken and another tenth part for his brother, the duke of York?"

Anthony nodded solemnly. "And will have it, else ye're all to be driven from the seas."

"By this Lord Marr?" scoffed van Ryker. "Who does he bring with him? The British fleet?"

"Ye're forgetting the Jamaica Squadron, Branch!"

"I'm not forgetting it. 'Tis a good force but overburdened. They must needs dash from place to place, for these colonies are defended by but a few coastal guns and a scattering of forts. D'ye mean to tell me this Lord Marr plans to focus the Jamaica Squadron on Tortuga? If so, he's rash indeed, for the guns of the Mountain Fort will blow him out of Cayona Bay before he's loosed a shot at the town!"

Anthony bit his lip. "I but wished to warn you, Branch," he said in an altered tone. " 'Tis but what I hear."

"I will consider myself warned." Van Ryker turned his attention to his food, ate as if famished. Imogene was reminded that he was a strong violent man in his prime and found a diet of fruit insufficient for his strenuous lovemaking.

"Whence do you hail?" asked Anthony, turning to Imogene as if in relief.

"The Scilly Isles. I was born in Penzance, but after my

parents perished in the Civil Wars, I went to live on Tresco with my guardian.''

"I did not know Branch had frequented the Scillies," murmured Anthony.

Van Ryker's dark head came up. "I met the lady elsewhere," he said sternly, and his forbidding tone made Anthony forbear to inquire further.

"Your sister Esme," asked Imogene suddenly. "Do you hear from her often?" She was looking at him coldly— this was the man who had described her as a "dockside whore"!

Van Ryker shot her a glance but Anthony, unaware of any friction, seemed eager to answer. "From time to time. Esme is an infrequent correspondent." He turned to van Ryker. "She is living in London now, Branch. She has left Jules."

"I feared she would not be happy with that Frenchman," sighed van Ryker. "But you were there, Charles. You wrote me that she *would* marry him, wrong choice though he has turned out to be."

"She has asked that I forward her some money for her support," murmured Anthony tentatively. "If you could spare some, Branch?"

"I will take care of the matter later," said van Ryker. "After this voyage. Her creditors can wait until then." He lifted his big head and listened. "I think I hear our guests now."

"I don't hear anything," muttered Charles. "Do you, Tony?"

Anthony shook his head and motioned Charles to be silent.

"No need to rise, Tony. I'll go and bring them in." Van Ryker rose and left the room. When he came back, he was ushering in two gentlemen. One, whom he introduced with a warning frown at Imogene as Raoul de Parnasse, she recognized with surprise as the rakish French doctor from the *Sea Rover,* Raoul de Rochemont. The other, a short, stoutish gentleman in a tall hat with a thick white beard cropped square to widen a thin face, he was about to introduce when Charles sprang forward.

"Mr. Gibbons," he cried, regarding the minister in astonishment. "I did not mean to put ye to the trouble of coming upriver to collect the money I borrowed!"

"He is not here to collect that," said van Ryker coolly. "Although of course I shall recompense him for any out-of-pocket expenses you have cost him. He is here for another reason. Have you brought the license, Raoul?"

The rakish Frenchman nodded.

"Then let us be about it. For it has come to my attention that there are some"—van Ryker's gaze played coldly over his brothers—"who do not consider our marriage a binding one, nor believe a certain governor to be authorized to issue a license." Charles turned beet red but Anthony's gaze was watchful; he had begun to frown.

"*I* never said that, Branch," he muttered argumentatively.

"What ye said or did not say about it is of no account now," said the tall buccaneer. "We are here to rectify the situation. Raoul here has brought Mr. Gibbons upriver to perform a Christian ceremony and unite Imogene and myself in holy wedlock—I, Branch Ryder, and this lady who already bears my name. Ye are all my witnesses."

Imogene's heart gave a lurch. Van Ryker had taken note of how she felt when she read that snatch of letter from Esme. He was not willing to go away to sea—very possibly to his death on some slippery deck—and let her union with him be contested. She felt a sudden dazzling pride in him, just as she had felt on a night in Tortuga when he had explained, with a naked sword lying on the table, all that he had done to win her.

Proudly she stood beside him in the candlelight. Proudly she took his hand. Proudly she faced the near-sighted minister Gibbons, who had no need to read the ceremony—he knew it by heart. And so, on a hot night in Jamaica, Imogene, who had been a buccaneer's bride known everywhere throughout the Caribbean as "van Ryker's woman," became wife to Branch Ryder, gentleman of Devon.

Gibbons, she realized, never dreamed he was uniting a famous buccaneer with a woman about whose head scandals had swirled since her early teens. Plainly, de Rochemont had

not told him; like the rest of them, de Rochemont was sailing
under false colors. The stoutish minister with the cropped
white beard beamed as he pronounced them man and wife,
and afterward, as the rest of them celebrated the wedding
with wine, forgot any questions he might have had and
pounced upon the good food on the table and ate ravenously.

But for Imogene this merry celebration did not last long.
Hardly was it well begun before her buccaneer bridegroom,
studying her from beneath dark brows as he lounged at the far
end of the table, rose and abruptly proposed a last toast to the
bride's health "for we must be abed"—which caused a ripple
of laughter to circle the table and brought a smiling blush to
Imogene's face.

"And once again I'll carry my bride across her threshold,"
declared the tall buccaneer gallantly. Imogene rose and twined
her arms about his neck and de Rochemont applauded as van
Ryker scooped her up and carried her out into the courtyard
and upstairs.

There in the bedchamber Anthony had assigned them, he
laid her down carefully upon the bed, bent over her with a
face of yearning.

"Imogene, Imogene," he whispered ruefully. "Ye're more
woman than I deserve."

"Nonsense," she scoffed, and would have pulled him
down to her. When he resisted, stepping back with a sigh, she
jumped up and began undoing the hooks of her bodice.
"Help me," she said impatiently—for the thought was ever
in her mind that she would so lure him from his intentions
that he would end up abandoning this voyage altogether, sell
the Sea Rover, or turn it over to his men—anything, just so he
did not prowl these dangerous seas again.

Van Ryker obliged by undoing the last of the hooks.

"You could at least remove your sword," she murmured,
feeling it swing against her thigh.

He did not answer but cupped her breast with his hand and
pressed a kiss upon her white shoulder, let his lips prowl her
neck as he breathed deep of the heady lemon scent of her
hair. Then the dress went over her head; Imogene unfastened

her petticoat and let it glide down over her hips to the floor and looked up smiling.

Van Ryker had stepped back and she saw that the expression on his dark face was one of great indecision, for the sight of his twice-wed bride was breathtaking. The candlelight played over her golden hair, rippling down it, and turned her delicate peachbloom skin to gold. Her lips were softly parted and her blue eyes promised everything. As he watched she pulled the silken drawstring, shrugged her tempting body free from her chemise and stood before him naked in all her glorious womanhood.

Amused at the intentness of his stance, she gave him a mocking look, turned slightly and bent to remove her shoes and stockings, her bare bottom flashing at him as she did so. "I'll be in bed before you!" she taunted him over her shoulder.

But before the second shoe was off she heard the bedchamber door close. And then a key turning in the lock.

"Van Ryker!" She whirled in alarm. "You're not leaving!"

His voice came to her from the other side of the door. "I *must* leave, Imogene. If I stay with you longer, God knows I may never leave your side."

"But why must you leave *now?*" she wheedled, pressing her naked body against the door. "This is our wedding night—our second, true, but to be paid some attention to, none the less!"

His sigh reached her through the sturdy door. "We'll have it later—when I return."

She began to batter on the door. "I will *not* be left in Jamaica!"

"Imogene," he said ironically. "I intend to leave you where you will be safe—no matter how it galls you!"

Her voice rose dangerously. "I will not be cheated out of my wedding night!"

She heard his laughing "Good-bye, my lady," and the sound of his boots clattering down the stairs. She beat against the door angrily. "Come back!" she shouted. And kicked the wooden panel—winced, and seized her shoe and began beating against it. "Let me out!" she screamed. "Let me out, do you hear? I will not be left in Jamaica!"

Boots pounded on the stairs, but they were strange footsteps, not van Ryker's. Then Anthony Ryder's voice, sounding solicitous.

"Pray do not excite yourself. Branch swears he will be back—intact, and meantime we will do our best to entertain you here."

"Let me out!"

"I have promised Branch that I will not unlock this door tonight. He fears you may try to follow him."

"Then I will go out the window!"

"If you choose." He sounded cheerful. "But it is rather a long drop. And if you *do* land safely on the ground without breaking a leg, you will find two of my servants waiting to bring you back inside."

Imogene's shoe struck the door and she heard him laugh. "Branch said you were spirited," he observed. "It would seem he was right!"

Downstairs a door closed—that would be van Ryker and de Rochemont going out into the night. Imogene's naked body sagged against the door. He was gone. Gone into the wilds of the Caribbean, where Spanish guns might find him. Perhaps he was never coming back.

She went over and threw herself face down upon the bed. She had never felt so alone.

CHAPTER 9

In the darkness below, just outside the house—for they did not want the minister Gibbons to hear them—van Ryker was having a last conversation with his brother.

Anthony murmured that they'd need to bring Imogene's luggage ashore.

"Time enough for that later." Van Ryker brushed that aside.

Anthony blinked. "But won't ye need the boat if ye're going back downriver?"

"There's another boat waiting for us."

So van Ryker had been followed upriver by a crew of buccaneers who were even now waiting for him? That would certainly explain his hurry to leave! Anthony tried to concentrate on what his brother was saying.

"Ye'll send the minister downriver tomorrow, Tony," he was being instructed. "No need for him to know I have any other name than Branch Ryder."

"What? Oh—right." Anthony's mind was still on Imogene and the way she had fought to get out and accompany Branch. He gazed enviously at his brother, asking himself what it was about Branch that would make a beautiful woman so unshakably loyal to him.

"And you must care for Imogene in my absence," van Ryker was saying. "I'll be back for her—tell her that, for she fears for me greatly. Promise me ye'll guard her with your life, Tony."

"Ah, I will," cried Anthony. The light that flared in his murky lavender eyes seemed to van Ryker one of determination—how could he know that it was of sheer relief that van Ryker would be gone before tomorrow's dawn revealed the mighty strides the plantation had made? "Ye can count on me, Branch," he said heartily.

Van Ryker gave his brother's elegant shoulder a friendly cuff. "I'll make things right with ye, Tony," he promised. "Never doubt it."

"Yes, yes, but now 'tis best ye get ye gone," muttered Anthony, eager not to prolong the departure. "For this is English soil, Branch, and ye tread upon it at your peril."

If van Ryker winced inwardly at this reminder that he was a wanted man, he did not show it. He told Anthony to go back inside and allay the minister's astonishment that the groom would leave the bride so soon after the nuptials "for we want no suspicion there, Tony."

Anthony wanted none either and hastened away.

Van Ryker stood with his thumbs hooked in his belt, looking up at the house for a moment. It might be, he knew, the last time that he would ever see it—and the last time he saw the golden woman he had left here.

Then, ''If we hurry, Raoul, we can make tomorrow's tide,'' he muttered and turned away. At night the vegetation but a little way beyond the house rose up like a green wall, solid and dense. It was into this wall he plunged and disappeared into the darkness with Raoul following.

He might have turned back toward Gale Force had he known that down on the coast a lean pirate ship, *Le Sabre*, was just then gliding into Port Royal bay.

And he would certainly have turned back even though he had reached the coast, could he have heard the muttered conversation that took place between the brothers that night in the garden after the white-bearded minister was snoring in his bed and Imogene lay pensively in hers, staring out at a white moon and wondering if van Ryker would live to return to her.

''Well, Branch has done it now,'' Charles said gloomily, looking up at the house, which from here looked larger than it was, looming up above them in the moonlight. ''He's married the wench once and for all—in sight of God and all the people.''

''Not so,'' declared his brother, who now leaned against the bole of a tall coconut palm and also studied the house, behind whose walls Imogene lay abed. ''He has married her in *our* sight, Charles. For we were the only witnesses.''

''And that French doctor,'' pointed out Charles.

''I do not count him,'' said Anthony in a cold voice.

''D'ye not, Tony?''

''No. He's a Frenchman, a buccaneer, and easily lost track of.''

''Well, Mr. Gibbons is not so easily lost track of! For he's a minister in Port Royal.''

''Ye've hit the nail on the head, Charles.'' Anthony sighed and brushed a night-flying insect from his elegant sleeve. '' 'Tis Gibbons is our problem—not the Frenchman.''

His thicker-witted brother stared at him. "What d'ye have in mind?" he asked at last.

"A license was procured—but who will know that license was ever used if the minister is dead and you and I do not tell it?"

Charles recoiled. "Ye are not going to kill a man of the cloth, Tony?"

"No." Anthony smiled thinly. "*You* are going to do it, Charles." And at Charles's exclamation, his surly, "*You* aren't going to tell *me* to kill someone, Tony," he turned on his brother with a Machiavellian adroitness.

"You are not going to do it because I tell you to, Charles," he said suavely. "You are going to do it in your own enlightened self-interest. If Gibbons lives to return to Port Royal, he will make a record of this marriage—one we will be hard put to erase. But if he does *not* live to return to Port Royal, none will know of it—save you and I, and Branch and the Frenchman."

"And the woman."

"And the woman, of course."

"The servants, Tony?"

"They will do as I tell them. They fear not to. Besides, I kept them well back during the ceremony—they know not what went on. Tomorrow you will take Gibbons downriver—and you will lose him in the Cobre. You will drown him, Charles, and return with a sad story of how he fell overboard and you could not save him. None but you will know what really happened."

"I'll not! *You* kill him! I wash my hands of it."

"If you do *not* do it, Charles," Anthony's cold voice froze to ice, "*I* will wash my hands of *you*. And how will you make out, turned out into the commons with naught but the clothes on your back? Think on it. Ye've a liking for luxurious living, and if Branch is gone—and keep in mind he cannot live forever at his trade, he may not even survive this present voyage—then ye can sell Longview for enough to keep ye in style for the rest of your days."

Charles was silent. Then a long sigh emanated from his

flabby body. "I will do it," he said in a defeated voice. "Tell me how you think it should be done, Tony."

With a triumphant gleam in his eyes, his brother told him.

"But then there's still the woman to be taken care of, Tony."

"Yes." That dark wig nodded. "There's still the woman to be taken care of, but leave her to me, Charles. *I* will dispose of her."

Two weeks had passed since van Ryker had left and Charles had made his fateful trip downriver with the Reverend Gibbons and returned with the minister's hat and a tale of a terrible accident in which Gibbons had fallen overboard and drowned. Two weeks in which the burning jewel eyes of Anthony Ryder had played over Imogene, seeing her in sun and shade, pensive as she waited for van Ryker's return, but for all that a lustrous bird of plumage. He saw her now in the garden outside, a sunny vision in her yellow dress, and stood at gaze, leaning on the balustrade, to watch her.

Money had always been the thing that drove Anthony—money and power. He had itched to own, to possess, to control, to dominate. Women had had no real place in his life. A servant girl's skirts—even a slave's—had served well enough for his needs. But now as he studied this woman with hair of molten gold in the hot Jamaica sunlight, watched her as she bent gracefully to bury her face in the brilliant blossoms of the bougainvillaea, saw her turn with a light swirl of skirts and toss back her shimmering hair, he was forced to admit there were other things in life than money. . . .

Watching her now, he could imagine what life would be like if she belonged to him. He saw her strolling through Port Royal with all the buccaneers at gaze. Saw her sweeping all before her at Government House in Spanish Town. Saw her sitting at his candlelit table here at Gale Force with her beautiful delft blue eyes not brooding over Branch's fate, but filled with concern for *him*—Anthony.

And beyond that, he saw her in his bedroom in a filmy gown that left nothing to the imagination. Black, it should be, he thought critically, studying her slender form in the garden. Of black gossamer lace, fine as a spider web, with the moonlight peeking through it and silvering her peachbloom skin with its fine pale light. He would be divesting himself of his garments in that bedroom and she would lean against the bedpost in the heat, fanning herself lightly with a palm-leaf fan that would blow and ripple that gossamer that only half shielded her naked beauty.

And then as he approached her, naked now himself, she would of a sudden pull the black satin riband drawstring that held up her night rail and it would float down and away from her like a cloud. She would step out of it into his arms. Her warm damp flesh would press against his in sweet torment and her kisses would be like wine. Bodies entwined, they would fall into his great bed and he would have his way with her. He would steal from that fair body all its sweetness. He would—

His hot thoughts came to a crashing halt. This was Branch's woman and Branch, from the time they were boys, had always taken everything worth having. That these good things had come to Branch by blood and sweat and dangerous endeavor he counted for nothing; that Branch had been more than generous to his half-brothers and half-sister he counted for less.

For now he wanted Branch's woman—and Branch, whom the world knew as the dangerous buccaneer van Ryker, stood squarely in his way.

Anthony knew he should have tried to keep from Imogene the great strides he had made with the plantation—for any day Branch might appear and whisk her away, and if Imogene was kept in ignorance there might still be the chance to hoodwink Branch. But he had not been able to resist strutting before Imogene, proudly showing her the orchards he had caused to be planted, taking her riding over the cane fields, exhibiting the sugar mill that was going up, the increasing livestock—in short, parading before her his wealth.

The effect on the lady had not been quite what he had hoped. Two afternoons ago had been a fair example.

They had all been sitting on the long veranda, relaxing in the shade with cooling drinks. Imogene, her golden hair bound up and looking pensive in her light yellow calico dress, so suited to the tropics, was leaning back in one of three throne-backed woven reed chairs made on the island. She was toying with a glass of limeade that had been chilled in the spring near the house.

Across from her on the other thronelike reed chairs lounged van Ryker's half-brothers, Charles and Anthony. Charles was carelessly dressed, for he was of a careless nature and tended to be slovenly in appearance. His shirt was open in the heat and the lace at his throat looked wilted.

Anthony Ryder presented quite a different picture. Faultlessly attired in peach brocade, he seemed not to feel the heat at all. His grooming was meticulous—indeed he might have been seated on a marble bench at the Court of St. James rather than on a reed chair on a hibiscus-covered veranda in Jamaica.

"The furnishings here are lovely," Imogene was saying frankly. "I had not expected anything half so fine."

"Almost all are of rosewood," Anthony admitted proudly. "Some pieces are imported, of course, some things were made locally, for rosewood abounds here—'tis actually mahogany, but of so fine a grade that when the wood is fresh cut it emits an odor of roses. I have ordered carved mahogany doors to be constructed for the entire house."

"I am sorry van Ryker—Branch—" Imogene tripped apologetically over the name, for she could not rid herself of the habit of calling her husband "van Ryker"—"could not stay to see all that you have done with the plantation. I am sure he would have been delighted."

"Aye, Tony is a wonder," agreed Charles gloomily.

Anthony's chest expanded beneath his peach brocade doublet. "I have done fairly well," he admitted modestly.

"Better than that!" Imogene's voice was warm. "Had van Ryk—had Branch stayed overnight and seen it all, I think he might have been persuaded to leave off his voyage and settle down here at last." There was a wistful note to that, for it was what she most desired.

The brothers exchanged glances.

"Yes, he might," said Anthony with a quelling look at Charles. "But . . . I think the time is not yet, Imogene."

"Oh, how could it not be?" she demanded passionately. "Surely you, as much as I, would urge him to leave off his dangerous profession? For someday if he persists in it some Spanish shot will surely reach him!" A shudder went through her spontaneously at the thought.

"That could happen, I admit it," murmured Anthony. "But you are not to think on it, Imogene. Branch has always been lucky in such matters—he will surely live a long time."

"So we are to hope his luck holds," said Imogene bitterly. "Instead of persuading him to leave off!"

Anthony saw he was losing ground by taking this tack and hastily amended his stance. "Not at all," he said, and in an attempt to change the subject, "I have just heard from Esme."

"I didn't know you'd heard from her!" Charles looked startled.

Anthony gave his brother a silencing look and Charles fell back, realizing there had been no letter, that this was just another ploy of Anthony's devious mind.

"Esme writes from London," continued Anthony smoothly. "She begs to be remembered to you, Charles, and hopes your fortunes are improved. But it was what she had to say about Branch that interested me most."

Imogene, who remembered that part of a letter from Esme that she had snatched from Branch's table and read, lifted her head. She half expected Esme's quoted words to be something about Branch's marriage of which she so strongly disapproved, but Anthony's next words caused her to lean forward tensely.

"She is moving in lofty circles now, our Esme." Anthony leaned back, smiling at Imogene. "She had dined at Whitehall only the night before she penned the letter. She has friends well placed at court and she thinks it might be possible to secure a king's pardon for Branch." He watched her for effect—it was immediate.

"Oh, that would be wonderful!" breathed Imogene.

And Charles, who was half persuaded by Anthony's manner that the letter was genuine, demanded, "How? How does she say she can do it?"

"She does not say, Charles. She promises she will write to me at greater length about it." Anthony was bedazzled by the full power of Imogene's gaze, now bent upon him. "Perhaps I will be able to give her some guidance," he added expansively.

"Oh, do write to her," begged Imogene. "With a king's pardon, we could live anywhere we liked!"

"Yes, Tony, they could even choose to live in Jamaica," pointed out Charles gloomily.

"Yes—even in Jamaica!" In her happiness at this startling new development, Imogene missed the gloom in Charles's tone.

"I should very much like to have you live in Jamaica, Imogene," said Anthony, and she ascribed the sudden warmth in his voice to his delight at having a cloud removed from the family name, and not to the real reason. She could not know that at that moment Anthony was envisioning her as Branch's widow, now married to *him*. Had she known, she would have recoiled from him in horror. As it was, Esme's suggestion of a pardon for Branch seized upon her mind and she thought of little else, asking Anthony daily if anyone passing upriver had brought him a letter from Esme.

It was her preoccupation with the river—and the river traffic coming and going up and down the Cobre from Spanish Town to Port Royal, that led her to make a terrifying discovery.

From her upstairs window she saw a riverboat approach and saw Anthony down at the landing. Hurrying downstairs, she would have rushed out the front doors but that one of the slave girls was just dumping a large bucket of water over the tiles, preparatory to scrubbing the floor. Imogene elected to go out the back. She found herself in a tangle of uncut undergrowth and was just about to emerge from behind a screen of cascading vines that spilled down from one of the large trees, when she heard something that caused her to stiffen to stillness and listen.

Anthony had been dashing up the slope and on the other side of those vines he had obviously encountered Charles, for she heard Charles's gasping, "My God, Tony, what is it?" And then Anthony's low savage growl, and his, "How did ye think to fool me? Out with it!"

"Fool ye? I didn't!" She could hear Charles writhing in Anthony's grasp, for the older brother was by far the stronger. "What're ye talking about, Tony?"

"Did ye not?" A crash of broken branches as Anthony flung Charles from him. "The Reverend Gibbons sends you his regards. He says he forgives you for rowing away and leaving him in the stream but he would appreciate the return of his hat! *Why didn't you kill him as I told you to?*"

"But I thought he had perished," wailed Charles. "I did as you told me, I pretended to a seizure and managed to lurch against him and knock him overboard into the current—and I was sure his boots would drag him down. There was no one about. I just—"

"You just simply left him." His scorn lashed out at Charles. "You didn't make sure he was dead."

"Oh, I was sure of it. The river was terrible there!"

"You came back and told me he was dead," said Anthony bitterly. "And now there's this message delivered by Amos Whittel that tells us he is not. He has got himself back to Port Royal and entered the marriage in the record books!"

There was a sniveling sound from Charles. "'Twas too much to ask of me, Tony," he burst out. "I could not strike down a man of the cloth! Not while he floundered in the water! I could not watch, I seized the oars—"

"Damn your niceties, Charles!" Anthony's voice was laced with fury and with something else—something very like despair. "For you have forced on me a decision I did not want to make. For now there's no way out—we must kill Imogene—for if Branch dies and she lives, we are still lost. The will leaves everything to her—ye know that."

"Oh, we cannot—I will not be a party to it, Tony!" Charles's voice was filled with mounting horror.

"I will think on it." Anthony sounded tired. "I think I have the answer, Charles. We can neither of us afford to be a party to anything happening to her, for Branch would tear us to pieces in his vengeance. No, we must spirit her to London, Charles, and let Esme deal with her."

"Ye think she would?" Charles wondered fearfully.

"I know she would," sighed Anthony. "For Esme's a good head on her shoulders and she knows we'd share with her if she broke up this marriage for us."

"True, I do remember she hoodwinked Branch into taking the blame when you killed Vincent Dunworth," agreed Charles.

"Ye'd best forget that," said his brother sharply. "All the world believes Branch did it—he signed a confession, if you'll remember."

"Esme loves you well," sighed Charles. "I doubt she'd have done it for me."

"She was angry enough with Dunworth to kill him herself and well you know it. 'Twas a toss-up who'd kill him—Esme or me!"

"But he was her lover!"

"*And* was going to marry another woman and put *me* in debtors' prison for my tailor's bills, which he refused to pay!"

" 'Twas not enough to kill a man for, Tony—a tailor's bill! Ye should have found a way to pay it."

"How?"

"Ye could have asked Branch for the money."

"How, you fool? None of us knew Branch was back in England before he showed up that night at Dunworth Hall with pockets full of gold and Esme had the presence of mind to tell him Vincent had raped her and she'd killed him in defense of her honor!"

"But if Branch returns and finds we've spirited his bride away from him—"

"She'll go, Charles," came the gloomy response. "She'll go willingly to secure this pardon for Branch that I invented. Oh, damn ye, Charles!" His voice was of a sudden grief-stricken. "For I wanted the wench for myself and now I must lose her!" There was the sound of a hard blow and the vines bent back whiplike as Charles's flabby body careened into them.

But by now Imogene, who had stopped dead in her tracks at their first stunning words, was pressed tight against a tree bole, holding her breath. All that she had just learned resounded through her head like the sonorous beat of a great drum.

They were false, these half-brothers of van Ryker's—as Esme was false. Esme had probably never been near Whitehall—it was all Anthony's invention. Anthony and Charles and Esme—they had all fed on Branch's generosity, his greatness of spirit, his chivalry. They had all profited by it! Imogene yearned to burst out of the enveloping vines and accuse them—but she knew death awaited any such move, here in the hot Jamaican sunlight.

Instead she waited, breathlessly still, while Charles struggled up and dusted himself off and followed, complaining, after Anthony, who was striding toward the house. After they were gone she made her way at right angles to the house to a little spring-fed pool Anthony had shown her. There she took off her shoes and stockings and dipped a foot into the water.

Let them find her here wading! Let them put their minds to rest that she had heard nothing—nothing.

Anthony had said she'd go willingly—ah, indeed she would! For somehow she must get word to van Ryker, somehow she must tell him that some horrible plot was afoot to get him killed—for that was how she had interpreted Anthony's deadly "if Branch dies and she lives." Yes, and she must tell him of Esme's treachery, of his own chivalrous foolishness—oh, perhaps there would yet be a way to resolve it all in his favor!

So reasoned Imogene in desperation as she stared down at her reflection in the mirrorlike depths of the pool.

It was there Anthony found her, lying apparently relaxed by the pool with her shoes and stockings beside her, munching on a mango.

She saw he looked worried and came to a sitting position, as if in alarm. "Is something the matter?" she cried. "You look so—upset, Anthony."

His expression cleared as if by magic, for by her very startled manner he was assured that she had heard nothing.

"I *am* a bit upset." He studied her. "For I have just learnt that Charles deserted poor Mr. Gibbons in the river and rowed away, leaving him to his fate. Fortunately Gibbons made it to Port Royal. . . . "

Imogene gave him a suitably bewildered look. "Oh, Branch must not hear of it, for he would be doubly angry with Charles."

"I am glad you wish to keep peace in the family, Imogene."

"It is my greatest desire." She met his sharp gaze with an innocent stare. "What time is it, Anthony? Don't tell me I have whiled away the whole afternoon here?" Hastily she began to don her shoes and stockings.

"It is indeed time for dinner," he said more softly, watching her graceful movements with delight. It made him the more bitter toward Charles, as he escorted this winning woman back to the house. And it never occurred to him that the smiling face she turned to him was as full of guile as his own.

The High Seas, 1660

CHAPTER 10

A fresh wind billowed the sails of the *Carolina*, bound for London from Port Royal, Jamaica, but her captain, John Wilkerson, found nothing in that to comfort him.

"I like not the look of the weather," he said, shaking his head as he spoke to the ship's master, Curtis Watford. "What think ye of it, Mister Watford?"

From her place by the rail nearby—for she had been

walking up and down the deck as restlessly as a caged cat—Imogene turned to hear the answer.

She had lost a little weight in the two weeks the *Carolina* had been at sea. All morning she had been recalling every step of how she had come to be here—outmaneuvered and outgunned, she told herself bitterly.

It had all seemed so simple, the perfect solution, when Anthony had brought up at supper the day after she had heard the angry discussion between the brothers, the subject of her voyage. He had been dressed most correctly in apple green taffetas. He had taken snuff delicately and put away his enameled snuffbox before he had brought up the subject.

"I have this day heard from Esme again," he had announced in a portentous way.

It took a physical effort for Imogene not to curl her lip in scorn. "What does she say?" she managed.

"Gossip is rife through the court that there is to be a Spanish marriage for the king—and that could well mean the end of the buccaneers."

Imogene felt fear go through her. She was almost certain that Anthony was lying for his own ends, but suppose there was truth to the rumor?

"Esme feels the rumor is well founded and thinks we should move with all possible speed."

"We?" asked Imogene mechanically.

"Esme fears she will not be able to engineer Branch's pardon in time," Anthony elaborated. "But"— he lifted one of his long fingers—"there is still hope."

"I can hardly believe it," she murmured.

"If *you* go to London."

Imogene stared at him fixedly. "But what could *I* do there?" she wondered.

Anthony gave her a supercilious smile. "King Charles," he murmured, "is a notorious roué. He acknowledges a dozen or more mistresses and has God knows how many more."

Imogene stiffened. "Are you suggesting I become Charles's mistress?" she asked frostily.

For a moment he gave her an admiring look. Blast, the wench had style! Any ordinary woman would jump at the chance of being a king's mistress—would simper, indeed, at the mere suggestion of it! "No, I'm not suggesting that," he said. "But Esme says Charles is frequently deep in his cups. She hints that a woman with beauty such as yours could easily lure him to a private supper, ply him with drink, get the pardon signed and be gone before Charles woke up."

"Is that the way such things are done?" Imogene hoped she could keep the scalding fury out of her voice.

"That—and other ways. . . . The point is, Charles is susceptible to beauty, Branch is in need of a pardon—you will find a way."

"In London?"

"In London."

"Very well." Imogene rose as if the discussion had tired her. "When shall I go? Or do you not think I should wait for Branch's return before I go?"

"Oh, by no means. Do you think he would let you go to the court of a licentious king to plead his cause?"

"You are right," she agreed carelessly. "He would not." She frowned. "But how am I to go? I have not enough money for passage."

"I will advance all you need," said Anthony, frowning.

"Oh—would you do that?" Imogene gave him a bright, insincere smile.

"I will do more. I will take you to Port Royal and put you on the ship myself."

"To see that I am not mislaid on the journey downstream?" Her smile was quick to cover that, for her hatred of this pair was a palpable thing and she was constantly afraid that she would give herself away.

Anthony laughed tolerantly. "I would also satisfy myself that it is a stout merchant ship that you set your foot upon, for Branch would hold me accountable were I to let you embark upon some leaky barge."

"And what ship is this?"

"Her name is the *Carolina* and she sails day after tomorrow. I suggest you pack, for we shall be going downriver in the morning.''

"Does she go direct to London?"

"Such is her captain's plan."

Imogene began to feel hemmed in. "You are right," she said with decision. "I *should* go. Although for London, I shall need some things—no matter, I can always pick them up in Port Royal."

"Or wait till London for a better choice," agreed her host in as offhand a manner as her own, although his murky eyes had brightened. "I would be glad to guide you about Port Royal's shops."

"I can't think I'd need a guide in broad daylight!"

"Port Royal is too dangerous a place for a woman alone even in the daytime," he said smoothly, and she felt checkmated.

He suspects me, she thought, and a bright little flutter of fear rippled through her breast.

"A very sinful city, Port Royal," said Charles heavily. " 'Tis said to be the wickedest city in the world."

"I doubt it could triumph over London in that regard," said Anthony calmly. "But of course Imogene will have Esme to guide her through the maze there."

Yes, thought Imogene grimly. *I will have Esme there! I wonder if she'll let me disembark or send some cutthroat to stab me whilst I'm still aboard?*

But she knew her impulsive remark about shopping in Port Royal had sown seeds of doubt in Anthony's mind, and cursed herself for speaking out. She should have waited until she was already in Port Royal and found some excuse for leaving his side.

As it was, both brothers stuck to her like molasses until she was safe aboard the *Carolina.* Although she had looked about her carefully on the way to the ship, she had not seen any faces she recognized from Tortuga. There were plenty of strong-muscled men with cutlasses clanking, plenty of hard-eyed traders, but none to whom she could call out that she was being kidnapped—none to come to her aid.

She told herself that did not matter. The captain of the

Carolina was a kind-enough-looking Englishman—although his lips did tighten a bit at sight of her and he gazed at her watchfully as she came aboard. But he had an open-faced appearance and Imogene could not believe that he was in league with the Ryder brothers.

Ah, surely he would listen to reason! As soon as they had cleared the harbor, she would go to him, she would tell him she needed passage to Tortuga and that Captain van Ryker would reward him well for this change in plans and this short delay in reaching English shores.

Hardly had they cleared the harbor before she sought him out, telling him that she urgently desired passage to Tortuga and that he would be well rewarded.

"By whom, Mistress Wells?" wondered the captain, regarding her from beneath shadowed lids.

Imogene hesitated. His words had reminded her that Anthony had booked her passage on this voyage as "Imogene Wells," which was her maiden name. Was she now to give another name? She took a deep breath. "Captain van Ryker will reward you for bringing me there," she said quietly.

"'Van Ryker,' ay?" The captain gave a short barking laugh. "Mistress, I advise you to go to your cabin and keep to yourself this voyage. I've no mind to listen to rubbish, nor yet have my crew annoyed with it, either!"

Taken aback, Imogene left the captain to wander about distractedly. Eventually she cornered one of the ship's officers, who, although dazzled by her beauty, left her side abruptly when she asked him to deliver a message to Tortuga on his return voyage.

It was the same with the ship's doctor, save that he peered with clinical interest into her blue eyes and asked gently, "How *long* have you imagined this van Ryker?"

"I do *not* imagine him!" cried Imogene indignantly. "He is very real, as is his ship of forty guns! And if you can but help me persuade your captain to return me to him, he will reward all of you handsomely!"

The ship's doctor shook his head. "You sound miraculous honest," he sighed. "If ye have trouble sleeping, I've a potion might do the trick. But I'd not be bandying this story about, else the captain swears he'll have you in irons.''

" 'In irons'? For *what*? What is my crime?''

"No crime, mistress," sighed the doctor. "But ye might as well know that your uncle, who paid for your passage back to England, told us about your trouble, how ye were jilted and pined and now have imagined for yourself a real buccaneer for your lover—he warned us ye might insist on being taken direct to him. But we're sworn to deliver ye to your Aunt Esme unscathed—even though the captain does insist that if ye turn violent or rail at us, he'll put ye in irons for the whole voyage. So take my advice, mistress, and stay clear of the captain and the crew. Walk, pace about—exercise is good for these nervous complaints, I do believe, although some would disagree. The voyage will pass soon enough and you'll forget all about pirates.''

Imogene had turned away from that conversation with tears of exasperation in her eyes. Anthony had outfoxed her. He had spread word of her "insanity" until no one would believe her—indeed, all the passengers had been warned of her "condition" by the captain and steered clear of her. One woman in passing was heard to remark tartly that such a one "belonged in Bedlam!"

Looking out across the empty ocean, Imogene realized there was to be no escape. She was on her way to London.

Until now, when the captain's gloomy question of the ship's master made her prick up her ears. Foul weather could make the captain beat toward Bermuda perhaps—there was a chance of escape there.

"There does look to be a gale coming," agreed Watford, frowning at the southeast, where clouds seemed to be endlessly forming only to race over their heads and disappear again into the northwest. They were out in the Atlantic now and all of yesterday mare's tail clouds had whipped past them, even into the red sunset as nightfall approached. Now a great bank of clouds had appeared to the southeast and was moving toward them like a great wall, endlessly tall. And out of that wall, scudding gray clouds spun off, flew overhead, reeled over the northwest horizon.

"Perhaps if we headed for Bermuda?" suggested Imogene.

Both men turned to gaze sternly at a woman who had the temerity to suggest a course at sea.

"We'll not be heading for Bermuda to pile up on the reefs there," said Captain Wilkerson heavily, nodding to the ship's master to accompany him as he moved away.

Imogene sighed. Madwoman they thought her—and as a madwoman they treated her. She supposed she was fortunate to have the run of the ship.

Now she looked toward that ominous wall of clouds piling up ever higher. She thought she had glimpsed its beginning in the glow of yesterday's spectacular sunset. This morning the sun had risen like a ruby ball above the ocean and workaday sailors had muttered as they looked at the steady line of little swells that moved across the sea.

Imogene had never experienced what they called a "West Indian hurricane," but now—like the captain and his crew— she sensed that something large and dangerous was churning toward them, something that would dwarf the little wooden ship that had seemed so capacious back in Port Royal's harbor.

By noon the captain had reconsidered his position and decided to strike out for Bermuda after all, but the storm winds of the afternoon, blowing in gusts and striking the ship with sudden lashing spatters of rain, drove him away from it, into the open sea. Had he made landfall in St. George's harbor as he desired, Imogene would surely have been reunited with little Georgiana, for unknown to her, Georgiana had not gone down with the *Wilhelmina*. Elise had slipped ashore with the baby when the ship had made an unscheduled stop at Bermuda to take on fresh water and had been in hiding there ever since, for she had heard Imogene had died far to the north and she feared revenge still might be taken on the child. They still lingered in Bermuda—and Imogene was for a little while that day within striking distance of Bermuda.

But the winds that shape the destinies of men had decided that was not to be. They blew the ship fiercely away from Bermuda and Imogene was not to know how near she had been to a reunion with her lost daughter.

That night was a terrible one aboard the *Carolina*. After a frightening coral and ruby sunset, the sun had seemed to sink into a sea of blood. Then violent gusts of rain had battered the ship, threatening to strip her of her shrouds. All night the crew worked desperately to save the masts and keep the straining ship from foundering. Rain came down in continuous sheets, and the shrieking of the gale made it necessary for the passengers, already bruised by being thrown about their cabins in the lurching ship, to shout at each other to be heard at all.

Imogene, clinging to her bunk, felt the ship shudder from stem to stern as mountainous waves raked her from end to end. She felt she would go deaf with the hellish noise of the elements. And then one last rending collision tossed her from her bunk and sent her crashing against the opposite wall of her tiny cabin.

For a moment she was stunned and then it came to her that this last blow had not come from a wave—they had struck something.

After several tries, she managed to gain the deck and through the sheets of water that threatened to knock her backward, she saw that they had crashed into what looked to be a derelict. The men were working frantically, but the lines of the two ships had become hopelessly entangled and the waves were causing them to pound against each other like giant hammers.

Tied together thus, the two sturdy little wooden ships were breaking each other apart.

A wave of spray dashed into Imogene's face and blinded her, and then as she opened her eyes again a tall green wall of water that turned black as it swept closer reared over her head. She screamed and grasped something and when the wall of water had passed over her and subsided again, she came up like a drowned thing to discover she was enmeshed in a tangle of fallen rigging.

She was trapped in it! She would go down with the ship! With frantic fingers she fought to free herself but the tangled ropes were too heavy for her and each fresh wave seemed to send her deeper in. A brilliant flash of blue lightning showed her that the effort to cut loose from the derelict had been abandoned and the ship's boats were being hastily lowered. Dear God, they were abandoning ship!

Imogene screamed to them but her voice was lost in the roar of the storm. The passengers, drenched and wailing, were struggling toward the boats, being washed back again. Imogene fought to extricate herself, to join them, but with each wave she was being pounded more tightly into the rigging, every time the water subsided it seemed to make the snarls of rope around her worse.

The last boat was being loaded now, amid howls and shrieks as precious stuff was washed away, as loved ones were clutched, and sometimes clinging arms torn from the necks around which they tried to lock. Imogene, fighting for her life in the snarled rigging of a broken mast, saw children swept away from their parents and at least one sailor borne away on a broken spar.

"Cap'n—there's a woman over here!" It was the ship's master, who had discovered Imogene as he struggled across the deck carrying a small chest.

As Imogene watched, a tall green wave roared up and reared high above them—and swept chest and ship's master away with it.

The captain, hanging on for dear life, saw it happen and as the wave subsided he saw Imogene too. Half mad with the night's events, he shook his fist at her.

"Madwoman!" She could barely hear his bellow above the roar of the storm. "I should not have sailed with you—'tis *you* have brought this on us!"

But surely he would not leave her here! Imogene's frantic cry was whipped back into her throat by the wind. Horror-struck, she saw the captain turn his back and clamber into the last boat. It was not half launched before another wave turned it careening over on its side and spilled all its passengers out into the froth-whipped sea, which swept away their screams and themselves alike into the wild wastes of wind and water.

She was alone now, hopelessly entangled in the rigging,

hearing the ceaseless battering as the two ships strained apart and returned with tearing force to crash against each other. Alone with the wind and the sea. If the ship's first boats had made it—and how could they survive these seas?—they were far away by now.

She was alone in the storm. She would die alone.

There was no longer any real reason to try to free herself from the tangled rigging. In a way that rigging was aiding her at the moment, saving her from inevitably being washed overboard as mountainous waves battered the sturdy little wooden vessel.

And like others about to die, Imogene, gasping for breath beneath each wave's fierce assault, had time to think and remember, as her past life flashed before her.

Her thoughts were for van Ryker, somewhere afloat upon the Caribbean. She hoped he had not encountered this storm in its full fury, she hoped it had somehow passed him by. She wanted to think of him returning in triumph to Tortuga with the *Sea Rover's* golden hull blazing in the sun as he drove her before the wind into Cayona Bay.

Wind-driven rain whipped her face as she imagined him striding tall and purposeful toward his white-stuccoed house there—that house over which she had so briefly reigned as mistress. Behind him would come the heavy trunks of booty carried on the sailors' straining backs. King of the Buccaneers, they sometimes called him—and he would look every inch a king, returning home to his island stronghold.

If only he had taken her with him, she thought, gripped by a wave of yearning. Too late to ponder that, too late for regrets, for she would soon be joining Georgiana in some far-off Place of the Dead beyond the far horizon. She would sink down endlessly into these green depths. . . .

She tossed her head, shaking her long golden hair that lay like pale wet ropes across her shoulders. She would not think on death! She would think on life and on the times when she had lain in van Ryker's arms and felt complete—a loved woman lying beside the man in all the world she held most dear.

Green towering waves cascaded over her—but in her imagination she was swimming in the cool blue depths of a Jamaican spring and van Ryker, with a flash of white teeth and smiling gray eyes, was coming up beside her, cutting the water cleanly and shaking the drops from his heavy head of dark hair. And now his wet lips found hers in a soul-satisfying kiss.

Lightning flashed blue and terrible about her—but the blue flash was only an echo of the sultry flash of her delft blue eyes in that moment when she had swayed toward him, twined wet arms about his neck—and let her woman's body tell him what her stubborn mouth would not, that she was his, his forever.

The ship shuddered and groaned beneath the assault of yet another mountainous wave, but Imogene was hearing her own soft moans as van Ryker had taken her, wet and dripping, to the shore and made love to her—elegantly, with authority. The tremors of the ship seemed to her like the tremors of his lean body as explosions of fire ripped through him, and the assault of flowerlike eruptions of feeling shook her from head to toe—as the great ship was shaken, stem to stern.

The pounding roar of the storm was to her like the beat of his heart, throbbing strongly in his chest as he held her to him, communicating wordlessly that she was more than life to him, that he would love her always.

Tears mingled with the salt water striking across her face and somewhere out there through the shrieking blackness she felt she could almost see a golden-hulled ship with tall white sails sweep across the horizon—van Ryker, come to save her once again.

Only this time, the dice had fallen differently. The man who loved her so was far away and she was captive to the storm-swept sea. Remembering, aching, wishing she could hold him in her arms but one more time, she waited for that last horrendous crack of timbers that must come, and then—bound to the ship as she was—the inexorable sinking beneath the waves that would put an end to her.

The storm's grip held her fast, helpless in the fallen

rigging. She swayed with the motion of the ship, her long wet hair, fair as any mermaid's, whipping about with the violent assaults of the wind, her whole body disappearing from view as wild green seas crashed across the deck. From each assault she rose gasping from the foam and felt like a slash of thrown gravel the violence of the pummeling sheets of rain.

Oh, van Ryker, she murmured incoherently as she slumped in the enveloping tangle of ropes, *why couldn't you have taken me with you? For now I will never see you again....*

Even worse was the galling thought that she had not been able to warn him. Now he would walk unhesitatingly into whatever trap Anthony had set for him.

BOOK II
The Rakehell

Dare she trust him? Dare he love her?
Dare they now this moment take?
Drifting thoughts, tumultuous, sultry,
Draw her to this London rake!

PART ONE:
Out of The Frying Pan ... !

The cards are stacked against her now,
Her enemies closing in,
And now she knows in terror,
She has traded gold for tin!

THE HIGH SEAS, 1660

CHAPTER 11

Haggard now, resigned upon that storm-driven sea, Imogene hung trapped in the wet rigging and waited for the end to come.

But it did not happen. Morning came instead—a pale sallow dawn that crept over the horizon and found the hurricane—which after all had only lashed the *Carolina* with but half its force—screaming away to the northwest across the Atlantic to menace the shipping there.

Imogene, who had never expected to live to see another dawn, could not believe it. She gazed around her through saltwater-dazzled eyes and beheld an empty ocean with great rolling swells that changed the horizon to tipsy angles.

No—not empty! In the distance she could see a mast and a bit of frayed sail. It was a ship—and neither the *Carolina* nor the derelict to which she clung had yet gone down. If Captain Wilkerson had chosen to ride out the storm instead of abandoning ship, he would have been standing on the deck with her now, staring in wonder at that ship that could mean succor.

Blinking, with eyes that still smarted from the sting of all the blinding salt water that had poured over her last night, Imogene watched the ship beat toward her. Across the giant swells that billowed the sea's still angry face, it bobbed up and down like a cork—now she saw it, now a great mountainous swell obscured it. Each time it disappeared her heart dropped to her soggy slippers, for the *Carolina* was riding perilously low in the water—the miracle was that she had not already sunk.

She looked up. Against that grayish pall of sky she could see the terrible ravages the storm had wrought upon the ship. All three masts had been sheared away. One was completely gone, washed over the side. But two of them had splintered in a tangle of torn shrouds and entangling ropes and broken unidentifiable pieces of wood so that they still rode the deck like giant spears, moving restlessly with each motion of the ship. As the masts moved so did the hopeless tangle of ropes that held her move—gently sometimes, at other times with enough force to cut off her breathing and leave her gasping as the mast slid a little again with the next roll of the ship. With each playful tug on those ropes that bound her, she felt as if the ship were some great mindless beast—and that it was playing with her, enjoying her struggles.

All through the violence of the storm she had been calm but now hysteria threatened to claim her. She tried to push aside such wrenching thoughts and fix her gaze on the only hope there was—that little ship out there, so small it looked to be of toy proportions. She made another last desperate wriggling effort to force her body free of the entangling ropes and choked off a scream of pain as the mast moved again subtly and the viselike grip of the ropes tightened. The ship sidled in the water and the mast moved again grudgingly and let her breathe.

She hung there, limp and exhausted.

Now her gaze flickered to the side, for there was yet another crunch of wood—the fallen mast that was her main tormentor had poked out some of the ship's railing. Now the tugs against her body as the ship rolled were worse. Inevitably, she knew, that mast must slide through the open hole it had punched in the ship's railing into the sea—and take her with it.

No, it would not take a whole woman, for as it left the ship it must assuredly tear her in half.

Now in this last extremity, the courage she had always known rushed in to aid her. She lifted her chin defiantly. Even though there were none to hear her, she would not let the wind hear her go screaming to her end. She would die bravely.

Fastening her gaze upon that distant ship, she locked her jaw firmly and fought back a cry with every creak of the ship, every fearful tightening of the ropes about her frail body. Still unable to wrest herself free of the wet ropes that were threatening at any moment to cut off her circulation for good, and in terror lest the mast make an abortive last move and slide into the sea and the ropes that were still attached to that mast casually tear her to pieces, she watched the little ship grow larger and larger as it bobbed between the swells. As it drew closer she could see that it too had been vastly battered by the storm. Two of its masts had been sheared off, the third slanted at a crazy angle. Sick and dizzy from her terrible ordeal, she prayed it would not prove to be some derelict like the one to which the *Carolina* was still firmly attached. More likely, she thought dully, it would prove to be a stout merchant ship abandoned by her captain and crew that—like the *Carolina*—had weathered the storm alone.

It was not! Now as it drew closer she could see little figures pointing from the deck. And now a hail.

She answered with a hoarse scream that sounded thin and weak to her own ears, for the pounding of the night had drained her physically and she was near numb from being jerked this way and that against the rigging.

Now a boat was being put over the side. It was having trouble with the mountainous swells, but Imogene thanked God for it, and prayed for its safe arrival.

She saw the first man come over the *Carolina's* side and—overcome with exhaustion and relief—she fainted.

She was revived aboard the rescue ship, where a stout woman with red, work-hardened hands was rubbing her wrists and arms where the ropes from the *Carolina's* rigging had made raw weals.

"Who are you?" she asked, confused as to where she was.

The big woman smiled genially at her. "I'm Emma Tuck and this be the good ship *Bristol*."

"Have you picked up any other survivors?" Imogene asked weakly.

"From your ship? No, you was the only one," said Emma stolidly.

"But there were boats . . ."

"Only you," reiterated Emma. "Only you from the *Carolina*. The other one wasn't from your ship."

"The . . . other?"

Emma beamed at her. "Oh, we fished someone else from the sea before we found you—well, his boat was being swamped, he'd soon have been swimming. He was far gone, poor thing, and looked not like to live, out of his head from his terrible trials. He's resting now too, just like you be—but he wasn't from the *Carolina*, some Spanish name 'twas."

"A Spaniard?"

"Looked to be. Couldn't understand a thing he said—some foreign tongue. Captain said 'twas Spanish—he was half a mind to throw him back, such terrible things do the Spanish do to us when they catch us sailing 'their' seas. But Parson Smithers and the elders wouldn't hear of it, said 'twould be living like savages to do such a thing. We've been holding prayers that he recovers."

Spanish . . . there had been no Spaniards aboard the *Carolina* certainly. Imogene sank back.

"You were near gone when we found you," said Emma. "How'd it happen the men left you tangled up in the rigging like that? We were near to abandoning ship at the height of the storm but the captain of the *Bristol* would never have let a woman stay on board trapped like that if *he* had taken to the boats."

Imogene was about to say, "They thought me mad, and to blame like a jinx for the storm itself," but she thought better of it. "I fell on deck when we were abandoning ship," she lied, "and must have passed out, for when I came to I was snarled in the ship's rigging and everyone was gone. I thought to die there."

"And well you might!" The big woman clucked her tongue. "Well, 'tis over now, so just drink up—this broth will give you strength."

Imogene sipped the broth. It tasted good. Still haunted by the terrors of the past night, she had not realized she was so hungry.

It came to her suddenly that her clothing felt strange and rough. She tossed aside the blanket that covered her and looked down to see that she was wearing a homespun bodice and kirtle.

"Where did I get these clothes?" she wondered.

"They're mine," supplied Emma promptly. "And far too big, as you can tell. But I've tied the kirtle around your waist with a piece of braid and pinned together the neck of the bodice."

"But my own clothes—"

"Were half torn off ye when they took ye off that sinking vessel. Near naked ye were! I've spread them out to dry on the deck but I doubt they'll be much use to ye. 'Tis a pity, for they looked to be fine garments."

Not half so fine as I have at home in Tortuga, thought Imogene.

"Thank you for lending me yours," she said.

"Bodies should help one another," said Emma comfortably. She sat watching Imogene drink the broth.

"Where are we bound?" asked Imogene, for the broth had revived her interest in life.

"For Jamaica," replied the big woman promptly. "And if we'd known we'd have such a voyage, there's many of us as would have never left London. What's your name, dearie, and how come you were aboard the *Carolina*?"

Jamaica! That was the last place Imogene wished to go just now, for there the brothers waited. Still . . . they would not be expecting her, for they had sent her to London themselves. And if they did learn of the sinking of the *Carolina*, they'd logically presume her drowned.

"I am Imogene van Ryker," she said absently.

The name obviously meant nothing to London Emma. "Well, 'tis over now, the storm, the ship sinking, so finish up—and have a bit of bread too." She beamed as Imogene took a small bite. "And then when you've rested, you can come out on deck and take the air. We won't be much of a sight to see, for we're all a sodden mess on board after this terrible storm, but wait till tomorrow—you'll see, we'll be tidied up and all looking forward to making a safe landing in Port Royal!"

"And what brings you to Port Royal, Emma?" wondered Imogene.

"My man is there," confided Emma with a big smile. "A bondservant he's been these seven years and now he's free and has sent for me."

"He chose to stay in Port Royal and not return to England, then?" Somehow that surprised Imogene.

"Aye." Emma nodded her head violently. "And best he did, too. Things is gone terrible bad in London. Theaters opening up, bear-baiting, whores frolicking, people lurching about the streets drunk, dancing—you can hear coaches dashing by full of laughing people even on Sundays!" She rolled her eyes. "There's even rumors of a Spanish marriage for the king!"

There had been truth to the rumor, then, thought Imogene in alarm and felt icy fear for van Ryker.

"And so Parson Smithers said 'twas time we Godfearing people left, that England weren't no Christian place to be now the king with his trollops has been restored to the throne!"

"You won't find Port Royal so Godfearing," sighed Imogene.

"Maybe not, but my man has a house there now. 'Tis but one room, but we'll add to it!"

Imogene smiled at her. She hoped that hearty Emma and her ex-bondservant husband would make it.

"And now you be resting." Emma bustled out, pausing to say, "I'll leave the door open, for 'tis perishing damp in here."

Imogene found that open door a drawback. Once her name was noised around the passengers and associated with the buccaneer van Ryker, the females of the ship came by to visit her in a body and to denounce "infamous pirate ways" and the "sinkholes of Tortuga."

"And yet you're going to Port Royal," said Imogene grimly, rallying beneath this censure. "And what sinkhole greater?"

There were mutters of disapproval and the women filtered out. Imogene saw sadly that Emma, rolling her eyes, was among them. If she had hoped for help from that quarter, she realized she would be disappointed. She wondered how this group of Puritans would fare in Tortuga and supposed they would find any place burdensome, now that the Puritan Lord Protector was dead and King Charles with all his licentious royalist ways restored to the throne. But to seek a new life in Port Royal . . . she shook her head in wonder.

She looked up as a shadow fell across her bed from the open doorway. She was looking at a slim woman, dark against the light. Although Imogene could see her only in silhouette, that silhouette was the very mirror of fashion—tight-bodiced, full-skirted, big-sleeved, a head of dancing curls.

Imogene came alert, for if there was a lady of quality on board, there might be hope for her yet. She knew that there were handsome houses built on the sands of Port Royal, that money flowed there almost as freely as wine. What she needed was not a bevy of women who condemned buccaneering while knowing nothing about it, but a woman of quality who would be met by a carriage, someone who could get her past the dock and the possibly watching brothers, someone who would provide a temporary refuge while she waited for van Ryker to surface.

"Is it true that you are Imogene van Ryker, wife to the buccaneer, Captain Ruprecht van Ryker?" asked a high light voice. And at Imogene's nod, the fashionable lady swept into the room and advanced upon her. "Then we are kin by marriage, Imogene. For I am Esme Ribaud, bound for Jamaica to visit my brother."

Imogene caught her breath. Fate—which had whimsically snatched her from the deep—had played a dirty trick on her.

Of all the ships afloat, she had chanced to be rescued by the very one that was carrying scheming Esme to Jamaica!

The same hurricane that had driven the *Carolina* to her doom had brought van Ryker luck.

He had made rendezvous with the *Hawk* and the *Heron*, and at first the three ships had sailed over what seemed an empty ocean. A hot blue world with only the *Sea Rover*'s creaking timbers and the wilting crew lying at midday beneath a "roof" of canvas that had been erected on the deck. Stifling weather of the kind that presaged storms in these parts, as van Ryker knew only too well.

Narrowly he watched the sky—and congratulated himself that the house at Gale Force was so far inland. Even so, winds like those that could come out of the cauldron of these southern seas could rip that roof to shreds and scatter its tiles about the island. He hoped, if worse came to worst and a storm struck Jamaica, that Anthony would take Imogene and Charles and everyone from the plantation and go up into the higher hills, for he had once seen a storm wave, tailing on the mountainous seas a West Indian hurricane builds, rush through the wide mouth of a small bay and into the narrow cleft of a river. It had built to some seventy feet in height, that wave, before it had roared down on a tiny fishing village, and after it had passed there was no longer any sign that man had ever inhabited the place . . .

Somber were his thoughts as the first telltale mare's tail clouds scudded across the sky. He studied that first spectacular red sunset that met his gaze across the Caribbean's oddly disturbed surface as little swells came and went with great regularity. Then he turned to look at the great galleass that he had renamed the *Hawk*, riding the swells, and the dainty little caravel, the *Heron*. If a hurricane was coming—and he now had no doubt of that—the *Hawk* and the *Sea Rover* might ride it out, but not the fragile *Heron*. Abruptly he loaded his ships with all the canvas they could carry and set sail for the Windwards, meaning to seek shelter on the lee side of some island.

The admiral in command of the Spanish treasure *flota*, determined to outwit the many buccaneers who every year prowled the seas like a wolfpack in hope of plundering this golden quarry, had taken a new route. Instead of striking out toward Cuba and running the gauntlet of the Florida straits, he led his fleet almost due east from Panama, intending to slip around the Antilles and break out into the open Atlantic, free of any pursuit.

But the storm that caught van Ryker caught him also—and like van Ryker he too struck out for the Windwards.

He was unfortunate—the storm caught him first. Out of the twenty-seven proud ships that had put to sea, two ships of the *flota* were lost in the storm's first onslaught. The remaining twenty-five managed to find shelter on the leeward side of a nameless island's narrow-mouthed bay.

But West Indian hurricanes are tricky. This one recoiled on itself, turning and twisting, and caught the Spaniards in their bay. Unable to break out, there was naught for them to do but try to ride out the storm there before the wind's full fury. The same winds that trapped the Spanish *flota* there drove the *Sea Rover* back into the churning sea, but she was a stout ship, she was struck only a glancing blow by the storm, and she and her sister ships survived.

The Spaniards were not so lucky. As if to deliver one last great blow, a *coup de grâce*, the ocean seemed to pile itself up into a great mountain and that mountainous storm wave, borne by hurricane-force winds, roared into the bay. At the far end of that bay, where it narrowed, lay the Spanish vessels, close together. And now a rising cliff of water lifted them and hurled them like ninepins over a beach, which had disappeared beneath the churning waters, and tumbled them into the trees.

Wave upon wave licked at their broken hulls; screaming, clawing men were trapped and drowned within and beneath them. Not a quarter of the complement of men who had manned the *flota* survived that terrible night, and the island was littered with their bodies—and their booty.

It was into this garish scene that van Ryker, searching for

the scattered members of his own fleet, sailed the *Sea Rover*, cast anchor and stared about him.

There were galleons and pieces of galleons scattered as far as the eye could see—galleons far above his head, roosting on the broken-down remains of a forest. There were bodies floating in the water. In the now clearing waters of the bay he could see beneath his prow the glitter of a golden chain.

That day would stand out forever in buccaneer history. For that was the day when the Spanish treasure *flota*, almost intact, was taken by a single ship. The Spanish admiral was dead, drowned the night his *flota* died. His next in command promptly surrendered his sword in hope of food and aid and shelter.

Van Ryker gave them that. He disarmed those who were still armed and set them, under supervision of his own men, to making those galleons that were not too badly smashed seaworthy again. The *Hawk* and the limping *Heron* found them next day and the buccaneers on board stood at gaze at the sight of a busy beach, with van Ryker's men rounding up work crews of Spaniards.

A month it took them to salvage what they could—a month in which divers brought up heavy gold link money chains that had been spilled into the sand of the bay. A month in which hulls were shored up and shattered galleons cannibalized that others might sail again. A month in which de Rochemont worked himself gaunt tending the wounded, and the sand dunes were littered with rude wooden crosses. The galley slaves had had no chance at all—van Ryker cursed as he saw how they had drowned in their chains. The slaves housed below decks had drowned almost to a man. But enough ships' officers and crews were left to temporarily patch up a number of the ships for the voyage to Tortuga.

And day after endless day van Ryker supervised the reloading of the bullion and pieces of eight and golden doubloons and coffers of emeralds and Inca jade that had made their way by lumbering cart across Panama from Lima and the mines of Peru. Now it would make its way at the pace of the slowest vessel across the Caribbean once again toward the buccaneer stronghold of Tortuga.

The most valuable of the booty—and the highest-ranking captives—van Ryker took with him aboard his own ship. The *Sea Rover* would ride low in the water from the very weight of the treasure she carried when van Ryker sailed at last into Cayona Bay.

But, for Imogene, still reeling with the shock of her near escape from death, a new devil had been added to torment her. For here was a new and deadly enemy that she must face—Esme.

Now she studied that enemy. Esme carried her head imperiously on a slender neck and that head was crowned with a great wealth of shining dark hair. A pair of glowing gray eyes—Imogene thought they were gray as she strained to see against the light—rested upon her and there was a glimmer of jewels about that delicate throat beneath a small arrogant chin. With a rustle of taffeta and a ruffling of lace, Esme swept into the cabin toward her.

"I thought you were in London, Esme," Imogene murmured.

"And so I was. But I thought to hie me to Jamaica, for I am longing for the sight of my brother Anthony."

"He will be surprised to see you, for he had sent me to London that you might aid me in presenting a petition for pardon for Branch to the king."

There was a slight stiffening of that slender taffeta figure. "*Anthony* sent you?" With a wary emphasis on the name.

"Yes," said Imogene, pushing her luck as she tried to surprise some admission, some knowledge that might help her, out of Esme. "Because of what you had written to him, of course—he read it to me." She made herself smile into a pair of eyes she now decided were amethyst.

"Oh, yes," said Esme vaguely. "What I had written. . . . Well," her voice brightened, "I am glad we met on the high seas—even under such terrible circumstances—for now we can both return to Jamaica and make our plans to launch our offensive and see Branch cleared of those dreadful charges!"

"You will aid him in this?"

"Have I not always aided him?" Esme's silvery voice, the

voice of a consummate actress, could almost make you
believe it was true. "But of course I will!" She peered at
Imogene. "Anthony had written to me that you were reputed
to be very beautiful, but I had no idea *how* beautiful. *Mon
Dieu*, you are dazzling—no wonder Branch married you!"

"Van Ryker," corrected Imogene in a soft fierce voice.
"On this ship you must remember to call him that. You must
not divulge his real name—you endanger his life when you
do it!"

Esme gave her an amused half-smile. "Of course," she
said lightly. "I will call Branch what you please." She
paused with elaborate courtesy. "Would you prefer me to say
that *you* are my sister and Branch my brother-in-law?"

Imogene flushed. "That will not be necessary, so long as
you don't call him 'Branch Ryder.' Why can you not state
that your maiden name was van Ryker—if it comes up? I do
not see why anybody will ask. Unless you tell them, of
course."

"My, my, you *are* thorny where Branch is concerned. I
could almost believe that you love him?"

"Dearer than my life," said Imogene, still in that fierce
soft voice. "And I will not let you endanger him, Esme, by
careless talk aboard this ship! He has done enough for you
already!"

"Ah—so you know about that?" The lavender eyes that
rested on her in such amusement darkened suddenly to
tarnished silver.

"Yes. Branch—van Ryker told me." She sat up irritably,
for this unexpected encounter with Esme had given her
strength. "I feel better," she said, pushing the broth away.

"I am glad to hear it." That smiling inscrutable face never
wavered in its calm. *She is as steady as van Ryker*, thought
Imogene uneasily. *And in her way as deadly.* "Then perhaps
you would care for a turn around the deck to get away from
this mildewed atmosphere? And meet your fellow passengers?"

"I have already met them—a delegation of women who
have all consigned me to the devil because I am married to a
buccaneer!"

Esme laughed. "But the men will not. For all they are Puritans, they have an eye for a pretty face. And there is one gentleman aboard—indeed without him I should have had a desperately boring voyage."

"Your husband did not accompany you, then?" Imogene knew he had not, but she wondered what Esme would say.

"Anthony did not tell you?" Esme looked surprised. "I have left Jules. Left him in France to his debts—which are mountainous! We are ruined..." She shrugged.

She certainly *looked* far from ruined, for she was garbed with French elegance. Esme's company was the last thing Imogene wanted, but she felt reluctantly drawn to her as a moth might, flitting around a spider's web and staring in fascination at the dangerous creature in the center. She allowed Esme to urge her outside and followed that gliding taffeta figure as Esme introduced her newfound sister-in-law, bride to her errant brother, the famous buccaneer.

Imogene, who had been so miraculously snatched from death, for she had been told that the *Carolina* and its death-locked sister ship, the unknown derelict, had sunk beneath the waves but minutes after she had been removed, could not but wonder that everybody seemed so calm after the storm. She supposed it was because her own experience with the storm had been so devastating that she felt so.

To any but Imogene's eyes, who had seen worse on board the *Carolina* as the dawn came up, the appearance of the *Bristol*'s deck was a fearsome sight. Crewmen, haggard from their battle with the storm, were scrambling over piles of debris scattered about, in response to bellowed orders from the ship's officers. Shattered wood was being cast overboard, repairable items stacked up and saved. The task looked insurmountable.

The elderly, the women, the half-dozen children, the men of God—there were three on board, she was to learn—all shuffled about, getting in the way, being roared at, but unwilling to leave the clean-washed air of the deck for their musty holes below.

Through it all, Esme fluttered like a silvery moth, plucking

her way daintily over fallen timbers, determinedly urging
Imogene along with her. From group to group, Imogene
followed on slippers that were still damp from the waves that
had crashed over the dying *Carolina*'s deck.

"Oh, Captain Bellows," trilled Esme. "I want to present—"

"I haven't time now." The grizzled captain pushed by her,
roaring at a sailor, "Watch out for the mast there! Can't ye
see 'tis like to fall on ye?"

Esme sniffed distastefully but Imogene's gaze followed the
captain. She must find a way to speak to him later. As she
watched, another sailor, whom the captain knew as able
Seaman Starnes, scurried up to him, and at his words the
captain stiffened. Imogene and Esme were too far away to
hear, but had they or the other passengers been able to hear,
his words might have created a panic on a ship where near
hysteria had reigned throughout the storm.

"Cap'n, that Spaniard we picked up—I just left him. He's
burnin' up with fever."

"And no wonder, Starnes," his captain said irritably.
"Having been exposed in an open boat under such conditions!"

"He's out of his head, Cap'n, talkin' wild," insisted
Starnes. "I know a bit of Spanish, sir." He flushed as his
captain's glare raked him accusingly. "'Twas from a wench I
learnt it."

The captain, with his mind on desperately needed repairs,
was about to raise his voice and blast this simpleton back to
his duties when Starnes's next words silenced him.

"He was talkin' about being aboard a fever-rid ship, he
were, and the ship sinkin' because most all were dead and the
rest too weak to man her. I dunno if there be any truth to it
but I thought ye should know."

Fever! That was all he needed just now—a virulent fever
running through the disabled *Bristol*, laying good men low!
And that the gift of a damned Spaniard! The captain, who had
held back his language out of deference to his God-fearing
passengers, now made the air blue with a blast of profanity
that seared even the hardened ears that were listening atten-
tively for his instructions.

"Damn and blast!" he ended tiredly. "I should've thrown the fellow back into the sea, I knew it! 'Tis good ye told me of it, Starnes, and I'll remember it of ye. Put the fever-rid fellow in a separate cabin so he'll have no contact with the crew."

"That's another thing, Cap'n. This Parson Smithers and some of his congregation, they wants to go in and pray over him—"

"Damn Smithers!" exploded Captain Bellows. "Keep him out—keep them all out! Lock the fellow's door."

"The passengers'll wonder about it."

"Not a word to them or the crew, either. Tell them the man was injured, tell them anything, but keep him isolated." And when Starnes was about to say something more, "Do it now!" he barked. "Now!"

He watched the sailor's hastily departing back and began to curse again. Devil take it, why had he left harbor without a doctor on board? Why, with all the sea to choose from, had that single open boat carrying a fever-ridden man had to pick *him* out? Heartily he wished himself back at his small home outside Port Royal with his wife, Mary Ann. A broken spar fell, bringing down with it a tangle of rigging. He whirled and his roaring oaths caused a little group of his Puritan passengers to turn their heads and frown at him. Captain Bellows couldn't have cared less. He had begun to feel doomed.

Silenced by Esme's silvery flow of light conversation, Imogene had little to say to her fellow passengers beyond a brief nod. That they were curious about her was self-evident. Her beauty, and the fact that she was the new wife of a famous buccaneer, caused heads to crane. They seemed to her a dull enough lot, these Puritans—mostly small tradesmen, on their way out to the Colonies with their goods—and lamenting loudly the storm's spoilage of much of it.

But then Esme said smoothly, "And this is another of our fellow passengers—Darnwell Keating. Darnwell, this is my chance-met sister-in-law, whom it seems we have snatched from a watery grave—Imogene van Ryker."

Imogene came to a full stop before the tall striking man

who swept her the deep bow of a courtier and then rose to his full height to consider her from a pair of blazing green eyes as clear as seawater.

"The wife of the buccaneer?" he exclaimed in apparent delight.

"The same." Esme nodded airily, and turned to Imogene. "Darnwell misses London as much as I do—he has been bored the whole of the voyage! I have had to entertain him with tales of my adventurous brother."

Imogene gave her a bitter look. How like Esme not only to trick van Ryker but now to carelessly endanger him!

Perhaps Esme interpreted that look correctly, for there was a brief shaft of steel in her amethyst gaze. "I must have a look to my trunks and boxes," she announced. "For seawater splashed everywhere and I would not arrive in Jamaica with sodden ruined gowns. Will you not come with me, Imogene? I forgot to mention that the captain has set up a cot for you in my cabin, so we will be sharing a cabin for the rest of the voyage. Perhaps you would like to see it?"

Sharing a cabin . . . with Esme. Imogene had hoped for some safe even though disapproving cabin-mate, someone like good-hearted Emma. She moistened her lips for her answer.

"No, I need the air. I believe I will stay on deck awhile."

"Good," said Darnwell Keating coolly, as Esme left them with a taffeta rustle. "You must let *me* show you the ship— what there is left of it."

Imogene fell into step beside him, noting how handsome were his wide-topped boots, how jaunty the stride of his lean legs in their forest green satin trousers. In spite of their near shipwreck, Keating might have just stepped out of a tailor's shop in London, she thought—and told him so. "Were you born in London?"

He grinned. "Not London—Surrey. And I was the despair of my father, a bluff soldier who smelled of leather and bristled with pistols. He wanted a son just like him—and he got me instead. Ever since I could keep a seat on a horse he flayed me with invective—I was too foppish, too light of foot on the dance floor, too ready with a compliment, too quick to duel, too lucky at cards. In short, a disappointment. I am sure he would be glad to see me across the seas at last—if he were alive, which he is not. But tell me about this well-known buccaneer van Ryker, for I have always been curious about such men."

Something arrogant and condescending in his voice, something flippant too, made her break stride for a moment. "In truth you could be such a man yourself," she said, turning to him with an angry look. "For you have the look of a swordsman about you—and an adventurer."

"Is that how I impress you?" He chuckled and adjusted his broad shoulders suddenly so that his russet hair swung about them. It gleamed bronze in the sun.

"Yes—and I am a good judge of men."

"Are you, now?" His voice was easy. "But then, all women fancy themselves to be that." Those wicked sea green eyes challenged her.

"I think I would like to stop walking and stand by the rail for a while," said Imogene breathlessly. She felt suddenly light-headed and Darnwell Keating, sensing that, reached out and steadied her with a strong arm. He was very close now and there was a scent of good Virginia tobacco about him— much the same blend as van Ryker used. Those sea green eyes were smiling down at her curiously as if they would peer inside her golden head and divine what she was thinking.

And what she was thinking brought sudden color to her cheeks, for she was abruptly reminded of another tall gentleman of Devon who had sailed to the Scillies and broken her heart. He too had had green eyes—of a turquoise hue. And his hair had been copper, not russet. But there had been the same rakish look of the adventurer about him, the same stamp of the ne'er-do-well . . . She hated to admit it but she found this Darnwell Keating was dangerously attractive.

Imogene took a deep breath of the salt air and steadied her quickly beating heart. Attractive strangers had no place in her scheme of things just now. She was sailing back whence she had come—to a place where only death awaited her. Somehow she must break free before she reached there—but how?

She looked out across the empty ocean, she who had so

recently believed the sea would take her life. Like a remembered nightmare, that storm was over. But just over the horizon a new storm was brewing—for her. For the woman with the lavender eyes and the silvery laugh had come to Jamaica for but one reason—to destroy van Ryker and, incidentally, his bride. Nights were dark aboard ship, the sea silent and deadly, food easily poisoned—many died before ever reaching shore, and were consigned to the deep; accidents were commonplace.

Imogene shivered suddenly although the sun was warm. Three times in her eventful life she had been snatched from death: once by the man with copper hair, once by van Ryker, and once—she looked up at the calm blue dome of the sky—once by Fate. Or perhaps all three times by Fate.

This fourth time, would she escape? For she knew with a sinking feeling that if Esme had her way, she would never live to see Jamaica.

CHAPTER 12

Surprisingly, Emma Tuck's words proved true. The *Bristol*'s passengers and crew were obviously a resilient lot and by the next day much of the rigging had been repaired, wood splinters from fallen spars removed from the deck, water-logged clothing and stores were strewn about on deck in the sun to dry, and the passengers—some with wigs that still looked a bit damp and the worse for wear—were strolling about as if this were any other voyage, and uneventful.

But those next few days, as the *Bristol* limped southward under tattered sails, were a waking nightmare for Imogene. She was afraid to sleep with Esme so near. Half asleep, evil thoughts drifted through her mind—of Esme rising silently, finding a small vial she had hidden beneath her pillow, carefully letting a golden drop or two fall on Imogene's sleeping lips . . . perhaps a drop or two of golden manzanillo, that deadly poison of the tropics, so poisonous that even the Indians who stirred it in their kettles were cautious to stand well upwind of the steam that rose from it . . . So many ways to kill . . .

She tried desperately to stay awake but those nights when unwittingly she did fall asleep, she woke with a feeling of surprise and a determination to spend her day as much as possible out of Esme's company. So far she had accepted neither food nor drink nor sweetmeats from Esme's hand, which Esme seemed to regard with a kind of droll amusement.

Her days were spent in friendly camaraderie with Darnwell Keating, who went to great lengths trying to amuse her. He pointed out interesting sea life—dolphins and brilliantly colored fish and now and then a squid or an octopus and once a school of gray whales. He spun her tales of London court life, which she believed to be all fascinating fabrications.

But it was the entertainment he had provided for her that first day that had interested her most. For on that day, when Esme had come back up on deck and announced blithely that her trunks and boxes had survived the ordeal and she was now ready for a turn around the deck, Imogene had seized that opportunity to say she would go down and rest now.

"But there is nothing there to amuse you," protested Esme.

"*I* may be able to provide something," offered Darnwell. He fished in his pocket and came up with a pack of cards and a pair of dice. "You can return these to me tonight, for if the weather holds, we will be dining on deck." He made her a low bow.

Imogene was exhausted enough not to need entertainment but she smiled at this friendly gesture and accepted the cards and dice.

Esme struck Darnwell a mocking blow with her fan. "You will corrupt us yet!" she trilled. "Imogene, Darnwell is always trying to tempt me into a game—but I have not the knack.''

''Perhaps he will teach us—the knack,'' smiled Imogene, and left them.

The cabin was tiny and crowded with Esme's trunks and boxes. The addition of a cot had made it almost impossible to get through the door. But even tired as she was, Imogene felt wakeful. Perhaps it was the faint perfume that lingered in the cabin, the scent of Esme. Perhaps it was the lavender satin dressing gown carelessly tossed over the bunk ... Esme's color.

Restless, Imogene tossed the dice out once or twice, noting how they fell. And then in surprise she picked them up and hefted them and studied their corners very carefully.

One was very delicately shaved so that it had a rounded corner. The other had an almost imperceptible weight in one corner. Both fell predictably.

Even more curious now, she held the playing cards up to the light and studied them. They were a trifle dog-eared—and they were marked.

Imogene, so recently the pupil of Arne and de Rochemont in the ways of cheating at cards and dice, smiled grimly. Gentleman, Esme might call Darnwell Keating. Gentleman, the Puritan passengers on board this ship might believe him. But *she* knew, from her study of the cards and dice he had so carelessly lent to her, what his real profession was.

Darnwell Keating was a gambler and a crooked one at that. His reason for going to wealthy Port Royal at least was obvious, for its taverns and grog shops offered limitless opportunities to such as he. She wondered if he would survive the month without having a cutlass split him in half, for pirates and buccaneers took swift and bloody vengeance against those they perceived had cheated them.

It was, she decided after all, no business of hers. But she felt strangely comforted that everybody on board did not condemn buccaneers, and his very perfidy warmed her to Darnwell Keating.

Had she known herself better, she would have admitted that

rakehells had always attracted her. The first was a copper-haired Englishman long ago—and Darnwell Keating, in coloring at least, resembled him in a darker hue. And van Ryker—ah, he had been a rake when first she'd known him, she thought tenderly. Not like Keating perhaps—a daring adventurer he, wagering his life on the length of a sword on many a slippery Spanish deck.

At last, still holding the crooked dice, she sank into an uneasy sleep—and slept until suppertime when she woke to find Esme bending over her.

Imogene sat up with a start.

"I am sorry to have frightened you," said Esme with a frown. "But it is time for supper. There will be only cold food, I am afraid, for all the fires are out, but Darnwell requests that we join him on deck and sup with him. Of course, if you are too tired, I could always bring you something?"

To have Esme bring her supper was the last thing Imogene desired. She sprang up.

"Oh, you cannot wear *that*!" Esme frowned as she saw the ruined clothing Imogene was about to put on. Although hung up to dry, her garments were nearly in shreds from being pulled about by ropes in storm and seawater.

"I must," said Imogene quietly. "For I cannot continue wearing Emma's clothes, knowing how she now feels about me."

"Here, I will find you something."

Quickly Esme rummaged in her trunk, produced a shimmering French gray silk, its low-cut square neck trimmed with a flounce of white lace, its full slashed sleeves lined with black satin and caught up with black satin rosettes. "It is yours," she said, thrusting the gown at Imogene.

"It is very lovely," said Imogene slowly, surprised at the richness of the gift.

"I think it will fit you. Here—you will need these too." She scooped up a delicate white lawn chemise trimmed in gossamer lace, and a petticoat of rustling black taffeta. "I never wear this petticoat," she said carelessly. "Actually, I hate black. I have worn it only when I was in mourning for my husband's mother—and only kept it because it was too nice to throw away!'' She laughed.

Imogene was glad to put these nice clothes on, for she had felt some dismay in wearing ill-fitting homespun.

With a somewhat satirical look on her face, Esme watched Imogene dress. At last, she opened her trunk and held up a large mirror that Imogene might view herself.

Imogene drew a deep breath as she saw that reflection. She was reminded of the gown she had worn at that last party on Tortuga, when she had danced at the governor's house. She had worn gray and black then too and presented a silvery vision, as she did tonight. Esme's clothes were a near fit. The two women were of approximately the same height. The waist was just right, but Imogene's fuller breasts strained against the material of the shimmering gray silk bodice.

''Too tight at the bust, isn't it?'' said Esme with a sigh. ''Well, we can let out the seam there—so.'' Imogene flinched as a pair of small sharp scissors brushed her bare skin. ''And then''—Esme quickly threaded a needle—''anchor it so.'' She snatched up another black satin rosette. ''And cover the damage with this. Now no one will ever know it has been altered at all and''—her laughter trilled—''you will be able to take a deep breath once again.''

Imogene was indeed expelling a quick deep breath at that very moment, for she had half expected to be attacked by those scissors, so shining and sharp, held in Esme's determined white hands. ''I cannot believe you have altered the dress so quickly—and while I was wearing it,'' she marveled.

''I am very deft with a needle,'' said Esme. ''Indeed I was chief fitter for my cousins' wardrobe at Dunworth Hall.'' She gave Imogene a sharp look. ''But I suppose Branch has told you about that?''

''Not all.''

''Many the time I have had to make sudden repairs to my cousins' ball gowns—yes, and their guests' gowns too, when they had great balls.'' Her voice turned bitter. ''Indeed it was to have been my destiny to spend my life in that manner, serving my wealthy cousins' whims.''

"But that Branch rescued you," murmured Imogene.

"Yes, he saved me. He sent me to France, where"—she sighed and her winsome smile flashed—"I have made a disastrous marriage. Ah, well, we cannot all be so lucky as you."

Just at that moment Imogene did not feel so lucky. Esme was going out of her way to be friendly, but with a woman like Esme, what did that signify? She gave her hair a last pat, flung the clothes Emma had generously given her over her arm, and followed Esme to the deck.

There she found the passengers huddled among the piles of fallen rigging in damp little groups, attacking their water-soaked biscuit and salt pork and moldy cheese as best they could. Silently they watched the passage of these two birds of plumage through their midst—Esme in amethyst satin trimmed in yards of purple braid, and Imogene floating along behind her like a silvery moth.

Before the group that contained stout Emma Tuck, Imogene paused. "I do thank you for lending me these clothes, Emma," she said sincerely. "But as you can see, I am outfitted now."

With a disapproving grunt, Emma Tuck snatched back the homespun garments and turned her back.

"Come along," said Esme. "There is Darnwell—he is waving to us!"

Imogene sighed and picked her way over some tangled ratlines to a little space Darnwell Keating must have cleared for them. He rose as they approached and made them a sweeping bow. His heavy russet hair almost swept the deck and when he rose he was a picture of gallantry and fashion, for he had attired himself this evening in forest green taffetas, heavily trimmed in black braid and highlighted by a spectacular doublet of lime satin heavily worked in gold.

"Your sister-in-law has suffered a sea change from your wardrobe," he told Esme, smiling. "And for the better!"

"Yes, she is accustomed to nice clothes and her own were ruined beyond repair."

Darnwell's hot gaze passed caressingly over the bare expanse of bosom that dipped down to Imogene's deep-cut square neckline, wandered on along her bodice and lingered on her waist and hips. Imogene moved restlessly and that admiring green gaze returned to her face, telling her wordlessly that for Darnwell's taste, she could remove all and dine in her altogether.

"You have done well to provide such a feast," she said, surprised at the bottle of fine wine, the white linen tablecloth and the dry ship's biscuit and good cheese that was offered besides the usual salt pork.

"I suspect Darnwell always does well," laughed Esme, sinking down on the velvet cushion Darnwell had provided for her. "He is that kind of man!" She gave the tall rake a roguish glance.

"Is he indeed?" Imogene thought of the cards and dice, which she had forgotten in her room. She mentioned them as she sank down upon the wine velvet cushion Darnwell proffered her.

"Oh, you may keep them to amuse you during the voyage," he said airily. "I shall not want them back until we land."

Imogene suppressed a smile. *He will not want them back until there are better marks about than this stiff-necked Puritan crowd, who'd condemn wagering as a mortal sin*, she thought derisively. But she was well aware of his kindness in lending her these toys to take her mind off her shipwreck, and thanked him sweetly.

They sat on the cluttered deck like any other little knot of passengers, huddled together in the fast gathering dusk—but with a difference. They were like three fencers, making little jabs with their rapiers, testing one another out.

"You two had not met before this voyage?" asked Imogene.

"Oh, no," said Esme instantly. "Whilst I was in London, Darnwell was—"

"In Surrey," supplied Darnwell with a steady look. "In the bosom of my family." He gave a short laugh.

"But I thank God that he took this ship, else I would have been left with a pack of Puritans, which is hardly to my taste!"

"Why do they voyage to Jamaica?" wondered Imogene. "I would have thought Port Royal would be their last choice of a place to settle!"

"They seek to reform it," laughed Esme. "Really. You should hear them. They plan to thunder at the sinners from the pulpit and warn the buccaneers and pirates to repent or feel the flames of hell!" Her scoffing tone as she spoke of "buccaneers and pirates" irritated Imogene, for she had little doubt that a buccaneer's bounty had bought the very clothes Esme was wearing.

Darnwell seemed to sense that. He leaned forward, an elegant figure in dark green with an emerald flashing in the frosty lace at his throat. "How did you meet your buccaneer?" he wondered.

Imogene thought of that wild courtship, how the *Sea Rover* had paced her ship across the seas, how van Ryker had almost snatched her as a bride from her young husband's arms—and later saved her when those arms had turned against her. She thought wistfully of all the joy he had brought her.

"I met him on a sunny day in Holland," she said. "While I was shopping on the Kalverstraat." *With another man—my betrothed—beside me* . . . No need to tell them that!

"Really? How prosaic!" Esme's laughter tinkled. "I had half expected you to say he snatched you from the jaws of death."

"That came later," said Imogene.

Darnwell Keating had been watching her expressive face keenly as she spoke of van Ryker. He had caught all the nuances that said so much, so silently.

She loves him, he thought, and scoffed at himself for a fool that the realization should so disturb him.

"But you were married on Tortuga?" prodded Esme.

"Yes, a 'buccaneer's wedding.'" Imogene remembered the gaily colored lanterns, the deep-throated song of the buccaneers, that arch of raised cutlasses down which she had trailed as bride of the Caribbean's best blade and unofficial mayor of Cayona. "And again on Jamaica," she added softly.

"*Again?*" Esme looked startled.

Imogene had not really meant to divulge it, but she had not been able to resist thrusting at Esme. And she had found her mark.

"Why two weddings?" demanded Esme. "*Mon Dieu*, I should think that one would be enough to satisfy the most ardent!"

"Van Ryker was not certain the marriage on Tortuga was legal, so we were married again on Jamaica." She cursed herself for having spoken so thoughtlessly, for surely it was far better to let Esme believe—at least until they reached Jamaica—that hers was only a "buccaneer's wedding" and perhaps worthless in the sight of the law.

"So you are twice wed to the same man," murmured Darnwell. "He seeks to bind you with chains of gold, your buccaneer."

"This narrow band will suffice," said Imogene carelessly. She held up her finger so that he might see the plain band of gold that encircled it.

"Such a tiny thing—to hold a woman," he murmured.

"But adequate to the task."

He frowned. "Somehow I'd have expected a jeweled circlet from a man of such undoubted wealth."

"It was my own choice," she said sharply. "I have caskets of jewels in Tortuga!"

Esme and Darnwell exchanged glances.

"Then I am surprised he lets you roam about, since you could so easily be taken and held for ransom," said Darnwell suavely.

"I doubt the possibility has crossed van Ryker's mind." Imogene's careless shrug dismissed the idea as ridiculous. "Few would care to seize the wife of the best blade in the Caribbean and seek to hold her for ransom!"

"I see what you mean." Darnwell's green eyes gleamed. "Such a fellow would have a short life expectancy?"

"Undoubtedly. And if he harmed me—a slower death."

Esme shivered. "You make my brother sound monstrous, Imogene!"

"Not monstrous." Imogene considered Darnwell steadily,

in case the impudent rake was considering holding her for ransom himself. "Just—formidable."

Darnwell chuckled. "Well spoke," he said, eyeing her with grudging approval. *Ah, the wench has spirit*, he thought. *This buccaneer, whatever he is, is not deserving of her!*

"Now we have discussed *my* marital condition—and I am sure you already know Esme's," said Imogene with some asperity. "Perhaps you will be good enough to tell us yours?"

In the short silence that followed, the ship creaked and groaned and one of the hastily rigged sails gave a sharp crack.

"I am not married," said Darnwell.

Esme was eyeing him with interest. *Considering another disastrous marriage, no doubt*, thought Imogene scathingly. *This one with a rakehell gambler who will leave her in no better case than her Frenchman!*

"Not even betrothed?"

"Not even betrothed." Darnwell smiled into Imogene's eyes and raised his glass. "Although I might be persuaded to go that far if the lady were to my liking."

A little frown creased Esme's flawless forehead. "But you have roved the world, Darnwell. Surely there must have been *someone* to suit you?"

"Oh, at least a dozen," he laughed. "Pretty ladies all. But none of them would have me!"

"Liar!" She pouted at him. "You are having us on, Darnwell. Lean forward so that I can see your face—it is too dark to see your eyes."

"The moon will soon be up," he laughed. "And it will gleam upon my wolfish smile. Will you call me a liar then, I wonder?"

"Possibly not." Esme leaned back languorously and favored him with a shadowed look.

Imogene, watching, thought he kindled to that look, but perhaps, she told herself, she was fooled by the shadows that had fallen. All the little groups but one had retired to their cabins now, and that one was just rising to leave. It came to her that she was still very tired from her recent experience.

Fatigue had fallen on her like a cloak and she yearned to seek the cot that had been set up for her in Esme's cabin.

"I am afraid I must retire," she admitted, rising. "Else I will fall asleep here; for even though everybody else is, *I* am not yet recovered from the storm."

"Of course," said Darnwell sympathetically. He rose. "Let me escort you to your cabin."

"No, do stay. I can find my way over this stuff well enough, and I would not spoil your evening."

They let her go and as she picked her way carefully over tangles of fallen rigging, which the sailors would have to work on tomorrow, she could hear their voices murmuring companionably.

When she reached the cabin, she quickly set up a warning system—a brass candlestick with an already consumed candle, which would fall over with a crash when the door was opened. Then she quickly peeled down to her chemise and fell into bed, falling asleep almost as she touched the sheets.

Indeed, it seemed to her that she had only touched them when there was a clang and a rolling clatter as the candlestick was knocked over. She opened her eyes to see that the door was being pushed open and Esme was standing there in the dawn's pale light. She looked rumpled and her voice sounded hurried and excited.

"Whatever is that candlestick doing there?" she demanded. "I near stumbled over it and it has certainly made enough noise to rouse the ship!"

"I must have left it there—I was so sleepy," Imogene lied glibly. "At least, it has gone out safely."

"Yes, I can see that it has guttered out." Esme's cold voice sounded her disapproval. "To be careless with candles is to shorten one's life, Imogene. And to set a burning candle against a door!" She shuddered.

Imogene caught her meaning—one could be trapped inside a flaming cabin with the door alight. She was suddenly aware that the very mattress on which she lay was flammable, as was her sheer chemise and her long fair hair. She had a sudden horrendous vision of Esme, running from this burning cabin—a cabin that she herself had set afire—and of her own voice screaming as the waves licked at her while she pounded on a door that would not open.

Cold with perspiration from that vision, she got up.

"What are you doing now?" asked Esme with irritation. "Oh, I do hope you are not one of those people who prowls about all night?"

"No, I am arising," said Imogene loftily. "This cabin is too small and stuffy for two. I will seek the deck for a while."

"As you please." Esme shrugged and stifled a great yawn. "For myself I shall sleep until the sun is well up and maybe a trifle beyond. Pray do not wake me with your comings and goings."

Imogene, having quickly dressed, snatched a blanket against the damp morning chill and hurried out. She did not feel safe in that cabin with Esme.

On deck—a deck already alive with sweating sailors clearing away the wreckage of the storm—she found a quiet spot amid coils of rope, wrapped herself in her blanket and fell asleep again.

She waked to a yell and a thud as part of a broken spar crashed down beside her. At the sound of the impact, she rose with a short sharp scream and stood trembling, staring at the spar that had missed her by inches.

Darnwell Keating, standing by the rail, had turned at her scream and now he strode toward her. He looked very fit in the bright sunlight that poured down over his gleaming russet hair, turning it to the brilliance of a new copper penny.

"What's this?" he asked softly, staring at the blanket she clutched in her hands. "Don't tell me you've spent the night curled up in a pile of rope! I had thought you were sharing a cabin with Esme—with Madame Ribaud. Has she then turned you out?"

By now Imogene had stopped shaking and got hold of herself. "No, she has not turned me out—and after last night I think you might feel free to call her Esme." She stretched her sleep-cramped arms.

He chuckled. "Touché," he said pleasantly. "But consider it from another angle—I thought you might appreciate a little privacy in your cabin last night."

Imogene gave him a slanted look as she shook out her blanket and folded it. "Very thoughtful of you. Of course, Esme would kill you if she heard you say that."

Again that wicked chuckle. "So she would," he agreed. "But somehow I think she will not hear it—not from you, Imogene."

She had not given him leave to use her given name, but it sounded sweet rolling off his tongue like that. She decided not to chide him. After all, on this crowded vessel, they, the outcasts from this group of Puritans, must stick together if only for self-protection.

"No, Esme will not hear it from me," she said lightly. "How she spends her time and in whose cabin is no concern of mine."

"You are very liberal in your views of your sister-in-law's behavior. Somehow I would not have expected that in one who so cherishes a narrow band of gold."

Imogene yearned to tell him that Esme was her sworn enemy, but she bit back the words. Her foolish tongue, seeking to chastise Esme by letting her know that van Ryker had wed her lawfully in Jamaica as well as unlawfully in Tortuga, had already got her into enough trouble. "It is crowded with two piled into a cabin intended for one," she said. "And Esme chose to chide me for leaving a candle standing against the door while she was out."

"Lighted?" he asked softly.

"No," said Imogene.

Did she read a flicker of understanding in his eyes? "You are welcome to nap in my cabin today," he suggested. "If you fear to disturb Esme, who likes to sleep late?"

Imogene gave him a grateful look. "I believe I will do that," she said, "if you do not mind."

For answer he escorted her to his cabin, said quietly, "You may latch the door from within so that you will not be disturbed." And left her.

Somehow she had not expected such gallantry from this hard-eyed London rake.

Alone in his cabin she looked about her. His clothes were strewn about—plainly Darnwell Keating was not tidy. Idly she picked them up, folding them one by one and putting them into one of two trunks—the one that was open. The other one, somewhat smaller, was locked, as she discovered when the first trunk would not hold all the clothing she had folded.

Oh, well—let them pile up with the trunk lid open. She was folding a pair of detached green velvet sleeves when she felt something sharp. Inspection showed her a cleverly concealed clip with a spring that would hold cards and release them into the player's hand at a touch.

Imogene smiled grimly. Both Arne and de Rochemont had shown her such devices along with many others. She guessed that whatever story Darnwell Keating told about them would be false. He was a gamester, like many another, perhaps a dissolute son of the aristocracy, but long fallen from grace.

So that he might not know she had handled the big sleeves, she carefully replaced them on the chair where they had been flung and replaced the doublet that had been thrown across them. Keating had been kind to her. Let him flaunt his stories of high-placed friends and powerful connections—no need to let him know that she did not believe him.

She latched the door and lay down across the bunk and slept until a light knock and Darnwell Keating's voice told her it was time to sup. She came out refreshed to join him and met Esme's sharp, "Where have you been all day?" as they came out on deck.

"I found a quiet corner and rested."

"You might have come back to the cabin and rested!" Testily. "I half thought you'd gone overboard!"

"Be glad she did not disturb you," smiled Keating. "And let you have your beauty sleep."

Esme gave him the look of a caged animal, wary and untrusting. "Are you saying that you have spent the day together?"

Keating gave her a look of pure astonishment. "Would that

we had," he exclaimed ruefully. "For I have spent this entire day being instructed in the Puritan ethic by none other than"—he nodded toward Parson Smithers—"that sturdy old goat over there, whose name escapes me." He gazed with distaste at Smithers's black-hatted, homespun figure—even now haranguing a group of four who stood stolidly as he rained words upon them.

Esme looked mollified and was very merry at supper. That night Imogene used the same ploy, the candlestick. And again Esme, who had come in earlier this night, berated her for her carelessness.

This time Imogene did not rise but lay wakeful, listening to Esme's steady breathing. As she lay there, she decided what her course of action must be.

She would put it into effect in the morning.

CHAPTER 13

There in that small cabin, with her dangerous cabin-mate, Imogene had determined what she must do. She would go to the captain. She had not dared approach him yesterday, for she had observed him to be both busy and short-tempered as he directed the repairs to his storm-mangled vessel—but tomorrow when at least part of the work had been done and the rest well under way, she would speak to him.

The crippled ship was making slow progress toward Jamaica. It could be that the captain would be willing to drop her off in Tortuga. She *must* persuade him because if Esme was met by her brothers at the dock in Port Royal, they would see Imogene and would never let her go.

After breakfast she sought an audience with the captain in his cabin, went in and shut the door behind her.

"Leave it open, mistress," he sighed without looking up from his charts, which were spread out on the table before him. " 'Tis stuffy in here and reeks of mildew. Faith, I thought we were bound for the bottom in that gale!"

"So did I," said Imogene, reluctantly opening the door again. "Captain." She dropped her voice, mindful that other passengers might be passing by that open door. "I've a matter of importance to speak to you about."

"Speak up, mistress. I've so much water in my ears from that gale that I still can hear but the half of what's said to me. Near deafened me, the storm did!"

Desperately Imogene raised her voice and leaned forward. "By now you know that I am wife to the buccaneer, Captain van Ryker."

"Aye, I know it." From behind the table the stocky seaman's head came up to regard her with disfavor. "The passengers have apprised me of it."

And heaped them both with calumny, she had no doubt!

"Then you know that my husband is wealthy. He will pay you well to deliver me to Tortuga."

The captain raised bushy eyebrows. "But I'm bound for Jamaica," he said testily.

"I know, but—"

"And if I sail to Tortuga, there'll be further delay." He was thinking of the Spaniard he had taken aboard, sick of fever. "I might even encounter another storm." His voice rose argumentatively. "Nay, mistress, I was glad enough to snatch ye from the sea, and ye're welcome to accompany me where I go, but I'll not deviate from my course for ye—not for a thousand buccaneers, each with a purse of gold outstretched!"

She saw she could not move him. "At least," she asked desperately, "when we reach Port Royal, will you see me safe aboard a ship bound for Tortuga?"

The captain frowned. "And have ye gold to pay your passage on this ship ye would have me set ye on?"

"No." Reluctantly. "All I had was lost on the *Carolina.*"

"I know." He was gazing at her somewhat malevolently across the table now. "The ship was sinking so fast we had no time to bring anything off her save yourself. The miracle is that she had floated so long in the condition she was in. Nay, mistress, I cannot finance your voyage. There's a rumor about among the passengers that ye must have quarreled with your buccaneer and that he set ye on a ship bound for London to be rid of you!''

" 'Tis a lie! He wants me back.''

''Be that as it may, I will set you ashore in Port Royal with the other passengers and wash my hands of you, for I'll have duties to keep me busy unloading the ship and the owners will be at me to take on a new cargo. Ye've a sister-in-law aboard—ask her to help you.''

Her cheeks burning, Imogene left the captain's cabin—and met a pair of knowing green eyes that smiled into her own. Darnwell Keating was lounging against the wall near the cabin door.

''You were eavesdropping,'' she accused.

''Correct,'' he drawled. ''And heard the interesting thought advanced that you are presently estranged from your husband. Could this be so?''

''Certainly not! I merely wished to be set ashore at Tortuga, where I have a house and servants waiting.''

''And the captain would not do it?''

''He would not.''

As she flung away, Darnwell fell into step with her. ''You must not blame our captain too much,'' he counseled easily. ''He seeks to preserve his tranquility, our captain, and to that end he will whitewash over anything. You have just learnt his temper. He is not to be drawn in, no matter how noble the cause.''

Something in his voice made her suspect that he had sought to enlist the captain in some devious scheme of his own and been turned down as she had been. She gave him a sharp look but his expression was bland.

''I wish you would trust me,'' he said pensively.

Imogene looked away. She could hardly trust her desperate secret to Esme's lover!

''You are still welcome to use my cabin between breakfast and supper,'' he said quietly.

Imogene threw him a grateful look. He did not understand—could not understand, of course, but he was trying to help her. That much was clear.

The reason why he was so willing to help her was not quite clear, even to him.

"Imogene is beautiful—but in a shallow way, don't you think?" Esme had said enviously last night. She had been in his cabin then, posing seductively as she drew off her garters.

Darnwell had smiled an easy agreement as he lay propped up in bed, watching Esme undress. He was used to agreeing with women—it had paved his way to many delights. But in his heart he had thought the woman Esme sought to deprecate was anything but shallow. Imogene was lovely, she was—flawless. Her buoyant spirit, her rebellious, half-humorous moods . . . he was falling in love with Imogene and now on the deck, as she gave him a wry salute and retired to rest in his cabin to gain that sleep she could not gain by night, he admitted to himself that he was falling in love with her and envied the buccaneer, the very mention of whose name could make her blue eyes shine.

Darnwell Keating was a man who had mostly trod over women blithely, using them as suited his pleasure and flinging them away afterward. Close lasting relationships had never tempted him—until now.

Now his fertile, unprincipled, and very clever brain was intent on but one purpose—how to separate Imogene from her buccaneer lover and bring her thrilling to his arms.

It was not an easy task Darnwell had set for himself, for although Imogene was attracted to him—his masculine pride had assured him of that—and although he felt her pliant female body would respond to his overtures if he was allowed to make them, her heart, he knew, was elsewhere, sailing the Caribbean with her buccaneer.

Darnwell Keating, late of Surrey, envied van Ryker and most earnestly wished him dead.

Perhaps, he thought wistfully, the Spaniards would accomplish that purpose for him—it could not be too soon.

Imogene, unaware of the violence of feeling she had

aroused in the rakehell's masculine chest, remained intent
upon her own pressing problems, for the *Bristol* was slowly
limping south toward Jamaican waters.

Desperate, she decided to try the captain one more time.
He did not own the *Bristol*, she knew from conversation with
Darnwell. Suppose she were to offer—on behalf of van
Ryker—to buy him a part ownership in the vessel if he would
take her to Tortuga? Determined to chance it, she found him
alone at the rail, staring out to sea with his shoulders
hunched.

"Captain Bellows," she began hesitantly.

He turned about, fixed his burning gaze on her. He was
looking very stormy, she thought, but then when hadn't he
looked stormy? It was obvious he detested the passengers and
he hadn't had a civil word to say to her since she'd spoken to
him in his cabin—still, she had to try.

"Captain Bellows," she said more firmly. "If you would
reconsider dropping me off at Tortuga—" Her voice trailed
off, for the captain seemed to draw himself up. His cheeks
were bulging.

She could not know that the captain had been standing here
alone to collect himself. Indeed his head was still ringing with
an incident of a moment before when able Seaman Starnes
had come running up to him.

"I came to tell ye, Cap'n," Starnes had muttered. "That
Spaniard we picked up—he's dead."

A slight tremor had gone through Captain Bellows's thick
body. "Sew him in a sheet, Starnes," he said heavily. "We'll
bury him at sea. There's enough parsons aboard to say words
over him," he added in a bitter tone.

"But what'll we tell the passengers, Cap'n, when they ask
how he died?"

"Say a mizzenmast had cracked his ribs and he finally
coughed his life out!"

For a moment, after Starnes left, Captain Bellows's grizzled beard had sunk onto his chest. Fever . . . the man was
dead of fever. And Starnes and half the crew had had access
to the fellow before he knew what was wrong with him.
They'd be lucky, at the pace the *Bristol* was going, if they

arrived in Port Royal with half the passengers and crew alive.

It suddenly came to him that he, too, might die of it.

And that meant he would not live to see his Mary Ann again. Mere oaths would not serve to satisfy the sinking feeling that went through him at that thought.

He *had* to see her again! He had to make amends! He had to convince her that there was nothing between him and her friend Ernestine (What matter if there was, it was over now!), for he'd seen hatred and suspicion on Mary Ann's face when he was leaving, and he'd gone stomping out of the house in a rage without even telling her good-bye. And dammit, his whole life was wrapped around Mary Ann!

He couldn't die without seeing her again. Dear God, he had to make it home to Port Royal alive, if only to sweep her up in his arms and kiss her tears away and tell her she was the only woman he'd ever cared a shilling for—and now there was this damned fever aboard.

He was just rising up from his feeling of doom, determined to make the crew work twice as hard, for he knew it sometimes took time for fever to get its teeth into people and he meant to beat the fever to Port Royal. Just one night on shore to make amends—God, that was all he asked!

It was at this moment that Imogene, unaware of the crisis state of the captain's mind, chose to put her question to him.

She was shocked by the captain's wild accusing gaze and puffy face and how his sallow skin suddenly mottled.

"Take ye to Tortuga?" he roared. "I wish I'd left ye in the sea, woman—you and that Spaniard with you!" He brushed past her so furiously he almost knocked her down and left her staring after him open-mouthed.

It became clear to her then, if it had not before: she was going back—back to Port Royal, back no doubt to Gale Force.

Despondency settled over her—a despondency that was only heightened by the burial at sea that afternoon of the Spaniard, sewn tightly in canvas. "Had his chest caved in by a mizzenmast, poor fellow," Emma Tuck was heard to remark. "And his sufferings so terrible we was all kept away from him!"

Imogene turned away. Burial at sea was a nightmarish reminder of the dangers van Ryker faced.

Time passed listlessly on board the *Bristol* until the day when, as she was walking toward Darnwell's cabin for her daily nap, she heard the captain announce proudly to one of the passengers that they would make landfall at Port Royal on the morrow.

She had only a few hours, then, to plot and plan.

And alone in Darnwell's cabin she did just that, for she had determined on a last desperate move.

When he called for her at suppertime, knocking on the cabin door, he thought her eyes glittered overmuch and felt that she was watching him, cat-a-mouse. It intrigued him even while it made him vaguely uneasy. She was a complex woman, he had decided, neither so direct and simple as Esme made her out to be, nor so wily and witching as the female passengers whispered her to be. She was—Imogene. Exquisite. Unique.

"Darnwell." Her lazy voice drew him to a halt before they reached the deck. "Stop a minute. Darnwell, I believe you to be a man of honor."

His russet brows shot up. It had been some time since anyone had called him that—his uncle but recently had said somewhat the opposite. He halted and waited.

"I believe that you would pay your debts of honor—your gambling debts," she continued. "Scrupulously."

"I have always done so."

"Good." Those delft blue eyes played over him brilliant as sapphires, like prisms almost, glittering, tempting. "I would play a game of chance with you tonight—in your cabin."

"A game of chance, you say?" His eyes lit up.

"Yes, I would play at cards with you and dice with you. I am lucky at cards. We will see who is the better player."

"And the stakes?" he asked softly, leaning nearer.

"We cannot play for coins, you and I, for I know all about you, Darnwell." For a moment he stiffened, but relaxed as her lazy voice went on, challenging him. "You cannot play for gold, for you have none—nor can I who left a sinking ship with naught but the torn garments on my back."

A smile curved his wide mouth. "Then we will play for golden promises, perhaps?"

"For something more solid, I think. My petticoat perhaps against your doublet. . . ."

He leaned so close his lips almost brushed her ear. "I am ready to play *now*, Imogene."

"No." She shook her head irritably and sighed. "I believe you have a prior engagement—I doubt you can get rid of her."

" 'Twill be easy," he said coolly. "Esme will declare herself to have a headache and retire to her cabin."

"And how will you accomplish *that*?" wondered Imogene.

He patted his sleeve. "I have a powder here which I will slip into her wine when she is not attending. It will not harm her but it will assuredly give her a headache."

Imogene, who hoped he gave Esme a violent headache indeed, favored him with a mocking glance. "It would seem you are a dangerous man, Darnwell, and equal to every occasion."

"I try to be." Modestly.

Supper was a taut affair. For Imogene was nervous beneath the brooding glance that rested on her from beneath russet brows. Esme watched them narrowly—and drank a trifle too much. And some of what she drank contained a white powder that Imogene thought she saw—just fleetingly—dropped into her wineglass as Darnwell laughed into Esme's eyes.

"I hear Jamaica is to have a new governor," said Imogene, making conversation.

"Yes. Lord Marr," answered Darnwell absently. "All London knows it." His gaze was on Esme.

"I am surprised he did not come out on this ship," she said.

"He will most likely come aboard a man-of-war," said Darnwell.

"Have either of you seen him?"

Esme seemed not to be listening but Darnwell answered quietly, "I have."

"What is he like?"

"Old, toothless, a model of propriety." He grinned. "The sort who would take neither of you ladies' fancy!"

Esme managed a rueful smile but Imogene sat silent. *Old, toothless, a model of propriety, and long at rakish young King Charles's side* . . . what hope for van Ryker from a man like that if ever he caught him?

She felt sad suddenly and when one of the sailors, standing by the rail, began singing a melancholy sailors' song, it suited her mood. He had a rich voice and they all fell silent, listening.

When they had finished they sat lazily on their cushions, lounging about the tablecloth spread on the deck that held the remains of their meal. There was no need for shawls, for the night was very warm and the stars were a thousand diamonds cast into the black recesses of space. The moon cast its white light upon the white bosoms of the women and gilded their hair with silver. A light breeze sang in the shrouds and one by one the little groups of passengers, who still ate on deck rather than in the still moldy recesses below, silently departed to toss upon their Puritan bunks and dream of earthly hells and sterile heavens.

"I do not feel well." Esme was rising unsteadily to her feet, one hand pressed against her temple. "My head is splitting."

"Perhaps you have had too much sun," said Darnwell solicitously. "It was very bright today."

Esme shook her head irritably. "Will you help me to my cabin, Darnwell?"

"Of course." He took her arm. "Are you coming, Imogene?"

"No," said Imogene carelessly. "The night is lovely. I think I will stay on deck for a while."

When Darnwell came back for her, she realized that he must have stopped by his own cabin on the way back, for he had changed his doublet. He was now wearing the resplendent one, of lime green satin, so heavily embroidered with gold threads that it seemed to be made of gold. And his big green velvet detachable sleeves—the ones that contained the secret spring that could release cards into the hands of the wearer.

Imogene gave him a swift secret smile. There were four or fives aces up those sleeves, she had no doubt.

"I have brought the cards and dice you lent me," she said impassively, and drifted along beside him to his cabin, where he opened the door with a flourish to let her in.

The cabin, she noted, was very neat. Obviously Darnwell had swept everything into his trunk and slammed the lid on it. He was very eager to make a good impression. . . .

"Now." He stood before her, tall and genial, smiling down at her. "What is your pleasure?"

"Cards, I think." Innocently she held out the deck, shuffled it flashily, asked him to cut.

"And what is the object?"

"High card wins," she said dispassionately, putting the deck back together with a slap. "Draw a card, Darnwell."

She saw his shoulders shrug and saw a moment of surprise go over his features. And knew a great satisfaction. This afternoon she had cleverly fixed the spring clamp in his sleeve so that it would not eject a card. Darnwell, sly gambler that he was, would have to take the luck of the draw. For herself, she had chosen another spring clamp in another pair of his sleeves and secreted it into her own. It contained all the aces in the present deck and beneath the aces, all the kings.

"For what do we play?" he asked, frowning.

"The doublets in that trunk against my petticoat."

"But you do not know how many doublets are in that trunk," he protested.

"I should. I have been putting away your clothes in that trunk every day since I have been using this room!"

She won handily.

"And now my petticoat against the trousers in that trunk," she said.

And won again.

"And now my petticoat against—"

"You are planning to open a haberdashery?" he inquired politely.

"I told you I am lucky," she said shortly. "And now my petticoat against that doublet you are wearing."

"You fancy it?" he asked, fascinated—and frowned when she won that too.

Thoughtfully Darnwell divested himself of his doublet but his eyes never left the lustrous lady so intent on the cards. He smiled as she won his boots.

"And you won them by another ace," he said softly. "There must be none left in the deck."

"How could there be?" Her expression was bland. "There are only four in any deck. And now let us play for your sleeves."

"Is it your intention," he asked in amusement, "to strip me down to my smallclothes only? Or to set me entirely naked into the world?"

"Neither."

"You cheat so awkwardly," he complained, "that I feel entitled at least to the petticoat."

She froze into immobility, staring at him.

His hand lashed out and seized her arm, reached up into the big capacious gray silk oversleeve and found the clip, pulled out four kings.

"A trove!" he said genially. "And I'll wager the deck has no kings at all."

"You would be right, Darnwell," she told him, leaning forward and suddenly pouncing on his sleeve. "And I'll wager your sleeve has four or more aces in it in a clip that will not disgorge them because I tightened it this afternoon so that it cannot!"

"We are a pair of cheats—well matched." He smiled down into her eyes and as suddenly drew her to him.

"No! Darnwell—" Her lips were silenced by his searching mouth and she found her body pressed warmly against his cambric shirt. She could feel his heart beating through it, a continuous steady throb, powerful, demanding. Just as his lips were demanding, just as his impudent tongue was demanding, pressing, now finding its way past her lips to nuzzle invitingly within. His hard arms tightened about her and she could feel her senses swirl. Darnwell was not only a congenial London rake—he was a handsome male animal, a vigorous man in his prime, an experienced lover who had set the heart of many a woman astir in his rovings.

He felt her sudden yielding, her quick indrawn breath, her guilty renewed struggle—and let her go with a low laugh.

"I but sought to test the temper of your spirit, Imogene, and 'tis plain you are not made of iron after all."

"Of steel," she whispered, furious that he had found her out—that she was a woman of tinder. "Well-tempered steel can bend."

"Ah—so you have bent a little and now snap back to your original position like a well-tempered blade." He studied her face. "What is it, Imogene, that you want of me?" he asked bluntly.

She moistened her lips. "I need your help, Darnwell."

"Then why," he asked softly, "did you not ask for it? Why this charade?"

"I suppose because I am become a woman of Tortuga and you—what you have become. A gamester."

"You are saying you have lost directness?"

Imogene's white hands clenched and unclenched. She was taking a terrible chance with him. "I am saying, Darnwell, that I am desperate. I know not which way to turn. You and Esme are lovers. I—"

"What has Esme to do with it?" he asked quickly.

She ignored that. "I hoped to win everything you brought with you—by fair means or foul. Foul was surer—and besides they are *your* spring clips."

"True. And what would you have done, had you won everything from me? Pretend you have won all that you wished, Imogene? What then?"

Imogene moistened her lips and gave him a wild look. She could not know how appealing she looked, with her white breast rising and falling, straining the shimmering gray silk of her bodice. "I would say to you then, 'Darnwell, you may have it all back—if only you will do me one favor. *One dangerous favor*.'"

His green eyes glinted. "I would do more than a favor for you," he said softly, reaching out to lift a lock of her bright hair from her throat and push it back over her shoulder.

She edged a little away from him. There was a feeling of summer lightning in the air tonight. She felt afraid of him—and of herself.

"I have feared death throughout this voyage," she said hoarsely. "For Esme has come out from London to kill me. Yes, it is true." She met his startled gaze squarely. "I need your help, Darnwell, so I am going to tell you a story. It is a story that will put my life in your hands—and perhaps van Ryker's too. May I trust you, Darnwell?" It was a wistful whisper.

"Of course." He gave her a wary amused smile. "Do I not look to be the soul of trust?"

"Not really." She sighed. "But as you overheard in my conversation with the captain that day, I am in sore need of getting me to Tortuga. I dare not return to Jamaica, where I am in peril of my life."

"Tell me about it," he said, "over a glass of wine." He found a pair of silver goblets in his trunk and a bottle of golden Canary, poured out for them both and sank back gracefully on his bunk, crossing his elegant legs in their silk stockings and wide boots. He cut a handsome figure, she thought, in his flowing white cambric shirt, open to the waist, his lean hips and long legs encased in forest green silk.

"First, tell me truthfully, Darnwell—why do you journey to Jamaica?"

He shrugged. "It is but one of the islands on my itinerary. I will tell you in confidence, since a woman in your position is not likely to reveal it—that I am here on a mission of some importance for the king himself."

"And what is that?"

He sighed. "It is confidential."

"So you are privy to the king?" Imogene studied him, uncertain whether to believe him. She frowned at this new development.

"To some extent," he said carelessly. "No man is very close to Charles, I think. 'Tis women he is close to."

And sports and games of chance. . . . Darnwell was undoubtedly one of those clever gamesters who amused the debonair king who had spent so many of his years in impoverished exile.

"Yes, Esme said as much," she murmured.

"Esme," he said dryly, "would know very little about it. I doubt me she has ever seen the king at close quarters—although she does pretend to some intimacies at Whitehall."

"But you have seen the king at close quarters?"

"Many times."

She felt her throat go dry and leaned forward. "Do you know the king well enough to seek a pardon from him?"

" 'A pardon'?" He frowned. "For whom?"

"For a man who has been done a great wrong."

He meditated on that. "It would depend, I suppose, on what the wrong was."

Imogene, uncertain that a gamester—even one who played at games of chance with the king—could engineer a pardon for van Ryker, took a deep breath.

"Esme's maiden name is not van Ryker—it is Ryder. She has two brothers, Anthony and Charles. The three of them have a half-brother, Branch Ryder. The world knows him as Captain Ruprecht van Ryker—my husband."

He was gazing at her keenly, his green eyes shadowed by russet brows that had drawn together in concentration.

"The three of them—Esme and Anthony and Charles—seek to dispose of me so that they may one day inherit van Ryker's wealth."

"How do you know that?" he interrupted.

"I heard it from Anthony's own mouth, in conversation with his brother Charles in Jamaica. Of course, they did not know I heard or that would have been the end of me. Believing Esme still to be in London, they dispatched me to her willy-nilly, so that she might dispose of me in London, and Branch—van Ryker—would never know their part in it. Doubtless they would have spun a web of lies about how I was set upon in some alley and killed by cutpurses. But Esme had already departed London for Jamaica when I was set perforce upon the *Carolina*, and as luck would have it I was picked up by the very ship on which she was journeying to Jamaica."

"A nasty coincidence," he agreed. "And that is why you have been so interested in sleeping away the days in my cabin?"

"Yes, because I dare not sleep at night lest Esme poison me or set my clothes afire or drive a knife through my ribs and haul my lifeless body to the rail and push me overboard."

"You have a vivid imagination," he murmured.

"I have seen a deal of life in my short years!"

"But why would Esme do it? I mean, it seems a long chance for her to take. A woman as handsome as Esme could find another protector. Why would she take such a risk?"

"For gold. And possibly to cover up a crime that was committed by Anthony Ryder long ago. For in England he killed a man named Dunworth and Esme persuaded van Ryker, who had just returned to England at the time, that *she* had killed Dunworth in self-defense after he had raped her. To save her from jail or worse, van Ryker signed a confession to the crime and disappeared—back to the Caribbean."

"How gallant of van Ryker," murmured Darnwell lazily. She was not sure there was not a note of derision in that lazy comment.

"He is *very* gallant," she flashed. "*And* chivalrous!"

"And well defended by his beautiful wife, which speaks better of him than all the fine words in the world."

"I need passage to Tortuga, Darnwell. Will you help me?"

"I'll do better than that," he told her, running a hand through his thick russet locks. "I'll even help you prove van Ryker's innocence."

She was startled, for she had not expected an offer so handsome. "I—I do not know how other you can help me than to set me on a ship bound for Tortuga, and to petition the king to clear my husband's name so that he may walk free on English soil again."

"But I cannot petition the king on mere rumors," he pointed out. "He will want proofs. Have you any? Or is this tale based on moonbeams?"

"It is the truth!" she cried angrily.

He studied her, smiling. "I know it is," he said softly. "I had deduced it myself some time past. When I thought over the character of Branch Ryder, I guessed that he would not plunge a blade in a man's back and leave him to die. A woman might—or a coward. And Branch Ryder is neither.''

"You know my husband?" she asked, bewildered.

"I know of him," he amended. "My commission is a strange one, Imogene. Among other things, I am to learn something of the buccaneers, their loyalties, their ways. You see, Imogene, they are becoming a power, stronger every day. They have set themselves up like independent princes on the island of Tortuga, and they may decide to extend their power to all of the West Indies. King Charles would like to know their intentions—he is a man who prides himself on being forewarned."

"So your mission is one of intelligence?"

"I am set to spy out the country," he admitted glibly.

And what better person to do that than a London rake? she thought, ruefully admiring the choice of England's cynical young king.

"And since your husband is the uncrowned king of the buccaneers, I set myself to learn all I could about him. He seemed to fit the description I had heard of an Englishman who had fled Devon some years ago on a charge of murder. I checked into the charge and found the facts did not fit the character of the man charged with the deed. It is a happy chance that led us to meet, Imogene, for I could not have ferreted it out alone."

"Then you *will* help?"

"I told you I will do better. I will make it my personal endeavor to see that Captain van Ryker receives the king's justice. I'll ask a pardon for Branch Ryder—that I promise you. But not unless you get me proof, Imogene."

"And how am I to do that?"

"I think ye must needs cultivate Esme," he said pleasantly. "If I could catch her or one of her brothers in some slip of the tongue—something that I could relay truthfully to the king—that, I think, would be enough."

"You mean—return to Gale Force?"

"With me along, of course, to chaperon you. Esme has already invited me." He touched his sword hilt lightly. "I promise you that no harm will come to you whilst you are under my protection."

Imogene moistened her lips and considered that. It would mean hurling herself back into the danger she had so recently left and she would have but one sword arm between herself and destruction. Still—it was a chance to give van Ryker back his name, his honor, his country.

She would do it!

She lifted her goblet in a reckless gesture and the man seated across from her saw another reason besides her beauty why the notorious buccaneer loved her—her valiant spirit.

"To the venture!" she cried. "We will bring them down!"

He gave her a grim smile and drank her toast, and then proposed another. "To a valiant lady," he said, and she smiled into his eyes as he drank.

But as they drank to the future they never guessed—nor did the other passengers, asleep in their bunks—the kind of ship they traveled in. For three of the crew were already down sick. They were on a fever-ridden vessel, bound for Port Royal.

PART TWO
...Into the Fire!

The memory of his kisses is sweet upon her lips
As her sheer chemise glides softly down below her silken hips.
She whispers to a pale white moon—she who's about to flaunt him:
Will my love ever forgive me? Or will this night ever haunt him?

Port Royal, Jamaica, 1660

CHAPTER 14

Even though the *Sea Rover* could not possibly be in Port Royal, Imogene could not resist studying the shipping as they approached. She kept telling herself that van Ryker never sailed into Port Royal, for he did not want his face to become known to the townspeople against that future day when he retired to his holding at Gale Force. But even that inner remonstrance could not keep her blue eyes from eagerly scanning every tall ship they passed as the *Bristol* sailed in toward that six-mile sandy strip of land the Spanish had christened Las Palizadas, negotiated the narrow strait that led between the shore batteries of Port Mayfield to port and Port Pelican to starboard, and arrived at last in the deep blue waters of majestic Port Royal bay.

Of all the shipping they passed, only one vessel did she know—and that one caused her to frown, for it was the dark hull of *Le Sabre*, anchored well out in the bay as if to make a ready escape. She wondered if *Le Sabre*'s captain, the dark Frenchman, Vartel, was aboard her or in the town.

Beside her at the rail Darnwell Keating, handsomely attired

in lime silks, turned to smile at her. Last night he had told her his interest in Esme had been fleeting—and she had believed him. Now he gave her hand a reassuring squeeze.

She needed that to help raise her spirits as the town of Port Royal loomed ahead, crowding down to the strip of white beach, with its handsome backdrop of the Blue Mountains rising behind. For she had spent another sleepless night in Esme's cabin and morning had found her feeling queasy. She ascribed it to nervousness over once again having to face the dangers that lurked at Gale Force and sternly rebuked herself, but she was grateful for Darnwell's helping hand as they went ashore into the New World's most sinful city.

Tortuga was a wild outpost, she now realized, but Port Royal was a city. The whole town, to her surprised gaze, seemed to be under construction, so many new buildings were going up—some of them quite handsome, with thick walls. Some of them, she saw, rested upon pilings driven into the sand at the water's edge, as if trying to creep out into the sea on stilts.

Once ashore, they found crowded, jostling, busy streets. There were the same swaggering cutlassed buccaneers here that she had grown used to in Tortuga, but there were more tradesmen here, more carriages. Handsomely gowned women rode past in carriages driven by grinning black men, some of them in livery. Women in silks and taffetas swayed like bright flowers into the shops. Important-looking men in beaver hats—despite the heat—strode about through a sea of straw hats worn by lesser mortals. Street vendors struggled through the crowds calling out their wares. Seabirds wheeled overhead. Everywhere was confusion.

Once, as Imogene missed a step and would have fallen had not Darnwell caught her, he said, "Aren't you feeling well? You look flushed. Would you like me to buy you some of those mangoes? Would you find that refreshing?"

"No—I don't know what's the matter with me," she said dizzily. "But I think—I think I should sit down."

Esme had accompanied them quietly, her keen attention centered on the town itself but now she turned to Darnwell. "What is the matter with her?" she asked sharply.

"She feels faint, I think."

"It is nothing," insisted Imogene. "It will pass if only I could find a place to sit down."

"There's an inn," said Darnwell, looking up the street. "The White Stag. I'll take you there. You can rest a while in the common room."

"Thank you," said Imogene faintly.

She could feel her legs wobbling under her as they made their way to the inn and she almost collapsed onto a bench in the common room. The uneven plaster of the walls and the rude beams of the ceiling seemed to swim around her and she leaned upon her arms on the unpainted wooden table, trying to fight off nausea.

"The lady ain't feeling well?" asked the landlord solicitously.

"She'll feel better after she drinks something," said Darnwell. "Ale? Brandy?"

"Oh, I couldn't," shuddered Imogene.

"Have you any lemonade?"

"I've got limeade."

"Fine, bring us some of that." And to Esme, "Why don't you stroll around the town and enjoy the shopping? Imogene plainly isn't up to travel just now, and as soon as she feels a little better, I'll let her rest here and go and make arrangements for a boat to take us up the Cobre River to Gale Force."

"Oh—would you do that, Darnwell?" Esme sounded relieved. "I hate dealing with these riverboat people—I'm never sure which ones are cutthroats and which are not!"

Darnwell Keating gave her a look that suggested she had never dealt with a riverboat person in her life. Esme flushed, and with her back a little stiffer, left them.

There in the coolness of the inn's high-ceilinged common room, Darnwell urged limeade on Imogene and to please him she took a swallow. It almost came up.

"No—no more," she said, pushing the pewter tankard away.

"There's no need for us to attempt the trip up the Cobre today," he said. "We can go tomorrow, when you feel better."

"I couldn't bear trying to stay awake all night, keeping an eye on Esme."

His mouth tightened. "You won't have to. I'll take a separate room for you and you can latch it from the inside."

"Darnwell, have you forgotten? We have no *money*."

"Not so loud," he muttered, looking about him. "A resourceful fellow should be able to get along without it."

"*How*?" she groaned.

"You'll see," he said cheerfully. "This inn looks second-class to me. I'm sure there must be a better one down the street—something for the gentry. Come, can you stand up? We'll just toddle down the street and find us a better inn. Then when Esme comes back, I'll tell her I took a room for you here and you're sleeping and not to be disturbed. Let her spend the night trying to find you!"

"Fine, fine," mumbled Imogene. She stumbled to her feet with her head whirling. "If only I can—" Her voice faded away as she slumped to the floor.

The landlord had left the empty room, for it was an off-hour and there were no patrons save Imogene and Darnwell, but a little servant girl was mopping in one corner. She gave a low screech as she saw Imogene slide to the floor and came running over.

"Did the lady slip?" she demanded anxiously. "Oh, lor', don't let 'im know she fell!" She jerked her head in the direction the landlord had gone. "He'll think sure I left the floor wet—and I didn't, did I?"

"No, of course you didn't," said Darnwell, who was cursing himself for not having realized Imogene could not stand alone, and leaping forward in time to catch her. "Is this the best inn the town affords?" he asked the girl. He was scooping Imogene up in his arms as he spoke.

"No, there's two better. But the Bell and Candle is the best one."

"How far?"

"Just around the corner a-ways."

"Good. You run ahead and tell the landlord of the Bell and Candle I'll be needing a room for the lady and myself. Tell him the lady's with child and has fainted and I'll want the bed turned down and everything ready. Run along—there's a penny in it for you." And when the girl hesitated. "And if you don't do it," he warned her pleasantly, rising with his limp burden in his arms, "I'll tell your master you deliberately left a puddle of water on the floor for the sheer pleasure of seeing people slip on it and fall and break their bones!"

The girl gasped, but she ran outside still carrying her mop, and sprinted down the street. Keating followed more leisurely, noting how childishly Imogene lay in his arms—it gave his heart a tug to see her thus.

People turned to look at the handsome young rake in lime green silks striding down the street with his well-dressed limp burden. Some paused to stare and one, a buccaneer with a black patch over one eye and a scarred face, drew his companion to a halt and watched Keating carry Imogene into the Bell and Candle.

"Lookee there," he muttered, digging his elbow into his companion's leathern-clad ribs.

"All I see is one o' the locals carrying his wife into that inn."

"No, that ain't all ye see! The dandy carrying her, I don't know who *he* is. But the woman I seen many a time in Tortuga. That's Cap'n van Ryker's woman!"

"Couldn't be!"

"It is, I say!" Wrangling, they went off down the street to repair them to the Bird and Bottle and continue their argument there among a group of their fellows.

With a lordly air, Keating carried Imogene into the inn, stared down the landlord, tossed a penny to the girl with the broom, who scurried away, and set his booted feet upon the wooden stairway that led to the second floor.

"Which room?" he inquired haughtily. "I'll need your best."

Those last words won the landlord. "First one to the right of the stairs," he beamed. " 'Tis ready for ye."

Darnwell Keating chuckled as he ascended those stairs. The fates that look out for children and fools for once had favored a rake. Imogene, whose fainting fit he had already assured himself came from days of worry and a missed breakfast, would come to presently and find herself in his bed—where he would comfort her alarms and incidentally seduce her.

So went his calm thoughts as he deposited his frail burden gently upon the big bed. He removed her shoes and stockings, felt her forehead—she seemed very cold to him. He had removed all her clothes but her chemise and was tempted to remove that when he reminded himself how cold she was, and tossed a coverlet over her even though he personally considered the room stifling.

It was his intention to remove his own clothes and join her in the big soft bed and with that in mind he went to latch the door. When he turned, Imogene had come to and was staring at him.

"What am I doing here?" she asked in confusion. "Darnwell, where is this place?"

" 'Tis an inn in Port Royal, the Bell and Candle. Ye had a fainting fit in the common room of the White Stag. You'll be safe here."

"But—my clothes! I'm—"

"I had the chambermaid put you to bed," said Darnwell smoothly. "Do not alarm yourself. You need a bit of rest."

"Where is Esme?" She had begun to shiver.

He frowned. For a moment there, thinking of the delights of joining Imogene in the big bed, he had forgotten Esme. "I'll go and see to Esme," he said. "And find her a room at the inn we left. Ye'll have nothing to fear from her. Try to rest—I'll be back soon."

He went out, striding through the downstairs, thankful the innkeeper was not about, and went directly to the White Stag. Esme, unused to the rigors of the tropics, had returned and was fanning herself with a small fan she carried, and looking most perturbed. She leaped up at sight of him.

"Darnwell, where have you been?" She ran over to him. "I was afraid to ask the landlord—afraid to call attention to myself!"

"Why?" His voice echoed his surprise.

"Haven't you heard?" she demanded in a low urgent tone. "There was fever on the ship that brought us here. One of the crew died just as we came into port. The authorities are combing the town looking for the passengers from the *Bristol*—they're going to quarantine all of them in some pesthole of a building. They even stopped *me*, but I told them I was off the *Lancaster*, which was the only ship's name I could remember seeing when we landed. They believed me, but they've yet to check the passenger list and my name is on it—yours too. Oh, Darnwell, you must *do* something!"

His brows elevated. "And what would you propose I do?"

Esme stamped her foot in exasperation. "You must get us away from here before they shut us up with a lot of dying people!"

Various possibilities occurred to Darnwell—none that he liked. Foremost among them was what it would be like to be sent to a pesthole. For himself—well, he could probably get away, but the women . . . his face went thoughtful.

"You must stay here, Esme," he said at last. "We can't risk trying to get upriver now, they'll be searching the boats."

Her hand flew to her mouth. "Oh, I hadn't thought of that."

"Well, do think about it." His smile was grim. "Take a room here. Don't use your married name. Tell the landlord you're Esme Ryder from Gale Force plantation upriver and that your brother Anthony will shortly be joining you. Keep to your room, don't mix about. There may be a search but if you keep your head, you should have no trouble. And remember, even though there was a case of fever on the ship, it may not spread."

"Imogene!" Esme's hand flew to her mouth. "*She* was feeling ill. Do you think—?"

"She has a chill, not a fever," said Darnwell roughly, for the same thought had occurred to him. "I've taken a room for her elsewhere, in any event."

"You'll be staying here? Or with her?"

"With her. Someone must keep an eye on her and—you'll have a better chance without her, Esme. Remember she's not feeling well and they could decide to take her along to a pesthouse anyway—in which case they'd very likely take you along as well!"

Esme shivered. "Pray God she doesn't have it, Darnwell, for we were both with her constantly."

"I do pray it." His mouth was grim. "I'll come by later, Esme." A new thought occurred to him. "Find out if the landlord knows your brother by sight."

"Oh, I'm sure he doesn't! Anthony seldom comes into Port Royal. He has written me that it's a terrible place, beneath contempt. When he needs something from the town, he sends for it. And he has no friends here."

"Good." Keating's face cleared. "Then I shall present myself as your brother, Anthony Ryder of Gale Force. All will know the name of the plantation and the owner, so none will question me. I can come and go at will."

"Excellent. Oh, Darnwell, do take care!" Esme watched him go, anxiously, then drew herself up and descended upon the landlord with all the airs of a great lady, demanding the best room in the house for herself, and chattering about her brother "who just left, didn't you see him?" and the magnificence of Gale Force plantation.

The landlord, duly impressed, gave her the best room in the house.

"I will want a bath sent up," Esme told him haughtily. "And I will desire to send a message. I will let you know when it's ready."

The landlord bobbed his head and went to order her bath brought up, but later when it came to the message he was adamant. "The authorities has just been here, mistress," he told her severely. "And 'twas only because I told them you was in the tub that they didn't come bustin' in. They's searching this whole city for the passengers off a ship just docked today—fever ship, they say."

" 'Fever ship'?" Esme managed to keep her voice from trembling.

"Aye, the *Bristol*. They's roundin' up the passengers and puttin' em back aboard her and makin' her captain sail her out. Got to stay out till all are dead or all are well, that's the order come down from the gov'ner. He's seen fever before, he says, and he don't want the town to be wiped out."

Not a pesthouse, then—a doomed ship.

"Orders from the governor? From Lord Marr?"

"Lord Marr don't be here yet. Comin' next month, I hear. 'Tis the old gov'ner give the order. He's in town hisself today, so he give it personal afore he went back to Spanish Town."

"That seems very cruel," she protested.

"Cruel it may be, mistress, but if it serves to preserve Port Royal from another dose of the fever, I'm for it and so's everybody else!" His bushy brows drew together. "Plagues do rage here, for this is hot country, this is, and 'tis best to nip them in the bud, I say, I do say!"

Esme was very pale. "Have they—found all the passengers?"

"All but one. Woman named Ribaud—French baggage, I take it, from the name. 'Tis thought she's left the city, but they're scouring house to house for her just the same."

"*All but one?*" Esme leaned forward. But that meant Darnwell and Imogene must have been seized and were back on board the *Bristol*!

"Got two of 'em just now, I heard. Man and woman, both of 'em dead drunk, but a tavern keeper identified them as bein' passengers."

Esme drew a deep breath. She had no doubt who had arranged *that!* Darnwell Keating was a clever fellow and could now lie low in safety—but he *might* have made similar arrangements for her!

"It is indeed a desperate situation and I am sure the authorities are doing the right thing," she said hastily. "But this message is really most urgent and I must insist—"

"No, no, mistress." The landlord was shaking his head stubbornly. "Insistin' won't do no good with me. I've shut the inn doors and locked them and nobody goes in nor out until the *Bristol* sails. Won't none o' my people be walking the streets this day bringin' us foreign plagues and fevers!"

"But I'll pay well," she cried. "Double whatever you ask!"

He gave her a jaundiced look. " 'Twill have to keep till morning, mistress, until I climb to the roof and make sure the *Bristol* no longer rides the bay. I just looked and she's still here. Once she's gone, 'twill cost ye only what ye care to

give the lad who carries it. But there's naught can compensate
a man for his life, and that's what ye could be askin'." He
left, shaking his head at the vagaries of the gentry, and a
dismayed Esme watched him go.

Meantime, Darnwell Keating, having arranged for suitable
"substitutes" for himself and Imogene, and seeing them hauled
off in the direction of the *Bristol*, went back to the Bell and
Candle, where he registered with a flourish as Anthony Ryder
and wife of Gale Force plantation. He then demanded that
food be sent up and the best of wine.

The real Anthony Ryder, had he known of it, would have
choked with fury.

Darnwell clattered up the stairs, gave a single knock to
announce himself, and entered the room.

A quick glance was enough to tell him all was not well.
Imogene, her face violently flushed, had tossed off the coverlet and was turning over in the bed, moaning as he entered.

With a low exclamation, he strode across the room, sat
down on the edge of the bed and felt her forehead.

She was burning up with fever.

He stared down at her, his handsome face mirroring the
horror he felt at this discovery.

"Oh, Imogene . . ." In consternation he sank down on his
knees by the bedside and took her limp feverish hand in his
own. Heedless of infection, he bent his head and rubbed it
gently against her flushed cheek. She was moaning softly, lost
in a world of her own. She did not hear him, did not even
know he was there. Darnwell closed his eyes and to his own
astonishment, began to pray.

And then he lifted his head and looked at her, really looked
at her. Her hair was a tangled mass of curls and damp with
perspiration. The bedclothes were soaked. Her sheer chemise
clung damply to her lovely body and had ridden up so that her
long, delicately made bare legs were exposed to his gaze.

Less than an hour ago he had been ready to crawl into bed
with Imogene, to let her wake up in his arms. He'd been quite
prepared for a scuffle, laughingly certain he would win. He had
thought her a target, a lustrous prize to be captured, won,

sported with, and later, if he chose, tossed aside. But now—now as he saw her lying there, racked with fever and like to die, it came to him with crushing force how very much he loved her.

She had worked her way into his heart and there was no going back—ever.

Like a lean buccaneer before him, Darnwell Keating looked at the beautiful woman on the bed and determined to make her live.

With all his being, he set out to do it.

She would need a doctor. It suddenly occurred to Darnwell that he dare not call a doctor. Nor could he care for Imogene here at the inn—that would be to invite speculation, and speculation could mean disaster for them both.

But Darnwell Keating was a man of many resources. Accordingly, he made swift arrangements. In his engaging way, he told the landlord that afternoon that his young wife was prone to miscarriage, that she had already lost two children to miscarriage and he was loath to see her lose another. He thought it best they not attempt the return voyage upriver, he said, best to stay near doctors. He explained to the landlord that he had come to Port Royal only to meet his sister, who had arrived on the *Lancaster*, and had not carried much cash with him. His factor would be down shortly to pay for their stay, plus a handsome bonus for the inconvenience.

So impressive was the London rake's manner, so sincere his obvious anxiety about his young wife, that the landlord believed him absolutely. He even helped Darnwell find a suitable house that he could carry her to. It was a house that belonged to his widowed sister, who had only this morning left for England and given him instructions to rent it out. He was sure she would thank him for having brought her such a desirable tenant as the master of Gale Force plantation.

CHAPTER 15

At the Bird and Bottle the argument was still going on as to whether the buccaneer with the black patch over his eye had actually seen Captain van Ryker's woman carried down the streets of Port Royal. Tempers were waxing hot about it.

"I would wager ten gold doubloons 'twas her!" roared Black Patch, incensed at the sly suggestion someone had just put forward that his sight in his good eye had deserted him. He brought his fist down with a crash onto the wooden table before him and upset his tankard of ale.

"We could send someone to ask the wench who she is," snickered someone.

General laughter greeted this suggestion.

"If she *is* Cap'n van Ryker's woman and he be out voyaging and she be holed up here with her lover, d'ye think she'll admit it?" jibed a red-bearded giant.

"I know her by sight," spoke up a new voice. "For I kissed her once."

All heads swung to survey the lad who had made this mad claim. Intent on the conversation, tow-headed Lark Saxon lounged against the broom he had just brought to brush away the spilled ale on the floor. " 'Twas in Tortuga," he elaborated.

Amid loud derision, Black Patch stood up unsteadily and pointed at young Saxon. "He speaks the truth! This is the lad who seized van Ryker's woman and kissed her on the quay at Cayona—I was there and saw him do it!" He tossed young Saxon a gold coin, which was eagerly caught in midair. "Go to the Bell and Candle, lad, for that's where she was taken, and have a look at her and come back and tell us who she is.

Meantime we'll make our wagers. My whole purse says I'm right."

"Ten gold doubloons says ye're wrong!" cried Red Beard instantly.

Amid general wagering, Lark Saxon laid aside his broom.

He had fled Tortuga the very day he had been fool enough to seize Imogene on the quay and kiss her—fled in fear of his life. For Lark Saxon had for a breathless moment looked down the barrel of Captain Vartel's dueling pistol and something in the face behind the pistol had told him that he was expendable. Vartel had hired him right enough, but Vartel meant to pay him in lead—not gold. Lark Saxon had not even tried to collect; instead he had fled to Port Royal and had been here ever since.

Stormy in his memory was the feel of Imogene van Ryker's sweet body crushed in his arms, the softness of her lips—but he had many times wished he had thrust his arms around nettles instead. For he had a strong suspicion that something more than womanizing was afoot here. Else why would Vartel have tried to kill him on the quay?

Young Saxon had quickly taken the only job he could find in Port Royal—sweeping the floor at the Bird and Bottle. And it had seemed to him Judgment Day had sounded its knell when he looked up from the dock and saw *Le Sabre*'s dark hull anchored in the harbor. After that he had kept his head ducked down and tried to escape notice—but he need not have bothered. *Le Sabre*'s lean captain was not after him—he was intent on bigger game.

Now the sight of gold on the tavern table—like Vartel's offer of yellow gold back in Tortuga—had overtempted Lark Saxon. He knew he might pay dearly for it, but he could not resist.

With the coin burning his pocket, he went directly to the Bell and Candle, seated himself in the common room, where he could observe all comings and goings, and expansively ordered himself supper and a tankard of ale.

Time passed, twilight came and went. Night had closed down and young Saxon was beginning to worry. It would do no good, he felt, to make inquiries. If Imogene was here and heard she was being searched out, she would doubtless quietly disappear. If only he could search the rooms—but of course that was out of the question. He had been so *sure* that anyone staying at the inn would be down for supper, for who would stay in those hot holes upstairs when they could dine in the coolness of the high-ceilinged common room?

In desperation he was about to try bribing a serving girl for information, when Darnwell Keating, handsome in the lime silks Black Patch had so well described, came down the stairs carrying Imogene limp in his arms.

Young Saxon leaned forward. There could be no mistake. Even though her unforgettable blue eyes were closed and long lashes brushed her cheeks, that flushed lovely face he glimpsed in passing could belong to no one but Imogene van Ryker. Drunk, he supposed.

Silently he rose and, keeping at a safe distance, he followed Darnwell Keating as he took his fever-stricken lady to a solidly built two-story house situated on a quiet street, where he let himself in with a key.

At that point, Lark Saxon went back to the Bird and Bottle.

" 'Tis Captain van Ryker's woman," he assured Black Patch. "I've seen her close up and I'd stake my life on it."

Wild howls greeted this pronouncement as wagers were snapped up amid rumbles of disappointment from the losers.

"Ye told the wrong man, lad." A scarred buccaneer with breath heavy with rum leaned toward him. "Twas Cap'n van Ryker ye should have told. He'd have given ye a whole stack of doubloons to find where his lady was hidin' out with her lover!" His laughter cracked like a pistol.

Lark Saxon's blue eyes widened. It came to him suddenly that he was possessed of very valuable information if he but had the chance to market it. The rest of them thought Imogene was still at the Bell and Candle. *He alone knew where she was now*. And his recent confrontation with van Ryker had reassured him that he was not the kind to shoot you down after you'd done the job—like the Frenchman, Vartel.

He presumed van Ryker to be in Tortuga and itched to

go there and market his dangerous knowledge. But he was prevented, of course, by the fever, for once the *Bristol* had cleared the harbor on her voyage to nowhere, the port was closed to all shipping—in or out.

But the fever watch could not prevent him from keeping a sharp eye on the bay. He even began to sleep on the waterfront, the better to keep watch, for he felt in his soul that—quarantine or no—the buccaneer captain would come storming into Port Royal looking for his lustrous lady. And he alone could tell van Ryker where she was!

Having brought Imogene to a "safe" house, it occurred to Darnwell Keating that he was no closer to getting her medical attention. To call a doctor in the usual way would be to invite disaster. The doctor could hardly be expected to keep his mouth shut, there would be an outcry and he and Imogene could well find themselves set into a sailboat and told to catch up with the fever-ridden *Bristol*—or worse, shut into some little hovel without air or light and left to suffer.

No, he dare not call a doctor in the usual way but—devil take it, he would have one anyway! Keating's always agile mind set to work on the problem and that night, having ascertained that a certain Dr. Jenkins frequented a certain waterfront tavern, he tied a scarf over his face, seized the good doctor from behind, bound his hands and gagged him and managed to get him into a rowboat at the quayside— where to any bleary-eyed lategoers they seemed to be a couple of harmless drunks, slumped down, trying to find their way home.

"I'm taking ye down the coast," he told the doctor in a muffled voice, "where ye're to see to my young daughter." He tried to sound old and ended up sounding merely fierce.

There was a terrified mumble from the bagged head beside him.

"Naught will happen to you if you forget what you see," Keating told the doctor and the mumble subsided gloomily.

After half an hour of rowing and drifting aimlessly about the bay, Keating decided the doctor was addled enough. He took him back ashore and marched him through dark alleys to the house he had rented, not removing the bag from the doctor's head or untying his hands until he was in Imogene's bedchamber.

As the gag left his mouth, Dr. Jenkins gasped, "But this woman is ill of the fever—she must be one of those from the *Bristol*!"

The man beside him gave him a deadly smile. His teeth gleamed through his scarf. "Think what ye will but if ye say it aloud, ye'll find your throat slit some fine night, for I've many friends in Port Royal who would deem it a privilege to do me such a small favor. Ye'd not escape them."

Had he lived in a more lawful town the doctor might have scoffed, but in buccaneer Port Royal such a threat was not to be discounted. Dr. Jenkins turned as pale as his collar.

"I'll not speak of it," he mumbled, and bent to examine Imogene.

She was delirious now, sometimes incoherent.

"But why *this* bay?" she was asking as she tossed and turned. "Why not Port Royal, when it's so close?" Something unintelligible and then, "They're planning to kill me," she muttered. "I must . . ." her voice became inaudible until suddenly she sat up with a piercing scream. "*Georgiana*! Oh, God, let it not be true!" She fell back quivering onto her pillow and sobbed brokenly.

The doctor's head lifted. Gravely he met Keating's searching gaze.

"Will she live, doctor?"

Dr. Jenkins shook his head and sighed. "I cannot say. She is very ill indeed."

Keating returned the doctor to Port Royal's waterfront in the same manner as his leavetaking and returned hurriedly to the sickroom he had so recently left. He had learned to his sorrow that there was little he could do. Rest, a sparing amount of food—and that mostly fruit. The medical profession was all but helpless before these fevers that lashed through tropical towns like a hurricane, leaving behind them a trail of death.

Port Royal, accustomed as were other low-lying cities of

the tropics, to being swept by plagues, was swift to put up its defenses. But—like the three aristocrats who had traveled here on board the doomed *Bristol*—there were always those who managed to escape the net.

Several ships in the harbor upanchored and sailed away on the evening tide, including the *Lancaster*, which had docked just before the *Bristol*, and Captain Vartel's lean *Le Sabre*.

When next morning a passenger count revealed that there were still three passengers missing from the *Bristol* and that the drunken pair who had been dragged aboard and left to sober up by the ship's rail were not the right passengers, it was assumed that all three had somehow managed to escape aboard those departing ships. Port Royal's authorities did not care. If the captains of those ships desired to take the fever elsewhere, so be it. The *Bristol* was hastily given fresh water and fresh stores and banished to sea again.

The *Bristol*'s captain now cursed himself that he had not put ashore in Tortuga as that woman had wanted, let this cursed fever ride itself out there, and sailed back to Port Royal with whatever crew still survived. As it was, he had these psalm-singing Puritans on his hands again until death did them part.

He thought of Port Royal, whose streets he had almost trod, he thought of the woman who waited inland, believing him unfaithful. He wept. And when one of the Puritans chided him for not joining them in prayer in this terrible hour, his face convulsed and he struck the fellow across the face and stomped off.

The Puritans looked at each other, appalled, and gathered in little groups. It was a judgment, they agreed, when a new squall struck and the leaky ship nearly foundered.

During the night of that wild squall, another crewman died and two of the passengers were taken.

The *Bristol* sailed on.

Now she was far from Port Royal, out on the broad Caribbean's uncaring face, and circumstances worsened. There was no doctor aboard, the supply of fresh fruit was soon exhausted, the water in this heat quickly turned bad. The

Puritans joined in mournful little groups on the deck and implored their deity to aid them.

The pitiless sun beat down.

On sailed the *Bristol*, losing a man a day and sometimes two. She had sailed into port a fever ship, but now she was a death ship limping along under canvas there was not manpower enough to handle. Her captain still steered, but he was not the man he had been. Gaunt and hollow-eyed, he gave the order to consign first this sheeted figure and then that one to the deep. He had given up all thought of Mary Ann. He would sail this ship to hell, by God!

Strangely, he alone survived. He woke one morning, half mad, and discovered about him a strange silence. He stumbled over two dead men as he went to get his morning coffee. A search of the ship revealed no one else. He pushed the dead over the side, unsheeted, and made what was to be the last entry in his ship's log: *All dead save me. Why am I spared?*

For a whole week the *Bristol* drifted, a derelict, but eventually she was picked up by a passing Dutch ship and towed to Curaçao, where she was refitted. Eventually her exhausted captain was to reach home and Mary Ann.

She was to find him greatly changed. Convinced that he had been saved by his Creator for some divine purpose, hard-drinking Captain Bellows would become a teetotaler, he would pray loudly and conspicuously in church, take a job on Port Royal's docks and never put to sea again.

Not only in Port Royal—at Gale Force they were worrying about the fever too.

"Like as not we'll die of it while Branch, who's lucky enough to be at sea, lives on to be ninety," remarked Charles gloomily as he lounged on the long veranda.

The same thought had occurred to Anthony and was already causing him to sweat. He turned irritably on his younger brother. "More likely he'll come sailing into Port Royal ignoring the quarantine and—"

"And die after he reaches us here, infecting us all," finished Charles with a sigh.

"No, he'd—" Anthony went suddenly reflective. "More like he wouldn't come through Port Royal at all. You remember Imogene insisted she'd never seen Port Royal? And that would hardly be possible if she'd come up the Cobre. . . . How *did* Branch reach here?"

"He could have landed anywhere on the coast."

"Yes, but he wouldn't. He's too cautious for that, he'd leave his ship somewhere safe, he'd land somewhere within easy striking distance of Gale Force, not too far that he couldn't get back to his ship in a hurry if need be . . . ." Suddenly he snapped his fingers. "I've got it, Charles. You know that bay I told you about?"

"The one Gale Force fronts on? You said it was almost impenetrable around there, that Branch had ordered that part of the holding kept wild."

"Exactly." Anthony was chuckling. "And why was that? To give him a back door to reach us, Charles. He sailed in and cast anchor there and brought Imogene here overland—no, not even all the way overland. There's a branch of the Cobre wanders down through there. It breaks up into rough rivulets as it nears the shore but—come on, Charles, we're going looking for a boat!"

Under protest, indolent Charles followed his elegant brother, who forthwith plunged into the brush. Cursing at every bramble that snagged his finery, Anthony followed the path Branch must have taken to reach the bay—and found at last the narrow dugout Branch had hidden.

"We've found it, Charles." Anthony slapped his thigh. "This is how he did it—this is how he'll do it again!"

"Found what, Tony? All I can see is a boat."

"We've found more than that. We've found the answer to our problem, for when Branch comes back to that bay he'll find more than lemon trees—he'll find the Jamaica Squadron waiting for him. We won't wait to inherit, Charles. Imogene has gone to London, where Esme will see she's never heard from again—and the Jamaica Squadron will finish Branch off right here!"

Charles blanched. "I'll have naught to do with it, Tony."

He backed away into the brush. "Branch would kill us both if he found out."

"'Found out'?" scoffed Anthony. "How's he to find out? 'Tis neither of *us* will set the Jamaica Squadron on him. No, 'twill be one of his own."

"Who?" wondered Charles, jumping as a flying insect stung him.

Anthony gave him a droll look. "You'll not have heard of him, Charles. His name is Jacques Vartel."

"The buccaneer?" Charles had indeed heard of Vartel; Reverend Gibbons had referred to the Frenchman as "one of the scum that infest Port Royal." It made him curious. He sucked the bee sting on his wrist. "What did ye offer him, Tony?"

"Half," said Anthony dispassionately.

"'Half'?" exploded Charles, seeing himself stripped of half of the Carolina holding before ever receiving it.

His brother turned a laughing face toward him. "There is no need to take that attitude, Charles. Vartel will never live to collect. Remember what he is, Charles—a pirate. He has thrice attacked English ships—I checked."

"Then why is he at large, Tony? 'Tis well known he has the run of Port Royal harbor!"

"Aye." His brother nodded. "But Vartel was careful to spread the word the deeds were done by others—and he left no survivors. He slipped up there, for I have found one. And that one can testify about the others, for he heard Vartel brag of it. No, Charles—Vartel will not trouble us. For as soon as I hear Branch is taken, I will bring Vartel's crimes before the governor and the Jamaica Squadron will be set upon *him*!"

At Gale Force the spider had spun his web well.

In that room of fever in Port Royal where Imogene lay, out of her head and raving, reliving past moments, there was a feeling of death in the air.

Darnwell Keating sat hunched and exhausted and unshaven beside her. He had learned so much about Imogene these past days from her disjointed ravings. So many hurtful secrets, what the world had been like that had trod her down. He had been hard put not to weep.

Now suddenly, with fever-bright unseeing eyes, she sat up and her voice rose hysterically. *"Don't leave me in Jamaica!"* Her clutching hands reached out—reached out to van Ryker, whom she could see in her scalding imagination, van Ryker, strong and wonderful and—leaving her. "Don't leave me, don't leave me," she cried brokenly.

And Darnwell Keating, that sometime London rake, took her fragile body in his arms, let her golden hair spill down over his chest, and tried to comfort her.

"I won't leave you, Imogene," he choked. "I will never leave you. *Never.*"

Imogene could not hear him, of course. She was lost in a world of her own, a bright and terrifying world. She did not even feel the hot tears that fell upon her face.

Esme detailed what she could glean of Darnwell's actions in a letter she wrote and eventually dispatched.

I fear our plans must be changed, she wrote. *Darnwell has become enamored of Imogene and will not leave her side. She is ill of fever and he has chosen to nurse her—imagine that! So he now presents a danger to us, for I am satisfied that he will allow nothing to happen to her. Wait till you hear from me before attempting anything. She may die and if she does we may wish to conceal it—at least for a while. I need time to think.*

She had time and aplenty to think, had Esme, for she was afraid to wander abroad. In the town, while no fever victims had appeared (none knowing of Imogene's plight), all strangers were suspect. Had they contacted the people from the fever ship *Bristol?* Everyone wondered. And rumors flew about of people coming down of fever in Spanish Town and elsewhere on the island. Esme kept to the inn, fretting, and waited eagerly for Darnwell's infrequent calls, even though she was half afraid to have him near her—after all, might he not come down with fever at any moment?

Darnwell was thinner now. Constantly working with Imogene had worn him down. He was by her side every moment, sponging her hot face, forcing liquids down her protesting throat, bathing her, caring for her. He slept on a pallet on the floor by her bed, exhausted in the heat, rousing himself groggily to care for her needs.

Had he been able to view himself objectively, as a stranger might, the rake would have been astonished at himself. He had found at last someone he loved dearer than himself, dearer than life even—and she was about to be snatched away from him. There was the smell of death on her; terrified, Darnwell could scent it. She was very weak, she slipped in and out of consciousness, she moaned and called for van Ryker—which made him wince—and for Georgiana, who seemed to be a child, and for someone named Elise. But mostly she called for van Ryker. Sometimes, in fleeting moments of reality, she seized his arm and urged him to send a message to van Ryker in Tortuga, warning him.

It cut Darnwell Keating to the quick. But always he promised.

But she would be well soon, he told himself firmly. *He would make her well*! And she would turn to him then—after all, a gently bred lady like Imogene could not really enjoy living the uncertain life of a buccaneer's woman! Thus he buttressed himself. That his own life had been hardly less uncertain was a fact he brushed cavalierly aside. He would change, adjust, improve. He would enoble himself for her—if only she would live!

For the first time in his dissolute life he stared earnestly up at the ceiling past which lay heaven, impenetrable, awesome—and, characteristically, he offered God a deal. He would become at last the man his uncle had so fervently wanted him to be, the man his father had despaired of his ever becoming, the man who would be worthy of this lovely, frail, dying woman—if only a merciful heaven would spare her.

Someone Upstairs must have heard his plea, for in a night of wild raving when it seemed he must surely lose her at any minute, the crisis passed and Imogene gradually—so slowly that sometimes Darnwell could not convince himself it was true—got better.

She could care for herself now—a little. She was able to bathe herself in the metal bathtub he filled with water for her—no more of those sponge baths he had given her so lovingly when she was burning up with fever. She was able to sit up and to dress herself. And although she had at first been startled when he had told her there had been no woman to care for her, that he had personally attended to all her needs, when he explained how desperate their situation had been in a town panicked by fever, she smiled on him very tenderly.

It gave Darnwell hope.

"Has Esme gone upriver?" she asked.

"No, she still resides at the White Stag."

Imogene frowned. "That seems very strange. I would have expected her to go at once to Gale Force—and for Anthony and Charles to descend upon me here . . . or at least to tell the authorities that I was a fever victim from the *Bristol*."

"You have not thought it through," he said wryly. "If the authorities had seized *you* as a fever victim, then Esme herself would have been in danger—for she herself was a passenger on board the *Bristol*."

"I would not have given her away," sighed Imogene. "For my chances of living through the fever would have been even slimmer had Esme been beside me!"

"Ah, but she would not have realized that—she would assume you to be vindictive, to guess who had given you away, and to take your revenge by setting the authorities upon her as well."

"And you, Darnwell—you took a long chance for me." Again she gave him that pensive tender look and again his heart leaped.

He sat down upon the bed beside her and took possession of both her hands. She gave them to him very readily, for she had every reason to trust him.

"These last weeks have made you very dear to me," he told her.

For we hold closest that which we are about to lose, she thought, remembering van Ryker in a situation that had had its similarities.

"I am indebted to you, Darnwell," she said softly. "And although I know you ask nothing but my regard, nevertheless van Ryker will reward you."

He stiffened and she saw that she had affronted him. "I do not *want* him to reward me, Imogene. That is not the reward I seek."

"What, then?" But she knew the answer.

"We have grown close during your illness," he said caressingly, and his voice grew rich and deep. "I know ye regard me as a rake and past saving, but that is not the case. For you I would change, Imogene. I will be whatever you want me to be, a man heaped with honors."

A little laugh caught in her throat at the thought of Darnwell, the London rake, "heaped with honors."

"Darnwell," she said, trying to keep it light. "Tomorrow you'll be sorry you said all this. And next week you'll look back in horror and thank your stars that I didn't take you up on it."

"Ah, don't joke, Imogene." He sounded aggrieved. "Can't you see how much you mean to me? Haven't you guessed?"

She had guessed—she just hadn't chosen to admit it.

His face—perhaps the second most attractive she had ever encountered—pressed closer. His very heart was in his eyes—she could feel like a touch the pressure of that gaze. His lips brushed her ear and his voice was intense, passionate. "Ah, Imogene, forget him. Come make a new life—with me."

She edged away nervously and gave him a rueful look. "'Tis true I owe you my life, Darnwell. I freely admit it. But van Ryker is my husband and—I love him."

He winced and looked away. For a long time he was silent. Then, "You would forget him," he muttered. "In time."

"Never," she said softly. "When two people love as van Ryker and I do, there can be no forgetting. There is a great bond between van Ryker and me—a bond that only death will sever."

She had a side view of his face as she said that and she saw his jaw harden perceptibly. "So be it," he said harshly, and rose. But his tortured gaze came back to her. "Why must ye be so damnably beautiful?'' he burst out. "Why must your face haunt me so?''

"I cannot be beautiful now," she told him in a practical tone. "For I've been ill of fever. My hair comes out in combfuls, I'm thin and there must be great dark circles under my eyes! Come," she tried to cajole him. "Admit it! This 'beauty' you speak of is but a figment of your imagination!"

"Would it were true," he muttered, his caressing gaze sliding over her ruefully, as if loath to leave each feature. "For you have an ethereal beauty now that haunts the mind. Imogene, Imogene, think on what I say. I can give you a better life than van Ryker—think on it!"

"I will think," she promised sadly. "But I will come to the same conclusion, Darnwell."

Abruptly he fled the room. When he came back, bringing hot broth, his green eyes were shuttered, watchful. Not by the flicker of an eyelash did he betray the storm that had rocked him but moments ago.

But as he leaned forward to set down the tray he had brought, the lace at one of his cuffs was brushed back against the bedclothes and Imogene saw what she was not supposed to see. He had taken a golden combful of her hair that had been combed out after her high fever and twisted it into a little braid and now wore it around his wrist.

Imogene's blue eyes fell on that and she swallowed. A moment later the full lace cuff fell down and hid it from view. She looked up mistily at Darnwell and laid her hand, feather-light, upon his own. She felt a shudder rock him.

"Darnwell," she said sadly, "I do believe you really love me."

A muscle worked in his cheek. "And does this make a difference?"

"To me it does."

"Then you have considered?" he asked eagerly. "You have thought upon what I said?"

"No." She shook her head and her bright hair rippled in what he considered to be maddening beauty. "I will never change, Darnwell. But I am grateful to you—so grateful."

"Eat your broth," he said roughly, and went to stand before the window. She saw his silhouette there, dark and brooding.

"I have promised to see you upriver," he flung over his shoulder. "And I will do it."

"You do not need to keep that promise," she said bleakly. "You have done enough for me. You have sent a message to Tortuga—I remember your telling me that. Van Ryker has been warned—he will not fall into a trap."

His shoulder muscles rippled slightly. There was a long silence.

"You *did* send a message to Tortuga?" she asked fearfully.

He turned upon her a haggard face. "No, I did not. For it meant you would be the sooner taken from me."

Imogene's face whitened. "Oh, Darnwell," she whispered. "What have you done? Van Ryker may be even now sailing into a trap!"

Darnwell ran a distracted hand through his russet hair. His voice was ragged. "Very well, write out a message. I will see that it reaches van Ryker if I have to hand it to him myself!"

The glow of gratitude that shone in her blue eyes almost broke his heart.

"And since you are so set on clearing van Ryker's name," he added hoarsely, "I will take you upriver as I promised and give you your chance. And if you manage to get hard evidence that van Ryker was innocent of Dunworth's murder, you have my word as a gentleman that I will petition the king on his behalf."

"Oh, Darnwell," she breathed, reaching out her arms to hug him, "there was never a friend like you! Bring me a quill and an inkwell and parchment that I may write to van Ryker and warn him!"

Darnwell broke free from her grasp as if he could not bear the contact with her sweet flesh. "For no other woman," he said bitterly, "would I go to such lengths."

It was the truth.

Tortuga, 1660

CHAPTER 16

A greeting such as Tortuga had never known awaited van Ryker when at last, with his ships riding low in the water from the very weight of the treasure they carried, he sailed into Cayona Bay. For word of his success had flown ahead of him, word had long since reached the buccaneers of Tortuga that the "king of the buccaneers," Captain van Ryker, had captured with a single ship the entire treasure *flota* of Spain.

Such a feat was unheard of. The quay was jammed with shouting well-wishers as van Ryker strode ashore, and his heavy back muscles ached from being joyously thumped, his hand grew weary from endlessly clenching those hands so determined to grip his.

All Tortuga rejoiced that night, and it was a drunken night of brawling in the taverns, for enough of the booty had been distributed that every man felt himself a king for a night. They were hours bringing the most valuable stuff ashore. Most of it had not even been counted and van Ryker set a heavy guard around his house, which had become the repository of that wealth.

For himself, he was glad that it was over—that it was all over, his whole buccaneering career. For now with what he had taken, he could set himself up a new life, no matter how badly things had fared at the two plantations managed by his brothers.

Tired from arranging housing for his prisoners, tired from
making arrangements to contact Spain for their ransoms and
eventual return, from supervising the endless succession of
trunks and strongboxes that seemed about to crush his house
with their weight, van Ryker sat that night in his chart room
drinking from a captured goblet of jade-studded gold a
measure of captured Canary wine before he betook himself
down to the town to accept the plaudits of the multitude.

It was there Captain Flogg found him.

Van Ryker heard the disturbance at the door, heard Flogg's
heavy voice insisting he "must see the cap'n quick-like," and
frowned.

Flogg's ship, the *Barracuda*, had been one of those lost to
the hurricane. Leaking like a sieve, she had managed to stay
afloat, drifting helplessly about the ocean. It was sheer
happenstance that one of the galleons that had followed the
Sea Rover home to Tortuga had picked up Flogg and his crew
just before the disabled *Barracuda* had sunk beneath the
waves. Van Ryker, who detested Flogg, had felt no necessity
to invite him aboard the *Sea Rover,* as he might have done in
some other case. So this was the first time Flogg had had a
chance to speak to the now doubly famous buccaneer.

"Let Flogg come in," he called to Arne, for there was a
scuffling sound at the door and he saw no need for loyal Arne
to have to fight the fellow.

His normal caution caused him to rise and loosen his sword
in its scabbard before Flogg burst into the room.

"I been tryin' to see you all day, Cap'n," said Flogg in an
aggrieved voice. "I'm here to straighten somethin' out."

"My sword is at your disposal," said van Ryker coldly.

"No, no." Flogg lifted both hands hastily, as if to show he
was not about to reach for his weapon. "Ye don't rightly
understand me, Cap'n. 'Tis about that little incident on the
quay that involved your lady that I wanted to speak."

"There's no need to discuss it. I was there on the quay that
day. Even assuming ye were drunk when ye sent the lad,
ye can't have expected me to let the matter pass unchallenged!"

"Damme, Cap'n, hear me out!" Flogg was so excited his
face empurpled. "*I* didn't send ye no message. I never heard

of the lad who brought it! 'Twas a nasty joke someone played on us both, and that's what I've come to tell ye."

Van Ryker considered Flogg narrowly. Drunkard and coward he certainly was, and doubtless a liar too when it suited him. "So?"

"That's all I got to say, Cap'n. I had nothin' to do with it. I never even looked crossways at your lady, and that's the Lord's truth." He sounded abused. "And if ever I catches up with that young lad what says I did—!" His teeth ground.

Van Ryker was looking at him more alertly. Every word, every gesture of heavyset Flogg seemed straight from the heart.

"Could you suggest who might have done it, then?" he wondered. "For I'm as eager as you to learn his name."

"Not unless'n we catches up to the lad," said Flogg morosely. "But I wanted no bad blood between us, so I came to see you as soon as I made port and heard the story what was circulatin'."

Silently van Ryker poured out a glass of Canary, offered it to Flogg, who downed it at a gulp.

"I didn't want ye to be thinking ill of me, Cap'n van Ryker," said Flogg earnestly, wiping his mouth with his hand. Van Ryker might have grinned, but he did not, for Flogg was a surly fellow who cared little what anybody thought of him. "And I thought since ye've brought home so many fine galleons and I've lost my ship. . . ."

There was the reason for this call—Flogg wanted command of one of those ships!

"I'll think about it," van Ryker said.

"Good, good!" Flogg rubbed his thick hands together. "Ye know ye can trust me, Cap'n."

Van Ryker knew he could not. With a grim smile, he showed Flogg out.

But this news had put a new face on things.

For a time, van Ryker sat drumming his fingers on the table, an intent frown on his face. Then he rose.

"Arne," he called. And when big Arne was standing before him, "Has Captain Vartel sailed, or is *Le Sabre* still about? I didn't see her in the bay when we sailed in. Is she being careened somewhere?"

"Vartel sailed the week after you left, Cap'n. I heard he was in Port Royal, but the news may be stale."

In Port Royal . . . van Ryker's heart gave a lurch. Imogene was in Jamaica, just an easy march from Port Royal!

The most famous buccaneer in all the Caribbean that night did the unthinkable. He failed to appear at any of the festivities held in grog shops and taverns—he even failed to accept the governor's invitation for a later supper. Instead he left a heavy guard on his treasure and marched himself to the quay. But half provisioned, he set sail on the *Sea Rover* with Barnaby and de Rochemont and a hastily formed crew, out of the harbor.

He was bound for Jamaica. For Imogene.

He did not know what treachery waited for him in Port Royal harbor, where Captain Vartel had just received a message from upriver—a message that would bring down on van Ryker the whole might of the Jamaica Squadron.

True to his promise—perhaps driven by it—Darnwell Keating made swift arrangements for the three of them to be transported up the Cobre River. Imogene went along willingly enough, but before she left she cast a somber look toward Port Royal bay and checked the shipping. The golden-hulled *Sea Rover* was not among them, but dark and lean, *Le Sabre* still rode the bay. She did not know that the ship had been gone all during her illness, that Vartel had returned but yesterday, for he feared the fever and had waited until well after the quarantine was lifted to return.

As they got into the boat that was to take them upriver, Esme, rustling in lavender taffeta, leaned toward Imogene.

"I hear Darnwell has taken *excellent* care of you," she said in a voice rich with innuendo. "And all by himself!"

"To have brought in others would have been to announce to all that I had the fever," said Imogene quietly. "And *you* would have been dragged down with me. Indeed I believe he did it for all our sakes!"

Esme's dark brows rose but she held her tongue. *As I hope she will hold it when she meets van Ryker, if that should come to pass*, thought Imogene uneasily, remembering the jealousy of her lean buccaneer.

"Have you written to Anthony to expect us?" she asked, and was surprised when Esme shook her head with a careless, "I thought we would surprise him."

Imogene shot a quick look at Darnwell, but he was busy studying the bank, pointing things out, showing interest in all that they passed.

"Anyone would think you were a planter," chided Esme with a yawn. "Who cares which are the pepper trees and which the lime?"

That trip upriver was for Imogene a dreaded journey and she responded mechanically to their small talk. She knew she was embarked on a dangerous venture and one she might not be able to carry off, but she yearned to do it for van Ryker's sake. To give him back his honor, his good name. . . . She sighed and set her hopes on her ever inventive mind and on Darnwell's broad shoulders in the event of need. Still her mind drifted along dark passageways, for every slap of the oars carried her closer to Gale Force and Anthony Ryder.

Had she looked—and she did not—she would have seen a boat following them, hovering usually just out of sight, lying back so that they might not notice its presence. It was manned by a couple of cutthroats and once Esme looked back and smiled a secretive smile. Although she could not make them out from this distance, she had a very good idea who was in that boat.

Imogene had begun to wish she had insisted Darnwell put her on a ship bound for Tortuga—even that she had slipped away from them and taken her chances in Port Royal's alleys—when Gale Force hove in sight. Her palms were damp as Darnwell helped her from the boat and she walked once again up the green incline toward the magical house rising from amid the palm-strewn jungle.

They had almost reached the house when Anthony Ryder threw open the door and stepped out. He seemed to totter as he peered at the newcomers. Imogene thought she had never seen so shocked an expression on a man's face.

"Esme," he stammered. "And Imogene! Odd's blood, Esme, I thought ye were in London!"

"In truth I was, Anthony." Esme rushed forward, taffeta skirts skimming the ground, and threw her arms about her startled brother's neck. In that moment of greeting she must have muttered something, Imogene decided, for Anthony came away from that embrâce shaken but in control of himself. Could she but have heard it, the words Esme had muttered were, "Trust me."

"And who is this?" Anthony eyed Darnwell Keating.

Darnwell came forward with all the grace of a practiced courtier. "Darnwell Keating," he said, with a sweeping bow.

Anthony looked to Esme for help.

"Darnwell is the gentleman who made my voyage tenable," she smiled. "Without Darnwell it would have been a disaster."

"*My* voyage *was* a disaster." Imogene found her voice, for she knew she must not falter in the role she was to play. "The *Carolina* foundered in a great storm, and I was taken off by Esme's ship, the *Bristol*. Indeed I was the last to leave, for I had become tangled in the fallen rigging and the boats had left without me. Had the *Bristol* not happened along, I must surely have perished."

"How fortunate the *Bristol* happened along when it did." There was a detectable note of falseness in Anthony's voice, but Esme was quick to interrupt with, "Was it not? And besides it gave me the chance to get to know my new sister-in-law." She gave Imogene a charming little hug. "But you have done wonders with this plantation, Tony. Can all those banana trees and pimento and lime trees we passed really be your doing?"

Anthony nodded sourly. "I trust ye'll be visiting with us?" he told Darnwell in as hearty a voice as he could muster. "We have few visitors here at Gale Force and a new face is always welcome."

"For the night only," smiled Darnwell. "For I must go on to Spanish Town in the morning. There's an old friend of my uncle's there that I have promised to greet. But I will be back no later than three days hence and will be more than glad to avail myself of your hospitality then."

Imogene shot Darnwell an alarmed look. He was leaving? But he had promised to stay and guard her! The look he returned was bland. Her heart lurched. Could Esme have...won him over?

Esme walked ahead of them, with Anthony beside her. His chest in its handsome saffron doublet expanded as she exclaimed over the miracles he had wrought in this wilderness. Imogene leaned toward Darnwell and managed to mutter an accusing, "You promised to stay!"

"I will return," he promised in a low tone. Then, "Careful!" he warned as Esme turned with a graceful gesture to wave them forward to admire a carved rosewood table and again a tall carved chair in which she flung herself with childish delight.

"But you live like a prince here, Tony!" she cried.

With a little complacent bow, her brother acknowledged the truth of that remark. Very courteously he showed them all to their rooms and Imogene sat down on the bed in hers and looked blankly at the walls she had left such a short time ago and wondered what would become of her if Darnwell did not make good his promise to return. Suppose he simply said good-bye and left her here? They were three against one....She pressed her fingers to her throbbing forehead and tried to think.

Nothing occurred to her. Van Ryker was on the high seas—still living, she hoped, but too far away to do her any good in her present situation.

She felt forlorn as she went down to dinner.

They were all waiting for her—Esme resplendent in a ball gown of rich purple changeable silk overlaid with silver tissue that made her a creature of light. Her heavy black hair was caught up with a rope of pearls and an amethyst pin gleamed at her throat. Wife to a debt-impoverished wastrel she might be, but she looked more like a reigning queen, thought Imogene irritably, well aware that the gown she herself was wearing—and even that gown was, gallingly, part of Esme's largess—was the only gown she owned in Jamaica.

Darnwell's fiery gaze told her she could depose Esme

anytime and assume the throne. That hot look lifted her spirits, for she could not believe he would look at her like that and then desert her. Holding that thought, she managed to be almost lighthearted at supper, listening to Anthony go on and on about the plantation. It was almost as if he wished to keep any other subject from being brought up.

She shot a look at Charles across the table. He had not surfaced till dinnertime, and he had been, obviously, well briefed by his smarter brother and sister. The lace at his throat was snarled as if trembling hands had tied it, his hair stuck up a bit at the back as if he had forgotten to comb that which he could not see, and his whole manner was glum. When his gaze rested on Imogene, it was one of foreboding, for Charles was superstitious and believed that bad pennies always turned up again. And hadn't this one done so, to prove it?

Anthony was explaining to Darnwell about bananas. "A plant produces but a single stem in a twelve-month. At harvest that stem is cut down with a machete."

"You do not eat them tree-ripened like apples?" asked Darnwell innocently.

Anthony laughed. "If they ripen on the tree it impairs the taste. No, the stem of green bananas must be removed to ripen. Later the trunk is cut to the ground and a single shoot, which we call a ratoon, emerges. The next year that ratoon will grow another stem of bananas."

"Interesting." Darnwell ate his chocho meditatively. It was the first time he had tasted this squashlike vegetable. "Would you say bananas are your most important crop?"

Anthony shrugged. "Oh, no. We have many coconut trees and plant more each year. Our pimentos and limes are doing well, and also our breadfruit."

"Do you consider this plantation average for the island?"

His host drew himself up in annoyance. "Far *above* average. Our slaves—"

"Do twice the work per man," cut in Charles gloomily. "Tony sees to that."

Darnwell's russet brows lifted. "A nice trick that. How do you accomplish it?"

"With a whip," said Charles.

Anthony cast him a lowering look. "My little brother is squeamish," he said testily. "I only lay open the backs of those who will not work—and then but lightly, for an injured man does a poor day's work."

"That must have accounted for the screams I heard the second night I was here," Imogene said, fixing Anthony with a level look. "I was told that someone had been bitten by a snake."

Charles thought back. "That would have been the new slave who stole Tony's best plumed hat. He had enough weals on his back to keep him from working for a month! Anthony thought your ears too tender for the story."

"Did he recover?"

"No. He died—but of infection, not the whipping."

Across the table Anthony had a look of pure vexation on his face. He reddened as Darnwell, taking another bite of chocho, asked innocently, "Doesn't the government take an interest in these matters? I mean, theft of a hat is deplorable but do they really allow such strong measures?"

"The hat was extremely valuable. It bore three ostrich plumes and a jewel of price," said Anthony in a suffocated voice. "And the man's death was an accident—'twas not intended." When Darnwell said nothing, he burst out, "The governor is old and sick and little interested in internal matters on the plantations."

"Do your neighbors agree with your position?"

"Yes," shouted Anthony. "They do agree!"

"But then how would ye know?" murmured Darnwell lazily. "Since by your own admission ye seldom see them?"

Anthony leaned forward. His saffron doublet rose and fell, his murky lavender eyes were bloodshot, his face mottled with rage. Imogene half expected him to leap up, overturning his chair, and challenge his impudent guest to battle there and then.

Instead Esme, with a silvery trill of laughter, stepped into the breach.

"I have news," she announced merrily. "And I have saved

it for this moment when we are all together, have finished our supper, and are sitting here companionably sipping our wine.'' She raised her glass and the billow of lace fell away from her slender forearm. ''A toast is in order. For I heard in Port Royal from the captain of a ship just in and bursting with the news that that famous buccaneer, Captain van Ryker—*our brother*''—she turned to Imogene apologetically—''you understand I had to tell Darnwell Branch's real name when he decided to bring us here to Gale Force—that *our brother* has captured the entire Spanish treasure fleet!''

''The *flota*?'' gasped Charles.

''The *flota*,'' affirmed Esme.

''But he could not!'' cried Imogene. ''He set out with but three ships and the *flota* has—how many? Twenty or thirty?'' Her heart had lurched in her chest at Esme's words, for such a battle would have been terrible and bloody. Van Ryker could be injured, dying . . . or, terrible thought, already dead . . . for how many captains had won the day only to perish, themselves? ''Do they say he is all right?'' she implored.

''They did not say but I suppose he must be.''

''Oh, Esme, how could you not have told me when we were in Port Royal? I must go to him!''

She was rising from her chair when Darnwell reached out and gently eased her back into it again. ''All in good time,'' he murmured, and held up his glass. ''The same rumor has reached me. I doubt 'tis true, but I hope it is, for if van Ryker has managed to take the treasure fleet, it will go far to break the power of Spain in these waters.'' He lifted his glass. ''To your brother. May the rumor prove true!''

All of them emptied their glasses save Imogene, who was so upset she could manage only a swallow.

''Did they say how he had done it, Esme? Did they say where? Oh, they must have told you something that would lead us to know whether he was safe?''

Esme smiled her winsome smile. ''They said he had scored a great victory over the Spanish—an almost bloodless victory, for he caught the Spanish fleet wrecked on some nameless island, and that he was on his way to Tortuga with all the galleons that he could refloat and his own ships riding low in the water from the weight of silver and gold bullion.''

Imogene gave a gasp of relief. ''He is alive then, thank God,'' she whispered.

Darnwell gave her an irritable look. ''Not only alive but prospering!''

A new thought occurred to Imogene and her eyes widened in horror. ''He will hear that I went down aboard the *Carolina*—he will believe me dead!'' For she knew her hastily written note would not have had time to reach him.

''Nonsense,'' said Darnwell roughly. ''He will believe you living, since you were rescued by the *Bristol*.''

''You could have sent him word from Port Royal,'' said Esme brightly. ''There were buccaneers there who would surely have been shortly in Tortuga!''

Darnwell cut smoothly through Imogene's instant ''Oh, I did!'' with a drawling, ''I've no doubt of it. But has it occurred to you that those same buccaneers might have seized Imogene and held her for ransom? For van Ryker—if this story proves true—is now one of the richest men in Christendom. And who could doubt he would pay a king's ransom to get her back?'' He beamed his sunny smile on Esme. ''Doubtless *you* thought of that?''

''Oh, yes,'' dimpled Esme. ''I thought of that. As Imogene's sister-in-law, I am ever ready to protect her.'' She turned to Imogene. ''You would be well advised to wait for van Ryker here, Imogene. Port Royal is too filled with dangers for you.''

''But he will be in Tortuga for weeks, just dividing up the treasure and refitting the Spanish galleons!''

''Even so.'' Esme shrugged. ''You will be quite comfortable here.''

'' 'Comfortable'?'' said Imogene tartly. ''When I have but one dress to my name and that one only through your largess!''

''Then you shall have others,'' said Esme promptly. ''Tomorrow you may choose from my wardrobe.''

Imogene felt checkmated. It was, of course, tempting to

change into a different dress, tempting to let matters slide, tempting to wait until van Ryker came for her. She decided on a bold move.

"I am glad van Ryker did not lose too many men in the venture," she sighed, "for the buccaneers set a ceiling on what a fallen comrade's heirs can receive. They believe a widow should receive her mite—but that it should not be too large, as that will encourage remarriage!"

All heads swung toward her. She had their full attention.

"And others?" cried Charles. "What of other heirs?"

"Children are shared out, share and share alike—other heirs are ignored."

"But—but that's preposterous!" cried Charles, aghast. "What of—of elderly parents?"

"Yes," said Imogene, telling herself God forgave those who lied in a good cause. "And brothers and sisters! Nephews and nieces, aunts and uncles—I have always thought it most unfair, but remember, the Articles were written by buccaneers—not lawyers. They do not hold probate as they do in England."

"I had not heard that about the buccaneers," said Anthony thoughtfully. "You say a man's children inherit—"

"All he died possessed of. His widow less. Others—nothing." Imogene spoke in a self-assured voice. Now she touched her bare white throat with tentative fingers. "I suppose I will be wearing captured Spanish pearls and emeralds when next I visit Gale Force—and I am sure van Ryker will be very generous with you all." Her smile flashed at them.

"Assuredly!" Esme's voice was lightly malicious. "For now he can buy and sell all of us!"

"He always could," said Charles. He, of them all, looked delighted. "He can buy me a new plantation!" he cried.

Anthony gave his brother a crushing look. "Stop thinking about what he'll give ye, Charles," he said testily. "More like, he'll give ye a boot on the rump and send ye packing!"

Charles's hopeful expression lapsed into sullenness, but Imogene spoke up again, for if she could cause dissension between them, she would be buying time that could save her life.

"Of course he won't do that, Charles," she said sweetly. "Has Branch ever been other than generous? It would be more like him to give you all fine holdings!" She included Esme in her general smile. "I would suppose that he would give Longview to you, Charles—unless you preferred something else. And that he would give Gale Force to you, Anthony, since you have managed it so well."

Charles's eyes lit up again but Darnwell looked startled, and she realized he had not known that van Ryker was the true owner of Gale Force.

Imogene felt she had done what she could. Hopefully she had given them food for thought which they would gnaw over until Darnwell returned. She gave Darnwell a look and rose.

"You must all excuse me—I'm for bed," she declared. "And you should be too, Darnwell, if you're thinking of going on to Spanish Town in the morning."

She had hoped he would take the hint that she wished to speak to him in private but he did not. Instead he smiled meaningfully into Esme's lavender eyes. "Ah, yes. Early to bed makes one . . . wiser?"

Esme tossed her head archly. "I'm a bit tired, too," she murmured, rising in a sinuous way and returning Darnwell's look with a provocative glance through her lashes. "Although I doubt I'll be up to see you off tomorrow, Darnwell."

As Imogene closed her bedroom door, she saw Darnwell turn at the stair head and follow Esme down the hall. So he was up to his old tricks, spending his nights with Esme as he had at sea. Of course it was unreasonable to expect him to be faithful to her when she had turned him down but—she frowned, feeling puzzled. It was impossible to figure Darnwell out. He had seemed so—honest, when he had told her of his love. He had promised to bring her to Gale Force and protect her and now—now he was blithely leaving her here while he went on to Spanish Town!

She had earlier been surprised to learn that her bedroom at Gale Force had a lock but no key. Lost, Anthony had explained pleasantly. They were still searching for it. Now that lack of a key became a major calamity, for she feared to go to sleep. She was tempted to drag a heavy piece of

furniture in front of the door to block it, but that would make
a scraping noise and probably bring the whole household to
her door—and how would she explain it?

Fretful and barefoot, she paced the floor. The moon on that
hot Jamaican night cut a bright path across the floor, and there
were strange rustles without as palm fronds scraped against
each other. Down the hall Esme and Darnwell were no doubt
locked in a fond embrace while downstairs, doubtless still
lounging about the long dining table, the brothers plotted.

Tired at last, she decided to lie down on the bed. Hardly
had she done so when her senses were alerted by a little
sound just outside her door. What was it? A soft padding
footstep? Tense, she lay there peering into the darkness.

Suddenly the door was opened a crack. Imogene lay still as
death. She could not see who stood there, but she kept her
lashes low, peering through them at the interloper.

As silently the door was closed again and there was once
again a light padding footstep—on the stair?

Imogene guessed who it was: Esme, on her way downstairs
for a council of war with her brothers.

Swiftly she rose and on silent bare feet padded to the door,
opened it a crack. From here she could view the iron
balustrade, the columns of the encircling covered walkway
that served as a corridor—it was empty. So was the open
courtyard below. Silent as a wraith, she fled downstairs. Just
as she had expected, there was a light coming from the dining
room. She edged toward the dining room door and even
before she reached it, she could hear Esme's voice.

"Of course, I'm sure. I left him sleeping like a baby and
looked in on Imogene as well. She was lying there fast
asleep. We're safe enough to talk, Tony."

"Is there truth in what she said about other relatives not
inheriting?"

"No," scoffed Esme. "Of course not. I think she said that
merely to twit us. We all know that Branch is alive! And
she's expecting him to come and get her—here."

"Still it could be true."

"I've *checked* and it *isn't*."

Imogene's heart sank. So Esme had not bought her lie about the buccaneers. She pressed closer to the door.

"The woman seems to have more lives than a cat," complained Anthony. "She should have died aboard the *Carolina*, she should have died of fever—and now instead she's here." He heaved a heavy sigh.

"Yes, but I've the answer. You were right to send her to me, Tony—I'd have disposed of her in London."

"Aye, but now she's back in Jamaica."

"Why is there any need to dispose of her at all?" Charles's voice, sounding petulant. "Ye talk like ghouls, you two. Branch is rich now, *he* can take care of us!"

"Ye're assuming he'll want to." Anthony's voice grated. "And we've no hope at all that he will. More like, he'll retire *here* and take over, leaving us both to rot."

"If Branch has seized the Spanish treasure fleet—and I've no doubt the rumor is true," came Esme's cool voice, "then there's no better time than now to cut him down. For as you've pointed out in your letters, Tony, the buccaneers are quite scrupulous about turning a man's share over to his heirs."

Imogene felt her nails cut into her palms. She yearned to go in there and tear Esme's hair out. But she froze at Anthony's calm, "I've already arranged to bring the Jamaica Squadron down on him when he comes for Imogene."

"Then you should *un*arrange it," put in Charles heatedly. "Branch alive would probably give us more than we'd inherit from his death. For scrupulous or not, those who settle estates have sticky fingers."

"No." Esme's voice was cold and definite. "Anthony is right. And Imogene must be disposed of too. She'd be a never-ending danger to us."

"I can't help you kill a woman." Imogene could almost feel Charles's eloquent shudder.

"*Kill* her?" Esme again, sounding contemptuous. "Who said anything about killing her? I said *dispose* of her, Charles, not kill her!"

"But then how—?" Slow-witted Charles could not follow this.

"We'll have to wait until Darnwell is gone—he mustn't suspect, because he's half in love with her."

"What about *you*?" gasped Charles. "I thought you just left him asleep in your bed!"

"Oh, he's attracted to me, yes." Imogene could imagine that small dainty shrug of a delicate shoulder. "Darnwell and I have much in common, but he'd stick at letting anything happen to Imogene, nor must he guess we had anything to do with it."

"I still don't understand what's to happen to her." Charles sounded aggrieved.

"Keep your voice down," reproved Anthony fiercely. "Do you want to wake the house? What *do* you propose, Esme, for I'm bound to admit I don't follow you, either?"

"She will take the same route as other women who have boarded *Le Sabre*," laughed Esme.

"*Le Sabre?* But that's Vartel's ship!" exclaimed Anthony. "What do you know of him?"

There was a light delicious laugh on the other side of the door. "You forget I spent near a month in Port Royal, Tony, before coming here. I am now well acquainted in the town!"

There was a moment of silence during which Anthony weighed whether to tell Esme that they had chanced on the same man to do their tasks for them. He must have decided against it because when he spoke again he still sounded puzzled. "*What* other women boarded *Le Sabre*? I don't follow that."

"You don't need to, Tony," came Esme's airy voice. "For I've made all the arrangements. Tomorrow night I'll give Imogene some drugged wine—"

"I refuse to be present." Anthony sounded stubborn. "If your plan goes wrong—and I fear 'tis too elaborate to work, for I know the complicated way your mind works, Esme— then Branch must have no inkling that *I* had any part in it."

"Gallant as always, Tony," she mocked.

"Gallantry be damned!" Testily. "Can you handle it alone?"

"Yes, of course I can—at least the drugging part. I must rely on you and Charles to carry her down to the shore."

"I told you I refuse to be involved!"

"Would you prefer the servants to see men creeping up to the house, and sound the alarm? They will gossip about it and we will soon be the talk of Port Royal!"

"I see what you mean." Imogene could almost see Anthony frown. "Very well." Reluctantly. "Charles and I will carry her down to the boat but after that she is your responsibility."

"No, after that she will be Captain Vartel's responsibility," laughed Esme. "Oh, do not look so stormy, Tony. It will all be very simple. I intend to be very charming to Imogene tomorrow—indeed I may give her half my gowns!" Her laughter trilled again. " 'Twill not matter since she will have them only for a day."

Imogene felt chilled. She bent forward wondering what indeed Esme *did* intend for her.

"Once she is drugged, I will push her into a wicker trunk which will be conveniently to hand. Then you and Charles will carry the trunk to a boat which is even now waiting, out of sight of the house. She will be rowed downriver by two men who followed us up here in a boat—there can be no mistake, no slip-up, the men are here now, Tony—I looked back and saw them following. When Darnwell returns, we will tell him that we could not stop her, that she seized a boat and ran away downriver, hoping to find a ship to take her to Tortuga and a rendezvous with van Ryker. He will believe it—and we will all search for her. And van Ryker, when he arrives, will believe it too. He will believe that she was set upon in the streets of Port Royal—everyone knows it is a dangerous town—and spirited away. He will look for her, but—he will not find her."

"Well, where will she *be*?" wailed Charles.

Esme's casual laugh reached Imogene with the sudden chill of a bucket of ice water. "She will be in Tangier being sold in the marketplace to the highest bidder. Once in some sultan's harem—and I've no doubt she'll land in one eventually, even if she reaches there by way of a brothel, for she's marvelous-looking—she'll be guarded by far better watchdogs than you and Charles, Tony. They have eunuchs whose sole duty is to keep the gentlemen *out* and the ladies *in*."

Imogene felt a wash of pure horror pour over her. So *that*

was the fate of Captain Vartel's Spanish captives! Those beautiful women, never seen, never heard from again. . . .

Panic seized her. She must find Darnwell, beg him not to go, to get her away from here—now!

She ran soft-footed to the stairs, made it to the top. She would have turned down the hall to Esme's room but as she reached her own door she heard Esme's light laugh and realized they were all coming out of the dining room. In another moment they would be climbing the stairs.

She had only time to go through her own door and close it soundlessly behind her. She leaned against it with her heart thudding. Had she delayed another moment they might have come out of the dining room and found her spying on them. And then she might not have lived to be drugged tomorrow night—Anthony might have killed her on the spot lest she escape and go carrying tales to van Ryker.

Frightened as she was, she was sure she would not fall asleep, but her exhausted body, run down by its bout with fever, betrayed her. She woke to find the sun shining brightly in through the windows.

With a little cry, she leaped up and tore into her clothes. She ran downstairs and looked about her. All the rooms seemed empty. They must be down at the landing bidding Darnwell good-bye!

She ran outside and sure enough, there they were, gathered on the landing. Darnwell's boat was just gliding out into the current. He saw her and gave her a jaunty wave.

Imogene, seeing she could not reach him, stopped in her tracks.

Her last chance of escape was gone.

Port Royal, Jamaica, 1660

CHAPTER 17

Fog lay heavy over the sea and around the shore when van Ryker hove in sight of Lemon Bay—for he intended to reach Gale Force by his usual route and assure himself of Imogene's safety. Wild alarm for her had coursed through his veins all this voyage—some premonition of disaster. He could not rid himself of the feeling that something had happened to her. Sometimes he had almost felt he could hear her calling him. His lean body had broken out in a cold sweat at the terrors that haunted his mind and he had loaded on canvas until the great masts of the *Sea Rover* could bear no more.

He was standing at the prow as they approached the shore—and suddenly the drifting fog blew open like a curtain and revealed the hulls of two lean ships riding restlessly at anchor.

Van Ryker drew in his breath. He knew those ships—they belonged to the Jamaica Squadron. And what would they be doing so near the mouth of Lemon Bay?

Quickly, silently, he put about. It was flawlessly done. Buccaneers were used to silent running, for not a man here but had sailed tense and silent through the darkness beneath the fixed guns of shore batteries, hoping to escape their attention.

Once farther out to sea and well concealed by the fog, van Ryker sent a young buccaneer in a rowboat to spy out the coast and tell him how many ships were there. The fellow came back with the words he had dreaded.

"The whole Jamaica Squadron's there, Cap'n—every ship of 'em."

That meant they knew about his secret road to Gale Force. They'd be waiting for him there too.

And that must mean they had Imogene.

Never one to panic, van Ryker now decided upon a bold plan. He would sail boldly into Port Royal, take his men swiftly up the Cobre River in a flotilla of small boats to Spanish Town and there seize the old governor—for he doubted the new one had had time to arrive. Garbled reports had reached him about elderly Lord Marr, reports evenly divided that Lord Marr was dead and that he was soon to arrive in Jamaica. In any event the old governor should prove a good hostage. He would take the governor down the Cobre and carry him to Tortuga, leaving word that he would exchange the governor for Imogene and his brothers—for he was sure Anthony would have defended her and been taken; Charles had most likely run away.

It was the best plan he could arrive at on short notice.

It was somewhere between midnight and dawn when he reached Port Royal bay and the fog had lifted. Van Ryker's gray eyes narrowed when he saw *Le Sabre*'s dark hull riding at anchor in the moonlight. So Vartel was still here. . . .

In longboats he brought half his force ashore. In his impatience to find some smaller boats, he outstripped them, striding along the dark waterfront when a voice suddenly stopped him.

"Cap'n, could I speak to ye, sir?"

Van Ryker whirled at the sound of a voice coming to him out of the darkness. His hand was on his basket-hilted sword.

"Show yourself," he growled.

A figure emerged hesitantly from the shadow of a pile of kegs.

"Come out where I can see you," he directed.

It was a tall lad who came into view and suddenly van Ryker's eyes snapped open wider. It was Lark Saxon, the lad who had seized Imogene and stolen a kiss that day on the quay. A very bedraggled Lark Saxon, thinner and quite dirty, who shuffled forward.

"Cap'n van Ryker, I know where your lady is."

Van Ryker stood thunderstruck—but only for a moment. He seized the lad urgently by the shoulders, as he had once before in Tortuga.

"And where is that?" he grated.

Again Lark Saxon paled before the violence he read in the buccaneer's dark countenance.

"I meant your lady no harm that day in Cayona," he gasped. "I was paid by Captain Vartel to say Flogg sent me—and then Vartel tried to kill me to keep me quiet!"

"Vartel? What's he got to do with this?"

"Nothing—I mean, I don't know. But a month or so ago—'twas at the time the fever struck—I did see a gentleman carry your lady out of the Bell and Candle to a house in the town."

"Carry her?"

"Yes. She didn't look to be hurt—more like asleep. I thought"—he swallowed—"I thought she was most likely drunk."

Van Ryker's frown deepened. "Imogene's never been drunk in her life," he said harshly. "Who was this fellow?"

"I never saw him before but I did inquire careful-like at the Bell and Candle and they told me he was Anthony Ryder of Gale Force plantation."

Relief poured through van Ryker. It was easy to envision what had happened. Spirited Imogene had probably been trying to join him. She had run away from Gale Force and Anthony had caught up with her in Port Royal and slipped something into her drink so that he could bring her back quietly.

But he had to make sure.

"What was the fellow like?" he demanded.

Lark Saxon considered. "Tall."

Anthony was tall.

"Well-dressed."

Anthony was well-dressed.

"Sort of reddish hair and eyebrows."

Van Ryker's thoughts skidded to a violent halt. Anthony's hair and eyebrows were very dark indeed. And so were Captain Vartel's.

"He carried her like he liked her," volunteered Lark Saxon helpfully.

Those words did nothing to reassure van Ryker. He beckoned his men to follow and then turned back to Saxon.

"This man took her to a house, you say?"

The lad's head bobbed. "Private house."

"Are they still there?"

"Should be. They was still there yesterday morning. I saw her leaning out the window. She was calling to him to hurry."

Van Ryker's strong features became very set. "Take me to this house," he said stonily. "There's gold in it for you, I can promise, if you've led me aright!"

Lark Saxon's eyes brightened. "Yessir, Cap'n!" He leaped ahead, showing the way.

Van Ryker strode forward, never dreaming Imogene had gone upriver the day before, that she had been calling to Darnwell to hurry and make the arrangements for their departure when Lark Saxon had seen her at the window.

Had he come yesterday, he might have caught her before she went upriver—but now he would be too late.

Gale Force, Jamaica, 1660

CHAPTER 18

Imogene stared at Darnwell's departing figure, waving from the boat. *Traitor!* she thought, her shoulders drooping. *You are the light-minded rake I always thought you to be!* No, that wasn't fair because she would have died of fever in Port Royal or aboard the *Bristol* had it not been for Darnwell. But to be spared—for life in some harem in Tangiers? Never to see van Ryker again?

She was hard put to keep angry tears from her eyes as Esme hurried up.

"Darnwell said we were not to wake you—that you needed your sleep," she said solicitously.

I need more than sleep—I need rescuing, thought Imogene desperately. Aloud she said, "How thoughtful of Darnwell. I came out to tell him good-bye, for I doubt I'd have survived were it not for him."

"Yes, you do owe him a great deal," agreed Esme cheerfully. "Have you breakfasted?" And when Imogene shook her head, Esme took her arm. "There's the most delicious tropical fruit—and conch. I'd never tasted conch before I came to Jamaica!"

Imogene did not really want breakfast, but she could not think of a good excuse to refuse. She needed to think, to plan, for today she must make her escape—before night fell and she was drugged and carried aboard *Le Sabre* for a journey to Tangier and oblivion.

If she could but slip away...she knew the way to the deserted bay where the *Sea Rover* had cast anchor—and doubtless would again. Still...she could not carry much food with her, and once there, where would she be? At the mercy of the elements, as lost as if she were on some desert island. No, she dared not try to hold out there until van Ryker sailed back from Tortuga.

If she tried going down the Cobre, they would surely catch her—for it was in that direction that they would search, believing she would strike out for Port Royal and some ship to reunite her with van Ryker.

Would her chances be any better in Spanish Town? Yes, her heart told her, for Darnwell would be there. And rake-hells, she knew from experience, wielded wicked blades. To travel inland, not toward the coast, was her best clear chance.

She had been thinking furiously as Esme guided her in to breakfast and then joined her for a bite. Now she looked up as Esme asked her, "How do you like the conch?"

"What? Oh, it's very good." Hastily she stuffed a piece of conch into her mouth but her anxiety was such that she could hardly taste it. "I'm worried about van Ryker," she said, to cover up the real reason for her preoccupation.

"Why?" Esme nibbled a bit of cassava bread smeared with honey. "He's the richest man in the Caribbean now—I shouldn't think you'd worry about *him*!"

There was a spiteful edge to her tone that sharpened Imogene's own voice. "And what of the Spanish?" she flashed. "Do you think they will take this insult lying down? Or will they be even now mounting an expedition against Tortuga?"

Esme shrugged. "I should think that Branch had annihilated their entire fleet when he took the treasure *flota*."

Imogene gave her sister-in-law a bitter look. "And so you think they will lie supine after but one engagement? Really, Esme! We are speaking of a country, not some single pirate like—like Captain Vartel!"

She had named the first name that had come into her mind and having spoken she could have bitten her tongue, for Esme frowned. "Why did you mention him?" she asked suspiciously.

"Because I have met him, I suppose. Because he"—she threw caution to the winds—"because he would have fought for me on the quay at Tortuga had not van Ryker intervened."

"*Fought* for you?" Esme's amethyst eyes were incredulous.

"Oh, it was nothing. A cabin boy, a mere stripling, seized me at the open-air market and kissed me. Vartel would have killed him with his dueling pistol but van Ryker struck the gun away and spanked the lad with the flat of his sword. It was really nothing."

"Vartel would have killed him?" repeated Esme as if she could not believe it. She leaned forward, the honeyed cassava bread forgotten. "Tell me about this Captain Vartel. What is he like?"

Imogene shrugged. "A womanizer, always chasing this one or that one. When I left Tortuga, he was laying siege to the younger daughter of Tortuga's French governor. He will be thwarted there, I can tell you, for Esthonie Touraille has other plans for little Georgette!"

"And did he lay siege to *you*?" wondered Esme.

"Of course." Imogene thought it best to divert Esme from any thought that she had overheard them talk last night. "But van Ryker does not like him, so I see little of him."

"But he does pursue you?" Esme's voice sharpened.

It came to Imogene suddenly that if she could make Esme believe Vartel was in love with her, Esme might decide against sending her down the Cóbre with Vartel's buccaneers lest she surface again where van Ryker would find her—and time was her ally.

"I will tell you in confidence." She leaned forward and lowered her voice to a confidential whisper. "But you must promise not to tell van Ryker?"

"Oh, I promise." Esme was hanging on her words.

"Very well, then—it is the scandal of Tortuga the way he pursues me. Van Ryker has reason to dislike him, for Vartel turns up everywhere I go, always bowing and paying me extravagant compliments, but then"—she lifted an eyebrow knowingly—"you know Frenchmen!"

"And that is all there is to it, a few extravagant compliments? I wonder that Branch is so exercised, for surely there must be many who pay you extravagant compliments?"

"Well, that's not quite all. . . . " murmured Imogene. Her eyes sparkled as she leaned toward Esme. "At Esthonie Touraille's party the night before we left Tortuga, Captain Vartel removed the large amethyst he always wears in his hat and put it in my hand and closed my fingers about it and asked me to study it in secret and think of him. He said that if I would but leave van Ryker, he would take me to France—anywhere. We would live any life I chose."

Esme drew in her breath. "He is in love with you!" she cried accusingly.

Modestly, Imogene inclined her head. "But I want you to know, Esme, that although I *did* keep the stone—I lost it aboard the *Carolina*, it is at the bottom of the sea by now—I have *never* let Captain Vartel take any liberties with me, although he has urged me endlessly to meet him...anywhere." Her voice became dreamy.

Esme jumped up and gave her a withering look. "I should think you'd best look to your wayward instincts," she warned. "Lest Branch find out which way the wind is blowing. Charles!" She waved to Charles, who was just passing the dining room door. "Come here and entertain Imogene. I must go and speak to Tony."

So that was the way it was to be, thought Imogene. *Guarded, watched, passed from hand to hand*. Plainly, the Ryder clan did not intend to let her out of their sight!

Charles stayed with her through breakfast and, afterward, when she insisted on going back to her room to "freshen up," he accompanied her, chattering up the stairs, and lounged about outside the door "waiting to take her to see the new banana trees."

Imogene looked out the window. Anthony and Esme were pacing about in the overgrown garden below. Their voices could not reach her but they both looked excited and Esme was waving her arms.

She wondered grimly if they were working out some new way of "disposing" of her.

As she and Charles returned from "seeing the new banana

trees,'' Anthony strode up and took her in tow. Imogene tried to excuse herself, but he stuck to her like court plaster. They were not going to relinquish their grip on her for a moment, she saw—and guessed that they had decided to go ahead with their original plans. And now Esme was wafting toward her.

"Imogene, I'd clean forgot—I promised you a new gown!''

It irritated Imogene that Esme should seize her and all but drag her to her room, but of all her captors Esme was the frailest—there was some comfort there. She strolled along, only half hearing Esme's chatter, to Esme's bedchamber, there to watch Esme spread out before her on the bed a variety of handsome gowns.

"What I need most,'' she told Esme truthfully, "is a new chemise—yes, that one would do nicely.'' She held up the sheer lawn garment, deliciously trimmed in point lace. "And something cool and simple to wear here at Gale Force by day.'' For she must not let Esme suspect that she knew what was planned for her!

"This voile, perhaps?'' And then, regretfully, as Imogene reached for it with tentative fingers, "No, perhaps not *that* one.'' Esme caressed the lovely voile dress with its lavender bodice laced shepherdess style and its wide lovely flowered skirt billowing in soft shades of lavender and blue and pink. "I do think I'll wear it this evening—nights are so hot here, don't you think?''

Esme doesn't want that particular dress transported to Tangier, thought Imogene grimly. Of a sudden a new and malicious plan occurred to her. It was a desperate plan, but did not desperate plans fit her situation? And why should she shudder in fear of Esme? Her natural courage had returned to her and with it her buoyant spirit.

"I believe I'd like something more—distinctive,'' she murmured.

Esme shrugged. "Take your choice.''

Thoughtfully Imogene sorted through purple velvets, shimmering violet satins, rustling amethyst-toned silks—oh, no, she didn't want anything that *rustled*, in case she should be able to get away!

"I like this one best.'' She held up a cheap, brilliantly

colored, thin lawn dress that for all its sheerness was very
covered up—high-necked, with long full sleeves and a not-
too-tight bodice. Its large diamond design was of rich purple
and flashing magenta and white—all of it tastefully muted by
reason of its sheerness and many folds.

"But that's my domino dress," protested Esme. "I wear it
only for costume parties."

"Of course, if you don't *want* me to have it?"

Esme flushed. "No, no, if you want it, you may have it. I
just thought..." She let die what she had just thought
and Imogene guessed satirically that perhaps of all her wardrobe Esme was most ready to part with this particular dress.
She smiled grimly, for that too suited her purpose.

"And perhaps a wide-brimmed hat?" she suggested.

"Here, would you like this one?" Esme held up an
amethyst-plumed felt. Her manner was reluctant. Imogene
guessed she really hated to give it away.

"No-o-o..." She lifted the hat and considered it from all
angles. "Too heavy for this climate. Perhaps I'll buy a straw
hat from one of the servants."

Esme choked back her amusement and with relief snatched
back the hat from Imogene's casual grasp. "That—might
please you better," she agreed, and Imogene could almost
hear Esme's thoughts: *This life has brought her so low that
she would prefer a straw hat to a plumed one!*

It was exactly what she wanted Esme to think.

With some coins she got from Anthony, Imogene—with
Esme still hovering in the background—went out to ask
among the servants until finally she found a hat that suited
her. It was of wide-brimmed straw, island-made and ideally
suited to the hot Jamaican climate.

"Here, you try it on so I can guess at how it will look on
me." She thrust the hat toward Esme, who shuddered delicately and shrank away from it as if she feared contamination.
With a light laugh, Imogene tried it on.

"Oh, yes, it shades my face nicely from the sun." She
turned and gave the eager servant girl the coins.

"Really, Imogene—a servant's hat? I am amazed you'd try

it on, much less wear it," muttered Esme irritably as she dragged Imogene away, making for the house.

Imogene gave her sister-in-law a wry smile. "Beggars," she said cryptically, "cannot be choosers." That remark, she promised herself, would have a bitter significance for Esme later.

She wanted to safeguard against her wine at supper being drugged, for that would have spoiled her plans. So just before supper she drew Esme aside.

"I do hope we will have time to talk awhile alone after supper," she said earnestly. "For there are things about Branch that I would tell you."

Esme gave her a speculative look. "What things?"

"Important things. You are his sister and his favorite. Branch and I have no children and if anything happened to us—"

"But why should anything happen to you?" drawled Esme with elaborate unconcern. "Branch, I could understand, for his profession is a dangerous one, but *you*, Imogene—oh, I grant you that you had a narrow escape on the *Carolina* and again from the fever, but once you are back in Cayona with Branch, what harm could come to you?"

"It is this life we lead," sighed Imogene, watching Esme for effect. "But a week before we left Tortuga, some buccaneers got into a brawl at one of the taverns and came out shooting at each other. One bullet went through the crown of my hat."

Esme stared at her.

"It is true," said Imogene quietly. "Tortuga is a dangerous place. Captain Flogg sent word to van Ryker that he intended to kidnap me *and he'd be in no case to prevent it*! Drunken buccaneers swagger about, dueling—van Ryker has fought three duels since our marriage alone! And if Branch dies"—she gave Esme a tragic look—"it is not my intention to survive him."

Esme's smile froze. "You mean you would do away with yourself?" she demanded in amazement.

"Yes. Oh, yes." Imogene bobbed her head. She hoped to inspire Esme to change the plan and instead arrange to have word brought up from Port Royal by some "reliable" party that van Ryker was dead—anything to buy time.

Esme did not buy that. "You believe that now," she stated bluntly. "But you would not do it. Why should you? You'd be the richest woman in the Caribbean if anything happened to Branch—no, forget about the 'widow's mite' the buccaneers would let you have, that is only a share of booty yet undivided. You'd have all his wealth, Imogene. You could return to England, you could be the toast of Europe!"

Imogene abandoned that tack. She decided to try another way to eliminate the chance of drugged wine at supper.

"Still, in case the worst happened," she sighed, "I know Branch would want you and his brothers to inherit his fortune, for as you know, we are but recently wed and have no children of our own."

"Go on," said Esme thoughtfully.

"Most of Branch's gold is hidden—and I have no doubt that he will secrete much of this new-gotten wealth in the same locations. I feel that you should know the location of his strongboxes, Esme—in case anything should happen to us."

Esme caught her breath. "Oh, yes, indeed—you are right, Imogene. It would be best all around if I knew."

"Very well. I will tell you after supper."

"Tell me now," prodded Esme.

"No, the locations are difficult to find. I will have to draw you maps. Perhaps after supper, when Anthony and Charles are ready for bed—for I do not wish to be rude to my host—you and I might go into the drawing room and I might sketch for you the location of these strongboxes."

"Do you know the location of all of them?" Casually.

"Oh, yes, for van Ryker wishes me to be well cared for should he die in some engagement with the Spanish."

"I think—" Esme hesitated and frowned. "I think it might be best not to tell Anthony and Charles of this."

"Yes." Eagerly. "I thought it best that it be our secret, for Charles talks overmuch and how can we know that Anthony will not tell him?"

"Yes, Charles talks overmuch," murmured Esme. Her

expression for a moment was scornful but it was quickly papered over with a bright smile. " 'Tis time we change for supper, don't you think? You can wear your new domino gown.''

Imogene took a deep breath. *You can wear your new domino gown.* . . . As plainly as any signal, Esme's sly inflection told her that tonight was indeed the night. They were playing for keeps now. Whatever happened, she knew she would not be spending another night beneath the terra-cotta roof tiles of Gale Force!

But somehow the very nearness to the brink only gave her confidence. She dressed slowly, taking her time about it, for she wanted the evening to drag on and the night to become very dark before she made her move. She looked into the mirror and her reflection gave her back a fiery woman, for the reckless girl had become indeed a reckless woman and tonight against all odds she meant to take her world back again!

Charles was waiting outside her door. That was no surprise, she had expected him. Halfway down the stairs she floated before she stopped and said, "Oh, I've forgotten my fan! I must run and get it."

"I'll get it for you," he offered.

"I doubt you could find it." Her voice was airy. Picking up her skirts she ran back upstairs and Charles, wild-eyed, ran after her, for he had explicit instructions from Anthony to keep Imogene in sight at all times until he had her safely down to supper.

She rummaged about idly, letting Charles wait interminably beside the open door. Eventually she found the fan—which was exactly where she had placed it earlier this afternoon. A cheap fan of painted wood that she had borrowed from Esme, she slipped its little chain around her wrist.

"Oh, and I must not forget my straw hat!" she said merrily.

"Your straw hat?" Charles blinked.

"Yes, I am going to consult Esme after supper about how to add a plume and give it some style. Or perhaps flowers would be better?"

Charles shook his head at the foolishness of women and Imogene, in her gown of multicolored diamond design, glided downstairs beside him.

In the open courtyard Anthony and Esme were waiting for them—waiting impatiently if the quick swish-swish of Esme's ivory fan was any indication.

"What have we here?" wondered Anthony gallantly, stepping forward. "A domino, no less!"

"It was her choice—of all my wardrobe," said Esme, frowning as Imogene pirouetted blithely for Anthony's approbation.

"A capital choice—capital," approved Anthony—but his approval was not for the gown but for the delectable figure the gown encased.

Esme hid a sniff but Imogene smiled directly into his eyes. "How nice of you to say so, Anthony." She turned to Esme. "Has Anthony told you that he has ordered carved rosewood doors for the house, Esme? I am sure there will be nothing in Jamaica to match them!"

Anthony gave her a proud and rather wistful look. He was as usual shaken by her beauty and wished they could postpone her departure.

Esme caught that regretful look. "We have been waiting supper for you, Imogene," she said sternly.

"Oh, have you?" Imogene was suitably contrite. "Well, then we must go in, mustn't we? Oh, you are looking at my hat, Esme. I brought it down so that after supper, while Charles and Anthony talk about women over their wine, you and I may retire to the drawing room and you can suggest how I may decorate it to make it more elegant. A plume perhaps, or flowers?"

Esme's face cleared. She saw at once that the hat would be an excellent excuse for a private conversation with Imogene.

"I am sure we will think of something," she agreed warmly.

At supper Imogene chatted merrily over the gungo-pea soup and fish and curried goat and bammies—which, she was informed, were made with cassava flour. She dawdled over her food, keeping up a running flow of repartee with her host, who sat at the head of his table, resplendent in wine satin and gold braid. Charles was hardly less elegant in sky blue silk adorned with lemon ribands, but he was worried and kept his touseled head ducked down. Esme, in her shepherdess voile, ate as if the devil were after her and tapped her foot impatiently. That slight movement set the brilliants in her hair dancing. Imogene knew they were meant to draw all eyes to Esme's gleaming dark hair and beautiful oval face, and it amused her to make herself the center of attention. She gave Anthony arch looks and lifted her glass to him in little toasts, and seemed to admire him and all his works. Anthony was charmed and refused to heed Esme's black looks or the impatient kicks she delivered to his silk-stockinged shins with her slipper under the long dining table.

At last they had finished their supper and a fresh bottle of wine was brought. Imogene toyed with her glass, half afraid that Esme had tricked her.

She lifted her glass. "Perhaps we should take our glasses into the drawing room now, Esme. You remember I wanted to consult you about my hat?" She gave Esme a significant look and picked up the hat.

"Oh, no," cried Esme, rising instantly. "Leave your glass here, for there's a decanter and fresh glasses in the drawing room."

This instant response told Imogene what she wanted to know. Well content, she made a toast—this one to Gale Force—sipped her wine and considered them all: these three who, next to herself, should have been closest in all the world to van Ryker, and who schemed only his downfall and death....

She would find a way to destroy them! Alone!

So long had they talked that the moon was high when at last—most impatiently—Esme got her alone. "I thought you would linger at table forever," she complained.

"I could not be rude," murmured Imogene, tossing the hat onto a chair. "And besides, after Port Royal I feel so *safe* here in the bosom of Branch's family." She looked about her with what she hoped appeared to be a feeling of contentment, and noted the large wicker trunk that reposed conspicuously at one side of the room. "What is that doing here?" she asked innocently.

"Oh, I plan to pack my winter things in it—you are right, this climate is too ungodly hot for velvets and stiff brocades."

"Yes, I have found it so." Imogene stifled a yawn. "I feel half giddy from the wine. Perhaps I should wait until tomorrow to draw the charts?"

"No, you had best do it now," said Esme crossly. "For Tony and Charles will become very curious if they find us constantly closeted alone with ink and paper!"

"Perhaps we should have a glass of wine first." Imogene seized the decanter that rested on a small gateleg table and poured it out into the two waiting glasses. She proffered one to Esme. "And toast our fortunes?"

"No!" Hastily Esme took the glasses from her. "I perceive that you are getting drunk," she said crossly. "If you drink any more you will not be able to draw a straight line. Oh, do sit down and draw your charts, Imogene!"

"Very well." With a slight but realistic stagger, Imogene snatched up the glass and moved toward the little writing desk. And to Esme's protest, "I promise you I will not drink it until I have done." She paused halfway to the desk, swayed unsteadily. "Would you bring me that larger sheet from over there, Esme? One of the maps will be rather elaborate, since the location is well outside the town of Cayona."

Esme sighed. She brought the larger sheet, bent to put it down on the little writing desk—and stiffened as she felt a sharp blade pressed against her back.

"This is a letter opener, but it will serve as well as any dagger," murmured a soft dangerous voice in her ear. "Sit down, Esme—sit down and write as I tell you. Write *This is my sworn confession. I, Esme Ribaud, who was born Esme Ryder, now of France but late of England, do swear that I, and I alone, murdered my lover, Vincent Dunworth.*"

CHAPTER 19

Esme sat down but she did not lift the quill pen. "It isn't true, you know," she murmured. "I didn't kill Vincent."

"I know," said Imogene ruthlessly. "But I want you to take the blame for something you didn't do just as Branch has done all these years!"

Esme's oval face turned to study Imogene obliquely. Although pale, that face bore a cold expression. "Why should I write that?" she asked quietly.

"*To save your life*," whispered Imogene, controlling herself with an effort. "For I yearn to drive this knife through your ribs and into your black heart!"

Esme's face went a shade paler. "There is no reason to be so dramatic about it—I will write your confession. But I will write the truth, how Anthony killed Vincent."

"And add how by lies and trickery you persuaded a man who had never even laid eyes on Vincent Dunworth to take the blame!"

"Very well," sighed Esme. "Although"—her courage, still with her, made her add mockingly, "you must realize that I will repudiate it later."

"I don't doubt it," said Imogene grimly. "*Write!*"

In the large flowing scrawl Imogene remembered, Esme put quill to paper. As if in amusement, she wrote not only what Imogene dictated, she wrote the whole bizarre story, adding details Imogene had no knowledge of.

She has found someone to brag to about her secret triumph, Imogene realized in amazement, and her fingers tightened on the knife.

But Esme hesitated when it came time to sign. "If I sign this," she said in an uneasy voice, "then you will kill me, right?"

"Wrong. I will not kill you—although you well deserve it. Sign, Esme, and then drink. Drink the wine!"

Revelation flashed over Esme's face. "You *knew*," she whispered. "You knew all the time?"

"All the time," echoed Imogene grimly.

"But why?" cried Esme in a low tone as she affixed her signature. "Why did you not strike me down in my bed-chamber and make your escape? Why did you stay when you *knew*?"

"I stayed to save van Ryker. With this document—now that you've signed it"—Imogene set the wine down and snatched up the incriminating paper—"he'll be a free man. He can go back to England or wherever he chooses. *Drink the wine!*"

"You know you can't escape," murmured Esme maliciously. "Tony will find you, he'll destroy this paper—"

"*Drink!*" grated Imogene, pressing the point of the paper knife deep enough that it pricked Esme's back.

Esme winced but she did not cry out. Instead, she drained her glass.

"How long before it takes effect?" wondered Imogene.

"Very soon," said Esme calmly.

"And how long will you sleep?"

Esme shrugged. "Long enough. I think I had best sit down." And then petulantly, "You can put that knife away— you will not need it."

"It will keep you from crying out—for you know that if you do, I will drive it into your heart up to the hilt," warned Imogene.

"Oh, stop being dramatic," said Esme. "You have your confession, and as soon as I am asleep you can run away to Port Royal. That *is* where you're going, isn't it? Or do you plan to pursue Darnwell to Spanish Town?"

"I think I will stay here," said Imogene, "and wave this paper under Anthony's nose and take over Gale Force."

"Oh, do that," said Esme conversationally. "I am sure he will find that very interesting." Her eyes were glazing over and she moved unsteadily. "I hope I didn't put too much drug into the wine," she muttered, and slid sidewise in her chair.

Imogene caught her as she fell, for she did not want any sudden thump to alert the brothers, who still lingered in the dining room.

Swiftly she eased Esme to the floor, and began to remove her outer garments. Then she removed her own, down to her sheer lawn chemise, and set about changing clothes with Esme. She dressed Esme in the cheap domino gown and then fastened Esme's pale blue lavender petticoat around her own waist and donned the wide flowered voile overskirt. Now she slipped into the separate shepherdess bodice. She fastened two of the hooks—it opened in the back—and then impatiently thrust the paper containing Esme's confession deep down into the bodice. Taking a deep breath she forced it past her breasts so that it lay spread out across her smooth stomach.

"That was a nice trick," said an amused masculine voice behind her. "How about letting me try it?"

With a gasp, Imogene swung round—reaching for the letter opener as she did so.

"Oh, no need to attack me—I'm on your side," said the amused voice.

Silhouetted in the candlelight against the hot Jamaican darkness, the tall figure of Darnwell Keating lounged in the open casement window.

"You near frightened me to death," accused Imogene. "I thought you were Anthony come to collect me!"

"I've been here for the past few minutes watching you operate," said Darnwell genially.

"Then why on earth didn't you make yourself known?"

"What? And spoil your fun? I couldn't have done it better myself!"

"This is not a game, Darnwell!"

"Oh, no?" His smile was wicked.

Imogene gave a sniff and again bent her efforts to fastening the hooks at the back of her bodice.

"Here, I'll help with that," he offered.

In exasperation, Imogene swung on him, hands on hips. "Darnwell, how long have you been watching through that doorway?" she demanded in a fierce low voice.

"Every minute." He lounged before her, smiling lazily. "I had hoped you would change chemises with Esme, but I guess that was too much to hope for. Let me say that you look most appealing in your chemise!"

Imogene, flushing pink at the thought that he had seen her often enough without that chemise—had indeed bathed her and cared for her for many days—whispered sharply, "We must hurry. Fasten these hooks—I can't reach them."

"It's one of the things I do best—fastening bodice hooks," he said impudently. "The only thing I do better is undo them."

She gave him a warning look and he hastened to get her hooked up.

"And now we must get Esme into that wicker trunk— quietly. Darnwell, how do you happen to be here?"

He bent down to pick up Esme's limp form, now clad in the cheap domino gown. "When Esme went downstairs in the middle of the night, I knew something was afoot, so I vaulted out the window, swung down on a branch, and listened at the dining room window. I heard the three of them make their plans, including"—he nodded at the wicker trunk—"this interesting arrangement."

"*I* was listening from the courtyard outside the dining room door."

"So I gathered. They should post sentries, these Ryders!"

"Darnwell, we haven't time for jokes." Imogene picked up the straw hat that she had earlier flung onto a chair and dropped it on Esme's body so that it hid her face and her dark shining curls. Then she tossed the cheap painted fan on top of her. "That's in case they open the trunk and peek in—they'll see something they recognize, things I was wearing that Esme wouldn't touch!"

"They won't be taking time to peek in," said Darnwell grimly. "There's a boat and men waiting."

Imogene gave Esme's prone figure, curled up in the big wicker trunk, a last look. It did her heart good to know that Esme would wake up aboard a departing ship clad in a cheap dress she despised and a servant's straw hat. On her way to Tangier.

"When I slam this trunk lid shut and lock it, we must be quickly away," she warned Darnwell. "We'll go outside and they'll think Esme felt she had done her part—and left them to do theirs."

Darnwell nodded, his gaze thoughtful. "A pity to send her such a distance," he murmured. "She was a delightful bedfellow."

Imogene gave him a look of annoyance and slammed down the lid, threw the makeshift lock.

"After you." He struck a courtly pose and threw wide the door.

"Oh, hurry, can't you?" She ran from the room, caught his hand and dragged him chuckling after her.

They were well hidden in the bushes of the overgrown garden when Anthony and Charles, having heard the trunk lid slam, opened the door.

"I suppose Esme couldn't stand it, seeing Imogene carted away," said Charles glumly, looking about the room.

"More like she wanted to be sure not to be asked to help!" said Anthony in a crisp voice. "The boat is waiting, Charles. I could see it from the window. Lift up, man!"

"This wicker trunk is heavier than I thought," panted Charles, who was unused to any physical exertion more strenuous than lifting a tankard. He struggled to follow Anthony through the courtyard and outside but his end of the trunk was sagging. "I didn't realize she'd be so hard to carry," he complained. "Are ye sure she won't smother in there?"

"Lift up on your end, Charles, before ye drop it," said Anthony testily, with a fierce look back at his younger brother. "I can assure ye she won't smother. This cursed thing is made of wicker, can't you see? Ye could pack it with geese and they wouldn't smother!"

Breathing hard, Charles managed to carry his end of the

trunk down the slope, dropping it only once to the accompaniment of his brother's low-voiced but heartfelt curses.

"Branch will never believe our story," said Charles gloomily, staring at the wicker trunk he had just put down with such relief.

"Branch won't need to believe it. Branch will"—Anthony's voice cut off, knifelike, for a half-dozen men had emerged from the gloom by the riverbank where Anthony had expected but two. He stepped back, reaching for his sword hilt. Beside him, Charles, affrighted, whirled and broke into a run up the hill. It made no difference. Two of the silent men sprinted after him and brought him down, sobbing. They thrust a gag into his mouth and dragged him back to where Anthony, taken by surprise, had already been wrestled to the ground and a gag stuck into his mouth as well.

"We might as well take this pair as well as the woman," said a dispassionate voice, and both brothers turned, perforce silently, to look at the speaker. "True," he continued, "the woman will bring a better price in Barbary, but the men are fair specimens and will bring something as slaves in the market there. Also, it is better to leave no one behind us to tell who did this night's work. We'll stop on our way back downstream and pick up the others."

A mutual shudder shook the brothers and Charles could be heard whimpering through his gag as they were dragged on to the boat, along with the wicker trunk that contained their sister.

As silently as it had come, the boat slid away into the darkness.

Back in the dark overgrown garden, Darnwell seemed loath to go. "A handsome plantation house this," he mused, staring up at the walls in the moonlight. "One would hardly expect to find one so well built in this Godforsaken hole!"

Imogene clutched his arm. "Darnwell," she muttered fiercely. "When Anthony and Charles come back up that hill, they're going to go looking for Esme—and when they don't find her, they're going to realize that I'm not the woman in the wicker trunk! Do you want that to happen while we stand here talking?"

"You're right," he agreed. " 'Tis time we took our leave." With a flourish he pushed aside a large palm frond that barred their passage. "This way, Imogene—I've had an entire day to find all the best hiding places this plantation affords. This is one of them!"

She was grateful for his help through the thick underbrush.

"How do you propose that we get away?" she demanded.

"I've secreted a boat a little ways downriver," he murmured, and led her circuitously down what was scarcely a path until at last, half hidden by a growth of palmetto, she saw its prow sticking up. It was small, she saw, but adequate.

As they were about to push off, he said, "Sh-h-h," and gripped her arm, pulling her back behind a clump of huge cabbage palms.

Imogene, chilled by the pressure of his grip, peered out. In the darkness—for the moon had gone overcast—she could see a boat going silently by. It had a number of men in it—she did not try to count them—and vaguely she could see the shape of what looked to be a large box toward the stern.

The wicker trunk! These were the cutthroats who were taking Esme downriver! And *she* could well have been the woman in that trunk! She felt faint for a moment and swayed against Darnwell, who clamped a quieting hand over her mouth.

When the boat had receded into the darkness, he let her go.

"I think we'll just let them get well ahead of us," he said comfortably.

"Darnwell," she cried, quivering. "Don't you feel anything at all? The woman in that wicker trunk was Esme—a woman you've held in your arms! A woman you've made love to—"

"I doubt me any sultan of Araby can stand against her," said Darnwell coolly. "If Esme ends up in a harem, I'll wager you guilders to oranges she ends up ruling it!"

Imogene shuddered away from him. It had suddenly come over her what it would be like to wake up on a pirate ship with no hope at all—for whatever their arrangements had been before, she was sure that would make no difference to Captain Vartel—what it would be like to be sold in the marketplace like cattle, and then... after all that... She turned her head away.

" 'Tis the fate *she* had arranged for *you*," Darnwell said silkily. "I am surprised you could mope over a woman who duped your cherished van Ryker to his ruin."

That was true! In that moment of horror she had forgotten that! She turned back to face Darnwell. "You are right," she said in a steadier voice. "I had forgotten how she ruined van Ryker."

The man beside her smiled grimly into the verdant darkness. Just at that moment he would have given the fortune he did not possess to be that "ruined" van Ryker and have this lovely woman yearn for him.

"They misjudged van Ryker's temper," she said as they got into the boat and cast off. "He would not simply let me disappear—he would tear the Caribbean apart to find me."

"I don't doubt it," Darnwell murmured, picking up the oars. "I know *I* would—if you were mine."

Something yearning in his voice caused her to lift her head.

"I had given you up," she said sternly.

His back was moving rhythmically as he rowed. "But I told you I would be back," he chided.

"Yes, but when you did not come...." She shuddered.

"Actually," he told her in a conversational voice. "I never left. I went but a-ways upriver and came immediately back."

She stared at him in the darkness. They were passing beneath the overarching branches of some great trees and it was too dark to see his face.

"But why did you not tell me?" she cried. "Why did you leave me alone there? I thought I was deserted!"

"I'm of the opinion you did very well for yourself. I stayed in the background, waiting to lend a hand when you came a cropper—but you didn't. Indeed, I doubt me I could have forced such a confession from Esme!"

"She only 'confessed' because she believed Anthony would soon have both the paper and me and she could snatch and burn it!"

"Yes," he said gravely, "but had I been there, she would

not have done it. She is a brave woman and she would have stood her ground and dared us to do our worst.''

"Yes," said Imogene reflectively, "I suppose she might have.''

"You wanted to get your confession—I let you get it.''

"And with it, I can win van Ryker a pardon? Can I not, Darnwell?''

"I should think it would be possible," he said. "For it is concrete evidence, signed and''—his white teeth flashed in a grin as he and Imogene came out from under the trees.—''of course, witnessed by me when I get around to affixing my signature, that Anthony Ryder and not his brother Branch killed Dunworth.''

"You'd do that?'' she breathed.

"Of course. Did I not hear her confess it and watch her write and sign it as well?''

It was with a lighter heart that Imogene sat back in the boat and let the current and Darnwell's oarsmanship carry them downriver to Port Royal.

"Where will we go?'' she wondered, as they approached. "To some inn? For I must get me quickly on the first ship bound for Tortuga.''

"I made arrangements before leaving Port Royal," he told her coolly.

"I cannot believe it! Darnwell, you have thought of everything.''

"I have tried," he said modestly. "There may be some small details that I have overlooked, but as to the main elements, I believe them to be well under control.''

Imogene fought back a desire to laugh—and managed it. Darnwell was entertaining, he was droll—and he was competent. She had been reluctantly forced to admit it.

To her surprise, he took her not to an inn but to the same solidly built two-story house she had occupied during her bout with fever. He brushed by a fellow who seemed to be lounging near the entrance and pushed open the door.

Imogene was about to comment on its being unlocked, but at Darnwell's slight silencing shake of the head, she held her peace and let him lead her in and close and latch the door behind him.

It was dark where they stood in the entrance hall and Darnwell's booted feet echoed on the stone flooring as he guided her toward another door beneath which a line of light showed.

"There is something in here that will interest you," he said, flinging the door open and suddenly sweeping her with him into the room, closing the door with his boot.

A moment later Imogene had whirled and was trying to surge back through that door, but Darnwell grasped her by the arm and held her fast.

Her stricken gaze went from the single candle guttering in a brass holder on the table to the wicker trunk in the center of the room, and seated on the floor, flanking it with their hands and feet tied and gags stuck in their mouths, the figures of Anthony and Charles Ryder.

"And here in this room we have," said Darnwell in a voice gone suddenly ruthless, "a murderer and his two accomplices and"—his voice softened, became caressing—"a most delightful buccaneer's woman—sure bait to bring van Ryker storming to Jamaica, where he'll be shot to pieces by the Jamaica Squadron."

As those cold words trickled over her, Imogene steadied herself. Flight was no longer possible. She had reached the end of her rope. Her stricken gaze flew to the grim face of the suddenly formidable man who towered over her.

"Who are you?" she whispered, for this was not the casual whim of a rakehell, but a well-thought-out scheme, expertly crafted and carried out.

"Who am I?" he drawled. "Why, I thought by now you'd have guessed. I'm Darnwell Keating, as I told you. I'm also Lord Marr—the new governor of Jamaica."

"I don't believe you!" cried Imogene. "You're not the governor of Jamaica—Lord Marr is an old man. You said so, Anthony said so, all the world says so!"

Darnwell kept his grip on her. "I said *Lord Marr* was an old man—and so he was. He was also my uncle. He died just before I set sail, died commending me to my new post, which was supposed to reform me and for which he'd paid a pretty penny to the king. I would to God he had given the coin to me instead of to Charles, for I'd much have preferred the gaming hells of London to exile in the Caribbean. But then I'd never have met you, would I? So there's a bright side after all!''

''You—a *governor*?'' She still could not believe it.

He gave a short laugh. ''It's all too true, Imogene. My uncle said before he died he was going to give me a chance to mend my wild ways, for he'd be dead soon and I'd inherit his title. He used to think a good woman could do it, but he flung several my way and I promptly misled them all. He came to believe that a firm seat of power would hold me on the paths of righteousness. What do you think about it?''

He was laughing at her—laughing as she stood here amid the ruin of all her hopes, laughing as he planned van Ryker's death! Imogene's fists clenched.

''Come,'' he said, urging her toward the door. ''I've something to say to you in private.''

''But—'' she looked back at the three of them. ''You can't leave them here in this condition. Esme could smother in that trunk if she moves about and gets her sleeves over her face—those full sleeves could easily smother a person! And those huge gags—Anthony and Charles could choke to death, Darnwell!''

Darnwell, now come into his own as Lord Marr, heaved a heavy sigh.

''Your soft heart will be your ruin, Imogene.'' But he went over and threw open the lid of the wicker trunk, which revealed Esme's limp form, sleeping peacefully. He lifted the straw hat and Imogene saw again that beautiful petulant face.

''We'll leave the hat,'' said Imogene quietly. She wanted Esme to wake up feeling straw scratching her cheeks, to look down and see herself clad in the domino, to find herself in the trunk—even if she wasn't sailing to Tangier!

''As you wish.'' Darnwell reached out and yanked the gags from the mouths of the two brothers. ''Keep silent,'' he warned them. ''For if ye make any disturbance at all, the men behind that door''— he jerked his head toward the only way out—"have orders to slit your throats without benefit of trial; we'll try you posthumously and hang your corpses!"

Charles gave a great shudder and his eyes rolled heaven-ward as if seeking aid. But Anthony leaned forward with all the fury of a striking cobra. "Having your men say ye'd have us sold as slaves in Barbary! And now talking of hangings! Ye'll pay for this!" he snarled.

"Doubtless." Darnwell placed a boot casually against Anthony's thigh and sent him sliding to the other side of the room, where he ended up with a thump against the wall. "But *you'll* not live to see it!" He turned at the door and gave them all a nasty smile. "Rest well, gentlemen. I leave ye to contemplate your sins, which doubtless will occupy ye until your trials."

He took Imogene by the hand and firmly escorted her upstairs, back to that room where she had spent long weeks burning up with fever. She felt at a disadvantage in that room, for it reminded her that she was beholden to this man.

"*You* were financing Esme," she murmured. " 'Twas *you* made her give me that gray silk gown on shipboard. *You* were the reason she did not try to kill me on board the *Bristol. She* knew you were the new governor. She sold van Ryker to you—and me as well!"

He did not bother to deny it.

"All the time you were scheming." Dark and accusing, her level blue eyes looked into his. "I cannot believe it—that you could have been so false to me."

His muscles quivered as if she had struck him a hard blow. "I have not been false to you, Imogene," he said hoarsely. "I told you I came here on a mission. That mission was to clean out this nest of buccaneers that infest this part of the Caribbean."

"And give the colonies back to Spain?" she said scornfully.

He shook his head. "The English fleet will patrol these seas. The Jamaica Squadron is being enlarged, refitted. We will no longer *need* the buccaneers."

"These colonies could not have survived without them!"

He gave her an angry look. "Can we not forget politics?"

"*Politics?*" She looked about to explode. "We are speaking of my husband's *life*, Darnwell!"

"Yes, but it is a worthless life," he sighed. "You deserve better—and I will give you better, Imogene. Once he is dead, I will marry you. You will be wife to the governor of Jamaica, a woman respected, looked up to, protected. Nor will we have to languish long in this accursed outpost. Once my mission is accomplished, I will petition the king for some better post—something in the West Country perhaps. We may have to make our way back to London by circuitous routes— but make it back we will!"

Imogene was staring at him as if he were a monster. She had not heard his last words. Her mind had come to a dead stop with *Once he is dead, I will marry you.*

"If you harm van Ryker," she told him in a level voice, "I will find a way to kill you—so help me God!"

He saw he had taken the wrong tack with her. She was an emotional woman, given to storms. He looked past her at the big bed where she had lain tossing with fever.

"Then you can buy him his life," he said slowly. "And he can sail to hell, for all of me."

Fear crackled inside of her. " 'Buy his life'? How?"

"You can become *my* woman."

The room held a sudden stillness, a tense waiting. It was as if they had always known it would come to this, these two. They stared at each other raptly. They might have been alone in the world.

"Van Ryker would hear of it," objected Imogene in an altered voice. "He would tear Port Royal apart stone by stone to find me—yes, and Spanish Town too!"

That russet head was nodding in agreement. "But if he does not hear of it?"

"How could he *not* hear of it?" she demanded bitterly. "I would be seen at the marketplace, riding about in a carriage, attending balls!"

He made himself harden his heart, although the hurt look around her mouth tore at him. What Imogene had not chosen to give, he would now take—for he could not bear to lose her.

"He would not hear of it if you kept yourself to this house, if you lived here as cloistered as a sultan's favorite in some harem in Barbary."

She flinched. "I could not do it!"

"Not even for van Ryker?" he taunted.

A storm seemed to shake her, blowing her this way and that. Pain throbbed through her as she thought of van Ryker. Never to see him again? A dry sob racked her body. Van Ryker's tall commanding figure floated up before her. He seemed to be staring down at her, fierce and hawklike, demanding that she reject this insolent offer and let him take his chances. . . . And then another vision intervened. She saw him suddenly in her mind's eye, mounting a tall gallows erected between the high tide and the low. She saw him giving a last look out to sea. . . .

"You mean—live here *always?*" she whispered.

Darnwell's eyes gleamed. He had her now! Her love for van Ryker had been her undoing. *She would be his at last!*

"Always," he said calmly. "As long as I am here in Jamaica. When I leave you will go with me. Meantime you will live here. With me. And as long as you accept me, Imogene, I promise not to harm a hair of van Ryker's head. You have the word of a gentleman."

"I have the word of a dissolute rake from the gambling hells of London," she said bitterly, her face very white. "I don't doubt your uncle urged this governorship for you on King Charles 'to make a man of you'—it is not likely to happen. You will never change."

He nodded urbanely, his eyes veiled. "What you say has more than a grain of truth," he admitted. "But it is beside the point, whether I reform or no. Do we have a bargain?"

She swallowed. It was hard for her to speak.

"*Do we have a bargain?*" Fear that he would weaken and let her go hardened his voice.

"Yes," she whispered.

Darnwell Keating, late of London, drew a long ragged breath. He had won. He had forced from her a promise. And he knew in his heart that she would keep it. Why then did he not feel better about his victory?

"I will leave you alone now," he said. "For I have matters to attend to. There is no escape from this room, so I pray you, do not try it. *If you try*, I may change my mind about not harming van Ryker—I may decide to loose the Jamaica Squadron on him after all."

And van Ryker, suspecting nothing, would sail into a trap. Imogene's hands clenched.

"I will be ready," she said steadily, "when you come for me."

"Good." He bent and pulled her dress down from her shoulder—a shoulder he now felt belonged to him. Fire rushed through him as he brushed that smooth, enticing skin gently with his lips. "They call you the Jewel of Tortuga, did you know that, Imogene?" he asked hoarsely. "And sometimes its queen."

"Ridiculous," she scoffed, although her shoulder quivered under the pressure of his lips, for against her will she found this man desirable. "Tortuga has no queen. It has a governor sent by France." She decided to try once more. "Van Ryker would pour over you a shower of Spanish gold," she said wistfully, "if only you would let me return to him."

His hands slid down her shoulders, freed her breasts from her tight bodice, his fingers eased beneath her chemise. He cupped her silky breasts in his hands, toyed with them gently. Imogene stood her ground, for to cross him was to watch van Ryker die.

"My rewards will be even more golden," he told her, looking deep into her eyes. "And more joyous."

She caught her breath. For him, she saw, there was no turning back. Nor for her.

She was trapped.

"All I ask is that van Ryker be kept safe from harm," she said in a breathless voice.

"Then I suggest you undress. I would prefer to find you in bed when I get back."

He gave her an impersonal smile and strode away, closing the door behind him.

Port Royal, Jamaica, 1660

CHAPTER 20

In silent bitterness, in shame, in utter soul-wrenching defeat, Imogene looked about her at the big bedroom in which Darnwell had left her. It had memories for her, this room—and well Darnwell knew it. For it was here that she had fought for her life, here that he had cared for her so tenderly.

He must have guessed she would not be able to hate him in this room.

Reluctantly, feeling every garment rasp her skin like a lover's sigh, she removed her shoes, her stockings, the shepherdess bodice, which was half down anyway—her shaking fingers tore the hooks loose when they gave her difficulty. She slid down the flowered kirtle with a sob and loosed the blue-lavender petticoat so that it joined the flowered voile overskirt in a heap around her feet.

She stepped out of that colorful heap of material feeling this had all been ordained, intended, that her short, fierce love for van Ryker had not been meant to last. They had been wrested apart once before—now it would happen again. And this time it would be permanent.

All this, so that he might live. . . .

Dry-eyed, remote, she faced the fact that she would not see her lean buccaneer again. He would sail his seas—without her. He would come home to his handsome house in Tortuga—without her. He would receive his king's pardon—ah, she would force Darnwell into that—and he would perhaps leave the buccaneering life and return to England, become again a tall gentleman of Devon—and all without her. . . .

She sat there in her light chemise, with her lovely body silvered by the moonlight pouring in the window, and considered seriously hurling herself out, to land upon the hard stones of the street. But—that was unlikely to kill her, she would at the most break her leg . . . and be unable to leave at all.

She looked about her absently, peering into the dark corners the candlelight did not reach. A bit of glass to slash her wrists perhaps and bleed her life away before Darnwell came back? The windows? No, they were unglazed.

There was nothing of glass in the room.

Still . . . her gaze grew dreamy . . . there was no way for Darnwell to keep her alive—not if she chose to die. Tonight, tomorrow, she would find a way.

But, for now, she dared not even attempt escape. Who knew, even now the *Sea Rover* might ride anchor in that sheltered bay up the coast, the one van Ryker had christened Lemon Bay in her honor, even now her buccaneer might be striding toward Gale Force, fully expecting to find her.

He would find instead an empty house, his brothers, herself, all mysteriously gone, and the servants would know nothing—he would not be able to wring from them what they did not know.

He would search for her, long and hard, she knew. *And in that search he would be careless of the Jamaica Squadron.* She shivered and bent her head. She *must* live—if only to protect van Ryker! For who knew what would happen if she died? Would Darnwell honor his word to her then? She had good reason to doubt it.

A sob caught in her throat.

She must become—as she had once before—a bird in a golden cage. And this time without even a chance of escape.

She shivered, and her chemise fell down over one shoulder. She let it remain there—it would be leaving her body soon enough. A new pair of arms would hold her, caress her—the arms of Lord Marr, new governor of Jamaica. His lips would rain kisses upon her unresponsive mouth—*no, she dared not be unresponsive,* that too might spell van Ryker's ruin!

Racked by her turbulent emotions, she sat there tense upon the bed and stiffened as she heard the door behind her open.

Her back was turned toward the man who stood there in the candlelight and her beautiful naked shoulder and sheer chemise was all that he could see besides a cascade of long golden hair that reached below her waist.

"I want you to know this, Darnwell," she said in a low bitter voice, "that I will always love van Ryker, and that I do this only to save his life. If you cross me in this, if you turn loose the Jamaica Squadron on him after all, if you do not strive to secure his pardon as you have promised, I swear to you on all I hold dear that I will slide a knife between your ribs one night. For no matter what I owe you—and I admit my debt to you is great—I am van Ryker's woman and I will never cease to love him."

"I am glad to hear it," said a deep masculine voice—a voice she had not expected to hear again. "For when I found you in your chemise in the governor's bedchamber, I was inclined to doubt it!"

"Van Ryker!" Imogene leaped up and swung round to face him with glowing eyes. "They did not take you!"

He laughed and tossed back his dark hair with a careless hand. In two strides he had crossed the room and she was in his arms, pressed against him vibrantly, laughing, crying—she could not believe her luck.

"Did you think I was taken?" he murmured against her hair.

"I was afraid you might be," she whispered. "But"—her head lifted—"what of the governor?"

"He will be my guest on Tortuga for a while," van Ryker told her. There was something ruthless in his voice, a sound she had not heard before.

She laughed softly. "I dare say Lord Marr will object to that!"

"He has already made his objections known." Van Ryker's strong hands caressed her shoulders. "But I could not seem to hear them over the din in my ears screaming *This man has Imogene—he has held her in his arms, he has made love to her!*"

"Not so! Although"—reluctantly—"I must admit I was *about* to let him take me, for he had promised me that if I did not, he would greet you with the Jamaica Squadron when you came to get me."

"The Jamaica Squadron," said van Ryker lazily, "has already received 'word' from the governor. They have streamed away on a wild-goose chase and are far over the horizon by now. 'Twill be some time before they realize they have been hoodwinked. And by then we'll all be well on our way to Tortuga."

"I wish we were on board the *Sea Rover* right now," she sighed, leaning against him.

"And so ye shall be soon enough," van Ryker promised her. "But since we were cheated out of a wedding night but recently, as I remember, and since the governor so kindly offered to allow you to spend a night in his bedchamber"—he gave the room around him an ironic glance—"I think it might be fitting that ye get to spend this last night ashore in that bedchamber after all. See to my Lord Marr, will ye, Raoul?" he called over his shoulder through the open door, "In case he becomes restless? For my lady and I are off to test the softness of his bed!"

From the next room she could hear de Rochemont's soft laughter. A Frenchman, he'd be thinking, could not have arranged it better.

"How did you learn," she asked, "that Esme and Anthony and Charles had betrayed you?"

"Betrayed me?" He looked taken aback. "But I've just this moment set them free!"

"Then get them back!" She broke away from him and ran barefoot in her chemise into the next room, entered it tempestuously with her golden hair flying.

Raoul de Rochemont, the ship's doctor, gave her an admiring glance. He thought she looked a very angel.

"Where are they?" she cried. "Where is Esme? And Anthony? And Charles?"

"Esme is just waking up," said de Rochemont. "But Anthony and Charles confessed to the need of some fresh air after their ordeal. We insisted they have a drink first and—"

"Seize them!" cried Imogene. "For it is they who plotted to bring down on you the Jamaica Squadron!"

Doctor he might be, but de Rochemont was also a buccaneer. He left the room with the speed of a running cat and they could hear some bickering and several blows in the hall below as the brothers were again trussed up, while Imogene poured out to van Ryker, who had followed her, the whole outrageous story: how Esme had tricked him, how Anthony and not Esme had killed Dunworth, how she had been put willy-nilly aboard the *Carolina* and almost died there, how she had been picked up by the *Bristol* and found it a fever ship. She was just tearing through the telling of how Esme happened to be waking up inside a wicker trunk when she realized she and van Ryker were not alone in the room.

Over in a corner, listening with a cynical expression on his worldly face, was the new governor of Jamaica. His sword remained by his side but his arms were bound.

In the rage he had felt at learning of the treachery of his close relations, van Ryker too had forgotten that they were not alone. Now he stepped between them to shield the lovely disheveled sight of her from Lord Marr's devouring gaze.

"Get your dress, Imogene," he said absently, for his mind was still upon the other matter.

"It does not matter," said Imogene impatiently, "for Darnwell has seen me in my chemise—and less!"

Van Ryker fingered his sword. His expression grew wicked in the extreme. "Has he, now?" he asked softly.

She tugged impatiently at his arm. "Oh, you are not to harm him for it! For it was Darnwell who saved my life when I had the fever. He cared for me here—right here, day and night until the fever was broken."

"Alone?" Van Ryker was thunderstruck.

"All alone," murmured Darnwell with a sigh.

"And there were no women about? Only himself?"

"Van Ryker, he dared not bring in a woman—he had to blindfold the doctor he brought to see me and make him think he'd been dragged somewhere down the coast. Darnwell fed me, bathed me—"

"*Bathed* you?" Van Ryker's voice rose thunderously.

"Yes—and why are *you* so scandalized? You did the same thing aboard the *Sea Rover* when you thought I was like to die."

"You see?" murmured Lord Marr, from his seated position. "The lady's logic is beyond reproach." His mouth still smiled but his eyes looked tired, as if he had fought some great inner battle.

"Darnwell gave me back my *life*!" cried Imogene. "I'd not be standing here now without him. Oh, 'tis ridiculous to keep him tied up, van Ryker. Your men are here to prevent his escape." She went over and began untying Darnwell's bonds.

Darnwell gazed at the buccaneer. "As you've observed, she sweeps all before her!" He gave van Ryker the benefit of his engaging smile. "It was my original intention to capture you, make a great stir about it and bring myself to the favorable attention of the king—hoping by that new-gained favor to rid myself of this abominable post and get me back to England and some position at court. But then I met your lady . . ."

Van Ryker was considering him narrowly. They could hear oaths as footsteps sounded on the stairs. "And what did you have in mind for my brothers?" he wondered.

Imogene had run into the next room and was hastily pulling on her petticoat and overskirt, but she heard clearly the next words.

"I had in mind to hang them," said Lord Marr cheerfully. "Anthony for the murder of Vincent Dunworth in England. Charles for the attempted murder of the Reverend Gibbons. Imogene would not have been involved."

Imogene smiled and came out, pulling on her lavender shepherdess bodice.

"And Esme?" Van Ryker's frown deepened. Imogene could see that in spite of all that Esme had done, he was remembering her as a little girl—he still felt protective toward her as he had long ago. "What were you going to do with her? Hang her with the others?"

Lord Marr sighed. "No, I was not. As you once so aptly pointed out"—he turned to Imogene with a crooked grin—"Esme was a woman I had held in my arms. I could not face the sight of her big amethyst eyes staring down at me from a gibbet. No, I had something else in mind for Esme, I will admit. I was going to turn her over—in the wicker trunk—to the French pirate, Captain Vartel, to do with as he pleased."

"To Vartel?" cried Imogene indignantly. "But he'd have sold her in Tangier!"

Van Ryker ripped out an oath and his blade came up.

Lord Marr gave them a jaded look. "She would not have been hurt—nor sold in Tangier, either." He faced the tall buccaneer. "You are not the only man who sails under false colors, van Ryker. Other men than you have taken new names to suit their new roles in life. Captain Vartel's real name is not Vartel but Ribaud—Jules Ribaud. He is Esme's husband."

Imogene's jaw dropped, and van Ryker looked thunderstruck.

"I assure you it is true," said Lord Marr coolly. "As true as that your sister Esme sold your body to me for future delivery here in Port Royal. She did not want her brothers to know of it—and I now realize that was because she planned to eliminate them as well and thus secure for herself your entire estate. You have a nice sister there, van Ryker."

"Half-sister," growled van Ryker, "and soon to be no sister at all."

"Oh, you won't kill her?" cried Imogene, looking up in alarm as she struggled with her hooks.

Van Ryker turned on her with a frown. "I seem to remember you asked me the same question about a fool of a cabin boy on the quay at Cayona! 'Tis plain this buccaneering life doesn't suit you, which is the reason you're leaving it. I've no intent at all to harm Esme or Charles or Tony—nor do I plan to see them hang."

The brothers had just arrived, urged on by the point of de Rochemont's blade.

"I'm sending them all to Vartel, tied in one package, and he can transport them to whatever port he chooses. But when I cut these ropes"—van Ryker's blade slashed out and severed the ropes that bound the wrists of a cringing Charles—"I sever all connections as well. Ye're no longer kin of mine. As for you, Tony"—his blade adroitly cut the ropes that bound his eldest brother—"I was sailing in intending to *give* you Gale Force for you and Charles to enjoy perpetually, and was going to make a London agent guardian of Esme and her fortunes, but now—!"

"Branch, you don't understand!" Anthony, to his last breath, would try to recoup.

"I understand well enough," growled van Ryker. "Take them away. Get them from my sight!"

"You realize what this will do to the pardon you'll no doubt be seeking?" interposed Lord Marr politely. "I mean, you've just helped several notorious criminals escape punishment for their crimes."

The countenance van Ryker turned on him was stern. "Well do I realize it. Ask yourself, in my place, could you do otherwise?"

Lord Marr's worldly face turned thoughtful. "Perhaps not," he admitted reflectively. "And with such store of treasure as you have amassed, I doubt me not you can buy a king's pardon at will."

"Give me leave to doubt it," said van Ryker heavily. "For I've no mind to pay a king's ransom for a king's pardon for a crime I never committed!"

"But confessed to," pointed out Lord Marr.

Van Ryker gave him an angry look. "Beside the point," he growled.

"However, I do confess I'm obliged to you for ridding the island of such ill-doers as these," said Darnwell affably. He looked at Imogene. "She's having trouble with that last hook, van Ryker—it's a tricky one." His smile was bland. He watched as van Ryker bent to secure the recalcitrant hook.

"We need strong intelligent planters here—men such as yourself, van Ryker. I've seen your goodly plantation at Gale Force. I would like to see you occupy it—with your bride." He gave Imogene a blithe smile. "As governor here I have some leeway, and 'tis my intention to forward my own request to the king for the pardon of one Branch Ryder, to whom I perceive some past wrongs have been done—supported of course by the confession of one Esme Ribaud, which confession I had the good fortune to witness. Since I have never laid eyes on the buccaneer van Ryker—who sails not into Port Royal for personal reasons of his own—no one can expect me to recognize him among the planters here. Especially since he will use a name which will by then have been cleared." He gave the surprised van Ryker a cheerful look. "I will send word to you in Tortuga when your pardon comes through."

"I cannot believe it," said van Ryker softly. "Ye would do this for me after—" He cast a significant look at Imogene, just now fluffing out her hair, which she realized was very disheveled.

"A man will do what he must to win a woman," sighed Darnwell. "And must take his licks when he loses."

Van Ryker regarded him with some sympathy. He remembered well to what lengths *he* had been willing to go to win Imogene.

"If you would care to look on the writing desk downstairs," added Darnwell casually, "you will find a packet with your request for pardon already written out. And you may add your half-sister Esme's confession—once I have witnessed it." His crooked smile flashed again. "That message you had me pen to the Jamaica Squadron—twas unnecessary. I had already sent word to them to be about their business elsewhere."

Van Ryker stared at him. "*Why*?"

Darnwell turned a suddenly wistful gaze toward the resplendent woman who shone like a candle as she watched them quietly. "Need you ask?" he murmured.

Van Ryker sheathed his sword and suddenly offered his

hand. "Though 'twas for my lady that you did it, it is I who will profit. For now I can add the promise of some gold and the king is like to grant my petition."

"Aye, that he is—for Charles loves gold."

Cynical green eyes looked into cynical gray ones—in complete understanding.

"May I tell the lady good-bye?" asked Darnwell. There was a yearning in his voice van Ryker understood—and sympathized with. Long go he had had to leave this lady, and it had turned knives in his heart.

He nodded and moved away from them.

In two strides Darnwell was beside Imogene. "Say the word," he murmured, "and I'll rid the world of your buccaneer, for behind that door unknown to him stand a dozen armed men ready to burst through and take him. And then you and I . . . " He let the words, fraught with meaning, trail off.

Looking up at him, Imogene's wide lovely eyes were very steady, but she swayed toward him and his gaze kindled and flared up.

Until suddenly he realized that she had drawn his sword. She flung away from him, holding the point very steadily against his chest.

"If there are armed men outside," she said softly, "you will not call them. For if you seek to destroy van Ryker, 'tis *I* who will put a blade between your ribs!"

Across the room van Ryker's big muscles rippled and he was about to spring forward when he saw the sudden wry smile that lit his rival's face.

"Imogene, put the sword away," sighed Darnwell. "Van Ryker is safe from me because you love him and"—he gave her a rakish grin—"there *are* no armed men. You understand, I had to try. For if I thought you could learn to love me, I would turn about on that great fellow yonder and have at him—despite all his buccaneers!"

Imogene gave him an uncertain look, but she let the sword point sink to the floor. "In all this world, Darnwell, I think you would have been my second choice," she said frankly.

"And I think that in another time, another place, we would have been lovers."

"Ah, yes." He sighed. "Another time, another place . . . "

"Before I met van Ryker. But you must understand, Darnwell, that I am his—I will always be his."

The London rake smiled down on her, a very loving glance. He told himself he would not have her otherwise than honest and clear-eyed and forever true. For she was all of these things and more. Her wild spirit had called out to him and he had answered that call, deep and full. But she was bound by wings of the wind to another man. Eternally. He had to face it.

Darnwell Keating, once a London rake and now Lord Marr, new governor of Jamaica, lifted Imogene's hand to his lips and smiled deep into her delft blue eyes. "Whenever I lift my glass," he said, drowning in their blue depths, "I will drink to another time, another place."

Imogene's lashes were wet with unshed tears. "I will remember you, Darnwell," she whispered mistily. "*And always wish you well*. Silently she gave him back his sword.

Across the room, van Ryker watched with narrowed eyes as his rival sheathed that sword. He guessed that Lord Marr was still half a mind to spring at him and settle the contest there and then.

But Darnwell Keating, black sheep of his illustrious family, was for once bent on doing the Right Thing.

"Do not forget your packet," he sighed, his wistful gaze roving over Imogene. "For it holds the key to another life for you." He turned moodily to the tall buccaneer. "And I would have that life for you, van Ryker—not for your sake, you understand, but to pleasure a lady."

Green eyes glinted into gray again.

"About my plantation here in Jamaica," said the buccaneer frankly. "Are ye saying I may occupy it freely without being bothered by English law?"

"While I am governor ye may—but not right yet. Wait a few months. For I'm a man of hot blood and tomorrow if I saw Imogene walking through Spanish Town or strolling the quay here in Port Royal, I might forget my promise and loose the Jamaica Squadron on ye yet.''

"I understand," grinned van Ryker. "Time heals all. Good luck to you in your governorship. Jamaica's a fine place, but hard to govern. And if ye choose to come to Tortuga, send me word and I'll furnish ye safe passage into Cayona Bay."

Van Ryker could afford to be generous, thought Lord Marr, sighing in his heart, *for he had the woman. . . .*

That night on board the *Sea Rover* on their way to Tortuga, Imogene and van Ryker held their own celebration.

They conducted it in the wide bunk of the great cabin with their arms about each other and their bodies locked in warm embrace. That they should be together again seemed the stuff of miracles.

Van Ryker's voice was deep with triumph as he told her of his success with the Spanish treasure fleet, and softened as he added, "Now I can give you all your heart desires."

"You could have given me that without capturing the treasure fleet, van Ryker," she murmured. "For all I ever wanted was to linger in your arms."

"As you shall do," he promised her hoarsely, fitting his big body to her slight one.

"Promise that you will never leave me."

"That is a promise."

"And that you will give up this buccaneering life?"

"Granted."

"And take me with you wherever you go."

"Always."

"And promise"—she was whispering now, softly against his lips—"that you will always, always love me."

"Imogene," he murmured, as he had once before, "how could you ever doubt it?"

She clung to him wordlessly and let his lean body tell her more vividly than words that he would never cease to love her. Together they sighed and swayed and embraced and let their feverish bodies rise and fall to a rhythm older than time. Tears of joy were wet upon her cheeks, for she had thought for a time tonight that she would never hold him in her arms again—and now he would be hers. Forever.

Such a woman was Georgiana's mother—little Georgiana, who was being brought up in Bermuda as Anna Smith.

BOOK III
Anna

On the day her mother bore her,
A sighing bitter wind
Swept sear across the rooftops
And promised her—to him!

PART ONE
The Little Princess

Like the reckless lass who bore you,
You will fling yourself at life.
Will you end up, island beauty,
Mistress, chatelaine, or—wife?

The Bermuda Islands, 1673

CHAPTER 21

In the diamond-clear weather the crests of those giant submarine mountains shipwrecked British sailors had named the Summer Islands rose from the sea to sparkle like emeralds in the sun. To the high-flying gulls the low rounded green hills of those islands must have seemed like jeweled links in a frilly necklace of foaming coral reefs—and all of it surrounded by crystalline depths of brilliant blue that rivaled the sky in intensity. The gulls saw other sights too, for from the air an occasional cruciform plantation house cut its white stone cross into the green.

In heat unseasonable to early June, humid heat that seemed to oppress and smother the white manor house of Mirabelle Plantation, seated on the broad stone front steps that widened out in a graceful curve to form what everyone called "welcoming arms," young Mistress Anna Smith was holding court. Her thick shining hair, of a burnished gold so deep it was copper in some lights, was fashionably caught up and her curls shimmered and danced in the sun. Just beyond the toe of one strawberry pink satin slipper that peeked from her pale strawberry silk skirts, a grinning little black slave boy languidly waved a big palm-leaf fan mounted on a broomstick, meant to keep cool the young lady and the two ardent suitors who importuned her on either side.

The young lady was but fifteen but she was tall for her age and beautiful and, by the standards of her day, eligible for marriage. Indeed, most of her friends were wed already— Anna had been bridesmaid to one who'd been wed two years ago at the ripe old age of twelve.

Young Mistress Smith smiled indulgently at the boy waving the fan—she was well liked by all the staff on the plantation— and her dark-lashed turquoise eyes flashed as she vividly recounted to the two enraptured youths who flanked her pale strawberry skirts on either side how this morning she had ridden her new silver mare, Floss, up under the giant cedars that rose on the hill behind the house and thundered down to the white beach to ride gaily through the foaming surf. Her light voice bubbled with laughter as she told them how Belize, one of the black servants at that moment engaged in whitewashing the thick coral stone roof slabs an even more sparkling white, had stood up on the roof and yelled, "Mis' Anna, you goin' to kill yourself on that horse!" as she flashed by the house on her wild descent to the sea.

"He almost fell off the roof," she laughed. "And wouldn't Papa Jamison have taken a switch to me if I'd caused poor Belize to fall into that big clump of pink oleanders he prizes so!"

"That clump would have broken his fall," declared Ross Wybourne, a tall lad of seventeen summers who sat on her right on the stone steps. "He'd have walked away from it none the worse." As he spoke he caught a whiff of the lime scent with which young Mistress Smith had rinsed her hair that morning. It was a heady fragrance and made him slightly dizzy—as Mistress Smith's nearness always did.

"Ah, but the oleanders wouldn't have survived it! And Papa Jamison imported them by ship and coaxed them to grow—sometimes I think he treasures those oleanders more than anything at Mirabelle!"

"He treasures *you*, Mistress Anna, the most of anything at

Mirabelle," declared Lance Talbot, the tall young gentleman in apricot satins on her left. His fascinated gaze was not on the young lady's face however, but on the exposed flesh of her deep-cut square neckline. That skin was very fair and seemed to tease him. He swallowed.

Mistress Smith had noted with a touch of amused cynicism the direction of Lance's avid glance. She was wary of sandy-haired Lance Talbot, even though she could not but admire—as did all her friends—the sight of his tall figure swaying in the saddle as he spurred his roan stallion to victory over the other island lads in the impromptu horse races that were so popular. Lance was given to dalliance, to swift dangerous flirtations, and island matrons had taken to warning their marriageable daughters against him ever since two young ladies of St. George had married hastily after having hot flirtations with Lance. Lance was saved from being foppish by an unruly shock of sandy hair that never looked truly combed.

He's false, thought Anna distastefully, as he gave her his most winning smile. For hadn't she caught him herself with Gilly Carter, and the Carter girl's skirts up half over her head? And when Anna almost tripped over them as she helped search for Old Bowzer's puppies, Gilly had blushed scarlet and cried in a half-hysterical voice that they thought they'd seen one puppy beneath the hedge and were trying to crawl through to it! In the face of this patently ridiculous excuse, Anna had maintained a suitable gravity. She had turned tactfully away but not before she had glimpsed Lance's frantic embarrassed struggle to adjust his trousers. And the Carter girl's mother had come out and found them just then and shrilled to her daughter to "Come in the house at once!" And a month later Gilly Carter had found herself mincing to the alter with a doddering third cousin once removed!

Lance might be false—but he was fun, Anna admitted grudgingly as she smiled into his merry green eyes so alive now with overheated interest in her. A superb rider, he was always cantering over on Cavalier, his big roan stallion, and if he found her out strolling he'd sweep her up before him on the saddle and gallop away—for Lance loved riding above all

else. Only yesterday he had taken her for a long ride along
the deserted white beach. They had walked their horses
companionably along the lacy edge of surf, watching it
endlessly advance and retreat. As usual, Lance had been
talking about marriage, but Anna had hardly heard him. His
eager voice had blended into the boom of the ocean and the
crunch of the horses' hooves grinding into the talc-soft coral
sand. She had thrown back her bright head and let the wind
take her hair and watched the wheeling cahows and gulls
swooping overhead. She had looked out to sea at the lazy red
sails of a little fishing boat tacking perilously near the reefs
and felt a deep content with her island. All the world had
seemed a blue and white shimmer in her turquoise eyes.

She had almost forgotten Lance when he suddenly interrupted
his latest impassioned proposal with a critical, "Your stirrup's
loose."

Anna had kicked her foot negligently. "No, it isn't."

"It is. I can see it is. Here, stop and let me tighten it."

Beside a twisted gnarl of coral rock, battered by wind and
wave, they had halted their horses and Lance had dismounted,
ostensibly to tighten her stirrup, which he still insisted was
loose, but actually to find an excuse for taking hold of her
dainty foot and ankle that he might caress them as he talked.
He was pressing his courtship, urging her to marry him and
when she had leaned down, laughing, to free her ankle from
his warm hand, her burnished gold hair had spilled across his
narrow face. The blood had rushed to his face at the contact
with those silken strands and his grip had tightened on her
ankle as he told her in excited terms that their union would be
a wondrous one—for would it not combine their stables? If
she had no care for him—and ah, but she'd learn to love him
in time—she should think of the two equine bloodlines that
would be thus united! Floss mated with Cavalier! Bonny Joe
with Jezebel! While Anna laughingly protested, still trying to
pry his fingers loose from her ankle, he had leaned closer.
With his hot breath blowing on her cheek, he had extolled the
virtues of Cavalier, his big roan stallion. What a mate for
dainty Floss!

"There's no need for us to get married just to mate Floss with Cavalier!"

"Of course not, Anna." He had nipped playfully at her—exactly as Floss had done only that morning. He smelled like horseflesh too—but wasn't that logical? He spent all his time in the stables. "Just wait till we're married—you'll agree then!"

"You may wait a long time for that," she warned dryly.

His confident laugh rang out, for her heady nearness had inspired in him the mistaken belief that she favored his suit. "Not long. I dare say we'll be married before the summer's over."

"Would you care to wager on it?" Anna had given him a determined push that had at last freed her ankle.

Staggering backward a step, Lance had looked dashed. His long sandy hair fell over his face like a disconsolate mane. "Don't be hasty, Anna," he pleaded. "When you think it over, you'll realize how right we are for each other. Combined, we'd have the best stable on the island—and remember, you love horses as much as I do!"

"Not as much as you do, Lance," Anna had sighed. "Nobody could!"

She had nudged Floss with her knee and galloped away from him over the sand, leaving him to spring to Cavalier's back and thunder after her crying, "I'll keep on asking you, Anna!" As the warm breeze from the ocean whipped against her face, Anna had felt vaguely sorry for the girl who would eventually marry Lance, for after the first flush of honeymoon joy was over, Lance would spend his time not in her bed but in his beloved stables, and Lance's wife would find herself slightly above his dog in his affections—but far below his horse!

And to Anna Smith that thought was appalling. In whatever she did, Mistress Smith had a burning need to be first. As much as Lance, who usually finished first in a race, she was imbued with the will to win. And to come second in the affections of a husband?

Now, seated on the stone front steps, the very thought

made her shudder, but she covered that brief involuntary
tremor with a shrug that made her delicately molded young
breasts, trapped in the tight bodice of her strawberry gown,
move appealingly before Lance's delighted gaze.

"It's so hot," she murmured. And to the grinning little
black slave boy who was languidly waving his broomstick fan
over the heads of the company, "Boz, can't you fan a little
faster? No, never mind—a breeze is coming up. You can go
round to the bakehouse and see if the cakes are ready. Tell
Mossy we'd like them served out here with tankards of
limeade."

Hot baking cakes! The palm-leaf fan was flung down and
little Boz was up and circling the house on the run. He almost
crashed into Belize's ladder on his way to the bakehouse.
Belize, just descending that ladder, splashed the white lime-
wash paint onto his homespun trousers and shook his big fist
at Boz as he streaked by. "You, Boz, you knock over this
ladder and I tan your hide for you!"

But sprinting Boz was already out of hearing. He arrived
out of breath at the bakehouse to inquire, panting, into the
readiness of the cakes. Boz had no fear of Big Belize, whose
bark was far worse than his bite, nor of kindly Mistress
Anna, whom all the house servants adored. When Mossy
turned her back, Boz reached out and snatched a bit of cake,
yipped as he burned his fingers. Mossy shouted epithets at
him, but Boz laughed and ran away. With Tobias Jamison
away and Mistress Anna in full charge, nobody was about to
punish *him*!

As the cakes were served hot with honey by wide-hipped
smiling Mossy in her brilliant pink turban and magenta skirts,
the conversation lapsed into, "Oh, this is good!" and "Watch
out, you'll burn your fingers!" and Lance's jovial "Ross,
you're dribbling honey on your trousers!"

"Look out, Lance, you will too!" laughed Anna, glancing
at those resplendent apricot breeches glowing in the afternoon
sun. "What were you saying, Ross?"

"I asked, How long will Mr. Jamison be gone this voyage,
Mistress Anna?" Ross was licking the finger that he had
burned on a too hot cake.

"I don't know," she told him frankly. "He's never spent this long a time in Jamaica before. I'd expected him back long before this. I do hope nothing's happened to him."

"His ships are sound, his captains all good seamen," Ross assured her.

But over Anna's bright head, bent over the tray of cakes as she selected another one, the two young fellows looked at each other with a wild surmise. If widowed Tobias Jamison was dead, his ship foundered in some storm off Jamaica where he had been bound, then young Anna Smith, who was mistress of the plantation when he was gone, would become sole owner of Mirabelle—for Tobias Jamison had often enough announced publicly his intention of leaving all he owned to the young girl he thought of affectionately as a daughter. And Mirabelle was a wealthy holding, including not only rich pastures and cultivated lands on which Tobias Jamison had lavished his wealth and his endeavor, but tall stands of the native cedars for which these islands were famous, a massive stone house of the admired cruciform style that were flung like white crosses all across these green islands, handsome furniture—some of it imported from England and France— much plate, as well as a number of slaves and bondservants, indentured for varying periods of servitude.

If Tobias Jamison did not survive this journey to Jamaica, in short, Anna Smith would be an heiress—and the catch of Bermuda.

Neither lad meant to lose such a golden opportunity.

So now on the front steps of the big cross-shaped house at Mirabelle, two bedazzled young fortune hunters were vying for Mistress Smith's wandering attention.

"How white your lace is, Mistress Anna!" exclaimed Lance admiringly, his gaze not on the froth of white lace that spilled from her full puffed sleeves to cascade down over her slender forearms, but on Mistress Smith's ripe young breasts so round and fascinating beneath the supple silk.

"It's new," Anna told him carelessly. "Papa Jamison bought it for me from Captain Tygart of the *Shallot,* who said he'd bought it in the marketplace in Tortuga along with a lot of braid and ribands. He said it came from France."

"By way of Tortuga?" Lance's gaze lifted from Mistress Smith's ravishing breasts to encounter her mocking smile. "Then it will be pirate loot, and the buccaneers—"

"Will have had it from some Spanish galleon who stole it from a French merchant ship peacefully sailing these waters," said Anna calmly.

"The lace *is* uncommon white," chimed in Ross, thrusting out his broad chest in his determination not to be left out of the conversation. Before he could comment on the long pink riband that trailed down through Mistress Smith's gleaming curls, Lance echoed, "White as snow. Have you ever seen snow, Mistress Anna?"

"You know I haven't!" she laughed.

"Well, I have. Last winter in Philadelphia it snowed and snowed. People made great balls of it, white like cotton. They built snow forts and pelted each other. And they harnessed horses to their sleds and glided about on long iron runners, and skated on the ice."

"I wish I'd been there to see it," said Anna pensively. Snow was something she had only heard of but never seen; it never snowed in Bermuda. She had seen pictures of snow-covered landscapes, of course, with icicles dripping from the eaves, and heard what it was like from people like Lance, who had voyaged to England and America. It was strange, but the very word "snow" evoked in her a kind of shivery expectant feeling. She could not know that her copper-haired father had loved the snow and spent long days ice-skating and evenings by a roaring fire as big white flakes drifted down outside. This love of the snow country was in her blood, but young Anna did not know that—yet.

"I've just learned that my father's having the *Leeward* refitted and we'll be sailing her to Turks Islands for salt next spring," cut in Ross, determined not to be outdone.

"You are?" cried Lance, for the moment forgetting the tempting feminine charms beside him. "And will you be going trading through the islands, Ross? I'm told there's some fine horses to be had!"

"Oh, yes—though maybe not for horses." Ross gave a

careless shrug. He had the long-sighted look of the deep-water sailor about him and he'd spent so much time on ships that he walked with a slight roll. "Mostly we'll be going for salt."

"I envy you, Ross! You won't have to stay and rake up salt in the pans yourself?"

"No. We'll go out with a cargo of cabbages and onions and whale oil and building stone and leave most of our crew—and all of our bondsmen and slaves—on Turks to rake up the salt."

Anna frowned. It seemed to her that ever since the Bermudians had taken over Turks Islands all the eligible young men were always gone. "But you'll be gone from May to October, then," she protested.

"Longer! For we'll trade our cargo in the islands for rum and sugar and then make a run to the American coast and trade *that* for Indian corn. After we've brought the corn home, we'll load up again and pick up the salt and the men and go trading again through the islands before we come home for good."

"You'll be gone for months, Ross!"

Ross nodded proudly and Lance, dazzled by the prospect, felt quite eclipsed by the anticipated voyage. "I'll ask my father," he said. "Perhaps he'll let me sign on with you."

"Perhaps he will," agreed Ross, who was a great friend of Lance's, competing with him only for Mistress Anna's affections. "I hope so."

"Of course, both my mares will be foaling this summer and I'd hate to miss that—but think what stock I might pick up trading in the islands!" His green eyes sparkled at the prospect.

"Ho, ho, 'tis I who'll be going trading to the islands—not you," his friend jibed. "If you do sign on, you'll have to stay and rake salt on Turks!"

"Not if my father puts in a share of the money for the cargo," protested Lance.

They were happily wrangling now and Anna bent to pet the big tortoiseshell cat, Coral, who was rubbing her black and white and orange sides against Anna's ankles and purring. Ross, she thought, had a wife already—the sea. He would always love the sea more than he loved any woman. And like most sailors, he'd seldom be home. Only last week at a garden party given by Gilly Carter, Ross had separated Anna from the pack and in the shade of a towering oleander bush most earnestly declared his love. The corners of Anna's lips twitched with amusement as she remembered how he had launched from there directly into a description of a ship he'd seen last year on Turks. A real beauty, she was—and for sale! With her dowry, they could have the ship for their wedding voyage!

Anna gave him a rueful but affectionate look. Ross, bluff sailor that he was, felt that she should feel about the sea as he did—that it was mother, father, mistress, wife. . . . Perhaps someday some woman would share that feeling with him, but Anna knew she was not that woman.

She turned at a flutter of cloth down the drive and saw a lone horseman approaching down the long green alley of trees. Although she could not see the face of the rider, whose mop of yellow curls was bent over a piece of parchment as he rode, there was no mistaking the tall lanky form in that tasseled doublet of popinjay green.

This would be Grenfell Adams with another sonnet. The last one he had written to her eyelashes—perhaps this time he would make so bold as to address her entire face.

Anna chuckled inwardly. Grenfell's awkwardly coltish appearance was made ludicrous by clothes two sizes too large, for Grenfell's doting mother—despite the fact that her little lad was all of twenty-three—incessantly badgered the tailors with her prattle that Grenfell was but a "growing boy." Studious Grenfell, more interested in the flight of a butterfly than in his appearance, never stood against her in this matter or any other.

As Grenfell approached, Anna saw that his lips were moving; he was talking to himself. Nearing the house, he slid off his handsome mount, almost tripping himself up with the stirrup, and absentmindedly left the beast unhitched to fend for himself in the driveway. The sleek sorrel horse looked about, decided the grass at the driveway's edge would do well enough, and began to munch it as his beaming master, flush-faced, ambled toward the front steps and gave Anna a sweeping bow.

"Mistress Anna!" Grenfell's myopic hazel eyes peered at her from his thin eager face. "What luck I've found you at home!" He sounded as surprised and delighted as if this were not her residence. He nodded tolerantly at the two lads, who stopped wrangling to frown at him, for each considered him a dangerous rival—nothing to look at, of course, but with money and an annoying knack for making rhymes.

"I'm usually here," sighed Anna. "Sit down and have some cakes. Boz"—to the little boy lurking in the bushes—"go fetch another tankard from Mossy. How are you, Grenfell?"

"Fine as silk, Mistress Anna." Grenfell remained ceremoniously standing.

"And your father?"

"Fell off his horse, laid up now for a week or two in splints. Gave me time to canter down here to see you. And wait till you discover what I've brought you!"

"*I* brought roses," muttered Lance.

"And I brought a fine bottle of Canary," said Ross with some asperity.

Grenfell gave them both a quelling look. "Material things," he scoffed. "*I* bring Mistress Anna something far better. I bring her verse!"

Anna nearly choked with amusement at the indignant faces that flanked her on either side. "Read on, Grenfell," she said with composure.

"No, I know not if I should." Grenfell hesitated. "Poetry speaks best when spoke in private."

"No doubt," she told him dryly. "But as you see, I have guests. Either you must read your verses to us all or leave them for me to peruse later."

That he should not be heard and at once was unbearable to Grenfell. "I'll recite them now," he said hastily. "For I did commit them to memory on my way here: "*The sea-depths*

*cannot match your matchless eyes. / The breaking surf, it
cannot match your sighs.''*

Lance snickered and nudged Ross. Anna gave him a
reproving look. Grenfell seemed not to notice. He went on:
''Your hair is sunlight and you are so wise!''

"I'm not wise," objected Anna.

"But it rhymes!" cried Grenfell. He hurried on:*''Your little
foot has trod upon my heart, / Made me your slave and set
us both apart!''*

"Her little foot!" muttered Lance. "Blast you, Grenfell,
how does that set you apart?"

"Why, Mistress Anna and I are set apart by our love of
verse!" cried Grenfell in a wounded tone. "Wait, there's
more! *For your vast beauty I am sore beholden / And brave
I stand before your hair so golden!''*

" 'Vast beauty'?" cried Ross. "You make Mistress Anna
seem a whale and not a woman. Let's see how brave you are!
Here, Ross, let's set this fool backward upon his horse and
see if the animal can find his way home, for the rider
assuredly cannot!"

Inwardly convulsed by Grenfell's ungainly lines uttered
with such fire and fervor, Anna leaped up before Lance could
lay hands on Grenfell and caught him by the arm. "You
forget that Grenfell is my guest!" she gasped. She was
red-faced and sparkling-eyed from her effort not to laugh, for
to laugh at his verse would have been to crush Grenfell
utterly. "You'll not lay hands on him here at Mirabelle or
I'll—I'll not speak to either one of you until after the Waites'
ball. That's a fortnight away. Nor dance with you at the ball,
either!"

Aghast at the thought, Lance fell back from a distraught
Grenfell. "But, Mistress Anna, surely I'm squiring ye to the
Waites' ball!"

"No, I am!" shouted Ross, standing up to shoulder Lance
aside.

Anna stood up and stamped her foot. "Both of you, sit
down! You asked me, Lance, but I have not said I'd go with
you." She shook her head at him reprovingly and her burnished
gold curls danced against her white neck. "Ross has asked

me too and so has Grenfell here and''—she gave a happy sigh—''half a dozen others, but I've yet to make up my mind in whose carriage I'll ride! Indeed, I may decide to take my own—in case I get a headache and decide to leave early.''

''But you've never had a headache in your life!'' exclaimed Ross in astonishment. ''Mistress Alma Waite—she has them all the time, but never you, Mistress Anna!''

Anna secretly thought it rather overdone, the way Alma Waite was always having the ''vapors'' at strategic moments, but pretty Alma did have a very fetching way of touching her forehead with rosewater and declaring herself unable to cope with the inequities of life. She had been pondering on imitating Alma and this outburst of Ross's irritated her.

''How would you know whether my head aches or not, Ross Wybourne? I see you not twice a week!''

'' 'Tis my father keeps me away!'' cried Ross. ''I mean—'' his honest ruddy face reddened—'' 'tis my duties at home.''

Anna knew exactly what he meant. Ross's seafaring father was skeptical that little Anna Smith would ever actually inherit Tobias Jamison's plantation and his ships. Ross's father had an eye for his son's future; let the lad marry some likely girl whose father had but one ship—and but one daughter to leave it to, and she of his own flesh and blood.

As for Lance, she thought cynically, his parents probably didn't know that he was riding constant attendance on Anna Smith. And Grenfell—well, it was rumored that his family would finally be sending him off to Oxford—if his mother could bear to part with her darling little boy, where he would become, Anna supposed affectionately, an educated fool. But perhaps—she chuckled inwardly—better at composing verse!

But although all three had asked for her hand in marriage and Anna was thoroughly enjoying their pursuit, she had no real intention of marrying any of them—even if Papa Jamison would let her, and he insisted that Anna was far too young to think seriously of betrothal.

Someday, of course, she told herself she would be married . . . perhaps in St. Peter's Church, the white limewashed parish church of St. George with its lighthouselike square belfry, where Papa Jamison and Anna attended ser-

vices, sweeping grandly into their box pew. Sometimes on
Sundays in the days when Mamma Jamison had been alive,
she had sat between Mamma and Papa Jamison with her
hands demurely folded in her silken lap, her feet that yearned
to be dancing peeping out from beneath her fancy silk
petticoats, and briefly closed her eyes. She would forget the
stern sermon being intoned from the three-deck cedar pulpit
and imagine that wedding.

How merrily the wedding party would sweep into the
church! Or perhaps . . . perhaps she would decide to be married at home, in the great cruciform house at Mirabelle. In
either case, she would wear a white dress of delicate imported
lace brought by one of the ships that dared the reefs to make
harbor in St. George. And around her slender neck would be
a necklace of West Indian pearls. She pictured herself standing
before the high-flung paneled cedar fireplace of the main
drawing room. The fireplace's big wooden double doors
would be closed because it was summer and the light streaming in through the deep-silled windows that flanked it on either
side would turn her hair with its circlet of myrtle to a blaze of
light, almost as brilliant as the shining polished brass candlesticks that caught the sun's rays and cast dancing light up past
the handsome cove moulding to the higher reaches of the high
slope-sided "tray ceiling" that gave the big room such
airiness.

She would stand before that fireplace in bridal white,
smelling the faint pungent scent of the cedar fireplace, the
carved cedar furniture, and she would take her vows to be
faithful always to—somehow she could never see his face.
She imagined him tall and dark but his face eluded her.

Usually at this point she would receive a small nudge from
the toe of Mamma Jamison's velvet slipper and her turquoise
eyes would fly open and she would be back again in the
familiar box pew in the familiar church and find the minister's eyes fixed on her sternly, for he too had noticed Mistress
Smith's frequently closed eyes and firmly believed she caught
"catnaps" sitting up during his sermons. He might have done
more than just give her a chiding look, but since he frequent-

ly took supper at Mirabelle and greatly fancied Tobias Jamison's stock of metheglin and Canary, he prudently overlooked this inattention of what amounted to a daughter of the house.

Anna abandoned her daydreams of marriage and came back to the present. All three of her guests were glaring at one another.

"I'll challenge all of you to a race!" cried Lance. "And the winner squires Mistress Anna to the ball!"

Grenfell, who had the best horse but was a sorry rider, demurred. "My horse was near to losing her shoe on the way over. I must have her to a blacksmith before she throws the shoe."

Lance, recognizing this as a weak excuse, gave Grenfell a look of pure contempt. "Then you're out of it," he declared flatly. "How about you, Ross? Down to the bend and turn around and the first one back here, Mistress Anna shall declare the winner?"

Anna's turquoise eyes sparkled. She enjoyed being wrangled over, contested for.

"Gentlemen, mount your horses!" she cried, tearing free the light kerchief, or whisk, around her neck that was intended to keep prying eyes from the lowest part of her square-necked gown, and waving it in the air. "When I bring down this whisk, you will start—and may the best man win!"

"The best man will win!" growled Lance, running to unhitch his roan stallion even as Ross unhitched his bay mare. As one man—for they were both excellent horsemen—they vaulted to the saddle, sat impatiently waiting for Anna's signal.

"Go!" Anna brought the light whisk down dramatically and the two young men were off, neck and neck, in a cloud of dust.

"Mistress Anna." It was Grenfell at her side.

"Yes, Grenfell?" Anna was impatient at this interruption, for her gaze was glued to the racers, thundering down the driveway toward the turn, which was obscured by a clump of trees at the far end.

"I told ye a falsehood, Mistress Anna. My horse was shod

only yesterday. 'Twas my way of having a moment alone with you.''

Anna turned to him in astonishment. "Since your sorrel is the best horse, Grenfell, you might have won—and then we could have had lots of time alone as we danced together at the Waites' ball.''

"But that's not alone, Mistress Anna," he insisted. "I mean—well, *alone*. I would speak with you privately.''

"Well, speak!" she said impatiently, for the riders were fast approaching the turn.

"Then look at me, Mistress Anna," said Grenfell plaintively. "You well know my love for you and—"

"No!" cried Anna. "Stop!" she shouted, and Grenfell fell back, his face paling in alarm. But his heart's desire was already dashing away from him. Now she had seized his horse's bridle, for Grenfell had not bothered to hitch the gentle animal but let her graze nearby. Anna vaulted aboard in a swirl of flying strawberry skirts and gave the sorrel mare a kick on the flanks. She was off down the course in pursuit of the two young men just now disappearing around the turn.

And now Grenfell, standing in open-mouthed bewilderment, saw what Anna's sharp eyes had already seen. So intent had they been upon their quarrel that none of them had observed a carriage flashing in and out between the big trees that flanked the narrow driveway beyond the blind turn, a carriage gay with color. Grenfell's horrified gaze focused on it—Ross and Lance were catapulting around that blind turn, and now the carriage, bent on a collision course with them on the narrow drive and all unknowing, had disappeared into the trees just ahead of them. *A carriage with ladies in it!*

He too began to run, pelting down the driveway after the girl, with her pink skirts flying, aboard the sorrel mare.

CHAPTER 22

The ladies in the carriage—and there were four of them, the Waite sisters—had been singing "Greensleeves." Their big pastel skirts overflowed the carriage sides and bounced merrily as the wheels jolted along the roughest part of Mirabelle's driveway. Their light voices, raised in song—and laughter too, for there wasn't a one among them who could carry a tune—had so diverted the elderly black driver in his stovepipe beaver hand-me-down hat that he had turned his grizzled head to look at them and was letting the horses find their own way down the familiar drive.

Thus it was that none among them had noticed the thud of oncoming hooves fast approaching—until it was too late.

The two young gentlemen, charging down their makeshift race course, rounded the blind turn neck and neck—and parted in surprise and horror as they found themselves faced with a head-on collision with a rearing horse and a carriage full of screaming women.

Ross managed to come to a skidding halt, pulling his bay mare's head back so hard that the poor beast slid along on her haunches. Lance, swerving to avoid the oncoming carriage, shot off his careening roan's back like an arrow to land unhurt but crestfallen in a clump of underbrush.

The ladies were not so lucky.

With their horse plunging and rearing up into the air, their delicate vehicle overturned and sent them off in a colorful heap, legs and arms waving, into the dusty road.

Into this scene rode Anna Smith.

"Are you hurt?" she cried, dismounting with a flash of silken legs that for once nobody noticed.

"Oh, Mis' Chloe!" the driver was moaning. His black face had gone ashen and he was down on his knees in the blue velvet trousers of which he was so inordinately proud, kneeling beside a rather large young woman in pastel green silk who was struggling ineffectually to rise. Now she fell back with a moan.

"Ross Wybourne and Lance Talbot, you have caused me to break my ankle!" she shrilled in the strident voice that had frightened off all the young men of the island and left her at eighteen an "old maid." Her face reddened until it was almost the color of her russet hair. "And I hold *you*, Anna, responsible!"

"Oh, Chloe, perhaps it isn't broken." Anxiously, Anna pushed the wailing black driver aside and bent to touch the injured ankle.

Chloe gave an angry moan. "Of course it's broken—and it's *your fault* for letting this pair of rakehells tear down your driveway as if they were leading a cavalry charge!"

"They were only racing to see who would take me to the ball at your house," protested Anna. "None of us saw you in time. There—does this hurt?" She was testing the ankle with gentle fingers.

"Of course it hurts!" snapped Chloe.

"Here, Mattie, Alma, Sue—help me get her up."

"I'll do that," cried Ross. "Lance, take her other side—we can boost her up gently."

"You'll not touch me, either one of you!" shouted Chloe.

"Let them help you," insisted Anna. "They're stronger than we are."

Over violent protests, as the other young ladies dusted themselves off and muttered, Chloe was helped to her feet. Gingerly she tested her right foot.

"Can you stand on it?" wondered Ross.

For answer, Chloe gave a sharp shriek and staggered—but remained upright.

"She can stand on it," said Anna with satisfaction. "It

isn't broken after all. Do you think you boys can right the carriage?"

Lance nodded. He was still somewhat shaken from being flung headfirst into the bushes and his handsome face was scratched. The nervous gray hitched to the carriage was still pawing the ground and shaking, but the black driver seized the reins and began to soothe the beast as the two young gentlemen set their broad shoulders to raising the fallen carriage.

Once it was back on its wheels they assisted the complaining Waite sisters back into it.

"Now lift Chloe back in," directed Anna, who had become used to command with Papa Jamison away so much.

This was accomplished with a large amount of groaning and several shrieks from Chloe.

"Now we'll all go back to the house," Anna looked at Grenfell, who had just come up to them and was staring helplessly about him. "Mount and help me up before you, Grenfell. We'll lead the way."

Grenfell complied with alacrity, for any contact with Mistress Smith's delicious body was more than welcome. He was quite flushed as he helped her up before him on the horse and she could feel him trembling as they led the carriage down the driveway to the front steps with Ross and Lance, thoroughly sobered and disheveled, bringing up the rear.

Ignoring Grenfell's look of mute appeal as they reached the steps—he had actually considered tightening his grip on her, wheeling the horse and running away with her for all time despite what his mother or anyone else might say—Anna dismounted and turned a level look on Ross and Lance. "We'll bring Chloe into the drawing room and let her rest on a couch—you two can carry her. Boz"—to the avid-eyed boy who had come to watch—"go get some brushes from Tessie. We'll brush the dust off the girls' dresses and if any seams are torn out Tessie will stitch them up for you. And we'll all eat these little cakes Mossy just baked and have some limeade."

"I think I need something stronger than limeade," complained

Chloe, who had a secret passion for rum and often stole a nip from the dining room at home.

"We'll break out a bottle of Canary," decided Anna, noting the sudden shake of Sue's head, for Sue was aware of Chloe's secret nipping and disapproved. "Boz, before you go for the brushes, run tell Mossy we need some glasses and a bottle of Canary." She led the way into the house, through the cool dim hallway into the main drawing room, where Chloe was deposited on a couch with her sprained ankle propped up on green velvet pillows.

"At least, if you had to hurt your ankle, Chloe, this is a fine place to lie in state!" laughed pretty, scatterbrained Alma. "This house always impresses me, Anna. All that forest of silver—" She nodded toward the arched doorway that led to the dining room. "And especially"—she gave a heavy theatrical sigh—"those *candlesticks*! There's nothing like them on the island—they look like *pillars*!"

Anna glanced toward the huge square-based candlesticks that dominated the heavy sideboard. They stood like Grecian columns, three feet tall and ornamented with fat cupids and twining vines. She knew Alma's remark was occasioned not by their beauty, which was considerable, but because they were worth a fortune.

"Mamma Jamison told me I could have them for my dowry when I marry," she said in an altered voice. "They were part of *her* dowry when she married Papa Jamison."

"You'll have to marry an earl at least to find a table massive enough to support them!" giggled Alma.

"They do look too heavy for an ordinary table," frowned Sue, studying the candlesticks. "One gets the feeling ordinary table legs would buckle under their weight. Do you ever use them, Anna?"

"Not on the dining table—they dwarf it," admitted Anna. "They look too big even on that enormous sideboard. Mamma Jamison came from a huge house in Sussex. It had tremendous rooms and tremendous furniture."

"I love everything at Mirabelle," sighed Mattie, Deborah Waite's third daughter, and quite plain. "Especially this room—now that you've taken down the black hangings."

Anna tried not to wince at this reminder of Mamma Jamison's death two years ago, and of the long period of mourning during which she and Papa Jamison had worn unrelieved black, and the house had been somber with black funereal hangings and all the mirrors turned to the wall as was the custom in mourning. But her voice as she answered Mattie was not quite steady, for she'd loved Mamma Jamison with all the fervor of her young heart and had felt lonely and bereft when she died.

"Yes, it is a lovely room." Her somber gaze took in the familiar high tray ceiling and the big paneled cedar fireplace with its double wooden doors closed for the summer months. "Mamma Jamison ordered these drapes herself," she said softly, looking at the handsome flowered brocade hangings that flanked the windows. "She didn't have time to get them hung before she died."

"You've certainly added some nice touches," declared Sue Waite, settling her buff-colored skirts down on a high-backed chair. "That pair of carved stools and all these velvet cushions and those andirons are new, aren't they?"

"Yes," smiled Anna. "I think Mamma Jamison would have liked what I've done with the room."

"Anna has put her touches over the whole house," Sue told the others. "You should see her bedroom, what she's done with *it*! A new coverlet all the way from France!"

"I loved the old coverlet," sighed Anna. "But last Guy Fawkes Day, when my horse balked at jumping over a bush and threw me, and the doctor said I must rest in bed until we found out if I'd really got out of the fall scot-free, Doubloon was carrying in my dinner and she tripped on the Turkey carpet and spilled a whole trayload over the coverlet."

"And so you had a coverlet full of sweet potato pudding!" Sue's laughter pealed as she spoke of the traditional fifth of November dish.

Anna's nose wrinkled in remembrance. "And fish chowder and shark pie and cedar berry beer! We tried everything but the stains wouldn't come out. Then on his last trip to Jamaica, Papa Jamison found a wonderful embroidered coverlet that was almost a match for the wall hangings. So it was his good taste, really—not mine.''

"What a lot of trouble to go to, redecorating everything!" chimed in Mattie wonderingly. "I mean, his new wife will change everything when he remarries."

Everyone turned to look at her.

" 'Remarries'?" asked Anna in an odd voice.

In the face of their startled attention, Mattie had the grace to blush. "Well, I mean it's bound to happen *sometime*, isn't it?"

"Not anytime soon," murmured Anna. "He loved Mamma Jamison very much and misses her even more than I do."

"Men change," Chloe said in a spiteful voice that reminded them all she'd been jilted at the altar last year. Her mother had arranged the marriage by mail, with a friend of hers who dominated her sons just as Deborah Waite dominated her daughters. He had arrived by ship a week before the wedding, but that one week of constant criticism by Chloe, who thought him too short, too frail, too mousey, too unlettered, and too poor, had been enough. On the day of the wedding he fled and had not been heard from since. "Men aren't faithful like women," pronounced Chloe, glaring about her.

"Ah, come now, Mistress Chloe," cried Grenfell in an aggrieved voice, for he was sure in his heart that *he* would be faithful to young Mistress Smith forever. "That's not fair, to condemn us all!"

Before Chloe, whose jilting still smarted, could snarl an answer, Anna cut in, for Mossy had arrived carrying a tray containing a wine bottle and glasses. "Grenfell, will you help us get this cork out?"

Offering wine to her guests averted open warfare between Chloe and Grenfell, but Anna insisted on limeade for herself. "It's too hot and sticky for anything that isn't instantly cooling!" she laughed. "I live on limeade all day long—Boz can testify to that!"

"What's this about you two racing for the chance to squire Anna to our ball, Ross?" Alma's dark head was bent as she played with apparent absentmindedness with a yellow riband on her sleeve.

Ross, who had kissed Mistress Alma behind the hedge at a party only a fortnight ago, and would have gone further had not his hostess stumbled over them, gave her a hunted look.

"Unless of course you've already forgotten!" Alma's face as she looked up at him was a model of innocence, but her light voice had an edge to it.

Ross looked from Alma, whom he had always fancied, to his young hostess, heiress to Tobias Jamison's fortune. He was not much given to flights of fancy but behind her for a moment he seemed to see a tall white ship of which he would be master—such a ship as her dowry would bring him!

"Yes, Mistress Anna," he said. "Ye should declare a winner, and I'll remind you that I was as yet unhorsed when we met the carriage, whilst Lance here was airborne, barreling headfirst into a bush—and see, he bears the marks of it." Indicating Lance's scratches with a nod of his dark head.

Anna, witnessing Alma's red-faced discomfiture, gave him a level look.

"I declare Grenfell the winner, Ross," she said sweetly. "For his horse was first to reach the front steps."

"But *you* were riding with him!" protested Ross.

" 'Tis true Grenfell started late—"

" 'Started late'?" cried Lance. "He ran the first half of the course on foot!"

Anna frowned at him. "I distinctly heard you challenge the others to 'a race'! You said nothing about disqualifying any who entered on foot. Grenfell started late and carried extra weight—myself. But he did finish first. I'm to the Waites' ball with him."

Both Ross and Lance shared a look of discomfiture and turned to glare at Grenfell, whose popinjay green velvet doublet swelled at this unexpected piece of luck.

Pretty Alma could hardly conceal her delight. "Nonetheless we'll expect you both at the ball," she told the two young men scoldingly. "With ladies or without them. Ross, I'll even take pity on you and let you be *my* escort—if you ask me nicely enough!"

"Why, thank you, Mistress Alma." Ross rose to the

occasion and considered the smiling girl in lemon taffeta, who lifted her glass coquettishly.

Anna smiled too. She knew how Alma felt about Ross—indeed the whole countryside did, for Alma pursued Ross everywhere; Anna strongly suspected that Alma had found out Ross was calling on her this afternoon and that was the reason for the Waite sisters' pilgrimage to Mirabelle. But even though she and Alma weren't exactly close—it was taffy-haired Sue Waite who was her special friend—she wished Alma joy of him, for she herself had no intention of becoming engaged to Ross Wybourne.

"Have you heard the news?" asked Alma, eager to bring the center of attention back to her own pretty face. "Clara Beecham is marrying again—Chad Wright, of all people!"

"When?" came a general chorus.

"In the spring."

"I should think Chad would be afraid to marry her," cried Ross. "For Beecham was as dark as Chad is blond, and they'll have all black-haired children and none of them to look like him!"

"Oh, I don't think—"

"Come now, Mistress Alma. Everybody knows that if a woman marries more than once, her children by her second husband may look like her first husband. 'Tis called telegony!"

In the face of this generally held belief, Alma fell silent but Mattie said, her brown eyes big as saucers, "Let's hope she doesn't have all children with smashed-looking noses like poor Henry Beecham!" She looked awed.

In the ensuing lively discussion of whether Henry's nose had been born that way or knocked that way, Anna thought of frail Clara Beecham at whose wedding two years ago they'd all been bridesmaids. Poor Clara—a bride at twelve, a widow at thirteen, and now at fourteen a second wedding in the offing. "Perhaps they'll be lucky," she murmured, and turned to Sue for agreement.

Sue was looking down with anxiety at her buff-colored silk skirts. "I do hope I'll be able to wear this dress again," she muttered.

"It *is* torn, I can see that," said Anna quickly, peering at he rip in the hem. "I'll have Tessie sew it up for you. Meantime, why don't you choose one of my dresses, since we're almost the same size? No, really, Sue, I do insist because I feel to blame for this whole thing."

On the couch Chloe stiffened. "Remember, neither blue or green become you, Sue!" she shrilled.

"Not any shade of pink!" put in Mattie in her high insistent voice.

"And certainly not yellow!" cried Alma in alarm.

Anna gave them all a pleasant look. How well she knew that the Waite sisters had divided up the rainbow. Chloe, the oldest and most forceful—so forceful she frightened suitors off with her square jaw and the straight dark line of her thick brows—had chosen all the blues and greens as her domain. Mattie, with her mousey hair, had delightedly claimed the entire spectrum of red through pink and wine and coral. And anything even remotely yellow was claimed exclusively by pretty Alma, who thought the yellow shades set off her dark hair and had been reinforced in that belief when no less a personage than the governor had beamed at her and told her she looked splendid in her best lemon silk.

They had left kindhearted Sue with nothing but gray and buff and brown.

"If Sue does not choose something from my wardrobe—yes, and wear it to the ball—I will be very much put out," said Anna sweetly, taking Sue by the arm.

"Remember, gray is your best color!" called Chloe stridently as Anna led Sue off toward her bedroom.

"You *can't* choose gray," whispered Anna. "For I've nothing gray in my wardrobe except a dove gray riding habit—and you certainly can't wear *that* to the ball!" She gave her friend's arm a friendly squeeze.

In her bedroom, she threw open the big press, bursting with fashionable clothes. "Here, Sue, let me choose something that will suit you." She pulled out a delicate pastel pink tissue gown that overlaid a shimmering soft rose satin.

Instinctively Sue's hand went out toward it. Then, "Oh, I couldn't—it's pink," she demurred, and drew back.

Their eyes met and they both laughed. Each girl was well

aware that mousey unassuming little Mattie, bookish and wrapped up in her girlish daydreams, would ordinarily not have demanded colors of her own like the owner of a racing stable—Mattie was far too shy for that. But ever since Mattie had read *Passion's Perilous Price*, a luridly romantic novel by the countess of Wakefield, her whole life had been changed, for its heroine, Prunella, had worn shades of red on every flaming page—pink and coral and rose and wine. Although the novel had been passed by Anna to Sue and had been read voraciously and in private by each giggling Waite sister save Chloe, who had tossed it aside as "trash," only Mattie, bookish and unworldly, had been so affected. She had loved the novel. She read it six times and by the sixth reading every shade of red had become inescapably connected in her impressionable mind with sex and desire and passion and fulfillment. That accounted for her newly formed and passionate devotion to the red side of the spectrum. Women who wore red and pink got their man, Mattie firmly believed—and everything else worth having.

From that day, she had never worn anything but pink or red or coral, she had wept when her mother suggested any other color to her, and she had ruthlessly gone through her older sisters' wardrobes and appropriated to her own use—shortened and let out for her shorter, plumper figure—every dress they owned on the red side of the spectrum.

For wearing pink brought women everything and Mattie's one desire was to have an exciting life.

Not that she ever would, of course—she was too plain, too dull. The droll look that passed between Anna and Sue acknowledged that. But they both liked harmless little Mattie and giving up a color to her seemed little enough to generous Sue.

"I was wrong to suggest pink," agreed Anna hastily. "It would break Mattie's heart. And anyway *this* would be a far better choice." She drew out a delicate blue silk ball gown that exactly matched the color of Sue's china blue eyes.

"Chloe would be furious!" demurred Sue, taking a step back in alarm.

"Never mind that," said Anna briskly. "Put it on." In jolly fashion, she bullied her friend into changing into the blue silk and then brought forth the fashionable big puffed separate sleeves she had had made to match the dress and tied them on Sue.

"Oh, its *beautiful*!" sighed Sue, staring at this unexpected vision of herself in the mirror. Her everyday self seemed to have changed dramatically.

"And just suits you," declared Anna energetically. "Especially if you wear your best white petticoat."

"The one I embroidered with blue peacocks against Chloe's wishes?" giggled Sue.

"The very one."

"But I thought—didn't you say you were going to wear blue to the ball, Anna? Oh, don't tell me this is the new dress you meant to wear?" Sue looked dismayed.

It was indeed the gown she had had made for the ball, but Anna promptly denied it. "I realized it didn't suit me," she declared cheerfully. "Amber is *my* color, and I've an amber silk that just sets off my hair. See?" She reached into the press again and pulled out a changeable silk that shimmered from lemon to copper. The effect was amber, rich and gleaming as her own burnished gold hair. "*And* it's trimmed with gold lace," she added triumphantly, "and the bodice is embroidered with gold threads, as you can see. Oh, I shall be very grand and outshine you, Sue!"

"Oh, I know you will," cried Sue with a rush of gratitude. "And I'm so grateful, Anna. I'm so tired of buff and gray and brown, and every time I even suggest wearing anything else, there's such a howl at home!"

"I'm sure there is," agreed Anna dryly.

"And now I can wear some other color without actually *wounding* anybody!"

"You're too good to them, Sue. Mattie is the only one of your sisters with a heart tender enough to be really 'wounded.' You know, I thought she seemed a little quenched."

"She's sulking because mamma says her face is mottled and insists on using puppy dog urine to clear up her skin.

Mattie shrieks every time anyone brings the stuff near her—but Mamma's tried everything else already and Mattie's skin is still mottled. She howls almost as badly as Chloe did when Mamma used boiled stone lime and barrel soap to remove that wart on her nose—and it did remove the wart, but of course it left a permanent scar," she added pensively.

Lye and slaked lime to burn one's skin! Silently and devoutly, Anna thanked God for her own blemish-free peachbloom complexion, which had saved her from these horrors.

"I'm surprised your mother's giving another ball so soon, Sue," she said in an attempt to change the subject. "I mean, you gave one only last month."

"Oh, but that was before Mattie—" Sue stopped, looking undecided.

"Before Mattie what?" prodded Anna.

Sue shook her taffy curls and looked conspiratorial. "Well, I'll tell you but you mustn't breathe a word because it's all supposed to be a great secret. We're giving the ball to announce Mattie's betrothal. That's why Chloe is so waspish today—it isn't her ankle; she's furious because she's the eldest and Mattie, who's younger, is getting married first. *I* don't care a pin who marries first, so long as I get the man I want—and neither does Alma. But Chloe—!''

"But who's Mattie marrying?" cried Anna in amazement. "I mean, I've never seen anyone even notice her!" She stopped, reminding herself that it was Sue's sister she was talking about.

"I know." Sue nodded wisely, her china blue eyes solemn. "And nobody ever had noticed her—until yesterday. Old Mr. Trimble came over to sup and after dinner he was closeted with Mamma and Papa and they called Mattie in and she came out in tears, crying that they were going to make her marry Mr. Trimble's nephew Abner, and her face got all mottled and that's why mother was using—"

Anna didn't feel she could go through the "puppy dog urine" treatment again. "But Abner's not—" she interrupted and stopped, looking uncomfortable.

"I know he's not very bright, Anna, but he *will* inherit all

Mr. Trimble's property when he dies, and it seems Mr. Trimble's health is worse and worse and that means Abner could inherit any day—at least Mamma thinks so.''

Anna's head was awhirl. Poor Abner, with his vacant face, could barely find his way home from church. What kind of life would Mattie have? No wonder she'd been so subdued today!

"Mattie begged and pleaded with Mamma to wait, and Chloe wailed that she was the oldest and they *should* wait until she got married. Mamma agrees with Chloe in most things—but not this; I think it's because Chloe got jilted— she *blames* Chloe for it and I guess she really is to blame because she kept *picking* at the poor fellow so that it's no wonder he ran away. Anyway Mamma said it was all arranged between Papa and Mr. Trimble and what with Mattie's skin being so blotchy, and having naught but a scant dowry, she'd be lucky not to be an old maid and Abner would probably be her only chance. So 'tis all arranged and just waiting to be announced to the world.''

The price of a blotchy skin! "I think I'd *rather* be an old maid than marry Abner,'' said Anna frankly.

"So would I,'' shuddered Sue. "So I'm hoping that by the time Mamma gets to me I'll already have made my own arrangements!''

Anna hoped fervently that she would.

"Although perhaps 'tis all for the best,'' sighed Sue. "For Mamma likes not poor Mattie's front teeth, which she says are too prominent and make Mattie resemble a rabbit. She has been told by Captain Souers that there is a dentist in London who advertises that if a gentleman has lost his teeth, he can have them replaced by the teeth of impoverished youths—and a dentist in Williamsburg is advertising the implanting of teeth as well for those who have lost them. Mamma says she is considering having Mattie's perfectly good front teeth removed and others put in which she likes better.''

Anna joined her friend in an involuntary shudder. She noticed that Sue's wistful gaze had fallen on the velvet jewel case that stood open on a little washstand, revealing a glimmer of blue.

"Would you like to borrow my blue lapis necklace to wear with your blue gown, Sue?" After all, she might as well go all the way—this was the necklace she had meant to wear herself with the blue dress that now adorned Sue's back.

"Oh, could I?" breathed Sue. "I've always admired it ever since Mr. Jamison gave it to you last Christmas, and as you know I've nothing but a jet mourning ring given me at Aunt Agnes's funeral, and some agate set in silver."

"I know," said Anna. "Gray agate."

"And some 'fairy stones' from Virginia," added Sue, punctiliously honest.

"Crosses. Brown. Wouldn't do at all with this blue dress."

Sue smiled shyly. "If I look like this"—she smoothed the blue silk of her skirt self-consciously—"do you think Lance might notice me?"

Anna, just lifting the blue beads out of her velvet jewel case, turned to look at her friend in surprise. "You and Lance, Sue? I didn't know."

"Well, he—he never notices me. I think it's because we're neighbors and we grew up together. Lance just doesn't *see* me, if you know what I mean. It's as if I'm invisible."

"In that dress, he can't overlook you," said Anna dryly.

"That's what I'm hoping. Oh, Anna, *you* aren't interested in him, are you?"

"Never," said Anna. "And I warn you that if you snare him, you'll run second to his horse!"

"Just so long as I'm running second to a horse and not a wench," muttered Sue. She looked upset. "You mustn't say anything, Anna. Chloe, Mattie, Alma—none of them know."

"Of course I won't, Sue. Your secret's safe with me." Anna clasped the blue necklace around her friend's slender neck and stepped back. "Looks better on you than it ever did on me," she said critically. "It's yours, Sue."

Impulsively Sue kissed her, and her blue eyes filled with tears. "If you ever need anything, just ask me!" she said in a choked voice. "For I shall never forget this—never."

"Well, you could pay me back—one way."

"How?"

"By insisting your next dress be yellow and the one after that purple!"

Sue's laughter bubbled up. "Let's see if I survive this blue one first!" She hugged Anna and together the two tripped back to the big drawing room, where Lance was standing—posing actually—against the double-doored cedar mantel so that his jutting jaw caught the light.

Everyone turned in surprise at the vision of dowdy Sue so suddenly transformed into a peafowl.

"Why, Mistress Sue—you're beautiful!" Lance blurted.

"That color doesn't become you at all, Sue!" Chloe's voice rasped. "You must give it right back to Anna. Anyway, 'tis a ball dress. Why are you wearing it now?"

"She is wearing it," said Anna, who had Sue's buff-colored gown slung over her arm, "so I can take *her* dress to Tessie to be mended." She left the room to give Tessie the dress and when she returned Lance was gazing at Sue as if he had never seen her before. Could this be the grubby little girl he had taught to ride, the tomboy who had climbed trees and fallen into his hedge? Sue, conscious of this new interest, arched her slender neck and tossed her head coquettishly, making her taffy curls bounce to great advantage.

"Mistress Sue, if ye are not otherwise engaged, may I be your escort to the ball?" he asked breathlessly.

To Anna's delight, Sue did not intend to let him off easily for his failure to notice her before. "I shall have to think about it," she said with a pensive look. "For it has come to my attention that I am not your first choice."

"Ah, Mistress Sue, I had not seen ye then as a blue vision." His hot gaze rested on her neckline, which Anna had had cut mercilessly low to fire the blood of every man in sight. Sue had lovely skin and now the blood came and went in her cheeks, giving them a glow.

"I will not give you my answer until tomorrow, you know." Sue's lashes fluttered in a way that would have done flirtatious Alma credit. "And not then unless you call upon me to take me riding."

"I will do so!" he cried, inspired both by her beauty and

by her refusal to fall like a ripe apple into his arms. Here on the island Lance had been very successful with women. It had surprised him somewhat that Anna had not readily succumbed to his irresistible masculine charms.

"You can't mean to wear that dress to the ball, Sue!" Alma, sounding shocked, had decided to reinforce her older sister. "You know Chloe's wearing blue and two of us can't!"

Sue gave Anna a stricken look and Anna lifted the bottle of wine and refilled Chloe's held-out glass before she spoke. "If Sue doesn't wear that dress—my gift —to the ball," she told Chloe clearly, "I shall not invite a one of you to the big ball I'm going to give to celebrate Papa Jamison's return. In fact, I may never speak to any of you again." Serenely, she began pouring wine for the others. "And my blue lapis necklace too," she added succinctly. "For I gave it to Sue also."

Complete silence greeted the announcement of this further gift.

"But since you're wearing blue also, I wonder if you'd like to borrow my blue lapis earrings that you admire so much—for they do match your eyes, Chloe?"

"Oh, Chloe, you'll look beautiful," cried Sue eagerly. "For your dress is deep blue too!"

Caught between a threat and a promise, Chloe's dark blue eyes went crafty. "Could you get them now?" she wondered.

Anna saw where this was leading. Chloe was planning to get the earrings in hand and then find a way to prevent Sue from wearing the dress. "They're locked away," she said carelessly, "and I've somehow mislaid the key. But I'll find it in time for the ball and bring them along with me," she promised, sipping her limeade.

Chloe subsided, looking frustrated. Anna knew she had won—Sue would wear the blue dress to the ball.

She was glad when the conversation shifted to politics. And to whether Peter Howes had won the kite-flying contest unfairly last Good Friday with his unusual high-flying kite with its sagebrush mast. And whether old Sean O'Toole really was a wrecker who rigged false lights to run ships on the reefs—most were of the opinion he was, for he looked fierce enough that owls might nest in his beard! And whether muscadine was really better than malmsey. And whether "Old Badie," the "witch" who'd been tried last year for practicing witchcraft on Mistress Jenkins's children and causing them all to break out in warts, would have been hanged if she had floated instead of sinking like a stone when she was ducked in the water.

"Witches always float!" insisted Grenfell importantly. "You see, they aren't really human—like us."

"She bled when she fell into the thornbush," remembered Anna, her eyes clouding. She had been glad indeed when Papa Jamison, after "Old Badie" had survived her ordeal, had taken her aboard his ship and transported her to Jamaica, where no one knew Badie had ever been charged with witchcraft.

Over more wine, the argument grew spirited over whether women should leave off—in the scandalous way of the London court—the whisks they wore for modesty's sake over their bosoms. That argument was still unresolved when the party rose to go, Chloe being carried out to her carriage in style by the two young men who had caused her accident.

From the flaring stone front steps of the white plantation house, Anna watched them go—the three young men on horseback following the carriage full of girls in pastel dresses, walking their horses down the drive in the soft afternoon air.

She stood for a long time on the steps after they had disappeared, drinking in the peaceful scene. She smiled as she stood there breathing the scented air, looking at the glory of the bougainvillaea in full flower, and hearing all about her familiar sounds—Coral purring as she rubbed her furry sides against Anna's skirts, Mossy singing a lullaby in a voice like liquid honey, the wild cry of the cahows and gulls wheeling overhead. And it seemed to her there was a magic here, that Mirabelle was an enchanted place and the islands of Bermuda the most wondrous in all the world.

She had forgotten that in Bermuda it was the season of storms.

CHAPTER 23

Certain that Grenfell, who had been encouraged beyond all measure by her promise to let him escort her to the Waites' ball, would rush over to spend the next afternoon with her, after lunch the following day Anna put on her gray riding habit and cantered down the drive. She would elude him, she told herself with some amusement, and not spend a boring afternoon listening to his endless sonnets!

She gave her carefully combed curls a rebellious toss that set the gray plumes of her wide-brimmed silver-banded hat atremble. She might even chance to ride by Lilymeade, the estate belonging to the Meade family, which bounded Waite Hall on the north as the Talbots' Shatterwood did on the south. For the Meades had an interesting guest, a handsome cousin from Boston named Arthur Kincaid, who dressed like a fop and swore like an Englishman and had a mouth half cruel, half smiling. Arthur Kincaid had shown a marked interest in Anna. On the one occasion when she had met him, his fascinated gaze had not strayed from her bodice.

Anna, enjoying the power of her young feminine wiles, had been amused by that. Yes, she might just ride past Lilymeade. . . .

With her mind so occupied, she cantered down the driveway toward the front gates of Mirabelle. She was riding beneath a leafy green ceiling where the branches met overhead. With a wicked smile she turned Floss's head in the direction of Lilymeade.

Halfway there, to her annoyance, she ran into Grenfell. He was ambling toward Mirabelle on his sorrel mare, blundering along through the hot afternoon and reading a book as he went.

"Grenfell!" Anna hailed him sharply. "You aren't paying attention to the road—you'll be thrown if the mare shies at anything!"

"Mistress Anna!" Grenfell closed his book and gave her a broad smile. "I was just on my way to Mirabelle."

That was self-evident, since nothing else lay at the end of this road. Feeling frustrated that she should have met him like this and unwilling to take him back to Mirabelle for a long boring afternoon, Anna said, "I was just on my way over to"—she hesitated, for she couldn't say "Lilymeade," for that was an entirely male establishment and would be sure to bring a torrent of questions from Grenfell—"Waite Hall," she finished unhappily.

"You shouldn't ride alone, Mistress Anna," he reproved her. "Where's your maid? Why isn't she with you?"

"Oh—Doubloon's off somewhere," shrugged Anna.

"Well, you should not be riding alone. There's a rumor about of a new slave revolt."

Anna sighed. "There are always rumors of slave revolts, Grenfell." She remembered how last year martial law had been enforced throughout the islands and armed patrols had marched the night to make sure no dangerous slaves were lurking. "But we've never had any trouble at Mirabelle."

"There's always a first time," warned Grenfell repressively. "And you're a woman alone—easy prey. Luckily, I'm here to protect you." His popinjay green doublet expanded masterfully.

Anna gave him a cynical look. She wasn't sure she wouldn't have to protect Grenfell if they ran into trouble!

"And besides you're so beautiful," he added. "Mistress Anna"—his voice grew breathless—"I do think you are the most beautiful thing I have ever seen!"

"But then you haven't traveled very widely," she scoffed. "Not even so far as Jamaica. Papa Jamison tells me Jamaica is filled with pretty girls."

"Not half so pretty as you, Mistress Anna—couldn't be," Grenfell declared loyally. "Although there is talk . . ." He hesitated.

Anna gave him a sharp look. "Talk about what, Grenfell?"

Grenfell moved his shoulders and the tassels on his popinjay green doublet stirred alarmingly. He had reddened to the roots of his fair hair. "Well, some people do say that the reason Mr. Jamison stays so long in Jamaica is because of a woman."

" 'A woman'?" Anna was startled.

"Well, he's been widowed now these two years past and that's a respectable length of time, and it's said—oh, but you don't want to hear such gossip, Mistress Anna."

"Indeed I do," insisted Anna. "Tell me what they say, Grenfell."

"Well, they say there's this widow that he met there last year and she has two daughters."

"Do they say he's in love with her?"

Grenfell shrugged his shoulders helplessly and set his tassels astir again. Love at their age? He couldn't credit it. To callow Grenfell, love was the exclusive province of the young. "They say he stays at her house in Port Royal when he's in Jamaica and that's why he's gone so long, longer each trip he makes."

Not the reefs, then. Anna gave a sigh of relief. "It would be nice to have another woman at Mirabelle," she said thoughtfully. "And two daughters, you say—perhaps they're near my age?"

"I don't know."

"Yes," she said decisively. "I think I'd be very glad if Papa Jamison married again."

Grenfell's mouth dropped open. "But that means you—you could lose your inheritance, Mistress Anna!" The very thought horrified him. It would be like being cast out of Eden! "You couldn't maintain a library or have leisure to read or—"

Anna smiled at Grenfell's vehemence. "I'm sure Papa Jamison will give me a very generous dowry in any event, and perhaps the man I marry will have a plantation as fine as Mirabelle—or finer."

"Oh, I doubt me that could be," said Grenfell reverently, for he had an enormous respect for Mirabelle Plantation.

Anna found herself laughing aloud at this honest comment. She found herself warming to Grenfell. She could ride to Lilymeade some other day! "Whatever happens, Papa Jamison won't cast me out," she told him humorously. "If that's what you fear, Grenfell."

"Oh, no, I didn't mean he would." Too eagerly. Grenfell thought second wives had tremendous influence. Look at his Uncle Archibald—he had cut the children of his first wife off with a shilling and left everything to that odious William!

"I'm out of the mood for riding, Grenfell. Will you stay to supper? We're having cassava and pork pie."

"Oh, I'd like to," sighed Grenfell with a shake of head and tassels. "But I'm expected back. My mother's in a state—father insists she take woodlice steeped in wine for her asthma and *she* says she prefers the ailment to the cure!"

"I don't blame her," shuddered Anna.

"I left her gasping for breath, and no doubt she'll be no better until she follows his advice. In any case, she'll want me to read her my sonnets until she falls asleep."

Which should happen very speedily, thought Anna with a rueful look at Grenfell. Grenfell's sonnets would put anyone to sleep. She gave an inward sigh. Life at Great Grenfell, which was the ambitious name of the Adams's estate, was so unutterably dull. She wondered now why she had accepted Grenfell's invitation to the ball. She might have accepted several others—or even waited to see if Arthur Kincaid would ask her. Arthur was tall and traveled; he spoke French and Spanish and played the new game King Charles enjoyed so much—tennis. He had promised to teach her. His wicked brown eyes had told her he'd like to teach her other things as well. Yes, she really should have waited for Arthur.

She sighed. "Well, if you can't stay to supper, let's ride down to the shore, Grenfell."

They rode through the pleasant afternoon, with Grenfell reciting verse and her mind wandering. She went back to Mirabelle feeling thwarted. Grenfell was monopolizing her time! Two days later when she saw Mr. Porter, the factor, heading into St. George in a carriage, she hailed him and impulsively climbed in beside him.

"I've some shopping to do," she told him blithely. But her real intention was to stay away from Mirabelle all day to discourage Grenfell's constant visits.

The factor gave her a tolerant look. Like everyone else on the plantation, he was very fond of Anna.

In St. George Anna wandered about the waterfront, which was endlessly fascinating to her. She enjoyed seeing the goods of the world unloaded and the tall ships that had been everywhere—and were about to go again!

She jumped as behind her Mr. Porter said, "I'm sorry, Mistress Anna, but the horse has thrown a shoe. 'Twill take some time to fix it, for the blacksmith has work ahead of him."

"Oh, that's all right." Anna looked up to see the Waite carriage with all four Waite sisters just pulling up down the street. "I'll find my own way home." She waved to Sue Waite, who had jumped out of the carriage and was hurrying toward her.

"We were just over to see you at Mirabelle," Sue told her blithely, with a nod to the departing factor. "And Belize told us you'd gone to town."

Anna blinked. "Surely you didn't come all the way in to St. George just to find me?"

"Oh, no, we had some shopping to do—ribands and pins and such for Mattie's trousseau. It was Chloe's idea to come calling again so soon—I really think she hoped to collect the blue earrings!" Sue's laughter pealed.

"Like as not that was her reason," agreed Anna lightly.

Sue gave her a roguish look. "Tell me, Anna, are you going to marry Grenfell?"

Anna gave her friend a startled look. "Of course not, Sue!"

"We found him sitting on your front steps waiting for your return and he implied as much." Sue's blue eyes sparkled.

"Oh, no," groaned Anna. "He comes over every day now!"

"Of course, I don't care who you're after—just so long as it isn't Lance," declared Sue merrily.

Anna stopped in her tracks. "Boz, go and catch up with Mr. Porter," she instructed the little boy with the parasol. "You can ride home with him." She took the parasol from him and turned to Sue. "I'm not really 'after' anyone, Sue. Why can't anybody believe that?"

"Because of the way you look," Sue told her frankly. "You're so beautiful that men just stop stock-still in their tracks when they see you coming their way. Arthur Kincaid says you have the face of an angel."

"Does he, now?" Anna turned away so that Sue might not see how pleased she looked. New conquests always interested her. She twirled her parasol. "And what else did he say?"

"That you must be the greatest 'catch' in Bermuda!" laughed Sue. "And he wondered why the local bucks were so foolish as to let you slip through their fingers."

"And that"—she shot a cynical look at Sue—"was just after one of you had told him that I was sole heiress to Mirabelle."

"Like as not," Sue shrugged. "We *were* discussing Mirabelle at the time as I remember."

Anna's lip curled. Once again, it was Mirabelle a man wanted and not her. "Would you want to be married because you were an heiress, Sue?" she asked quietly.

"If the man were Lance, I'd take him on any conditions." Sue's frankness surprised her. "Any way at all," she repeated softly. "But—the question's not likely to come up, Anna." She gave a rueful laugh. "I'm the youngest in a family of four daughters and there's likely to be no dowry left by the time Chloe and Alma and Mattie are taken care of!"

"Chloe may never marry."

"You may be right. Her sharp tongue does scare away men."

"And Alma's after Ross—and she may never get him. *You* may be the next to marry, Sue."

"Don't even think it!" shuddered Sue. "Chloe would kill me!"

By now the rest of the Waite sisters had joined them and the conversation had become general.

After a search for pins and ribands at the shops, it was decided that Anna would ride home with the Waite sisters in their overcrowded carriage—no, they would not take no for an answer!—then borrow a horse and ride back to Mirabelle.

"You should have brought your maid into town with you, Anna," Alma told her after she had enjoyed some light refreshments at Waite Hall and was mounting her borrowed horse for the short return ride to Mirabelle. "Ross told me there are rumors of a slave uprising."

"And you think," Anna wondered on a note of faint derision, "Doubloon would protect me?"

"*I* think she might lead the rebellion," said Chloe crisply.

"Nonsense! She's my maid—and my friend."

"Then you make a reckless choice of friends," muttered Chloe. "I have seen the way that woman looks at us—when she thinks we're not observing her!"

"We should send a groom with you," said Sue apologetically, "but we just don't have one handy at the time. Both our grooms are helping Father work up in the cedars. Why don't you change your mind and stay the night?"

"This is a nervous island," Anna sighed. "I can find my way home without assistance, thank you. I'll send the horse back tomorrow."

She waved to them all and cantered down the driveway away from Waite Hall. At the front gates she took the familiar road home, through walls of green with sea grapes dangling.

But all this talk of slave uprisings preyed on her mind, and when her horse shied at the front gates of Mirabelle, Anna called out sharply, "Who's there? Whoever is lurking in the bushes, come out where I can see you!"

A moment later the bushes parted and a golden-skinned young woman sauntered out into the road.

"Doubloon!" cried Anna. "What are you doing?"

The slim-hipped young woman in her loose island clothing fixed a pair of liquid almond eyes on Anna and shrugged. She was walking with her usual slight swagger that made her bright calico skirts sway provocatively, and she had a rakish assurance that was better than style. Anna saw that Doubloon's bare feet were dusty; she must have walked a long way.

"Where have you been, Doubloon?" demanded Anna in exasperation. "You're never here lately when I want you and now you've been gone two days! I was wondering if I should organize a search party—I thought you might have been eaten by sharks!"

Doubloon gave her a lazy look. "I was off on important business, Mis' Anna," she drawled.

" 'Important'?" Anna's imperious young brows shot up. "Don't ever let Papa Jamison hear you say that, Doubloon! He'll have your hide for it!"

Doubloon's golden shoulder twitched in a knowing shrug. "But he gone," she pointed out. "And you don't have nobody whipped—you too softhearted for that."

"I see you have found me out." Anna's lips fought back a smile and failed. "Now tell me, where have you been that was so important? All the house servants roll their eyes when they speak of you these days."

"I been to get me a love potion from old Tarwus," said Doubloon.

"But Tarwus lives up in the cedars somewhere. How did you know how to find him?"

"I find him. I always know where to find him. I bring him cedar berry beer. He sick and I stay and make him Hoppin' John out of chicken and peas and rice, and conch soup. He tired of eatin' prickly pear. And he give me love potion. You want I give you some? I got enough for two."

A potion? To make some man love her? Anna laughed reluctantly and shook her head. "I want some man to love me for myself and not because I tricked him into it."

Doubloon gave her a scornful look. "Then you a fool. Men not like that. They love, they leave. This potion"—she patted the big bandanna tied turbanlike around her shiny black hair, where she had obviously stashed the potion—"make him stay as long as you like. Never leave you."

Never leave you. . . . Had there ever been a potion that could make a man do that? Didn't they stay because they wanted to? And leave because they wanted to?

"I wish you luck with your potion, Doubloon," sighed Anna. "Last time you got a love potion you said it was for that big new fellow Papa Jamison bought on his trip to Jamaica—the giant who ran away during the slave revolt, what was his name?"

"Temera."

"Yes—Temera. I remember how you kept swaggering out of the house every time he came in from the fields. Who is it you're after this time?"

Liquid eyes old as time considered her. "New fellow—you don't know him. He live on another plantation."

"Oh? If you want to marry him, Doubloon, I'll get Papa Jamison to buy him so you can live together here at Mirabelle."

Doubloon gave an irritable shrug. "No need marriage. Love good enough."

Perhaps it was, thought Anna. If you could only find it!

Doubloon was pleased that Anna believed her. It protected Temera, and she wasn't ready for Anna to know about Temera yet—not until Tobias Jamison came back, not until she'd killed him.

For it was not a love potion she had got from old Tarwus—it was poison.

"You sure you don't want love potion?" she prodded Anna. "You want someone? Love potion bring him to your bed real quick. Old Tarwus say so and old Tarwus never wrong."

Anna's sigh deepened. "I wish I had your faith in potions, Doubloon. Well, don't let me catch you sleeping by the driveway again—remember, you're a house servant, not a field hand!"

Doubloon was unperturbed. "I walk a long way from old Tarwus's place. I need rest." As if to emphasize the point, she sat down insolently on her haunches by the side of the road. Lazily she plucked a grass stem and bit into it.

Anna gave her an irritable look. Doubloon in one of her stubborn moods was hard to handle. Doubloon in love was impossible!

"If you've been here for a while, Doubloon, you must have

seen who came and went. Did Grenfell leave or is he still waiting for me at the house?''

"He come, he go." Doubloon gave her an inscrutable look. "Waite sisters, they come, they go too. Mis' Alma lost her hat comin' out the gates, and the carriage, it stop, while the driver go get it. They were talkin' 'bout you."

In spite of herself, Anna felt her curiosity piqued. "What did they say?" she asked when Doubloon failed to continue.

"They call you the little princess." Doubloon chewed on the grass stem and spat. "That's what I hear them say—the little princess."

"Did they, now?" Anna felt pleased. For once an eavesdropper by proxy had heard something good about herself.

"And they say you better take care or you be *de*throned!''

"That would be Chloe, I don't doubt!" Anna's laugh rang out.

"You right. That Mis' Chloe was talkin'. You could hear her a long way." Doubloon nodded her head vigorously. She turned her curious almond gaze full on Anna. "What happen to you if you get *de*throned, Mis' Anna?"

Anna felt strangely uncomfortable before that penetrating golden gaze. Doubloon had a way of saying things that put you in your place.

"I don't know," she said. "I suppose I'd get along—I always did."

"But you didn't get along none so well, did you, Mis' Anna?" asked Doubloon bluntly.

"No, I guess not," admitted Anna.

She was sober as she went into the house to change clothes for supper. *The little princess* . . . a pretty turn of phrase.

But it had not always been so for Anna Smith.

CHAPTER 24

Anna had come to Bermuda as a babe in arms in 1659, borne on a winter gale. The ship *Wilhelmina,* bound for Jamaica, had fouled her water casks and made an unscheduled stop at Bermuda for fresh water. There Eliza Smith and her small niece Anna Smith had come ashore and later that year Eliza had abruptly indentured herself as a bondservant on Mirabelle Plantation for a term of seven years.

No one knew why Eliza Smith, who had seemed to have enough money to keep her and the child at the inn in St. George, had suddenly signed Articles of Indenture. Eliza had never even told Anna. But in later years Anna had secretly speculated that Eliza might have been lured by the beauty of Mirabelle. Built of the native coral limestone by a sea captain in the island's early days, the great house lay gleaming white against the lush tropical vegetation that sought to overpower it. Steep terraced roofs caught the precious rain, for this was a land without wells or springs or streams, and water was caught from the whitewashed rooftops and ran down stone gutters to be stored in huge stone cisterns—each kept clean of algae by a busy goldfish. Mirabelle also had paved catchments on the hillsides that caught the rain. It was a local landmark, its lime-washed walls and roof gleaming against the verdure surrounding it so that it looked like a great monolithic white stone cross, flung by heaven into the emerald countryside.

But past its beauty, all resemblance between Mirabelle and heaven ended, as Eliza Smith discovered to her sorrow. Its only advantage to her was that due to the crowding of the servants in the great house, she was allowed to live in a tiny hut by the sea. For although Mirabelle's great house was set well back from the sea and its storms, the property included a long sweep of coastline and along that coast was a broken-down fisherman's hut, half ruined, with a leaky palmetto thatch for a roof. Such were the living quarters, a long distance from the main house, that were assigned to Eliza, whose eyes gleamed when she saw it, for she had grown up by the sea and had always loved it.

Mirabelle was then owned by a dour family named Martinson, and gaunt Eliza Smith, no longer young and with no prospects of marriage, was not long in learning that she had made a bad choice. Forced to work long hours in the big house and in the nearby stone buttery where food was stored, Eliza had little time for the baby. The child grew up wild and free, her fair skin kissed golden by the sun, her long burnished gold hair tangled by the wind, her running bare feet learning the warm sands of all the nearby beaches. There was no future for little Mistress Anna Smith—then.

In some ways Eliza Smith was a harsh taskmistress. She insisted the child learn dainty table manners, taught her to curtsy, corrected her speech as best she could. But she never hugged her or caressed her, never showed her affection in little ways—not even when she was combing that thick thatch of gleaming golden hair.

It almost seemed as if Eliza shrank from physical contact with the little girl. She did not even face the truth herself—that she had given her heart to another child, Anna's mother, and had it broken to bits. She would never dare to love another child—it had been too painful the first time.

But Eliza could feel fear for little Anna, for her future. Sometimes she looked at the beautiful child, running carefree along the beach gathering seashells, or dancing in the surf, and felt an old pain strike through her heart.

Anna had handsome ways, like her father—quick to anger, quick to repent. And her mother's challenging spirit.

From them both she had inherited physical beauty, strength and health and joy of living. She had inherited some of their bad traits too—her father's temper, her mother's impulsive

recklessness. And Eliza knew in her quaking heart that Anna
would grow up to be a wondrous woman, as lovely as her
mother—and as lost.

It made her want to cry.

"We must be brave, Anna," Eliza told the little girl
gravely when food was short and they shivered against the
gales. "Somehow our deliverance will come."

The pretty child had smiled at her, not understanding.

Their "deliverance" had come in fact when Martinson,
supervising the felling of a great cedar tree for use as ship's
timbers, tripped unwarily over a root and had his leg severed
by an ax. He bled to death before they could transport him to
a doctor, and his widow, tired of Bermuda and longing for her
native Yorkshire, sold Mirabelle complete with furniture,
slaves and bondservants, to Tobias Jamison, a ship owner in
St. George who had long had his eye on the plantation.

Jamison had bought the plantation as a "surprise" for his
wife, Samantha, who had taken their only daughter Beatrice
to London three years previously to be treated by the physi-
cians there for a stomach condition, a lingering malady no
local doctor could seem to diagnose. Samantha had written to
him that the child was much improved, had gained weight,
and they would be home soon. That was in the spring of 1665
and Tobias Jamison had labored mightily to make Mirabelle
all that a loving wife and child could want.

Samantha Jamison reached Bermuda that fall—but it was a
tearful Samantha garbed in black who disembarked. She
brought with her the bitter news that a Great Plague was
raging in London and little Beatrice, recovered from her
lesser malady, had been one of its victims. St. George was
shocked by her tales of pesthouses and carts and a city filled
with brimstone. But the shock of her little daughter's death
(Beatrice was then seven) had almost killed Samantha Jamison
and darkened their lives permanently, for they were both well
along in years and had little hope of producing another child.

Samantha spent hours brooding over the scalloped Jacobean
crib that had been her daughter's in infancy, and idly rocking
it with her foot. She sat slumped in her Cromwellian rocker,
with its finely turned spool back, and seemed to pine away.

It was a miracle to Samantha Jamison, sitting listlessly on the broad shaded veranda, being fanned by a little black slave boy whose attention kept wandering to a chameleon about to drop from the blue morning glory vine that shaded the veranda from the morning sun, to look out and see a golden-haired child approaching.

Samantha had leaned forward, puffing out her fat cheeks in surprise and clutching her hands to breasts like sofa pillows. The same burnished gold hair, the same—no, of course not. Not the same at all. Beatrice was dead. Dead and entombed in far distant London with the other plague victims.

Still this was a golden-haired little girl of winsome beauty and she had not seen her before. Not a neighbor child surely, for her simple shift was too short and of cheap material and patched. But her bones had a delicacy, her skin a sheen, her turquoise eyes a frank intelligent clarity.

Who was this child? On impulse, Samantha leaned forward and waved a fat arm, setting all her ribands in motion. "What is your name, child?" she called. "And where do you come from?"

"My name is Anna," said the child gravely. "I am Eliza's niece."

"Oh, yes, of course—Eliza, the upstairs maid." Samantha Jamison sank back, quivering like a bowl of jelly, her heavy body enervated by even this small endeavor. "Come closer, child." She held out a soft white hand—doubly soft, for she wore gloves made of chicken skin at night to keep them so—and her jeweled rings flashed. "Come here and talk to me."

So seven-year-old barefoot Anna, with her tangled mop of burnished gold hair, climbed up on a big reed chair and joined in polite conversation with the fashionably dressed billowy lady on the veranda. She enjoyed the slight breeze made by the languorously waving palmetto fan that wafted the lady's scents and pomades toward her, and talked gaily with the fresh enthusiasm of youth of all that she would see and do when she was a woman grown and the whole world opened up to her.

So entertained was Samantha Jamison, so taken by the

barefoot child's easy talk and graceful manners, that they were still conversing when Eliza, her upstairs chores finished, spied them through the dining room window. Eliza's heart leaped at the sight of the two of them together . . . It was what she had dreamed of, that these new people who had bought the place would take an interest in little Anna.

Stifling a cough—for her lungs, never strong, were failing her now and she had to pause for breath and sometimes spit blood just from climbing the broad flaring front steps outside—Eliza hurried away unnoticed. Let them talk: she did not want to interrupt this welcome new development.

"What were you looking at, Eliza?" demanded a suspicious voice from the door and Eliza saw with alarm that Editha Jamison had come into the room. Editha was Tobias's older sister, who, as was the custom with impoverished relatives, lived with her brother and sister-in-law in the big house at Mirabelle. Eliza did not like Editha, who ordered her around in a snappish manner—and the feeling was mutual. Editha had never liked or trusted this tall, gaunt, noncommittal woman with the forgotten past who did her work overwell and confided in nobody. To Editha's way of thinking, Eliza Smith considered herself better than a servant and held herself above the others—she should be brought down a peg or two. Editha had often told her sister-in-law that but foolish Samantha refused to listen. She had even insisted she liked the tall gray-haired woman with the firm set to her mouth.

"I wasn't looking at anything," said Eliza impassively, hoping Editha would believe her. "I was just straightening the curtain."

"Don't look so innocent," snapped Editha. "I *saw* you staring out the window. What's out there? Some young lad you've got your eye on, I don't doubt—and you old enough to be his mother!"

At this unwarranted—and indeed imaginative—accusation, Eliza's mouth tightened to a straight line and she withdrew from the room, hoping Editha Jamison would follow to berate her and so leave the child a clear field with Samantha.

But Editha did no such thing. Her suspicions were fully

aroused, for she had sensed an unaccustomed tension in Eliza Smith's back as she peered out, and now she hurried her large limbs across the floor, moving her massive bulk in a heavy-footed way that would have shaken the house had the floor been of timber instead of stone.

What she saw was her billowy sister-in-law, Samantha, conversing with a child whose tumbled gold hair hung down like spun silk around an angelic oval face.

"Who *is* that child?" she demanded indignantly, noting the child's mended cotton shift and bare feet. But Eliza Smith had already gone.

Editha stormed out on to the porch and repeated her question to her sister-in-law.

Samantha Jamison turned to her with the most animation she had shown in weeks. "She is Eliza's niece, and isn't she a lovely little girl?"

"Well, Eliza must come and get her!" cried Editha, indignation sharpening her voice. "I can see she's tiring you."

"No, let her stay," said Samantha. "Up to now all I've had to interest me is what's for dinner. Don't run away, child—sit back down and talk to me."

Anna, who had been about to flee, sank back gingerly onto the reed chair. "Why do you wear black?" she asked innocently. "And that heavy black veil, isn't it hot wearing it?"

Editha sniffed but Samantha's large eyes filled with tears. "I wear black for a little girl who'd have been about your age—*my* little girl," she choked. "She's gone and I miss her."

"Oh," said Anna in a small voice. "I'm very sorry she's gone—and I didn't mean to make you cry."

"We're all sorry," snapped Editha. "Now get you gone. Don't you see you've upset the mistress of the house?"

The child jumped up and edged away but as she left, Samantha, dabbing at her face with a handkerchief, called to her, "Come back and see me tomorrow, Anna. I'll expect you."

It was the first of many long talks between the pretty child and the lonely woman. Before the week was out Samantha was taking an interest in something besides food and grief; she could be seen in the afternoons walking with the child through the gardens of Mirabelle, pausing to admire the flowers, explaining the different plants. Over Editha's protests that she was "raising that child above her station," Samantha had a dress made for Anna—a simple dress of white cambric trimmed in azure velvet ribands that set off her delicate beauty.

Clad in that dress, little Anna came to dinner in the long dining room at Mirabelle. Her lustrous hair was washed and combed and brushed to a high sheen by Eliza. With faultless manners and unstudied grace, she presented herself shyly at the door and was ushered in to sit speechless at a frosty white board covered with a sparkling array of gleaming silver.

Tobias was equally charmed with Anna and delighted that with her winning ways, the child was bringing Samantha back to life. Already it seemed to him Samantha had lost weight— some of the many pounds she had listlessly packed onto her medium-sized frame after Beatrice's death.

"I think you should leave off mourning," Tobias told his wife decisively. "Our little Beatrice—if she can see you now—wouldn't want you to grieve. She'd want you to wear the pretty clothes and bright colors you always loved."

Samantha looked down at her pale hands, with their jet mourning rings, for a long time without speaking. She never answered Tobias but the next morning she came down to breakfast in Tobias's favorite gown, which he had not seen since she left for London with Beatrice—a delicate mauve taffeta, very thin, with an overdress of violet tissue.

"Little Anna has had a good effect on you, Samantha," he beamed, and leaned down to brush his mustached lips affectionately against his wife's plump cheek.

And so Eliza's hopes were realized. She and Anna were moved from the seaside hut to the great house, where they occupied—once again over Editha's protests—one of the small guest bedrooms. Samantha began to redecorate her daughter's old room, using a great quantity of white lawn and commissioning a blue and white coverlet to be embroidered for the big square four-poster. Editha had a sinking feeling every time she looked in on the needlewomen stitching up the new flounced white curtains, for she had little doubt who would occupy this pretty bedroom—Anna Smith.

But for Eliza, triumph was short. As her health failed, so that at last Samantha decreed that she should have no more household duties and she kept to her room, coughing out her life's blood into a linen kerchief, so Anna's fortunes prospered.

Anna had been moved into the big, lovely, newly decorated bedroom on the shallow excuse that Eliza was sick and needed quiet. But everyone but little Anna knew that Eliza was sinking and would not last very long.

The day Samantha Jamison spoke to Eliza about Anna's education and how she and Tobias had plans for the child, if Eliza approved, found Eliza very weak and with her cheeks two red spots of color in her white face.

"I feel—I really feel you are too ill to be with the child so much," Samantha said hesitantly. "But if you will let us have Anna to raise as our own, we will be glad to transport you back to England, where there are better doctors."

The trace of a smile played over Eliza's wasted face. "There be no need to transport me anywhere," she said with a sigh, "for I'll not be here that long. And glad I am to give Anna to you, for I know you'll keep her and care for her—which I cannot. But there's something that must be writ down before I go, and I cannot write."

Samantha could see for herself that the woman was dying.

"My writing hand is so poor nobody can read it," she told Eliza apologetically. "And Tobias is gone for a fortnight to St. David Island. But I'm sure that Editha—"

From the bed Eliza held up her hand as if she were warding off something. "Not Mistress Editha."

"Oh—well." Samantha could understand how, with Editha's patent dislike of her, Eliza might very well not wish to dictate to Editha her dying words. "I know," she cried. "I'll send for Mr. Hunt, the minister. He's no doubt busy packing, for he leaves next week on the same ship that will bring our new minister, Mr. Cartmell, but I'm sure he can find time for such a small thing and he does write a nice neat hand."

"Would you see that we are not disturbed?" came that weak voice from the bed. "Would ye grant me that?"

"Why—why, of course." Samantha felt flustered.

"I mean," elaborated Eliza, "will ye keep Mistress Editha and the servants away from the door. I don't want them to be hearing what I'll be saying to him."

Samantha would have protested, but she reminded herself that Eliza was dying and the dying deserve some privileges. "I'll keep Mistress Editha with me the whole time Mr. Hunt is here and I'll see that the servants are all sent on errands that will keep them away," she promised.

"Thank you," said Eliza faintly. "You were always a good woman. I've got no regrets about leaving Anna with you, thank God, for I know ye'll treat her like a daughter."

"Yes," said Samantha Jamison in a smothered voice, "we will."

She hurried away, certain that Eliza's demand for secrecy was only a symptom of her dying condition; she must be out of her head. All that the woman could possibly want to do was to make some note of how her meager possessions should be left. Samantha told Mr. Hunt as much, after he was brought to her. So it was a surprise to the minister, on being left alone with Eliza Smith, to see her fix him with a stern gaze and say, "First off, ye must swear on the Bible that naught that I say tonight will be told to anyone—your solemn oath on it, sir."

Feeling foolish, Hunt placed his hand upon the Bible and swore.

Eliza sank back in bed. She had only this one chore left to make her peace with God and then it would be all over for her. But this one last effort she owed to a woman dead these seven years and more, a woman who—like her—had come from sunny isles across the sea and who had been like a daughter to her.

"You understand," Eliza told the minister solemnly, "the child's to know nothing of this. I've told her naught, for she's so young, no need to mark her life at this tender age."

"Then am I to understand this is not a will you wish me to draw up?"

Eliza shook her head. It cost her an effort—any motion did. "'Tis, in a way, the story of my life, and of Anna's mother—all things she will want to know when she is grown. And there's much else I need to say—about the necklace of pink Scottish pearls with its great silver links—how I got it and how I came to part with it."

For two hours Eliza dictated to the astonished minister, who wrote it all down laboriously in his labored hand by a candle's light as Eliza's own light ebbed away. At last he let her make her mark upon the last sheet of parchment, inscribed her name beside the mark—and then his own in testimony to her signature. In silence he sealed the parchment with dripping red sealing wax and took it away with him, promising "to keep it safe and not open it nor deliver it to anyone but Anna Smith on the day of her marriage."

"And here—" Eliza called him back in a faint voice as he started to leave. "Look in that chest yonder. There's a small book—a journal—that must go along with it. Ye must keep them both safe; fasten them both up and seal them both with sealing wax."

With a hand aching from writer's cramp, the minister did as he was told, making a bulky packet, which he stuffed into his saddlebag and took back with him to the town of St. George. He was very thoughtful on the journey and twice nearly turned back to speak to Samantha Jamison. He wondered if Eliza's claims could be true or if they were a fabrication. She was far gone, he could see that but—she had seemed sane enough.

He worried about it all that week, wrestling between his oath and what he considered his plain duty, and finally, with a weather eye on heaven and a Deity that kept count of the hairs on his head—thrust the packet into the hands of the new minister, David Cartmell, with a muttered instruction that he'd given his oath the packet was to be kept inviolate and delivered to Anna Smith only upon the occasion of her marriage. Young Cartmell, overwhelmed with the duties of this, his first church, had thrust the packet into the locked box in which he kept his own valuables and thought no more about it.

Eliza, exhausted from this chronicling of her adventures and all that had brought her to Bermuda, had died the day after the minister's visit, with a smile on her tired face.

And with her passing Anna Smith became, in all but legal fact, a daughter of the house. For the child whose only memories were sharing the barren fortunes of an upstairs maid, the move was a fabulous overturn.

CHAPTER 25

When Anna was eleven years old—and thus approaching marriageable age by the standards of her day—she was allowed to choose her own personal maid. That day she made a choice that was to affect her life, and the lives of all of them at Mirabelle, for she chose a new slave girl Tobias had just acquired from Barbados.

Her name was Doubloon. She told them all she had been named for the golden color of her skin but it was a lie. Actually one golden doubloon had been the price paid for her when she was a small child in Jamaica and expected to die. After that her past was murky. She spoke English and French—fluently if with bad grammar and erratically—and lied glibly in both languages. Her stories were as colorful as the brilliantly hued turbans with which she tied up her Indian-straight black hair.

Doubloon's wild beauty and wicked ways created a sensation among the slaves of St. George's Island. Especially during the gombey dancing at holiday time when, wearing a tall headdress of peacock feathers and a frightening mask, she leaped high into the air with a wild half-human scream or bent over backward with her red skirts riding up, as if her slim back were made of India rubber. She would tremble there, coiled like a spring, pulsing to a savage beat while the gombey drums throbbed louder and louder until the world seemed filled with their thrumming and a deep-throated roar rose from the onlookers. African steps, voodoo steps, West Indian steps—Doubloon knew them all and a few besides. She seemed made to dance and even Anna held her breath like the other onlookers and swayed to the music when supple Doubloon led the other slaves—she seemed born to lead them, like some pagan queen—down the narrow winding streets of St. George on Boxing Day or New Year's.

Her age was a matter of conjecture, for it changed every time you asked her. For a while after her arrival the slave quarters were abuzz with the stories Doubloon told about her past, but Anna believed implicitly the version Doubloon told her.

She was, Doubloon told Anna, the daughter of an Arawak Indian woman—and her coarse straight black hair and golden skin and almond-shaped eyes and Oriental features certainly bore that out—and an Irish sailor who got drunk one night in Port Royal and raped her mother. *That,* Anna firmly believed, accounted for Doubloon's violent temper and singing ability, for were not the Irish a tuneful and violent race?

Her mother had been won in a dice game by a French gambler who had loved both mother and child unstintingly. When the gambler's rich uncle had died, he had found himself suddenly possessed of a sugar plantation in Jamaica and Doubloon's mother had ruled the great house called Fleur-de-Lis as its mistress. The gambler would have married her if he could, Doubloon insisted, but he had a living wife in Paris and a daughter he had not seen since birth.

Young Doubloon, with her thick shining dark hair and scornful almond eyes and glowing golden skin, had been brought up as if she were indeed the plantation owner's own daughter. It was a heady life-style she had enjoyed—very similar to Anna's as it was now, she informed Anna loftily, for all had deferred to "Young Missy" and many—those who would not bend their spirits to her imperious will—had bent their backs to her whip. The gambler, who had blithely never given much thought to the future and spent his rum-money as lavishly as his sugar-money, indulged all her whims. She had her own horse, her own coach, even—and if the other plantation owners' wives shunned Fleur-de-Lis Plantation for its wild reputation and never included its owner or his mistress and her illegitimate daughter in their parties, what did that matter? Doubloon was young and headstrong and had her own way in all things.

But gradually, as her mother lost the bloom of youth, her father began to change. He drank more, lost at cards. He married an island heiress and—

"But he already had a wife!" Anna cried excitedly at this point. "You told me so!"

"*She* did not know that!" Doubloon replied scornfully with a fierce shake of her great mane of black hair.

"Oh," said Anna inadequately.

"You think he should have tell her, don't you?" cried Doubloon with scorn in her voice.

"Yes, I do!"

"But then he wouldn't have got her fortune, would he?" Doubloon's enigmatic smile flashed. "Besides he was a *man*."

"I don't see what that's got to do with it."

"*Men*," said Doubloon with an expressive shake of her golden shoulders.

" 'Men'?" Anna was puzzled.

"Men no damn good," elaborated Doubloon with heavy irony. "After he marry her, he change toward me. My horse is take away and sold. House servants don't listen to me no more—they listen to *her*. My mammy can't stand no more. Take poison. Die."

Anna shivered. "What did you *do*, Doubloon?"

"I cry, I beg my 'daddy.' First time—last time." Doubloon's glare was significant. "Then I get sent away to school—make lady of me, he say. Not good enough for new wife. Church school—strict. I run away, get caught, taken back, run away again. Now I learn my 'daddy' dead. I go back, tell about wife in Paris, daughter in Paris—they turn *her* out, say she no true wife."

"Who was turned out, the second wife?"

Doubloon nodded.

"Well, then—"

"I think everything be all right now, at least I have time till new wife arrive, and maybe she share with me because my testimony give her Fleur-de-Lis. So I wait for her to come across the sea to Jamaica."

"And did she?"

Doubloon shook her head. "Nobody come. Just a letter saying there was no wife, no daughter. Just a lie my 'daddy' made up so my mammy stop asking he marry up with her." Her face seemed to shrivel. *"Men,"* she whispered. *"No damn good."*

There was silence for a while and then Anna inquired in a small voice, "What happened then?"

"They come and say I lie to keep my 'daddy's' true wife from her inheritance. They say I no daughter, I a slave and I got to be whipped." She bared her back expressively and Anna flinched. It still bore criss-crossed ridges and long pale scars, compliments of the lash. "After that, you don't want to know what happen to me," said Doubloon gloomily. "I sold here, I sold there. Mr. Tobias, he buy me on Barbados. That all you need to know."

"I'm glad you told me this, Doubloon," Anna said earnestly. "It wasn't fair what happened to you. Do you want me to tell Papa Jamison about it?"

Doubloon gave her a scathing cynical smile that spoke volumes.

"Well, then"— Anna swallowed—"if you don't think *that* would help, I promise you this: I'll try to make it all up to you. You're *my* slave and *I'll* free you. I don't need a maid, I can dress myself and do my own hair!"

Doubloon's wide smile flashed and she looked at Anna with sudden real affection. "You a nice girl," said Doubloon. "A kind girl—but you a fool."

That was when Anna learned that Doubloon was *her* slave

insofar as ordering the girl to do her bidding, but Tobias Jamison's slave in fact. She could not free Doubloon; legally Jamison owned her.

"You'll treat the wench kindly, child," he told Anna in a soothing voice. He ruffled her hair fondly and gave her his gentle smile. "And Doubloon will come to love it here. After all, if she left us, what do you think would happen to her?"

"Why, she'd—she'd go her own way. She's beautiful—she'd marry."

Tobias Jamison sighed. "You're very young, little Anna," he told the child. "And your heart is tender. But the world is not. Pray God you never learn that." For already he thought of Anna as his own child.

Anna sought to enlist Samantha Jamison's aid, only to find she sided with her husband in this matter. Anna had been given a gift—but not a gift she would be allowed to part with.

After Anna's attempt to free Doubloon, Anna and Doubloon became inseparable. Doubloon, who was years older and of uncertain age—Anna always suspected Doubloon had the secret of eternal youth—adopted a protective attitude toward her young charge. She did not behave like a maid, but like a protective older sister. And she did her best to impart her cynicism, her worldliness, to Anna, but regretfully she had to admit to herself that it was useless, for Anna's joy of living overflowed everything.

Anna in those days was like a butterfly testing her wings. Lovely wings that could carry her anywhere. Even Editha's perpetual enmity was unable to quench her good spirits. She was growing up in beauty—and she was receiving the island equivalent of a genteel education. She was tutored by both Samantha Jamison and by a down-at-the-heel gentleman living impecuniously in St. George, and between them they taught Anna a genteel if scrawly writing hand, enough of reading to manage to enjoy a novel, and how to do simple sums.

But as the "daughter" of the doting Jamisons and the acknowledged heiress to Mirabelle Plantation, she learned so much more.

For Tobias Jamison was wealthy and, like it or not, Anna

Smith was accepted into local society. Daughters of the wealthy planters came to call in their carriages and sometimes stayed the night, and from the time she was ten young gallants with an eye to a fortune began to notice her.

By the time she was twelve Anna had been thrice a bridesmaid for brides but slightly older than herself and had already had two offers of marriage, both turned down rather grumpily by Papa Jamison on the grounds that Anna was "too young."

"What that old fool talking about? You *not* too young!" stormed Doubloon, who had had an eye herself on the last suitor and thought it would be grand if Anna married him; with a chance to live in the same house, who knew? She might end up his mistress!

"But I *am* too young," insisted Anna, laughing. "Besides, I don't want to get married! I want to go to parties and dance and have a good time."

"You don't need to stop havin' fun just because you marry!"

"Maybe not." Anna thought of a thirteen-year-old friend whose bridesmaid she had recently been. Her jealous bridegroom had ordered her to wear only high-necked dresses and never to go out unattended! "But you can never be sure what you'll get."

"That right," agreed Doubloon instantly. "Men no damn good."

It was a refrain Anna was used to hearing from her.

And of course Doubloon cursed both gentlemen roundly when she learned that they had cast their eyes elsewhere and become betrothed to other island girls.

It was through Doubloon's efforts that Editha, Tobias Jamison's sister, left Mirabelle. One day she came out to the big old kitchen where young Anna was watching cook make a fresh kettle of conch soup and before the scandalized kitchen help accused Anna of poisoning her.

"The soup you brought to my room this afternoon when I wasn't feeling well—there was something wrong with it!" she cried in a slurred voice.

"But I only brought it to you because Mamma Jamison

asked me to!'' cried Anna, bewildered by this unexpected accusation.

"That soup kind of old,'' insisted cook. "But it still good. We all ate it this noontime. Nobody get sick. Nobody!''

"You'll tell me what you put in it! You'll tell me right now! I won't be poisoned by a little chit who wants to usurp the place of my brother's dead child!'' Editha seized Anna and began to beat her.

Anna screamed, wrenching away and trying to protect her face from this unwarranted attack.

"Mis' Samantha, Mis' Samantha!'' shrieked Mossy, running from the room with her apron thrown up about her face. "Mis' Editha goin' to kill this child!''

Moments later a white-faced Samantha Jamison arrived upon the scene and with surprising strength tore a wailing Anna from her sister-in-law's angry grasp.

"What is the meaning of this, Editha?'' she cried.

"That girl brought me poisoned food!'' Editha pointed dramatically at Anna. "And it's not the first time!'' Editha's massive form seemed to tower over plump Samantha; she was beside herself with rage.

"Nonsense,'' said Samantha sharply. "You would do well to get hold of yourself, Editha. Tobias shall hear of this.''

"Hear of it he shall indeed!'' stormed Editha. "And from me!'' Charging around her sister-in-law, she dashed out of the kitchen like a ship in full sail and steered her course on a straight line for Tobias Jamison's ''office,'' where he kept his account books and dealt with plantation affairs.

Samantha and Anna were right behind her.

Tobias met this female onslaught blinking. "What's this to-do?'' he inquired mildly. "Speak one at a time, won't you? I can't make sense of what any of you are saying.''

"Your sister has accused Anna of poisoning her!'' cried his wife dramatically.

Tobias's jaw dropped. "Is this true, Anna?'' he asked sternly, turning to the child.

Anna shook her head helplessly, dragging a fist over her wet eyes. "I but took hot soup from the kitchen to her room, as Mamma Jamison asked me to do.'' In the shock of the moment she entirely forgot that she had met Doubloon on the stairs and set the soup down for a moment as Doubloon told her to go look out the window, the geese were making their annual migration north, as they did every year up the Great Eastern Flyway. Anna had gone to look, marveling as great waves of birds darkened the sky. ''It was good soup,'' she insisted. ''I had some myself for lunch.''

''And so did I!'' cried Samantha triumphantly, in a tone of *So there, Editha!*

''*Mine* was tampered with,'' insisted Editha. ''I felt dizzy afterward and fell to the floor. When I was managed to get up, I recollected that the child had brought it and came down and accused her to her face. She has no call to love me, you know, for I considered it a mistake to have brought her here and well she knows it. Treating her as if she were your own daughter! Why, poor little Beatrice would turn over in her grave!''

At this mention of Beatrice, Samantha covered her face with her hands and groaned. Tobias Jamison winced.

''There is no need to recall our loss to us,'' he told his sister sternly. ''We remember it all too well. But this child'' —he indicated Anna, standing woebegone before him—''has brought new sunshine into our lives. It has been all too plain that you resent her presence here, Editha, but I will remind you that this is my house and I will bring into it anyone I please, whether you approve or not.''

Editha drew back as if he had struck her and her mouth formed a straight line. ''Then, since that is the case, I will remove myself from your house, Tobias! I have no intention of staying here until I am put into a coffin like poor Beatrice!''

She turned on her heel and left them, her dark skirts billowing angrily. Samantha gave her husband an anguished look. ''I'll try to mollify her,'' she whispered. ''For she's your only sister and I do know how you feel about her. Stay here with Tobias, child,'' she told Anna, and fled down the hall after Editha's angry departing back.

But nothing would move the furious Editha. Two weeks

later she departed aboard the *Pandora*. A sudden squall came up and drove the *Pandora* upon the reefs, where she broke up. Strenuous efforts were made to save the ship's crew and passengers, but only a handful of them survived the lashing wind and water that drove them onto the jagged coral. Editha was not among them.

There was sadness at Mirabelle, but it was brief. Samantha had never liked her dour sister-in-law and only tolerated her out of consideration for Tobias, and Tobias was of a nature to consign all shipwreck victims to God. He had had dealings enough with the angry sea to believe that it was the hand of God that led men across the waves—and God had not chosen so to lead Editha.

Not for months did Doubloon confide the truth to Anna.

"She smart, that old Mis' Editha," she told the child one day, chuckling.

"How so, Doubloon?"

"She know I put something in her soup—not once but three times. But always she think I somewhere else. She blame *you* because *you* there. And nobody believe *you* do anything to her—you too young and sweet!" She laughed aloud.

"Doubloon, tell me you're joking," said Anna slowly. "You can't mean you really poisoned Editha? I thought she made it all up because she hated me!"

"Oh, she hate you, all right," said Doubloon with a careless shrug. "But I put something in her soup I get from old Tarwus. A little not kill—a lot do. And I only put in a little. I goin' make her sick slow so doctor not know what to do."

Beneath her sun-kissed tan, Anna's face paled. "Then you really—meant to kill her?" she faltered. "Eventually?"

The look Doubloon tossed her was affectionate but half contemptuous. "What you care?" she demanded. "She your enemy!"

"But I *do* care," insisted Anna. "I wouldn't have hurt her, you know that!"

"I have my own reasons for what I do." Doubloon drew

herself up as haughtily as any queen. "You not know it, but Mis' Editha, she always after Mr. Jamison to sell me off to some other plantation; she say I 'bad influence on the child!' " She gave a short wicked laugh. "But she gone now!"

"But you wouldn't really have killed her? Would you?" Anna asked haltingly.

Doubloon saw now that she had gone too far. "Of course not! You know they hang me in St. George if I do that, Mis' Anna. I just want to make her sick some because she try to get rid of me."

"Of course," murmured Anna, who couldn't imagine murder by stealth. "I knew you wouldn't." But, unaccountably, she found herself shivering. There'd been something in Doubloon's eyes for a moment—infinite malice, that was it. "I'm cold," she said abruptly. "I think I'll go back in the house."

Doubloon was frowning. "You not tell anyone what I say? You get Doubloon whipped!"

Anna shook her head wearily. "No, Editha died by drowning, not by poisoning. She was in good health when she boarded the *Pandora*. Whatever else you did, Doubloon, you didn't drive her ship onto the reef."

"That right," purred Doubloon. "Old Tarwus, he do that." She couldn't resist telling Anna, taking credit. "Old Tarwus, he put spell on ship, say: *Fly away, never come back, all die!*"

And they all had. Anna remembered Tarwus, old and bony and toothless, his wrinkled face scarred and evil. She shuddered. She didn't believe in Tarwus's powers, in which Doubloon believed so implicitly. But those few times she had seen him mingling with the gombey dancers, she had felt in him something dark and sly.

Abruptly she turned and fled and left Doubloon frowning after her.

For a long time her secret knowledge worried Anna. She couldn't bring herself to go to Papa Jamison with the story, for at the least it would have brought Doubloon a cruel whipping and at the most a trial in St. George and hanging for attempted murder. She reminded herself that Doubloon

often lied and loved to brag. She told herself Doubloon
wanted her to *think* that it was her doing that had rid the
island of Editha—to boost her own self-importance.

In the end she did nothing about it, except to have nightmares some nights in which old Tarwus, with his tribal
markings that disfigured his wrinkled face, sang and chanted
over a little fire deep in the cedars and chuckled as he made
up love potions and poisons, all of which he delivered to a
smiling, swaying Doubloon with instructions that this one
would cause love and that one would cause death. From these
nightmares Anna awoke silent and shuddering, wet with cold
sweat in the warm Bermuda nights.

After that conversation with Doubloon, Anna always felt
that she herself had killed Editha. For if Editha hadn't
guessed that she was being slowly poisoned and accused *her*
and quarreled over it with Tobias, she would never have taken
the ship that broke up on the reef, she would never have
drowned.

Although she still felt close to Doubloon, this guilty
knowledge she now shared had put a wedge between them.

And when next Boxing Day, with the twelve days of
Christmas in full swing, the Gombey dancers snaked through
St. George's streets and Anna saw Doubloon's golden form
writhing seductively, her almond gaze focused in a single
direction, Anna followed that gaze.

There stood old Tarwus, smiling at Doubloon's lithe golden
form, pulsing to the beat of the skin-covered gombey drums.
As she watched, Doubloon leaped high in the air and gave a
wild half-human scream and bent over backward so far that
her tall peacock headdress brushed the street. And Anna felt
for a moment that she did not know Doubloon at all. Beside
her, excited half-naked black figures were throwing axes and
bows high in the air and the crowd clapped and swayed in
rhythm to the drums.

All but Anna.

She felt a sudden savage loneliness. She felt she had lost a
friend.

Although young Anna had not noticed it, Samantha Jamison

had been gazing speculatively at Doubloon ever since Editha's abrupt departure. There was a glimmering of suspicion in her pale blue eyes. For slave revolts were always simmering in Bermuda, and slaves poisoning their masters was more common than one liked to think. She kept her silence because she had no real proof and it was plain that Anna was happy in Doubloon's company—but now her gaze followed Doubloon when the golden-skinned woman moved about.

Doubloon had an instinct for such things. She was quick to note Samantha Jamison's changed attitude toward her.

Anna never suspected Doubloon at all when Samantha Jamison had her heart attack and died. Samantha Jamison had a history of attacks and had been in delicate health ever since Beatrice was swept away by the plague. Samantha's death saddened them all, but it came as a surprise to no one.

And this time Doubloon kept her silence, patting her little vials and smiling.

Now at last her position was secure.

Anna grew closer to Papa Jamison after Samantha's death. Grieving, they strove to comfort each other. And for Doubloon these were golden days in the sun; she of them all was perfectly contented with her life. She had Temera, the wild new field hand, for a lover. On moon-drenched nights she stole away from a house draped in mourning, where the mirrors were turned to the wall, and Anna and Tobias wept in their sleep, stole away and lay with her ebony giant beneath the palms on the white beach—and plotted revolt.

These were dark days for the islands. Slave revolts simmered again and again. Sometimes a curfew was imposed on all slaves. But curfew or not, Doubloon could always slip away to Temera, finding her way silently through the rocks or through the tall grasses to some secret place where she could strain against his hard-muscled gleaming black body beneath the stars.

Anna knew Doubloon had a lover—it was the only explanation surely for the furtive way she slipped away each night. She never suspected that Doubloon was a leader in the coming slave revolt, that night after night she stood in a little clearing deep in the cedars, surrounded by a circle of shining black faces, screaming "Death to all the planters!"

She knew Doubloon was influential and catered to among the black house servants and field hands alike—but she never guessed the reason.

The slave revolt, when it came at last, failed. One of the cross-shaped manor houses on the other side of the island was set afire, three barns were burned, half a dozen white women and children slaughtered—and in retribution more than double that number of blacks. But Doubloon was not among them; she had come down with one of the fevers that periodically swept the islands and lay in bed, out of her head and burning up with fever, talking in disjointed fashion while Anna bathed her forehead and worried over her.

The revolt went on without her.

So it happened that by the time she recovered, a dozen of her conspirators were dead and Temera, who had escaped and was hiding out, was nowhere to be found.

Doubloon found him, of course, and managed to bring food to him surreptitiously. It was never enough, for Temera had a big appetite. He would seize the food she brought him and wolf it down, then wipe a hand over his mouth and fall upon the golden-skinned woman lying lazy and recumbent on the grass as she watched him eat. They would roll about in frenzy and afterward they would talk about stealing a boat and finding some island that would be all their own, but they never actually attempted it.

For Doubloon had had a new thought: If Tobias Jamison were dead, young Anna would inherit. Had she not heard Tom tell Josiah Waite that he had drawn up a will in Anna's behalf, leaving everything to her?

To Doubloon, whose conscience—if indeed she had ever had any—had long ago been beaten out of her by her changing fortunes, the solution to her problem was simple: She would poison Tobias, Anna would inherit, and softhearted Anna would give her her freedom and passage for her and Temera to Jamaica or Barbados, and enough money so that they could set themselves up there in style. For wouldn't Anna be grateful, Doubloon reasoned—judging Anna by her own lights—when she finally told her what she had done in killing off Tobias, to have come into all this great inheritance?

Anna would have fainted if she had guessed what was in Doubloon's mind.

But Doubloon knew she must be very careful what poison she used. Anna was too softhearted. She must suspect nothing.

So young Anna, mistress of all she surveyed, continued along her serene path. She rode Floss over the green hills and along the white beaches, she danced and flirted with likely lads. She was growing up a beauty and an island empire lay before her.

But sometimes she looked out over the wide blue sea stretching ever away and wondered pensively what the lovely young mother she had never seen had been like, and how she had lived her short life.

PART TWO
The Impatient Lover

Gather your forces and wait a bit,
Though you are hot to bed her.
This is no light-minded little chit!
To bed you first must wed her!

The Bermuda Islands, 1673

CHAPTER 26

Flashing downhill through the giant cedars from the hills behind Lilymeade, the fleet, sure-footed, silver mare fled before the wind like a shadow. Erect and slender in her dove gray riding habit with her big skirts billowing gracefully over the side saddle, Anna Smith was proving once again what a magnificent rider she was. Today—with this very ride—she was going to teach arrogant Arthur Kincaid a lesson!

Her turquoise eyes sparkled and the white froth of lace at her throat blew against her smiling mouth. Her gray-plumed hat had long since blown off and was lost somewhere back in the cedars. In the wild ride her bright hair had come unloosed and was streaming straight back behind her as she cried, "Faster, Floss! Let's teach him not to brag to us!"

Alert to Anna's command, the dainty mare cleared a hurdle of low brush and stones with mane and tail flying and increased her pace to a breakneck speed. Anna stole a glance behind her and gave a reckless laugh as she saw that Arthur Kincaid, who pursued her now on the fleetest horse in his

cousins' stables, a big charcoal stallion named Thunder, was
losing ground as he thundered along behind her.

The glimpse she caught of his face showed frustration and
anger. He too had lost his hat, brushed off by a low-hanging
branch, and she guessed that Arthur, who was mightily proud
of his wardrobe, was cursing that branch right now. With
deliberate intent Anna had led Floss under that low-hanging
branch, lying low on the mare's silky mane, hoping for just
such an outcome. That the branch had cost her her own hat,
lost somewhere in the cedars, mattered not to Anna, but she
knew the loss of his handsome plumed hat would infuriate
Arthur, who prided himself on looking his natty best at all
times.

The branch had not only swept off Arthur's hat—and his
involuntary effort to catch it had almost cost him his seat on
the horse—but it had given him a nasty slap across the face.
That he might have avoided this facial contact with the branch
if he had bent low enough over Thunder's dark mane did not
at the moment occur to Arthur. Angry at the loss of his
expensive hat—bought in Boston, but imported from London
—which he was gloomily sure he would never find again,
and smarting from the sharp stroke of the branch across his
face, he cursed his horse, he cursed the branch, and—he
cursed the girl, that devilish girl with her tempting slender
waist and her breasts like round apples, who flashed in and
out through the trees before him like a wraith. Riding like the
wind, taunting him to catch her!

Arthur could think of several things he would like to do to
Mistress Anna Smith if he caught her. Foremost among them
was a vision that made him suck in his breath through his
clenched teeth. He could see himself dragging the laughing
wench from the mare's back and flinging her down on the
ground before him, where she would lie, startled, at his feet
in that damnably smart gray riding habit, too surprised to leap
up. Her mocking lips would be parted in surprise and the lace
at her throat would flutter with her sharp indrawn breath. On
his booted feet, he would stand over her prone form, legs
spread apart, a sneer on his handsome face (Arthur was only

too well aware he was handsome; from childhood people had remarked on it and he confirmed their judgment in his mirror every day). She would try to rise and he would push her roughly back down with the toe of his dusty boot. She would protest, but what would her protests matter here in the wild? He would tear open his trousers, while she, cowering on one elbow, her turquoise eyes now wide and dark with fright, tried desperately to scramble to her feet and crawl away from him. A boot planted squarely on her stomach would put an end to that! And as she struggled desperately with the boot, which was threatening to crush her even as it pinned her down, he would fall upon her as inexorable as death and take what he wanted from this maddening wench who was so set to best him.

His breath sobbed in his throat and his eyes nearly glazed over as he pictured how he would go about it. A virgin she was—all those he had asked maintained no man had ever had her. A virgin...*But not for long!* She would find him an impatient lover. Fiercely he would grasp her in his arms, uncaring if his fingers left bruise marks across her white flesh. Her struggles would be a delight, only adding to his pleasure as he tore that blasted riding habit from her back! And then her chemise—ah, he could hear the fabric rip like sweet music in his mind. Naked now, panting above her, he would bury his face in those impudent young breasts, twine his hands in that lime-scented golden hair and ruthlessly hold her head in position while he worked his will on the body she flaunted, he would thrust deep within her and revel in her sudden cry of pain as he took her maidenhead!

And if, when he was done, she still had will and strength to resist, he would bring her to heel again. She would pay a price for inflaming him—by God, she would learn he was master! Pain struck through his groin and he felt almost sick with longing and frustration as he watched the slender figure in the tight dove gray riding habit increase the distance between them on this mad downhill run.

Anna would have been shot through with indignation if she had known what Arthur was thinking.

That he desired her, she well knew, for Arthur had been
pursuing her all week—but in another fashion from this wild
careen through the cedars. Having shouldered aside Grenfell,
Arthur now danced daily attendance on young Mistress Smith.
Grenfell might have protested Arthur's usurpation, but he was
in no case to. His father had made a fast recovery from his
injury; hobbling around again on a cane at Great Grenfell, he
required his son's constant attendance—mainly as a crutch
when going up and down stairs, Anna was sure, for he could
not depend on Grenfell for much else. Chagrined, Grenfell
was forced to confine his courtship to a series of overheated
sonnets, which were delivered to Mistress Smith twice a day
by laconic servants.

Anna found the change from meek Grenfell to arrogant,
overpowering Arthur exhilarating.

In the last week Arthur had all but camped out at Mirabelle, taking half his meals there. His shiny boots were to be
found more frequently tucked under the massive cedar dining
table at Mirabelle than under the long walnut board at
Lilymeade, and his handsomely embroidered gauntlet gloves
rested upon the rosewood hall table as if they belonged
there—indeed he would have spent his nights at Mirabelle
had not Mistress Smith firmly ushered him to the front door
when it was time for bed and closed it upon him, leaving him
to ride home in the moonlight brooding about her. Already
Arthur had assumed a proprietarial air with Mirabelle's servants, ordering them about as if he were their master. To a
man, they disliked him and obeyed him with reluctance.

Arthur had asked Anna to show him about the estate and
she had complied, for she loved riding over it herself. Talking
about the place, recounting with enthusiasm all the things
Papa Jamison had done to improve it, she walked her horse
beside his along the great sweep of coastline that was Mirabelle's, over its fertile fields and up through banks of wild
flowers into the magnificent forest of virgin cedars, some
measuring fifteen feet in circumference.

"These should be cut," Arthur muttered. "They would
bring a fortune for ships' timbers."

"They will not be cut while Papa Jamison is alive—for he loves them as much as I do." Anna gave Arthur a level look.

Arthur returned her a supercilious smile. "You will wait till after his death?" he drawled. "*Then* you will cut them?"

Anna colored. Arthur's lofty manner nettled her. "I do not desire money as much as all that," she said shortly.

Arthur made no comment and they rode in silence through the tall trees, listening to the sighing of the soft wind through the branches. Looking about her, Anna gave the beautiful trees, endlessly old, a look of real affection. To her they had always seemed like green castles rising against the vaulted blue of Bermuda's skies. The winding paths between them were like the church aisles of some lofty open-air cathedral, and the sunlight streamed through their branches as magnificently as through tall stained-glass windows, sending down filtered shafts of light in green and lemon and gold—and at sunset, when the air was hushed, shafts of rose and coral and red and orange and violet. The cedars were a heritage of these islands, an heirloom, if you please, of Mirabelle itself. It would be sacrilege to cut them!

Of a sudden, impulsively, she wanted to share this wonderful feeling the cedars gave her. She tried to tell Arthur how she felt about the cedars, this lovely forest where she loved to ride, but she saw that he was not listening. He was muttering to himself and it came to her with a sense of shock that he was actually tallying up their worth!

It had marked him down considerably in Anna's estimation.

Still he was a stranger with the glamour of far places, he was handsome above the ordinary, he was reputed to be wealthy—and indeed his clothes bore out that impression for he had arrived with an unconscionable number of trunks, his silk stockings always matched his trousers and he was seldom seen in the same doublet twice. And he was in love with her. If you could call it love—that heat that glowed in his eyes when he looked at her, the intentness with which he followed her about. And Anna had to admit she found his pursuit an entertaining summer pastime.

Thrice a day Arthur importuned her to marry him. Thrice a

day she went her laughing way and refused him. On wine-velvet bended knee—and that knee on the Turkey carpet of the drawing room while Mistress Smith's yellow silk skirts were spread out decorously on a long settee—Arthur implored her to consider his suit. Across sparkling glasses of Mira-belle's best wine, he urged on her the joys of Boston, which he insisted were unending. On horseback—and Arthur cut a handsome figure on a horse—he told her that in America there were endless forests for riding—she need never take the same trail twice if she did not choose to—compare that to a handful of paths on some dot of an island in the Atlantic!

With heated passion, for nearness to Mistress Smith's knees even in two layers of silk caused the blood to rush to his head and his nervous fingers to loosen the lace at his throat, he described, on Mirabelle's long veranda, Boston's streets and shops and the bustle of trade that was ever present—in Boston she'd have a vast continent behind her instead of this fragile fishhook island chain!

"Ah, but these are very special islands!" she rallied him. Daintily she took a sweetmeat from a silver compote atop a little cedar stretcher table with turned legs. "They are the tops of volcanic mountains, Arthur. Submarine mountains rising from the blue depths. Has Boston *that* to offer?"

"You'd like America, Anna," he insisted stubbornly. "There are endless forests, wide deep rivers, springs, wells—Bermuda has nothing like it."

"We have the cedars—and we have an entire ocean!" she scoffed.

"But no fresh water!" he was quick to point out.

In retribution for his wanting to cut the cedars, Mistress Smith considered him with malice. "We *do* have fresh water, Arthur," she told him with wide innocent eyes. "It comes from the sky. We call it rain."

Arthur, who lacked any sense of humor, pounced on that. "It falls from the sky indeed—and goes down catchments, into cisterns to be saved and drunk later. But it isn't like a broad river flowing by that you can swim in, sail upon, skate on in winter when it freezes. And where are your blue lakes or gushing springs with clear cold water to drink?"

No, she thought suddenly, looking out past the brilliant bougainvillaea vines to the vivid ultramarine sky, these lovely islands caught at your heart but hillside catchments and slave-whitewashed stone roofs to catch rainwater for the cisterns—that *wasn't* like having a blue lake or a river flowing by or clear cold gushing springs where you could stop and drink.

And for the first time really she contemplated life in an entirely different background, with different vegetation and climate—a different way of life.

It made her look at Arthur with startled turquoise eyes and from his expression she could see he felt he was making headway with her—an impression she quickly sought to dispel by informing Arthur that she could not spend the afternoon with him today, for she had to go over the plantation books with Mr. Porter, the factor.

"But I could do that for you!" protested Arthur. " 'Tis a man's job and not suitable for a woman."

Anna gave him a scathing look and her silk skirts rustled as she rose from her big thronelike woven reed chair. "Not at Mirabelle," she said crisply. "Papa Jamison has taught me to manage the affairs of the plantation so that I can take care of things while he is away and I go over the books regularly."

"Then I will stay and help you!"

She shook her head. "Doubtless they are wondering at Lilymeade where you are," she said dryly. "And why you, their houseguest, spend so little time with them!"

"Oh, no, they know where I am."

That was undoubtedly true! thought Anna, who was beginning to tire a little of Arthur's constant and demanding presence.

She might have been more impressed with his zeal had she not chanced to learn from Sue that Arthur had spent the week previous learning the extent of Tobias Jamison's holdings and just how great an heiress this Anna Smith was. He had even, Sue whispered, tittering, asked her father *if Anna was a virgin!*

Now Anna's turquoise eyes gleamed with malice as she saw how far in the lead she was on this race to the sea.

At first—like everyone else—Anna had been attracted by Arthur's flashy good looks and charmed by his easy flattery. But that he had made sure of the extent of her wealth before he had declared himself besotted—! And to dare call that *love!* And to have actually *asked* someone if she was still a virgin!

Anna had come away from that conversation with Sue determined to humble Arthur if it was the last thing she did. The chance had come sooner than she had expected when he had asked her to go riding with him. She had been quick to accept and if her eyes had burned unnaturally bright, Arthur had thought that but a natural female reaction to his masculinity—and not the fiery resolve to humble him it really was.

She had gazed at Arthur on the mighty stallion, calculated his weight and the power of Thunder's long legs, and cast a glance at dainty Floss beneath her, tossing her silver mane. And then she had turned her turquoise gaze up at the cedars, rising lofty on the hills above them and chosen her terrain well. Although the big charcoal stallion had more staying power on a long straightaway where his long legs might run away from Floss, supple Floss, with only Anna's light weight on her back, would wind through the tree trunks like a silver arrow.

With a sweet smile on her face, Anna had led Arthur to the top of one of these low hills and flung him her challenge to a downhill race.

Now as she glanced back, taking joy in his vain efforts to catch her, she caught her breath. Weaving in and out of the giant cedars, Arthur had reached the barrier of brush and rocks Floss had cleared so easily. But Arthur was not possessed of Anna's superb horsemanship, nor did he have the confidence of the horse beneath him. At the brink of the low barrier of brush and rocks she saw the big horse shear off and rear up, refusing the jump. Arthur, caught unaware, slid ignominiously over Thunder's charcoal mane to sprawl head-first into the brush.

That sight sobered Anna, who up to now had been wickedly

enjoying her lead over pompous Arthur. She brought the silver mare to a halt, gave her trembling neck a pat and wheeled her about.

"We must go back, Floss, and see if Arthur's hurt," she whispered to the mare, who tossed her head as if she understood and would brook the disappointment of not being allowed to race untrammeled all the way down to the sea.

More sedately now the silver gray mare picked her way back to the spot where Arthur, red-faced and with his plum velvet trousers torn, was cursing his mount, the terrain, and the world in general as he struggled to his feet.

Anna could see from the pettish way he moved, and the angry way he was brushing leaves and twigs from his torn trousers, that all that was hurt was his pride.

"I think I have won my wager," she said gaily, smiling down on him without malice. "For I'd surely have beaten you in our race to the sea. Once you were thrown, you could never have caught me."

Arthur's face was dark with humiliation as he looked up at this slight, smiling figure with the disheveled mass of burnished gold hair falling down around her slim shoulders. In the past week Mistress Smith had beaten him at cards, defeated him at bowls, roundly shellacked him at all the popular parlor games, and even yesterday had taken a set from him in tennis, a sport she had learned but this week—and from him!

Now she had beaten him in a downhill race—he, Arthur Kincaid, who prided himself on his horsemanship! This mere slip of a girl had beaten him! His ignominy was complete.

"I'll kill this damned beast!" His voice was thick with venom as he raised his whip to strike his trembling mount.

Anna came alive to Thunder's danger.

"If you do, your Cousin Walter will turn you out," she declared crushingly. "For Thunder's his favorite mount."

"Then I'll pay Cousin Walter whatever damages he chooses to name—but *afterward!*" The whip was about to be brought down when Anna swung her own riding crop and struck it from his hand.

"If you touch that horse, Arthur," she said through clenched teeth, "I'll have *you* horsewhipped! Next to Floss, Thunder's the best horse on these islands and I won't have you abusing him!" She herself was terribly fond of the big charcoal stallion and had often asked Walter Meade to sell him to her.

"No wench will tell *me* what to do!" roared Arthur. He would have reached down to seize his whip again but that Anna, her anger now matching his own, brought down her riding crop with stinging force across his face, marking it with a red weal.

No woman had ever before raised a hand to Arthur Kincaid.

And having marked him—had she known more about Arthur's background—Anna might have followed the prudent course and wheeled Floss about and fled.

For Arthur had not come to Bermuda because he was eager to meet the relatives he had never seen, as he smoothly told everyone. Arthur could not have cared less if he never laid eyes on the Meades, and especially his cousin Walter Meade, who was as strong as an ox and looked as if he might put Arthur in his place if he went too far.

Arthur had left Boston because of a wrangle with a tavern maid. Arthur had lured her to his house on the pretext of a post with better pay and promptly tried to bed her. When she had resisted his advances, Arthur, far gone in drink, had flung his tankard, which was half filled with brandy, at the girl. The brandy had splashed over her skirt and the terrified girl, with Arthur bawling at her to get out, had slipped and fallen in her hurry to escape the room. Arthur, already pelting her with curses, followed by hurling a pewter candelabrum at her. The candles thus hurled should have gone out in transit, but one of them unfortunately had ignited the alcohol that had already saturated the girl's skirt and she had run from the house screaming, with her skirts afire. An alert passerby had seized her and promptly plunged her into a mud puddle and got the fire out, but a crowd had collected around the crying girl, observed the ugly burns on her legs and muttered when they heard her story. There was talk in Boston of arresting Arthur. Money changing hands in the right places had scotched the chance of arrest, but friends warned Arthur that the girl's burly sailor sweetheart, home on shore leave, had threatened to pour a whole bucket of brandy over Arthur's head and ignite it.

Thoroughly frightened, for he was at heart a coward, Arthur had fled the town until the girl's burns should heal, her sailor sweetheart sign up on another ship and clear port, and the whole thing blow over. He could not really see the importance of the matter. The girl was a nobody—as he had, with a yawn and a pinch of snuff, explained to the officials he'd bribed—and her burns were minor. He had—although he did not acquaint the officials with that fact—done worse to chambermaids who tried to flout him—not that many had. In Arthur's household chambermaids—indeed all the defenseless female help—had gone in deadly fear when Arthur was growing up. For had he not tripped Ruth when she was carrying that heavy laundry basket and caused her to fall downstairs and break her leg? And had he not poured the pot of scalding molasses down Moll's back? Of course, he had sworn both were accidents but *they* knew. For hadn't Ruth refused him the night before her "accident"? And hadn't Moll, weeping, told him she'd have to leave off going to his bedroom of nights because she feared she'd become pregnant— and the very next day met a torrent of hot molasses that had left her scarred and near killed her? And going to Arthur's parents was no avail. His father was a drunken bully who cared for no one and came to the assistance of none, his mother an indifferent lady of fashion who had borne Arthur reluctantly and forgotten him the day after, leaving him in the care of maids whom he terrorized as soon as he was old enough. She turned a deaf ear to all cries for help.

In Boston Arthur was allowed to go his own way. As a child he tormented birds and dogs and cats with happy abandon. When he learned to ride, it was horses he punished— laming three and injuring another so badly it had to be destroyed.

When Arthur reached puberty and discovered girls, life for the help in his home became one long nightmare. He lay in wait for them in dark corners, he bedded the willing and raped the unwilling, he deflowered the innocent. He saw to it that the chambermaids' rooms had broken latches or he had

keys made, whichever suited his purpose, and the tired girls
stumbled up to their attic rooms only to be wakened in the
night by a pillow smothering them as Arthur in a level deadly
voice gave them instructions—for he tried out on the servants
all the cruel sadistic things he heard whispered about at
school.

As a child he had been a callous bully. As an adult he was
a monster.

But not one bit of the evil that was in him showed on his
handsome face—unless one counted the slightly cruel look
around his mouth, which few noticed, or the sudden look of
cunning that would come into his brown eyes.

The Meades, of course, had no idea what Arthur was really
like. They had taken him in because he was a kinsman and
had written to them that he was coming for a visit to meet his
cousins at Lilymeade. They had introduced him to their
neighbors and handsome Arthur, who could be pleasant
enough when he wanted to be, had made an instant hit with
the ladies.

Eager not to lose this safe berth in Bermuda until his
friends wrote that Boston was safe for him again, Arthur had
been circumspect in his treatment of the chambermaids at
Lilymeade, but every day he grew more irritable. Surmising
that need of a woman was at the base of his irritability, Walter
had taken him whoring in a St. George brothel but it had not
helped much. Arthur preferred targets of opportunity.

He had considered Anna Smith one of those targets, once
he had learned that she was not a true daughter of the house
but the niece of a bondswoman, and had been shocked when
he realized that to get lustrous Mistress Anna into his bed, he
needs must marry her.

Determined to have her even at such a price as marriage,
he had made careful inquiry into her financial status and had
been more than pleased at what he had learned. A wife with
such beauty and such wealth—for he'd been told Tobias
Jamison was an old man and given to dangerous sea voyages—
what a figure he could cut in Boston if he brought back such
a prize!

To his astonishment and chagrin Anna had scoffed at him,

beaten him at every sport, nettled him—and with a casualness that stung, refused to consider him seriously as a husband.

All his life, when denied anything he wanted, Arthur had cruelly wrested it from whoever had it—be it a toy from another lad when he was small, or the last ounce of strength from a dying horse, or virginity from an unwilling maid. And he had been building up a mountain of frustration and anger against spirited Anna Smith.

And it was on such a man that dauntless Anna, alone in the cedars and in defense of a big charcoal stallion, brought down her whip.

CHAPTER 27

Anna had fully expected her stinging blow to bring Arthur to his senses. His anger she was prepared to confront, but she was taken aback by the look of demonic fury that came over Arthur's handsome face.

He turned white and the mark of her riding crop was a red weal against that whiteness. She sat transfixed as his hand came up for a moment and caressed that red weal.

Then his mouth worked, his face went mottled and he flung himself toward Floss with a strangled cry. He dashed the riding crop from Anna's hand with a blow that numbed her wrist, seized her around the hips and dragged her precipitately from the saddle. She screamed as her foot caught in the stirrup and Floss reared up before Arthur, with a violent gesture, wrenched it free.

"You're but the niece of a bondswoman! A servant who's been raised up!" His hoarse voice came gaspingly in her ear, so great was his fury, and his hot breath raked her face. "You'll take no airs with me!"

Even as he spoke he kicked her feet out from under her, caught her as she fell and before she could move to stop him, his hot angry mouth had closed down crushingly over hers and his hard arms tightened about her with a pressure that threatened to break her ribs.

Anna was stunned by the violence of Arthur's assault. Although all week she had been teasing him unmercifully with apparently inadvertent displays of breast or stocking as she leaned over to pick up things she'd dropped, giving him a glimpse of silk-stockinged leg as she did so or an even more tempting peek down her bodice—for Anna was unmerciful in this respect and enjoyed watching her flushed-faced swains squirm and redden—it had never occurred to her that it might come to this. She struggled furiously in his grasp. But Arthur, off his tennis game though he might be, was entirely capable of holding an angry squirming young woman immobilized while he forced his tongue through her sputtering lips.

Struggling against him as he bent her slender frame backward, Anna found her weight now balanced precariously on one foot, tried to right herself and felt herself falling. With Arthur on top of her she went down heavily in the brush, feeling twigs snap against her back as she broke through them to the friable red earth, damp and fragrant beneath the cedars. Her breath was nearly knocked out of her and the crushing weight of Arthur's long-limbed form pinned her painfully to the ground.

Fighting for breath, she was only half aware of a ripping sound as Arthur's impatient fingers tore the gray broadcloth of her doublet, rending off one of the detachable sleeves and ripping the neckline open nearly to the V-shaped waistline. Now the delicate lawn of her lace-trimmed chemise was all that stood between those strong fingers and Anna's delicately molded young breasts. The thin material proved no barrier, ripping easily, and Anna felt with sudden shock Arthur's damp hands ranging over her suddenly bared upper torso, gasped as he squeezed her breasts with hot insolence.

Choking with rage at these rough caresses, Anna knew bright fear as she felt him seize her dove gray broadcloth skirts, petticoats and all, and roughly drag them upward. She clearly heard her chemise skirt rip as they came. Now his knee was firmly inserted between her thrashing bare thighs, now his long body rested upon hers more insistently.

Inner screams tore through her brain, screams of fury, screams of fear. The twigs were digging painfully into her back through the doublet of her riding habit, but she was powerless, with all her strength, to dislodge him. She could not even cry out or remonstrate with him, for the cruel pressure of his mouth, his sucking intake of air from her lungs, was making the world spin dizzily about and lights seem to crash in her brain.

She felt as if she were dying.

Arthur moved abruptly. His fumbling effort to wrest his trousers open had not succeeded and he must needs shift his position to achieve his purpose. As he moved, his mouth left Anna's for a second and his body lifted from hers. It gave her her chance.

In that moment Anna wrenched free and rolled violently away from him. Still suffocated, with her breath sobbing in her throat as she gasped for air, she could not speak. Her sudden move was involuntary, catlike in its swiftness. With her rent gray broadcloth doublet spilling out a delicate cascade of sheer white lawn and torn lace and revealing a long expanse of bare flesh and a round, pink crested, pearly breast, Anna gained a crouch on all fours. White-faced now and desperate, she was prepared to bolt—to escape him at any price.

But escape was not to come.

Now Arthur had his trousers open and saw that his prey was escaping him. With a howl of rage he plunged for Anna. She darted to the side, chose the wrong direction, collided with Arthur's heavy body—he was on her again, knocking her to the ground she had so recently left.

With her burnished gold hair spread out in a bright tangle in which twigs and leaves were caught, Anna looked up into a face she would not have recognized, a face that lust and rage had combined to contort into what seemed an evil mask.

Gone was the handsome countenance all the girls sighed over. In its place was another face—the true Arthur: brutal, remorseless, bent only on satisfying his lust.

"You can't take me like some tavern wench!" she choked. "You'd hang for it! I am not your whore!"

"Ye've teased me long enough!" The words were a hoarse growl as he held her bare white shoulder to the ground with one big hand while he eased his now half-naked hips into a more comfortable position down on top of her squirming body. "Now I'll take what's mine!"

With what air was left in her gasping lungs, Anna screamed. Her scream was short and sharp and carrying—but that scream too was promptly cut off by the suffocating slap of her gray broadcloth skirts, which Arthur promptly and callously tossed over her head and held over her face with a big suffocating hand.

His impassioned gaze raked over the cool beauty of her naked figure, bared now to his lascivious contemplation, and his brown eyes gleamed. He had wanted Mistress Smith with a pain that knifed through his groin—and now he would have her! He would enjoy her charms to the fullest!

Faced with real suffocation now, sure she would not survive to see Mirabelle again, Anna clawed at the material Arthur held so oppressively over her face but it was held there with remorseless pressure.

But one thought—one thought only—was held uppermost in Anna's whirling brain. Through reeling senses she clung to it, for a savage ripple of unwanted pleasure had gone through her suddenly as his masculine hand roved along her stomach.

Let me not respond to him, she prayed silently. *Though I die of it, let me not respond to him!*

Intent on what he was doing now, lost to all else, Arthur never heard Anna's frantic muffled cries—or cared not if he did. Always a handsome lad, Arthur was endowed with a great sense of his own worth. It had never occurred to him in his wildest dreams that a girl he deigned to offer marriage might actually decline to marry him. And that the wench be of low antecedents—a bondswoman's niece! It was unthinkable. Arthur had been fighting all week the dim realization that Mistress Anna Smith was doing the unthinkable—she was toying with him. It was blazoned before him now in letters of fire. But he would have her anyway! For now he meant to make her his in an old, time-honored fashion. He would put the insolent wench in her place, he would strip away these airs she took, he would make her pregnant and she would come whining to heel soon enough!

Moans rose in Anna's throat as with grim determination he set about his task.

Until an ungentle hand closed over his straining shoulder and he was jerked away from the brink of entering the wildly struggling girl.

"What devil's work is this?" cried a rough booming voice. "Let the wench go!" And as Arthur was fetched willy-nilly to his feet and Anna was able at last to dash the suffocating gray broadcloth away from her face, "My God, 'tis Mistress Anna! Are ye mad, Arthur? Tobias Jamison would have ye whipped across the island at the tail of a cart for this day's work—if he was generous enough not to have ye hanged!"

It was Walter Meade with his deep chest and broad back and rippling muscles, Walter Meade, Arthur's cousin, whose shock of wheat-colored hair was falling over his blue eyes, which were filled with a combination of consternation and disbelief as he hauled his houseguest away from the disheveled girl on the ground.

Anna was thankful to her bones that it should be a man as powerful and heavy-muscled as Walter who had come to her rescue, for she didn't doubt Arthur might have attacked some lesser rescuer and very possibly won. Numbly she came to a sitting position. Her face was still flushed dark with the exertion of trying to draw breath into her heaving lungs while being suffocated and now she bent her head, gasping in air as she tried to pull herself together.

"Mistress Anna and I were only frolicking," began Arthur defensively, at sight of his Cousin Walter's dismay.

" 'Frolicking'! Is that what ye call this—frolicking? With the girl's head covered up with her skirt to keep her screams from being heard?"

"You don't understand!" shouted Arthur. "And it's none of your business anyway, what I do with Anna!"

"We were racing downhill." Anna found her voice, albeit she was still gasping. She had swished her skirts down over her silk-stockinged legs and was trying to pull her torn doublet up over her deliciously bared breasts from which Walter—gentleman that he was—was careful to avert his gaze. "Arthur was thrown," she added tersely. "It seemed to madden him. He said he would kill Thunder and when I struck his whip away—"

"Aye, and struck me! She left this welt on my face!" cried Arthur, thrusting out his jaw the better that Walter might view the damage.

Anna gazed on that red weal with distaste. "Yes, and did that too," she agreed. "And might have done worse had he persisted in his attack on Thunder." She gave Arthur a dangerous look. "It was then that he lost his temper, dragged me from Floss's back, threw me on the ground and tried to rape me. I think," she added dispassionately, "that he was going to kill me as well, for he cut off my breath with my skirt."

Walter's honest face darkened. "Ye're a disgrace to the family, Arthur. Ye come to us from Boston and make light of all that we say and do, calling it 'rustic,' and yet ye have no more common sense than to attack a lady!"

Arthur, who had managed to hitch up his trousers as the others talked, gave Walter's broad shoulders a gloomy look. Too broad. He'd seen that rippling back, made muscular by chopping down the big cedars to make sloops. He was tempted to throttle Walter and proceed with Mistress Smith as planned, but he realized with regret that he'd never make it. At his first move Walter would bear him to the ground and perhaps further injure his already stinging face.

"My intent is to marry Mistress Anna," he said sulkily. "Ye know that well enough, Walter."

"Yes, but my God, man, this is rough courting!"

"'Tis no courting at all," declared Anna. She gave Arthur an icy look and turned back to Walter. "And 'tis grateful I am that you came along, Walter, for a moment later would have

been too late!'' She paused significantly. ''But I'll thank you
to forget what you have seen, Walter, for I've no mind to
become the scandal of these islands.''

''And what shame is there in lying with the man ye're to
wed?'' demanded Arthur passionately.

''None,'' agreed Walter. ''But it would seem you brought
her to earth unwillingly. Ye're supposed to get permission,
Arthur, before you rend a young lady's doublet, toss her
skirts over her head and pierce her maidenhead.''

At this graphic description of events, the flush deepened in
Anna's already hot face. ''You are lucky Papa Jamison is
away,'' she told Arthur darkly.

Having realized that he was losing this battle, Arthur threw
caution to the winds. ''Am I so? He'd do naught but have me
marry you!''

''I think not.'' Anna gave him another cold look. ''I think
he'd prefer to shoot you.''

''What! And have ye bear a bastard child?'' sputtered
Arthur, to whom the idea was inconceivable.

''No child of mine would need lack for a father,'' Anna
retorted. Her tone was like a slap.

''Mistress Anna is right,'' agreed Walter severely. ''She
lacks not for suitors, Arthur, and there are plenty of men on
this island who'd stand up with her, ruined or not!'' He
turned to Anna. ''I thank you from the bottom of my heart,
Mistress Anna, that ye've decided not to pursue this matter,
for Arthur here is still our kinsman and our guest and my
mother would near die of shame if a guest in our house was
brought up on charges of raping a neighbor's daughter.''

''She's not Jamison's daughter, and I didn't rape her!''
cried Arthur, maddened.

''Near enough!'' Walter gave him a savage cuff on the ear
that sent Arthur staggering backward. He reached for Thunder's bridle and beckoned to Anna. ''Come mount up, Mistress Anna. I'll see you and Floss safely home and Thunder
safe in his stall. As for my Cousin Arthur here, he can walk
home. The exercise may work off some of his spleen.''

By now Anna had managed to regain her breath and even
to regain some of her aplomb. She realized that she was

actually unhurt although her back was scratched and Arthur had pinched her breasts hard enough to turn them black and blue. Her riding habit was ruined and her chemise would have to be discarded but her virginity was still intact—indeed she had emerged triumphant from a terrifying encounter.

She vaulted to the saddle, unmindful of the flash of bare curves and white skin as she did so. A second later she had caught up her gray doublet with her fingers, held it together with one hand.

"I leave you with this warning, Arthur," she called over her shoulder. "If you bother me again, or if you speak out against me and slander me, I will have Walter here call you to account—and if that is not enough to quiet your tongue, I will charge you with attempting to rape me!"

"No court would believe you!" howled Arthur. "You are a notorious tease, a flirt—you *invite* assault!"

That there was some truth in his last remark stung Anna.

She turned in the saddle. "And if I *do* charge you, and the case comes to trial and you are acquitted, be certain that if Papa Jamison does not shoot you himself—which is likely—I will have certain gentlemen of my acquaintance find you some dark night and drown you in the sea. You will not live to see Boston again, Arthur, if you dare to make free with my reputation!"

There was no truth in this latter remark. Anna did not know anyone who would do such a deed for her, but she hoped sincerely that Arthur would believe it. She could not hear Arthur's strangled reply, for she had already urged Floss forward and the underbrush crunching under the hooves of the three horses drowned out what he said as she and Walter departed.

It was a pity she did not look back, for the sight would have done her heart good. Arthur stood there with a mixture of emotions fighting for mastery of his handsome countenance— a turmoil of wild rage and self-pity and frustration. His features were contorted, his eyes bulged, his breath heaved raspingly in his throat. He looked as if he were about to burst.

She had escaped him! The damned slippery wench had escaped him! Blast the luck that Walter should come riding by at just the wrong moment! Blast Walter for daring to interfere in what was no affair of his! Blast Walter for being so powerful in build that only a man demented would attack him with his bare hands in broad daylight! He cursed himself for not having brought his sword along, for he could have slashed to ribbons an unarmed Walter Meade and left him in the cedars—aye, and the wench too if she protested too much! As it was, Walter would go back and tell the Meades all about it and Arthur would no longer be welcome in their home.

Arthur felt dismally sorry for himself. And to make it all worse, a pain knifed miserably through his groin, reminding him vividly of what he had almost had—and missed.

With a despairing groan of pure self-pity, Arthur threw himself face down on the ground, hammered the turf with his clenched fists, and sobbed like a baby as the sounds of their hooves diminished and the riders disappeared. His self-love had been violently punctured.

Anna, had she looked back, would have given a scornful laugh. But she did not look back. She had fought Arthur valiantly—indeed she would have fought him to her last breath, and she had held her calm while she told Walter about it.

But now a nervous reaction had set in and as she rode, she discovered that she was trembling. She was ashamed that this should be so, and hoped that Walter would not notice her attack of "nerves." She tried to speak and was shocked to find her teeth were chattering.

"If ye'd care to stop and collect yourself for a moment, Mistress Anna?" Walter asked solicitously.

"Just—just for a moment, Walter." Anna reined Floss in and leaned forward along that long arched neck, buried her face in that familiar silver mane and told herself she was safe—safe. She was back aboard Floss, heading toward Mirabelle. Nothing could happen to her now—nothing.

Walter watched with compassion. He had the good sense to

keep silent. How he wished he had smashed Arthur's teeth for him! Indeed, if Arthur had the temerity to show up for dinner, he might do it yet!

"Mistress Anna," Walter hesitated. "Are ye sure he didn't—?"

"No—he didn't." Anna's voice was muffled and Walter gave her slender back, dirty and with twigs stuck to the broadcloth, a relieved look. For a moment there he'd thought...

After a few moments in which she managed to bring the four corners of her world back together again, Anna lifted her head. She was feeling better. She gave Walter a wan smile. "I'm all right now. We can go on again." As the horses began to move forward she said soberly, "I'm indebted to you, Walter. For had you not come along when you did—how *did* you happen to come along, Walter?"

"I was riding to find the work crew, felling a cedar up above us." Walter jerked his head toward the summit of the next hill. "And I chanced upon your hat. I recognized it by the silver buckle that caught up the gray plumes."

"Yes," murmured Anna. "'Tis hand-worked, with my initials graven upon it." For the first time she noticed that Walter had the hat attached to his saddle. Arthur's unexpected attack must have rattled her more than she had realized, she thought ruefully.

"I listened and I could hear a horse crashing through the brush below me—"

"That would have been when Arthur fell off."

"And then a little later I heard you scream and rode toward the sound as fast as I could."

"Lucky indeed for me."

"Lucky for Arthur." Walter's strong white teeth closed with a snap. "The men of this island would have strung him up if he'd raped you!"

"Oh, I doubt it," said Anna. "Arthur would have made up some awful story about how I lured him on and half the island would have believed him."

"And the *other* half would have strung him up!"

"You won't let Arthur ride Thunder again, will you,

Walter?'' Anna cast a worried look back at the big gentle horse following them.

"Indeed I will not.'' Walter's square jaw closed with a snap. "Nor any other horse from our stable! He may rent a nag in town to carry him about or use his legs, whichever he chooses.''

Anna thought that an extremely fair decision, one which would certainly bring humiliation to Arthur. Her eyes gleamed. Humiliation richly deserved!

"I feel I must apologize for Arthur's treatment of you.'' Walter's frown brought his wheat-colored brows together. "I'd thrash him save that he's our guest—and our kinsman.''

"You are not to blame for your relatives, Walter,'' said Anna crisply. They were now approaching Mirabelle and she reined in Floss.

Walter stopped and looked at her quizzically.

"You need not accompany me to the house, Walter. For my clothes are quite torn and I'd not like the servants to think that you—I mean you have a young wife, and servants tell such garbled stories, and for your sake I'd not like gossip—'' She stopped in confusion. "I will tell the servants I was racing Arthur to the sea and Floss tossed me and the tree branches tore my clothes and I rushed home instead of joining him because I didn't want him to see me in this condition.'' Her winsome smile flashed. "They'll believe me, for they're all convinced I'm bound to break my neck riding.''

Big conservative Walter, married a year now and with a baby scarce two months old, gave her a grateful look. He had been worrying about how it would sound to his jealous young wife, Coraline, to hear that he had squired Mistress Anna Smith to Mirabelle with half her clothes missing!

"You're a fine lady, Mistress Anna—and thoughtful too,'' he burst out. He gave her a troubled look. "Love can make a man do crazed things.'' He was thinking how during his courting days he had clambered to Coraline's balcony on a moonlit night, hanging onto some vines, and near broken his neck when they gave way at the top. "Arthur is a rash fellow and needs a firm hand but—''

"That firm hand should have been applied by his father before he was out of dresses!" said Anna with spirit, thinking of the even-handed justice applied to tots before the boys were separated from the girls by dressing them in little trousers while the girls remained in the same skirts both had worn up to that time.

"But it wasn't. Obviously," said Walter with a sigh. "Still," he added thoughtfully, "he *is* hot to wed you."

"Nonsense," scoffed Anna. " 'Tis Mirabelle he's hot for!"

"That too, I've no doubt. But Arthur's still a good catch and most men are set on a dowry and you can't deny yours will be a good one." He hesitated. "We can't cut him off from polite society, Mistress Anna, even though it should be done. He's our guest and he'll be coming to the Waites' ball tomorrow night with us. Mother's in poor health and—"

"And you're hoping I won't cut him dead at the Waites' ball," guessed Anna shrewdly. "And so bring on a storm of questions and upset your mother?"

Walter nodded miserably. His wheat-colored head hung.

" 'Tis true I'd intended to walk by him with my head in the air as if he were dust," she said truthfully. "But I'm beholden to you, Walter, for saving my virtue and so"—her smile dimpled at him, for she had recovered her aplomb—"I promise you I'll be civil to Arthur. Not that he deserves it."

"No—not that he deserves it," agreed Walter hastily. His friendly smile flashed. " 'Tis more than good of you, Mistress Anna." Hurriedly he took his leave. It had occurred to him that he'd best be back home when Arthur trudged in with whatever wild tales he might bring, so he could forestall tears and accusations from jealous Coraline.

Doubloon had seen Anna ride up. She was waiting for her at the front steps when she dismounted. Her almond eyes took in Anna's disheveled hair, full of leaves and twigs, her rent doublet, which she held together with one hand.

"I see you been ridin' with that Arthur," she observed.

Anna tossed her plumed hat to Doubloon, who caught it in one hand. She was in no mood for questions.

"He get what he want?" asked Doubloon bluntly. She

would have seized Floss's bridle but the gray horse shied away from her. Floss had never trusted Doubloon.

"No, but he tried hard enough," admitted Anna, dismounting. "You'll tell the servants I *fell*." She gave Doubloon a stern look.

Doubloon grunted. "You all full of twigs, been rolling on the ground," she said dispassionately, circling around Anna. "Your back scratched underneath too?"

Anna nodded, keeping a tight hold on her bodice as she swiftly climbed the steps.

"Boz!" hollered Doubloon. "You come take this horse to the stable, have Billy give him a rubdown, you hear?"

Boz appeared from nowhere and Doubloon followed Anna inside, trailed her to her bedroom.

"You goin' marry with him?"

Anna gave a contemptuous sniff. "Not if he were the last man alive."

Doubloon digested that. "You want me kill him?" she asked dispassionately.

Anna, whose face was turned away just then, didn't take Doubloon's calm offer seriously. She read nothing into that calm voice but the sound of friendship, awkwardly expressed. She shrugged. "Arthur may deserve killing but I'll let some other girl's father do that!" She groaned as she dragged her chemise over her scratched upper arms.

"You *sure* you not goin' marry with him?" Doubloon persisted. This time Anna didn't dignify that question with an answer and Doubloon said, "Here, let me help with that." She began carefully to rub ointment into the scratches on Anna's bare back.

Anna pulled away. "I want a bath first," she said with a shudder. She wanted to wash his very touch from her body.

"He no good for you," Doubloon told her, when the bath was brought. "I look into that Arthur's eyes. He bad."

Anna sighed as she sank into the warm water, felt it caress her abused body. "You always say that about men, Doubloon."

"That right." Doubloon shook her head so decisively that her long coarse hair rippled blue black in the late afternoon sun beaming through the windows. "Men no good."

"Even Temera?" Anna shot at her.

For a moment the sponge with which Doubloon was lathering Anna's bare back hesitated. "Maybe not Temera," she said reluctantly. "But he gone, you know that."

"No, I don't know it," said Anna. "But I don't want to know where he is. The authorities are still looking for him."

Doubloon gave one of the deep scratches an unnecessarily hard rub and Anna winced.

"Well, they *say* he may be the one who killed that Morgan woman during the uprising," she pointed out.

"Temera never kill no one," sniffed Doubloon. "He only run away."

"I believe you, Doubloon," said Anna quietly. "That's why I haven't told Papa Jamison or anybody else where I think you go at night."

"You don't know where I go. Nobody know where I go!"

"You go up into the cedars," guessed Anna. "No, don't bother to deny it. Temera's new here, you were too sick to guide him the night of the uprising when he ran away. I believe you when you say he isn't a killer. I saw him carry little Boz all the way back to the house for help that time Boz ran away and fell out of the tree—and I don't think Temera would hurt anyone, much less kill them!"

Behind Anna's wet back, Doubloon hid a smile. Anna was right. It was not Temera—it was she, Doubloon, who had the cool courage to kill anyone who stood in her way. But in her twisted way Doubloon loved this young girl who so staunchly saw good in almost everyone.

"You right," she agreed, sponging Anna's back more gently. "Temera good man—as men go."

"I know," Anna laughed ruefully. She mimicked the way Doubloon always said it, with a shake of her head. "Men no good!"

"Men no *damn* good," echoed Doubloon gloomily. "There, your back all washed. Now I rinse, put on ointment. Heal soon. No damage done. Now you stay way from that man!" She gave Anna a curious look. "You mark him?"

"Across the cheek with my riding crop," remembered Anna with satisfaction.

"Good!" Doubloon chuckled. "You learning," she approved, and addressed herself to the job of combing twigs and moss from Anna's lustrous hair.

Having bathed and changed her clothes, Anna went out onto the broad veranda. She felt restless. Her violent encounter with Arthur had waked banked fires in her—fires that had been slumbering, ready to ignite. Now she admitted to herself that she had teased him, goaded him. That was no reason for his control to snap like that, of course.

She bent to pet Coral, who rubbed luxuriously against her ankles. Then she seated herself in a big woven chair and looked about her. Around her Mirabelle stretched, lovely and rich and dreaming in the late afternoon. Even its soil was rich—so rich that if you stuck a twig into the ground it seemed at once to burst into bloom or rise into a great flowering hedge. The air was fragrant with blossoms and something new seemed to have invaded the air—a new wild scent of recklessness and passion.

Anna sighed and gave way to strange new thoughts about the world of men, thoughts that were interrupted by little Boz, who brought out a big blue and white earthenware bowl of smooth-skinned pink and yellow fruit. He set the bowl down beside Anna, snatched one and ran off laughing.

Thoughtfully Anna selected a mango. Arthur had enthusiastically called them the "peaches of the tropics" and said they wouldn't grow in Boston.

Arthur. Her pretty face hardened and she took an unnecessarily vicious bite of the luscious mango. Any headway Arthur had made with her, he'd certainly lost today!

But now in the late afternoon sun, she lazed on the broad veranda with her slippers resting daringly on the wooden railing—for after all, who could see? The luxuriant flowering vines hid her dainty legs from the view of anyone who might come suddenly round the corner of the house. And so, with scratches on her back from the rough wooing of an overheated suitor still smarting, Anna Smith leaned back and gave thought to her future.

She could, she knew, take her pick of suitors from among Bermuda's young men. So far she had not seriously considered any of them—not Lance or Ross or Grenfell or any of the others. And certainly not Arthur, the visitor from Boston. She was not even sure exactly what kind of man she wanted—only that she did not want those she had so far seen.

But today's events that had so nearly catapulted her from girlhood to womanhood had waked strange stirrings in her breast. What would he be like, this man she would desire above all others? How could she find him? Suppose—chilling thought—suppose he never came along?

Suppose—suppose she chose none of them, this pack of ardent swains who pursued her. Perhaps she could wheedle Papa Jamison into sending her away to school in London. There she might meet and marry an earl. Or perhaps even a duke.

Nothing is impossible to the young.

And so Anna lay back, luxuriously dreaming, letting the hours flow past her the way migrating birds, streaming along the Great Eastern Flyway, fled past Bermuda on the wing. She had no idea that for her the dream was ending, that the bright world she had known at Mirabelle would not last past tomorrow, that Bermuda would become her past, for her destiny lay elsewhere than these pleasant green islands—and perhaps it is kind that the future does not lift its veil to us, for Anna might have trembled had she known that her future would be decided by two incredible trials.

CHAPTER 28

An imposing sight in her flowered Italian silk overlaid with tissue (last year's best dress remade, but with all those black velvet ribands to accent it, who would notice that?), Deborah

Waite looked around her at the ball in progress at Waite Hall
with some satisfaction. She had the same coloring as her
eldest daughter, Chloe, the same aggressive personality and
air of a martinet—but there the resemblance ended, for
Deborah had a glow that Chloe would never achieve and none
of Chloe's spite. Married twenty years and not yet in her
forties, Deborah Waite had an enormous energy that swept all
before it. She engulfed her family with projects, involved
them in all the social doings of the island, and kept them in a
perpetual state of exhaustion—especially her husband, who
sometimes felt that Deborah, whom he loved with the devotion of a lost dog, was coming at him from all sides. Born
poor, Deborah—who might have had other "better" catches—
had waited to marry until Tom Waite came along. He was a
younger son with small expectations but he was, above all,
biddable, and Deborah had spent the last twenty years bossing
him and—now that her four daughters had reached marriageable age—imposing her will upon their futures.

Tom—dear foolish Tom. Deborah smiled ruefully as she
considered the awkward figure he cut slouching by the door
of their wide entrance hall. Tom would never stand straight,
he would never be able to push his way to the top, he would
never even be able to keep his stockings up—look at him now
with the black rosettes of his garters already giving way and
his mended stockings sagging down into his boots! His
clothes were shabby, for on one thing at least Tom Waite had
stood firm: he would not be got up like a peacock while they
were still heavy in debt. So Deborah and her daughters were a
handsome sight in gowns contrived from last year's finery,
but Tom Waite wore anything that was handy. It was a sort of
truce arrived at between man and wife.

Life had not been easy for Deborah. Tom had been lucky
enough to buy a considerable holding here in Bermuda with
the small sum his father gave him but he had never had any
capital to develop his acreage. He was an indifferent farmer,
allowing others to take advantage of him, and he spent most
of his days with a crew cutting and hauling the giant cedars
that were so in demand to make sloops. Deborah, by marshal-

ing her daughters to her aid, had been able to get by with a
minimum of servants and had gained an enviable position in
island society.

Take tonight: Who would notice in the glitter of home-
dipped candles (set in chandeliers and wall sconces neither of
silver nor crystal but simple pewter) that the rooms of Waite
Hall were rather small? On warm nights like this, humid and
flower-scented, the guests *preferred* to overflow from the twin
living rooms into the lush gardens riotous with hibiscus and
bright with the colored paper lanterns that Deborah's daughters had hung from the branches over the stone benches only
this morning.

Over to Deborah's right, stiff as a post in her coral taffeta,
stood her daughter Mattie, bravely displaying her toothy smile
to a new arrival. Deborah sighed. Poor overweight Mattie,
with her prominent front teeth and permanently anxious
expression, would never be a beauty or a belle.... Mattie
didn't want to marry Abner, of course, but for the moment
she was holding up very well. A few moments ago, when she
had looked at Abner Trimble, who stood aimlessly beside her
staring vacantly into space, Mattie's eyes had looked suspiciously
moist. Deborah Waite could only hope that when the betrothal was announced later this evening Mattie would not shame
them all by bursting into tears. Deborah had thought very
hard about Mattie's situation and reluctantly decided on
Abner, who, while he would have been no catch at all for
pretty Alma on whom she was pinning her hopes, would at
least inherit enough money to be able to take good care of
Mattie for the rest of her life. And what did it matter that he
shuffled along without taking an interest in anything? Mattie
could take over his affairs and she, Deborah, would instruct
Mattie as to how to guide him.

It had never occurred to Deborah Waite—indeed she would
have been shocked and outraged had she been accused of
it—that by the very weight of her dominance, she had warped
and bent and twisted her daughters' personalities.

Out of Chloe, her eldest, who so desperately wanted to
match her mother's overriding ways, Deborah had created a

harpy who might never land a man and who would probably make miserable anyone foolish enough to wed her.

Of Alma, by overemphasizing the girl's superficial prettiness, she had created a vain silly girl whose feet were planted firmly in the air. In an island filled with practical seamen and horsey planters, Alma was lost.

Mattie had suffered most of all, for she had a sweet rather buoyant nature and her mother's constant criticism had pushed Mattie into a shell from which she was dragged out quivering on occasions like tonight, braced to endure the blows of the world. Deborah's criticism of Mattie had been constant and harsh, for she had sensed that Mattie might have been so much *more*. Her mother's harshness had sent Mattie scurrying in feverish panic into the leaves of exciting novels and endless daydreams. From those she was being wrenched tonight, for as she stood there in her coral dress, perspiring in the heat, she knew that she would soon be thrust into a terrible meaningless marriage with a boy who would achieve age but not manhood. Numb with the shock of it, Mattie greeted the guests with a bright frozen smile that hid her shyness, and wished the earth would swallow her up before this unwelcome betrothal could happen.

Only Sue had not suffered ruinously under Deborah Waite's tutelage. Sue loved horses and the outdoors, she had a resilient spirit, and being the youngest she had escaped the brunt of her mother's pressure, for Deborah had always believed that once she had disposed of her three eldest daughters she could turn her attention exclusively to her youngest. Deborah had always considered Sue plain. But that plainness had suffered a transformation in the blue dress Anna had given her; the moth had become a butterfly. Tonight Sue looked distinctly pretty and—especially when Lance Talbot came into her field of vision—delightfully animated. Deborah gave Sue a narrow speculative look. The girl was growing up—it might not be too early to begin looking for a husband for her.

Forgetting Sue, Deborah's gaze wandered to her eldest daughter, Chloe, ramrod straight and furious to be wearing

her green velvet—too hot for the weather, and last year's
gown with only a small refurbishing of lace—but Deborah
had decreed she wear it because her daughters must look
different and Sue was wearing blue. That the glamorous pale
blue gown had been a gift of that little nobody, Anna Smith,
caused Deborah's patrician nose to wrinkle in distaste, but the
gown looked so well on Sue—as did the blue lapis necklace—
that Deborah had grudgingly decided to let Sue keep it. She
hoped sincerely that Anna Smith would arrive soon bearing
the earrings Chloe wished to borrow, for Chloe's expression
was vengeful and she had just snapped an angry retort to
something young Willis had said to her—and young Willis
was just about the only lad left on Bermuda with whom Chloe
had not crossed swords.

Ah, there was the little chit now! Anna Smith, making a
dramatic entrance in amber silks on the arm of Grenfell
Adams. Grenfell's mother planned to send him all the way to
Oxford to give the Smith girl time to marry in his absence—
she had told Deborah so. She had added that Anna Smith was
a bondswoman's niece with an uncertain future—for who
could tell what her fate would be if Tobias Jamison remarried,
and wasn't he spending more and more time in Jamaica with
that widow?

Deborah smiled pleasantly at Anna Smith and welcomed
her to Waite Hall. And wished in her heart that young
Mistress Smith was twenty leagues under the sea. For hardly
had Anna entered the hall than popular Alma lost more than
half the young gentlemen who surrounded her as they drifted
toward the far more lustrous Mistress Smith.

Sue, always impetuous, rushed forward to hug her. "Anna,
you're late!" she chided. "Grenfell, why didn't you bring her
earlier?" And as Grenfell muttered something unintelligible,
for his mind was already at work on his next sonnet and he
scarce knew where he was, she said in an undertone, "I do
hope you brought the earrings, Anna. Mamma made Chloe
wear her old green velvet because we couldn't both wear blue
and Chloe has been finding fault with me ever since!"

"Right here." Anna took the earrings from her bodice—a

casual gesture that caused young masculine necks to crane and young masculine eyes to sparkle avidly, for young Mistress Smith's gleaming bosom was a matter of consummate interest to them—and pressed the earrings into Sue's palm.

"I had thought Arthur would bring you," murmured Sue, pulling Anna along with her as Grenfell stopped to speak to Tom Waite. "But you're here with Grenfell after all!"

"I promised to come with Grenfell, remember? You were there!"

"Yes, but I do know how Arthur's been pursuing you and—" Sue peered into Anna's face. "Did you and Arthur have a falling out?"

"Something like that," murmured Anna.

"Oh?" Sue scented something amiss in the wind but couldn't quite nail it down. "Did you know that Arthur has left Lilymeade?"

Anna shook her head. Her turquoise eyes glinted and it was hard to keep silent.

"Well, he has. Moved out yesterday afternoon bag and baggage. No explanation at all. Went out riding and didn't even return to Lilymeade, so I hear, just walked into town and hired a cart and sent it—*sent* it, mind you, didn't go himself, for his things. Mamma asked the Meades where Arthur was, when he didn't arrive with them—you know how eager she is to have eligible men around—and they said they didn't know, they were just mystified by Arthur's sudden disappearance."

Anna frowned. "Did *Walter* say he was mystified?"

"Oh, Mamma didn't ask Walter. He didn't come. The baby took the colic and his wife wouldn't leave the baby, so Walter elected to stay home with her—she's a silly thing, don't you think?"

"Rather lucky, I should say, to have Walter."

"Yes—oh, look out, that awful Willis boy is bearing down upon us; his face is red, so I guess Chloe's been insulting him—yes, Walter is a tower of strength, but his wife could easily have had a nurse bring the baby along and *she* could have gone back to see how it was between dances!"

"Sue, you were born to be a social butterfly," laughed Anna, as Sue adroitly pulled her into the next room to avoid young Willis.

"Me? Not likely! Although my blue dress *has* been a great success—Lance has asked me to dance again and again. And Arthur said I looked like a great lady."

"I wouldn't credit what Arthur says, Sue."

Sue pounced on that. "You *have* had a falling out! Whatever happened? I'd had it from Walter that Arthur was never at Lilymeade, always over at Mirabelle dancing to your tune—I'd half thought we'd lose you to Boston!"

"You'll *never* lose me to Boston," said Anna ironically. "Count upon it!"

"I'm glad to hear it," laughed Sue, giving her hand with a tinkling laugh to young Willis, who had come to claim the next dance. "Well, Anna, I must get these earrings to Chloe. I can see her watching us across the room—and I suppose I can dance them to her as well as walk them!"

And Anna watched the blue silks sweep away from her, and gave Grenfell her hand as he trotted up to claim her first dance of the evening.

Anna had been in no hurry to arrive at the Waites' ball, for if Arthur intended to talk about her, she meant to give him full chance—and enough rope to hang himself—before she swept in and destroyed anything he might have said, with good reliable Walter to back her up. So she had kept Grenfell cooling his heels for some two hours. Grenfell had not minded the wait at all, for on arrival he had immediately pounced on the little writing desk in the corner with its India ink and goose quill pens, and when Anna trailed into the room at last in her amber silks, he turned to her, flushed-faced, and waved a piece of parchment.

" 'Tis finished, my verses are finished," he had declared triumphantly and nothing would do but that Anna must sit down and hear them all while Grenfell roamed back and forth across the room, declaiming.

As it was a very long poem, Anna's attention had wandered and it was a shock when Grenfell had, at the end, fallen upon his satin knees before her and implored her in an impassioned tone, "Promise me you'll wait, Mistress Anna!"

" 'Wait'?" Anna realized she hadn't been listening. "Wait for what, Grenfell?"

"Why, that's what I've been telling you—in verse." Grenfell looked rather dashed. "I'm off to Oxford in two weeks. I'll be studying at Oxford—at the university. And I want your solemn promise, Mistress Anna, that you'll marry nobody else while I'm gone."

"But you may be gone for years, Grenfell."

"Aye, that's true," muttered Grenfell. "But doubtless I'll come home on holiday." He gave her a wild look. "Oh, you *must* promise to wait!"

Anna smiled down into his intense boyish face. Grenfell looked so silly kneeling there. For all that he was twenty-three and might someday become a great scholar, Anna felt that in some ways he would never grow up. She felt—older, since yesterday's tussle in the cedars. Her brush with the harsher side of life, her flashing glimpse of what love should *not* be like, and yet what love *could* be like with the right man, had brought her flirtatious heart to a near awakening.

"You'll have forgotten me in Oxford, before the month is out," she said a little sadly, for she felt in her heart that it was true. Bookish Grenfell would fall in love with Oxford and would find scholarship a jealous mistress.

"Never!" protested Grenfell passionately, seizing Anna's gloved hand and pressing his ardent lips against the creamy kidskin. He looked up miserably. "*Do* promise you'll wait."

"Well, I can't promise that, Grenfell." Anna bent down and gave him a lightly teasing kiss that caused his young face to glow ruddily. She stood up, smoothing down her amber silk skirts with her gloved hands. "But I *will* promise you the first dance—which may be the last unless we leave soon." She walked to the door and called down the hall, "You can retire now, Doubloon. I won't be needing you any more tonight, I'll undress myself when I return."

"You're too good to your servants," complained Grenfell,

accompanying her out. "They do not obey you properly. My mother has noticed it."

And no doubt she has noticed a hundred other things in which to instruct a future daughter-in-law, thought Anna ironically. For to Grenfell's mother *no one* would ever be good enough for her darling boy.

"Doubloon has a lover," she whispered to Grenfell. "I think it's only fair that since I'm off to a ball, that she spend the night in his arms."

"Indeed I do not understand you, Mistress Anna." Grenfell was solicitous about helping her into the carriage. "Young ladies don't speak of such things!"

"Well, perhaps I'm just not a proper young lady," laughed Anna. "But many women, whether 'tis spoken of or not, take lovers—before or after marriage." And to his scandalized look, "Why, you know as well as I do that Captain Marney's wife has her bachelor neighbors to tea on alternate days when he's away and that often as not they stay the night."

Grenfell gulped and told his horse to "Giddap!" Captain Marney's wife's behavior was indeed an open scandal but he did not think it a suitable subject to discuss with Mistress Anna.

"And even you, Grenfell"—Anna could not resist a parting shot—"will admit that's rather long hours for a tea party!"

Happy that she had managed to thoroughly scandalize prim Grenfell on the ride over, Anna had swept into the Waites' front hall just as the musicians finished a strain. Past Sue's blue form that hurried forward, Anna could see the stir she had caused among the dancers in the Waites' long living room and felt she had made a regal entrance.

As Grenfell swung her out for the first measure, the candlelight from the wall sconces and the overhead chandelier shimmered excitingly along the changeable amber silk of Anna's ball gown, making her seem clothed in golden flames as with her movements the light material changed in hue from lemon to gold to copper, seeming to glow with its own light, and casting its glow over Grenfell's copper satin breeches and rich copper brocade doublet. And as always when such beauty came into a room, some vibrancy was imparted to the company so that the pace of the dancing increased, the laughter rose a little higher, and cheeks that had been but pink before deepened to a rosier hue.

Arthur Kincaid, who, at the far side of the room, was keeping a careful distance between himself and his former host and hostess, the Meades, was one of the first to note Anna's figure whirling across the living room floor. His brown eyes gleamed at the sight of her, for Arthur had now had time to think—and even to regret his suddenness. For it was only his suddenness that had alarmed Anna yesterday in the cedars, he had persuaded himself. She had been frightened for the horse and had struck out wildly—probably she had intended to miss him. The mark on his face did not show—his mirror had told him that—so he was inclined to forget the incident and continue his relentless pursuit of the maddening wench who looked so glorious as awkward Grenfell spun her around among the dancers.

He stepped out where he could see her better and Anna missed a step at sight of him. Her teeth closed with a snap, for Arthur was an even more splendid figure than Grenfell in a heavily ribboned plum silk with satin trousers of a violent shade of pink. From across the room he made her a sweeping bow. Anna was tempted to cut him dead, but over his shoulder she could see Walter's mother. She reminded herself grimly that Walter had rescued her and forced herself to give Arthur a civil nod.

Encouraged by that, Arthur swaggered over to claim the next dance.

Dancing with Arthur was *not* something that Anna felt she must endure.

"My dances are all taken this evening, Arthur," she told him distantly, her gaze moving on as if she hardly saw him.

Arthur, who had been prepared to forgive and forget—at least for the moment—now remembered all: his rage, his frustration, his humiliation. His hand shot out and on the wall side, where Anna's amber skirts would hide the sight from the room, he seized Anna's gloved hand in a numbing grip, squeezing so hard he seemed to crunch the bone. "Ye'll not shame *me* by a refusal," he muttered in a low furious tone. "Ye'll dance with me!"

Blank shock registered on Anna's face. Whatever else she had expected, it was not this. She almost cried out in pain at the hurtful pressure of Arthur's fingers as she found herself borne irresistibly out into the dancers. Fury came over her in a bright wave and she almost drew back her free arm to deal Arthur a stinging blow across his cruel smiling mouth but— just at that moment she met the gaze of Walter Meade's mother. A puzzled gaze in a fragile kindly face. Walter's mother—all knew it—was dying of something that doctors could not diagnose, wasting away before their eyes. And it was Walter who had saved her there in the cedars.

No, to strike Arthur would be to make a scene and ruin the Waites' ball. It would call for explanations and those explanations would send Walter's mother home in tears.

Anna looked steadily into Arthur's hateful face and tried to flex her numbed fingers.

"I do not know how you have managed to live so long," she said conversationally. "Surely in Boston there must be somewhere a big brother or a father who objects to your mauling their sisters and daughters!"

In spite of himself, Arthur winced. In Boston there had been several such who had menaced Arthur, and only his wealth and position and twice the hiring of waterfront thugs to beat them to the ground had kept him from their wrath. It was that mention that brought him back to his senses and made him realize, angry as he was, that he was in a civilized living room dancing with a young lady who was the toast of these islands and surrounded by rugged men who would not hesitate to beat *him* to the ground if he insulted her in public. He tried hastily to make amends.

"Mistress Anna!" He tried to make his voice ring with sincerity. "Ye must forgive my impetuous behavior—ye must! 'Twas only my deep love for you—and you must know by now that I love you—that made me behave so. I swear to you"—his voice grew so intense it crackled—"that ye are the only woman who has ever driven me to such excesses!"

That it was a lie made no difference to Arthur—he believed it himself at the moment, for his blood was stirred by the very touch of her—even through her glove.

"I am glad to hear it," snapped Anna. "For I still bear the scratch marks of twigs across my back where you forced me down upon the ground!"

Memory of what it had been like to hold her thus made Arthur's blood pound. He bent toward her with a roguish smile. "Not so loud, Mistress Anna, or others will hear and there'll be those who'll say we should marry."

" 'Marry'? You? An unlikely event, you'll agree." Anna's voice was sweet but her eyes held a dangerous light.

"No, I do *not* agree, Mistress Anna!" Arthur's voice heated up again. "I've much to offer ye—I can bring you the world outside these islands."

"The world of Boston? With you? Ha! I prefer Bermuda!"

"But ye would not, once ye had seen that world," he insisted. "I've a fine house. My parents are dead so there'd be no woman to boss you about. So I was an impatient lover—I admit my fault and beg ye to forgive me. And," he added handsomely, "I'll even do penance, if you please!"

" 'Penance'?" Anna's gaze drifted over the dancers to poor Mattie Waite, who stood like a little gatepost in her stiff coral taffeta dress beside a vacant-eyed Abner, whose stare wandered about. The announcement was about to be made. Although it was Sue and not Mattie who had always been her special friend, Anna felt a sudden rush of pity for the plain plump girl. Poor Mattie, whose head had been in the clouds while her feet were carrying her to disaster—she deserved better, she deserved a whirl at least with someone she admired!

Anna's speculative gaze drifted back to Arthur. "Penance, you say? Very well, Arthur, I'll let you do penance. I'll forget your attack on me in the cedars if you will leave my side at the end of this dance and march directly over to Mattie Waite and use all your charm and show her the most ardent attention all evening long and call upon her every day for a week."

"But Mistress Anna—" cried Arthur in distress, for he had meant only to make the offer, not to carry it out.

"Those are my terms, Arthur. If you do not do it—and

swiftly—this is the last measure I'll ever tread with you even if you break my wrist!''

The music came to a crashing halt. Arthur could see that she meant it. Determined not to lose the ''catch of Bermuda,'' Arthur turned and sprinted toward Mattie Waite. He bowed low with a flourish and requested the honor of the next dance.

Mattie was startled. Never before had the handsome Bostonian, whom she'd met on numerous occasions, been more than civil to her, let alone ask her to walk out on the floor with him. Trancelike, she extended her gloved hand and found herself whirling about the floor with the best-looking man in the room.

Anna watched with satisfaction. Not only was she freed temporarily from Arthur's unwelcome attentions but Mattie would have a glittering evening to remember.

Deborah Waite, whose attention had been for a time worriedly focused on what had threatened to become a shouting match between old Mr. Trimble and Clement Adams, which had now dissolved into mere thorny discussion, was surprised to see her daughter dancing with Arthur. Critically she noted how well Mattie's skirts swung as Arthur whirled her about—a credit to the seamstress who had cut the dress down from one of Deborah's old ones. And although the girl's face was more blotched than usual—it always was when Mattie was excited—surprisingly, Arthur seemed neither to notice nor care.

Really, her daughter looked very well dancing with Arthur; she was not an ungraceful girl and with her brown hair swinging like that—! Deborah turned to meet the bewildered stare of one of her better-off neighbors who, she knew, had designs on the handsome Bostonian for one of her own marriageable daughters. The look on that woman's face made her bridle with satisfaction. She decided indulgently to let Mattie bask in the glow of Arthur's attention for as long as it was focused on her—the betrothal announcement could wait a bit.

When Arthur claimed a flushed, excited Mattie for the next dance as well, Deborah's gaze grew speculative.

Across the room a new idea now occurred to Anna—a way perhaps to rescue Mattie from Abner Trimble. She detached herself from Grenfell and drifted over to her hostess. "They do make a lovely couple, don't they?" she murmured, nodding toward Mattie and Arthur as they swung across the floor.

"I suppose so." Deborah Waite gave Anna a wary look. She wielded her fan methodically and asked herself if it could be possible that beautiful Anna Smith could be jealous of plain little Mattie? Everyone in Bermuda knew that Arthur was madly pursuing Mistress Smith. Could they have had a lovers' quarrel?

"Arthur told me he was going to dance every dance with Mattie," said Anna with a small sigh. "If she would have him." She tried to look pensive.

"Did he indeed?" Deborah's look of astonishment was its own reward.

"She is all he talks about when he visits me," lied Anna glibly. "For he views me as her special friend. He needs must know what she likes, what she eats, where she will be tomorrow." She made her voice petulant. "I am very bored with Arthur's questions and I have told him to ask her himself!" She gave her hostess a rueful look as someone claimed her for the next dance and laughed inwardly at the stunned gaze that followed her.

Anna had not misjudged Deborah as a woman of action. Hardly had Anna's skirts cleared her path than Deborah closed her fan with a click and went over and had a little whispered conversation with her husband. Tom Waite looked out at his daughter dancing with Arthur, and shook his head in bewilderment. But he had never favored this loveless match between Mattie and Abner Trimble, so his step grew jaunty as he sought out old Mr. Trimble and had a short talk with him.

Anna watched this cynically. She had set something in motion. She never dreamed the far-reaching effects it would have on her own life.

CHAPTER 29

"Whatever can have gone wrong?" Sue, looking lovely in the blue dress Anna had given her, cornered Anna as Grenfell left to bring back a plate of refreshments. "Mamma is saying she wants to postpone the announcement of Mattie's betrothal, that after all Mattie *is* her third daughter and she owes it to Chloe and Alma to give them both a chance to make a match first. Papa has already spoken to Mr. Trimble and says he took it very well, for he had given up matching Abner with any of the island girls; Papa thinks Mr. Trimble will give Mattie up now and not push Abner's suit. But Mamma was so insistent on it. Whatever can have caused her to change her mind?" Her blue eyes widened. "Is that *Arthur Kincaid* dancing with Mattie?"

Anna laughed. "He's been dancing with her all evening. You'd have noticed if you hadn't spent your time hiding behind the bougainvillaea kissing Lance!"

A quick blush spread over Sue's expressive face and she cast a quick guilty look about her to make sure nobody had heard that. "Mamma would kill me," she admitted. "For Lance hasn't a farthing—he's land-poor, like us. Mamma says I should look for someone with tall ships to transport Papa's cedars, or with funds to back him in a venture. But Anna, everybody knows Arthur is going to ask for you as soon as Mr. Jamison comes home. What's he doing with Mattie?"

"Dancing with her, Sue. And I don't doubt he'll be bringing her some refreshments soon, which they'll eat together—see, there he goes now. Yes, he's preparing two plates.''

"And he'll be marching over here to share them with *you*," laughed Sue. "No, you're right," she gasped. "He's taking them to Mattie. I can't believe it."

"I can—and I don't doubt he'll be over tomorrow to call on Mattie."

"Oh, he wouldn't—he's never noticed her at all and she's been in his plain sight." Sue had turned suspicious. "This must be your doing, Anna. Why have you put him up to it? Was it—oh, I see, you wanted to make Mamma think Arthur was after Mattie?" Her gentle face cleared. "You wanted to free her from Abner! Oh, Anna, she'll be eternally grateful—just wait till I tell her!"

"You'll tell her nothing of the sort," said Anna irritably, conscious that such an admission, whispered in her ear by Sue, would send Mattie in tears from the room. In turn, Deborah's suspicions would be aroused, she would wring the truth from her tearful daughter, and the betrothal with Abner would be on again. "You'll keep your mouth shut about what you think, Sue, or you'll ruin everything!"

"But don't you realize," gasped Sue, "that poor Mattie is mad about Arthur, has been ever since he arrived on the island? Look at the way her eyes shine, she's absolutely dazzled by all this attention! And see, her face is more blotched than ever. Her blotches always deepen when she's excited—it makes Mamma livid!"

"Why should he not turn to Mattie?" demanded Anna in a cool voice. "*I'm* certainly not interested in him. Indeed, why should Mattie not spend a pleasant evening dancing with Arthur?" She shrugged, feeling she had brought more than one gift to the Waites' household this night, not only a blue dress and a necklace and earrings but a reprieve for Mattie. "You should concentrate on your own affairs, Sue!"

Sue giggled. "I do think I'm making headway with Lance," she whispered.

"You must be," observed Anna. "I see the lace on your bodice is torn. You must insist he be not so hasty!"

Sue blushed and tried to stuff the offending bit of lace down her cleavage. "You know I'd never permit anything like *that*, Anna!" she protested with sparkling eyes.

"Indeed I know you *would*," laughed Anna. "As would any girl in love. You *do* love Lance, don't you, Sue?"

"Oh, yes," sighed Sue. "And I must be so careful that Mamma and Papa don't see us, for they know Lance hasn't a penny nor any expectations and they'd never agree to a match between us."

"I wouldn't let that stop me, Sue. Not if I loved him. And Lance will probably inherit *something* from his parents."

"Not much. It will all go to the older married brothers. Oh, he'll receive a couple of horses no doubt, but nothing Mamma calls *substantial*." Sue looked about her. "Grenfell must have gotten lost—I'd expected him to bring you some refreshments by now."

Anna laughed. "He got sidetracked. I can see him over there in the corner with old Mistress Felton. She's got her good ear inclined toward him and he's undoubtedly shouting his sonnets into it."

Sue peered past Anna and laughed. "I'm surprised you didn't come with someone more dashing—like Flan O'Toole over there." She nodded at a showy lad who was surrounded by three laughing girls. "In fact," she added honestly, "I'm surprised you didn't come with Lance. I know he asked you and—well, up until tonight when I dazzled him with this blue ball gown you gave me, I was afraid he was in love with you."

"Not me, Sue—my fortune," said Anna easily. "No doubt his mother was pushing him in my direction, egging him on, telling him he'd be set for life if he married me!" It wasn't true, but Sue was so much in love with Lance that surely a small well-meant lie wouldn't hurt.

Anna had yet to learn that it was dangerous, meddling in the affairs of others.

"Yes, I'm glad I realized that," agreed Sue, eager to believe it. "But he might never have discovered me, Anna— not as a woman, I mean—if he hadn't seen me in this dress.

Anna, if there's ever anything you want of me, anything at all, you've only to ask.''

Anna laughed indulgently as Grenfell came up with two plates of refreshments and bore her away. But she was to remind Sue of that remark much sooner than she'd ever have thought.

The evening sped on—much like any ball on a hot night in Bermuda. Mothers worried that their daughters' gowns were cut too low; daughters worried that their gowns were not cut low enough. A suddenly blown-up love affair—Sue and Lance's—was almost but not quite consummated amid smothered giggles in the bougainvillaea, and they both agreed, gazing at each other raptly, that they would go riding tomorrow up in the cedars where they could have more—privacy. Both the Carleton brothers got stumbling drunk and had to be taken back and tossed onto one of the big four-posters to sleep it off. Ross, under the influence of rum, tried to call out Stu Baker, but was diverted by Alma's frantic efforts. And the political differences of old Mr. Trimble and Clement Adams eventually developed into a shouting match.

And lustrous Anna Smith, as usual, eclipsed Alma Waite and all the other island girls in the number of young men who vied for her dances.

But for Anna, this night was to be like no other.

The hour grew late and Anna found herself in the scented side garden with Flan O'Toole, who had sailed here from his home in Sandys Parish at the far end of Bermuda's fishhooked island chain. Flan, like the other young men, was drawn to Anna like a moth, mesmerized by her beauty and by her great expectations. Flan had yellow hair and dark eyes and a wild look about him. He had been betrothed to a pretty girl of his own parish, another Sandys girl, Lila Meddler, but Lila had perished on an outing with her betrothed when a sudden squall blew up and drove their light sailboat onto the rocks. That Lila's tragic end had coincided with her father's financial ruin had given Flan a slightly sinister reputation, for there were those who asserted he'd drowned his troubles. All of this had given him a gloss and a luster in the view of the maidens of St. George, for good-looking Flan had a bold and roving eye and who among them would believe it of him?

Anna, still smarting from her humiliation at being dragged out onto the dance floor by Arthur, was considering the possibility of turning the two young men against each other and letting the bigger and stronger Flan give Arthur a sound thrashing. With this in mind, she turned her dazzling smile on Flan and let him whisk her into the moonlit garden, where giggles and a soft, hurried, "Oh, no, you mustn't!" and a feminine squeal issued from the darkness behind one of the big bushes.

"Seems the place is already occupied," smiled Flan, veering off and leading Anna in another direction.

He would have led her into the deepest darkest part of the garden had not Anna stopped him. She stood in her amber silks, swaying in apparent hesitancy as if she could not quite make up her mind. And the sight of her standing there with the moonlight pouring down in a pale golden wash over her gleaming hair and slim shoulders and enticing figure brought a fiery light to Flan's dark eyes.

"Tell me, Flan," murmured Anna, giving the sturdy young man a slanted look from her turquoise eyes. "If someone had—*insulted* me—would you take my part?"

"Instantly!" declared Flan in ringing tones, delighted that Anna would consider him in the role of protector—which was, to his direct mind, but a fleeting step from passionate liaison beneath the bougainvillaea.

"And would you," she asked pensively, wondering if dancing with Flan the last four dances really had borne fruit, "*maul* him a bit to please me?"

"I'd drown him in the sea if you asked me!" cried her overheated suitor.

But his reckless offer was not to be taken up—that night. For there was a sudden commotion in the house and Chloe, a strangely mocking expression on her face, leaned out the door and caroled, "Anna!"

Anna turned in surprise at hearing her name called, just as Flan, his face pressing closer toward her lime-scented hair, asked huskily, "Who is it ye'd like mauled, Mistress Anna?"

"Later," murmured Anna. "I'll tell you later." She caught up her amber skirts and ran toward the house. "What's amiss?" she cried, for she had scented trouble in Chloe's mocking smile.

Without answer, Chloe swung wide the door for her and Anna entered into a breathless hush with everyone looking at her—and then everybody talked at once.

For it seemed that the noise and confusion she had heard in the garden had been caused by Alan Royston of St. George, who had leaped off his horse and plunged through the Waites' front door. Alan, who had been out fishing in the phospho-rescent waters this warm night and moored his boat so late he had not intended to attend the ball at all, had had his mind changed for him—by a piece of news so exciting it would not keep. Always one to enjoy shocking his neighbors, Alan had thrust his skinny legs into his best-cut velvet trousers and his bony shoulders into a stained satin doublet. Still trying to tie the lace at his throat, he had thrown a long leg over his horse and arrived bareback at Waite Hall at a dead run, to burst into the living room, pealing out,

"The *Annalee* has just made harbor and Tobias Jamison has brought a bride home with him!"

A new wife! Startled glances shot across the dance floor with a wild surmise, and fans suddenly flew up to hide what their owners muttered to the person nearest. For half the ladies of Bermuda had tried to snare the wealthy Tobias—and failed. And besides, what would this marriage mean to Anna Smith, who so far had swept all before her?

But Anna, who should have been warned by the narrow glances that came her way—could take in only the delightful news that Papa Jamison was home safe. New wives could be dealt with later. She must be there at Mirabelle to greet him—or should she instead hurry to the ship? Where would he be now, in transit? Could she catch him on the road?

"I must off," she caroled breathlessly to her hostess, and paused to hug Sue, who ran forward.

"I'll escort ye," cried Grenfell. "The carriage will be brought round in a minute."

"No—thank you, Grenfell, but I'd like faster transportation than that. Lance, you live but next door—could you lend me your mount? For I've a mind to race into St. George and see if I can catch Papa Jamison on the road.''

"Of course, I'll bring the horse round," cried Lance, making a dash for the door.

"But you can't ride into St. George alone by night," wailed Sue. *And certainly not with my Lance,* her sudden pout implied.

Anna's impatient gaze roved over the company, passed over Arthur, who sprang forward and now at her sudden frown, slunk back, and over Flan, who had sailed here and had no mount available. "I'll be all right," she insisted.

"But we can't let you!" cried her hostess, rushing forward. "Everybody knows the slaves are seething with unrest. This might be the night they choose to—"

But Deborah's words dwindled away, for her high-spirited guest had already cleared the door and was flinging herself aboard Lance's roan stallion with what Deborah considered a shockingly immodest display of ruffled chemise and long white leg. Before she could more than gasp, Anna was gone, riding away like the wind into the summer night, and one could almost hear the half-audible sigh that went up from the male contingent at her departure.

With snapping eyes, Deborah Waite turned back to her guests. "The dancing must not stop, just because we've lost a guest," she told them with forced merriment. "Come, musicians, strike up!" she cried, with a wave of her arm toward the two half-drunken young bondservants who sat in a corner, playing on violas and beating out a rhythm with their slapping shoe soles. And in an aside to Chloe, who had joined her near the door, " 'Twill be interesting to see who wins out—this new wife or Anna Smith!''

Chloe gave a scornful laugh that plainly showed whose side she was on, despite the loan of the blue earrings. With a bright, venomous smile she accepted her father's hand for the next dance.

It was a pity, thought her mother, frowning as she watched them, to have a daughter who—with all the young men circling this room—was forced back upon her father if she wished to dance a measure! Deborah tapped her fan in impotent fury, and decided ungenerously that if Anna Smith were plucked from the running, there would be more chance for everybody.

So Deborah reasoned as her young guest, with amber skirts flying, fled at a gallop down the moonlit road to St. George.

But Anna had not gone far before she was hailed by an onrushing rider. She pulled up the roan in surprise as she recognized the bony figure of James Prentice, a bondservant who had accompanied Tobias Jamison to Jamaica.

"Mistress Anna!" cried Prentice plaintively. "I've come to fetch you, but—how did you know, that I find you already on your way?"

"How did I know? Why, Alan Royston came riding to Waite Hall with the news that the *Annalee* had made harbor at St. George—and found me among the guests at the ball there."

"No, I mean not that!" Prentice's voice faltered.

"The new bride?" interrupted Anna with a laugh. "Well, Papa Jamison has been alone a long time. He deserves—"

"No, no, Mistress Anna," Prentice moaned. "The new bride is a widow who's been feasting Mr. Jamison on all the rich foods imaginable. He's gained much weight in Jamaica—indeed he's very portly now—and tonight he did eat half a roast duck, dripping in fat. He washed it down with four glasses of metheglin just before we made harbor. And he'd no sooner stepped ashore than he went down like a stone, fell to the dock, he did. Alan Royston didn't see *that*, for he took off running when I called to him from the ship that Mr. Jamison had remarried—I meant for him to warn you, Mistress Anna. But 'twas right after that that Mr. Jamison fell to the dock. He's had a stroke, Mistress Anna, and the doctor's with him now. I came to fetch you on my own account, for I know you care for him, and who knows whether he'll live or die?"

PART THREE
The Outcast

A lustrous lass finds many lads
To court her in the sun,
But in desperate need, indeed, indeed,
She may not find a one!

Mirabelle Plantation, Bermuda, 1673

CHAPTER 30

The weeks had passed and all had changed for Anna Smith. From a carefree island beauty, negligently ordering her slaves about, she had been turned into a drudge.

In the summer heat, clad in a gray homespun dress with a plain white linen apron, Anna sat by Tobias Jamison's bed, sponging the perspiration from his face. It caught at her heart to see a man she remembered as so energetic, so alive, lying so still, so pale, unable to speak, with only his alert old eyes following her movements. He had been this way since the night the *Annalee* had cast anchor in St. George's harbor.

Anna smiled to give him encouragement. "There'll be hot soup soon," she said softly. "And you must eat it. We'll take our time about it, but you need it to keep up your strength, for the doctor says time will heal all."

A tear of gratitude welled from Tobias Jamison's right eye and trickled down his face. He wished he could tell Anna how he felt, how real a daughter she was to him, but he knew in his heart he never could. This frail lass was all that held him back from the Great Beyond. Silently he thanked God for her.

Anna, catching sight of that tear, also caught his thought. She was sure he could hear her although only by blinking his eyes could he communicate with her at all, and one couldn't be sure even then because his eyes had a way of blinking spasmodically. "You've been a true father to me," she told him tenderly. "And even though everyone here would be glad to take my place by your bedside, I won't let them—I claim that right."

His eyes blinked his gratitude.

From the doorway came a slightly malicious voice. "What, still here, Anna?"

"Yes," said Anna shortly.

"Has there been any change?"

"No."

"And won't be," said Bernice crisply. "You might as well come away."

Anna turned silently to survey Tobias Jamison's new wife. *How could Bernice have said that where Papa Jamison could hear her?* She saw a tall commanding woman who had once had beauty and still kept the remnants like rags upon a scarecrow. Her dark eyes had faded but they were still fierce as some bird of prey, her complexion was creamy smooth but not so fair or sheer as it once had been, and the harsh black color of her thick hair was the result of mineral dyes meant to cover up the gray that had crept into her reddish brown locks. Her demeanor was intimidating, her manner had a callousness that appalled softhearted Anna, and her cold tone flicked the girl's raw nerves like a lash.

"I don't know what you mean by 'and won't be,'" said Anna stiffly. "Papa Jamison is better than he was yesterday— aren't you?" She turned with a caressing smile to the man who lay so still in the big four-poster. "And soon he will be up and around."

That possibility had occurred to Bernice too. She had best watch her tongue before Tobias—he might get well!

"Of course, of course," she agreed hastily, frowning at the

figure in the bed. Her voice turned oily. "I only meant you should not sit beside him these long hours; you are wasting away yourself."

"I'm well enough," said Anna indifferently. *As if Bernice cared what became of either of them!* she thought bitterly. She had known *that* since the day Bernice had arrived at Mirabelle.

Her first night ashore had been spent at the inn in St. George, for the doctor had feared to move Tobias. But the next day Bernice had announced that she and her two daughters, who were both near Anna's age, could not remain in the cramped quarters of an inn when there was a large plantation house waiting for them. Over Anna's protests, she had ordered Tobias moved and a jolting wagon had carried him inexorably over the familiar road to Mirabelle on what the doctor whispered might well be his last journey.

On arrival, Bernice had abandoned the supervision of carrying Tobias into the house to Anna and the servants while she herself stayed outside to give loud instructions about the unloading of her trunks and boxes, which had followed them in a large cart. Subdued, with frightened rolling eyes, her two daughters, Pris and Prue, scurried along after their mother as she swept up the wide "welcoming arms" front steps, giving everything about her a shrewd appraising glance as she passed.

While Tobias was closeted with the doctor, Anna had taken Bernice on a tour of the house. Bernice had inspected her new home without comment, although her gaze narrowed a little when she discovered that the second-best bedroom belonged to Anna. But she stood for only a moment in the center of the bright cheerful room with its jalousies that shut out the afternoon heat, its tall ceiling and fluffy curtains and handsome hand-worked blue and white coverlet on the massive cedar bed.

Although Bernice had said nothing, just stood gazing silently about her at Anna's room, there had been something condemning in her glance. Anna had felt acutely uncomfortable and suddenly conscious of all that, since coming to live at Mirabelle's great house, she had learned to take for

granted. They seemed to stare back at her—all the lovely gifts
Tobias and Samantha Jamison had showered on her. That
gilt looking glass in the corner came from London. On the
dainty French dressing table lay the ivory fan that she had
flung there carelessly when she had decided yesterday not to
take it to the Waites' ball. It came from London too. . . . And
the big press fairly bulged with her pretty clothes: dresses of
soft flowered cambric and brilliant India silks and one—her
second choice of what she would wear to the Waites' ball—
flung casually over a high-backed chair. How lovely it looked
there, all frosty pale aqua satin overlaid with silver tissue.

Bernice walked over and bent down to finger the shining
material. Now for the first time she spoke.

"This is new?" she asked in an expressionless voice.

"Yes," answered Anna in a strangled tone. She was
bewildered that Bernice, who sported a spray of ostrich
plumes in her wide fashionable hat, as did her daughters, and
whose gown was of the latest cut, should want to engage in
idle conversation about a ball gown while her new husband
lay more dead than alive just down the hall.

For a moment Bernice's brooding dark gaze passed over
Anna and the girl shrank back from something in it.

Although she did not know it then, she would never wear
that gown.

"You are very fond of Tobias, aren't you, Anna?" Bernice
asked Anna. And at Anna's vehement nod, "Then perhaps
you would like to be near him? There is a small antechamber,
I observed, off his bedroom. I could have a cot set up
in it."

"But won't *you* want to—?" Anna was about to say "be
near him" but Bernice cut in emphatically.

"No, I will not. I nursed one husband through a fatal
illness, I could not bear another." And lest this seem hard-
hearted, her mouth curved in a dry smile. "Perhaps you will
be better able to ease him."

Ah, she would try! Anna gave Bernice a grateful look.
Perhaps she had misjudged this cold proud woman, she
scolded herself. It had been after all a hasty first impression
and under the most trying conditions as a new wife in a new

land found her new husband incapacitated before she could even reach her new home.

Together they hurried back to the bedchamber where the doctor had just finished his examination of Tobias Jamison. He left Anna comfortingly gripping the old man's hand and beckoned Bernice into the hall and closed the door. His face was gloomy as he cleared his throat.

"I am afraid I must prepare you for some bad news," he said gently, choosing his words. "Yesterday I had hopes that the paralysis was but temporary, caused perhaps by striking his head when he fell on the dock. But today—" He cleared his throat again and went on to tell her that almost complete paralysis had set in, that Tobias could not even speak, all he could do was blink his eyes. Indeed, they would try to feed him but he might be unable to swallow very well and slowly starve to death.

At this point Bernice clasped her hands together and turned away, as if in trepidation. The doctor's gaze followed her sympathetically. That sympathy would have faded from his face if he could have seen her countenance at that moment.

For Bernice had not wanted the doctor to see the naked joy that had lit her ravaged features at his words. Her dark eyes blazed with triumph. Ah, she had chosen well! She, a widow in a man's world, had won the toss.

As the doctor left, Anna came out, closing the door behind her and Doubloon came up on silent bare feet and stood watching.

"Will he—will he live?" Anna asked in a quavering voice.

"That will be as God wills it," said Bernice, her impassive gaze passing over Anna's fair head to golden-skinned Doubloon, who stood silently studying her with a murky expression in her dark almond-shaped eyes. "Who is this?" she asked in a sharp voice, her critical tone saying clearly, *Why is this woman not working?*

"This is Doubloon. She's my maid."

"Your . . . *maid?*" There was a wealth of irony in Bernice's contemptuous voice. "Tomorrow morning, Doubloon, you will report to the overseer. Anna will be busy in the sickroom. She will no longer require your services."

"But Doubloon is a house servant," protested Anna indignantly, stepping between them as if to shield the sinuous golden-skinned woman from the tall imperious one. "She isn't strong enough for fieldwork! Artemis, the overseer, will tell you that!"

"Be silent," said Bernice in a crushing tone. "Henceforth this woman is not your concern. If she is useless in the fields, she will doubtless bring a price in the slave market."

"Oh, you wouldn't! Doubloon has made her home here. Papa Jamison gave her to me and I've—I've promised her her freedom when he dies!"

At Bernice's short hard laugh, a quiver went through Doubloon. Anna was very afraid Doubloon might spring at the new mistress and bring down a general calamity on all of them.

"Doubloon should help *me*," Anna insisted. "There will be more than one person can do, taking care of Papa Jamison in the condition he's in."

"And I take it you have volunteered to nurse him?"

"Of course!"

"Excellent. But you will not do it in a ball gown." Irritably Bernice studied the beautiful amber silk dress. "Go and take it off and put on something more suitable. A serviceable dress and apron for carrying chamber pots."

Anna drew in her breath as if she had been slapped. Only the lowest servants carried chamber pots!

Now Bernice turned her ruthless attention to Doubloon. "Did I not see a small room off the kitchen?"

"Yes," nodded Doubloon, glowering. "Cook sleeps there."

"Before you report to the overseer, put another cot in it. Anna will be sleeping there with the cook. I have decided against the anteroom."

Anna's body stiffened. "But my things—" she began.

"Your things?" Bernice stared down from her greater height. "Oh, you mean all those clothes and trinkets a lonely widower showered on you? They are not *your* things, my girl, they are *his* things—*his*, and only lent to you. And now that he is so ill and unable to explain that to you, *I* will take custody of those things. I will be taking over your room."

Stunned as she was at this broad attack across the whole spectrum of her life, Papa Jamison's plight was still uppermost in Anna's mind.

"No matter what you mean to do to me—and I can see that you hate me," she cried, "there's still Papa Jamison to think of. I will do all I can, of course, but when I am asleep someone must stay near him, Bernice, in case he needs something. Surely you'll not leave him just to servants?" Her face was hot with indignation.

The tall woman before her drew herself up to her full height and looked down her nose at this rash girl who had dared to question her. "I will say this just once," she said heavily. "Do not question my decisions. We will hear no more talk of 'Papa Jamison.' In future you will refer to my husband as 'Mr. Jamison.' And if you ever dare to use my first name again, you will be whipped for your disrespect. You will call me Madame Jamison and my daughters Mistress Prue and Mistress Polly. They will call you Anna—as I will." Her voice grew mocking. "You are fortunate that I do not turn you out, or give you over to the overseer to see what use might be made of your talents. Tobias told me how young and pretty you were and even in Jamaica I could see what a little schemer you were! You have put on airs, imagined yourself a daughter of the house, but let me tell you, in *my* household you will not find yourself so favored. Instead of possessing a maid, you will become a maid yourself—to my daughters, when Tobias no longer requires your services. I may decide to take Doubloon for my own maid if she proves worthy and the overseer speaks well of her."

For a moment hope flickered in Doubloon's dark liquid eyes—for Artemis, the overseer, had always treated her kindly.

"But you're talking as if Papa Jamison is dead!" cried Anna wildly. "He'd never let you do any of these things. And when he's better—"

"I shall overlook this outburst," said Bernice coldly. "Understandably you are overwrought. You do not seem to comprehend that he *is* dead—we simply have not set the funeral date."

She left Anna, stunned, standing helplessly by the door. But not for long!

Papa Jamison was not dead, Anna told herself firmly. And this new wife, even though she had seized the reins, did not yet own the horse! Artemis Johnson, the overseer, had been hired by Papa Jamison—he owed his allegiance to *him*, not to this new wife.

On flying feet, Anna ran down to the overseer's pleasant cottage, where Artemis "bached" it now that his wife had died this past summer.

The old man was surprised to see her. He had lost his straw hat somewhere and had just come in to find another, to shield his bald pate against the blazing summer sun. It was worn and tattered and he was just jamming it on his head when the girl burst in. "Mistress Anna!" he cried. And at sight of her troubled face, "There's no bad news, is there—about Mr. Jamison?" His face showed fear, for he was fond of the master.

"No, there's no change, Artemis. But—but we've another problem." Swiftly she outlined Bernice's threats, sought to enlist his aid.

Artemis sat down, looking doubtful. "I'll do what I can," he promised at last. "I'll do my best to persuade the new mistress to wait until Mr. Jamison recovers before she makes sweeping changes."

"And if she won't listen?"

Artemis sighed. "Well, she's in charge, Mistress Anna. She's a full-grown woman and wife to Mr. Jamison."

In charge. . . . Anna shrank from the thought. When she left, Doubloon was just sauntering toward the cottage, looking sullen. Anna stopped to comfort her. "All this will be straightened out when Papa Jamison is better," she told Doubloon.

Doubloon's lip curled and she shrugged off Anna's kindness as she might a lazily buzzing bee. "He don't get no better, you know that. *She* in charge now. Your good days all over—like mine. You'll see."

Anna drew back, quivering. Doubloon's liquid voice had

contained a venom that was almost like a physical slap. She watched the girl swagger away, hips swaying.

Stifling a sob, Anna stumbled back through the summer afternoon to the sick man's bedside and put gentle fingers on his brow. "Everything's going to be all right," she said with forced cheerfulness. "The doctor says you'll be better soon and I'm to stay and nurse you. Everyone wanted to, but I insisted."

If he really was dying, she thought, at least she could make his last days happy. She wouldn't tell him about her clash with Bernice or the life that Bernice intended for her.

That week was a terrible one for all at Mirabelle. Ruthlessly Bernice set out to make them all accept her reign.

Doubloon was caught "stealing" food from the big kitchen (actually she had been trying to poison Bernice's food, but none of them knew that) and received three lashes. One of the scullery maids screamed but Doubloon bore each blow stoically, although the words she muttered under her breath as she slunk away would have caused Bernice to give her a dozen more had she heard them.

Anna, hearing the commotion from the sickroom, arrived too late to help Doubloon. She was exhausted from lack of sleep as she cared single-handed for Tobias Jamison and weak from forgetting to eat as she brooded over her fate. She saw the whip coming down on Doubloon's naked back—and fainted.

When Artemis, the overseer, who had reluctantly wielded the lash—as lightly as he dared with Bernice watching—would have run to Anna, Bernice stopped him with a cold, "Let her be. She's only faking, can't you see it?"

It was too much for old Artemis. He told the lady of the house in ringing tones what Mr. Jamison would do to her when he recovered. He was past caring that he had gone too far; he'd a little nest egg saved up and by the Lord Harry, he'd go and live on Sandys before he'd take any more of this!

Bernice heard him out to the end, with arms folded. When he had finished, his old face as white from fury as his bald pate, she told him to pack his things, there'd be a new overseer coming out from St. George in the morning.

Artemis clapped his battered hat on his head and stomped away from the home that had been his ever since he'd sailed into St. George's harbor.

Anna awoke, choking, as cook splashed water in her face. At first she was bewildered and light-headed and amazed that she was lying on the grass, staring up at cook. Then she remembered how she had come running and found Artemis whipping Doubloon while Bernice watched with arms folded. She felt sick.

"You hungry, that's what the matter with you," said cook gruffly. She looked around her with flashing eyes now that Bernice had gone to spread dismay in some other part of the plantation. "How come you don't eat no more now that you spend all your time nursing?"

"I guess I—forgot," admitted Anna lamely. She struggled up off the ground and dusted herself off. "I came running when I heard a woman scream and the sound of a whip cracking. And I couldn't believe it when I saw—where's Doubloon?" Her voice crackled with fear as she looked around and saw neither Doubloon nor the overseer. "What have they done with her?"

"Ain't done nothin' with her," soothed cook. "Doubloon all right; she walk away. But Artemis, he speak up for you and that Mis' Bernice, she tell him to let you lie there, and she tell him to leave this plantation, she'll have a new overseer here tomorrow."

"Oh, no!" Numbed, Anna let cook lead her into the kitchen and set a wooden bowl before her on the kitchen table.

"Here now. This Hoppin' John do you good, put meat on your thin little bones!" Cook vigorously spooned out a big helping of the tasty rice, peas, and chicken dish.

"I can't eat all that," sighed Anna. She felt depressed by the cook's clucking noises as she hovered over her, and by the sympathetic looks the scullery maids gave her.

"What did Doubloon do to merit so fierce a punishment?" she asked as she ate.

Cook shrugged. "That Mis' Bernice, she found Doubloon pokin' about in the food and called her a thief. I couldn't see Doubloon took nothin'."

Anna put down her spoon. She was no longer hungry. These people were *her* responsibility—Artemis, Doubloon, cook, all of them—they had always been her responsibility when Papa Jamison was away, and now she could do nothing to help them, nothing. Even the taste of the delicious Hoppin' John that cook prepared so well was bitter in her mouth.

If only Papa Jamison would get well, he'd straighten everything out!

The next day he took a slight turn for the better. He could swallow more easily although he still could not speak.

In spite of herself, Anna began to hope.

CHAPTER 31

That terrible week had in it only one really bright spot—and even that was to have repercussions far beyond the event itself.

The afternoon after Doubloon had been given three lashes and Artemis had been dismissed, a day when Anna, fanning Tobias Jamison in the sick room, had felt herself now truly alone against a powerful enemy, Sue Waite called.

Like all Anna's other visitors she was about to be turned away at the door with the crisp message that Anna was nursing Tobias and could not be disturbed, but Sue, excited and sparkling-eyed, refused to take no for an answer.

She demanded to see Bernice and when that lady, purple-gowned and unsmiling, swept in, Sue dimpled her best smile at her. "You're Mr. Jamison's new bride I've heard so much about,'' she exclaimed, extending her hand. ''I'm delighted to meet you at last.''

Bernice, ramrod-straight, ignored the hand. Sue's smile wavered and then recovered to shine steadily. ''But I really must insist on seeing Anna,'' she rushed on. ''Because she's done so much for us and she'll be so interested in the news I bring her!''

'' 'Done so much'?'' echoed Bernice, uninterested in Sue's news. ''And what, pray, has she done?''

''Why—why, this lovely dress.'' Sue indicated the shimmering blue gown, which she had adapted to daytime wear. ''It was her new dress she'd intended to wear to the ball we gave the very night you arrived, and she gave it to me because''— Sue's voice stumbled; she could not very well tell this frowning stranger that her sisters had divided the rainbow between them and left her only gray—''because it matches my eyes! And this necklace too!''

Bernice frowned as she peered at the handsome blue gown Sue was wearing. ''You have come to return the necklace?'' she asked, not understanding.

''Oh, no, 'tis mine to keep. And Anna gave me the gown as well. But of course the lapis earrings Chloe borrowed for the ball—oh, dear, I'm such a scatterbrain—I was supposed to bring them with me but I forgot!''

So the little chit had given away not only an expensive new ball gown but a handsome lapis necklace and was lending other jewelry about! Wrath rose in Bernice and her hands went cold as ice.

''My daughters and I will be over to pay our respects to your mother at Waite Hall,'' she told Sue ironically. ''In the meantime, Anna is not to be disturbed, for my husband's health is precarious and only Anna seems able to care for him properly. If you will tell me your 'news,' I will convey the message.''

''Oh?'' Sue looked daunted. ''Well—never mind.'' She was making haste to leave the presence of this tall dour woman. ''It can wait until I see Anna.'' She turned as she reached her carriage, remembering to dimple prettily. ''We all hope you'll be very happy here at Mirabelle and we know you will be as soon as your husband's health improves—and we do look forward to receiving you and Anna at Waite Hall."

Bernice watched Sue's carriage start down the drive before closing the front door. The Waite girl was a nice enough little thing—she'd probably be a good companion for her own daughters, who needed bringing out. And the Waites were neighbors, even though some distance away, and landed gentry. Bernice retreated to the big living room, cool-shuttered against the afternoon sun, and sat down to plan her course of action.

But Sue's carriage had not gone far. Halfway down the drive she had spied Anna looking out the window and waved wildly to her. Anna waved back and Sue pointed with one gloved hand to the grove of trees at the blind turn in the drive.

Anna understood. She nodded, and slipped out of the house unnoticed. She wound her way circuitously, so that she could not be seen from the house, to the grove of trees.

There, past the blind turn, Sue's carriage was waiting for her, the driver already dozing in his seat in the heat.

Sue was standing impatiently by the carriage and she lifted her blue skirts and ran up to Anna as she arrived.

"Oh, Anna," she cried breathlessly, "you won't believe this but Arthur and Mattie are married!"

If anything was calculated to stop Anna Smith in her tracks, that announcement was. "What?" she cried in astonishment. "When?"

"This afternoon—at our home," said Sue importantly. "They got a special license. Mattie is ecstatic. She says they'll be going to Boston and—"

Anna felt dazed. "I mean," she interrupted, "when did Arthur propose? They haven't had time to become betrothed even if—" She stopped short of saying, *even if Arthur were willing to marry Mattie, which he certainly wasn't the night of the ball!*

"I *know!* It happened so *fast!*" Sue leaned forward conspiratorially and dropped her voice so the sleepy driver couldn't hear her. "I suppose I might as well tell you," she giggled. "You're bound to find out anyway, the way servants talk around here. Arthur's taken Mattie riding every morning since the ball—''

As I made him promise to do, thought Anna. I wanted him to show her attention—but *this!* She could hardly credit it.

"At first they'd be gone only a short time and then Arthur would bring Mattie back and talk to us all pleasantly and go back to the inn in St. George, but *this* morning"—her blue eyes danced—"it seems that as they passed under some cedars, Mattie got swept off her horse by a low-hanging branch and she fell into some brush and tore her dress pretty badly. And Arthur's Cousin Walter just happened to be riding along in the same direction."

Keeping an eye on Arthur! thought Anna grimly.

"And it wasn't but a moment or two before Walter came riding up and he saw Arthur trying to help Mattie up where she'd got herself tangled in the underbrush and"—Sue giggled—"Walter was sure Arthur was attacking Mattie—I can't imagine why—even though she insisted he was only trying to help her. But her dress and her chemise were torn pretty badly—Mamma said it was a scandal because Mattie's chemise was near rent from shoulder to waist—and Walter was so furious that he wouldn't even let Mattie try to repair her clothes. He just threw his cloak over her and dragged them both back home and informed Mamma that Arthur had ruined her daughter!" She choked back her laughter.

"I wouldn't put it past him to try," cut in Anna. "He certainly tried—" She stopped, coloring.

Sue dissolved in helpless laughter. "Oh, I doubt he did *this* time, no matter what he's tried with others. Because—you must never tell this, Anna, Mattie would kill me if you did, but she was so excited about Arthur dancing with her all night and then coming over every day to take her riding—I mean, no one has ever noticed her before. And she told me last night—I'll never forget how triumphant she looked, saying it—that she was *sure* Arthur was in love with her but was too shy to say so."

"Arthur—*shy?*" Anna fell back against a tree bole for support.

"And this you must *never* tell." Sue leaned forward conspiratorially. "You promise?"

"I promise." Solemnly.

"Well, last night Mattie said Mamma wouldn't have to worry about *her* being an old maid, she'd figured out how to bring things to a head!"

"No!" breathed Anna, her eyes widening in horror as she got the drift of what Mattie must have intended.

"Isn't it wonderful?" chuckled Sue. "Who'd have thought it of backward little Mattie? Wouldn't it be rich if that was the way it happened?"

Anna could think of nothing worse than being married to Arthur Kincaid, by fair means or foul! "But didn't your mother believe Mattie when she told her nothing had happened?" she asked slowly.

"Not the way Mattie told her," giggled Sue. "Oh, Mattie said the words, all right, while Arthur stood there white-faced with his big Cousin Walter's hand clamped down on his shoulder. Mattie said—between sobs—that Arthur had never touched her, oh, they weren't to think that of poor Arthur, oh, he mustn't be made to suffer—and on and on until even *I* almost believed he'd been out there tearing her clothes off and she was too softhearted to let him take his licks for it. Mamma was just beside herself. I was afraid she'd have a stroke. She stuck her jaw out at Arthur and she talked to him through her teeth and she said she'd see him married to Mattie or hanged—he could take his choice. And by then Papa was back and Mamma got *him* all excited and he roared that he'd rather see the boy strung up than married to flesh of his!"

"I would have liked to see Arthur's face when your father said that," admitted Anna weakly, succumbing to an imaginary vision of Arthur's furious white face. "I have no doubt Arthur made the right decision—and saved his life."

"Oh, yes, indeed. Arthur chose marriage and Walter and Papa dragged him into St. George and they got a special license and marshaled Arthur right back home between them and the marriage took place at our house *this afternoon!* And

they're off, spending their wedding night at his Cousin
Walter's, although Arthur looked as if he wanted to kill us
all—and Walter most of all. So he's back at Lilymeade after
leaving for no reason—although tomorrow he comes back to
us with his bride. Oh, I couldn't wait to tell you, Anna. Now
that it's all over and Mattie is married to what Mamma calls a
real 'catch,' Mamma is cool as a cucumber and planning to
stitch up some new clothes for Mattie before she goes to
Boston. She's even talking about *visiting* Mattie there—do
you think Arthur will have her?'' Again Sue collapsed with
heartless laughter. ''And Chloe is so furious that Mattie has
beaten her to the altar that she's taken to her bed and refuses
to eat.''

That reminded Anna how hollow her own stomach felt;
she'd forgotten to eat again as she cared for Papa Jamison.
She told Sue as much.

''I'd forgotten to ask,'' said Sue contritely. ''How *is* Mr.
Jamison?''

''A little better,'' said Anna slowly. ''But not very much.''

Sue gave Anna's shoulder a sympathetic pat. ''I forgot to
bring back the lapis earrings Chloe borrowed from you,'' she
said. ''They were in her jewel box when I took her some hot
broth. Mamma said I must somehow quiet her nerves or she'd
have the whole house in an uproar, and broth seemed the best
thing.''

''There's no hurry to return the earrings,'' shrugged Anna.
''I'll pick them up next time I call.'' No need to tell Sue the
humiliating truth—that she'd been reduced to the status of
maid around here!

''You're so generous, Anna,'' said Sue wistfully. ''I wish I
had your generosity—and even more than that, I wish I had
your *style!* Anyone else would have been brokenhearted to
lose Arthur. Mattie can't believe her good luck!''

''I hope it *is* good luck,'' sighed Anna. This, she thought,
would teach her not to meddle in other people's lives. Poor
Mattie would find she had traded a kindly halfwit for a brutal
young fop who did not love her. And the blame, Anna knew,
could be laid squarely at her door.

Sunk in thought, she roused herself at Sue's curious question. "How are you getting along with Bernice? I was astonished that she wouldn't let me see you."

"Bernice won't let anybody call on me," said Anna tersely. "I haven't had a single visitor since she arrived. I've seen people riding away that I know must have come to see me—Grenfell and loads of others. I don't know what she says to them, but she never tells me they called."

"She just brushes them off like she did me," Sue informed her. "I know because Grenfell rode by and complained to me about it—as if I could do anything about it! What's she like, Anna?"

"She's a terrible woman." Anna did not feel she could truly unburden herself to Sue; if she did she might burst into tears and never stop crying.

"Oh? What's she done?" Sue looked alarmed.

"She's dismissed Artemis, our overseer who's been here forever, for one thing. She's upset the whole household and turned Doubloon out to work in the fields!"

"I can't believe it!" breathed Sue. "But Doubloon is your maid!"

"Not anymore," flashed Anna. "If Papa Jamison doesn't get better soon. . . ." She shook her bright head hopelessly.

"Well, you can always come and live with us," Sue told her vigorously.

Anna gave her friend a bitter smile. Sue's mother would have something to say about that!

"Then you really aren't the least bit upset that you've lost Arthur?" prodded Sue.

"Not the least little bit. Will they be going to Boston soon?"

"No, I don't think so. Arthur doesn't want to leave until Mattie's dowry is all arranged and since we've no loose cash, it will all have to wait until Papa can sell his lumber in England. It may take months."

At least Mattie would be living at home, and if Arthur turned out too badly she could refuse to go to Boston with him, thought Anna with a shudder.

"I do hope," said Sue plaintively, "that I'm as lucky with Lance. I haven't seen him in the last couple of days." She gave her friend a sidewise look. "Have you seen Lance, Anna? I mean, I know Bernice hasn't allowed anyone to call but have you seen him riding away from the house?"

Now Anna knew the main thrust of Sue's call. She was checking up on Lance!

"Not since the ball," she told Sue. And that was almost true. Until today she had not seen Lance, although she'd heard through the servants that Lance had called and been turned away by Bernice, as had Grenfell and Ross earlier. Grenfell, undaunted, had been back twice. When Sue looked as though she didn't quite believe her, Anna added carelessly, "Perhaps there's work to do at home and that's why he hasn't called. He's only just next door, Sue. Why don't you find some excuse to look in on him? Get some advice about a horse or something?" That surely was the way to horsey Lance's heart!

"Oh—I have," admitted Sue. "But twice he was out . . . I just thought he might have come over here." Sue's face cleared as if that were a load off her mind. "But since he didn't, I guess he really did have work to do. I did expect him to come calling on me, but you're right, I suppose—he's just busy. I know the Talbots have received a new mare from England to breed with their big roan stallion. I haven't seen her but she's had a long voyage and I guess Lance feels he must exercise her and get her in good shape before she's bred."

Lance had left Mirabelle not an hour before. From the window Anna had seen him as he had ridden away on the dancing new mare.

"Why don't you go over as soon as you get back and say you couldn't wait to see the new mare, and ask Lance to tell you all about her?"

"That's a good idea," agreed Sue, springing back into her carriage without waiting for the sleepy driver to assist her. "If I hurry, I can be over there and back before suppertime."

Anna gave her friend a sympathetic look as the carriage rolled away with Sue waving gaily. What would it be like, she asked herself, to marry a man who loved money more than hot kisses? Or a plantation such as Mirabelle more than a woman? Or his horses better than his wife? She hoped she would never have to find out.

Whatever happened to her, she told herself passionately, she must be first with the man she loved. He must love her better than anything, better than anyone.

First . . . it was worth dying for.

CHAPTER 32

Through the long days of summer Tobias Jamison held on. Anna did too. She was tempted to run away, to stow away on one of the tall white ships that put in at St. George's harbor, a ship that could carry her away—anywhere. But it tore at her heart to leave the only father she had ever known—kindly Tobias Jamison. She could not do it.

Day after day she cared for him, tended him, read to him—and talked to him for hours, detailing not her troubles but her world as it might have been—if he had never sailed to Jamaica, if he had not married there and brought home a wife. . . . She spoke in laughing confidential whispers of suitors and parties—and always made some blithe explanation for her ragged tired appearance.

She did not know if Tobias believed her or not, for he never regained his power of speech, but if he was going to die—and of that she was now sure—then he was going to carry with him to the next world pleasanter last memories than those of a neglectful wife and careless slipshod servants.

So Anna smiled and lied glibly to Tobias—and when his eyelids flickered shut in sleep, she would steal away to her narrow cot and listen to cook's stentorous snoring, for Bernice had locked the antechamber where she might have slept, believing it to be full of valuable articles that Anna might make off with.

Tormented by cook's snores, on warm nights Anna often stole out onto the broad veranda and slept there, huddled in a corner lest Bernice, who patrolled the house like a watchful dog, look out and see her and forbid her this last small comfort, a little corner of her own, however humble.

Sometimes of nights on the veranda she looked up at the white moon sailing serenely overhead and asked herself how her world, which had seemed so secure, could have been overturned in a single night . . . and the white moon with its bland and ancient face gave her no answers.

August came and with it some rainy days. Anna woke on one such morning to see that rain last night had left the green leaves of the bougainvillaea and the oleanders dripping, rain had run in rivulets down the gleaming whitewashed roof slates, down the gutters into the big cistern, where the goldfish scurried about keeping the big stone catchment clean of algae. But by midmorning the skies had cleared and Anna, desperately in need of a change, slipped away, leaving one of the maids to tend Tobias.

She felt safe in doing this because Bernice had left while it was still drizzling, announcing that she would be going into St. George and would not be back till nightfall.

Such an opportunity was not to be missed. Anna had hurried out the back door, run to the stables and ridden Floss down toward the sea. When they reached the shore, she had let the dainty mare pick her way along the surf, shying now and then at an unfriendly-looking bit of driftwood or some sea creature cast upon the shore.

Dismounting, she lay on her face on the warm sand in the shadow of a battered stone promontory. Then after a while she sat up and sat with her knees drawn up and her chin in her hands and stared out toward the reefs. How changed her own world was and yet—how unchanging this one. These were still the green and pleasant islands discovered around 1515 by the Spaniard Juan de Bermúdez, those reefs out there were the graveyard of countless ships that had smashed their hulls in wild storms upon the sharp-toothed coral. She could almost wish herself out there, for treasure ships had gone down in that sea, Spanish galleons of the treasure *flota* striking out from the New World for Spain had left their bones there—and their gold and silver and jade and emeralds. Great wealth lay sunken in those depths but the turquoise blue waters kept well their secrets and who knew where it lay?

At the moment she felt that if she knew where one of those treasure ships lay she would dive on it, even if she were devoured by sharks or barracuda. It would be worth the risk, just the hope of rising from the foam gasping but with perhaps a salt-encrusted necklace in her hand—the price of passage away from this place.

Her descent into her private hell had not been gradual; it had been like falling downstairs—one hard thump after another.

The first week of Papa Jamison's illness Anna had been too numb, too busy to notice much of anything.

The second week she had come out into the hallway to see Juney, one of the house servants, staggering out of her room beneath a huge burden of velvets and silks and ruffles that she recognized, startled, as her own clothes.

"What are you doing with my things, Juney?" she had demanded.

Juney had stopped and rolled her eyes at Anna. "Mis' Bernice says we got to remake them to fit her daughters."

"She does, does she?" Anna had whirled and run outside to confront Bernice on the front steps, where the older woman was just coming in from riding. "How dare you take my things without asking me?" she had cried, her voice high and accusing. "Those dresses are *mine!*"

Bernice had not answered her—in words. Instead she had swung her riding crop in an arc to smash the slender girl before her. Just in time, Anna had realized what Bernice was about. Her arms had gone up in time to save her face but she had stumbled backward, hitting her head against the wall and sliding to the floor.

"Jarosh! Bennett!" Bernice's sharp voice rang out. "Take this girl back to my husband's room. She is supposed to be taking care of him. Lock her in!" And as the black groom's big hand seized Anna from one side and the white bondservant's gnarled grasp caught her from the other, Bernice stepped closer. "We will hear no more talk about your *things!*" she hissed. "Or I will have you whipped as any slave!"

Dragged back dazed to the sick man's bedchamber and pushed inside, Anna realized fully for the first time her predicament.

Bernice hated her—and meant to humble her. And Bernice was well and truly in charge—everyone feared not to obey her.

The door was not kept locked after that first long tiring day when Anna wondered if this was to be her eternal prison. The next day it was left invitingly open as if to allow its young prisoner to escape.

But Anna did not take that easy way out—she could not. For if she did, who would look after Tobias Jamison? She could guess what his chances of survival would be with Bernice—he would probably not outlast the week!

So Anna—surrogate daughter that she was—tried as valiantly as any true daughter to nurse her foster father back to health.

She would fail, of course. Bernice knew that, they all knew it—in her heart even Anna knew it. But she could not help trying. Something steely in her nature would allow no less.

And something in the old man's eyes as they followed her about the sickroom told her that he understood—and was grateful.

Her second terrible humiliation came when she looked out the window and for the second time saw Sue standing up in her carriage halfway down the drive, waving to her.

Sue knows she will be turned away if she comes to the door and asks to see me—just as she was before, thought Anna bitterly as she slipped out and ran to join Sue at the place they had met before, in the clump of trees just beyond the blind turn.

"Oh, Anna, that woman—she's terrible!" cried Sue as Anna approached.

From the direction of Sue's vengeful gaze, which was focused toward the house, Anna had no doubt Sue meant

Bernice. "You're right," she said, as Sue urged her into the carriage. "I'm surprised you came over without a driver," she remarked.

"I slipped away," admitted Sue, trying without much success to turn the horse and carriage around in the narrow driveway. "Oh, here, Anna, you do it—you're better with horses than I am," she said impatiently.

"You'd best learn to manage horses if you're going to marry Lance," observed Anna, glad to be talking to someone besides the servants, or an old man who couldn't answer, for a change. "For horses are very important to him." She took the reins from Sue and expertly turned the carriage around so that Sue would be aimed in the right direction when she left. "I'm glad you came over, Sue. I was dying to talk to somebody."

"Those daughters of hers—don't they talk to you?"

Anna shook her head. "Never. If I chance to meet them in the hall, they scuttle on by. Aside from greeting me when I met them, they've never said two words to me. I think Bernice has told them not to."

"I hope Mr. Jamison gets well soon and turns her out of the house!" cried Sue angrily.

Anna was surprised. *She* might have said that and with feeling, but—this much heat from Sue? "What has Bernice done?" she asked slowly, almost afraid to hear.

"She came over to our house yesterday." Sue was breathing hard. "And she told my mother that she understood that you had given me a new blue gown and a valuable lapis necklace and my sister a pair of expensive earrings—*none of which were yours to give!* She demanded them back. She said these things were all meant to be gifts to her and her daughters, that Mr. Jamison had so intended and had written to her about them!"

Anna's face whitened. "It's a lie!" she cried. "Papa Jamison gave me that necklace last Christmas, you know he did! And the earrings he brought home from his last trip, and the dress I had made up myself out of material he bought from Captain Tygart of the *Shallot*—it came from Tortuga, you know that as well as I do."

"Yes, I know you told us that," agreed Sue indignantly. "But the way that woman put it made *you* sound like a thief and *us* like knowing receivers of stolen goods! My mother was just beside herself. She went and snatched up the earrings from Chloe's jewel box and told me to go up and get the dress and the necklace, and when I brought them down she plumped them all into Bernice's lap!"

"And then I hope she told Bernice to leave Waite Hall and never come back!"

"Well, she was about to, when suddenly that awful Bernice broke out into all smiles and her voice almost purred and she said this wasn't what she'd intended at all, that she had just wanted her neighbors to know what kind of a person Anna Smith was, so they would understand the terrible time she was having at Mirabelle controlling her! Controlling *you*, Anna!"

Anna's lips tightened. "Did she tell you I'm Papa Jamison's full-time nurse?" she snapped. "I can get one of the maids to sit with him for an hour or two but that's all—I do all the rest! Day and night!"

"No, she didn't dwell on that. She was too busy winning Mamma over. She said that she just hoped that Mamma would accept these little things—the dress and the necklace and earrings—as gifts from *her!*"

My best earrings! thought Anna angrily. *And I only lent them to Chloe, I didn't give them to her!*

"And she said she hoped that Mamma's daughters and *her* daughters would become very close friends, and she explained that with illness in the house she couldn't very well entertain, but when she did give a ball, the very first one would be in honor of Chloe and Alma! Mamma was charmed with her, completely taken in. They went out to Bernice's carriage arm in arm. Oh, Anna, I'll never feel right about wearing that dress again—or the necklace either, although Mamma says I shouldn't feel like that. . . . Oh, Anna," she wailed, "can't you do something about that woman? She's turning everyone against you. She went to see the Adamses day before yesterday and told them Grenfell was making a fool of himself over you—a bondservant's niece—and she thought they ought to know. Perhaps you didn't know it—I guess I forgot to tell you—but Grenfell's mother had gotten cold feet about sending Grenfell away to Oxford, but now after Bernice visited her, she's arranged for him to go next week!''

"And Lance?" asked Anna, before she thought.

"Oh, yes." Sue bobbed her head. "She's been to see the Talbots too—and told them awful lies about Lance coming over to see you almost as often as Grenfell."

"Don't you believe it," said Anna cheerfully, glad she could match lie for lie with Bernice on this point at least. "Lance hasn't been over here but—I think—once, asking at the door about Papa Jamison's health and bringing a basket of cakes from his mother. I didn't see him," she added casually. "I was busy feeding Papa Jamison his noonday meal. But I could hear him speaking to Bernice at the door."

Sue, who had been afraid that Lance was still dangling after Anna, gave her friend's arm a commiserating pat. "Don't you care," she said. "If Mr. Jamison lives, he'll straighten it all out—and if he dies, well, he'll take care of you in his will."

If he dies . . . Somehow Anna had not thought about that. All her concentration had been focused on somehow making him live. But now the thought struck her forcefully: *If Papa Jamison dies, he always said he was leaving me everything. And if he hasn't had time to make out a new will—and he probably hasn't, since his solicitor, Christopher Marks, is in London—then I won't be left out. I'll be able to strike back at Bernice!*

CHAPTER 33

"I mustn't be gone too long." Anna jumped down out of the carriage and gave her homespun skirts a shake. She looked up to see Sue looking with pity at her worn clothing—things she would never have worn in the old days. Anna's proud head lifted—she did not like to be the object of pity. "Thank you for coming over, Sue; I need to be kept abreast of what's happening on the island. Next time you come, stop the carriage just before you reach the blind turn and wave your scarf—I can see it from the window of Papa Jamison's room if I'm looking out. Or send Lucas, who usually drives you, to the house. Tell him to ask for cook. She'll manage to give me the message that you're waiting for me."

"I'll do that." Sue looked pensive as she watched Anna go. For the first time it had occurred to Sue that this—this *slipping about* might constitute her friend's future.

Anna had slipped back to the house, padding in on soft worn slippers, and paused outside the dining room door as Bernice's strident voice came to her.

"You, Tessie, carry these big candlesticks for me—all right, carry them one at a time if you can't manage the weight. So much silver left out in the dining room is an open invitation to thieves! I intend to lock it all up in the great cupboard!"

Anna had waited until they finished moving the silver and then gone silently into the dining room and looked about her. It didn't look the same without the silver—all those empty polished surfaces looked naked and bare and expectant, as if they waited for the shining trove they had always borne.

Especially bare looked the long top of the massive sideboard where Samantha Jamison's great candlesticks had stood like twin pillars.

Anna closed her eyes painfully for a moment.

Those huge square-based candlesticks made of solid silver with fat cupids peering down from among twining silver vines heavy with silver grapes—they were part of her earliest memories of Mirabelle. She had sat primly at table the first night she had dined in this dining room and stared at them in awe, wondering how anyone could ever lift them.

She had heard admiring jokes about their size and grandeur almost every time she had entertained guests at Mirabelle, from the preacher's half rueful, "They must have near sunk the ship that brought them!" to Grenfell's starry-eyed, "They're like the pillars that hold up the world, Mistress Anna!"

Heartsick, she remembered the day Samantha Jamison had come upon her as she stood on tiptoe, leaning against the long sideboard, and reached up to touch with her childish fingers one of the graceful silver leaves at the base of one of the candlesticks. Samantha had come up behind Anna and hugged her. Anna had felt warm and safe and loved in that gentle embrace. "They *are* beautiful candlesticks," she had told the little girl wistfully. "They were part of my mother's dowry when *she* married. And mine when *I* married. And they will be part of *your* dowry when *you* marry, Beatrice."

Beatrice! Not Anna—*Beatrice!* The child had stiffened but Samantha Jamison had never even recognized her slip.

That was the day it was borne in solidly on Anna that she was only a surrogate daughter, loved by Samantha Jamison because her hair, her coloring, her smile were so like a little girl who had died in faraway London in the time of the Great Plague.

Tobias Jamison had come into the room just then and told his wife he must speak to her—something about the accounts, was this invoice right, had they really received this much earthenware? And what about the blue and white china? Had she checked it out? He had nodded carelessly to Anna and with the sensitivity of youth, the child had realized like a dart through the heart that Papa Jamison tolerated her only be-

cause having her about had brought his wife back to him—
that she wasn't Anna to them, loved for Anna's sake, but
only a surrogate Beatrice, substitute for the daughter who was
gone from them forever.

The realization that Beatrice was first, would always be
first in their affections, had struck deep into the little girl's
consciousness and had joined there another knowledge she
did not even realize she possessed, for buried in her subcon-
scious was a deep hurt that Eliza Smith, who until Samantha
Jamison had come along, had been the only mother young
Anna had ever known, had never really loved her, perhaps
had never *dared* to love her. All those times when the child
had tried to show affection, to hurl herself into the older
woman's arms for comfort over some trifling hurt, that thorny
barrier had always risen between them and Eliza would seem
to back off, saying gruffly, "There, there, child, 'tis but a
little thing. Ye must be strong and stand against things as your
mother would have wanted ye to."

Her mother . . . that unreal beautiful mother about whom
Eliza never spoke. Somehow the child had sensed that the
barrier between Eliza and herself was Eliza's greater love for
her mother, her real mother.

So she had never been first with Eliza, just as she was
never to be first with Samantha and Tobias Jamison, no
matter how much affection they showered on her.

Out of that perhaps had come her fierce need to be first
with the man she chose to be her lover.

And now with her empty heart, she stared at the long
sideboard's empty top, seeing the candlesticks in her mind.
Those great square-based candlesticks had been inextricably
intertwined with her childhood, with her young girlhood.
Instinctively, they had seemed to Anna the very heart of
Mirabelle. To her that pair of silver candlesticks represented
home and hearth and family.

And now those beautiful candlesticks were to be locked
away in darkness to molder—just as she herself was locked
away in the sickroom of a dying man.

For even Anna could not deny the truth now. As she came
back into Papa Jamison's big silent bedchamber, where she

had opened the shutters and tied back the drapes to let the sunlight stream cheerfully in, she could see his white still face—and the eyes that turned toward her in mute appeal.

His big cumbersome body occupied less space in the four-poster now. Almost unobtrusively, he had been dropping weight. If she had not known it herself, Anna could have told from the gloomy faces of the servants that his fate was sealed.

Still she kept on, hurling herself blindly against fate, determined to make him live. Beatrice, she told herself fiercely, could not have done more, had she lived.

Only of late Anna had become more practical. She knew she must eat to keep up her strength. She was thinner, but she was determined not to let herself waste away and be taken by any plague that wafted their way—*that*, she told herself, would be to let Bernice off too easily. For Anna meant to live to see the day that Bernice was turned out of Mirabelle—yes, and her daughters with her!

Not that she had much contact with the daughters. Sometimes she heard them laughing and talking in the hall. Once or twice Prue, the elder, who resembled her mother in features and manner, had sneered as Anna passed and flaunted the skirts of some dress that had been cut to fit her from Anna's things. Once Prue said something rude as Anna went by carrying a heavy slop jar, and Pris had giggled, but Anna had lifted her head and stonily ignored them. For the most part Bernice kept them away from Anna, as if any contact might contaminate them. Pris, the younger daughter, if she chanced to meet Anna in the hall alone, usually turned and ran like a scared rabbit. Anna wondered at those moments what ugly stories Bernice must have told them about her.

For the most part she did not think about them at all. She was endlessly busy on her daily round of chores with the sick man and her world had been reduced to four walls.

Only Sue brought her messages—and sometimes, not often, she saw Doubloon. A burning-eyed, vengeful Doubloon with hands callused and arms scratched from work in the fields, her sinuous body moving without its usual languor, her back straight and angry.

"You see these hands?" Doubloon had raged, shaking them in Anna's face one day when Anna had stepped onto the back porch and found Doubloon demanding bacon grease from the cook. Cook had retired as Doubloon held up her callused hands. "*Me*, Doubloon, working like a field hand!"

Anna had tried to comfort her. "If Papa Jamison gets well—" she began.

"He don't get well and you know it!" Doubloon had interrupted her savagely. "Only reason that man not dead already is you won't let him die!"

Anna had stepped back in the face of this blast, but she knew in her heart it was true. It was only because of her tender care that Tobias Jamison had lingered this long.

"I've seen the fires up in the cedars at night," she told Doubloon, in an effort to change the subject.

Doubloon's almond eyes went opaque. "What you see?" she demanded.

"Nothing. But some nights I can't stand it, I have to get away from the house. Sometimes then I slip down to the stables and get Floss and go down to the beach and ride along the sand and listen to the surf. But sometimes I ride up into the cedars—and twice I saw bonfires in little clearings."

"You forget what you see." Doubloon's voice was surly. "You stay away from the cedars at night. Ride along the beach. Safer." She gave Anna a significant, smoldering look.

"Doubloon, I'm afraid for you," Anna told the golden-skinned woman bluntly. "I know you were somehow mixed up in the last slave uprising and if you hadn't gotten sick, you might have gotten yourself killed!"

"Don't you worry none about how *I* get killed! What you think happen to *you* when that old man die?"

"I think—I think I'll be taken care of." Anna swallowed, for she hated to face the fact that Tobias Jamison would die.

Doubloon sniffed. Disbelief was plain on her face.

"How is Temera?" asked Anna, desperate for a new subject. "Don't look at me like that, Doubloon. I know you see him, take him food probably."

"Temera all right," mumbled Doubloon. "How that fellow

Aiken who come around calling on Mis' Bernice?'' she shot shrewdly at Anna.

Anna stiffened. She hadn't known that Doubloon, spending her days in the fields and her nights in the slave quarters or out stirring up revolt around some hastily built bonfire, was that conversant with the doings in the big house.

"Cook told me that Aiken fellow comes around two maybe three times a week to call on Mis' Bernice and take her riding. He out front now talking to her and her daughters.''

"He's a fortune hunter,'' said Anna bitterly. "He's hovering over us like a vulture waiting for Papa Jamison to die so he can marry the widow!''

Doubloon's dark eyes gleamed suddenly with a golden light. She laughed and the big green parrot who swayed on a hoop suspended overhead gave a sudden squawk. "Hush up, you no-good bird,'' said Doubloon, balling up her fist at the parrot. She turned to Anna. "You come with me. We talk.''

"I can only be gone a little while,'' protested Anna as she followed Doubloon off the porch. "Papa Jamison—''

"He die all right without you.'' Doubloon's voice was brisk. She led Anna down behind the stables and seated herself on a rotting log. "I not tell you real truth about me,'' she said abruptly. Anna's face mirrored her surprise. She was gazing into a cynical pair of dark eyes set in a knowing ivory face. "I tell you now because I want give you some advice. Now I tell you real truth and how I know so much about men.''

Anna sank down upon the grass beneath a tree that cascaded sea grapes and listened.

"My father big black buck from Dahomey,'' Doubloon told her carelessly, flicking a spider from the log with her fingers. Her lazy voice went on, telling Anna how her father had got her off a white serving maid who had been turned out and publicly whipped for bearing a child out of wedlock.

Anna listened in silence. That, of course, could account for Doubloon's skin, which was dusky gold, the color of old ivory . . . but her features were more like the Arawak Indians, as were her straight blue black hair and almond eyes. Learning about the world the hard way now, Anna listened and reserved judgment. This too might be another lie.

Born free in Barbados, Doubloon told her dispassionately, she had been seized while still a half-grown child by pirates and sold into a Tortuga brothel. She had escaped via a rich Jamaican planter who "did business" at Tortuga's teeming market of captured goods. The planter had aided in her "escape," since the brothel's madam had been loath to sell the golden-skinned beauty, and on the high seas as they headed for Jamaica, Doubloon had known the freedom of a mistress.

On landing she discovered that she had suddenly become his slave, that she must be obedient to his wife's wishes by day—and his by night. Young and proud and angry, she had twice attempted escape. And her back still bore the marks of the lash that had earned her. Sold and resold, she told Anna in a reminiscent, singsong voice, she had at last been bought by kindly Tobias Jamison.

Doubloon's liquid gaze dwelt on Anna with affection. She had a kind of thorny love for spirited Anna, and often advised her out of her vast "street knowledge" of the world. But since her wisdom had been gained on the Bridgtown waterfront, in a Tortuga brothel, and as the favored slave-mistress of a succession of wealthy planters, her earthy West Indian advice had in the past not seemed appropriate to the foster daughter of a rich household.

"You better marry any man who want you," she told Anna. "Marry him quick before that old man die. If you can't get young man, marry that old Silas Pillford that keep tobacco shop."

Anna was shocked. "Whatever made you think of Silas Pillford? It's even money he wouldn't be able to creep to the altar—besides, he's old enough to be my grandfather!"

"He have money enough to keep you, which is more than you got! And he *willing* to keep you—I see him looking at you when you pass by."

"If I were looking for money, I think I'd prefer Grenfell Adams!" flashed Anna, resentful that Doubloon should feel she should be shucked off like this.

"That remind me," said Doubloon. "Yesterday I meet Grenfell riding out of here. He say Bernice won't let him see you."

"That's right, he was here. I saw him ride away."

"Well, you not so smart. Because he say he come tell you good-bye. His ship sail early this morning. If you been smart, you would have run after him and beg him take you with him. He gave me this to give you."

She pulled out a piece of paper. Anna took it and smoothed it out, wondering what words Grenfell had chosen to leave with her. Another poem! That was Grenfell's answer to everything—verse!

> *My island love, I would be true,*
> *And every rapture share with you.*
> *My soul's delight, my spirit's joy,*
> *Come soar with me—*

Anna laid the parchment down. Nothing concrete, just boyish ardor awkwardly expressed. And words were not going to save her situation. Grenfell was gone, sent across the sea to Oxford, where he might forget young Mistress Smith.

And perhaps it was just as well, because if she were tempted by the extremity of her situation to marry Grenfell, she had no doubt he would promptly be cut off by his incensed parents. And some inner wisdom told her Grenfell couldn't make it on his own. He was soft, he was pampered, he was a dreamer. The real world would crush him. All that could keep him going would be the money he would one day inherit from his parents—and he couldn't have that and have her too.

She sighed.

Grenfell was not an alternative.

"You got a third choice," ventured Doubloon in a voice of cunning. Anna looked up into a pair of dark liquid eyes as old and sinful as time.

"And what is that, Doubloon?" she heard herself say.

"That Mr. Aiken, him that Mis' Bernice has got her eye

on, she'll marry him before the sod is green over old Mr.
Jamison, you'll see!''

Anna winced. It was true, she knew. It was impossible not
to help remarking Bernice's obvious infatuation with the
dissolute fortune hunter, Aiken.

"But Mr. Aiken got his eye on *you*," said that mellow
insinuating voice. "And he set you up proper once he in-
stalled here as husband and own this place. Perhaps he even
take a whip to Mis' Bernice to please you!" Doubloon's eyes
sparkled.

Anna's hand came up. The palm itched to slap that wicked
smiling mouth that would suggest she enter into something
like that! But her hand fell listlessly back to her lap instead.
There was a nagging truth to what Doubloon said. She had
been aware all along—but had not admitted even to herself—
how Aiken's sly hot gaze followed her about whenever he
thought Bernice wasn't looking. His stare had become so
uncomfortable that Anna had hesitated to fetch and carry
when he was around.

It would not be a week, she realized bitterly, before the
reed-thin, snuff-taking Aiken, as Bernice's new husband,
encouraged his bride to take her daughters visiting somewhere. And then some moonlit night with Bernice away,
Anna would see a dark shape loom up beside her bed and
hear a low possessive laugh and smell his snuff-laden breath
and feel that thin hard body grasp her slender form with a
grip she could not break.

And she would become his chattel.

Anna's nails bit into her palm so hard she winced.

"You think on what Doubloon tells you," said Doubloon
grandly. "Doubloon give good advice. You had three choices.
You already lost one of them."

"What about all those boys who were forever asking me to
marry them?" demanded Anna bitterly.

"They don't come around so much now, do they?" said
that purring voice.

Anna realized with shock that that was true. Almost imper-
ceptibly the visits of the swains who had pursued her had
slackened off . . . it was rare now that anyone called to see

her. Yet more and more carriages drew up to visit the new lady of the house—Bernice. From the sickroom she could hear their laughter tinkling and the clatter of tankards and teacups.

"You listen to Doubloon," Doubloon was insisting in her insinuating voice. "You only got two choices left. If you don't take *someone*—even that old man, Pillford—you gets the last one. You think you like that?"

But I haven't come to that! thought Anna resentfully. "And have you and Temera worked things out so well?" she asked resentfully, stabbing where it was sure to hurt.

Doubloon laughed. "Maybe we have," she said. "Better than you." She got up and ambled toward the house, calling out to cook she was ready for that bacon grease now. Anna watched her take the crock cook handed her and then with a shrug of her supple shoulders, Doubloon was gone, sauntering away from them with that walk that was a dare to any man.

"Don't you listen to her, Mis' Anna," said cook, staring after Doubloon indignantly. "She not like you—she fill your head with bad ideas." She turned her head to listen nervously. "I think I hear front door shut. That mean Mis' Bernice maybe coming back here. Best she not find you and me together, Mis' Anna. She say people plot against her!" Cook sniffed.

As she went back toward the sickroom, Anna could hear Bernice berating her younger daughter, Polly. "Why are you so mousey, Polly?" she snarled. "Stand up straight and answer when you're spoken to! Mr. Aiken thinks you're backward—he told me so." And then, most unfairly. "Just look at you, Polly—blondes are all the rage just now, no woman who isn't blond is considered beautiful anymore. Why couldn't you have been born blonde?"

For once Polly's voice struck back in a kind of hiss. "I have dark hair because you and my father both had dark hair! And I don't care what Aiken says about me—I caught him peering in the window at Anna Smith, trying to watch her undress!"

There was the sound of a slap as Bernice's palm cracked across her daughter's cheek, a screech, and then Polly's furious wail. "If you wanted a *bonde* for a daughter, why didn't you cuckold father with some yellow-haired Dutchman?"

Prue had now joined the fray, taking Polly's part, for she, too, was a brunette. Anna would have banged the sickroom door behind her had she not had consideration for Tobias.

Born blonde, indeed! *She* had been born a strawberry blond. What had *that* brought *her*? Nothing but the unpleasant prospect, pointed out by Doubloon, that she might end up a chattel in a house she'd considered her own—or to escape that, she might have to share a bed with an old man who powdered his beard and was reputed to sleep with it encased in a cloth bag!

There were men on this island who cast rapt glances at her, true. Married men, single men, men "above her station," who lusted for her, men "below her station"—no, what was that? She had no station. Child of two worlds, belonging to neither, passing the first days of her memory as a waif, and suddenly thrust into prominence as a "princess" on this plantation . . . and now dowryless, back to where she had started, now that she was of an age to marry.

But money, she knew, would not count with her if only there was one man among them for whom her soul yearned. . . . Yet there was not one of them on whom she could not turn her back with a lighthearted shrug, not one she could not oh-so-easily forget.

What had Tobias once told her? Each man and each woman needs a rudder as a ship needs a rudder, each of us needs a tall mast to lean upon and a North Star to steer by. *Someday, little Anna,* he had told her, *you will find some tall fellow you cannot live without. He will be your North Star and you will guide your life by him.*

Anna had not yet found her "North Star."

CHAPTER 34

On the first day of September, Tobias Jamison died. Quietly, in his sleep. He was down to ninety pounds and no one knew how he had survived this long, but to Anna, who had been expecting it all along, it came as a hard physical blow.

Tobias, the only father she had ever known, was gone.

She bent her bright head and wept, and as she did the heavens above the Bermudas opened up and rain poured down. It seemed to her the sky wept for him too.

His funeral, held in a pouring rain, was a numbing experience. All the household staff, Anna included, had been supplied with mourning garb by Bernice as a "correct" gesture. Anna hated hers. It was of coarse black stuff, indifferently dyed, and the rough fabric scratched and reddened her tender skin—a far cry from the supple black silk Bernice and her daughters affected.

Tobias was interred in the churchyard of St. Peter's Church in St. George. Anna, who had not been provided with a long black mourning veil such as swathed Bernice's cold impassive face and the faces of her daughters, felt the curious stares that came her way. Too proud to weep where she could be watched, she stood stiff and dry-eyed and tried not to think.

After they came home, Bernice told her sharply to take off her mourning garb and resume wearing the gray homespun housedress and linen apron she had worn during the time she nursed Tobias. There was no need, Bernice said in her crisp voice, for Anna to appear to mourn Tobias, since she had been, after all, no blood relation.

Wearily Anna bit back the words that sprang to her lips—

that of all at Mirabelle she had been the only one who truly loved Tobias or mourned his passing. She went to change her dress.

When she came back, bearing the black gown in her arms, she could hear Bernice in the black-draped living room. She was talking to Ralph Kilhenny, her solicitor from St. George, and when she heard her name mentioned Anna paused outside the door to listen.

" 'Tis best ye treat the girl Anna well, that's my advice to you," Kilhenny was saying.

"But I do treat her well," Bernice protested.

"Nay, but I mean she did look shabby at the funeral, her that was always so well got up, and there's been talk about that she's no better than a maid here in the house—and perhaps even a prisoner. No, do not be getting on your high horse, madame. I but speak what everyone's saying. There's every possibility that Tobias made a will—though it may have been left with his London solicitor, Christopher Marks, whom I've never met, for he's never yet set foot on these islands, transacted all his business with Tobias Jamison by letter. But if Tobias did make out a will, you may well find that he's left his property to you and Anna jointly, and 'twould be better for future arrangements if there were no friction between ye. D'ye take my meaning?"

"I take it." In a sour voice.

"So my advice is to let the girl live here—I know ye desire to turn her out, and ye can do it once it's established there's no will, for ye'll have a wife's dower right and there'll be a search for his next of kin as to what to do with the rest."

"But I thought it would all be mine!" Explosively.

"Not under the common law. If there's no will, one-third be yours for your lifetime or until you remarry and the rest do go to his next of kin, which I take it is likely to be someone in England."

"Tobias never mentioned any relatives, although I believe his wife had some."

"No, 'tis Tobias's kin we'll be seeking—if there's no will."

So Ralph Kilhenny thought there was a will—somewhere.

Even through her weariness and grief, Anna felt a little ray of hope. Perhaps she would not find herself dispossessed after all.

"I would suggest you let the girl live here quietly, free to go about—and not treat her as a servant," Kilhenny was saying. "Let her go her own way. Then if there should be litigation later, ye can point out that she was seen about by divers folks and appeared to be well treated."

There was a strangled sound from Bernice.

"I know it goes against the grain," Kilhenny was sympathetic. "But look at it this way—a few months and all will be resolved."

So Anna found a truce of sorts declared between herself and Bernice. No money was forthcoming, of course, and she had to eat in the kitchen with the servants. But she was allowed to come and go as she pleased now, to ride Floss whenever she liked, and no work was thrust upon her.

She needed the rest—and she got it, for no longer was she invited anywhere. Gradually the blue circles of weariness and the gaunt hollows in her pale cheeks disappeared and she looked herself again—and to Bernice's secret fury, breathtakingly beautiful.

A week after the funeral Anna rode over to Waite Hall. Her reception from Deborah Waite was cool.

"I see you're not wearing mourning," said that lady critically. She gestured with her ringed hand at Anna's gray homespun dress.

"I do not possess any, nor coins to buy such garments. Bernice took away the mourning gown she lent me and told me henceforth to wear this. All my other gowns have been remade to fit her daughters."

Deborah Waite looked somewhat taken aback at this frank statement of the facts. "*All* your clothes?" she exclaimed.

"All. My room as well. I am forced to sleep with the cook and take my meals with the servants." Anna saw no need to dissemble before Deborah Waite. Sue was her best friend.

"Well, I must say!" But what she must say was postponed as Sue entered the room and ran to Anna and hugged her.

"How nice you're not wearing black," she exclaimed

ingenuously. "It's so grim! But why are you wearing that housedress? Oh, I forgot—Bernice took your other clothes," she faltered.

"Sue," reproved her mother. "'Tis none of your affair what goes on at Mirabelle. Remember that."

"Yes—of course, Mamma. Anna, you must come with me to the garden. We're trying to plant some spring bulbs that just came from England. Do you think it's too late for them to thrive?" And when they were out of earshot, Sue exclaimed, "You're the talk of the island, Anna!"

"Why?" wondered Anna, looking blank.

"Everyone is wondering what will happen to you. Will you inherit or won't you? Is there a will or isn't there? And if there isn't, who will you marry?"

"So far no will has turned up," said Anna. "Ralph Kilhenny has written to Christopher Marks, who was Papa Jamison's solicitor in London, and Bernice has searched the house three times at least." She didn't add that she felt Bernice would have destroyed any document she found and that the thoroughness of her search was only to that end, but Sue guessed.

"*You* should have done the searching, Anna."

"Well, I wasn't allowed to," said Anna grimly. "She turned me out and told me to go riding or walking or whatever I chose, so long as I stayed out from underfoot while they searched for the will."

"Do you notice anything?" Sue waved her finger.

"Sue! A betrothal ring! You and Lance?"

Sue nodded, her eyes sparkling as she merrily waved the plain gold ring. "Father was against it and Chloe threw up, but Mamma said I'd probably do no better and Lance was, after all, one of only three sons and should inherit *something!*" Her voice bubbled with laughter.

"But your dowry? You said you were afraid that after Mattie's dowry was taken care of—?"

"Ah, that's the trouble. Father's not been able to raise Mattie's dowry yet and of course mine will have to wait till after that, so the wedding is some time off—no date is set. Which is perhaps why Mamma gave her consent, she thinks we'll quarrel and then she'll find somebody else for me. But if a date isn't set soon—'' Sue leaned forward and her voice dropped to a happy whisper—''we're going to elope!''

So Sue was likely to have no portion at all, and Lance, with two grasping married brothers already bleeding his father white, would like as not end up with a horse and saddle. Anna looked down at the basket of bulbs, imported from England and moldy-looking from their long damp trip across the sea.

''Have you heard from Grenfell?'' Sue asked.

''A long letter. Bernice paid the post for it by mistake and cook smuggled it to me. Most of it was in verse. He raved on and on about Oxford and the tall spires and the Great Tom Bell. He loves everything about it, says he plans never to return, and urges me to don cap and gown and join him there as his 'brother'!''

Sue's laughter pealed. ''As if you could! Well, at least you can be sure of one man, Anna—you'll always be first with Grenfell!''

Anna shook her head ruefully and nudged the basket with her toe. ''Not any longer. I've been replaced in Grenfell's life. He's discovered Learning. I think he'll go to school for the rest of his life if the money holds out.''

Sue gave her an uncertain look. ''And Ross?'' she asked more quietly. ''Do you ever see him?''

''No. Not since Papa Jamison took ill.''

''I heard he was squiring a girl on Sandys,'' muttered Sue. ''Before he left for Turks Islands, of course. He'll be gone for months. Does it upset you—about the girl?''

''Not in the least,'' shrugged Anna. ''There are plenty of other men.''

''That's good. Alma is furious about it. She always wanted him for herself, you know. I think she'd have gone with him to Turks if he'd asked her!''

''Is Mattie happy with Arthur?''

Sue bent to pick up two moldy bulbs that had spilled from the basket to the ground. ''I—don't know,'' she said diffidently. ''Oh, I may as well tell you.'' She straightened up and her words came out in a rush. ''I think he beats her! She had a bruise just under her eye last week and she said she'd run into the cupboard door. And yesterday I brushed by her and she cried out—she had a terrible bruise on her shoulder that looked like *fingers* had pressed down on it.''

Anna's lips tightened. ''Mattie shouldn't go to Boston. She should stay here.''

''Anna.'' Sue's sweet face grew earnest and troubled. ''I think Mamma would send Mattie to Boston with Arthur if he half killed her. She's so determined to 'launch' us, she forgets that even well-launched ships sometimes sink!''

''But not yours,'' smiled Anna. ''Have you thought about where you'll live after you're married?''

''With whichever family will have us, I suppose,'' said Sue frankly. ''And I'm sure mine won't so I guess 'twill have to be his—although his mother cares not a pin for me and his father little more.''

''When she gets to know you, Sue,'' said Anna affectionately, ''she's bound to see what a treasure Lance has in you.''

''Ha! *She* doesn't think so!''

''Where is everyone? I'd expected the house to be full of people.''

''Chloe is visiting friends in Smith's Parish, and Alma is visiting on Sandys—hoping to find out what that girl has that interested Ross! And Mattie and Arthur rode out somewhere—oh, there's Mattie now.'' Sue started to wave at her sister, who was running across the lawn from the stables, but she stopped when she saw that Mattie had a kerchief pressed to her face and was sobbing. ''What's the matter?'' she cried, sprinting toward her.

''Oh—nothing. Nothing at all.'' Stocky Mattie came to a dignified halt and turned her head away so that they might not see the red welt across her cheek. ''I got something in my eye, that's all. Hello, Anna, it's nice to see you.''

''Mattie,'' counseled Anna. ''Leave him. He isn't worth it.''

Mattie's quick indrawn breath gave her away.

''Would you like me to have a word with him?'' Anna asked quietly.

"It wouldn't help."

"It might."

"Nothing will help!" Mattie's courage left her and she dissolved in tears. "Arthur doesn't love me, he was forced to marry me, and he never lets me forget it!"

Anna turned on her heel and strode toward the stables, where Arthur was doubtless abusing the groom. She felt responsible for this marriage. It had not been made in heaven—it had been made through a series of blunders. And some of those blunders were her own.

Arthur whirled as she entered the stable, coming in out of the light into the dimness. She couldn't know how the sun haloed her hair, her whole body, so that she seemed radiant.

"Anna," he whispered, and the stableboy took that opportunity to slink away with the horses.

Anna stood with one hand resting on her hip. "I came to ask you, Arthur, if you knew that Mattie's father once horsewhipped a man who kicked his hound?"

"And what has that to do with me?" scowled Arthur.

"Only that if someone were to tell him that you were cuffing Mattie, he'd most likely break both your legs."

Arthur sprang forward out of the gloom. His face was savagely close and his strong hand closed down over her wrist with punishing pressure. "You got me into this!" he rasped. "I don't doubt you planned it between you! First *you* led me on and then, by God, you tricked me into marriage with that foul wench!"

"Hush," said Anna through her teeth, unwilling to let him know he was hurting her. "If you call Mattie that again, I'll strike you down myself!"

What might have happened then was anybody's guess, but Sue appeared in the doorway with a bright, "Oh, there you are, Anna. What, still out here, Arthur? Mattie's gone back to the house."

Arthur flung down Anna's wrist with a strangled sound and stalked away, his purple satins blazing in the sun.

"Do you think your little talk did any good?" murmured Sue. "When I heard him yelp like that, I thought I'd best interrupt before he blacked *your* eye!"

"I don't know. I told him your father once horsewhipped a man for mistreating his dog."

"Why, so he did, I'd forgotten that. He was fond of that dog. Father aroused is not a man to tamper with!"

"Perhaps if you can manage to impress that on Arthur, Mattie may have some portions of her body still left unbruised when Arthur sails away to Boston."

"It's a terrible world, isn't it?" sighed Sue. "Arthur buffeting Mattie, Chloe so miserable she can't hold her food down, Alma dangling after a man who doesn't want her, father unable to get a dowry together, Bernice doing terrible things at Mirabelle and practically turning you out—honestly, Anna, I feel so *guilty* at being so terribly happy!"

Anna gave an indulgent laugh and hugged her friend. A fool's paradise Sue might be living in but looking at that happy face, Anna prayed that it might last.

That night after supper Bernice called Anna into the long dining room. She did not suggest Anna sit down, but let her stand before her. They were alone in the room and Bernice drummed her fingers on the long dining table as she studied Anna.

"'Tis obvious no will is going to be found," she told the girl. "For none has turned up here and—"

"But what about Papa Tobias's London solicitor? I heard Ralph Kilhenny say he'd written to Christopher Marks and there's not been time to hear from him."

Bernice frowned. "I've read all his correspondence and there's nothing about a will. So I'll assume there isn't one. There'll be a search for kinsmen, no doubt, but that will not concern you. And since he never considered you a daughter at all—"

"*You* wouldn't know what he considered me!"

In the thronelike chair at the head of the table, Bernice stiffened. "I will overlook that," she announced with a look calculated to freeze the girl in gray homespun who stood so defiantly before her. "Tomorrow I will decide what's to be done with you. You may go now, Anna." She waved her jeweled hand. "I will let you know tomorrow."

With all the hauteur she could muster, Anna turned on her run-down heel and left.

All evening she planned feverishly what she must do. Bernice, now that her reign was firmly established, rarely stirred from her bed till noon. That gave Anna some time. But tomorrow's noon must not find her at Mirabelle—for only God knew what Bernice planned for her.

The *Annalee* had been sighted some distance from shore by a fast sloop that had come in harbor this morning. That meant the *Annalee,* barring bad weather, should make harbor tomorrow morning. The *Annalee* was one of Tobias Jamison's ships that had, under Bernice's orders, been doing a bit of interisland trading. Anna felt that Captain Withers, out of compassion, would let her hide on board and carry her away with him when he sailed to some other island where, whatever became of her, she would at least be beyond Bernice's reach.

It was late but she was still tense and keyed up when she went into cook's tiny airless sleeping closet. It was hot and stuffy and cook's loud snoring abraded her already raw nerves.

Restless, she got up and stole outside, walked aimlessly about the moonlit grounds. Her feet eventually carried her toward the overseer's cottage, a long distance from the house, for it was considered that he had best sleep near the slaves' quarters, to put down night disturbances.

The overseers had changed twice since Bernice's arrival. She was always dissatisfied that Tobias's easy-going slaves could not be driven to greater efforts. The last overseer was a New Englander named Silas Mather who spoke with a twang and whose gaze had followed Doubloon lasciviously as she swayed in from the fields, carrying a basket on her head, and walking with that seductive loose-hipped walk that was characteristic of her.

Anna, troubled, had noted that gaze. She had seen the look of raw animal hunger and unbridled passion in the overseer's pale eyes and been afraid for Doubloon, but days had passed and nothing had happened and she had forgotten about it.

Now before her in the moonlight she could see the overseer's small stone cottage with its pyramidal peaked stone roof. It was almost hidden in the trees but, like the slave quarters just to her right, she could almost feel its presence. A dim light reached her through the slats of Silas's window—she was surprised that he should still be up.

She would have approached no closer for she did not like Silas Mather and had never spoken more than two words to him, but as she turned to go back she was startled by a wild cry from the cottage—a woman's scream, sharply choked off.

Without thought, Anna followed her automatic reaction—for, after all, this plantation and everybody on it had been her sole responsibility for months on end when Tobias was away. She ran silently toward the cottage and stood on tiptoe, trying to peer in through the shutters. But a curtain had been drawn and she could see nothing save the flickering glow that came from a candle within.

That voice, she was certain, had been Doubloon's, and now from inside she heard a woman's soft crying—and something else, the flick of a whip.

Indignation welled up in Anna. That terrible Silas Mather was whipping Doubloon!

Anger drove her. She ran to the front door and wrenched it open, plunged inside. The wind had come up and the draft from the open doorway promptly extinguished the room's sole candle. Abruptly a man's hand shot out and swept the curtains back from the window she had tried to peer into. Moonlight came pouring in and that moonlight gleamed on the golden figure of a woman crouched naked on the floor and above her the threatening figure of a bony man with a short thonged whip in his hand.

Now the man turned toward her, a half-seen intimidating visage. Sweat gleamed on his naked chest and shoulders. He was wearing only the thin cotton breeches the slaves wore, with the legs hacked off for coolness. His heavily muscled legs stood planted as he glared at this intrusion.

"We don't allow whips around here!" cried Anna. "Papa Jamison threw the last overseer who used one off the place."

Silas Mather took a hulking step toward her. His gleaming chest muscles seemed to expand. " 'Tweren't Tobias who hired me," he jeered. "And his rules don't hold round here no more, little missy. That grand lady in the big house, she don't care what I do with this yaller wench—nor any of the rest of 'em, for that matter."

"She *does* care! She wouldn't let you do this to Doubloon if she knew," Anna insisted bravely, knowing it was a lie.

Silas's nasty laugh was cut into by Doubloon's low cry. "Go back, Anna. Go back afore he hurts you."

Silas's laugh cut off as if a knife had ripped through it. "She gives good advice, this slave girl," he told Anna menacingly. He spat and Anna jumped back, for the spittle had nearly landed on the toes of her soft slippers. "Pity the wench doesn't *take* good advice. It's for that I'm whippin' her, case you care to know. For lyin' with a black buck in the fields somewheres."

"Who she lies with is none of your affair!" Anna threw caution to the winds. "Bernice sent her down here to cook and keep house for you—she didn't *give* her to you!"

"The slut is here to comfort me," roared Silas. "And it don't comfort me none to find she's just been rollin' in the dirt with some sweaty field hand!" He raised his whip.

"Give me that!" cried Anna, leaping forward to take it from him.

Doubloon's scream echoed in her head as his big hand lashed out and caught Anna along the side of the head. For a crazy instant the world spun and darkened. Her body seemed to blow away from him, carried on a strong whirring wind. Sightless from the blow, Anna staggered backward through the open door and fell upon the grass outside, striking her head as she did so against the hitching post near the door.

A velvet blackness descended upon her, carrying her down, down, deep down. . . .

PART FOUR
The Bound Girl

The fiery loves of yesterday
That seemed to burn so bright,
Have smoldered through another day
And flickered out at night.

CHAPTER 35

It was hot. Sunlight was beating down on her. Anna opened her eyes into a kind of fog and, out of a dizzy haze, a face swam toward her: Sue's face.

"Ah, you're awake, Anna!" Sue cried joyfully.

The fog lifted and Anna could see that she was in a small room. At first she did not recognize it; then she realized that it was the bedchamber occupied by Sue and her sister Mattie—before Mattie had married Arthur and moved into the Waites' only guest bedroom.

"How did I get here?" Anna asked in a weak voice. "What am I doing at Waite Hall?"

Sue went over and closed the door. "Lance found you," she told Anna. "He was taking an early morning ride—well, it was still night, actually." Her pretty blush told Anna that Lance had slipped into this bedroom by night and departed before dawn by the window; to avoid questions he had circled around, cutting through Mirabelle Plantation, in order to approach his home from a different angle. "And he found you lying on the ground outside the overseer's cottage. He put you across his saddle and rode back here with you.''

"Thank God he didn't leave me with Bernice.''

"Yes.'' Sue frowned. "He knew what kind of trouble you were having and he was afraid—he was afraid that Bernice might have turned you over to the overseer and you'd been hurt trying to escape him.''

"As well she might,'' said Anna, trying to rise. "Only she didn't. I was out walking and I heard Doubloon scream and I burst through the cottage door and saw Silas Mather whipping Doubloon. When I tried to stop him, he attacked me. He must have knocked me senseless if Lance found me lying on the grass!''

Sue's eyes were big and dark. "That's what Lance thought— that he'd attacked you. He brought you back here and tapped on my window and I slipped out and opened the door and we brought you inside and I put you to bed. The next morning I told Mamma you had signed Articles of Indenture to me, and those Articles would represent my dowry, so Lance and I could be married sooner.''

"Did she believe you?'' Anna was astonished.

"Yes. You'd better lie back, you'll probably have an awful headache. The doctor said your head had taken one slight blow and one harder one. Anyway, my story about the Articles of Indenture kept Bernice from coming to get you, for I insisted you were now legally bound to me—so for heaven's sake, back me up on it.''

"I will. Of course I will. How long have I been here?''

"Almost a week.''

Then the *Annalee* was already in harbor—indeed she might have sailed again! This time Anna did sit up although the world spun around for a moment.

"I'm surprised Silas Mather didn't dispute Lance taking me away,'' she said.

"He couldn't dispute with anybody,'' said Sue quietly. "He was dead. Lance said the candle inside had guttered out and was smoking, but there was enough light for him to see Mather's body lying on the floor. At first he thought the man was drunk and that he had knocked you out, and he went over and stirred him with his foot—it was then he realized the overseer was dead.''

"Dead?" repeated Anna stupidly, holding her head. "But how?"

Sue hesitated. "At first Lance thought *you* might have killed him," she admitted. "He told me that when he brought you home to me but—you're not to worry, Anna. You won't be involved. All he told the doctor was that you took a bad fall in the garden here at Waite Hall. Nobody knows you were there that night."

"But—" Anna's head was reeling. *"How* did he die, Sue? When he struck me he was furious but in perfect health."

"Manchineel. In his liquor," said Sue significantly. "They caught Doubloon and she confessed to killing him. You're not to worry," she added hastily. "She didn't involve you. She never said a word about you being there."

Manchineel—those poison "apples" of the West Indies! And Doubloon had known so much about poisons . . . doubtless old Tarwus had supplied it to her.

"I'm not worried about myself," cried Anna. "I'm worried about Doubloon. They'll try her, of course? I must get up, Sue, and go down there and testify to what I saw—how she was crouched there naked and helpless and he was beating her."

Sue gave her a sympathetic look and pushed back a lock of her taffy-colored hair that had fallen down over her forehead. "There's no need for you to get up now," she told Anna. "The trial's already been held. Doubloon was hanged yesterday. And—there's something else, Anna. Before she died, Doubloon confessed that she'd poisoned Samantha Jamison as well."

The mounting horror on Anna's face was rent with a sudden indrawn breath. "I don't believe it!" she cried. "They must have tortured her, to make her say that! Why would she want to kill Mamma Jamison? She was always good to Doubloon."

Sue gave her friend a pitying look. "She said you had promised to free her—when the Jamisons died and you inherited. She was impatient."

Anna's head dropped into her hands with a groan. It had happened more than once, she knew, slaves poisoning masters who had promised to free them in their wills. But Samantha Jamison—sweet, kind Samantha. Anna had been only a surrogate daughter to Samantha, but she had loved her—and now to learn that through an act of generosity she had brought Samantha death!

Sue left her sobbing with her face burrowed into the pillow and quietly closed the door behind her. She understood. Anna had lost more than a friend. This dirty business about Doubloon had brought Samantha's death back to her and it was for *her* she grieved.

Later on they talked, and Sue told Anna over and over that she could not have known, she was not to blame. Later on Deborah Waite stopped by to frown at Anna in the big bed and ask her sharp questions and Anna, dry-eyed and silent now, confirmed Sue's story about signing the Articles of Indenture.

"But Sue and Lance have nothing to offer you!" exclaimed Deborah, puzzled by this startling arrangement.

"Sue told me Lance's parents were insisting on a dowry and—I am that dowry." She hated lying to Deborah Waite but there was no help for it. Across the room Sue looked gleeful.

Deborah left, shaking her head.

Arthur, still in residence at Waite Hall, took the news with glittering-eyed triumph. Anna tried to avoid him, but it was no use. He waylaid her in the garden, where she was working with the bulbs, and when she would have brushed by him, seized her by the arm.

"It's true, then?" he marveled. "Ye've sold yourself to Lance?"

"To Sue," corrected Anna, wincing as she tried to free herself.

"Why not to Mattie?"

"Because I've no desire to be—" she was wrestling with him now—"*your chattel!*" she gasped.

"D'you not know they'll sell your Articles of Indenture when they need money?" he demanded. "And a fine price they'll bring too!"

Arthur's comments always sent chills down Anna's spine. She fixed her gaze with contempt on that cruel mouth. "Sue wouldn't." She stated it flatly.

"Ah, would she not?" Arthur's brows shot up and Anna, freeing herself at last from his hateful grip with a violent wrench, wondered if that was the way things were done in Boston.

"No, she would not!" she burst out and ran down the path away from him, scattering bulbs as she went.

"You'll be coming to Boston with me," he called after her in a low voice, "or I'll bring action for the dowry I was promised but have not received and cast Mattie out if her father cannot raise it."

Anna's flying feet came to a halt. She turned and tried to consider Arthur, in his purple silks, calmly. "It is easy to see why you left Boston," she said at last. "For surely you can have no friends there."

A spark of anger flared in Arthur's eyes but he kept control of himself. "Insults will gain you nothing," he said sullenly.

"Nor will this kind of threat!" flashed Anna. "I feel sorry for Mattie, as indeed I would feel sorry for any girl who had the ill fortune to become your wife, but I would hardly wreck my own life to keep her beside you! Indeed, I think she would be the gainor if you rejected her—and if you do, you can never set foot in Bermuda again, for all would be on her side!"

She left Arthur red-faced and sullen, and tried to keep away from him after that. Dutifully she kept up her pretense of serving Sue—and indeed she was glad to mend Sue's clothes, in spite of her indifferent needlework, for it kept her mind off Doubloon and Samantha and Tobias and Mirabelle and everything that had gone wrong with her life. And sometimes she helped Sue work with the flowering plants and shrubs for which Sue had such a talent. Deborah Waite had always said indulgently that her daughter Sue had a "green thumb," that anything would grow for her.

"That's a talent that will stand you in good stead on your own plantation," Anna told Sue, smiling down at a bit of growing hedge that had looked like nothing more than a line of sticks stuck into the ground when Sue had planted it.

"*If* Lance and I ever get a plantation," sighed Sue. "It would mean so much to him to raise horses, and I've a mind for importing new crops but—'tis doubtful we'll ever have our chance."

"Could not Arthur lend you and Lance enough to start?" wondered Anna. "He is always bragging about his wealth back home and you would be glad to pay him handsome interest. I know Lance dislikes him but he *is* your brother-in-law—"

"Lance has already approached him," said Sue quietly. "Arthur laughed in his face. He said Lance and I had nothing to offer between us of collateral other than empty talk and hopes."

"I'm sure he told you you had one asset he'd consider buying—me," said Anna bitterly.

Sue gave her a stricken look. "Lance ought not to have told you," she said. "Arthur did offer to buy your Articles of Indenture, Anna. Lance turned him down, of course."

"Lance didn't tell me—Arthur did. In a roundabout way."

Sue shook her head in wonderment. "I cannot understand what poor Mattie sees in him. She lives in terror of him—and yet she weeps for hours if he stays away from her. Anna, I think I should tell you—Mattie is very grateful that you do not encourage Arthur."

"Encourage him?" A twig snapped in Anna's hand. "I only wish I had a brother—someone who'd challenge him for me!"

"Don't talk like that," chided Sue. "If Mamma were to hear you, she'd be very angry. She'll hear no word against Arthur, for she feels it's very handsome of him to be so patient about Mattie's dowry. I wonder..." Sue's voice lowered and her blue eyes seemed to darken. "I wonder if his patience in the matter of the dowry is because he is biding his time, trying to bring you to heel, Anna?"

Anna jerked a weed from the ground with such energy that she tore her finger on a thorn. "If so," she told Sue, as she sucked blood from her finger, "he will be staying with you for a long time, for he will *never* bring me to heel!"

Relief lightened Sue's sweet face. "Here comes Mamma," she murmured. "Quick, I must give you an order, for she does not half believe that you are really indentured to me!"

"Tell me to bring you a bucket of water for the plants," suggested Anna.

"Good. Anna—" Sue's voice rose—"will you bring me a bucket of water? Hurry now!"

Deborah paused beside Sue and turned to watch Anna lift her skirts and hurry away. "I still cannot believe it," she muttered. "I cannot. Anna Smith—*our bondservant?*"

"Mine," corrected Sue cheerfully. "Look at all the work we have done today, Mamma." She gestured toward the neat garden.

"Aye, neither of you lacks energy. I came to give you the news, Sue, which will be announced at supper. Arthur has taken passage to Boston and he and Mattie sail three days hence!"

"Without the dowry?" Sue was taken aback.

"Without the dowry," confirmed Deborah Waite, her face glowing with pleasure. "He says we can send it to him later."

"Where *is* Arthur?" wondered Sue.

"He has gone to Mirabelle to buy a horse," said Deborah shortly.

Sue's eyes widened. "Not Floss?" she whispered. "He has not gone to buy Floss?"

"Yes, I believe he has." Deborah gave her daughter a vexed look. "And I came out to ask you to keep Anna busy at some distance from the house—take a stroll with her if you must—for I do not wish her to see him come riding in with Floss. I am sure she will make a great scene, for she considers the horse her own despite the fact that Ralph Kilhenny has told Bernice that Anna has no legal claim to it or anything else Tobias gave her."

"Bernice is a vicious woman!" burst out Sue. "How do we know Kilhenny said that?"

"You had best abandon that tack," advised her mother sharply. "For she is like to be your neighbor as long as you live and you will find that she wields a bigger stick in the community than Anna Smith. The time may yet come when Lance will wish to seek a job as her factor.''

"Never! I'd let him beg first!"

Clucking her teeth at her daughter's foolishness, Deborah returned to the house, passing Anna, who struggled by with a heavy, sloshing, wooden bucket.

"What was your mother so angry about?" wondered Anna as she set the bucket down. "She said not a word but just glared at me!"

" 'Twas something I said," shrugged Sue. "Anna, after we pour that water on these plants, let's walk over to Lance's. I want to see how the new foal is getting on."

"You should go alone," smiled Anna.

"No—for it might be I'll need you for a lookout at the stable door," Sue told her archly. "Lance and I never have a chance to talk in private."

"And you'd rather have your conversation in a haymow!" Anna's laughter peeled.

"Come along," said Sue, red-faced. She gave Anna a guilty look, which Anna ascribed to embarrassment over her tryst with Lance. It never occurred to her that her friend was keeping something from her.

Sue was silent as they walked. She felt herself a traitor. But, she reasoned, if Arthur were trying to lure Anna to Boston by taking along her favorite horse, he would bring up the subject soon enough himself.

That night at supper the conversation was all about the impending voyage—nothing at all was said about Floss, although Sue slipped out to the stable through a light rain and found the silver mare was indeed standing in one of the stalls, contentedly munching hay.

Troubled, Sue stole back to the house and paused to shake out the shawl she had worn over her head. As she went inside, the patter of rain increased to a steady beat, falling like tears against the windowpanes, cascading down the white stone roof.

Like Mattie's tears, thought Sue suddenly. And remembered how excited Mattie had been at dinner, alternately pleased and—frightened? Sue hoped not.

That night the clouds rained themselves out and the next day dawned damp and clear. By afternoon the house was almost deserted. Deborah Waite and her two as yet unspoken-for daughters had taken the carriage into St. George. The overworked house servants were busy in the laundry and buttery. Arthur was off somewhere. Tom Waite was out in the woods with every hand that could be spared, supervising the felling of a stand of big cedars. Lance and Sue had ridden dreamily away to seek some isolated spot on the seashore where they could make love undisturbed and talk about elopement. So Anna found herself left alone in the house with Mattie, whom she found occupying herself with repacking her few possessions to make them fit into her big curved-top trunk.

"I thought you packed your trunk last night, Mattie," said Anna. "And here you are doing it again?"

"I did pack it," admitted Mattie. "But everything would not fit in and Arthur says I can take only the one trunk, that he will throw my books out as rubbish."

"But that's nonsense. You can't travel all the way to Boston with only one trunk. Explain that to Arthur. Surely he'll relent!"

Mattie shook her head woefully. "I don't think so, Anna. You don't really know Arthur." Her voice trailed off. *I didn't know Arthur either,* came the bitter thought. *Not till I married him.* She remembered how excited she had been when Arthur had first asked her out—something she had never in her wildest dreams expected to happen. For Mattie's life had been blighted by several comments she had overheard in her childhood and taken bitterly to heart.

The first cloud over a hitherto normal childish existence had come when her father's two sisters, Jude and Vinnie, had come to visit them. Both sisters had piercing voices, both had formed an instant dislike for Bermuda and for their brother's domineering wife, who did not intend to let either of them influence her one iota in anything she did. That dislike had filtered down to include the children.

The other children shunned them, but Mattie, more trusting

than the rest, had continued playing around their big skirts as they sat together, knitting on the big veranda.

"She'll certainly never be anything for looks, will she?" muttered Jude, with a distasteful glance at the child, playing with her doll at their feet.

"Who?" asked Vinnie, looking up from her flying needles.

"Mattie. She's got the worst features of both her parents, hasn't she? Poor Tom's plainness and Deborah's prominent teeth! Mark my words, they'll have trouble getting rid of *her* when she's grown!"

Little Mattie crouched there, listening. Her small fingers quivered as they held the doll, for every word had gone right through her. She scrambled up and ran away clutching the doll and when she was out of sight, burst into tears. And then she had crept into her mother's empty bedroom and stared woefully into the mirror with tears streaking down her cheeks and realized that her face *was* plain. Not pretty like Alma's nor winning like Sue's nor flashily dramatic like Chloe's.

From that moment on, Mattie began to criticize herself. Even her name, Mathilde, which she had thought beautiful— no one called her that, they called her Mattie, which always made her think of straw matting or matted hair. She hated it.

As she grew up, she lost herself in books. Self-effacing, she tried to keep in the background, and read and dreamed. And this behavior brought on a heartfelt overheard comment from her mother.

"I do fear Mattie will never amount to anything," Deborah had sighed to Tom Waite. "She reads too much."

Mattie, who chanced to be walking by the living room door as this was spoken, froze and pressed her body against the wall to hear.

"And what *should* she be doing at her age?" wondered Tom Waite, whose love of reading his daughter had inherited.

"She should be riding to improve her seat on a horse so that men will notice her! Or practicing her dance steps so that she may shine at the next ball instead of remaining a wall- flower! Or learning to play the harpsichord or to sing so that she may attract favorable attention to herself!"

Mattie, whose last desire would have been to attract attention to herself, favorable or otherwise, would have fled but she stayed to hear her father's defense of her.

"Mattie is afraid of horses," said Tom Waite bluntly.

"And I suppose you will add that she has no sense of rhythm and therefore always blunders through a dance?" came her mother's tart voice.

Tom's silence was answer enough. Mattie writhed. But when he spoke, it was a mild reproof to his wife. "Mattie does not care to learn the harpsichord and you yourself have said frequently that she has no voice, so why do you wish her to sing?"

"Oh, you're impossible, Tom! I want her to *try!* At this rate, she'll never amount to anything, she'll never get a husband, she'll be on our hands forever. Do you want that?"

Mattie might have been heartened by her father's cool, "I wouldn't mind that at all. I'm very fond of Mattie." But she didn't hear it—she had already bolted.

This time she ran out on the broad lawns, wet from a sudden hard summer rain. She ran through the grasses, not bothering to pull up her skirts so the wet wouldn't stain them, and threw herself against the bole of one of the big cedar trees, clasping its trunk as though it were a lover, and sobbed her heart out.

Never amount to anything . . . never get a husband . . . the terrible words kept ringing through her head.

They were the words she'd lived her life by, always stepping aside that others might go first, having no belief in herself whatever.

Arthur had seemed heaven sent.

That first magical day when he had asked her out riding— after dancing endlessly with her at the ball—Mattie had dressed herself with trembling fingers and danced out of the house on air. For the first time in her life, she rode light in the saddle, her back as proud and straight as Chloe's. Her heart sang and the shining face she turned toward Arthur transformed her.

But Arthur, grudgingly admitting to himself that Mattie

was not so homely as he had first thought, had seen only an overwilling wench, a flower bending toward him eager to be plucked.

He had been tempted to seduce her that first day, but common sense had held him off.

The second day he would have considered it but that Mattie's horse went lame as they went out the gate and they returned to Waite Hall to while away the time on the veranda, a place so public that Arthur was forced to resort to conversation with the ecstatic girl.

The third day he would certainly have had his way with her, but that they ran into a group from a neighboring plantation who refused to be shaken off and rode with them through the long, exhausting afternoon. As the jolly group accompanied them home for a "stirrup cup," Arthur, glowering, determined that tomorrow should be *the day*. It was not that he particularly wanted Mattie, but she was more desirable than the chambermaids at Lilymeade who were too old and heavy for his taste, and it had been a long time since he had debauched a virgin. He was curious what it would be like with Mattie: Would she weep? Would she cry out? Would she pretend she felt no pain? Would she fight him? Ah, that would be splendid! His dark eyes shone and he licked his lips.

Besides his curiosity to find what it would be like to bring Mattie to earth, the obstacles that kept arising to thwart him had whetted his appetite, always strong where women were concerned. Having determined that nothing should henceforth stand in his way—and Mattie, he was sure, was too timid ever to tell what he had done if he frightened her enough—he now squeezed her hand and whispered hoarsely into her ear that she was the most desirable woman in the world, *why was she teasing him like this? Zounds, a man couldn't know where he stood with her!*

Mattie was thrilled. She walked back to the house on a tilt, and that night she had lifted her small chin and told Sue in deepest confidence—for she couldn't bear not to tell *someone* —that she was sure Arthur was in love with her but was too shy to tell her so, and that Mamma wouldn't have to worry about *her* being an old maid, she'd figured out how to bring things to a head!

She'd meant every word she said. She'd meant to melt in Arthur's arms—gloriously. To give herself to him body and soul. He already desired her—had he not told her she was the most desirable woman in the world? That such phrases came easily to Arthur's lips never occurred to Mattie in her innocence. He had charged her with *teasing* him! Ah, she would tease him no longer! And all must be resolved before Arthur thought of returning to Boston, for, feeling as he plainly did toward her, she could not bear to let him go. In her mind she breathlessly traced and retraced every handsome feature of Arthur's face. She missed the cruelty there and saw only the fire. Mattie went to bed and shivered against the sheets. She could hardly wait for tomorrow. Tomorrow in some lovely woodland glade Arthur would declare his love—and she would reward him for it! She would fling herself against him with a glad cry and melt against his tall frame. She was not sure just what would happen then, but she had great confidence that whatever happened, it would be splendid. And afterward—afterward with bodies glowing and eyes fierily locked, he would hurry her back to the house and demand her hand! He would carry her away to Boston in a great white ship and they would live happily ever after, just like the heroines of her favorite novels!

It had not worked out quite that way. They had never reached that romantic woodland glade. Mattie, with her starry gaze fixed on Arthur, had not watched where she was going. She had been swept from her horse by a low branch and landed heavily, with the breath nearly knocked from her body. As she lay there in her torn dress, dizzy from the fall, Arthur had bent over her.

What might have happened next she was never to know, for Walter, who had been shadowing them unseen on every ride, determined that what had happened to Mistress Anna should not happen again, had descended on Arthur like the vengeance of God and herded them both back to Waite Hall,

Valerie Sherwood

where Deborah Waite had furiously accused Arthur of ruining her daughter. Arthur's indignant protests of innocence had been ignored, all Mattie's tears unavailing. The special license had been procured—and the preacher. That afternoon in the living room at Waite Hall, Mattie had married a white-faced, furious Arthur.

She might have refused to go through with it if she had thought Arthur's fury sprang from any source other than having his gallant attempt to save her misunderstood (for his bending over her had assumed that status in Mattie's romantic mind) and at· being made to proceed faster than he had intended. For it never occurred to innocent Mattie with her ignorance of the world that a man who seized her hand and told her vibrantly how desirable she was, did not love her—and loving her and being a houseguest next door, a gentleman who moved in their own circle, that he would offer her anything less than marriage.

Mattie went through the ceremony in a dream.

A dream from which she waked that night at Walter's house as Arthur, impatient and still seething from this enforced marriage, called her a spineless slut who had trapped him, tore the clothes from her trembling back, tossed her headfirst into bed, and took her virginity with all the delicacy of a raging bull. Torn and frightened and in agony from Arthur's rude treatment, Mattie had tried to escape him when he turned over to throw from the bed a pillow that annoyed him. Halfway to the door, a naked Arthur had overtaken· her and struck her such a blow on the temple that she had slumped to the floor.

Whatever else happened on her wedding night was mercifully withheld from her, for she woke slowly, dizzily, with an aching head and groaned as she tried to move her loins.

Arthur was gone. Remembering, Mattie thanked God that he *was* gone and hoped he would never return.

Unfortunately he was only downstairs devouring his breakfast with the same speed, efficiency, and violence with which he had last night devoured her virginity, for all that exercise had made him exceedingly hungry.

Ashamed of what she considered her own failure—for Arthur had not hesitated to call her cold, inept, blundering, and any number of other things worse—Mattie had kept the events of her wedding night to herself.

Afterward things had gone from bad to worse. Although Arthur was usually careful to strike her where the bruise could not be viewed—and she often walked heavily, limped, or seemed to hobble from these blows—of late he had been less careful.

Her life had become one long nightmare. She was terrified when Arthur was around and wept when he was away. But Sue had been mistaken in the reason for those tears—Mattie wept for her own failure. She flooded her pillow with tears for what might have been—and was not.

Now, watching Mattie wearily repack her trunk, Anna leaned down to stare at the girl's face. For Mattie had been absent from the breakfast table, pleading a headache, and hidden in her room all morning.

"Where did you get that bruise on your jaw, Mattie?" she asked, frowning.

Mattie looked away, her lips about to form the lie that Arthur had invented for her: *Tell them you slipped and fell against the chest and struck your jaw.* Instead she turned about and said with a rush, "Oh, Anna, are all men monsters after they come to bed? I cannot please Arthur, everything I do seems to be wrong and he—he is so cruel to me!"

She began to weep—helplessly, like a child. Anna, filled with indignation and feeling guilty too that she had thrown them together, gathered the girl in her arms. "He struck you, didn't he?"

Mattie's brown head bobbed an assent.

"Have you told your mother?"

"No," whispered Mattie. "I am ashamed to. She will think me a failure."

"Then tell your father. *He* will know what to do. He will give Arthur a thrashing!"

She could feel Mattie's shudder. "And what would Arthur do to me afterward?"

"Yes, I see what you mean." Anna pushed Mattie away and began to pace the floor. "Perhaps if *I* spoke to your mother?"

"Oh, no, you must not!" Mattie's voice rose in a wail. "I am *so* afraid of him, Anna. If anyone meddles—oh, promise me you will not say anything!"

Anna opened her mouth—and closed it again unhappily. Mattie needed help yet she was unwilling to let anyone speak up in her defense. She sighed. "I advise you to speak to your mother, Mattie. She could insist you stay here and not accompany Arthur to Boston."

Mattie only continued to cry.

Exasperated by Mattie's tears, Anna would have gone outside but as she peered out the window she saw Arthur pacing through the garden with his hands clasped behind him, turning to shoot an occasional glance toward the house. At that point she decided to stay indoors even though it was stuffy. Arthur would be here but another two days and with most of the family gone, she had no intention of giving him a chance at her.

The sultry afternoon dragged on. Anna began idly to polish the silver—after all, she owed the Waites something for her keep! The windows were open and a bee droned lazily in. As she turned to watch it, she saw, out past a clump of trees, a thin column of dark smoke rising.

Anna frowned. All that lay in that direction was a dilapidated old shed in which produce was sometimes stored, but one could not have any of the farm buildings catching fire; it could well spread and damage valuable trees.

Her sense of property aroused, Anna hurried outside, and ran toward that column of smoke. As she neared the shed her eyes lit up with horror, for she could plainly hear a horse's terrified whinny and the crashing sound of hooves striking against boards.

The Waites' stables lay well to her left. Could one of the horses, tethered and left to graze sometimes in this area, have got into that old shed and knocked over something flammable?

She had almost reached the shed. From within it rose a

horse's frenzied scream and the shed door shook as heavy hooves struck it.

That door was bolted from the outside.

Anna ran to it, shot the bolt and threw it wide. She was greeted by a thick billow of smoke and she could feel the heat of the flames at the back of the shed.

"Why, it's Jemmy!" she cried, recognizing Deborah Waite's elderly saddle horse, a gentle brown mare with affectionate ways that endeared her to everyone. "However did you get in here, Jemmy?" She reached forward and tried to seize the terrified animal's bridle, but poor Jemmy shied away from her, kicked and reared up.

"Easy, Jemmy!" Smoke rolled over her as she edged gingerly into the shed and tried to soothe the horse, but terrified Jemmy only rolled her eyes, milled around and stamped, jerking up her head. She refused to come out even though Anna pulled at her bridle.

Anna was now choking on the thick black smoke. Sobbing with fear for the gentle old horse, she tore off her kirtle and tossed it over Jemmy's head—and was narrowly missed by a pair of flailing hooves as the mare reared up in fright.

Now that she could no longer see the flames, the horse turned docile and Anna was able to lead her from the shed, even as the fire raced along the rafters and ignited the thatched roof. As Anna tethered Jemmy's big trembling form to a tree—for she had no intention of letting the hysterical horse turn and plunge back into the burning shed—she heard a crash and turned to see the entire shed collapse in a fiery funeral pyre.

"Oh, Jemmy!" Horror at what had so nearly happened overcoming her, Anna pulled the kirtle from the mare's eyes and threw her arms around her neck and pressed her face against that silky mane. After a minute during which she soothed the horse, she stepped back. "Let's see if you're hurt, Jemmy. No, I don't believe so but it was a near thing. Who could have fastened you in there?"

"I did," said a sneering voice.

Anna turned to confront Arthur, who had stepped out from

behind a tree and now stood with his arms folded, relaxed and resplendent in his green silk knee breeches, watching her with a sardonic gaze.

"You?" Anna was so taken aback that she forgot she was standing there in her petticoat, holding her kirtle in her hand. "But even you"—she pushed the thought from her—"no, you wouldn't have!"

"I knew you were in the house and I thought by the smoke to bring you out to me."

"Ah, don't jest!" she cried. "Poor Jemmy could have died in there—burned alive! Whoever did this must pay for it!"

"I do not jest, Anna." Arthur moved toward her, swaggering a little. "The mare was grazing. She follows anyone who calls her by name." That was true, Deborah had often remarked it. "I locked her in and then set fire to a pile of dry straw I had already stacked behind the shed—although I will deny it, of course, when you race to tell the Waites about it. I had the devil's own time making the shed catch, for the timbers were damp from the rain, but"—he yawned—"it finally did catch and made a nice billow of smoke—and here you are. In your petticoat."

Anna, who had stood transfixed at his outrageous admission, recoiled at that last remark and quickly threw her kirtle around her. She jumped as the last timbers of the shed collapsed with a shower of sparks.

"I was sure you would arrive in time to save the horse," he added lazily.

"And if I had not?" she cried. "What then?"

He shrugged. "The beast is not worth much."

Rage made Anna feel her head was melting. "What kind of a monster are you, who would destroy a kind animal like Jemmy who has never done you any harm?" She was shaking with anger. "I will tell the Waites you have gone mad and belong in Bedlam!"

"Ah, I am sure you will." Arthur laughed nastily. "Just as I am sure you will now rush into the house and confront Mattie with this new proof of my bad character. But you will find Mattie too concerned with her own skin to back you up in this, for I have told her in vivid detail what I will do to her if she stands against me.''

''Mattie—knew what you were going to do? I don't believe it!''

''She did not know—but she does not care what I do.'' Arthur's words had the brutal finality of falling stones. ''So long as I leave her in peace.''

Anna drew in her breath. ''Someone should break your bones,'' she said between her teeth.

Arthur laughed and swaggered toward her but made no move to touch her. Instead he stood with legs spread apart, arms akimbo, and studied her. ''So now I have tested you, Anna, and I have learnt how to control you.'' His bold eyes raked over her slight figure, seeming to lift the skirts from her legs and peer beneath. ''You have a weakness and that weakness is your soft heart—you could not let this old horse burn even though you might have lost your life in the shed, been kicked insensible or set ablaze yourself.''

Anna swiftly untethered Jemmy; she was not going to leave the horse alone with this monster. ''You're a criminal!'' she flung over her shoulder. ''You don't deserve to live!''

''I care not what ye call me.'' His voice rang like flint on steel. ''But I've a mind to humble ye, Anna. Ye played with me, led me on, ye tricked me into a worthless marriage—and I'll humble ye for that. Aye, and I'll have that sweet body in the bargain!''

Anna gave an angry sniff and began to lead the trembling mare away. But—like the horse—she felt a pervading wave of fear wash over her.

Arthur's mocking voice followed her. ''Now that ye have learnt that I set this shed afire with a horse inside, ye know my temper. If you do not go with me to Boston, Anna, before I leave I will chain Floss in a shed piled high with hay and set it alight!''

Anna's feet came to a dead halt. She closed her eyes. A terrible picture rose up before her: Gentle Floss being led into a shed like this one, locked in, smelling the smoke, hearing the fire crackle, realizing she was trapped—gentle Floss with

her mane alight, screaming in agony and trying to break out
as the flames bit into her body and no one came to help. . . .

"*You would not,*" she whispered.

"Before God, *I would!*"

"Anyway," she cried, trying to push away that terrible
vision of Floss burning, Floss dying, "you do not own
Floss!"

"I bought her yesterday from the new owner of Mirabelle.
If you will look in the stable, you will find her already
there."

So Bernice had sold him Floss. Anna felt her world waver.

"If God does not find a way to punish you," she said
thickly, "*I will!*"

"Do not imagine that you can leap upon Floss's back and
ride away and escape me, Anna." His drawl flicked the raw
wound. "For 'tis a small island and I will surely find you."

A sob caught in Anna's throat as her silent scorn burned
back at him.

Nettled by her hatred, Arthur gave a short laugh. "I bid
you think on what I have said, Mistress Anna," he said with
an attempt at jauntiness. "You have some time left—but not
much. Mattie and I embark for Boston two days hence. I have
already spoken to Lance about buying your Articles of Indenture but he balks—he insists you must give your consent to
the sale. I believe you will agree I have found the way to win
that consent?"

He brushed by her, rudely reaching out and pinching her
breast as he went by. Anna spun away from him like a
spitting cat and struck his impudent hand away. She could
hear him laughing as he swaggered back toward the house.

CHAPTER 36

As long as Arthur was in sight, in case he should turn around, Anna stood proud and contemptuous. But when he had gone she collapsed against Jemmy's sleek brown side, her face gone damp with fear. She felt as if Arthur had locked *her* in a burning shed and she was fighting to get out.

"Jemmy, Jemmy," she whispered to the still trembling mare, "I cannot let Floss burn and he knows it. I *cannot.*"

Anna found Floss in the stable and spent the afternoon with her, hugging her, petting her, promising her nothing bad was going to happen—and fighting back her own dread.

Arthur, mercifully, did not come near the stables.

When Deborah Waite returned, she found Anna waiting for her in the living room—a very resolute Anna. Deborah looked at the girl and sighed. But she listened, pulling off her kid gloves, as Anna poured out Jemmy's story to her—poured it out in impassioned ringing tones—just as Arthur had predicted she would. And just as he had cleverly foreseen, she was not believed.

"Really, it's too ridiculous, Anna," scoffed Deborah, who was used to brushing aside high drama—usually imagined—from Chloe. She took off her hat and ran her fingers through her hair, damp from the heat. "You're obviously overwrought. It's a hot day—you must have had a touch of the sun. Why would Arthur want to harm my horse? Poor old Jemmy is everybody's friend!"

"Not everybody's," Anna corrected her bitterly. "Just watch her shy away from Arthur, if you don't believe me!"

"Of course! Jemmy's had a terrifying experience, she was

nearly burned up! One of the servants must have passed by
and seen the door open and having no idea that Jemmy was in
there, shot the bolt to keep the door from swinging in the
wind and breaking its hinges. But *no one* would deliberately
lock Jemmy in! Arthur met our carriage and told us what had
happened as we rode back home.''

Anna gazed at Deborah steadily. She saw a shallow energetic woman who usually took the easy way out. For a
moment she was glad she had told Deborah only about
Jemmy—nothing about Floss. She couldn't have borne to
hear *that* pooh-poohed!

Deborah Waite fidgeted under Anna's unblinking stare.
''Arthur told us how he saw the smoke and hurried up just in
time to see you pulling Jemmy from the stable with your skirt
over the poor thing's head. And indeed I'm most grateful to
you, Anna, for saving Jemmy at such risk, for I'm very fond
of her. But your account of the matter *does* conflict with
Arthur's.''

''I don't doubt it,'' said Anna grimly. ''Next he'll be
saying *I* set fire to the shed.''

''He believes you may have done it accidentally,'' said
Deborah in a distant tone. She held up her hand. ''I'm not
accusing you, mind you''—as Anna took an impulsive step
forward—''and even if you did, the shed was of little value
and you did manage to save Jemmy, so no real harm was
done. But this wild tale about Arthur—really, Anna, I cannot
have you accusing my daughter's husband of such vile things!''

Anna turned away feeling hopeless. Deborah Waite did not
even *want* to understand. She began to realize what it must be
like to be Mattie.

As she turned she saw Mattie go through the hall like a
wraith, beckoning to her as she disappeared. She followed
and caught her down the hall.

''You were listening at the door, weren't you, Mattie?'' she
accused.

Mattie nodded. ''I saw Arthur go out toward the shed and
then I saw the smoke rise,'' she whispered. ''*I* know you are
telling the truth, Anna.''

"Then why did you not speak up?" asked Anna wearily. "Instead of skulking about outside the door?"

"I was afraid." Mattie shivered and looked behind her. "Arthur has told me terrible tales of things they do to women in the Arab countries. He has warned me that he will do those things *to me* if ever I cross him *in any way*." She gave Anna a look of mute appeal. "Oh, Anna, you do understand?"

"Yes, yes, I understand," sighed Anna.

"But I *am* going to tell Mamma how he treats me—right now!"

Anna waited, leaning against the wall, while Mattie crept in to speak to her mother. It gave her time to think. If Deborah believed Mattie, there might still be a chance, for Deborah aroused would be a powerful ally. Like as not she would lock Floss away from Arthur and tell Tom Waite to boot her son-in-law aboard ship!

But Mattie returned bent over and looking crushed. She was twisting her hands together. "I told Mamma how Arthur treats me and she said pish-tush, I was making it all up to get attention and that if I let Arthur go to Boston without me I will fade away on the vine here, a deserted wife whose husband left her because she made vile accusations, and that I cannot look to her for help if that happens!"

Anna gave her a pitying look. "I am sorry for you, Mattie, but you must break away from Arthur now. *Now,* before he takes you away from Bermuda. There are dark nights at sea. Do you think that on some night when he is angry with you that he would hesitate to push you overboard?"

Mattie fell back, her cheeks whitening to the color of the ceruse whitening that hid her blotchiness. Her cringing gesture showed that she was losing weight, for the material of her formerly tight bodice rippled. "He would not," she whispered.

"A man who would lock a horse in a fiery coffin would stoop to anything," said Anna tersely.

"I know that he—that he desires you," stammered Mattie. Beneath the white ceruse her face flamed.

"'Tis hardly a secret," muttered Anna, too angry to be

properly sorry for Mattie's humiliation. "He strips me with his eyes every time I walk through the room!"

Mattie closed her eyes for a moment and her head drooped.

Anna would have left her then but that Mattie caught at her arm. "Arthur tells me"—Mattie's hand dropped away and she began to twist her gold wedding ring with her fingers—"that you are coming to Boston with us, Anna. That he is buying your Articles of Indenture from Lance. Is it true?"

"No, Mattie," Anna said pityingly. "You need not worry about that. I will not spoil your life." *Arthur will do that!* "Somehow, I promise you, I will manage not to go."

"But you must!" Mattie's words came out in a wail. "Oh, Anna, you must! Who else has the courage to protect me?"

Into what depths had life plunged poor Mattie, thought Anna. "I cannot protect you, Mattie," she told the other girl sadly. And suddenly she felt defenseless, too. "I cannot even protect myself." *And perhaps not Floss. . . .* It was a bitter realization.

With a sob, Mattie ran away from her and Anna wandered to a window and stood drumming her knuckles on the sill, looking out through the open casements at the gathering dusk.

There *was* someone who could help her—Flan O'Toole, the wrecker's son.

The next morning early found her in a borrowed boat, sailing down to Sandys, and the squat stone house Flan lived in.

She found everything there in confusion, for Flan was packing his gear to leave Bermuda. He had signed up with a privateer whose lean ship—a pirate ship if ever Anna had seen one, only waiting to clear land before hoisting the Jolly Roger—waited for him now in the bay. He would not be coming home for a long time—indeed, nobody knew how long these voyages would take. But he was very glad to see her. He shut the door on his weeping mother, who was dabbing at her eyes with a damp apron, hoisted over his shoulder a big knapsack full of the possessions he meant to carry aboard, and took Anna outside. He led her down to the white beach and listened as she poured out her story.

When she had finished, he looked torn and cast a hunted look about him. "I'd be more than glad to break his bones for him, Mistress Anna, but I've no time. The ship is leaving!"

"But—Floss!"

The glowing sight of the excited girl with her bright hair billowing about her shoulders in the sea wind near unmanned him. "It will have to wait," he muttered.

"Wait? *Wait*, you say? Why, Arthur will be trying to rape me next—he's tried already!"

"Tom Waite won't stand for that!"

"Not while I'm in his house, but Arthur threatens to burn my horse if I do not accompany him to Boston."

"He'll not do it." Flan's voice carried authority. No one burned horses—they were too valuable.

"He *will!*" It was a cry of anguish, torn from Anna.

"No, he will not," insisted Flan. "You must not let him threaten you this way. Ah, I'd love to crack his skull for him but I'm set to leave, as you can see—you understand how it is, Anna?"

"Too well!"

The bitterness of her tone took him aback. " 'Tis not that I don't love ye, Anna," he protested.

"Oh, no." Anna's voice was brittle. "I've no doubt you love me, Flan. In your fashion."

He looked upset. "I'd thought if I married you—"

"That I'd inherit from Papa Jamison and give you one of his ships and you could set yourself up as a privateer and sail away adventuring."

His dark eyes lit up and he seized her hand, squeezed it warmly. "I knew you'd understand, Anna. But when—"

"When it seemed there was to be no tall ship," she supplied ironically.

"Ah, Anna, that's not fair!" he protested.

" 'Fair'?" She gave a bitter laugh. "What's fair?"

Flan hesitated. Bare feet planted in the sand, legs spread apart, his body seemed already to have a slight roll—as if already he stood on the deck of that ship that waited for him in the bay. His sunny yellow hair blew into his sunburned face as he gnawed at his lip. "Well, this is the only way I can strike out for myself, Anna," he admitted. "Else I'll always be under my father's thumb."

And that, Anna could see for herself, could not be pleasant. A wrecker's life, was that really how Flan lived? Clubbing and killing exhausted men in the surf to claim their cargo? People called him "the wrecker's son" but she herself had never really believed it of him. . . . Overhead a seabird screamed. The sun seemed very bright.

"So you'll not help me?" Her voice had gone dull, hopeless.

"Ah, Anna, do not ask it. When I come back—"

"I'll be gone."

"I'll find you," he insisted eagerly. "Even if you be gone to Boston. I'll go there and find you, Anna."

Anna peered into his anxious sunburned face. She felt as if she had never seen him before. "Does it make no difference to you, Flan, that Arthur will be taking me to Boston as his mistress? Do you think he will ask my permission? No, he'll simply break down my door in the night and beat me senseless and ravish me. Doesn't that bother you, Flan?"

Red color rose in Flan's cheeks. He could not meet her steady gaze. "Aye, of course it does. And if he does that, I swear I'll avenge you—tell him that! 'Twill make him stop and consider!"

"I don't want to be avenged, Flan. I want to be rescued."

"But the ship leaves within the hour!" cried Flan. "And I must be aboard. Even now I see the captain waving at me from the rail—he cannot understand what's keeping me. Anna—" he turned and would have taken her in his arms but she backed away from him, holding her arms straight out in front of her, palms up, to fend him off. "Anna," he pleaded. "Be reasonable. 'Tis only for a voyage that I'll be gone and I'll come back rich. Rich! I can come to Boston and snatch you from him—yes, and kill him too, if you like."

"And are you then so used to killing?" she asked stonily.

"Yes!" He stopped, wincing. She had surprised that admission out of him.

"It's true, then," she said in a level voice, "what they say about you. You *are* a wrecker. I'd hoped you weren't—I'd believed you weren't.''

"I know not what men say," he said roughly. "And care less." But he was plainly ruffled; he stood, uncertain whether to go or stay. *"What* do they say?" His face was belligerent.

"They say—" She cast a contemptuous look toward the house and Flan's father, Sean, a gaunt skeletel figure on the beach, watching them with a lowering gaze. "They say your father is a wrecker, moving the lights at night so that passing ships will pile up on the reefs. They say no shipwrecked sailor reaches shore alive here—only their goods." Suddenly she wondered about Flan's betrothed, who had also drowned on those reefs. Lila might have been a little easy in her morals but she wasn't the kind to countenance murder. Had she found out about the O'Tooles' nighttime activities? Had she threatened to tell? " 'Twas not you but your father who took Lila out to the reef that day, wasn't it? The day she drowned?''

It was a shot in the dark but Flan was startled and his sudden guilty look confirmed her suspicions. "I know not how ye found out, Anna," he said stiffly. "But my father—"

"Was interested in the girl too," said Anna bluntly. "I heard the gossip. You *shared* her!"

"It would have broken my mother's heart to know my father had taken Lila out in the boat. The squall came up sudden and the boat was swamped. 'Twas an accident could have happened to anyone. 'Twas best my mother think *I* was in the boat, for she'd not have believed my father if he'd said he was only taking Lila to see me."

No, and I would not have believed him, either, thought Anna, turning back to stare at that shifty evil face watching her from a little distance down the sand. *Perhaps the girl had seen something and threatened Sean that she would tell it. Perhaps she had grown tired of being shared by father and son and given the older man an ultimatum. Perhaps her drowning was not an accident after all. . . .*

It was all there in her eyes, plain for him to see.

Flan stared at Anna, baffled. Of all the girls in Bermuda, he preferred this one—aye, and he'd have married her too if she could have set him up with a ship of his own. Although he did feel he was too young to settle down—he'd told Lila that when she'd pressed him to set the wedding date and take her away from here. But his father had said he couldn't leave, he and Lila must live here, for in their profession they couldn't afford to bring in outsiders. Their profession! Faith, he had no love for it—beating half-drowned men back into the water to drown in order to seize their goods "legally." He had had enough of the wrecking game and never meant to return to Bermuda—except perhaps for Mistress Anna. Her story worried him. He itched to smash Arthur Kincaid to the ground— ah, if he only had Arthur in the surf and could go after him with his belaying pin! But he itched even more to try the life of a privateer—a man could grow rich! And see strange places, new sights, have endless adventures!

A deep frown settled over his strong sunburned features. He cast a worried look at the sea and the waiting ship. "Stay here and wait for me, Anna," he pleaded at last. "My mother will take you in." *His mother, who locked herself in during storms and covered her ears against the human screams that rose above the shrieking winds.* "And when I come back, I promise you I'll spit Arthur like a chicken if you desire it!"

Anna had no doubt this brawny, fierce-faced lad would do it—but it was plain he hadn't time to do it now. There were other more enticing demands on that time—a tall ship, a reckless life ahead. She cast a long look toward his squat stone house, built to weather any gale, and thought of his mother, scuttling about with her head down and never meeting anyone's eyes—*she* knew how her menfolk made their living! And she thought of Lila, the young girl who had drowned, and of Sean's evil face watching her. She turned to give Flan a wondering look.

"Stay *here*?" she whispered. *"And be shared as Lila was?"*

"Ah, but that would not happen!" Flan protested. "Lila was different!"

"*I* am different too," Anna said sadly, backing away from him.

Impulsively he took a step toward her, reached out a hand to stay her going, but she avoided it as if his touch might scorch her.

"Anna," he cried in sudden panic. "Please wait!"

Anna shook her head. "When you return," she said, "I'll be far beyond your reach. Good-bye, Flan."

She turned then and ran away from him across the soft sand toward the point where she had beached her light sailboat. She glanced back once and saw him standing there, a sturdy figure against the shimmering blue. For a moment she thought he was going to run after her because he took an indecisive step forward. Then he straightened his broad shoulders and walked down toward the waiting longboat.

Anna leaped into her sailboat and cast off, watching Flan row out to sea toward his destiny. She felt the spray in her face and watched sadly as the tall ship cast anchor. The wind took its sails and it was carried majestically away from her.

She had been so sure that Flan would help her, but once again she had equated a hot look in a man's eyes with love.

They all coveted her beauty—but it came second with them.

Lance preferred horses, Grenfell preferred learning, Ross preferred ships—and Flan preferred adventure.

It seemed to her that she would never be first—with anyone.

And now she knew, as she set her sails for St. George and let the rising wind skim her across the blue-green water, that she was on her own.

Nobody was going to help her.

If she saved Floss—and God only knew how she was going to do it—she would have to do it herself.

Sue had hurt her ankle the day before when she came down awkwardly off her horse in the driveway at Lilymeade where she and Lance had ridden, and the Meades, always solicitous and hospitable, in spite of the fact that Walter had strained his back and was laid up, had insisted Sue spend the night. So Anna had had no chance to talk to her.

But now when Anna returned to Waite Hall, she found Sue hobbling about the grounds. "I always manage to look awkward before Lance,'' Sue sighed ruefully. "What's wrong, Anna?'' For she had caught a glimpse of Anna's worried face.

Anna told her of yesterday's events, and Sue's indignation matched her own. "Arthur should be flogged!'' she cried.

"Indeed he should, but which of us is to do it? You and I, whom he can overpower? Your father, who certainly won't believe my story now that your mother has been at him?''

"Lance! Lance will do it!''

Yes, Lance might do it because he loved horses better than women. But—if Lance assaulted Deborah's son-in-law, Anna knew Sue's hopes of marrying him would go out the window. There would be bad blood between the Waites and the Talbots then.

A sudden thought occurred to Anna. "Lance *can* help us,'' she said thoughtfully. "He can sell Arthur my Articles—I will make them out and sign them—and I will use the money to transport myself and Floss on any ship that will take us!''

"But you would be stealing Floss, now that Arthur has bought her,'' pointed out practical Sue. "Suppose you were caught?''

Anna gave a harsh laugh. "Would my fate be better with Arthur?''

Sue fell silent. "I will find a parchment,'' she said. "We will contrive to write up the Articles of Indenture.''

"Thank you, Sue.'' Anna felt older. Life was rushing past her at a furious rate that made every day seem a month. What lay in store for her, she had no idea. She only knew that she was faced with a terrible choice that she refused to make. She meant to take a third path—wherever it led.

There was no use now in asking Captain Withers of the *Annalee* to take her aboard. He might have taken *her*—but a stolen horse? Never!

Night found Anna Smith slipping into the town of St. George. She had left Floss some distance from the town, secure in a little grove of trees. She had fed and watered Floss well but she had had to wait till Arthur was abed before taking the mare stealthily from the Waites' stables. By this time tomorrow if her luck held, they would both be far away.

In her shabby clothes at this late hour, she hoped she wouldn't be noticed. And she had thrown a scarf over her head—ostensibly against the salt wind that promised rain, but actually to hide her highly identifiable golden hair. Her worn, nondescript homespun dress managed to half conceal her luscious figure. Sue had urged her to take one of her dresses but Anna had refused, for Arthur's ship sailed in the morning and Anna had no intention of being recognized, caught and dragged back.

Her heart was pounding as she slipped into the crowded, smoky waterfront tavern, noisy with the clanking of tankards and rowdy sailor voices. She turned quickly away from several faces she knew from the crew of the *Annalee* and hoped they would not recognize her.

Only hours before she had made out her Articles of Indenture to Sue and signed them with a flourish. In turn Lance had sold the papers to a gleaming-eyed Arthur, who had been a little taken aback when Lance had told him flatly that what he did with Anna once they were aboard ship was his own concern, but here at Waite Hall he'd have to let the girl decently alone.

Sullen, but sure now that his conquest of Anna was only hours away, Arthur had assented.

That sale of her Articles of Indenture had given Anna the money to transport herself and Floss across the sea. And the hard-won promise to let her alone that Lance had wrung from Arthur had given her time to slip into St. George and make the arrangements.

She had left Waite Hall after a hurried hug from Sue and a worried "I doubt me I should let you do this" from Lance, who had wanted to make the arrangements for her passage himself. Anna had turned down this kindly gesture as too risky.

"You'll be in enough trouble over this night's work when it's discovered I'm gone," she warned him. "For Arthur will believe you and Sue helped me—as indeed you have. But to involve yourself further in my affairs is to risk jail or worse."

Now with her heart thumping she looked about her through

the smoke and din and half regretted her decision to go it alone.

"Well, little lady!" said a whisky-roughened voice behind her. "Come share a tankard with me."

Startled by the voice so close to her ear, Anna turned to be almost overwhelmed by the big man's whisky breath. "I seek an officer from the *Running Gull*," she said, naming the only other ship in the harbor, besides Arthur's, that was bound for Boston, that she knew to be sailing on the morning tide.

"Ah, I'm from the *Running Gull*," said the big man, with a flash of yellow teeth. "But why would ye seek an officer, little wench, when there be good strong seamen like me to take care of y'er every need?"

What her "need" might be was made abundantly clear as he reached out for her arm.

Anna flinched back, fighting back the urge to cry out that his manner was as offensive as his breath. She knew she could not wander about the room asking for an officer of the *Running Gull*, for that was sure to attract attention. Chance had brought her one of the *Running Gull*'s seamen and she must make do with him.

"I—I seek passage," she muttered.

"Aboard the *Gull?*" He looked her up and down in some surprise. "And why would ye be leaving this paradise for Turks Islands? For that's where the *Gull* be going."

"She only stops off at Turks, I'm told," said Anna desperately. "Then she goes on to other islands."

"True, true." The big man nodded his head of matted hair. He seemed to sober a little, for his eyes focused on her better. "But we know not yet to which island her captain will take her. Could it be that ye care not where you go?" His bloodshot eyes grew crafty. "I think *I* could be of more help to ye than the *Gull*'s captain, little wench, for he's a mean-spirited, overreligious man who'd want your father's permission before taking ye aboard."

The jibe struck home and Anna winced. The big man, cunning now, was quick to notice it. He laughed and jerked his head at her. "Come over here to the corner table," he said, making way for Anna through the roistering crowd, "and we'll talk about it."

Anna hesitated for a moment, then she followed.

At the corner table, which was carelessly heaped with empty tankards that several revelers just now departing through the door had left behind them, sat another man. This one was smaller, with a wizened countenance, and a long clay pipe on which he pulled as he looked up at Anna with bleary eyes.

"I'm Burke and this here be Bender," said the big man by way of introduction. "Sit ye down, little wench. She wants to take passage on the *Gull*, Bender," he told his friend.

Bender's bushy pale eyebrows rose. "Why?" he asked dully.

"I have money for my passage," interrupted Anna.

Money? The wench had money? Burke stared at the worn dress, the kerchief that hid her hair, the strained look on her face. Even in this poor light, she did not look prosperous. He judged her by his own lights and decided she was lying. "Let's see your coin then, wench," he grunted.

"You've not told me yet there's a cabin available," protested Anna.

"'A cabin'?" Burke's coarse laughter pealed. "Listen to Her Ladyship here! If ye've money for a cabin, little wench, ye'll be off to see the captain o' the *Gull*, who'll ask ye to bring your father down to make the arrangements, for he'll have no part of helping a runaway!"

"I'm not a runaway," insisted Anna.

"Over there's the Captain," said Burke laconically. He pointed.

Anna turned to look across a pall of smoke at the *Gull*'s captain. Although far gone in drink, he still had a very severe look to him. Burke might well be right in his assessment—and there was no other ship leaving at the right time. "Still—I do seek passage *quietly*," she admitted reluctantly.

"'Quietly'? And why is that?"

"I would elude an unwelcome suitor," Anna told him primly.

"Ah-h-h." Burke looked as if that were very instructive. "A runaway," he said comfortably. "Just as I thought."

Anna's face reddened. "Are you saying there's no way?"

Big Burke considered her. "No, I'm not saying that. And could be even that ye'd have a cabin after all—if ye've money to pay. For there's a stripling traveling with us who's been seasick the whole voyage and kept to his cabin." Burke frowned as Bender gave him an astonished look. He gave Bender a sharp kick under the table and Bender grunted. But Anna, her attention caught by the word "cabin," did not notice. Oh, she *must* have a cabin to herself—she could not bear to be thrown into some common quarters with the kind of woman who would travel on the *Gull* to Turks Islands!

"Where is this man?" she asked eagerly.

"He's staying at the inn."

"I'll go to him," cried Anna, starting up. "What's his name?"

"Not so fast, lass." Burke's big hand settled down on her forearm.

"But if he's been as seasick as you say, then might he not be willing to let me have his cabin and take a later ship?"

"That was my thought," said Burke heavily. "But 'tis not such a simple matter. There's the Captain to be thought of—*he* won't take it lightly that he's got a new passenger trading places with the old—and without his permission!"

"Then how—" faltered Anna.

"Sit ye back down, wench." By pressure on her arm, Burke urged her back upon the bench. "I'm kickin' that around in me mind. 'Tis true the lad's loath to go further. And for a price the lad might be persuaded to let you go aboard in a suit of his clothes—they'd near fit ye—and make the trip in his stead. You'd be safe from people poppin' in, for the lad ain't popular, he ain't, and no one goes near him, save to leave food at his door and empty the slops when he pushes out the pail!"

Bender was looking at him in awed admiration. Burke frowned. The wench mustn't see that—she might catch on to the web that was being spun for her.

"Oh, I'd be glad to pay him for his passage on another ship and a handsome price for his clothes, no matter what their condition!" she cried, for to her this seemed the perfect solution. To cast off from Bermuda dressed as a man—Arthur would never find her!

Burke looked at Bender, who hung on his words, and played his master stroke. " 'Twould take a right sharp mite extra," he said, stroking his matted beard. "For the lad's on the run and might have to leave here sudden-like—and that might cost him. Ye see, he killed a wench in Jamaica and had to run for it—that's the reason he's so unpopular. The Captain, he don't know what the lad done but the crew do."

Bender's bleary eyes had lost their vacant look. He was tempted to strike his thigh and guffaw but Burke's warning look stayed him.

"Oh." Anna felt a little chilled and considerably less eager to seek out the "stripling" at the inn. "I do not know if I have enough gold for that," she said, troubled.

Burke's hard eyes kindled with mirth. He did not for a moment believe this little wench had any gold at all—if she had, she'd not be bargaining with the likes of them, she'd be off to the captain like a shot with it! She was trying to gull them, she was, into passage money or some such. But she'd find herself the one who was gulled, she would! He pretended to think over what Anna had said. "Perhaps he'd do it anyway—just for passage money," he acceded.

"There's a horse as well. I want to pay passage for my horse."

The pair exchanged significant glances, for Bender had by now figured out what Burke meant to do. Burke's grin told him this sly wench had stolen a horse and meant to make off with it.

"That can be arranged," Bender cut in, in an oily voice. "For we can say the young lad bought the horse here and wants to transport him, can't we, Burke?" He rubbed his damp palms together. He was beginning to drool a little and his wizened face was hot, for it was not his sweaty palms he felt in his imagination but the girl's ripe young breasts pressed between his eager fingers.

"Well, we'd best be off to see the lad," said Burke, rising.

"Can he not come here?" asked Anna, wary at the thought of accompanying these men out into the night.

"Sick as he be and already gone to bed? He'd refuse."

"Well, I—I could go alone, then. I know my way to the inn. I could tell him you sent me."

Burke gave her a wide grin that displayed his yellow teeth. "And he'd no sooner let ye in than he'd have ye'r clothes off and into his bed—for he's a rough hand with the wenches!"

"But if I told him—"

" 'Twouldn't do no good. We'd best go with ye." And as Anna still hesitated, he frowned. "The captain won't be drinking much longer. If we're to get ye stowed safe aboard the *Gull* before he leaves, there's no time to stand here debatin'."

Against her better judgment, driven by desperation, Anna accompanied them outside.

There was no one on the street. Noise carried to them through the tavern's small windows and a snatch of raucous song rent the air.

"Look there!" cried Bender, taking three steps forward and peering ahead. "I think I see the lad we want on board the *Gull* already—ain't that him, Burke, there by the rail?"

Burke beckoned Anna impatiently and moved ahead, peering into the darkness. "It is," he agreed solemnly, studying the vague shape by the railing, which at this distance looked to Anna not to be a person at all, but a bale. "He's come aboard already. Ye'll have to step smart now, little wench, for the Captain must not catch us striking a bargain!"

He strode up the street. Anna almost had to run to catch up with him.

" 'Tis hot," muttered Bender, who had fallen back slightly behind Anna now. Anna hardly noticed him, or what he was doing with the short cloak he carried over his arm.

A moment later, just as they reached a dark alley, Burke turned and seized her. Even as she screamed, Anna felt Bender's short cloak thrown over her head and she was swept up, half-smothered, trapped as if she were in a bag, onto Burke's heavy-muscled shoulder.

Hot and scalding, horror overcame her.

Poised on the brink of the frying pan, she had catapulted herself into the fire.

BOOK IV
Coralita

Now that my bridges all are burned,
Now that the die is cast,
I wonder, is my love returned?
I wonder . . . will it last?

PART ONE
The Tall Stranger

Wistful lass, lift up your head—
The world is passion's mart.
Someday the fates will send to you
A rogue to break your heart!

St. George, Bermuda, 1673

CHAPTER 37

Brett Danforth was tired. Although his ship, the *Dame Fortune*, had cast anchor in St. George's harbor this morning, Danforth, who had been rowed ashore by a longboat that had returned speedily to the mother ship, had passed the day neither making new friends nor enjoying the sights of Bermuda. Indeed Danforth had paid the ship's captain a handsome sum to carry him into English territory. For despite the name freshly painted on her hull, the *Dame Fortune* was a Dutch ship and ever since Charles II had abandoned his allies and suddenly taken the side of the French, England and Holland had been at war.

The *Dame Fortune*'s captain, one Paaterzoon, uneasy over the freshly daubed paint and the English colors his ship carried for this mission, had warned Danforth that a longboat would call for him tomorrow night and would wait no longer than an hour. Danforth must have finished his business on the island by then or he would be left cooling his heels in Bermuda. For Captain Paaterzoon had no desire for the British authorities to take an interest in the merchantman that rode far out in the bay, for that well might result in a British man-of-war being sent out to intercept him and blow him out of the water.

Danforth, well aware that the time was short, had taken a room at the inn in St. George and sent a messenger to look for Alexander Timmons. After that he had repaired himself to the inn's common room with a tankard of ale and sat down to wait.

Many tankards later he was still waiting, drumming his knuckles on the table's thick cedar top and wondering what had happened to Timmons. For it was he who had sent Timmons to Bermuda, and when the brass coat button had come back inserted inside a letter that Danforth had given to Timmons already addressed to himself (for Timmons, while reliable, could neither read nor write), he'd clasped the button in his strong hand, his face had split in a wolfish grin, and he'd set out to find a captain in New Amsterdam willing—for a price—to sail in English waters. No easy task, for in midsummer a Dutch fleet had anchored off Staten Island, taken back New York and christened it New Amsterdam once again, and Danforth, an Englishman with holdings in newly reconquered Dutch New Netherland, was pursuing a dangerous path.

Captain Paaterzoon of the *Haarlemmer* had proved willing, and cool enough when gold was offered. When they neared Bermuda, he had ordered the name *Haarlemmer* painted out, replaced by *Dame Fortune,* and hoisted English colors.

A good man—but he had warned that he would not wait.

Not till late afternoon—and by then Danforth had had plenty of time for self-evaluation and liked not what he saw—the messenger had brought back word that Alexander Timmons was dying, not expected to last the night, that he lay some miles away in a fishing shack, victim of a gunshot wound from unwise wenching.

At Danforth's raised eyebrows, the messenger had elaborated tersely: " 'Twas a quarrel over Tess, the tavern maid. Her husband found them together and shot him."

Danforth had jammed his hat down irritably on his head.

He was not surprised that Timmons, a notorious wencher, had been shot at last.

" 'Tis the kind of end comes to us all," he told the messenger grimly. "Is a doctor with him?"

At the messenger's dolorous shake of the head, Danforth had cursed under his breath. "Give me directions how to find this fishing shack where he lies. You go bring us a doctor." He had slapped enough coin in the boy's outstretched hand to bring all the doctors in Bermuda and set out.

He had had a devil of a time finding the place, but even at that he had gotten there before the doctor. Timmons had gasped out the information Danforth sought and died in his arms. When the doctor arrived, puffing in quite winded from the exertion, Danforth had silently handed him money enough to bury Timmons and departed.

Back to the inn, he had thought. *And only tomorrow left to do the thing!*

And it was something he was suddenly loath to do, although back in New Netherland it had seemed a fine idea.

Now as he approached the waterfront street that would lead him to the inn, he loosened his sword in its scabbard and walked more warily. For while Brett Danforth was new to St. George and new to Bermuda, he was not new to the waterfronts of the world and the night was velvety dark.

Suddenly, as he rounded the corner onto that deserted waterfront street—for it was very late and all but the hardiest revelers had already sought their beds—a woman's scream tore the air. And was as suddenly hushed.

But the sound brought Danforth's determined booted stride to an abrupt halt and his heavy dark hair swung like a shawl about his hawklike head as he looked about him. Behind him lay St. George's harbor, where a handful of ships lay at anchor beneath the stars. Before him stretched the little town of St. George with its scattering of stone houses and its ring of forts, designed to beat off the Spanish. The night was uncommonly dark, for the moon had retreated behind some scudding clouds and the street was lit only by the glow of guttering candles from a tavern some doors away whence issued loud laughter and a raucous song. But dark as it was, the keen gray eyes of the tall Englishman caught a slight movement in the shadows of a nearby alley.

Danforth leaned forward, hand now upon the burnished hilt of his sword, and peered into the darkness. Someone was huddled against the stone wall of that building—no, two figures skulking and one of them, the bigger of the two, carrying a large bundle. As Danforth watched, his eyes growing accustomed to the darkness, the bundle seemed to come alive and there was the sound of a yelp and a smothered curse from one of the two men as the moon came out and a pair of dainty white legs suddenly broke free amid a froth of white lace, and a shoe—from a small foot viciously kicking at the man who held her—was launched into the street.

The shoe landed not half a yard from Danforth, whose countenance had gone from watchful to exceedingly grim as he observed the nature of the bundle the big man was trying to control.

An obviously unwilling bundle.

Never a man to hesitate, Danforth snaked out his sword and launched himself at the men in the alley.

At this point Anna got free of Bender's smothering cloak. Clawing herself loose from Burke's suddenly relaxed hold, she landed on her feet in time to witness Danforth's charge.

What she saw was remarkable.

A tall man seemed to be leaping at them from out of nowhere—and even in her paralyzing fear, Anna caught her breath at the sight of him. This oncoming warrior had a mighty wingspread of shoulder, and that breadth seemed magnified by the sinewy twist of his body as he lunged. For even as he hurled himself forward, Danforth was engaging Bender. Tardily, Bender tried to drag out his cutlass—even as a sharp blade slashed his arm. With a cry of pain the wizened but tough and wiry Bender staggered back—and collided with Burke.

Big Burke, a bully with a hundred successful tavern brawls to his credit, had no fear of his oncoming foe. *These gentlemen were flashy fighters,* he had often hiccuped contemptuously on his way to working his way through a keg of ale, *but they*

hadn't got staying power; the idea was to wear them down.
So he shouldered the bleeding Bender into the stone wall
behind him and stepped forward eagerly to meet his opponent.

That necessitated clearing the road of Anna, who had
landed squarely in front of him, and Bender did that by
throwing out his left arm to sweep her from his path. Since
she was just in the act of turning her head to watch Bender
sag back against the stone wall, Burke's knuckles glanced
painfully across her cheekbone. The contact served its purpose, for it knocked Anna sideways and she landed, gasping,
on her hands and knees in the street, while Burke brought up
his cutlass to meet the stranger's challenge.

Anna gained her feet just as Bender, lamenting as he
clutched his bleeding arm, lurched away from the battle. Her
scarf had been lost in the struggle and had blown somewhere
down the dark alley, and now her golden curls cascaded down
her shoulders as she lifted her head to watch the battle. Rapt
with fascination, she saw the long lean stranger's sword crash
against Burke's hastily drawn cutlass with a ring that carried
into the tavern and brought the occupants pouring out into the
street. He seemed to her in that moment larger than life, as he
thrust and parried light-footedly, borne back momentarily by
Burke's greater weight and the heavy cutlass.

Anna watched him, riveted. His cold gray eyes were ablaze
and his face had a steady intent concentration—she would not
have called it ruthless though others had—that surpassed any
intentness she had ever seen on a man's face. Steadily,
resolutely, inexorably, he was dominating his foe, now driving Burke this way, now that—*there*, it was over! As Anna
gasped, the long blades had flashed like lightning along each
other's cutting edge, the very hilts had crashed together and
somehow, magically, the cutlass had gone winging to clatter
along the stones almost at Anna's feet.

"Care to give up?" came a deep sardonic voice. It was the
first time Anna had heard the stranger speak. A little shiver
went through her at the resonant timbre of that deep voice. It
had in it the faraway sound of the sea rolling onto the shore.
A deep, masculine sound, and to Anna strangely comforting....

Big Burke stepped carefully back, walking almost on his

toes, easing away from that singing blade that now snaked
almost playfully at his doublet, now flicked off his wooden
buttons one by one.

"Not if I had my blade again!" he snarled.

"Well, you'll never have this one!" cried Anna. She
scrambled to the cutlass, picked it up and tossed it with all
her strength into a long arc that ended in the sea.

A drunken cheer went up from the crowd that had gathered.

"That's showin' him, lass!" called someone.

The stranger laughed. "It would seem the battle is over,"
he told Burke. "Unless you enjoy seeing your blood run. As I
view it, ye've a simple choice—either your blood runs or you
do." He gave Burke's shoulder a sudden jab that made the
big man jump back, cursing.

Ah, he was magnificent, thought Anna, thrilling to the
sight of the stranger, tall and lean and purposeful. *And he was
fighting for her!* Something no other man on the island had
recently volunteered to do—unless one could count Flan's
promise to do future battle!

She was hopping around on one foot, looking for her shoe,
when Burke broke and ran, disappearing into the darkness
after Bender.

Someone kicked Anna's shoe toward her and as she bent to
pick it up she heard someone cry, "Why, look who the wench
is!"

Anna gave a start. She had been recognized, word would
filter to Arthur and early tomorrow morning there would be a
search for her. She must find a hiding place and stay well
hidden until Arthur's ship had sailed, she must not let these
people cluster around her, she must get away!

But—first she must thank him, this man who had saved her
from those cutthroats. She could not go without at least doing
that. She turned her glorious turquoise eyes on Danforth with
a look of mute appeal.

"I—can't thank you enough," she said in a trembling
voice, and for a moment was held by the intent look on the
smiling sardonic face that was turned toward her—a face she
knew would be etched forever in her memory.

Then she snatched up her shoe, pulled it on with a single

tug and took to her heels, running away from the crowd, away from the town. And although she would not admit it, not even to herself, she was running as much from the man as from the ogling, jostling crowd from the tavern. For there was that about this lean stranger that had shaken her, like the first felt rumblings of an earthquake deep inside the earth, unheard by human ears but causing keen-eared animals on the surface to panic.

Anna knew in a blind, unreasoning way that if she stayed, she would belong to this man.

And *that*, she who had always been her own woman, who had laughed and taunted and led men on with no care for the future—*that*, this wild daughter of the islands was not ready to accept.

So Anna ran, blown like a leaf before the wind, her light skirts whipping about her slim legs and her long bright hair streaming behind her in the moonlight.

The huddled houses of St. George were far behind her when Brett Danforth, running lightly, caught up with her. His long arm shot out and caught her by the arm to stay her flight, spun her around toward him.

"Faith, you run like a deer," he laughed. "Here now, there's no one about to frighten you, lass. What are you running from?"

"I—I cannot stay," she gasped. Her cheeks were flushed, her eyes fever bright from another reason besides her flight, for Danforth's very touch sent fiery sparks shooting up her arm. Anna tried to disengage her arm—unsuccessfully. She turned her head away lest he see in her face how that touch affected her.

"And why not?" The dark face above her was calm, but his grip on her arm was inexorable. It demanded an answer. And she knew she owed him one.

Slowly Anna turned her head to face her rescuer. The sight shook her.

Broad of shoulder, narrow of hip in his russet doublet and trousers, Brett Danforth's sinewy leanness had the swaying grace of a finely tempered Toledo blade. Light of foot, even in his wide-topped leather boots with their fashionable splash of white lawn and point lace, his serviceable sword, whose lightning touch she had already witnessed this night, and plain doublet and trousers of sensible russet cloth marked him as no dandy. Indeed his twenty-eight years had stamped a certain watchfulness over his keen hawklike features, a watchfulness that Anna in the moonlight remarked. She was sure this man had met many obstacles in his eventful life and overcome them all.

She was sure of something else as she stared, mesmerized, up into the dark interested countenance that gazed down at her. She was certain that many women had run their cool questing fingers through the thick shock of dark hair that fell in a gleaming mass to rest on the mighty wingspread of his broad shoulders, women who thought they saw their dreams reflected in his light gray eyes. She knew with a kind of instant divining that those dreams had soon faded as this tall fellow strode away, rode away, sailed away. The manner of his going might be different, the good-bye kisses wild or sweet, but he always went—intuitively she knew that. Out of their lives forever.

That daring face above her was the face of a man no woman had ever held—for long.

And Anna, looking up, knew a bright current of fear, for she knew with a woman's sure instinct that this was a face she could come to love, blindly, unreasoningly, beyond all turning back.

"There, there." Danforth's voice was soothing, as if the girl were some nervous colt he must break to saddle. With his free hand he lightly lifted the tangled mass of hair from her shoulders. As he did so, his fingers brushed the back of her neck and a quiver went through her slight frame. "Don't be frightened," he said softly. "Come, lass, I'll take you home safe. It's over."

Anna shook her head and her curls bounced. She tried to pull away from him. "For me it's not over," she whispered fiercely. "And I *have* no home—not anymore. I do thank you for what you did for me this night but now you must let me go. And of your kindness, forget you ever saw me."

The dark brows lifted. No young woman on such short acquaintance had ever asked Danforth to forget her. Especially one he had gone chasing through the moonlight to catch! His next words were laced with amusement.

"Come now, lass. If you've no place to go, I'll find a place for you at my inn."

"That—that I cannot do."

"Why not?" There was irony in his deep voice. " 'Tis not my custom to force myself upon unwilling women!"

Her blush deepened. "Oh—'tis not that," she protested hastily. She meant him to understand that she trusted him—as a gentleman; it was just that she could not go to the inn. But Danforth mistook her meaning. He thought this lass in her homespun dress and worn shoes was telling him that she was experienced enough with men—as was the case with many a lass of younger years than she—and that she wanted him to understand that she was not rejecting him as a bed partner, but for some other reason.

"Well, then?" he prodded.

"I cannot go to the inn," Anna admitted uncomfortably. "For I'm too well known in St. George."

Danforth's interest quickened. What had the lass done?

"That pair who were carrying you off?" he demanded. "What were they to you?"

"They were strangers," she said sharply. "Let me go!"

"Tarry a bit." Danforth kept his hold on her. The gray eyes studying her had gone thoughtful. "A man who's just shed a stranger's blood likes to have his curiosity satisfied as to why he's done it!"

Yes, he deserved to know, of course....

"They were sailors from the *Running Gull*," sighed Anna. "Their names were Burke and Bender. They had promised to arrange passage for me aboard the *Gull*." Best not tell him how! "But once we were outside the tavern, they threw a cloak over my head and tried to make off with me." A shudder went through her, a shudder he could feel in his hand and forearm. "I do not like to think what would have happened to me if you had not come along when you did."

Danforth did not like to think of that, either.

The moon was well out now and he could see her clearly. She was a vision of loveliness that might well startle a man. So lovely she looked unreal. The bruise beneath her eye from the rough handling she'd just received only made her the more appealing. Her burnished hair was pale shimmering gold in the starlight and her upturned turquoise eyes were lustrous and deep as the sea. Her soft lips were slightly parted and gave her a breathlessly expectant look and a little pulse beat in the hollow of her white throat. Danforth's gaze passed caressingly down that throat, noting the satin smoothness of her skin, crossed her white bosom and relished the molded perfection of her young breasts, straining against the worn material of her bodice.

A lovely wench, this. And she had a wild look to her. If she was so eager to get off the island, she might try something foolish again—as she had tonight.

"And if I'd not come along and they'd got you aboard ship and out to sea, what would you have done?" he asked bluntly.

She drew herself up to her full height and gave him a dauntless look. "I'd have escaped, of course!"

A smile played around Danforth's wide mouth. *Over the side and damn the barracuda!* This fiery little wench might have done just that. He judged her to be all of sixteen.

"I can't leave you here alone, lass."

"Why not? 'Tis a warm night."

"That pair might yet come looking for you."

She gave a shiver of revulsion. "They'll never find me. I know these shores. I'll find a place somewhere in the rocks to hide."

"And tomorrow? What will you do tomorrow?"

She gave him a miserable look. Tomorrow there was Floss to think about, Floss who must be fed, watered—and kept hidden away, for horse thievery on this island was severely punished and Anna had no wish to have the flesh torn from her back by a cat-o'-nine-tails.

"Tomorrow," she said in a soft hurried voice. "Tomorrow

I'll have to decide what to do. Each day must take care of itself.''

Her words had a mute appeal that called to Danforth. In a life that had been, to say the least, eventful, Danforth had gone through long periods when each day must indeed take care of itself, when every man's hand seemed turned against him and he had hungered and faced death in alien territory.

Those memories softened his voice. "I'll not let ye do it, lass. Not alone.'' Forgotten for the moment was his detestable mission, forgotten was the longboat that would arrive tomorrow night and would not wait, forgotten was everything but this lovely child-woman, hurt and frightened and needing him. "I'll go with you to the beach,'' he decided. "Tomorrow we'll decide what's to be done with you.''

And Anna, who had given orders imperiously to a whole plantation of slaves and bondservants and had them obeyed without question, Anna whose will had been sole rule of a little island empire, let her hand slip into his and walked beside him as docile as a child.

The touch of his hand seemed to communicate something to her, something unspoken. Her senses were tumbling, her awareness of the night heightened. The sky held a distant glow that seemed more than just the moon behind the clouds, the sea wind seemed to caress her hot face in a special way and twine gentle fingers in her long hair and blow her light skirts intimately against her young thighs, brushing, tingling. . . .

For in that crazy tangle that her thoughts had become, Anna *knew*, she knew without question that this man could reach her, thrill her, make her his . . . *if she let him*.

By now she had adjusted her stride to his and was taking two steps to each of his long ones as they strolled toward the sea.

"Why did ye seek passage aboard the *Running Gull?*'' he shot at her.

"I'm leaving Bermuda,'' said Anna tersely.

Danforth chuckled. This walk through the pleasant night promised to be entertaining. "Does your family know of your impending departure?'' he hazarded.

"I have no family. Not anymore." There was a sadness in her voice that made him wish he'd not asked. Still, he wanted to satisfy himself about the wench.

"Your employer, then?"

Her voice hardened. "I have no employer! Although—" She stopped, for had she not signed Articles of Indenture and let those Articles be sold to Arthur, intending to dupe him, to elude him?

Danforth digested her answer. It was possible the girl was running from the law. Possible, he thought, but not likely.

"So ye've run away from home?" He stated it as a fact.

Her stubborn silence told him he was right.

They were walking under the shelter of tall cedars now and a pungent fragrance filled the air. Danforth brushed aside a dangle of sea grapes that barred his path. They parted like a curtain. He could see that they were coming out onto a promontory of rocks. They had reached the sea.

"Where were ye bound?"

"Some other island." She shrugged. "America perhaps." She was clambering over the rocks as she spoke and suddenly she gave a sharp outcry. "I've broken my heel!" she wailed.

Danforth bent down and lifted up her ankle and inspected the shoe. He couldn't know how that slight contact made her heart pound.

" 'Tis a fine ankle, but the shoe's hardly worth fixing," he said, noting that the leather was badly scuffed, the sole nearly worn through.

"But they're my last pair," she told him sadly.

"I'll buy you a new pair in St. George," he offered.

"I—I couldn't let you do that," she said breathlessly—and the breathlessness came from his caressing grip on her ankle. "Give me back my foot!"

He let it go with a smile. A proud lass, this—she wanted no favors. He couldn't remember when he'd met a girl with shoes as worn as this one who'd have turned down a new pair. He followed as she walked unevenly ahead of him.

"And what would ye do in America, lass, if ye reached there?"

Anna had not really thought about that. She wended her

way through the big rocks and frowned. "I'd—I'd get a job, I suppose."

"As a cook? A chambermaid?"

"I am no cook," she admitted, turning to flash a sweet smile at him as they emerged onto the open beach. "But with most household chores I'm familiar."

She meant she'd supervised them, but Brett surmised that she'd been a house servant somewhere. Or perhaps, as her fresh face would seem to indicate, some farmer's daughter, brought up on cream and fresh eggs and curds. Disaster came easily to these islands, he knew. Diseases swept in and laid the populace low, diseases brought aboard the very ships that carried the things these islanders needed to live—perhaps her family had been one of those wiped out by the fevers that visited periodically.

"Who are you?" she asked curiously, coming to a stop on the sand in the shadow of the gray looming rocks. "And what are you doing in Bermuda?"

He answered her easily, thinking how lovely she was with the sea's dark glitter behind her. "Forgive me for not introducing myself earlier, my lady. My name is Brett Danforth. Off the *Dame Fortune*, anchored in the bay." He swept her a low, slightly mocking bow. "And I'm here on personal business. And you'll be—?"

Personal business . . . unspecified. A pirate doing business with the wreckers? Anna asked herself. He might be one of those shadowy unknowns who came on tall white ships and went away again and asked no questions . . . she had seen men like that more than once in St. George and heard whispers that these were men who dealt with the wreckers, men like Flan's father, Sean O'Toole. Best not to give her true name, she thought uneasily, for he might have heard it bandied about.

"My name is—Coralita," she said whimsically, naming the lacy pink flowers that spilled in tumbled masses throughout the West Indies, climbing bravely even into tall trees.

"Coralita," he repeated softly. "How well named you are!" He was thinking of the delicate heart-shaped flowers as he cupped her heart-shaped face in his palms. "Did you know that in Mexico that flower is called *Cadena de Amor*, which means Chain of Love?"

Anna's heart gave a lurch. He was close and bending closer, closer. In a moment his lips would be on hers.

And she wanted them there, yearned for them. Her whole being cried out to this man. She did not realize how all of her life—and especially her harsh recent experiences—had led her to this breathless moment. Her bittersweet childhood, her life as a surrogate daughter, all had carved in her a terrible need to be loved. And although she did not realize it, it was love she had sought so desperately from among the island's young men, and love she had not found. She had found that she ran second.

And Anna had a terrible, deadly, consuming need to be *first*. First in a man's heart, first above everything.

It was a need that could destroy her.

And now, poised trembling on the brink, she felt Brett's lips crush down on hers, felt herself enfolded tenderly in a pair of strong arms, felt her soft breasts flatten against a russet doublet—and melted, let it happen.

Without reserve, there on the white sand in the shadow of the age-old rocks the sea had carved and pounded, Anna gave herself to the stranger.

She let his warm lips trail down her throat, slide along her bosom. She made no move to stop him when he gently eased her bodice down over her young breasts—nor outcry when the worn material ripped. She trembled as expert fingers quested over her breasts, testing a nipple here, sliding over roundness there.

Dizzy and transported with a feeling she had never fully known existed, a feeling so overpowering that it swept her before it like a leaf before the tide, Anna let her clothing leave her, urged downward from her body by gentle insistent fingers.

"Coralita," a reckless voice murmured in her ear, a deep voice timbred with feeling. "Whatever your problem, I will solve it somehow—and I promise, I will take you to America."

It was a commitment! A commitment she had so yearned to

hear! A little sob rose in the girl's throat and she pressed her body fiercely against him. She would be his! His! This wonderful stranger who had come out of nowhere in her hour of need to save her.

"Brett," she whispered. "Oh, Brett. . . ." And sank with him to the sand.

He felt her surrender and was surprised and touched. She was so young, so vulnerable. A kind of triumph stole over him and he held her closer, let his arms tighten about her quivering form. Lovely wench that she was, he felt something for her that he had never before felt for a woman. Well, almost—once. But *she* had proved unworthy. He had no name for it, but it was there. Some inner sympathy perhaps, some kinship, a comradeship that was more than sex.

It never occurred to him to call it love.

But whatever it was, on that warm Bermuda night, he wanted this golden wench more than he had ever wanted anything. She was worth risking his mission for—with all that that entailed. She was worth the ruin he faced if that mission failed. She was worth dying for.

Although Brett Danforth did not know it, that night he gave his heart to a girl whose true name he did not even know.

A gift he would shortly come to regret.

But not at that moment, not as their passions mounted. Anna's dress was a tumble of cloth now, pillowed under her head. Her delicate, expensive chemise was a wedding sheet on which to lie. The tall sculpted rocks that rose above them were a cathedral to enshrine their union, the soft thrumming of the ocean as it broke along the reefs a chorus of angel voices pealing out a wedding march.

To Anna, who had given a false name and with it her heart, this night was sacred—and unforgettable.

Thrillingly she felt Brett's hands explore her hips, her thighs—and felt they belonged there. She caught her breath as his male hardness entered her and gave a short sharp cry as sudden blinding pain raced through her loins.

"I'm sorry," she heard him say with some surprise. "I didn't know you were—"

"Don't be," she heard herself gasp. "And don't stop. I—I can stand it." With a warm flood of emotion, she held on to him tightly and gritted her teeth. She would not cry out again!

But Brett, realizing now that she was a virgin, untried, had become gentleness itself. He retreated from his attack, he caressed her tense young body, so beautiful and glowing there in the shadow of the rock castles rising above, he ran tender exploring hands along her skin and nuzzled gently, expertly with his lips, the gleaming curves of her soft rounded breasts— teased her and caressed her until she relaxed again, trusting and pliable in his arms.

And then, as the sweet delights of her fresh young body goaded him to deeper passion, as his own body tensed and all his senses leaped and soared, he made her fully his with one last swordlike thrust that left her gasping and weak but thrilling in his arms, for unexpectedly her own passions had risen and peaked and she found herself enjoying one long delicious sensation after another, unfolding, flowering. Sensations raced through her body like sudden puffs of smoke, rising ever to greater heights. Her senses reeled and tumbled and found their way again, always cresting upward until it seemed to her that she had reached a height unimaginable, upflung into the clouds.

And all in the arms of a lover who had made many women his—and left them all.

She cared not. With tears and smiles blending on her cheeks, with soft endearments sobbing in her throat, she clung to her newfound lover and knew with tingling certainty, in the very depths of her being, that this night, this night of nights, she had given her heart—forever.

CHAPTER 38

An hour and more had passed since Brett had reluctantly slipped away from her yielding warmth and stretched out beside her to sleep. But Anna's tingling body, so full of newfound wants and needs, so ablaze with newfound desires and newfound bliss, would not let her sleep.

She sat up restlessly and moved her buttocks a little from side to side, trying to accommodate her bottom more comfortably to the sand. Beneath her naked body, her chemise was a shambles. Her wedding sheet. . . . She reached down and idly brushed sand from it, dusted the sand from her hands and cast a brooding look at the man beside her.

Two hours ago she had not known he existed. It seemed incredible that he should be there. She, Anna Smith, haughty island beauty that she was, had given herself to a stranger. All she knew about him was his name. She studied his long relaxed form, the lean hard muscles of his thighs, his forearms, the sleek heavy muscles of his upper arms, the flat stomach and narrow hips, the depth and breadth of shoulder and chest, all bared to her in the moonlight.

They had been together such a little time. It was hard not to think of him as a wild, fleeting dream that had come to her out of the night and would be gone with the dawn. She needed to see him there, to touch him, to realize he was real and substantial and human and would still be there when the sun came up. The wind blew her bright hair over her face in a cloud and when she tossed it back, arching her neck, she could see the dark glittering surface of the sea. It reflected the myriad stars and the moon—big and bright, like her hopes.

For Anna had left despair behind her. Hope had risen in her and blazed like the sun. She was alone no longer! At last, at last, she had found her lover.

She gave the man beside her a tender look. He was tall and strong—and understanding. *Whatever your problem, I will solve it somehow,* he had said. Which, translated, meant of course that he loved her. . . .

Naked and defenseless now, he lay beside her, this formidable warrior who had beaten down two men in her behalf. His dark hair was rumpled as a boy's, his determined face was relaxed in sleep. One of his sinewy arms was flung forward, pinioning her chemise—she had not had the heart to pull it from beneath that arm and perhaps wake him up. Nor her homespun dress, which had somehow got pillowed beneath his dark head. So she sat beside him naked as a water sprite, a glowing figure against the white surf beating in across the moonlit beach.

Anna sighed and hugged her slender naked body with her arms against the sudden stiff breeze that had sprung up. That breeze would be dancing in the shrouds of the big merchantmen who rode the bay—and one of them, fleet and beautiful, would be the *Dame Fortune*, which had brought Brett Danforth to Bermuda. She imagined that ship now, with her furled white sails, looking like a gull about to take flight. Would they sail away on her, she wondered? Or on some other tall white ship?

Dreamily, she who had thought herself lost, contemplated her future, for now everything had changed for her—everything.

This daring man, met tonight, loved tonight, would take her to his America and there they would have a wonderful long life together. . . .

With a bare toe she traced a pattern in the sand, the pattern of a castle, a fortress with tall walls and frowning battlements—forgetful that castles built of sand would soon crumble.

Morning found him smiling down at her, for she had fallen fast asleep after her moonlight vigil. She felt a soft tug of the chemise on which she lay—for the material had caught at his foot as he got up—and came awake. She looked up and saw him standing there, naked and smiling, above her. She caught her breath at that dark sardonic face, that wickedly gleaming smile, and felt a sudden wave of embarrassment that she was naked before his gaze. Instinctively she rolled over on her side to shield her breasts and stomach from his view—and then remembered last night and all that had passed between them. She tingled with the memory.

"Time to rise, lass," said that deep, timbred voice.

Anna rolled over on her back and felt the sun hot on her body. She stretched luxuriously, like a kitten not quite yet willing to be waked, flexing her soft paws and arching her dainty neck. She sat up—and fell back sleepily again. "I'd rather stay," she sighed—and stretched out her arms to him.

"So would I," he laughed, and bent to bury his face in her soft neck. He let his lips drag along her white skin, sending waves of rippling feeling everywhere they touched, down across her bosom to her trembling breasts, whose rounded crests he nuzzled expertly until she gasped with delight.

"Faith, you're enough to lure a man from his intentions," he murmured. "But yet I've a mission that must be accomplished." He gave her soft stomach a last kiss that caused her breath to intake sharply, and straightened up with decision, pulling on his shirt. "Have ye thought on what ye'd like to do today?"

"I'd like to go with you," she said instantly. "Wherever you're bound."

His smile broadened. "Well spoke," he said. "Especially since you don't know where that is. Suppose I told you I was a pirate, what then?"

She shrugged, by her very indifference telling him that she had chosen, and his way would be her way, his life her life.

"Are you saying you don't care what I am?" The question was blunt and his gray eyes were wondering. And when she nodded, "No woman has ever told me that," he said slowly. "At least none that meant it."

"Have you known so many, then?"

"A few." She guessed that was a terrible understatement.

"Were any of them—important?" Her voice was hurried, soft.

"'Important'? Yes—one of them."

She was desperately anxious to know about that one and when he did not elaborate she managed to wait a few seconds before she burst out, "And what of her?"

"Oh, nothing of her. She goes where she pleases—as do I. She leaves me and she comes back. We quarrel and she leaves again."

Anna swallowed. "You're not—*married* to her?"

He gave her a startled look. "I'm not married to anyone, lass!"

That made her feel better. For a moment there she had been afraid to think.

"But you *do* care for her?" she prodded.

He shrugged, pulling on his trousers. "It is an on-and-off relationship and no longer important to either of us. She meant a great deal to me once but she ran me over the shoals once too often. I saw in her"—he chose his words carefully, for he owed the truth at least to this lovely young girl who had given herself to him so unreservedly—"I saw in her something that wasn't there." His gaze rested on her curiously. For he had found it again in this girl—and this time he was sure it was real and true and lasting.

So there was no one who stood in her way. . . . After all, she couldn't have expected him to have lived a celibate, waiting for her to come along! But what he was telling her was that there was no one important, that she had a clear field. Her spirits rose and the sea wind caressing her white body felt delicious and fresh. Oh, they would have a wonderful life together! She wished Brett would state his intentions in words and get it all settled between them, but she supposed some men did not do it that way—they just let things happen with marriage understood but unspoken.

"I think I will like your America," she said shyly.

Brett had sat down and was tugging on his boots. Now he turned to look at the girl and felt again that new deep stirring inside him. A tenderness heretofore unknown to him possessed his body as his eyes roved caressingly over that bright shawl of burnished gold hair that fell over her bent head as she drew a pattern in the sand with her fingers. This slight, reckless, lighthearted wench had reached a spot within his secret heart never before touched by woman.

Brett Danforth looked at her—and wanted her for his own. To have, to hold, to keep. Not for an hour, a day, a season, as he had wanted other women. Not to enjoy and tire of and cast away. He wanted her for a lifetime, to share not only his bed but his life as well. In that blinding moment of self-revelation, he faced the fact that this trifling island girl meant more to him than self or fortune.

It was with difficulty that he dragged himself back to reality. He had come to these islands for a purpose. And that purpose was staring straight at him now, hardening his resolve.

He reached out and caressed a lock of her long falling hair, felt her move subtly at his touch.

As if in answer to the inward pull he felt toward her, she spoke. Shyly.

"Perhaps," she said, and her soft voice seemed to caress him in return, "in years to come, we'll come back here someday—with our grandchildren. And show them the place we met and loved for the very first time."

A kind of tremor went through him at her words and when she looked up he flinched before the sudden dazzle of her smile. It was such a smile as would catch at the heart—and it caught at his.

His face went sober and he stood up and drew on his doublet, buckled on his sword. He stood indecisively and he seemed loath to answer as he frowned down at her. Finally he spoke.

"I cannot marry ye, Coralita." His voice was a hoarse whisper but it went through the girl's head like a shout. "If that is what you desire."

Anna's back stiffened. Never one to ask for quarter, her bright head lifted proudly. "And what makes you think *I'd* marry *you?*" she asked loftily. "About our grandchildren—I was but jesting!"

Danforth gave her a rueful look, sensing rather than seeing the hurt behind that challenging turquoise gaze. " 'Tis true I'm no bargain, but I'd have asked ye to wife save for . . . other matters."

He'd have asked her to wife.... The words poured like strong wine over Anna's tumultuous senses.

"*What* other matters?" she asked with a great feigned carelessness, looking away from him. What would he tell her, she wondered. That he had taken some great oath not to wed until he had made a fortune? That he was the sole support of a widowed mother and ten brothers and sisters? That he was just escaped from debtors' prison and would not take her down with him?

Danforth drew a deep sighing breath. What he had to say to her now might well close that proud young heart against him—forever.

"Ye see before you a man bedeviled. An unwilling suitor."

Anna turned to give him an astonished look.

"A *suitor?*" she faltered, wondering what he could mean.

He nodded. "You asked me why I had come to Bermuda and I told you I was here on personal business. Now I will tell you what that personal business is: I have come to these islands to marry."

To marry! Anna could not believe her ears. She had not expected that he would seize her and drag her to the altar direct, but she had certainly believed that in time....

"And who"—she could hardly keep her voice from shaking—"who is your intended?"

His answer could not have rocked her more.

"I am come to a plantation called Mirabelle," he told her bluntly. "To marry the heiress there."

Surprise washed all expression from Anna's face. Brett Danforth had come to Bermuda to marry one of Bernice's homely daughters—the heiresses to Mirabelle! Having held her in his arms, having shared her deepest secrets, having lain with her through the long scented night, he would now take to his bed either despicable Pris or infuriating Prue—he would share his life with those who had supplanted her, driven her out! Shock and rage and pain all seared through her being at once and she was beyond speech. Well, she had heard Bernice bragging to callers that "great" marriages were being arranged for her daughters—doubtless this was one of them. Blindly, she turned away.

"Coralita." Brett's voice knifed through the hurt confusion of her thoughts. It had in it a call, a caress, a plea for forgiveness. "Try to understand. I do not choose this marriage—I *must* marry her."

"Why? Why must you?" She flung the words at him like stones. Her back was still rigid from the blow his revelation had given her.

She could hear him sigh. "My reasons need not concern you now, little one. 'Tis but a marriage of convenience, and need make no difference between us. Wait for me here and I'll come before the sun is down. Sail with me, Coralita."

How dare he say this marriage need make no difference? Fury welled up in her. She who had so lately in her despair considered a number of desperate measures—she had even contemplated marriage with Flan, for all his wrecking background—she who had gone, willing and unwed, into a stranger's arms last night now found herself like any other indignant virgin, enraged that she should be offered the part of mistress rather than wife. It was one thing to enter into a romantic love affair that could—oh, that *would* culminate in marriage, and quite another to be asked to play second fiddle to a new bride. Especially one she had reason to hate! *That* would be unbearable.

"I do not expect you to understand," he said hopelessly.

"Oh, but I understand very well!" Anna snatched up her chemise, ignoring the fact that it was full of sand, and donned it with a violence that made it rip. Her petticoat was hooked around her waist in record time. Her homespun dress came next and she yanked it over her head with fine abandon. Too much abandon—the bodice hooks caught in her tangled gold hair and jerked her head back. Not caring whether she pulled out her hair or not, she tore the hooks free and began to fasten them in desperate haste with fingers that shook so they half refused to obey her.

Brett was looking at her in alarm. "Here, let me do that."

She struck his hand away and jammed her sandy feet into her shoes. "I'll be on my way," she told him through her teeth, "and let you be about your unwelcome courting!"

"Wait. Coralita." He reached out and caught her wrist, for

he feared to let her go in this mood. Last night had been an example of her rashness. She could well repeat it! He sought to reason with her. "I said only that I could not offer ye marriage. But—"

Her turquoise eyes blazed at him like burning copper. "And what makes you think I'd accept less, Brett Danforth?" She gave a great wrench to jerk her arm away and almost fell when she found his hand opening to let it slip away like water from his grasp.

" 'Tis all I have to offer—at least for the time."

"What am I to wait for, then?" she taunted. "The death of your wife, perhaps?"

"I know not in what condition I'll find her. But offer for her I must. Should she later choose to divorce me, to retire to these islands, I'd marry you *then*."

Anna could not believe she was having this conversation here on Bermuda's wild northern shore. "And if she does not choose to give you up?" she flung at him.

"Then I'd spend as much time with you as I could. I'd care for you and protect you."

"A liar and a cheat as well," flashed Anna. "You'd cheat some poor girl you don't even know—and you're cold-blooded too, that you'd plan such a thing before you even saw her!" She shot a suspicious look at him. "You *haven't* seen her, I take it?"

"No," he sighed. "I've not laid eyes on her yet. And all that you say is true." His voice was imperturbable. " 'Tis a less than perfect world, as I keep learning to my sorrow. Still . . ." His voice softened, subtly tantalizing her. "Even should she choose to go to America with me, there's a river sloop I own. She's called the *River Witch*. You could make your home there and we'd be man and wife aboard her."

Man and wife . . . She shook her head to clear it. No, some other woman was going to be his wife, some other woman was going to stand beside him, first in all things—*he had offered her second place!*

As that ground in on her, Anna stared at him. "When I marry, Brett Danforth, 'twill be a man who will love me more than land and more than gold—and not some idle fool who cannot divorce one from the other!''

Danforth stepped back in surprise and reached out again to stay her but she eluded him and in passing, her palm cracked across his face. "Oh, damn you—damn you!" she cried, and turned and ran from him, fleet-footed in spite of her broken heel, across the familiar landscape.

He stood in silence and watched her go, disappearing from sight through the rocks. There was a rueful look on his sardonic face. Never had a woman's slap so touched his heart.

But, he reminded himself, he was still a man with a purpose. After one irresolute step after her, he got himself together. In the now brilliant sunlight from the hard blue sky overhead, he turned his face resolutely toward St. George, where he would freshen up and hire a horse. He must be presentable and not too dusty when he pled his suit with this lady he had yet to meet.

And, he decided, while in St. George he would also procure a special license. It would expedite matters if the bride were willing, and if she were not—as well might be the case after she learned who he was and where he came from—he would be no worse off. *Perhaps better off,* came the guilty thought, *for he could go seek Coralita then.* In either event the longboat would call for him tonight and wait no longer than an hour—and he must be there to meet it.

Whether he boarded that longboat wed or unwed was yet to be seen. With resolute steps and with a face so determined it seemed carved from stone, Brett Danforth strode off toward St. George and told himself he would deal later with the wench with the burnished gold hair.

But to Anna the sunlight had turned dark as she tumbled over the rocks, dashing from her long lashes angry tears that ran down her face unchecked. She had given her heart to a casual stranger—and he had chosen to break it, like a carelessly dropped vase. It was shattered now into a thousand shards and nothing would ever make it right again. . . .

Yet even as she ran away from him, she knew that she was

running also from herself and from her treacherous, almost overwhelming desire to return to him, to accept him on *his* terms.

No, she would not!

She never saw him take that step after her, then pause, irresolute and frowning. It would have made her feel a little better if she had—and perhaps a little worse. Half blinded by tears, she took the wrong path, collided with some bushes, forced her way through them and into the cedars with the twigs tearing her dress and scratching her arms. Midway into the thicket, when she was sure she was out of sight and out of hearing and in a place he would not find her, she pushed aside a dangle of sea grapes and flung herself down on the ground and hugged her knees and wept stormily into her petticoat.

She had found a lover—and lost him.

And all in the space of a day.

And through her turbulent mind kept drumming Doubloon's soft insidious voice. *Men no good . . . men no good. . . .*

After awhile Anna roused herself. Arthur's ship would have sailed by now, taking Mattie and Arthur with it. Anna gave a great sigh of relief. At least one enemy had left the field. Now there was only Bernice—and very possibly the law. For she had no idea what her present status might be—Arthur had no doubt made a great to-do over not finding her, he would have reported her as a runaway bondswoman and waved her Articles of Indenture in the face of the magistrate. Anna came up hard against something she had not heretofore considered. Under the law, she was now Arthur's property—for seven long years. Arthur might even have posted a reward for anyone who found her. A dread possibility loomed up before her: It was possible she would be seized and loaded onto a ship bound for Boston, and delivered to Arthur in irons!

Or did magistrates send runaway indentured servants skimming across oceans after their departing masters? Did they confine them to jails instead? Anna had never concerned herself with such things—now she was regretting it.

Suddenly she remembered Floss. Poor Floss was tethered

in a little grove of cedars, she had been there all night. Floss would be hungry and thirsty and it was a long walk to the place where Anna had left her, for she had wanted to be sure to secrete the silver mare where—whatever happened—Athur Kincaid would not find her.

Anna straightened her back and started walking across the spongy red earth. She would have to face whatever came. What would be, would be.

Floss was tethered in a grove near Mirabelle, for that was the country Anna knew best. Now it was toward Mirabelle that her feet led her, out from the cedars, running down into the meadows.

Anna fled on into the sunshine, prisoner of her tangled past, undreaming of her wild destiny.

PART TWO
Chains of Gold

The burning rhythm of yesterday's passion
Throbs white-hot through her veins
And now she knows she is bound to him—
Bound by golden chains!

Mirabelle Plantation, Bermuda, 1673

CHAPTER 39

Anna knew now where she was going. She was going to feed and water Floss and then ride to Waite Hall. Deborah Waite might disapprove of her actions, but Anna could not imagine Deborah actually handing her over to the law—and it was unlikely she would meet anyone on the way there. Sue had been right, it was best that Lance make the arrangements for her passage. She would give him back the gold he had got from Arthur for her Articles of Indenture and let him arrange for her passage on a ship to some other island, as he had offered to do—Jamaica perhaps, some place where Arthur would never find her.

The gold, those gold coins she had stuffed into her shoe. Anna came to a sudden stop. It had come to her suddenly that both her shoes, save for the missing heel, now that she had brushed away the sand, were very comfortable to walk in. That was odd, for they certainly had not been so when she had stuffed the gold coins Lance had given her beneath the lining of her right shoe—she had felt inclined to hobble when first she put that shoe on. It was worse than odd, she must have lost some of them!

In panic, she sat down and pulled off her right slipper, felt beneath the lining, which was loose. All of the coins were gone.

And now she remembered what in her haste and excitement last night she had forgotten: It was her right foot that she had used to kick at Burke as he was carrying her away, her right shoe that had come loose and hurtled into the dark street. When the shoe had struck the street, the lining must have come loose and the thin gold coins had spilled out—lost in the dust. She had not even thought of them when, rapt after watching the swordplay and fearing questions from the crowd, she had snatched up her fallen slipper and tugged it on. And last night's breathless events had swept her on a wild emotional tide that had made shoes and coins seem far away and unimportant, and this morning's overturn of her expectations— all had conspired to keep her from remembering the coins.

But now as the weight of her loss was borne in on her, Anna's slender body sagged against a tree bole. There was no use going back to St. George after all these hours had passed to look for the coins in the street—they would have been found long since by passersby or urchins and surreptitiously tucked into pockets or aprons or purses with feigned innocence, or dropped with a smile down a bodice cleavage.

The gold to buy her passage was gone, vanished.

Dismayed, she cast about for what to do.

After a few disconsolate moments in which she felt herself the unluckiest girl in the world, her head came up and her chin lifted.

Damn them all! She would not spend her life skulking about like a thief in the night! She would find Floss and take her boldly back to Mirabelle—it should be an easy thing to slip her back into the stables right under Bernice's nose—and feed her and water her and rub her down! And then she would make her way into the big house and take as much silver as she could carry—it was all part of her inheritance that she had been cheated out of, was it not? And with that silver she would find some sea captain who would not care if the plate be monogrammed with a "J," which stood for neither "Anna" nor "Smith," but would carry her and Floss far away from here—and at the moment any place at all would be better!

And why should she run away dressed like a beggar when all of Mirabelle was rightfully hers? Bernice would have destroyed the will by now, of course, so there would be no way she could ever claim the plantation but—Anna's chin lifted defiantly—she would steal into the bedrooms and find one of her handsome gowns that had not yet been cut down for Pris or lengthened for Prue; she would roll it up into a bundle—yes, and some of the jewelry too, if she could get to it! She would not walk out destitute into the world. She would change her clothes somewhere in the shelter of the cedars and after telling Sue good-bye, she'd be off to exchange her loot for passage from some strange sea captain who'd up-anchor and away without caring too much about where she got it.

She dashed away the tears and tossed her head.

She'd show them! She'd show them all—and especially Brett Danforth.

She found Floss glad to see her, nuzzling and affectionate. She hugged and patted the gentle silver mare and rode her nearly to the stables of Mirabelle, dismounted and led her under shelter of the trees inside the big doors. There was no one about, for it was Bernice's habit, after the early morning chores were done, to send the stable boys into the cedars to help with the work crews who were ruthlessly felling them. With Bernice money came first and animals second. It made Anna heartsick to see the unkempt look of the horses and the filthy condition of the stables. She not only fed and watered Floss but she gave the rest of the horses another meal, for she thought they looked thin.

Then she made her way under cover of the thick hedges up to the big house. Bernice, she saw with relief as she approached, was out in the back fully occupied with bullying the servants as they did the laundry. They were bent sullenly over the heavy washtubs and both Bernice's daughters were standing

beside her primly, watching intently and drinking in the way
their mother handled the menials under her rule. They were
receiving instructions in how *not* to run a plantation, to
Anna's way of thinking!

As she fled unnoticed past the little tableau a malicious
thought occurred to her—Brett would have Bernice for a
mother-in-law!

It was easy to slip into the deserted unlocked house, for
Bernice made multiple use of her servants so that she might
keep them busy almost around the clock. The maids had
cleaned up earlier and were now out laundering clothes or in
the cookhouse assisting cook prepare lunch.

Anna had wound around and come in from the front.
Moving warily, she came up the "welcoming arms" of the
wide stone stairway and opened the big front door. It took her
but a moment to reach her old room, to rummage in the big
clothes press and find a pale yellow voile gown, vastly
becoming, and trimmed with yellow satin ribbons of a deeper
gold. There were pins around the hem—obviously it was the
next of Anna's lovely gowns to be shortened for stout little
Pris.

Rummaging grimly, Anna found two lovely chemises and a
petticoat of lemon satin—and from a bag that was undoubtedly
to be sent to Boston or some other likely place to be sold, she
retrieved three pairs of her slippers, all too small for Bernice
and her daughters. She thrust all of these things into a big
white silk shawl she found at the bottom of the press.

Her pearls—the ones Tobias had given her on her last
birthday before his illness—lay carelessly on the dressing
table. Anna itched to take them, but she felt that unlike the
clothes their loss would be instantly noted and reported. She
abandoned the idea of taking any jewelry as too risky.

Not so the silver!

How well she remembered the flourish with which Bernice
had locked away the last piece of heavy silver into the big
cupboard. And the key to that cupboard should be—yes,
there it was tucked into the bottom of the woman's overflowing
jewel box. On silent feet, Anna ran to the big cupboard and
unlocked it.

There were many things she might have taken, silver bowls and salts and goblets, easy to carry, easy to sell—but Anna knew what she was looking for. There in the bottom were the great candlesticks that had graced the long sideboard from the first day she saw it, those candlesticks that had been part of Mamma Jamison's dowry when she had married Papa Jamison, and that had been promised to Anna for *her* dowry. To take the rest of the silver might seem like stealing, but not these candlesticks—*they* were *hers*, just as Floss and her clothes were hers. Too tall to stand upright in the big locked cupboard, they had been carefully wrapped in white linen and laid side by side on the cupboard floor, for Bernice had felt their weight might break the wooden shelves. To Anna those candlesticks were the very heart of Mirabelle—Mirabelle at its best—and she meant to take them with her. With desperate haste, she rolled them out on the floor. They were so heavy she had to carry them separately to the front door. She staggered down the steps with them, one by one, and managed to get unnoticed to the stables, taking two trips, one with each candlestick and her big bundle of clothes. There she saddled one of the horses, a strong gelding named Runalong, and tied the wrapped candlesticks and clothes onto his back. Then she leaped aboard Floss, and with Runalong, with his heavy load of silver, following along on a lead, she took herself off to Waite Hall.

She was almost there when she ran into Sue, riding Jemmy at breakneck speed out of the front gate. Sue brought Jemmy to a sliding halt at sight of Anna.

"Oh, God," she cried. "I've been looking everywhere for you, Anna! When Arthur couldn't find you this morning, he nearly went crazy. He let the ship sail without him and stormed over to Mirabelle and accused Bernice of hiding you! She threw him out and he's in the house swearing he'll have both Lance and me up on charges for swindling him! Where have you been, Anna? The only ships that sailed this morning went to Turks Islands and to Boston and we knew you couldn't have been on either of those! Anna, we must give him back his gold. Else he will surely—"

Arthur . . . still here. Anna's face lost some of its color.

"Where I have been, Sue, is no matter," she interrupted.
"What matters is that I have lost the gold. Can he really do
it, have you and Lance up on charges?"

"I don't see how, but he swears he will do it! Papa is up in
the timbers and knows nothing about all this—and Mamma,
when she learned Arthur was not taking the ship but going
instead over to Mirabelle, said coldly that she had acquired an
idiot for a son-in-law and went into St. George and took the
girls with her. I can't cope with it, Anna. Arthur wasn't so
bad as long as he thought to find you at Mirabelle, but when
he came back without you—he is beside himself. He followed
me about the house, insisting that I knew where you were!
This is the first time I have been able to slip away. I meant to
go find Lance and—"

She stopped abruptly.

Arthur himself, a smiling vindictive Arthur handsomely
dressed in puce satin, had stepped out from behind the hedge
that lined the drive. And he was carrying a long whip.

"So I have found you, Anna," he drawled. "And my horse
as well." He emphasized "my" with an evil look at Floss.
"Be good enough to dismount."

Anna reacted fast. With a nudge of her knee, she made
Floss whirl about to run—but not before the long whip Arthur
carried snaked through the air, curled around her slender
waist and lifted her like a feather from Floss's back to send
her tumbling and rolling into the dust of the driveway.

Dimly she heard Sue scream. And from somewhere the
sound of pounding hooves.

And then, surprisingly, the sound of a blade being drawn
and a deep masculine voice she had not expected to hear ever
again.

"You there!" called that commanding voice. "You with
the whip! Leave off!"

Anna struggled up from the driveway to see that Brett,
whose horse had just come to a skidding halt in their midst,
was dismounting—hurling himself off his horse actually with
his blade already drawn and flashing in the sun. His arrival
had had something of the irresistible forward rush of a cavalry

charge and before it Arthur stood uncertainly in the driveway with the long whip upraised.

"I am but chastening my bondswoman!" he howled, astonished and indignant that his actions should be questioned by a stranger.

"You are attacking my betrothed!" roared Brett—and by now his boots had taken him within range of Arthur's whip.

Arthur wielded the whip savagely. Anna moaned and covered her eyes, expecting when she opened them to see Brett writhing in the dust, his sword wrenched from his grasp.

But that was not the sight that met her turquoise gaze.

Astonishingly, when she dared to look, she saw that Brett was still standing, sword in hand. The whip had snaked around him but he had hold of it and with it he had jerked Arthur off his feet.

Arthur lost hold of the whip as he went down, and scrambled up with a curse. "No man dares to come between me and my property!" he snarled. "And the horse she rides is mine too! The law will take care of you for this day's work!"

"*Not today!*" Brett's voice rang out. He had cast the whip from him and had the point of his blade at Arthur's throat even as Arthur gained his feet. He seemed to tower over the shrinking Arthur. "Today *I* am the highest court. It is to *me* you must appeal. Give me one good reason why I should not take your life!"

"Oh, stop!" cried Sue, wringing her hands. "Stop! Arthur is married to my sister!"

Anna thought privately that Mattie would be much better without him, but Sue's words brought Brett—his blade still menacing Arthur—to a halt. "This lady is a friend of yours?" he asked Anna politely.

By now those magical words *You are attacking my betrothed* had sunk in on Anna. With shining eyes, she looked up at this daring stranger who had now saved her—twice. *His betrothed!* He had turned his back on Mirabelle's heiresses and come to find her! Only, how had he known where to look?

But this was no time to find out. Anna found her voice. "Of course she's my friend—the best friend I've got."

"Don't bother to explain, Anna." The point of Brett's sword still hovered close to Arthur's shrinking person. His voice was cool. "I've been to Mirabelle and found out who you really are—I saw your picture there and was told where to find you."

Of course, the painting! The one Papa Jamison had had commissioned for her birthday before he had his stroke. Bernice had kept it because she felt it might be valuable.

"I'm indebted to Bernice for telling you where I might be found."

"Oh, I paid her well for doing so." He flicked her a wry look, then turned his attention back to Arthur. "She's given her consent to our marriage."

Indignation welled up in Anna. "I don't need Bernice's permission!"

"No," bellowed Arthur, driven too far by this exchange. "You need mine, by God, and I'll not give it!"

"Don't keep tempting me to kill you," chided Brett in a silky voice. His blade crept a few inches closer to Arthur and Arthur blanched and fell back a pace.

"I'll have you know that Anna Smith is my bondswoman," exploded Arthur. "Ask her and she'll tell you so. You can't come between a man and his—"

"You certainly can't come between a man and his betrothed. Not mine, at any rate," interrupted Brett. His voice crackled. "If she's your bondswoman, then you must have paid for her. How much?"

"Pay him nothing!" cried Anna, outraged. "He bought my horse and threatened to lock her in a shed and burn the shed over her head if I would not travel to Boston with him as his mistress!"

The gray eyes turned a shade colder. Brett's jaw seemed harder chiseled than before. "Faith, a man eager to die!" he said softly.

Arthur recognized that look. There was death in those gray eyes that bored into his. "Have mercy!" he breathed. "Can ye not see I've been wronged? Bilked of my money?"

"I'll buy her from you," said Brett tersely. "And the horse too. Name your price."

"She's not for sale," gasped Arthur.

"She is," Brett corrected him. "I'll buy her from a living man or take her from a dead one. The choice is yours. Make it quickly."

"I'll tell you what he paid for them both," cried Sue, when Arthur seemed unable to speak. She named the figure and Brett, still keeping his sword at arm's length and a watchful eye on Arthur, reached into his pocket with his free hand and drew out a handful of gold coins, counted them by flicking them contemptuously at Arthur one by one. Arthur flinched as each coin struck him—each small stinging impact was another blow to his lacerated pride.

"Now she's paid for," Brett said coldly, when he had flung the last coin at Arthur. "I'll have her Articles—and a bill of sale for the horse."

"I can write you out a bill of sale but I can't give you her Articles," said Arthur hoarsely. "For I tore that paper to bits and burnt the pieces when I learned she was gone."

Considering the state he was in, they could well believe it.

"Then we'll to the house," said Brett, "and ye'll write out a bill of sale for them both!"

"I'll pick up your money for you, Arthur," offered Sue quickly, bending down to pick the coins from the dusty driveway. "You two go on ahead. There's parchment and ink at the little writing desk in the dining room. The pens may be broken but there's a supply of goose quills there, Anna. You can cut a fresh one."

"Thank you, Sue," breathed Anna. "For everything." She turned and fled after the two men. Brett was already striding toward the house and before him Arthur moved reluctantly, being herded along, prodded by the point of Brett's sword.

At a walnut writing desk in the Waites' dining room, the deed was done. With a shaking hand, Arthur made out two documents—one for the girl, one for the horse—and Sue came in in time to witness his signature.

Anna snatched the papers from him the moment they were signed. "Thank God I'm my own woman again. And Floss is mine again. Oh, Brett—'' Her heart was so full she could not speak.

"You took Anna from me under duress," cried Arthur. Some of his courage had come back and he was smarting under this cavalier treatment. "And Sue here is my witness."

"I'm witness to the fact that you've got back all your money and there'll be no more talk of bringing Lance and me up on charges for your loss!" said Sue tartly. She spilled the coins she had gathered up from the driveway onto the writing desk in front of him. "And when Mamma hears the things you called me, she may turn you out of the house!"

"Ye've bilked me!" cried Arthur. "You're all together in this thing—'tis a plot!"

Brett moved closer to Arthur. His sword was sheathed now and he supposed that was what gave the other man his newfound temerity.

"If you seek to cause my lady any further trouble," he said softly, "here's a reminder that I stand between her and you."

Without warning, his balled fist crashed into Arthur's mouth. There was an anguished yell and the sound of smashing bone as Arthur's front teeth cracked. He fell back, clutching his bloody mouth, his eyes filled with horror.

"Unless you'd care to lose the rest of your teeth, ye'll take that as a warning," Brett told him conversationally. "Shall we go, ladies? There's a wedding ceremony to be gone through, for which I've acquired a special license." He patted his doublet.

Anna gave him an adoring look, but as Arthur stumbled away to find water to ease his bleeding mouth, Sue spoke. "Would you like Lance to give you away?" she wondered.

Anna had eyes only for Brett. "I will give myself away," she told Sue gaily. "In fact I have already done so—but I'd be delighted to have you and Lance at the wedding."

"Which will be held at the church of your choice," smiled Brett.

"Then 'twill be at St. Peter's, for I have always fancied myself wed there."

"But we must be quick," he warned, "for my ship will not wait and we must be aboard her tonight."

CHAPTER 40

The wedding held that afternoon at St. Peter's was not at all the kind of wedding Anna had anticipated in the days when she was heiress to Mirabelle. Instead of wearing the handsome gown of white Italian satin and seed pearls imported from London that she had always imagined, she wore the pale yellow voile trimmed in gold ribands she had snatched up this morning from her big press at Mirabelle. And the slippers that peeped out from beneath her lemon satin petticoat were red—for red and black were the colors of the slippers she had found bagged up for shipment. And her bridal circlet, which she wore around her head, was a garland of hastily wound together pink Chain of Love flowers that they had snatched up from the roadside and Sue had woven on the way to the church.

Instead of a wedding party that included most of the eligible youth of the island, she was attended only by Lance—whom Sue had sent a servant to fetch—and Sue, and the minister's voice echoed hollowly in the empty parish church. He had been loath to perform the ceremony without proper crying of the banns, but Sue persuaded him that Danforth's ship would not wait and he took note of the special license Brett thrust into his hand.

Instead of a great reception held at Mirabelle, where the entire genteel population of Bermuda might toast the bride, the four of them clinked glasses of indifferent Madeira at a local tavern (for Sue had said that with Arthur still on the premises it would be impossible for the bridal couple to be entertained at Waite Hall, and Anna hesitated to impose on Lance's parents, although he offered handsomely).

But all of it went by Anna in a lovely golden haze. To her it was the most wonderful of weddings, for it was a wedding she had despaired of in the morning—and embarked on in the afternoon. Brett wore the same russet doublet and trousers he had worn when she first saw him. But he had earlier returned to the inn for a change of linens and the flowing sleeves of his cambric shirt were as frostily white as the careless ruffle of Mechlin at his throat.

He stood straight and tall and forceful beside her, concentrating on the minister's words, and he took her as his wife in deep resonant tones as behind them Sue sobbed audibly.

Anna was proud of him. And more—she loved him.

And as the minister pronounced them man and wife she felt a special surge of joy—for Brett had broken off whatever arrangement he had had to marry one of Mirabelle's heiresses, to wed *her*. *A girl with nothing to offer but herself!* To him, she came first. First above all other women! For that, if for nothing else, she felt she would have loved him.

Anna was young, and for all her self-vaunted sophistication, very innocent of the world. . . .

"Oh, Anna!" Still misty-eyed, Sue hugged her as she and Lance and Anna emerged into the sunlight, which struck blindingly against the white lime-washed walls of the church. "You're *married!* I can't believe it!"

Anna couldn't believe it, either. She didn't feel married, she felt confused. "Where's Brett?" she demanded merrily, looking about her. "Don't tell me I've already lost him!"

"He stayed behind to pay the minister," laughed Sue. "And I don't think you need worry about losing him, the way he looks at you! Lance, why don't *you* look at me like that?"

Inside the church, Brett was hastening to give the minister a suitable sum. He was in a hurry, for evening was coming and he had yet to arrange to get Anna's horse aboard.

"Ah, wait, I almost forgot," cried the minister as Brett turned to leave. "There's a packet put in trust with me by my predecessor, which was to be given to Mistress Anna on her wedding day. I'll get it.''

Brett waited impatiently while the packet was found and thrust into his hand. He studied the thick bundle. "Who gave you this, did you say?''

"My predecessor, who had it, I believe, from Mistress Anna's Aunt Eliza on her deathbed.''

"Her Aunt Eliza?'' asked Brett sharply.

"Eliza Smith, the bondservant—the woman who brought Mistress Anna to this island as a baby.''

Brett relaxed but he frowned at the packet in his hand. *It was a Pandora's box,* he thought grimly; *open it and all the troubles of the world would spill out.* For he had no doubt what the packet contained—it would tell about a dead woman, Anna Smith's mother. . . . Well, he would not let sad stories and old tragedies spoil this wedding trip! Anna could have the packet later—much later. He stuffed it inside his doublet and went out into the sunshine to join his bride.

They might have asked what had taken him so long but that Sue was asking wonderingly, "Anna, isn't that the dress you wore to a party at the Soames' two seasons ago?''

Anna laughed. "The very same.''

"But—how did you get it? I thought Bernice had confiscated all your lovely things?''

Anna leaned over and whispered in Sue's ear, "I went by there this morning and slipped in and snatched up a few clothes that hadn't yet been altered for her daughters!''

"Wonderful!'' Sue clapped her hands. "Mark you, I'll never tell it.''

Lance leaned toward them. "Danforth and I are off to see if we can arrange a means to get Floss aboard ship,'' he told them. "We'll meet you at the tavern.''

"There's no hurry, then,'' laughed Sue, strolling along beside Anna in the sunlight. "How Bernice will wonder what's happened to that dress and petticoat! I don't doubt me she'll beat the servants.'' She looked behind them at the three horses following them on leads. "Isn't that Runalong you brought along with Floss?''

Anna nodded. "I borrowed Runalong from Mirabelle's stables. Will you take him back with you, Sue, and feed him well before you turn him loose to go home? I think Bernice is starving the animals."

"Then you'll probably want to pick up Coral and take her along?"

"I'd like to, Sue," sighed Anna, "but I dare not go back there." She cast a quick glance at Runalong's heavy load.

Sue caught that glance. "But you told Brett that load on Runalong's back is only an iron popcorn popper and some fireplace tools and other iron utensils Eliza had given you. Surely they wouldn't be valuable enough for Bernice to make trouble over! Tell you what, I'll take Runalong back tomorrow myself and tell Bernice I found the horse on the road and recognized him. And on my way back I'll just snatch up Coral and take her home with me—you needn't worry, Anna, the cat will be well cared for."

Anna gave her a grateful look. "I hadn't thought about Bernice blaming the servants and beating them," she said, troubled. "So you must be sure to tell her *I* took the dress and the chemise and three pairs of slippers. Make a point of describing my gown—which you'd no idea how I came by! And also mention"—her voice slowed thoughtfully—"that I had a couple of long, well-wrapped, heavy objects with me."

"The fireplace tools?" gasped Sue.

Anna leaned toward her. "The candlesticks," she whispered.

"Those huge ones from the sideboard? Oh, Anna, you didn't?"

"They were given to me long ago. She stole Mirabelle from me but I gave myself a dowry!"

They were giggling when they reached the tavern and looked around for Brett and Lance, who would soon be toasting the bride.

But as Anna had left the church she had looked back and a sudden pang went through her. There had been one thing missing . . . no father to give the bride away, no mother to weep and kiss her and smile bravely through her tears.

Perhaps never again would she long so much for the mother she had never known, as she did at that moment. . . .

* * *

And far away in the Carolinas, by merest chance, Imogene was going through a trunk of old clothes. And in that trunk she found packed away carefully in lavender her own wedding dress—the gown of shimmering silk she had worn at her "buccaneer's wedding" on Tortuga when she had walked with van Ryker beneath an arch of cutlasses held on high by his buccaneers from the *Sea Rover* and heard their deep-throated cry of exultation as their captain claimed his woman.

She held up the dress and studied it wistfully . . . so many memories, so many. Then on a whim she decided to try it on. It still fit her lovely figure and as she turned before the mirror, puffing out with casual fingers the puffed virago sleeves caught with gold satin rosettes that cascaded into frosty lace at her elbows, she caught up the wide skirt and tucked it into billowing panniers to show her petticoat of shimmering Chinese gold. The low square neckline displayed her magnificent bosom to perfection.

No timid innocent bride she! she thought ruefully. When she had trailed down those stairs in Tortuga, she had fully intended to marry another man, waiting at the foot of those stairs, but van Ryker, bold as always, had made her his. . . . And in spite of all the wild adventures that life with him had brought her, these had been wonderful years. She felt she had lacked only one thing for perfect happiness—her firstborn, Georgiana, the daughter who had been wrenched from her arms so long ago.

She had other children now, of course, but they were in school in England and would be gone for months. She missed them terribly. And perhaps that was why, fingering the lovely material of her wedding gown and sighing as she studied her beautiful reflection in the mirror, her brooding thoughts came back to the child she had lost—Georgiana.

She would be of marriageable age now, that daughter—if she had lived. Imogene imagined her wistfully: a glamorous beauty with copper hair and turquoise eyes like her father's, for even as a babe in arms there had been a touch of burnished gold to the fair silky hair on that little head and a shading of turquoise in those blue, blue eyes. She would have had her choice of men of course—for was she not Imogene Wells's daughter? And Imogene had never lacked for suitors.

Georgiana would have chosen the best man among them, of course. A handsome rakish blade and yet a man of worth—someone her mother could approve of. Imogene gave a little inward laugh that caught in her throat in a sob.

Her daughter Georgiana would not have known the dangers and trouble that had beset her own girlhood. She would have grown to young womanhood here in the Carolinas, enjoying garden parties and balls at neighboring plantations. She would have had Imogene's love and van Ryker's protection.

She would have been happy.

And . . . once she had decided on the man she would marry, there would have been a wonderful wedding—not a "buccaneer's wedding" as she had had, of course, but a plantation wedding with the bride trailing in snowy white down the wide curving stairway of Longview and van Ryker, rakish as ever but with silver wings in his dark hair, giving the bride away.

Imogene's reflection blurred. She dashed a hand over her blue eyes to sweep away the tears that clung to her lashes.

At that moment she would have given anything—*anything* to have watched Georgiana grow up, to have stood by, dabbing at her eyes, while Georgiana was married, to have waved to her wistfully as her triumphant groom carried her away.

And at the very moment her tears were shed, on faraway Bermuda, her daughter Georgiana, just wed, was strolling away from the church.

Night found Anna and Brett aboard the *Dame Fortune*, and Floss and the candlesticks safely stowed away for the voyage north. Anna was perplexed to find that Captain Paaterzoon and his crew spoke only Dutch.

"How can that be?" she demanded. "An English ship flying English colors, and we're at war with Holland and yet—"

"A Dutch ship," Brett corrected her. "The *Haarlemmer*. She's only masquerading as English. And we're bound for

New Netherland, which has been English New York for some years past but is now Dutch once again.''

"I don't understand," puzzled Anna. "I thought when you said you were taking me to America that you meant an English colony. I mean, you're—"

"English," supplied Brett. "Yes, I am. And while New York was under English rule I bought land along the Hudson—which the Dutch, by the way, call the 'North River.' 'Tis a large holding lying along the eastern bank with a goodly mansion on it."

"But your position—an Englishman in Dutch-held territory—now that England and Holland are at war, must be untenable!"

"It may become so," said Brett grimly. "They call me 'the English patroon.' It has a scoffing ring to it."

And he had planned to marry an heiress to help cement his position, no doubt. Anna felt strangely guilty—and yet triumphant.

"Which had you asked for, Pris or Prue?" she asked him when they arrived at their cabin, wondering which of Bernice's daughters had been jilted. "I'm surprised Bernice let you off so easily," she added frankly. "I'd have expected her to rage and storm and threaten suit if you dared break your engagement with one of *her* daughters!"

"It took me a while to realize I came to Bermuda to marry you—only you," he said, his voice deepening. "You are my fate, Anna. Try to remember that."

She did not understand, she did not even try to understand, for by now Brett had swung open the cabin door, he was sweeping her up into his arms and carrying her across the threshold. Now he had closed the door with his boot and he was removing the white silk shawl she had worn against the brisk sea wind and—at Sue's suggestion—against the curious stares of the *Dame Fortune*'s crew, for Anna's yellow voile dress was cut unconscionably low; she had half expected the minister, who had frowned at sight of her, to refuse to perform the ceremony until she went to get a whisk!

And now she forgot his words altogether, for Brett's lips were roving over her hot face, he was kissing her eyelids, her cheeks, her mouth. And now—her heart gave a sudden irregular lurch—his tongue was probing past her soft parted lips.

A feeling as if she had drunk warm wine flowed over Anna, and the world became hushed, breathless. There was something she wanted to remember and it was fast slipping away under the insistent masculine pressure of that probing tongue.

Brett felt her slight movement away from him and lifted his head quizzically. Anna felt hypnotized by the depth and meaning she read in his gray gaze, bent so intently upon her.

"Let—let me remove my bridal circlet," she said in a soft rushing voice. "I want to press it between the leaves of a book and keep it—oh, where is it? It's gone!"

Brett smiled indulgently as he let her go. He bent down and scooped up the circlet of pink flowers and handed it to her with a flourish. "I hear they call these flowers 'Chains of Love,'" he said lightly. "But they seem too fragile to hold a man."

Anna, taking the flowers from him, looked up into his face. "They hold only those who wish to be held," she said softly. "Do you wish to be held, Brett?"

"By chains of love?" She could not read the smile that played around his mouth. "What man would not?"

Anna gave him a winsome smile as she laid aside the circlet of pink flowers. She shrugged provocatively. "Did you remember to latch the cabin door?"

"I latched it after I kicked it shut—while you were preoccupied with something else."

Yes, she had been carried away by the pressure of his lips. Anna's color heightened. "Then you can help me get unhooked." She turned her back to let Brett unhook her bodice. When he had done he eased the soft yellow voile over her shoulders and all the way down her arms it seemed to move as softly, as silkily as a promise. When his big hands brushed her arms and back she tried to control the tremor that went through her.

He laughed. "I believe you are anticipating, little one."

"Nothing of the kind!" But her face, flushed a guilty scarlet, gave that the lie.

"I think," he said, turning her about to face him and looking deep into her wide turquoise eyes, "that you desire me as much as I desire you." His deep voice was a caress. High above them a vagrant breeze caught and billowed the sails and the wooden ship, flying now—for her captain had not hesitated to cast off once they were on board—creaked and sighed.

The ship's sigh was mingled with Anna's as she murmured, "Oh, I do desire you, Brett. I do." And melted into his arms.

"But first let us get the rest of these clothes off." Deftly he unhooked her petticoat—it occurred to her fleetingly that he must have had a great deal of practice to do it so handily. But that thought too left her as she felt the shiny material glide luxuriously down her hips to fall in a lemon satin heap around her ankles.

"Now the chemise," he said. He smiled broadly at her obvious embarrassment, but to Anna it was all very different. Last night on the soft sands of Bermuda's north shore there had been only the moonlit stillness of the beach with the ocean moaning its endless song in the background. It had seemed heavenly, unreal.

Tonight there were sturdy ship-cabin walls around them and a swaying ship's lantern overhead.

"Put out the light first," she objected.

"Ah, so we're going back to maidenhood?" he teased. "I thought we'd been through all that last night."

She gave him a quelling look and he subsided, chuckling. "Anyway, we wouldn't want to tear this pretty thing in the dark!" With practiced fingers he untied the ribbon that held her chemise.

"You do that as if you'd done it before," she said sweetly.

"A time or two," he admitted with a grin. "And aren't you glad? For you're not the girl to want a bumbling boy!" With one swift gesture he pulled the drawstring at the top and caused her delicate white lawn chemise to float down around her body, down past her throbbing breasts, down over her tingling stomach, down over her rounded hips, the material rasping ever so lightly, just enough to set her senses stirring.

"Lovely," he said softly, stepping back to view her. "You seem to be bathed in the sun and standing in the surf. 'Tis a delight just to look at you."

Anna stepped out of the "surf" of her fallen chemise and bent over to pick up chemise and petticoat. As she did so, her long golden hair cascaded down around her arms. She made a pretty picture bending there in the lantern light and Brett's hard gaze softened.

"I'd best get these off the floor," she explained, her voice muffled by her hair as she picked them up. "For who knows when I can get more?"

"For my taste ye need wear nothing at all when we're alone," he told her lightly. "But in yon sea chest over there you'll find a few swatches of material and a petticoat or two that I picked up in New Amsterdam—for bait."

"For *bait?*" Anna rose slowly, holding her chemise up before her. She looked at him in astonishment as she parted the golden curtain of her long bright hair. Forgetful now that she was naked save for her stockings and shoes, she tossed her dress and petticoat and chemise over her shoulder and padded over to the sea chest he indicated and opened it, touched with amazement the articles inside, while he undressed.

The chest was filled with feminine finery. A fan of delicate white lace embroidered with seed pearls—and another of black lace trimmed in black ostrich plumes. Two velvet purses, a repoussé silver comb, two silver-handled brushes, half a dozen petticoats each handsomer than the last, a length of peach-colored velvet and yards and yards of apricot satin, chemises trimmed in fine Belgian lace, a loose flowing dress of amber silk—the trove went on and on.

"I can't believe it," she said, turning to him. *"Why?* Did you feel you needs must provide your bride with a trousseau?"

He shrugged. "I thought my charm might not be enough— so as you can see, I came bearing gifts. I doubt if much of it will fit. I brought assorted sizes, for I knew not what size my bride would be."

Anna's lips parted in true amazement. What kind of man was this, who would accept any size bride as his portion? And how—determined as he was—had she ever made him change his mind and seek her out instead of one of Mira-belle's heiresses?

"I think there is something you should tell me, Brett," she said slowly. "Isn't there?"

"Yes." He had taken off his clothes while she rummaged in the big chest and now he turned to her, a formidable figure clad only in his light drawers. The muscles of his chest and shoulders rippled as he moved toward her, and the lantern light gilded his dark hair. Light-footed as some big jungle cat he walked, and he moved with the calm certainty of the strong and purposeful. Her heart beat faster at the sight of him, and she only half heard his answer above its insistent drumming. "I came to Bermuda to marry Anna Smith—only I was under the impression at the time that she was the heiress to Mirabelle."

"I don't understand," she murmured. She was still holding her clothes over her arm.

He reached out and took them from her, tossed them over a chair, and pulled her bare body close to him so that her nipples brushed his chest and set her atingle. "I came here to marry *you*, Anna," he said quietly. "And I thank God that I did, for you're something I'd like not to have missed."

A lovely lie, she thought, swaying against him happily, feeling her breasts crushed like flowers against his chest. *A lovely, lovely lie.* For how could he have known anything about her in far New Netherland? But whatever he was holding back, what could it matter? He had fought for her, saved her, wed her, bought Floss for her, broken Arthur's teeth for her—what did it matter *why* he had come to Bermuda? She kicked off her shoes, and standing on one foot as she leaned against him, began to ease her stocking down with the other foot.

"What are you doing?" he asked. "You're squirming so!"

"Just trying to remove my stockings," she murmured.

He gave a low laugh and lifted her up in his strong arms

and bore her to the narrow bunk and laid her down. Still laughing, he lifted her right leg and with both hands eased her stocking down. He took his time about it and Anna squirmed and protested, for his handling of her made a feverish excitement course through her veins. She tried to tumble away from him but he pounced on her and removed the stocking from her left leg in the same teasing manner. He seized her bare foot and tickled it and Anna, gasping and laughing, lurched up toward him, threw her arms around his neck and dragged him down to her.

As she seized him, his expression changed and softened and he caught her in his arms with a terrible tenderness that seemed to be wrenched from the heart of him. Anna looked up mistily into his grave eyes and promised herself that whatever he was holding back from her, she would never ask him again—it did not matter. Nothing mattered but this man and this moment—nothing could change or alter the way she felt about him.

Last night there had been a fierce urgency to their lovemaking, a drive, a boldness—as if both knew the morrow might wrench them apart.

Tonight was different. Tonight they could see all their tomorrows stretching before them, each more breathless than the last. Tonight there was time—time to be gracious, time to be elegant, time to explore, to taste, to savor.

Tonight their bodies would mingle in fire, but with the certain knowledge it was not the last time.

Anna felt that difference as Brett gently lowered his long form down over hers. His hips—naked now—brushed lightly, playfully, against her own while he rested his weight on one strong arm, using the other to lift her up toward him. With his free arm cradling her back he swung her torso lightly back and forth against him. *Like the pendulum of a big clock!* she thought, amazed at his supple strength. And as she was swung, her nipples slid lightly, fiery across his chest—back and forth, back and forth. She could feel the tension in her building, building, threatening to explode in a burst of feeling.

Playfully, she tried to resist, to pull away.

As if in answer to an unspoken cry, he eased her back down against the sheet and dipped his head so that his heavy dark hair fell like a thick fringe over her neck and shoulders. She gasped as his lips nuzzled a nipple to hardness, teased the other in turn—and squirmed as his fingers toyed with her stomach, roved over her thighs, lost themselves in the silky triangle of hair at the base of her hips.

She settled more sinuously into his arms and Brett was glad he had not chosen this night to answer her questions.

Tomorrow—and all their tomorrows—was time enough to explore what was in the packet, to tell her of her fiery beautiful mother, around whose golden head so many scandals had swirled. Tomorrow, some pushed-away tomorrow, she could pout and question him and poke among old bones. Tomorrow could take care of itself, for all he cared tonight! With strong authoritative ease he drew her pliant naked body to him. For this night, more than any signed document, would seal their bargain and meld them forever together.

"I still don't understand," she murmured breathlessly, "why you chose me when you could have had Mirabelle?"

How could he tell her now that she was heiress to far more? To a manor that far surpassed Mirabelle? And all of it through a scandal that had driven her mother's name into behind-hand whispers in New Amsterdam? How could he tell this lovely, winning, trusting creature melting in his arms that she was not Anna, but Georgiana, heiress to far Wey Gat? Georgiana, found at last? How could he tell her all that and yet make her realize that he loved her for herself alone?

He decided not even to try to tell her—*he would show her.* By the very force and gentleness of his lovemaking. Every kiss, every touch, every murmur, every endearment, every caress would tell her how he felt about her, how he would always feel about her.

"Anna, Anna, ye've much to learn of the ways of life and men," he murmured. And set out to teach her.

He had the whole of this golden voyage, a whole life ahead, to prove how very much he loved her.

The magic world that lovers know
They will now discover
And he will give his heart to her
And never cease to love her!

Watch for WILD WILLFUL LOVE, the
thrilling sequel to Imogene's story
and for RICH RADIANT LOVE, the stirring
conclusion of Georgiana's stormy
love affair.

INTRODUCING
THE RAKEHELL DYNASTY

The bold, sweeping, passionate story of a great New England shipping family caught up in the winds of change—and of the one man who would dare to sail his dream ship to the frightening, beautiful land of China. He was Jonathan Rakehell, and his destiny would change the course of history.

THE RAKEHELL DYNASTY—
THE GRAND SAGA OF THE GREAT CLIPPER SHIPS
AND OF THE MEN WHO BUILT THEM
TO CONQUER THE SEAS AND CHALLENGE THE WORLD!

Jonathan Rakehell—who staked his reputation and his place in the family on the clipper's amazing speed.

Lai-Tse Lu—the beautiful, independent daughter of a Chinese merchant. She could not know that Jonathan's proud clipper ship carried a cargo of love and pain, joy and tragedy for her.

Louise Graves—Jonathan's wife-to-be, who waits at home in New London keeping a secret of her own.

Bradford Walker—Jonathan's scheming brother-in-law who scoffs at the clipper and plots to replace Jonathan as heir to the Rakehell shipping line.

BEST OF BESTSELLERS FROM WARNER BOOKS

THE CARDINAL SINS
by Andrew M. Greeley   (A90-913, $3.95)
From the humblest parish to the inner councils of the Vatican. Father
Greeley reveals the hierarchy of the Catholic Church as it really is, and its
priests as the men they really are. This book follows the lives of two Irish
boys who grow up on the West Side of Chicago and enter the priesthood. We
share their triumphs as well as their tragedies and temptations.

RAGE OF ANGELS
by Sidney Sheldon   (A36-214, $3.95)
A breath-taking novel that takes you behind the doors of the law and inside
the heart and mind of Jennifer Parker. She rises from the ashes of her own
courtroom disaster to become one of America's most brilliant attorneys.
Her story is interwoven with that of two very different men of enormous
power. As Jennifer inspires both men to passion, each is determined to
destroy the other—and Jennifer, caught in the crossfire, becomes the
ultimate victim.

SCRUPLES
by Judith Krantz   (A30-531, $3.95)
The ultimate romance! The spellbinding story of the rise of a fascinating
woman from fat, unhappy "poor relative" of an aristocratic Boston family to
a unique position among the super-beautiful and super-rich, a woman who
got everything she wanted—fame, wealth, power and love.

CHANCES
by Jackie Collins   (A30-268, $3.95)
                              (August 1982 publication)
Handsome, hot-blooded, hard-to-handle Gino Santangelo took chances on
the city streets where he staked his guts and brains to build an empire. He
used women, discarded them at will . . . until he met the woman of his
dreams. The greatest chance he ever took led him to America to escape
prosecution when he entrusted his empire to Lucky Santangelo. Jackie
Collins' latest is a real sizzling, sexy, action-packed national bestseller!

If you liked RASH RECKLESS LOVE, you'll want to read these other Valerie Sherwood bestsellers...

HER SHINING SPLENDOR
by Valerie Sherwood   (D85-487, $2.75)

Lenore and Lorena: their names are so alike, yet their beauties so dissimilar. Yet each is bound to reap the rewards and the troubles of love. Here are the adventures of the exquisite Lenore and her beauteous daughter Lorena, each setting out upon her own odyssey of love, adventure, and fame.

THIS TOWERING PASSION
by Valerie Sherwood   (D33-042, $2.95)

They called her "Angel" when she rode bareback into the midst of battle to find her lover. They called her "Mistress Daunt" when she lived with Geoffrey in Oxford, though she wore no ring on her finger. Wherever she traveled men called her Beauty. Her name was Lenore—and she answered only to "Love."

THESE GOLDEN PLEASURES
by Valerie Sherwood   (D33-116, $2.95)

She was beautiful—and notorious and they called her "That Barrington Woman." But beneath the silks and the diamonds, within the supple body so many men had embraced, was the heart of a girl who yearned still for love. At fifteen she had learned her beauty was both a charm and a curse. It had sent her fleeing from Kansas, had been her downfall in Baltimore and Georgia, yet had kept her alive in the Klondike and the South Seas.

THIS LOVING TORMENT
by Valerie Sherwood   (D33-117, $2.95)

Perhaps she was *too beautiful!* Perhaps the brawling colonies would have been safer for a plainer girl, one more demure and less accomplished in language and manner. But Charity Woodstock was gloriously beautiful with pale gold hair and topaz eyes—and she was headed for trouble. She was accused of witchcraft by the man who had attacked her. She was whisked from pirate ship to plantation. Beauty might have been her downfall, but Charity Woodstock had a reckless passion to live and would challenge this new world—and win.

ESPECIALLY FOR YOU
FROM WARNER